Becker

THE BEST KNOWN WORKS OF
IVAN TURGENEV

THE
BEST KNOWN WORKS OF
IVAN TURGENEV

Including *Fathers and Sons; Smoke;*
and nine short stories.

BLUE RIBBON BOOKS
Garden City, New York

1942
BLUE RIBBON BOOKS

CL

PRINTED IN THE UNITED STATES OF AMERICA

CONTENTS

FATHERS AND SONS

"Well, piotr, not in sight yet?" was the question asked on May the 20th, 1859, by a gentleman of a little over forty, in a dusty coat and checked trousers, who came out without his hat on to the low steps of the posting station at S——. He was addressing his servant, a chubby young fellow, with whitish down on his chin, and little, lack-lustre eyes.

The servant, in whom everything—the turquoise ring in his ear, the streaky hair plastered with grease, and the civility of his movements—indicated a man of the new, improved generation, glanced with an air of indulgence along the road, and made answer:

"No, sir; not in sight."

"Not in sight?" repeated his master.

"No, sir," responded the man a second time.

His master sighed, and sat down on a little bench. We will introduce him to the reader while he sits, his feet tucked under him, gazing thoughtfully round.

His name was Nikolai Petrovitch Kirsanov. He had twelve miles from the posting station, a fine property of two hundred souls, or, as he expressed it—since he had arranged the division of his land with the peasants, and started a "farm"—of nearly five thousand acres. His father, a general in the army, who served in 1812, a coarse, half-educated, but not ill-natured man, a typical Russian, had been in harness all his life, first in command of a brigade, and then of a division, and lived constantly in the provinces, where, by virtue of his rank, he played a fairly important part. Nikolai Petrovitch was born in the south of Russia like his elder brother, Pavel, of whom more hereafter. He was educated at home till he was fourteen, surrounded by cheap tutors, free-and-easy but toadying adjutants, and all the usual regimental and staff set. His mother, one of the Kolyazin family, as a girl called Agathe, but as a general's wife Agathokleya Kuzminishna Kirsanov, was one of those military ladies who take their full share of the duties and dignities of office. She wore gorgeous caps and rustling silk dresses; in church she was the first to advance to the cross; she talked a great deal in a loud voice, let her children kiss her hand in the morning, and gave them her blessing at night—in fact, she got everything out of life she could. Nikolai Petrovitch, as a general's son—though so far from being distinguished by courage that he even deserved to be called "a funk"—was intended, like his brother Pavel, to enter the army; but he broke his leg on the very day when the news of his commission came, and, after being two months in bed, retained a slight limp to the end of his day. His father gave him up as a bad job, and let him go into the civil service. He took him to Petersburg directly he was eighteen, and placed him in the university. His brother happened about the same time to be made an officer in the Guards. The young men started living together in one set of rooms, under the remote supervision of a cousin on their mother's side, Ilya Kolyazin, an official of high rank. Their father returned to his division and his wife, and only rarely sent his sons large sheets of grey paper, scrawled over in a bold clerkly hand. At the bottom of these sheets stood in letters, enclosed carefully in scroll-work, the words, "Piotr Kirsanov, General-Major." In 1835 Nikolai Petrovitch left the university, a graduate, and in the same year General Kirsanov was put on the retired list after an unsuccessful review, and came to Petersburg with his wife to live. He was about to take a house in the Tavrichesky Gardens, and had joined the English club, but he died suddenly of an apoplectic fit. Agathokleya Kuzminishna soon followed him; she could not accustom herself to a dull life in the capital; she was consumed by the ennui of existence away from the regiment. Meanwhile Nikolai Petrovitch had already, in his parents' lifetime and to their no slight chagrin, had time to fall in love with the daughter of his landlord, a petty official, Prepolovensky. She was pretty, and, as it is called, an "advanced" girl; she used to read the serious articles in the "Science" column of the journals. He married her directly the term of mourning was over; and leaving the civil service in which his father had by favour procured him a post, was perfectly blissful with his Masha, first in a country villa near the Lyesny Institute, afterwards in town in a pretty little flat with a clean staircase and a draughty drawing-room, and then in the country, where he settled finally, and where in a short time a son, Arkady, was born to him. The young couple lived very happily and peacefully; they were scarcely ever apart; they read together, sang and played duets together on the piano; she tended her flowers and looked after the poultry-yard; he sometimes went hunting, and busied himself with the estate, while Arkady grew and grew in the same happy and peaceful way. Ten years passed like a dream. In 1847 Kirsanov's wife died. He almost succumbed to this blow; in a few weeks his hair was grey; he was getting ready to go abroad, if possible to distract his mind . . . but then came the year 1848. He returned unwillingly to the country, and, after a rather prolonged period of inactivity, began to take an interest in improvements in the management of his land. In 1855 he brought his son to the university; he spent three winters with him in Petersburg, hardly going out anywhere, and trying to make acquaintance with Arkady's young companions. The last winter he had not been able to go, and here we have seen him in the May of 1859, already quite grey, stoutish, and rather bent, waiting for his son, who had just taken his degree, as once he had taken it himself.

The servant, from a feeling of propriety, and perhaps, too, not anxious to remain under the master's eye, had gone to the gate, and was smoking a pipe. Nikolai Petrovitch bent his head, and began staring at the crumbling steps; a big mottled fowl walked sedately towards him, treading firmly with its great yellow legs; a muddy cat gave him an unfriendly look, twisting herself coyly round the railing. The sun was scorching; from the half-dark passage of the posting station came an odour of hot rye-bread. Nikolai Petrovitch fell to dreaming. "My son . . . a graduate . . . Arkasha . . ." were the ideas that continually came round again and again in his head; he tried to think of something else, and again the same thoughts returned. He remembered his dead wife. . . . "She did not live to see it!" he murmured sadly. A plump, dark-blue pigeon flew into the road, and hurriedly went to drink in a puddle near the well. Nikolai Petrovitch began looking at it, but his ear had already caught the sound of approaching wheels.

"It sounds as if they're coming, sir," announced the servant, popping in from the gateway.

Nikolai Petrovitch jumped up, and bent his eyes on the road. A carriage appeared with three posting-horses harnessed abreast; in the carriage he caught a glimpse of the blue band of a student's cap, the familiar outline of a dear face.

"Arkasha! Arkasha!" cried Kirsanov, and he ran waving his hands. . . . A few instants later, his lips were pressed to the beardless, dusty, sunburnt cheek of the youthful graduate.

II

"Let me shake myself first, daddy," said Arkady, in a voice tired from travelling, but boyish and clear as a bell, as he gaily responded to his father's caresses; "I am covering you with dust."

"Never mind, never mind," repeated Nikolai Petrovitch, smiling tenderly, and twice he struck the collar of his son's cloak and his own great-coat with his hand. "Let me have a look at you; let me have a look at you," he added, moving back from him, but immediately he went with hurried steps towards the yard of the station, calling, "This way, this way; and horses at once."

Nikolai Petrovitch seemed far more excited than his son; he seemed a little confused, a little timid. Arkady stopped him.

"Daddy," he said, "let me introduce you to my great friend, Bazarov, about whom I have so often written to you. He has been so good as to promise to stay with us."

Nikolai Petrovitch went back quickly, and going up to a tall man in a long, loose, rough coat with tassels, who had only just got out of the carriage, he warmly pressed the ungloved red hand, which the latter did not at once hold out to him.

"I am heartily glad," he began, "and very grateful for your kind intention of visiting us. . . . Let me know your name, and your father's."

"Yevgeny Vassilyev," answered Bazarov, in a lazy but manly voice; and turning back the collar of his rough coat, he showed Nikolai Petrovitch his whole face. It was long and lean, with a broad forehead, a nose flat at the base and sharper at the end, large greenish eyes, and drooping whiskers of a sandy colour; it was lighted up by a tranquil smile, and showed self-confidence and intelligence.

"I hope, dear Yevgeny Vassilyitch, you won't be dull with us," continued Nikolai Petrovitch.

Bazarov's thin lips moved just perceptibly, though he made no reply, but merely took off his cap. His long, thick hair did not hide the prominent bumps on his head.

"Then, Arkady," Nikolai Petrovitch began again, turning to his son, "shall the horses be put to at once, or would you like to rest?"

"We will rest at home, daddy; tell them to harness the horses."

"At once, at once," his father assented. "Hey, Piotr, do you hear? Get things ready, my good boy; look sharp."

Piotr, who as a modernised servant had not kissed the young master's hand, but only bowed to him from a distance, again vanished through the gateway.

"I came here with the carriage, but there are three horses for your coach too," said Nikolai Petrovitch fussily, while Arkady drank some water from an iron dipper brought him by the woman in charge of the station, and Bazarov began smoking a pipe and went up to the driver, who was taking out the horses; "there are only two seats in the carriage, and I don't know how your friend . . ."

"He will go in the coach," interposed Arkady in an undertone. "You must not stand on ceremony with him, please. He's a splendid fellow, so simple—you will see."

Nikolai Petrovitch's coachman brought the horses round.

"Come, hurry up, bushy beard!" said Bazarov, addressing the driver.

"Do you hear, Mityuha," put in another driver, standing by with his hands thrust behind him into the opening of his sheepskin coat, "what the gentleman called you? It's bushy beard you are too."

Mityuha only gave a jog to his hat and pulled the reins off the heated shaft-horse.

"Look sharp, look sharp, lads, lend a hand," cried Nikolai Petrovitch; "there's be something to drink our health with!"

In a few minutes the horses were harnessed; the father and son were installed in the carriage; Piotr climbed up on to the box; Bazarov jumped into the coach, and nestled his head down into the leather cushion; and both the vehicles rolled away.

III

"So HERE YOU ARE, a graduate at last, and come home again," said Nikolai Petrovitch, touching Arkady now on the shoulder, now on the knee. "At last!"

"And how is uncle, quite well?" asked Arkady who, in spite of the genuine, almost childish delight filling his heart, wanted as soon as possible to turn the conversation from the emotional into a commonplace channel.

"Quite well. He was thinking of coming with me to meet you, but for some reason or other he gave up the idea."

"And how long have you been waiting for me?" inquired Arkady.

"Oh, about five hours."

"Dear old dad!"

Arkady turned round quickly to his father, and gave him a sounding kiss on the cheek. Nikolai Petrovitch gave vent to a low chuckle.

"I have got such a capital horse for you!" he began. "You will see. And your room has been fresh papered."

"And is there a room for Bazarov?"

"We will find one for him too."

"Please, dad, make much of him. I can't tell you how I prize his friendship."

"Have you made friends with him lately?"

"Yes, quite lately."

"Ah, that's how it is I did not see him last winter. What does he study?"

"His chief subject is natural science. But he knows everything. Next year he wants to take his doctor's degree."

"Ah! he's in the medical faculty," observed Nikolai Petrovitch, and he was silent for a little. "Piotr," he went on, stretching out his hand, "aren't those our peasants driving along?"

Piotr looked where his master was pointing. Some carts harnessed with unbridled horses were moving rapidly along a narrow by-road. In each cart there were one or two peasants in sheepskin coats, unbuttoned.

"Yes, sir," replied Piotr.

"Where are they going,—to the town?"

"To the town, I suppose. To the gin-shop," he added contemptuously, turning slightly towards the coachman, as though he would appeal to him. But the latter did not stir a muscle; he was a man of the old stamp, and did not share the modern views of the younger generation.

"I have had a lot of bother with the peasants this year," pursued Nikolai Petrovitch, turning to his son. "They won't pay their rent. What is one to do?"

"But do you like your hired labourers?"

"Yes," said Nikolai Petrovitch between his teeth. "They are being set against me, that's the mischief; and they don't do their best. They spoil the tools. But they have tilled the land pretty fairly. When things have settled down a bit, it will be all right. Do you take an interest in farming now?"

"You've no shade; that's a pity," remarked Arkady, without answering the last question.

"I have had a great awning put up on the north side over the balcony," observed Nikolai Petrovitch; "now we can have dinner even in the open air."

"It'll be rather too like a summer villa. . . . Still, that's all nonsense. What air though here! How delicious it smells! Really I fancy there's nowhere such fragrance in the world as in the meadows here! And the sky, too."

Arkady suddenly stopped short, cast a stealthy look behind him, and said no more

"Of course," observed Nikolai Petrovitch, "you were born here, and so everything is bound to strike you in a special——"

"Come, dad, that makes no difference where a man is born."

"Still——"

"No; it makes absolutely no difference."

Nikolai Petrovitch gave a sidelong glance at his son, and the carriage went on half-a-mile further before the conversation was renewed between them.

"I don't recollect whether I wrote to you," began Nikolai Petrovitch, "your old nurse, Yegorovna, is dead."

"Really? Poor thing! Is Prokofitch still living?"

"Yes, and not a bit changed. As grumbling as ever. In fact, you won't find many changes in Maryino."

"Have you still the same bailiff?"

"Well, to be sure, there is a change there. I decided not to keep about me any freed serfs, who have been house servants, or, at least, not to intrust them with duties of any responsibility." (Arkady glanced towards Piotr.) "*Il est libre, en effet*," observed Nikolai Petrovitch in an undertone; "but, you see, he's only a valet. Now I have a bailiff, a townsman; he seems a practical fellow. I pay him two hundred and fifty rubles a year. But," added Nikolai Petrovitch, rubbing his forehead and eyebrows with his hand, which was always an indication with him of inward embarrassment, "I told you just now that you would not find changes at Maryino. . . . That's not quite correct. I think it my duty to prepare you, though . . ."

He hesitated for an instant, and then went on in French.

"A severe moralist would regard my openness as improper; but, in the first place, it can't be concealed, and secondly, you are aware I have always had peculiar ideas as regards the relation of father and son. Though, of course, you would be right in blaming me. At my age . . . In short . . . that . . . that girl, about whom you have probably heard already . . ."

"Fenitchka?" asked Arkady easily.

Nikolai Petrovitch blushed. "Don't mention her name aloud, please. . . . Well . . . she is living with me now. I have installed her in the house . . . there were two little rooms there. But that can all be changed?"

"Goodness, daddy, what for?"

"Your friend is going to stay with us . . . it would be awkward . . ."

"Please, don't be uneasy on Bazarov's account. He's above all that."

"Well, but you, too," added Nikolai Petrovitch. "The little lodge is so horrid—that's the worst of it."

"Goodness, dad," interposed Arkady, "it's as if you were apologising; I wonder you're not ashamed."

"Of course, I ought to be ashamed," answered Nikolai Petrovitch, flushing more and more.

"Nonsense, dad, nonsense; please don't!" Arkady smiled affectionately. "What a thing to apologise for!" he thought to himself, and his heart was filled with a feeling of condescending tenderness for his kind, soft-hearted father, mixed with a sense of secret superiority. "Please stop," he repeated once more, instinctively revelling in a consciousness of his own advanced and emancipated condition.

Nikolai Petrovitch glanced at him from under the fingers of the hand with which he was still rubbing his forehead, and there was a pang in his heart. . . . But at once he blamed himself for it.

"Here are our meadows at last," he said, after a long silence.

"And that in front is our forest, isn't it?" asked Arkady.

"Yes. Only I have sold the timber. This year they will cut it down."

"Why did you sell it?"

"The money was needed; besides, that land is to go to the peasants."

"Who don't pay you their rent?"

"That's their affair; besides, they will pay it some day."

"I am sorry about the forest," observed Arkady, and he began to look about him.

The country through which they were driving could not be called picturesque. Fields upon fields stretched all along to the very horizon, now sloping gently upwards, then dropping down again; in some places woods were to be seen, and winding ravines, planted with low, scanty bushes, recalling vividly the representation of them on the old-fashioned maps of the times of Catherine. They came upon little streams too with hollow banks; and tiny lakes with narrow dykes; and little villages, with low hovels under dark and often tumble-down roofs, and slanting barns with walls woven of brushwood and gaping doorways beside neglected threshing-floors; and churches, some brick-built, with stucco peeling off in patches, others wooden, with crosses fallen askew, and overgrown graveyards. Slowly Arkady's heart sank. To complete the picture, the peasants they met were all in tatters and on the sorriest little nags; the willows, with their trunks stripped of bark, and broken branches, stood like ragged beggars along the roadside; cows lean and shaggy and looking pinched up by hunger, were greedily tearing at the grass along the ditches. They looked as though they had just been snatched out of the murderous clutches of some threatening monster; and the piteous state of the weak, starved beasts in the midst of the lovely spring day, called up, like a white phantom, the endless, comfortless winter, with its storms, and frosts, and snows. . . . "No," thought Arkady, "this is not a rich country; it does not impress one by plenty or industry; it can't, it can't go on like this, reforms are absolutely necessary . . . but how is one to carry them out, how is one to begin?"

Such were Arkady's reflections; . . . but even as he reflected, the spring regained its sway. All around was golden green, all—trees, bushes, grass—shone and stirred gently in wide waves under the soft breath of the warm wind; from all sides flooded the endless trilling music of the larks; the peewits were calling as they hovered over the low-lying meadows, or noiselessly ran over the tussocks of grass; the rooks strutted among the half-grown short spring-corn, standing out black against its tender green; they disappeared in the already whitening rye, only from time to time their heads peeped out amid its grey waves. Arkady gazed and gazed, and his reflections grew slowly fainter and passed away. . . . He flung off his coat and turned to his father, with a face so bright and boyish, that the latter gave him another hug.

"We're not far off now," remarked Nikolai Petrovitch; "we have only to get up this hill, and the house will be in sight. We shall get on together splendidly, Arkasha; you shall help me in farming the estate, if it isn't a bore to you. We must draw close to one another now, and learn to know each other thoroughly, mustn't we?"

"Of course," said Arkady; "but what an exquisite day it is to-day!"

"To welcome you, my dear boy. Yes, it's spring in its full loveliness. Though I agree with Pushkin—do you remember in Yevgeny Onyegin—

> *'To me how sad thy coming is,*
> *Spring, spring, sweet time of love!*
> *What . . .'*

"Arkady!" called Bazarov's voice from the coach, "send me a match; I've nothing to light my pipe with."

Nikolai Petrovitch stopped, while Arkady, who had begun listening to him with some surprise, though with sympathy, too, made haste to pull a silver matchbox out of his pocket, and sent it to Bazarov by Piotr.

"Will you have a cigar?" shouted Bazarov again.

"Thanks," answered Arkady.

Piotr returned to the carriage, and handed him with the match-box a thick black cigar, which Arkady began to smoke promptly, diffusing about him such a strong and pungent odour of cheap tobacco, that Nikolai Petrovitch, who had never been a smoker from his youth up, was forced to turn away his head, as imperceptibly as he could for fear of wounding his son.

A quarter of an hour later, the two carriages drew up before the steps of a new wooden house, painted grey, with a red iron roof. This was Maryino, also known as New-Wick, or, as the peasants had nicknamed it, Poverty Farm.

IV

No CROWD of house-serfs ran out on to the steps to meet the gentlemen; a little girl of twelve years old made her appearance alone. After her there came out of the house a young lad, very like Piotr, dressed in a coat of grey livery, with white armorial buttons, the servant of Pavel Petrovitch Kirsanov. Without speaking, he opened the door of the carriage, and un-buttoned the apron of the coach. Nikolai Petrovitch with his son and Bazarov walked through a dark and almost empty hall, from behind the door of which they caught a glimpse of a young woman's face, into a drawing-room furnished in the most modern style.

"Here we are at home," said Nikolai Petrovitch, taking off his cap, and shaking back his hair. "That's the great thing; now we must have supper and rest."

"A meal would not come amiss, certainly," observed Bazarov, stretching, and he dropped on to a sofa.

"Yes, yes, let us have supper, supper directly." Nikolai Petrovitch, with no apparent reason, stamped his foot. "And here just at the right moment comes Prokofitch."

A man about sixty entered, white-haired, thin, and swarthy, in a cinnamon-coloured dress-coat with brass buttons, and a pink neckerchief. He smirked, went up to kiss Arkady's hand, and bowing to the guest retreated to the door, and put his hands behind him.

"Here he is, Prokofitch," began Nikolai Petrovitch; "he's come back to us at last. . . . Well, how do you think him looking?"

"As well as could be," said the old man, and was grinning again, but he quickly knitted his bushy brows. "You wish supper to be served?" he said impressively.

"Yes, yes, please. But won't you like to go to your room first, Yevgeny Vassilyitch?"

"No, thanks; I don't care about it. Only give orders for my little box to be taken there, and this garment, too," he added, taking off his frieze overcoat.

"Certainly. Prokofitch, take the gentleman's coat." (Prokofitch, with an air of perplexity, picked up Bazarov's "garment" in both hands, and holding it high above his head, retreated on tiptoe.) "And you, Arkady, are you going to your room for a minute?"

"Yes, I must wash," answered Arkady, and was just moving towards the door, but at that instant there came into the drawing-room a man of medium height, dressed in a dark English suit, a fashionable low cravat, and kid shoes, Pavel Petrovitch Kirsanov. He looked about forty-five: his close-cropped, grey hair shone with a dark lustre, like new silver; his face, yellow but free from wrinkles, was exceptionally regular and pure in line, as though carved by a light and delicate chisel, and showed traces of remarkable beauty; specially fine were his clear, black, almond-shaped eyes. The whole person of Arkady's uncle, with its aristocratic elegance, had preserved the gracefulness of youth and that air of striving upwards, away from earth, which for the most part is lost after the twenties are past.

Pavel Petrovitch took out of his trouser pocket his exquisite hand with its long tapering pink nails, a hand which seemed still more exquisite from the snowy whiteness of the cuff, buttoned with a single, big opal, and gave it to his nephew. After a preliminary handshake in the European style, he kissed him thrice after the Russian fashion, that is to say, he touched his cheek three times with his perfumed moustaches, and said "Welcome."

Nikolai Petrovitch presented him to Bazarov; Pavel Petrovitch greeted him with a slight inclination of his supple figure, and a slight smile, but he did not give him his hand, and even put it back into his pocket.

"I had begun to think you were not coming to-day," he began in a musical voice, with a genial swing and shrug of the shoulders, as he showed his splendid white teeth. "Did anything happen on the road?"

"Nothing happened," answered Arkady; "we were rather slow. But we're as hungry as wolves now. Hurry up Prokofitch, dad; and I'll be back directly."

"Stay, I'm coming with you," cried Bazarov, pulling himself up suddenly from the sofa. Both the young men went out.

"Who is he?" asked Pavel Petrovitch.

"A friend of Arkasha's; according to him a very clever fellow."

"Is he going to stay with us?"

"Yes."

"That unkempt creature?"

"Why, yes."

Pavel Petrovitch drummed with his finger-tips on the table. "I fancy Arkady *s'est dégourdi*," he remarked. "I'm glad he has come back."

At supper there was little conversation. Bazarov especially said nothing, but he ate a great deal. Nikolai Petrovitch related various incidents in what he called his career as a farmer, talked about the impending government measures, about committees, deputations, the necessity of introducing machinery, etc. Pavel Petrovitch paced slowly up and down the dining-room (he never ate supper), sometimes sipping at a wineglass of red wine, and less often uttering some remark or rather exclamation, of the nature of "Ah! aha! hm!" Arkady told some news from Petersburg, but he was conscious of a little awkwardness, that awkwardness which usually overtakes a youth when he has just ceased to be a child, and has come back to a place where they are accustomed to regard him and treat him as a child. He made his sentences quite unnecessarily long, avoided the word "daddy," and even sometimes replaced it by the word "father," mumbled, it is true, between his teeth; with an exaggerated carelessness he poured into his glass far more wine than he really wanted, and drank it all off. Prokofitch did not take his eyes off him, and kept chewing his lips. After supper they all separated at once.

"Your uncle's a queer fish," Bazarov said to Arkady, as he sat in his dressing-gown by his bedside, smoking a short pipe. "Only fancy such style in the country! His nails, his nails—you ought to send them to an exhibition!"

"Why, of course, you don't know," replied Arkady. "He was a great swell in his own day, you know. I will tell you his story one day. He was very handsome, you know, used to turn all the women's heads."

"Oh, that's it, is it? So he keeps it up in the memory of the past. It's a pity there's no one for him to fascinate here, though. I kept staring at his exquisite collars. They're like marble, and his chin's shaved simply to perfection. Come, Arkady Nikolaitch, isn't that ridiculous?"

"Perhaps it is; but he's a splendid man, really."

"An antique survival! But your father's a capital fellow. He wastes his time reading poetry, and doesn't know much about farming, but he's a good-hearted fellow."

"My father's a man in a thousand."

"Did you notice how shy and nervous he is?"

Arkady shook his head as though he himself were not shy and nervous.

"It's something astonishing," pursued Bazarov, "these old idealists, they develop their nervous systems till they break down . . . so balance is lost. But good-night. In my room there's an English washstand, but the door won't fasten. Anyway that ought to be encouraged—an English washstand stands for progress!"

Bazarov went away, and a sense of great happiness came over Arkady. Sweet it is to fall asleep in one's own home, in the familiar bed, under the quilt worked by loving hands, perhaps a dear nurse's hands, those kind, tender, untiring hands. Arkady remembered Yegorovna, and sighed and wished her peace in heaven. . . . For himself he made no prayer.

Both he and Bazarov were soon asleep, but others in the house were awake long after. His son's return had agitated Nikolai Petrovitch. He lay down in bed, but did not put out the candles, and his head propped on his hand, he fell into long reveries. His brother was sitting long after midnight in his study, in a wide armchair before the fireplace, on which there smouldered some faintly glowing embers. Pavel Petrovitch was not undressed, only some red Chinese slippers had replaced the kid shoes on his feet. He held in his hand the last number of *Galignani*, but he was not reading; he gazed fixedly into the grate, where a bluish flame flickered, dying down, then flaring up again. . . . God knows where his thoughts were rambling, but they were not rambling in the past only; the expression of his face was concentrated and surly, which is not the way when a man is absorbed solely in recollections. In a small back room there sat, on a large chest, a young woman in a blue dressing jacket with a white kerchief thrown over her dark hair, Fenitchka. She was half listening, half dozing, and often looked across towards the open door through which a child's cradle was visible, and the regular breathing of a sleeping baby could be heard.

V

THE next morning Bazarov woke up earlier than any one and went out of the house. "Oh, my!" he thought, looking about him, "the little place isn't much to boast of!" When Nikolai Petrovitch had divided the land with his peasants, he had had to build his new manor-house on four acres of perfectly flat and barren land. He had built a house, offices, and farm buildings, laid out a garden, dug a pond, and sunk two wells; but the young trees had not done well, very little water had collected in the pond, and that in the wells tasted brackish. Only one arbour of lilac and acacia had grown fairly well; they sometimes had tea and dinner in it. In a few minutes Bazarov had traversed all the little paths of the garden; he went into the cattle-yard and the stable, routed out two farm-boys, with whom he made friends at once, and set off with them to a small swamp about a mile from the house to look for frogs.

"What do you want frogs for, sir?" one of the boys asked him.

"I'll tell you what for," answered Bazarov, who possessed the special faculty of inspiring confidence in people of a lower class, though he never tried to win them, and behaved very casually with them; "I shall cut the frog open, and see what's going on in his inside, and then, as you and I are much the same as frogs, only that we walk on legs, I shall know what's going on inside us, too."

"And what do you want to know that for?"

"So as not to make a mistake, if you're taken ill, and I have to cure you."

"Are you a doctor, then?"

"Yes."

"Vaska, do you hear, the gentleman says you and I are the same as frogs—that's funny!"

"I'm afraid of frogs," observed Vaska, a boy of seven, with a head as white as flax, and bare feet, dressed in a grey smock with a stand-up collar.

"What is there to be afraid of? Do they bite?"

"There, paddle into the water, philosophers," said Bazarov.

Meanwhile Nikolai Petrovitch, too, had waked up, and gone in to see Arkady, whom he found dressed. The father and son went out on to the terrace under the shelter of the awning; near the balustrade, on the table, among great bunches of lilac, the samovar was already boiling. A little girl came up, the same who had been the first to meet them at the steps on their arrival the evening before. In a shrill voice she said—

"Fedosya Nikolaevna is not quite well; she cannot come; she gave orders to ask you, will you please to pour out tea yourself, or should she send Dunyasha?"

"I will pour out myself, myself," interposed Nikolai Petrovitch hurriedly. "Arkady, how do you take your tea, with cream, or with lemon?"

"With cream," answered Arkady; and after a brief silence, he uttered interrogatively, "Daddy?"

Nikolai Petrovitch in confusion looked at his son.

"Well?" he said.

Arkady dropped his eyes.

"Forgive me, dad, if my question seems unsuitable to you," he began, "but you yourself, by your openness yesterday, encourage me to be open . . . you will not be angry . . . ?"

"Go on."

"You give me confidence to ask you. . . . Isn't the reason Fen . . . isn't the reason she will not come here to pour out tea, because I'm here?"

Nikolai Petrovitch turned slightly away.

"Perhaps," he said, at last, "she supposes . . . she is ashamed."

Arkady turned a rapid glance on his father.

"She has no need to be ashamed. In the first place, you are aware of my views" (it was very sweet to Arkady to utter that word); "and, secondly, could I be willing to hamper your life, your habits, in the least thing? Besides, I am sure you could not make a bad choice; if you have allowed her to live under the same roof with you, she must be worthy of it; in any case, a son cannot judge his father,—least of all, I, and least of all such a father who, like you, has never hampered my liberty in anything."

Arkady's voice had been shaky at the beginning; he felt himself magnanimous, though at the same time he realised he was delivering something of the nature of a lecture to his father; but the sound of one's own voice has a powerful effect on any man, and Arkady brought out his last words resolutely, even with emphasis.

"Thanks, Arkasha," said Nikolai Petrovitch thickly, and his fingers again strayed over his eyebrows and forehead. "Your suppositions are just in fact. Of course, if this girl had not deserved. . . . It is not a frivolous caprice. It's not easy for me to talk to you about this; but you will understand that it is difficult for her to come here, in your presence, especially the first day of your return."

"In that case I will go to her," cried Arkady, with a fresh rush of magnanimous feeling, and he jumped up from his seat. "I will explain to her that she has no need to be ashamed before me."

Nikolai Petrovitch, too, got up.

"Arkady," he began, "be so good . . . how can . . . there . . . I have not told you yet . . ."

But Arkady did not listen to him, and ran off the terrace. Nikolai Petrovitch looked after him, and sank into his chair overcome by confusion. His heart began to throb. Did he at that moment realise the inevitable strangeness of the future relations between him and his son? Was he conscious that Arkady would perhaps have shown him more respect if he had never touched on this subject at all? Did he reproach himself for weakness?—it is hard to say; all these feelings were within him, but in the state of sensations—and vague sensations—while the flush did not leave his face, and his heart throbbed.

There was the sound of hurrying footsteps, and Arkady came on to the terrace. "We have made friends, dad!" he cried, with an expression of a kind of affectionate and good-natured triumph on his face. "Fedosya Nikolaevna is not quite well to-day really, and she will come a little later. But why didn't you tell me I had a brother? I should have kissed him last night, as I have kissed him just now."

Nikolai Petrovitch tried to articulate something, tried to get up and open his arms. Arkady flung himself on his neck.

"What's this, embracing again?" sounded the voice of Pavel Petrovitch behind them.

Father and son were equally rejoiced at his appearance at that instant; there are positions, genuinely affecting, from which one longs to escape as soon as possible.

"Why should you be surprised at that?" said Nikolai Petrovitch gaily.

"Think what ages I have been waiting for Arkasha. I've not had time to get a good look at him since yesterday."

"I'm not at all surprised," observed Pavel Petrovitch; "I feel not indisposed to be embracing him myself."

Arkady went up to his uncle, and again felt his cheeks caressed by his perfumed moustache. Pavel Petrovitch sat down to the table. He wore an elegant morning suit in the English style, and a gay little fez on his head. This fez and the carelessly tied little cravat carried a suggestion of the freedom of country life, but the stiff collars of his shirt—not white, it is true, but striped, as is correct in morning dress—stood up as inexorably as ever against his well-shaved chin.

"Where's your new friend?" he asked Arkady.

"He's not in the house; he usually gets up early and goes off somewhere. The great thing is, we mustn't pay any attention to him; he doesn't like ceremony."

"Yes, that's obvious." Pavel Petrovitch began deliberately spreading butter on his bread. "Is he going to stay long with us?"

"Perhaps. He came here on the way to his father's."

"And where does his father live?"

"In our province, sixty-four miles from here. He has a small property there. He was formerly an army doctor."

"Tut, tut, tut! To be sure, I kept asking myself, 'Where have I heard that name, Bazarov?' Nikolai, do you remember in our father's division there was a surgeon Bazarov?"

"I believe there was."

"Yes, yes, to be sure. So that surgeon was his father. Hm!" Pavel Petrovitch pulled his moustaches. "Well, and what is Mr. Bazarov himself?" he asked, deliberately.

"What is Bazarov?" Arkady smiled. "Would you like me, uncle, to tell you what he really is?"

"If you will be so good, nephew."

"He's a nihilist."

"Eh?" inquired Nikolai Petrovitch, while Pavel Petrovitch lifted a knife in the air with a small piece of butter on its tip, and remained motionless.

"He's a nihilist," repeated Arkady.

"A nihilist," said Nikolai Petrovitch. "That's from the Latin, *nihil, nothing*, as far as I can judge; the word must mean a man who . . . who accepts nothing?"

"Say, 'who respects nothing,' " put in Pavel Petrovitch, and he set to work on the butter again.

"Who regards everything from the critical point of view," observed Arkady.

"Isn't that just the same thing?" inquired Pavel Petrovitch.

"No, it's not the same thing. A nihilist is a man who does not bow down before any authority, who does not take any principle on faith, whatever reverence that principle may be enshrined in."

"Well, and is that good?" interrupted Pavel Petrovitch.

"That depends, uncle. Some people it will do good to, but some people will suffer for it."

"Indeed. Well, I see it's not in our line. We are old-fashioned people; we imagine that without principles, taken as you say on faith, there's no taking a step, no breathing. *Vous avez changé tout cela*. God give you good health and the rank of a general, while we will be content to look on and admire, worthy . . . what was it?"

"Nihilists," Arkady said, speaking very distinctly.

"Yes. There used to be Hegelists, and now there are nihilists. We shall see how you will exist in void, in vacuum; and now ring, please, brother Nikolai Petrovitch; it's time I had my cocoa."

Nikolai Petrovitch rang the bell and called "Dunyasha!" But instead of Dunyasha, Fenitchka herself came on to the terrace. She was a young woman about three-and-twenty, with a white soft skin, dark hair and eyes, red, childishly-pouting lips, and little delicate hands. She wore a neat print dress; a new blue kerchief lay lightly on her plump shoulders. She carried a large cup of cocoa, and setting it down before Pavel Petrovitch, she was overwhelmed with confusion; the hot blood rushed in a wave of crimson over the delicate skin of her pretty face. She dropped her eyes, and stood at the table, leaning a little on the very tips of her fingers. It seemed as though she were ashamed of having come in, and at the same time felt that she had a right to come.

Pavel Petrovitch knitted his brows severely while Nikolai Petrovitch looked embarrassed.

"Good morning, Fenitchka," he muttered through his teeth.

"Good morning," she replied in a voice not loud but resonant, and with a sidelong glance at Arkady, who gave her a friendly smile, she went gently away. She walked with a slightly rolling gait, but even that suited her.

For some minutes silence reigned on the terrace. Pavel Petrovitch sipped his cocoa; suddenly he raised his head. "Here is Sir Nihilist coming towards us," he said in an undertone.

Bazarov was in fact approaching through the garden, stepping over the flower-beds. His linen coat and trousers were besmeared with mud; clinging marsh weed was twined round the crown of his old round hat; in his right hand he held a small bag; in the bag something alive was moving. He quickly drew near the terrace, and said with a nod, "Good morning, gentlemen; sorry I was late for tea; I'll be back directly; I must just put these captives away."

"What have you there—leeches?" asked Pavel Petrovitch.

"No, frogs."

"Do you eat them—or keep them?"

"For experiment," said Bazarov indifferently, and he went off into the house.

"So he's going to cut them up," observed Pavel Petrovitch. "He has no faith in principles, but he has faith in frogs."

Arkady looked compassionately at his uncle; Nikolai Petrovitch shrugged his shoulders stealthily. Pavel Petrovitch himself felt that his epigram was unsuccessful, and began to talk about husbandry and the new bailiff, who had come to him the evening before to complain that a labourer, Foma, "was deboshed," and quite unmanageable. "He's such an Æsop," he said among other things; "in all places he had protested himself a worthless fellow; he's not a man to keep his place; he'll walk off in a huff like a fool."

VI

BAZAROV came back, sat down to the table, and began hastily drinking tea. The two brothers looked at him in silence, while Arkady stealthily watched first his father and then his uncle.

"Did you walk far from here?" Nikolai Petrovitch asked at last.

"Where you've a little swamp near the aspen wood. I started some half-dozen snipe; you might slaughter them, Arkady."

"Aren't you a sportsman, then?"

"No."

"Is your special study physics?" Pavel Petrovitch in his turn inquired.

"Physics, yes; and natural science in general."

"They say the Teutons of late have had great success in that line."

"Yes; the Germans are our teachers in it." Bazarov answered carelessly.

The word Teutons instead of Germans, Pavel Petrovitch had used with ironical intention; none noticed it, however.

"Have you such a high opinion of the Germans?" said Pavel Petrovitch, with exaggerated courtesy. He was beginning to feel a secret irritation. His aristocratic nature was revolted by Bazarov's absolute nonchalance. This surgeon's son was not only not overawed, he even gave abrupt and indifferent answers, and in the tone of his voice there was something churlish, almost insolent.

"The scientific men there are a clever lot."

"Ah, ah. To be sure, of Russian scientific men you have not such a flattering opinion, I dare say?"

"That's very likely."

"That's very praiseworthy self-abnegation," Pavel Petrovitch declared, drawing himself up, and throwing his head back. "But how is this? Arkady Nikolaitch was telling us just now that you accept no authorities. Don't you believe in *them?*"

"And how am I accepting them? And what am I to believe in? They tell me the truth, I agree, that's all."

"And do all Germans tell the truth?" said Pavel Petrovitch, and his face assumed an expression as unsympathetic, as remote, as if he had withdrawn to some cloudy height.

"Not all," replied Bazarov, with a short yawn. He obviously did not care to continue the discussion.

Pavel Petrovitch glanced at Arkady, as though he would say to him, "Your friend's polite, I must say." "For my own part," he began again, not without some effort, "I am so unregenerate as not to like Germans. Russian Germans I am not speaking of now; we all know what sort of creatures they are. But even German Germans are not to my liking. In former days there were some here and there; they had—well, Schiller, to be sure, Goethe . . . my brother—he takes a particularly favourable view of them. . . . But now they have all turned chemists and materialists. . . ."

"A good chemist is twenty times as useful as any poet," broke in Bazarov.

"Oh, indeed," commented Pavel Petrovitch, and, as though falling asleep, he faintly raised his eyebrows. "You don't acknowledge art then, I suppose?"

"The art of making money or of advertising pills!" cried Bazarov, with a contemptuous laugh.

"Ah, ah. You are pleased to jest, I see. You reject all that, no doubt? Granted. Then you believe in science only?"

"I have already explained to you that I don't believe in anything; and what is science—science in the abstract? There are sciences, as there are trades and crafts; but abstract science doesn't exist at all."

"Very good. Well, and in regard to the other traditions accepted in human conduct, do you maintain the same negative attitude?"

"What's this, an examination?" asked Bazarov.

Pavel Petrovitch turned slightly pale. . . . Nikolai Petrovitch thought it his duty to interpose in the conversation.

"We will converse on this subject with you more in detail some day, dear Yevgeny Vassilyitch; we will hear your views, and express our own. For my part, I am heartily glad you are studying the natural sciences. I have heard that Liebig has made some wonderful discoveries in the amelioration of soils. You can be of assistance to me in my agricultural labours; you can give me some useful advice."

"I am at your service, Nikolai Petrovitch; but Liebig's miles over our heads! One has first to learn the a b c, and then begin to read, and we haven't set eyes on the alphabet yet."

"You are certainly a nihilist, I see that," thought Nikolai Petrovitch. "Still, you will allow me to apply to you on occasion," he added aloud. "And now I fancy, brother, it's time for us to be going to have a talk with the bailiff."

Pavel Petrovitch got up from his seat.

"Yes," he said, without looking at any one; "it's a misfortune to live five years in the country like this, far from mighty intellects! You turn into a fool directly. You may try not to forget what you've been taught, but—in a snap!—they'll prove all that's rubbish, and tell you that sensible men have nothing more to do with such foolishness, and that you, if you please, are an antiquated old fogey. What's to be done? Young people, of course, are cleverer than we are!"

Pavel Petrovitch turned slowly on his heels, and slowly walked away; Nikolai Petrovitch went after him.

"Is he always like that?" Bazarov coolly inquired of Arkady, directly the door had closed behind the two brothers.

"I must say, Yevgeny, you weren't nice to him," remarked Arkady. "You have hurt his feelings."

"Well, am I going to consider them, these provincial aristocrats! Why, it's all vanity, dandy habits, fatuity. He should have continued his career in Petersburg, if that's his bent. But there, enough of him! I've found a rather rare species of a water-beetle, *Dytiscus marginatus;* do you know it? I will show you."

"I promised to tell you his story," began Arkady.

"The story of the beetle?"

"Come, don't, Yevgeny. The story of my uncle. You will see he's not the sort of man you fancy. He deserves pity rather than ridicule."

"I don't dispute it; but why are you worrying over him?"

"One ought to be just, Yevgeny."

"How does that follow?"

"No; listen . . ."

And Arkady told him his uncle's story. The reader will find it in the following chapter.

VII

PAVEL PETROVITCH KIRSANOV was educated first at home, like his younger brother, and afterwards in the Corps of Pages. From childhood he was distinguished by remarkable beauty; moreover he was self-confident, somewhat ironical, and had a rather biting humour; he could not fail to please. He began to be seen everywhere, directly he had received his commission as an officer. He was much admired in society, and he indulged every whim, even every caprice and every folly, and gave himself airs, but that too was attractive in him. Women went out of their senses over him; men called him a coxcomb, and were secretly jealous of him. He lived, as has been related already, in the same apartments as his brother, whom he loved sincerely, though he was not at all like him. Nikolai Petrovitch was a little lame, he had small, pleasing features of a rather melancholy cast, small, black eyes, and thin, soft hair; he liked being lazy, but he also liked reading, and was timid in society. Pavel Petrovitch did not spend a single evening at home, prided himself on his ease and audacity (he was just bringing gymnastics into fashion among young men in society), and had read in all some five or six French books. At twenty-eight he was already a captain; a brilliant career awaited him. Suddenly everything was changed.

At that time, there was sometimes seen in Petersburg society a woman who has even yet not been forgotten, Princess R——. She had a well-educated, well-bred, but rather stupid husband, and no children. She used suddenly to go abroad, and suddenly to return to Russia, and led an eccentric life in general. She had the reputation of being a frivolous coquette, abandoned herself eagerly to every sort of pleasure, danced to exhaustion, laughed and jested with young men, whom she received in the dim light of her drawing-room before dinner; while at night she wept and prayed, found no peace in anything, and often paced her room till morning, wringing her hands in anguish, or sat, pale and chill, over a psalter. Day came, and she was transformed again into a grand lady; again she went out, laughed, chattered, and simply flung herself headlong into anything which could afford her the slightest distraction. She was marvellously well-proportioned, her hair coloured like gold and heavy as gold hung below her knees, but no one would have called her a beauty; in her whole face the only good point was her eyes, and even her eyes were not good—they were grey, and not large—but their glance was swift and deep, unconcerned to the point of audacity, and thoughtful to the point of melancholy—an enigmatic glance. There was a light of something extraordinary in them, even while her tongue was lisping the emptiest of inanities. She dressed with elaborate care. Pavel Petrovitch met her at a ball, danced a mazurka with her, in the course of which she did not utter a single rational word, and fell passionately in love with her. Being accustomed to make conquests, in this instance, too, he soon attained his object, but his easy success did not damp his ardour. On the contrary, he was in still more torturing, still closer bondage to this woman, in whom, even at the very moment when she surrendered herself utterly, there seemed always something still mysterious and unattainable, to which none could penetrate. What was hidden in that soul—God knows! It seemed as though she were in the power of mysterious forces, incomprehensible even to herself; they seemed to play on her at will; her intellect was not powerful enough to master their caprices. Her whole behaviour presented a series of inconsistencies; the only letters which could have awakened her husband's just suspicions, she wrote to a man who was almost a stranger to her, whilst her love had always an element of melancholy; with a man she had chosen as a lover, she ceased to laugh and to jest, she listened to him, and gazed at him with a look of bewilderment. Sometimes, for the most part suddenly, this bewilderment passed into chill horror; her face took a wild, death-like expression; she locked herself up in her bedroom, and her maid, putting an ear to the keyhole, could hear her smothered sobs. More than once, as he went home after a tender interview, Kirsanov felt within him that heartrending, bitter vexation which follows on a total failure.

"What more do I want?" he asked himself, while his heart was heavy. He once gave her a ring with a sphinx engraved on the stone.

"What's that?" she asked; "a sphinx?"

"Yes," he answered, "and that sphinx is you."

"I?" she queried, and slowly raising her enigmatical glance upon him. "Do you know that's awfully flattering?" she added with a meaningless smile, while her eyes still kept the same strange look.

Pavel Petrovitch suffered even while Princess R—— loved him; but when she grew cold to him, and that happened rather quickly, he almost went out of his mind. He was on the rack, and he was jealous; he gave her no peace, followed her about everywhere; she grew sick of his pursuit of her, and she went abroad. He resigned his commission in spite of the entreaties of his friends and the exhortations of his superiors, and followed the princess; four years he spent in foreign countries, at one time pursuing her, at another time intentionally losing sight of her. He was ashamed of himself, he was disgusted with his own lack of spirit . . . but nothing availed. Her image, that incomprehensible, almost meaningless, but bewitching image, was deeply rooted in his heart. At Baden he once more regained his old footing with her; it seemed as though she had never loved him so passionately . . . but in a month it was all at an end: the flame flickered up for the last time and went out forever. Foreseeing inevitable separation, he wanted at least to remain her friend, as though friendship with such a woman was possible. . . . She secretly left Baden, and from that time steadily avoided Kirsanov. He returned to Russia, and tried to live his former life again; but he could not get back into the old groove. He wandered from place to place like a man possessed; he still went into society; he still retained the habits of a man of the world; he could boast of two or three fresh conquests; but he no longer expected anything much of himself or of others, and he undertook nothing. He grew old and grey; spending all his evenings at the club, jaundiced and bored, and arguing in bachelor society became a necessity for him—a bad sign, as we all know. Marriage, of course, he did not even think of. Ten years passed in this way; they passed by colourless and fruitless—and quickly, fearfully quickly. Nowhere does time fly past as in Russia; in prison they say it flies even faster. One day at dinner at the club, Pavel Petrovitch heard of the death of the Princess R——. She had died at Paris in a state bordering on insanity. He got up from the table, and a long time he paced about the rooms of the club, or stood stockstill near the card-players, but he did not go home earlier than usual. Some time later he received a packet addressed to him; in it was the ring he had given the princess. She had drawn lines in the shape of a cross over the sphinx and sent him word that the solution of the enigma—was the cross.

This happened at the beginning of the year 1848, at the very time when Nikolai Petrovitch came to Petersburg, after the loss of his wife. Pavel Petrovitch had scarcely seen his brother since the latter had settled in the country; the marriage of Nikolai Petrovitch had coincided with the very first days of Pavel Petrovitch's acquaintance with the princess. When he came back from abroad, he had gone to him with the intention of staying a couple of months with him, in sympathetic enjoyment of his happiness, but he had only succeeded in standing a week of it. The difference in the positions of the two brothers was too great. In 1848, this difference had grown less; Nikolai Petrovitch had lost his wife, Pavel Petrovitch had lost his memories; after the death of the princess he tried not to think of her. But to Nikolai, there remained the sense of a well-spent life, his son was growing up under his eyes; Pavel, on the contrary, a solitary bachelor, was entering upon that indefinite twilight period of regrets that are akin to hopes, and hopes that are akin to regrets, when youth is over, while old age has not yet come.

This time was harder for Pavel Petrovitch than for another man; in losing his past, he lost everything.

"I will not invite you to Maryino now," Nikolai Petrovitch said to him one day, (he had called his property by that name in honour of his wife); "you were dull there in my dear wife's time, and now I think you would be bored to death."

"I was stupid and fidgety then," answered Pavel Petrovitch; "since then I have grown quieter, if not wiser. On the contrary, now, if you will let me, I am ready to settle with you for good."

For all answer Nikolai Petrovitch embraced him; but a year and a half passed after this conversation, before Pavel Petrovitch made up his mind to carry out his intention. When he was once settled in the country, however, he did not leave it, even during the three winters which Nikolai Petrovitch spent in Petersburg with his son. He began to read, chiefly English; he arranged his whole life, roughly speaking, in the English style, rarely saw the neighbours, and only went out to the election of marshals, where he was generally silent, only occasionally annoying and alarming land-owners of the old school by his liberal sallies, and not associating with the representatives of the younger generation. Both the latter and the former considered him "stuck up"; and both parties respected him for his fine aristocratic manners; for his reputation for successes in love; for the fact that he was very well dressed and always stayed in the best room in the best hotel; for the fact that he generally dined well, and had once even dined with Wellington at Louis Philippe's table; for the fact that he always took everywhere with him a real silver dressing-case and a portable bath; for the fact that he always smelt of some exceptionally "good form" scent; for the fact that he played whist in masterly fashion, and always lost; and lastly, they respected him also for his incorruptible honesty. Ladies considered him enchantingly romantic, but he did not cultivate ladies' acquaintance. . . .

"So you see, Yevgeny," observed Arkady, as he finished his story, "how unjustly you judge of my uncle! To say nothing of his having more than once helped my father out of difficulties, given him all his money—the property, perhaps you don't know, wasn't divided—he's glad to help any one, among other things he always sticks up for the peasants; it's true, when he talks to them he frowns and sniffs eau de cologne." . . .

"His nerves, no doubt," put in Bazarov.

"Perhaps; but his heart is very good. And he's far from being stupid. What useful advice he has given me especially . . . especially in regard to relations with women."

"Aha! a scalded dog fears cold water, we know that!"

"In short," continued Arkady, "he's profoundly unhappy, believe me; it's a sin to despise him."

"And who does despise him?" retorted Bazarov. "Still, I must say that a fellow who stakes his whole life on one card—a woman's love—and when that card fails, turns sour, and lets himself go till he's fit for nothing, is not a man, but a male. You say he's unhappy; you ought to know best; to be sure, he's not got rid of all his fads. I'm convinced that he solemnly imagines himself a superior creature because he reads that wretched *Galignani*, and once a month saves a peasant from a flogging."

"But remember his education, the age in which he grew up," observed Arkady.

"Education?" broke in Bazarov. "Every man must educate himself, just as I've done, for instance. . . . And as for the age, why should I depend on it? Let it rather depend on me. No, my dear fellow, that's all shallow-ness, want of backbone! And what stuff it all is, about these mysterious relations between a man and woman? We physiologists know what these relations are. You study the anatomy of the eye; where does the enigmatical glance you talk about come in there? That's all romantic, nonsensical, æsthetic rot. We had much better go and look at the beetle."

And the two friends went off to Bazarov's room, which was already pervaded by a sort of medico-surgical odour, mingled with the smell of cheap tobacco.

VIII

PAVEL PETROVITCH did not long remain present at his brother's interview with his bailiff, a tall, thin man with a sweet consumptive voice and knavish eyes, who to all Nikolai Petrovitch's remarks answered, "Certainly, sir," and tried to make the peasants out to be thieves and drunkards. The estate had only recently been put on to the new reformed system, and the new mechanism worked, creaking like an ungreased wheel, warping and cracking like home-made furniture of unseasoned wood. Nikolai Petrovitch did not lose heart, but often he sighed, and was gloomy; he felt that the thing could not go on without money, and his money was almost all spent. Arkady had spoken the truth; Pavel Petrovitch had more than once helped his brother; more than once, seeing him struggling and cudgelling his brains, at a loss which way to turn, Pavel Petrovitch moved deliberately to the window, and with his hands thrust into his pockets, muttered between his teeth, "*mais je puis vous donner de l'argent,*" and gave him money; but to-day he had none himself, and he preferred to go away. The petty details of agri-cultural management worried him; besides, it constantly struck him that Nikolai Petrovitch, for all his zeal and industry, did not set about things in the right way, though he would not have been able to point out precisely where Nikolai Petrovitch's mistake lay. "My brother's not practical enough," he reasoned to himself; "they impose upon him." Nikolai Petrovitch, on the other hand, had the highest opinion of Pavel Petrovitch's practical ability, and always asked his advice. "I'm a soft, weak fellow, I've spent my life in the wilds," he used to say; "while you haven't seen so much of the world for nothing, you see through people; you have an eagle eye." In answer to which Pavel Petrovitch only turned away, but did not contradict his brother.

Leaving Nikolai Petrovitch in his study, he walked along the corridor, which separated the front part of the house from the back; when he had reached a low door, he stopped in hesitation, then pulling his moustaches, he knocked at it.

"Who's there? Come in," sounded Fenitchka's voice.

"It's I," said Pavel Petrovitch, and he opened the door.

Fenitchka jumped up from the chair on which she was sitting with her baby, and giving him into the arms of a girl, who at once carried him out of the room, she put straight her kerchief hastily.

"Pardon me, if I disturb you," began Pavel Petrovitch, not looking at her; "I only wanted to ask you . . . they are sending into the town to-day, I think . . . please let them buy me some green tea."

"Certainly," answered Fenitchka; "how much do you desire them to buy?"

"Oh, half a pound will be enough, I imagine. You have made a change here, I see," he added, with a rapid glance round him, which glided over Fenitchka's face too. "The curtains here," he explained, seeing she did not understand him.

"Oh, yes, the curtains; Nikolai Petrovitch was so good as to make me a present of them; but they have been put up a long while now."

"Yes, and it's a long while since I have been to see you. Now it is very nice here."

"Thanks to Nikolai Petrovitch's kindness," murmured Fenitchka.

"You are more comfortable here than in the little lodge you used to have?" inquired Pavel Petrovitch urbanely, but without the slightest smile.

"Certainly, it's more comfortable."

"Who has been put in your place now?"

"The laundry-maids are there now."

"Ah!"

Pavel Petrovitch was silent. "Now he is going," thought Fenitchka; but he did not go, and she stood before him motionless.

"What did you send your little one away for?" said Pavel Petrovitch at last. "I love children; let me see him."

Fenitchka blushed all over with confusion and delight. She was afraid of Pavel Petrovitch; he had scarcely ever spoken to her.

"Dunyasha," she called: "will you bring Mitya, please." (Fenitchka did not treat any one in the house familiarly.) "But wait a minute, he must have a frock on," Fenitchka was going towards the door.

"That doesn't matter," remarked Pavel Petrovitch.

"I will be back directly," answered Fenitchka, and she went out quickly.

Pavel Petrovitch was left alone, and he looked round this time with special attention. The small low-pitched room in which he found himself was very clean and snug. It smelt of the freshly painted floor and of camomile. Along the walls stood chairs with lyre-shaped backs, bought by the late general on his campaign in Poland; in one corner was a little bedstead under a muslin canopy beside an iron-clamped chest with a convex lid. In the opposite corner a little lamp was burning before a big dark picture of St. Nikolai the wonder-worker; a tiny porcelain egg hung by a red ribbon from the protruding gold halo down to the saint's breast; by the windows greenish glass jars of last year's jam carefully tied down could be seen; on their paper covers Fenitchka herself had written in big letters "Gooseberry"; Nikolai Petrovitch was particularly fond of that preserve. On a long cord from the ceiling a cage hung with a short-tailed siskin in it; he was constantly chirping and hopping about, the cage was constantly shaking and swinging, while hempseeds fell with a light tap on to the floor. On the wall just above a small chest of drawers hung some rather bad photographs of Nikolai Petrovitch in various attitudes, taken by an itinerant photographer; there too hung a photograph of Fenitchka herself, which was an absolute failure; it was an eyeless face wearing a forced smile, in a dingy frame, nothing more could be made out; while above Fenitchka, General Yermolov, in a Circassian cloak, scowled menacingly upon the Caucasian mountains in the distance, from beneath a little silk shoe for pins which fell right on to his brows.

Five minutes passed; bustling and whispering could be heard in the next room. Pavel Petrovitch took up from the chest of drawers a greasy book, an odd volume of Masalsky's *Musketeer*, and turned over a few pages. . . . The door opened, and Fenitchka came in with Mitya in her arms. She had put on him a little red smock with embroidery on the collar, had combed his hair and washed his face; he was breathing heavily, his whole body working, and his little hands waving in the air, as is the way with all healthy babies; but his smart smock obviously impressed him, an expression of delight was reflected in every part of his little fat person. Fenitchka had put her own hair too in order, and had arranged her kerchief; but she might well have remained as she was. And really is there anything in the world more captivating than a beautiful young mother with a healthy baby in her arms?

"What a chubby fellow!" said Pavel Petrovitch graciously, and he tickled Mitya's little double chin with the tapering nail of his forefinger. The baby stared at the siskin, and chuckled.

"That's uncle," said Fenitchka, bending her face down to him and slightly rocking him, while Dunyasha quietly set in the window a smouldering, perfumed stick, putting a half-penny under it.

"How many months old is he?" asked Pavel Petrovitch.

"Six months; it will soon be seven, on the eleventh."

"Isn't it eight, Fedosya Nikolaevna?" put in Dunyasha, with some timidity.

"No, seven; what an idea!" The baby chuckled again, stared at the chest, and suddenly caught hold of his mother's nose and mouth with all his five little fingers. "Saucy mite," said Fenitchka, not drawing her face away.

"He's like my brother," observed Pavel Petrovitch.

"Who else should he be like?" thought Fenitchka.

"Yes," continued Pavel Petrovitch, as though speaking to himself; "there's an unmistakable likeness." He looked attentively, almost mournfully, at Fenitchka.

"That's uncle," she repeated, in a whisper this time.

"Ah! Pavel! so you're here!" was heard suddenly the voice of Nikolai Petrovitch.

Pavel Petrovitch turned hurriedly round, frowning; but his brother looked at him with such delight, such gratitude, that he could not help responding to his smile.

"You've a splendid little cherub," he said, and looking at his watch. "I came in here to speak about some tea."

And, assuming an expression of indifference, Pavel Petrovitch went out of the room.

"Did he come of himself?" Nikolai Petrovitch asked Fenitchka.

"Yes; he knocked and came in."

"Well, and has Arkasha been in to see you again?"

"No. Hadn't I better move into the lodge, Nikolai Petrovitch?"

"Why so?"

"I wonder whether it wouldn't be best just for the first."

"N—no," Nikolai Petrovitch brought out hesitatingly, rubbing his forehead. "We ought to have done it before. . . . How are you, fatty?" he said, suddenly brightening, and going up to the baby, he kissed him on the cheek; then he bent a little and pressed his lips to Fenitchka's hand, which lay white as milk upon Mitya's little red smock.

"Nikolai Petrovitch! what are you doing?" she whispered, dropping her eyes, then slowly raised them. Very charming was the expression of her eyes when she peeped, as it were, from under her lids, and smiled tenderly and a little foolishly.

Nikolai Petrovitch had made Fenitchka's acquaintance in the following manner. He had once happened three years before to stay a night at an inn in a remote district town. He was agreeably struck by the cleanness of the room assigned to him, the freshness of the bed-linen. Surely the woman of the house must be a German, was the idea that occurred to him; but she proved to be a Russian, a woman of about fifty, neatly dressed, of a good-looking, sensible countenance and discreet speech. He entered into conversation with her at tea; he liked her very much. Nikolai Petrovitch had at that time only just moved into his new home, and not wishing to keep serfs in the house, he was on the lookout for wage-servants; the woman of the inn on her side complained of the small number of visitors to the town, and the hard times; he proposed to her to come into his house in the capacity of housekeeper; she consented. Her husband had long been dead, leaving her an only daughter, Fenitchka. Within a fortnight Arina Savishna (that was the new housekeeper's name) arrived with her daughter at Maryino and installed herself in the little lodge. Nikolai Petrovitch's choice proved a successful one. Arina brought order into the household. As for Fenitchka, who was at that time seventeen, no one spoke of her, and scarcely any one saw her; she lived quietly and sedately, and only on Sundays Nikolai Petrovitch noticed in the church somewhere in a side place the delicate profile of her white face. More than a year passed thus.

One morning, Arina came into his study, and bowing low as usual, she asked him if he could do anything for her daughter, who had got a spark from the stove in her eye. Nikolai Petrovitch, like all stay-at-home people, had studied doctoring and even compiled a homœopathic guide. He at once told Arina to bring the patient to him. Fenitchka was much frightened when she heard the master had sent for her; however, she followed her mother. Nikolai Petrovitch led her to the window and took her head in his two hands. After thoroughly examining her red and swollen eye, he prescribed a fomentation, which he made up himself at once, and tearing his handkerchief in pieces, he showed her how it ought to be applied. Fenitchka listened to all he had to say, and then was going. "Kiss the master's hand, silly girl," said Arina. Nikolai Petrovitch did not give her his hand, and in confusion himself kissed her bent head on the parting of her hair. Fenitchka's eye was soon well again, but the impression she had made on Nikolai Petrovitch did not pass away so quickly. He was forever haunted by that pure, delicate, timidly raised face; he felt on the palms of his hands that soft hair, and saw those innocent, slightly parted lips, through which pearly teeth gleamed with moist brilliance in the sunshine. He began to watch her with great attention in church, and tried to get into conversation with her. At first she was shy of him, and one day meeting him at the approach of evening in a narrow footpath through a field of rye, she ran into the tall thick rye, overgrown with cornflowers and wormwood, so as not to meet him face to face. He caught sight of her little head through a golden network of ears of rye, from which she was peeping out like a little animal, and called affectionately to her:

"Good-evening, Fenitchka! I don't bite."

"Good-evening," she whispered, not coming out of her ambush.

By degrees she began to be more at home with him, but was still shy in his presence, when suddenly her mother, Arina, died of cholera. What was to become of Fenitchka? She inherited from her mother a love for order, regularity, and respectability; but she was so young, so alone. Nikolai Petrovitch was himself so good and considerate. . . . It's needless to relate the rest. . . .

"So my brother came in to see you?" Nikolai Petrovitch questioned her. "He knocked and came in?"

"Yes."

"Well, that's a good thing. Let me give Mitya a swing."

And Nikolai Petrovitch began tossing him almost up to the ceiling, to the huge delight of the baby, and to the considerable uneasiness of the mother, who every time he flew up stretched her arms up towards his little bare legs.

Pavel Petrovitch went back to his artistic study, with its walls covered with handsome bluish-grey hangings, with weapons hanging upon a variegated Persian rug nailed to the wall; with walnut furniture, upholstered in dark green velveteen, with a *renaissance* bookcase of old black oak, with bronze statuettes on the magnificent writing-table, with an open hearth. He threw himself on the sofa, clasped his hands behind his head, and remained without moving, looking with a face almost of despair at the ceiling. Whether he wanted to hide from the very walls that which was reflected in his face, or for some other reason, he got up, drew the heavy window curtains, and again threw himself on the sofa.

IX

ON THE SAME DAY Bazarov made acquaintance with Fenitchka. He was walking with Arkady in the garden, and explaining to him why some of the trees, especially the oaks, had not done well.

"You ought to have planted silver poplars here by preference, and spruce firs, and perhaps limes, giving them some loam. The arbour there has done well," he added, "because it's acacia and lilac; they're accommodating good fellows, those trees, they don't want much care. But there's some one in here."

In the arbour was sitting Fenitchka, with Dunyasha and Mitya. Bazarov stood still, while Arkady nodded to Fenitchka like an old friend.

"Who's that?" Bazarov asked him directly they had passed by. "What a pretty girl!"

"Whom are you speaking of?"

"You know; only one of them was pretty."

Arkady, not without embarrassment, explained to him briefly who Fenitchka was.

"Aha!" commented Bazarov; "your father's got good taste, one can see. I like him, your father, ay, ay! He's a jolly fellow. We must make friends though," he added, and turned back towards the arbour.

"Yevgeny!" Arkady cried after him in dismay; "mind what you are about, for mercy's sake."

"Don't worry yourself," said Bazarov; "I know how to behave myself— I'm not a booby."

Going up to Fenitchka, he took off his cap.

"Allow me to introduce myself," he began, with a polite bow. "I'm a harmless person, and a friend of Arkady Nikolaevitch's."

Fenitchka got up from the garden seat and looked at him without speaking.

"What a splendid baby!" continued Bazarov; "don't be uneasy, my praises have never brought ill-luck yet. Why is it his cheeks are so flushed? Is he cutting his teeth?"

"Yes," said Fenitchka; "he has cut four teeth already, and now the gums are swollen again."

"Show me, and don't be afraid, I'm a doctor."

Bazarov took the baby up in his arms, and to the great astonishment both of Fenitchka and Dunyasha the child made no resistance, and was not frightened.

"I see, I see. . . . It's nothing, everything's as it should be; he will have a good set of teeth. If anything goes wrong, tell me. And are you quite well yourself?"

"Quite, thank God."

"Thank God, indeed—that's the great thing. And you?" he added, turning to Dunyasha.

Dunyasha, a girl very prim in the master's house, and a romp outside the gates, only giggled in answer.

"Well, that's all right. Here's your gallant fellow."

Fenitchka received the baby in her arms.

"How good he was with you!" she commented in an undertone.

"Children are always good with me," answered Bazarov; "I have a way with them."

"Children know who love them," remarked Dunyasha.

"Yes, they certainly do," Fenitchka said. "Why, Mitya will not go to some people for anything."

"Will he come to me?" asked Arkady, who, after standing in the distance for some time, had gone up to the arbour.

He tried to entice Mitya to come to him, but Mitya threw his head back and screamed, to Fenitchka's great confusion.

"Another day, when he's had time to get used to me," said Arkady indulgently, and the two friends walked away.

"What's her name?" asked Bazarov.

"Fenitchka . . . Fedoysa," answered Arkady.

"And her father's name? One must know that too."

"Nikolaevna."

"*Bene*. What I like in her is that she's not too embarrassed. Some people, I suppose, would think ill of her for it. What nonsense! What is there to embarrass her? She's a mother—she's all right."

"She's all right," observed Arkady,—"but my father."

"And he's right too," put in Bazarov.

"Well, no, I don't think so."

"I suppose an extra heir's not to your liking?"

"I wonder you're not ashamed to attribute such ideas to me!" retorted Arkady hotly; "I don't consider my father wrong from that point of view. I think he ought to marry her."

"Hoity-toity!" responded Bazarov tranquilly. "What magnanimous fellows we are! You still attach significance to marriage; I did not expect that of you."

The friends walked a few paces in silence.

"I have looked at all your father's establishment," Bazarov began again. "The cattle are inferior, the horses are broken down; the buildings aren't up to much, and the workmen look confirmed loafers; while the superintendent is either a fool, or a knave, I haven't quite found out which yet."

"You are rather hard on everything to-day, Yevgeny Vassilyevitch."

"And the dear good peasants are taking your father in to a dead certainty. You know the Russian proverb, 'The Russian peasant will cheat God Himself.' "

"I begin to agree with my uncle," remarked Arkady; "you certainly have a poor opinion of Russians."

"As though that mattered! The only good point in a Russian is his having the lowest possible opinion of himself. What does matter is that two and two make four, and the rest is all foolery."

"And is nature foolery?" said Arkady, looking pensively at the bright-coloured fields in the distance, in the beautiful soft light of the sun, which was not yet high up in the sky.

"Nature, too, is foolery in the sense you understand it. Nature's not a temple, but a workshop, and man's the workman in it."

At that instant, the long drawn notes of a violoncello floated out to them from the house. Some one was playing Schubert's *Expectation* with much feeling, though with an untrained hand, and the melody flowed with honey sweetness through the air.

"What's that?" cried Bazarov in amazement.

"It's my father."

"Your father plays the violoncello?"

"Yes."

"And how old is your father?"

"Forty-four."

Bazarov suddenly burst into a roar of laughter.

"What are you laughing at?"

"Upon my word, a man of forty-four, a *paterfamilias* in this out-of-the-way district, playing on the violoncello!"

Bazarov went on laughing; but much as he revered his master, this time Arkady did not even smile.

X

ABOUT a fortnight passed by. Life at Maryino went on its accustomed course, while Arkady was lazy and enjoyed himself, and Bazarov worked. Every one in the house had grown used to him, to his careless manners, and his curt and abrupt speeches. Fenitchka, in particular, was so far at home with him that one night she sent to wake him up; Mitya had had convulsions; and he had gone, and, half joking, half-yawning as usual, he stayed two hours with her and relieved the child. On the other hand Pavel Petrovitch had grown to detest Bazarov with all the strength of his soul; he regarded him as stuck-up, impudent, cynical, and vulgar; he suspected that Bazarov had no respect for him, that he had all but a contempt for him—him, Pavel Kirsanov! Nikolai Petrovitch was rather afraid of the young "nihilist," and was doubtful whether his influence over Arkady was for the good; but he was glad to listen to him, and was glad to be present at his scientific and chemical experiments. Bazarov had brought with him a microscope, and busied himself for hours together with it. The servants, too, took to him, though he made fun of them; they felt, all the same, that he was one of themselves, not a master. Dunyasha was always ready to giggle with him, and used to cast significant and stealthy glances at him when she skipped by like a rabbit; Piotr, a man vain and stupid to the last degree, for ever wearing an affected frown on his brow, a man whose whole merit consisted in the fact that he looked civil, could spell out a page of reading, and was diligent in brushing his coat—even he smirked and brightened up directly Bazarov paid him any attention; the boys on the farm simply ran after the "doctor" like puppies. The old man Prokofitch was the only one who did not like him; he handed him the dishes at table with a surly face, called him a "butcher" and "an upstart," and declared that with his great whiskers he looked like a pig in a stye. Prokofitch in his own way was quite as much of an aristocrat as Pavel Petrovitch.

The best days of the year had come—the first days of June. The weather kept splendidly fine; in the distance, it is true, the cholera was threatening, but the inhabitants of that province had had time to get used to its visits. Bazarov used to get up very early and go out for two or three miles, not for a walk—he couldn't bear walking without an object—but to collect specimens of plants and insects. Sometimes he took Arkady with him. On the way home an argument usually sprang up, and Arkady was usually vanquished in it, though he said more than his companion.

One day they had lingered rather late; Nikolai Petrovitch went to meet them in the garden, and as he reached the arbour he suddenly heard the quick step and voices of the two young men. They were walking on the other side of the arbour, and could not see him.

"You don't know my father well enough," said Arkady.

"Your father's a nice chap," said Bazarov, "but he's behind the times; his day is done."

Nikolai Petrovitch listened intently. . . . Arkady made no answer.

The man whose day was done remained two minutes motionless, and stole slowly home.

"The day before yesterday I saw him reading Pushkin," Bazarov was continuing meanwhile. "Explain to him, please, that that's no earthly use. He's not a boy, you know; it's time to throw up that rubbish. And what an idea to be a romantic at this time of day! Give him something sensible to read."

"What ought I to give him?" asked Arkady.

"Oh, I think Büchner's *Stoff und Kraft* to begin with."

"I think so too," observed Arkady approvingly, "*Stoff und Kraft* is written in popular language. . . ."

"So it seems," Nikolai Petrovitch said the same day after dinner to his brother, as he sat in his study, "you and I are behind the times, our day's over. Well, well. Perhaps Bazarov is right; but one thing I confess, makes me feel sore; I did so hope, precisely now, to get on to such close, intimate terms with Arkady, and it turns out I'm left behind, and he has gone forward, and we can't understand one another."

"How has he gone forward? And in what way is he so superior to us already?" cried Pavel Petrovitch impatiently. "It's that high and mighty gentleman, that nihilist, who's knocked all that into his head. I hate that doctor fellow; in my opinion, he's simply a quack; I'm convinced, for all his tadpoles, he's not got very far even in medicine."

"No, brother, you mustn't say that; Bazarov is clever, and knows his subject."

"And his conceit's something revolting," Pavel Petrovitch broke in again.

"Yes," observed Nikolai Petrovitch, "he is conceited. But there's no doing without that, it seems; only that's what I did not take into account. I thought I was doing everything to keep up with the times; I have started a model farm; I have done well by the peasants, so that I am positively called a "Red Radical" all over the province; I read, I study, I try in every way to keep abreast with the requirements of the day—and they say my day's over. And, brother, I begin to think that it is."

"Why so?"

"I'll tell you why. This morning I was sitting reading Pushkin. . . . I remember, it happened to be *The Gipsies* . . . all of a sudden Arkady came up to me, and, without speaking, with such a kindly compassion on his face, as gently as if I were a baby, took the book away from me, and laid another before me—a German book . . . smiled, and went away, carrying Pushkin off with him."

"Upon my word! What book did he give you?"

"This one here."

And Nikolai Petrovitch pulled the famous treatise of Büchner, in the ninth edition, out of his coat-tail pocket.

Pavel Petrovitch turned it over in his hands. "Hm!" he growled. "Arkady Nikolaevitch is taking your education in hand. Well, did you try reading it?"

"Yes, I tried it."

"Well, what did you think of it?"

"Either I'm stupid, or it's all—nonsense. I must be stupid, I suppose."

"Haven't you forgotten your German?" queried Pavel Petrovitch.

"Oh, I understand the German."

Pavel Petrovitch again turned the book over in his hands, and glanced from under his brows at his brother. Both were silent.

"Oh, by the way," began Nikolai Petrovitch, obviously wishing to change the subject, "I've got a letter from Kolyazin."

"Matvy Ilyitch?"

"Yes. He has come to—to inspect the province. He's quite a bigwig now; and writes to me that, as a relation, he should like to see us again, and invites you and me and Arkady to the town."

"Are you going?" asked Pavel Petrovitch.

"No; are you?"

"No, I shan't go either. Much object there would be in dragging oneself over forty miles on a wild-goose chase. *Mathieu* wants to show himself in all his glory. Damn him! he will have the whole province doing him homage; he can get on without the likes of us. A grand dignity, indeed, a privy councillor! If I had stayed in the service, if I had trudged on in official harness, I should have been a general-adjutant by now. Besides, you and I are behind the times, you know."

"Yes, brother; it's time, it seems, to order a coffin and cross one's arms on one's breast," remarked Nikolai Petrovitch, with a sigh.

"Well, I'm not going to give in quite so soon," muttered his brother. "I've got a tussle with that doctor fellow before me, I feel sure of that."

A tussle came off that same day at evening tea. Pavel Petrovitch came into the drawing-room, all ready for the fray, irritable and determined. He was only waiting for an excuse to fall upon the enemy; but for a long while an excuse did not present itself. As a rule, Bazarov said little in the presence of the "old Kirsanovs" (that was how he spoke of the brothers), and that evening he felt out of humour, and drank off cup after cup of tea without a word. Pavel Petrovitch was all aflame with impatience; his wishes were fulfilled at last.

The conversation turned on one of the neighbouring land owners. "Rotten aristocratic snob," observed Bazarov indifferently. He had met him in Petersburg.

"Allow me to ask you," began Pavel Petrovitch, and his lips were trembling, "according to your ideas, have the words 'rotten' and 'aristocrat' the same meaning?"

"I said 'aristocratic snob,'" replied Bazarov, lazily swallowing a sip of tea.

"Precisely so; but I imagine you have the same opinion of aristocrats as of aristocratic snobs. I think it my duty to inform you that I do not share that opinion. I venture to assert that every one knows me for a man of liberal ideas and devoted to progress; but, exactly for that reason, I respect aristocrats—real aristocrats. Kindly remember, sir" (at these words Bazarov lifted his eyes and looked at Pavel Petrovitch), "kindly remember, sir," he repeated, with acrimony—"the English aristocracy. They do not abate one iota of their rights, and for that reason they respect the rights of others; they demand the performance of what is due to them, and for that reason they perform their own duties. The aristocracy has given freedom to England, and maintains it for her."

"We've heard that story a good many times," replied Bazarov; "but what are you trying to prove by that?"

"I am tryin' to prove by that, sir" (when Pavel Petrovitch was angry he intentionally clipped his words in this way, though, of course, he knew very well that such forms are not strictly grammatical. In this fashionable whim could be discerned a survival of the habits of the times of Alexander. The exquisites of those days, on the rare occasions when they spoke their own language, made use of such slipshod forms; as much as to say, "We, of course, are born Russians, at the same time we are great swells, who are at liberty to neglect the rules of scholars"); "I am tryin' to prove by that, sir, that without the sense of personal dignity, without self-respect— and these two sentiments are well developed in the aristocrat—there is no secure foundation for the social . . . *bien public* . . . the social fabric. Personal character, sir—that is the chief thing; a man's personal character must be firm as a rock, since everything is built on it. I am very well aware, for instance, that you are pleased to consider my habits, my dress, my refinements, in fact, ridiculous; but all that proceeds from a sense of self-respect, from a sense of duty—yes, indeed, of duty. I live in the country, in the wilds, but I will not lower myself. I respect the dignity of man in myself."

"Let me ask you, Pavel Petrovitch," commented Bazarov; "you respect yourself, and sit with your hands folded; what sort of benefit does that do to the *bien public?* If you didn't respect yourself, you'd do just the same."

Pavel Petrovitch turned white. "That's a different question. It's absolutely unnecessary for me to explain to you now why I sit with folded hands, as you are pleased to express yourself. I wish only to tell you that aristocracy is a principle, and in our days none but immoral or silly people can live without principles. I said that to Arkady the day after he came home, and I repeat it now. Isn't it so, Nikolai?"

Nikolai Petrovitch nodded his head. "Aristocracy, Liberalism, progress, principles," Bazarov was saying meanwhile; "if you think of it, what a lot of foreign . . . and useless words! To a Russian they're good for nothing."

"What is good for something according to you? If we listen to you, we shall find ourselves outside humanity, outside its laws. Come—the logic of history demands . . ."

"But what's that logic to us? We can get on without that too."

"How do you mean?"

"Why, this. You don't need logic, I hope, to put a bit of bread in your mouth when you're hungry. What's the object of these abstractions to us?"

Pavel Petrovitch raised his hands in horror.

"I don't understand you, after that. You insult the Russian people. I don't understand how it's possible not to acknowledge principles, rules! By virtue of what do you act then?"

"I've told you already, uncle, that we don't accept any authorities," put in Arkady.

"We act by virtue of what we recognise as beneficial," observed Bazarov. "At the present time, negation is the most beneficial of all—and we deny——"

"Everything?"

"Everything!"

"What, not only art and poetry . . . but even . . . horrible to say . . ."

"Everything," repeated Bazarov, with indescribable composure.

Pavel Petrovitch stared at him. He had not expected this; while Arkady fairly blushed with delight.

"Allow me, though," began Nikolai Petrovitch. "You deny everything; or, speaking more precisely, you destroy everything. . . . But one must construct too, you know."

"That's not our business now. . . . The ground wants clearing first."

"The present condition of the people requires it," added Arkady, with dignity; "we are bound to carry out these requirements, we have no right to yield to the satisfaction of our personal egoism."

This last phrase obviously displeased Bazarov; there was a flavour of philosophy, that is to say, romanticism about it, for Bazarov called philosophy, too, romanticism, but he did not think it necessary to correct his young disciple.

"No, no!" cried Pavel Petrovitch, with sudden energy. "I'm not willing to believe that you, young men, know the Russian people really, that you are the representatives of their requirements, their efforts! No; the Russian people is not what you imagine it. Tradition it holds sacred; it is a patriarchal people; it cannot live without faith . . ."

"I'm not going to dispute that," Bazarov interrupted. "I'm even ready to agree that in that you're right."

"But if I am right . . ."

"And, all the same, that proves nothing."

"It just proves nothing," repeated Arkady, with the confidence of a practised chess-player, who has foreseen an apparently dangerous move on the part of his adversary, and so is not at all taken aback by it.

"How does it prove nothing?" muttered Pavel Petrovitch, astounded. "You must be going against the people then?"

"And what if we are?" shouted Bazarov. "The people imagine that, when it thunders, the prophet Ilya's riding across the sky in his chariot. What then? Are we to agree with them? Besides, the people's Russian; but am I not Russian, too?"

"No, you are not Russian, after all you have just been saying! I can't acknowledge you as Russian."

"My grandfather ploughed the land," answered Bazarov with haughty pride. "Ask any one of your peasants which of us—you or me—he'd more readily acknowledge as a fellow-countryman. You don't even know how to talk to them."

"While you talk to him and despise him at the same time."

"Well, suppose he deserves contempt. You find fault with my attitude, but how do you know that I have got it by chance, that it's not a product of that very national spirit, in the name of which you wage war on it?"

"What an idea! Much use in nihilists!"

"Whether they're of use or not, is not for us to decide. Why, even you suppose you're not a useless person."

"Gentlemen, gentlemen, no personalities, please!" cried Nikolai Petrovitch, getting up.

Pavel Petrovitch smiled, and laying his hand on his brother's shoulder, forced him to sit down again.

"Don't be uneasy," he said; "I shall not forget myself, just through that sense of dignity which is made fun of so mercilessly by our friend—our friend, the doctor. Let me ask," he resumed, turning again to Bazarov; "you suppose, possibly, that your doctrine is a novelty? That is quite a mistake. The materialism you advocate has been more than once in vogue already, and has always proved insufficient . . ."

"A foreign word again!" broke in Bazarov. He was beginning to feel vicious, and his face assumed a peculiar coarse coppery hue. "In the first place, we advocate nothing; that's not our way."

"What do you do, then?"

"I'll tell you what we do. Not long ago we used to say that our officials took bribes, that we had no roads, no commerce, no real justice . . ."

"Oh, I see, you are reformers—that's what that's called, I fancy. I too should agree to many of your reforms, but . . ."

"Then we suspected that talk, perpetual talk, and nothing but talk, about our social diseases, was not worth while, that it all led to nothing but superficiality and pedantry; we saw that our leading men, so-called advanced people and reformers, are no good; that we busy ourselves over foolery, talk rubbish about art, unconscious creativeness, parliamentarism, trial by jury, and the deuce knows what all; while, all the while, it's a question of getting bread to eat, while we're stifling under the grossest superstition, while all our enterprises come to grief, simply because there aren't honest men enough to carry them on, while the very emancipation our Government's busy upon will hardly come to any good, because peasants are glad to rob even themselves to get drunk at the gin-shop."

"Yes," interposed Pavel Petrovitch, "yes; you were convinced of all this, and decided not to undertake anything seriously, yourselves."

"We decided not to undertake anything," repeated Bazarov grimly. He suddenly felt vexed with himself for having, without reason, been so expansive before this gentleman.

"But to confine yourselves to abuse?"

"To confine ourselves to abuse."

"And that is called nihilism?"

"And that's called nihilism," Bazarov repeated again, this time with peculiar rudeness.

Pavel Petrovitch puckered up his face a little. "So that's it!" he observed in a strangely composed voice. "Nihilism is to cure all our woes, and you, you are our heroes and saviours. But why do you abuse others, those reformers even? Don't you do as much talking as every one else?"

"Whatever faults we have, we do not err in that way," Bazarov muttered between his teeth.

"What, then? Do you act, or what? Are you preparing for action?"

Bazarov made no answer. Something like a tremor passed over Pavel Petrovitch, but he at once regained control of himself.

"Hm! . . . Action, destruction . . ." he went on. "But how destroy without even knowing why?"

"We shall destroy, because we are a force," observed Arkady.

Pavel Petrovitch looked at his nephew and laughed.

"Yes, a force is not to be called to account," said Arkady, drawing himself up.

"Unhappy boy!" wailed Pavel Petrovitch, he was positively incapable of maintaining his firm demeanor any longer. "If you could only realise what it is you are doing for your country. No; it's enough to try the patience of an angel! Force! There's force in the savage Kalmuck, in the Mongolian; but what is it to us? What is precious to us is civilisation; yes, yes, sir, its fruits are precious to us. And don't tell me those fruits are worthless; the poorest dauber, *un barbouilleur*, the man who plays dance music for five farthings an evening, is of more use than you, because they are the representatives of civilisation, and not of brute Mongolian force! You fancy yourselves advanced people, and all the while you are only fit for the Kalmuck's hovel! Force! And recollect, you forcible gentlemen, that you're only four men and a half, and the others are millions, who won't let you trample their sacred traditions under foot, who will crush you and walk over you!"

"If we're crushed, serves us right," observed Bazarov. "But that's an open question. We are not so few as you suppose."

"What? You seriously suppose you will come to terms with a whole people?"

"All Moscow was burnt down, you know, by a farthing dip," answered Bazarov.

"Yes, yes. First a pride almost Satanic, then ridicule—that, that's what it is attracts the young, that's what gains an ascendancy over the inexperienced hearts of boys! Here's one of them sitting beside you, ready to worship the ground under your feet. Look at him! (Arkady turned away and frowned.) And this plague has spread far already. I have been told that in Rome our artists never set foot in the Vatican. Raphael they regard as almost a fool, because, if you please, he's an authority; while they're all the while most disgustingly sterile and unsuccessful, men whose imagination does not soar beyond 'Girls at a Fountain,' however they try! And the girls even out of drawing. They are fine fellows to your mind, are they not?"

"To my mind," retorted Bazarov, "Raphael's not worth a brass farthing; and they're no better than he."

"Bravo! bravo! Listen, Arkady . . . that's how young men of to-day ought to express themselves! And if you come to think of it, how could they fail if they followed you! In old days, young men had to study; they didn't want to be called dunces, so they had to work hard whether they liked it or not. But now, they need only say, 'Everything in the world is foolery!' and the trick's done. Young men are delighted. And, to be sure, they were simply geese before, and now they have suddenly turned nihilists."

"Your praiseworthy sense of personal dignity has given way," remarked Bazarov phlegmatically, while Arkady was hot all over, and his eyes were flashing. "Our argument has gone too far; it's better to cut it short, I think. I shall be quite ready to agree with you," he added, getting up, "when you bring forward a single institution in our present mode of life, in family or in social life, which does not call for complete and unqualified destruction."

"I will bring forward millions of such institutions," cried Pavel Petrovitch —"millions! Well—the Mir, for instance."

A cold smile curved Barazov's lips. "Well, as regards the Mir," he commented; "you had better talk to your brother. He has seen by now, I should fancy, what sort of thing the Mir is in fact—its common guarantee, its sobriety, and other features of the kind."

"The family, then, the family as it exists among our peasants!" cried Pavel Petrovitch.

"And that subject, too, I imagine, it will be better for yourselves not to go into in detail. Don't you realise all the advantages of the head of the family choosing his daughters-in-law? Take my advice, Pavel Petrovitch, allow yourself two days to think about it; you're not likely to find anything on the spot. Go through all our classes, and think well over each, while I and Arkady will . . ."

"Will go on turning everything into ridicule," broke in Pavel Petrovitch.

"No, will go on dissecting frogs. Come, Arkady; good-bye for the present, gentlemen!"

The two friends walked off. The brothers were left alone, and at first they only looked at one another.

"So that," began Pavel Petrovitch, "so that's what our young men of this generation are! They are like that—our successors!"

"Our successors!" repeated Nikolai Petrovitch, with a dejected smile. He had been sitting on thorns, all through the argument, and had done nothing but glance stealthily, with a sore heart, at Arkady. "Do you know what I was reminded of, brother? I once had a dispute with our poor mother; she stormed, and wouldn't listen to me. At last I said to her, 'Of course, you can't understand me; we belong,' I said, 'to two different generations.' She was dreadfully offended, while I thought, 'There's no help for it. It's a bitter pill, but she has to swallow it.' You see, now, our turn has come, and our successors can say to us, 'You are not of our generation; swallow your pill.' "

"You are beyond everything in your generosity and modesty," replied Pavel Petrovitch. "I'm convinced, on the contrary, that you and I are far more in the right than these young gentlemen, though we do perhaps express ourselves in old-fashioned language, *vieilli*, and have not the same insolent conceit. . . . And the swagger of the young men nowadays! You ask one, 'Do you take red wine or white?' 'It is my custom to prefer red!' he answers, in a deep bass, with a face as solemn as if the whole universe had its eyes on him at that instant. . . ."

"Do you care for any more tea?" asked Fenitchka, putting her head in at the door; she had not been able to make up her mind to come into the drawing-room while there was the sound of voices in dispute there.

"No, you can tell them to take the samovar," answered Nikolai Petro-vitch, and he got up to meet her. Pavel Petrovitch said *"bon soir"* to him abruptly, and went away to his study.

XI

HALF an hour later Nikolai Petrovitch went into the garden to his favourite arbour. He was overtaken by melancholy thoughts. For the first time he realised clearly the distance between him and his son; he foresaw that every day it would grow wider and wider. In vain, then, had he spent whole days sometimes in the winter at Petersburg over the newest books; in vain had he listened to the talk of the young men; in vain had he rejoiced when he succeeded in putting in his word, too, in their heated discussions. "My brother says we are right," he thought, "and apart from all vanity, I do think myself that they are further from the truth than we are, though at the same time I feel there is something behind them we have not got, some superiority over us. . . . Is it youth? No; not only youth. Doesn't their superiority consist in there being fewer traces of the slave-owner in them than in us?"

Nikolai Petrovitch's head sank despondently, and he passed his hand over his face.

"But to renounce poetry?" he thought again; "to have no feeling for art, for nature . . ."

And he looked round, as though trying to understand how it was possible to have no feeling for nature. It was already evening; the sun was hidden behind a small copse of aspens which lay a quarter of a mile from the garden; its shadow stretched indefinitely across the still fields. A peasant on a white nag went at a trot along the dark, narrow path close beside the copse; his whole figure was clearly visible even to the patch on his shoulder, in spite of his being in the shade; the horse's hoofs flew along bravely. The sun's rays from the farther side fell full on the copse, and piercing through its thickets, threw such a warm light on the aspen trunks that they looked like pines, and their leaves were almost a dark blue, while above them rose a pale blue sky, faintly tinged by the glow of sunset. The swallows flew high; the wind had quite died away, belated bees hummed slowly and drowsily among the lilac blossom; a swarm of midges hung like a cloud over a solitary branch which stood out against the sky. "How beautiful, my God!" thought Nikolai Petrovitch, and his favourite verses were almost on his lips; he remembered Arkady's *Stoff und Kraft*—and was silent, but still he sat there, still he gave himself up to the sorrowful consolation of solitary thought. He was fond of dreaming; his country life had developed the tendency in him. How short a time ago, he had been dreaming like this, waiting for his son at the posting station, and what a change already since that day; their relations that were then undefined, were defined now—and how defined! Again his dead wife came back to his imagination, but not as he had known her for many years, not as the good domestic house-wife, but as a young girl with a slim figure, innocently inquiring eyes, and a tight twist of hair on her childish neck. He remembered how he had seen her for the first time. He was still a student then. He had met her on the staircase of his lodgings, and, jostling by accident against her, he tried to apologise, and could only mutter, "*Pardon, monsieur,*" while she bowed, smiled, and suddenly seemed frightened, and ran away, though at the bend of the staircase she had glanced rapidly at him, assumed a serious air, and blushed. Afterwards, the first timid visits, the half-words, the half-smiles, and embarrassment; and melancholy, and yearnings, and at last that breathing rapture. . . . Where had it all vanished? She had been his wife, he had been happy as few on earth are happy. . . . "But," he mused, "these sweet first moments, why could not one live an eternal, undying life in them?"

He did not try to make his thought clear to himself; but he felt that he longed to keep that blissful time by something stronger than memory; he longed to feel his Marya near him again to have the sense of her warmth and breathing, and already he could fancy that over him. . . .

"Nikolai Petrovitch," came the sound of Fenitchka's voice close by him; "where are you?"

He started. He felt no pang, no shame. He never even admitted the possibility of comparison between his wife and Fenitchka, but he was sorry she had thought of coming to look for him. Her voice had brought back to him at once his grey hairs, his age, his reality. . . .

The enchanted world into which he was just stepping, which was just rising out of the dim mists of the past, was shaken—and vanished.

"I'm here," he answered; "I'm coming, run along." "There it is, the traces of the slave owner," flashed through his mind. Fenitchka peeped into the arbour at him without speaking, and disappeared; while he noticed with astonishment that the night had come on while he had been dreaming. Everything around was dark and hushed. Fenitchka's face had glimmered so pale and slight before him. He got up, and was about to go home; but the emotion stirred in his heart could not be soothed at once, and he began slowly walking about the garden, sometimes looking at the ground at his feet, and then raising his eyes towards the sky where swarms of stars were twinkling. He walked a great deal, till he was almost tired out, while the restlessness within him, a kind of yearning, vague, melancholy restlessness, still was not appeased. Oh, how Bazarov would have laughed at him, if he had known what was passing within him then! Arkady himself would have condemned him. He, a man forty-four years old, an agriculturist and a farmer, was shedding tears, causeless tears; this was a hundred times worse than the violoncello.

Nikolai Petrovitch continued walking, and could not make up his mind to go into the house, into the snug peaceful nest, which looked out at him so hospitably from all its lighted windows; he had not the force to tear himself away from the darkness, the garden, the sense of the fresh air in his face, from that melancholy, that restless craving.

At a turn in the path, he was met by Pavel Petrovitch. "What's the matter with you?" he asked Nikolai Petrovitch; "you are as white as a ghost; you are not well; why don't you go to bed?"

Nikolai Petrovitch explained to him briefly his state of feeling and moved away. Pavel Petrovitch went to the end of the garden, and he too grew thoughtful, and he too raised his eyes towards the heavens. But in his beautiful dark eyes, nothing was reflected but the light of the stars. He was not born an idealist, and his fastidiously dry and sensuous soul, with its French tinge of cynicism was not capable of dreaming. . . .

"Do you know what?" Bazarov was saying to Arkady the same night. "I've got a splendid idea. Your father was saying to-day that he'd had an invitation from your illustrious relative. Your father's not going; let us be off to X——; you know the worthy man invites you too. You see what fine weather it is; we'll stroll about and look at the town. We'll have five or six days' outing, and enjoy ourselves."

"And you'll come back here again?"

"No; I must go to my father's. You know, he lives about twenty-five miles from X——. I've not seen him for a long while, and my mother too; I must cheer the old people up. They've been good to me, especially my father; he's awfully funny. I'm their only one too."

"And will you be long with them?"

"I don't suppose so. It will be dull, of course."

"And you'll come to us on your way back?"

"I don't know . . . I'll see. Well, what do you say? Shall we go?"

"If you like," observed Arkady languidly.

In his heart he was highly delighted with his friend's suggestion, but he thought it a duty to conceal his feeling. He was not a nihilist for nothing!

The next day he set off with Bazarov to X——. The younger part of the household at Maryino were sorry at their going; Dunyasha even cried . . . but the old folks breathed more easily.

XII

The town of x—— to which our friends set off was in the jurisdiction of a governor who was a young man, and at once a progressive and a despot, as often happens with Russians. Before the end of the first year of his government, he had managed to quarrel not only with the marshal of nobility, a retired officer of the guards, who kept open house and a stud of horses, but even with his own subordinates. The feuds arising from this cause assumed at last such proportions that the ministry in Petersburg had found it necessary to send down a trusted personage with a commission to investigate it all on the spot. The choice of the authorities fell upon Matvy Ilyitch Kolyazin, the son of the Kolyazin, under whose protection the brothers Kirsanov had once found themselves. He, too, was a "young man"; that is to say, he had not long passed forty, but he was already on the high road to becoming a statesman, and wore a star on each side of his breast—one, to be sure, a foreign star, not of the first magnitude. Like the governor, whom he had come down to pass judgment upon, he was reckoned a progressive; and though he was already a bigwig, he was not like the majority of bigwigs. He had the highest opinion of himself; his vanity knew no bounds, but he behaved simply, looked affably, listened condescendingly, and laughed so good-naturedly, that on a first acquaintance he might even be taken for "a jolly good fellow." On important occasions, however, he knew, as the saying is, how to make his authority felt. "Energy is essential," he used to say then, "*l'énergie est la première qualité d'un homme d'état;*" and for all that, he was usually taken in, and any moderately experienced official could turn him round his finger. Matvy Ilyitch used to speak with great respect of Guizot, and tried to impress every one with the idea that he did not belong to the class of *routiniers* and high-and-dry bureaucrats, that not a single phenomenon of social life passed unnoticed by him. . . . All such phrases were very familiar to him. He even followed, with dignified indifference, it is true, the development of contemporary literature; so a grown-up man who meets a procession of small boys in the street will sometimes walk after it. In reality, Matvy Ilyitch had not got much beyond those political men of the days of Alexander, who used to prepare for an evening party at Madame Svyetchin's by reading a page of Condillac; only his methods were different, more modern. He was an adroit courtier, a great hypocrite, and nothing more; he had no special aptitude for affairs, and no intellect, but he knew how to manage his own business successfully; no one could get the better of him there, and, to be sure, that's the principal thing.

Matvy Ilyitch received Arkady with the good-nature, we might even call it playfulness, characteristic of the enlightened higher official. He was astonished, however, when he heard that the cousins he had invited had remained at home in the country. "Your father was always a queer fellow," he remarked, playing with the tassels of his magnificent velvet dressing-gown, and suddenly turning to a young official in a discreetly buttoned-up uniform, he cried, with an air of concentrated attention, "What?" The young man, whose lips were glued together from prolonged silence, got up and looked in perplexity at his chief. But, having nonplussed his subordinate, Matvy Ilyitch paid him no further attention. Our higher officials are fond as a rule of nonplussing their subordinates; the methods to which they have recourse to attain that end are rather various. The following means, among others, is in great vogue, "*is quite a favourite,*" as the English say; a high official suddenly ceases to understand the simplest words, assuming total deafness. He will ask, for instance, "What's to-day?"

He is respectfully informed, "To-day's Friday, your Ex-s-s-s-lency."

"Eh? What? What's that? What do you say?" the great man repeats with intense attention.

"To-day's Friday, your Ex—s—s—lency."

"Eh? What? What's Friday? What Friday?"

"Friday, your Ex—s—s—s—lency, the day of the week."

"What, do you pretend to teach me, eh?"

Matvy Ilyitch was a higher official all the same, though he was reckoned a liberal.

"I advise you, my dear boy, to go and call on the Governor," he said to Arkady; "you understand, I don't advise you to do so because I adhere to old-fashioned ideas of the necessity of paying respect to authorities, but simply because the Governor's a very decent fellow; besides, you probably want to make acquaintance with the society here. . . . You're not a bear, I hope? And he's giving a great ball the day after to-morrow."

"Will you be at the ball?" inquired Arkady.

"He gives it in my honour," answered Matvy Ilyitch, almost pityingly. "Do you dance?"

"Yes; I dance, but not well."

"That's a pity! There are pretty girls here, and it's a disgrace for a young man not to dance. Again, I don't say that through any old-fashioned ideas; I don't in the least imagine that a man's wit lies in his feet, but Byronism is ridiculous, *il a fait son temps*."

"But, uncle, it's not through Byronism, I . . ."

"I will introduce you to the ladies here; I will take you under my wing," interrupted Matvy Ilyitch, and he laughed complacently. "You'll find it warm, eh?"

A servant entered and announced the arrival of the superintendent of the Crown domains, a mild-eyed old man, with deep creases round his mouth, who was excessively fond of nature, especially on a summer day, when, in his words, "every little busy bee takes a little bribe from every little flower." Arkady withdrew.

He found Bazarov at the tavern where they were staying, and was a long while persuading him to go with him to the Governor's. "Well, there's no help for it," said Bazarov at last. "It's no good doing things by halves. We came to look at the gentry; let's look at them!"

The Governor received the young men affably, but he did not ask them to sit down, nor did he sit down himself. He was in an everlasting fuss and hurry; in the morning he used to put on a tight uniform and an excessively stiff cravat; he never ate or drank enough; he was for ever making arrangements. He invited Kirsanov and Bazarov to his ball, and within a few minutes invited them a second time, regarding them as brothers, and calling them Kisarov.

They were on their way home from the Governor's, when suddenly a short man, in a Slavophil national dress, leaped out of a trap that was passing them, and crying, "Yevgeny Vassilyitch!" dashed up to Bazarov.

"Ah! it's you, Herr Sitnikov," observed Bazarov, still stepping along on the pavement; "by what chance did you come here?"

"Fancy, absolutely by chance," he replied, and returning to the trap, he waved his hand several times, and shouted, "Follow, follow us! My father had business here," he went on, hopping across the gutter, "and so he asked me. . . . I heard to-day of your arrival, and have already been to see you. . . ." (The friends did, in fact, on returning to their room, find there a card, with the corners turned down, bearing the name of Sitnikov, on one side in French, on the other in Slavonic characters.) "I hope you are not coming from the Governor's?"

"It's no use to hope; we come straight from him."

"Ah! in that case I will call on him too. . . . Yevgeny Vassilyitch, introduce me to your . . . to the . . ."

"Sitnikov, Kirsanov," mumbled Bazarov, not stopping.

"I am greatly flattered," began Sitnikov, walking sidewise, smirking, and hurriedly pulling off his really over-elegant gloves. "I have heard so much. . . . I am an old acquaintance of Yevgeny Vassilyitch, and, I may say—his disciple. I am indebted to him for my regeneration. . . ."

Arkady looked at Bazarov's disciple. There was an expression of excitement and dulness imprinted on the small but pleasant features of his well-groomed face; his small eyes, that seemed squeezed in, had a fixed and uneasy look, and his laugh, too, was uneasy—a sort of short, wooden laugh.

"Would you believe it," he pursued, "when Yevgeny Vassilyitch for the first time said before me that it was not right to accept any authorities, I felt such enthusiasm . . . as though my eyes were opened! Here, I thought, at last I have found a man! By the way, Yevgeny Vassilyitch, you positively must come to know a lady here, who is really capable of understanding you, and for whom your visit would be a real festival; you have heard of her, I suppose?"

"Who is it?" Bazarov brought out unwillingly.

"Kukshina, *Eudoxie*, Evdoksya Kukshin. She's a remarkable nature, *émancipée* in the true sense of the word, an advanced woman. Do you know what? We'll all go together to see her now. She lives only two steps from here. We will have lunch there. I suppose you have not lunched yet?"

"No; not yet."

"Well, that's capital. She has separated, you understand, from her husband; she is not dependent on any one."

"Is she pretty?" Bazarov cut in.

"N . . . no, one couldn't say that."

"Then, what the devil are you asking us to see her for?"

"Fie; you must have your joke. . . . She will give us a bottle of champagne."

"Oh, that's it. One can see the practical man at once. By the way, is your father still in the gin business?"

"Yes," said Sitnikov, hurriedly, and he gave a shrill spasmodic laugh "Well? Will you come?"

"I don't really know."

"You wanted to see people, go along," said Arkady in an undertone.

"And what do you say to it, Mr. Kirsanov?" Sitnikov put in. "You must come too; we can't go without you."

"But how can we burst in upon her all at once?"

"That's no matter. Kukshina's a brick!"

"There will be a bottle of champagne?" asked Bazarov.

"Three!" cried Sitnikov; "that I answer for."

"What with?"

"My own head."

"Your father's purse would be better. However, we are coming."

XIII

THE small gentleman's house in the Moscow style, in which Avdotya Niki-tishna, otherwise Evdoksya Kukshin, lived, was in one of the streets of X——, which had been lately burnt down; it is well known that our pro-vincial towns are burnt down every five years. At the door, above a visiting card nailed on all askew, there was a bell-handle to be seen, and in the hall the visitors were met by someone, not exactly a servant, nor exactly a companion, in a cap—unmistakable tokens of the progressive tendencies of the lady of the house. Sitnikov inquired whether Avdotya Nikitishna was at home.

"Is that you, Victor?" sounded a shrill voice from the adjoining room. "Come in."

The woman in the cap disappeared at once.

"I'm not alone," observed Sitnikov, with a sharp look at Arkady and Bazarov as he briskly pulled off his overcoat, beneath which appeared some-thing of the nature of a coachman's velvet jacket.

"No matter," answered the voice. "Entrez."

The young men went in. The room into which they walked was more like a working study than a drawing-room. Papers, letters, fat numbers of Russian journals, for the most part uncut, lay at random on the dusty tables; white cigarette ends lay scattered in every direction. On a leather-covered sofa, a lady, still young, was reclining. Her fair hair was rather dishevelled; she wore a silk gown, not perfectly tidy, heavy bracelets on her short arms, and a lace handkerchief on her head. She got up from the sofa, and care-lessly drawing a velvet cape trimmed with yellowish ermine over her shoulders, she said languidly, "Good-morning, Victor," and pressed Sitni-kov's hand.

"Bazarov, Kirsanov," he announced abruptly in imitation of Bazarov.

"Delighted," answered Madame Kukshin, and fixing on Bazarov a pair of round eyes, between which was a forlorn little turned-up red nose, "I know you," she added, and pressed his hand too.

Bazarov scowled. There was nothing repulsive in the little plain person of the emancipated woman; but the expression of her face produced a dis-agreeable effect on the spectator. One felt impelled to ask her, "What's the matter; are you hungry? Or bored? Or shy? What are you in a fidget about?" Both she and Sitnikov had always the same uneasy air. She was extremely unconstrained, and at the same time awkward; she obviously regarded herself as a good-natured, simple creature, and all the while, whatever she did, it always struck one that it was not just what she wanted to do; everything with her seemed, as children say, done on purpose, that's to say, not simply, not naturally.

"Yes, yes, I know you, Bazarov," she repeated. (She had the habit—peculiar to many provincial and Moscow ladies—of calling men by their surnames from the first day of acquaintance with them.) "Will you have a cigar?"

"A cigar's all very well," put in Sitnikov, who by now was lolling in an armchair, his legs in the air; "but give us some lunch. We're awfully hungry; and tell them to bring us up a little bottle of champagne."

"Sybarite," commented Evdoksya, and she laughed. (When she laughed the gum showed above her upper teeth.) "Isn't it true, Bazarov; he's a Sybarite?"

"I like comfort in life," Sitnikov brought out, with dignity. "That does not prevent my being a Liberal."

"No, it does; it does prevent it!" cried Evdoksya. She gave directions, however, to her maid, both as regards the lunch and the champagne.

"What do you think about it?" she added, turning to Bazarov. "I'm persuaded you share my opinion."

"Well, no," retorted Bazarov; "a piece of meat's better than a piece of bread even from the chemical point of view."

"You are studying chemistry? That is my passion. I've even invented a new sort of composition myself."

"A composition? You?"

"Yes. And do you know for what purpose? To make dolls' heads so that they shouldn't break. I'm practical, too, you see. But everything's not quite ready yet. I've still to read Liebig. By the way, have you read Kislyakov'e article on Female Labour, in the *Moscow Gazette?* Read it, please. You're interested in the woman question, I suppose? And in the schools too? What does your friend do? What is his name?"

Madame Kukshin shed her questions one after another with affected negligence, not waiting for an answer; spoilt children talk so to their nurses.

"My name's Arkady Nikolaitch Kirsanov," said Arkady, "and I'm doing nothing."

Evdoksya giggled. "How charming! What, don't you smoke? Victor, do you know, I'm very angry with you."

"What for?"

"They tell me you've begun singing the praises of George Sand again. A retrograde woman, and nothing else? How can people compare her with Emerson? She hasn't an idea on education, nor physiology, nor anything. She'd never, I'm persuaded, heard of embryology, and in these days—what can be done without that?" (Evdoksya even threw up her hands.) "Ah, what a wonderful article Elisyevitch has written on that subject! He's a gentleman of genius." (Evdoksya constantly made use of the word "gentleman" instead of the word "man.") "Bazarov, sit by me on the sofa. You don't know, perhaps, I'm awfully afraid of you."

"Why so? Allow me to ask."

"You're a dangerous gentleman; you're such a critic. Good God! yes! why, how absurd, I'm talking like some country lady. I really am a country lady, though. I manage my property myself; and only fancy, my bailiff Erofay's a wonderful type, quite like Cooper's Pathfinder; something in him so spontaneous! I've come to settle here finally; it's an intolerable town, isn't it? But what's one to do?"

"The town's like every town," Bazarov remarked coolly.

"All its interests are so petty, that's what's so awful! I used to spend the winters in Moscow . . . but now my lawful spouse, Monsieur Kukshin's residing there. And besides, Moscow nowadays . . . there, I don't know— it's not the same as it was. I'm thinking of going abroad; last year I was on the point of setting off."

"To Paris, I suppose?" queried Bazarov.

"To Paris and to Heidelberg."

"Why to Heidelberg?"

"How can you ask? Why, Bunsen's there!"

To this Bazarov could find no reply.

"*Pierre* Sapozhnikov . . . do you know him?"

"No, I don't."

"Not know *Pierre* Sapozhnikov . . . he's always at Lidia Hestatov's."

"I don't know her either."

"Well, it was he undertook to escort me. Thank God, I'm independent; I've no children. . . . What was that I said: *thank God!* It's no matter though."

Evdoksya rolled a cigarette up between her fingers, which were brown with tobacco stains, put it to her tongue, licked it up, and began smoking. The maid came in with a tray.

"Ah, here's lunch! Will you have an appetiser first? Victor, open the bottle; that's in your line."

"Yes, it's in my line," muttered Sitnikov, and again he gave vent to the same convulsive laugh.

"Are there any pretty women here?" inquired Bazarov, as he drank off a third glass.

"Yes, there are," answered Evdoksya; "but they're all such empty-headed creatures. *Mon amie*, Odintsova, for instance, is nice-looking. It's a pity her reputation's rather doubtful. . . . That wouldn't matter, though, but she's no independence in her views, no width, nothing . . . of all that. The whole system of education wants changing. I've thought a great deal about it; our women are very badly educated."

"There's no doing anything with them," put in Sitnikov; "one ought to despise them, and I do despise them fully and completely!" (The possibility of feeling and expressing contempt was the most agreeable sensation to Sitnikov; he used to attack women in especial, never suspecting that it was to be his fate a few months later to be cringing before his wife merely because she had been born a princess Durdoleosov.) "Not a single one of them would be capable of understanding our conversation; not a single one deserves to be spoken of by serious men like us!"

"But there's not the least need for them to understand our conversation," observed Bazarov.

"Whom do you mean?" put in Evdoksya.

"Pretty women."

"What? Do you adopt Proudhon's ideas, then?"

Bazarov drew himself up haughtily. "I don't adopt any one's ideas; I have my own."

"Damn all authorities!" shouted Sitnikov, delighted to have a chance of expressing himself boldly before the man he slavishly admired.

"But even Macaulay," Madame Kukshin was beginning . . .

"Damn Macaulay," thundered Sitnikov. "Are you going to stand up for the silly hussies?"

"For silly hussies, no, but for the rights of women, which I have sworn to defend to the last drop of my blood."

"Damn!" but here Sitnikov stopped. "But I don't deny them," he said.

"No, I see you're a Slavophil."

"No, I'm not a Slavophil, though, of course . . ."

"No, no, no! You are a Slavophil. You're an advocate of patriarchal despotism. You want to have the whip in your hand!"

"A whip's an excellent thing," remarked Bazarov; "but we've got to the last drop."

"Of what?" interrupted Evdoksya.

"Of champagne, most honoured Avdotya Nikitishna, of champagne—not of your blood."

"I can never listen calmly when women are attacked," pursued Evdoksya. "It's awful, awful. Instead of attacking them, you'd better read Michelet's book, De l'amour. That's exquisite! Gentlemen, let us talk of love," added Evdoksya, letting her arm fall languidly on the rumpled sofa cushion.

A sudden silence followed. "No, why should we talk of love," said Bazarov; "but you mentioned just now a Madame Odintsov . . . That was what you called her, I think? Who is that lady?"

"She's charming, charming!" piped Sitnikov. "I will introduce you. Clever, rich, a widow. It's a pity, she's not yet advanced enough; she ought to see more of our Evdoksya. I drink your health, Evdoxie! Let us clink glasses! Et toc, et toc, et tin-tin-tin! Et toc, et toc, et tin-tin-tin! ! !"

"Victor, you're a wretch."

The lunch dragged on a long while. The first bottle of champagne was followed by another, a third, and even a fourth. . . . Evdoksya chattered without pause; Sitnikov seconded her. They had much discussion upon the question whether marriage was a prejudice or a crime, and whether men were born equal or not, and precisely what individuality consists in. Things came at last to Evdoksya, flushed from the wine she had drunk, tapping with her flat finger-tips on the keys of a discordant piano, and beginning to sing in a hoarse voice, first gipsy songs, and then Seymour Schiff's song, "Granada lies slumbering"; while Sitnikov tied a scarf round his head, and represented the dying lover at the words—

> *"And thy lips to mine*
> *In burning kiss entwine."*

Arkady could not stand it at last. "Gentlemen, it's getting something like Bedlam," he remarked aloud. Bazarov, who had at rare intervals put in an ironical word in the conversation—he paid more attention to the champagne —gave a loud yawn, got up, and, without taking leave of their hostess, he walked off with Arkady. Sitnikov jumped up and followed them.

"Well, what do you think of her?" he inquired, skipping obsequiously from right to left of them. "I told you, you see, a remarkable personality! If we only had more women like that! She is, in her own way, an expression of the highest morality."

"And is that establishment of your governor's an expression of the highest morality too?" observed Bazarov, pointing to a ginshop which they were passing at that instant.

Sitnikov again went off into a shrill laugh. He was greatly ashamed of his origin, and did not know whether to feel flattered or offended at Bazarov's unexpected familiarity.

XIV

A FEW DAYS LATER the ball at the Governor's took place. Matvy Ilyitch was the real "hero of the occasion." The marshal of nobility declared to all and each that he had come simply out of respect for him; while the Governor, even at the ball, even while he remained perfectly motionless, was still "making arrangements." The affability of Matvy Ilyitch's demeanour could only be equalled by its dignity. He was gracious to all, to some with a shade of disgust, to others with a shade of respect; he was all bows and smiles *"en vrai chevalier français"* before the ladies, and was continually giving vent to a hearty, sonorous, unshared laugh, such as befits a high official. He slapped Arkady on the back, and called him loudly "nephew"; vouch-safed Bazarov—who was attired in a rather old evening coat—a sidelong glance in passing—absent but condescending—and an indistinct but affable grunt, in which nothing could be distinguished but "I . . ." and "very much"; gave Sitnikov a finger and a smile, though with his head already averted; even to Madame Kukshin, who made her appearance at the ball with dirty gloves, no crinoline, and a bird of Paradise in her hair, he said *"enchanté."* There were crowds of people, and no lack of dancing men; the civilians were for the most part standing close along the walls, but the officers danced assiduously, especially one of them who had spent six weeks in Paris, where he had mastered various daring interjections of the kind of— "*zut*," "*Ah, fichtr-re*," "*pst, pst, mon bibi*," and such. He pronounced them to perfection with genuine Parisian *chic*, and at the same time he said "*si j'aurais*" for "*si j'avais*," "*absolument*" in the sense of "absolutely," expressed himself, in fact, in that Great Russo-French jargon which the French ridicule so when they have no reason for assuring us that we speak French like angels, "*comme des anges*."

Arkady, as we are aware, danced badly, while Bazarov did not dance at all; they both took up their position in a corner; Sitnikov joined himself on to them, with an expression of contemptuous scorn on his face, and giving vent to spiteful comments, he looked insolently about him, and seemed to be really enjoying himself. Suddenly his face changed, and turning to Arkady, he said, with some show of embarrassment it seemed, "Odintsova is here!"

Arkady looked round, and saw a tall woman in a black dress standing at the door of the room. He was struck by the dignity of her carriage. Her bare arms lay gracefully beside her slender waist; gracefully some light sprays of fuchsia drooped from her shining hair on to her sloping shoulders; her clear eyes looked out from under a rather overhanging white brow, with a tranquil and intelligent expression—tranquil it was precisely, not pensive—and on her lips was a scarcely perceptible smile. There was a kind of gracious and gentle force about her face.

"Do you know her?" Arkady asked Sitnikov.

"Intimately. Would you like me to introduce you?"

"Please . . . after this quadrille."

Bazarov's attention, too, was directed to Madame Odintsov.

"That's a striking figure," he remarked. "Not like the other females."

After waiting till the end of the quadrille, Sitnikov led Arkady up to Madame Odintsov; but he hardly seemed to be intimately acquainted with her; he was embarrassed in his sentences, while she looked at him in some surprise. But her face assumed an expression of pleasure when she heard Arkady's surname. She asked him whether he was not the son of Nikolai Petrovitch.

"Yes."

"I have seen your father twice, and have heard a great deal about him," she went on; "I am glad to make your acquaintance."

At that instant some adjutant flew up to her and begged for a quadrille. She consented.

"Do you dance then?" asked Arkady respectfully.

"Yes, I dance. Why do you suppose I don't dance? Do you think I am too old?"

"Really, how could I possibly. . . . But in that case, let me ask you for a mazurka."

Madame Odintsov smiled graciously. "Certainly," she said, and she looked at Arkady, not exactly with an air of superiority, but as married sisters look at very young brothers. Madame Odintsov was a little older than

Arkady—she was twenty-nine—but in her presence he felt himself a school-boy, a little student, so that the difference in age between them seemed of more consequence. Matvy Ilyitch approached her with a majestic air and ingratiating speeches. Arkady moved away, but he still watched; he could not take his eyes off her even during the quadrille. She talked with equal ease to her partner and to the grand official, softly turned her head and eyes, and twice laughed softly. Her nose—like almost all Russian noses—was a little thick; and her complexion was not perfectly clear; Arkady made up his mind, for all that, that he had never before met such an attractive woman. He could not get the sound of her voice out of his ears; the very folds of her dress seemed to hang upon her differently from all the rest—more gracefully and amply—and her movements were distinguished by a peculiar smoothness and naturalness.

Arkady felt some timidity in his heart when at the first sounds of the mazurka he began to sit it out beside his partner; he had prepared to enter into a conversation with her, but he only passed his hand through his hair, and could not find a single word to say. But his timidity and agitation did not last long; Madame Odintsov's tranquillity gained upon him too; before a quarter of an hour had passed he was telling her freely about his father, his uncle, his life in Petersburg and in the country. Madame Odintsov listened to him with courteous sympathy, slightly opening and closing her fan; his talk was broken off when partners came for her; Sitnikov, among others, twice asked her. She came back, sat down again, took up her fan, and her bosom did not even heave more rapidly, while Arkady fell to chattering again, filled through and through by the happiness of being near her, talking to her, looking at her eyes, her lovely brow, all her sweet dignified, clever face. She said little, but her words showed a knowledge of life; from some of her observations, Arkady gathered that this young woman had already felt and thought much. . . .

"Who is that you were standing with?" she asked him, "when Mr. Sitnikov brought you to me?"

"Did you notice him?" Arkady asked in his turn. "He has a splendid face, hasn't he? That's Bazarov, my friend."

Arkady fell to discussing "his friend." He spoke of him in such detail, and with such enthusiasm, that Madame Odintsov turned towards him and looked attentively at him. Meanwhile, the mazurka was drawing to a close. Arkady felt sorry to part from his partner; he had spent nearly an hour so happily with her! He had, it is true, during the whole time continually felt as though she were condescending to him, as though he ought to be grateful to her . . . but young hearts are not weighed down by that feeling.

The music stopped. "*Mercy*," said Madame Odintsov, getting up. "You promised to come and see me; bring your friend with you. I shall be very curious to see the man who has the courage to believe in nothing."

The Governor came up to Madame Odintsov, announced that supper was ready, and, with a careworn face, offered her his arm. As she went away, she turned to give a last smile and bow to Arkady. He bowed low, looked after her (how graceful her figure seemed to him, draped in the greyish lustre of the black silk!), and thinking, "This minute she has forgotten my existence," was conscious of an exquisite humility in his soul.

"Well?" Bazarov questioned him, directly he had gone back to him in the corner. "Did you have a good time? A gentleman has just been talking to me about that lady; he said, 'She's—oh, fie! fie!' but I fancy the fellow was a fool. What do you think, what is she?—oh, fie! fie!"

"I don't quite understand that definition," answered Arkady.

"Oh, my! What innocence!"

"In that case, I don't understand the gentleman you quote. Madame Odintsov is very sweet, no doubt, but she behaves so coldly and severely, that . . ."

"Still waters . . . you know!" put in Bazarov. "That's just what gives it piquancy. You like ices, I expect?"

"Perhaps," muttered Arkady. "I can't give an opinion about that. She wishes to make your acquaintance, and has asked me to bring you to see her."

"I can imagine how you've described me! But you did very well. Take me. Whatever she may be—whether she's simply a provincial lioness, or 'advanced' after Kukshina's fashion—any way she's got a pair of shoulders such as I've not set eyes on for a long while."

Arkady was wounded by Bazarov's cynicism, but—as often happens—he reproached his friend not precisely for what he did not like in him . . .

"Why are you unwilling to allow freethinking in women?" he said in a low voice.

"Because, my boy, as far as my observations go, the only freethinkers among women are frights."

The conversation was cut short at this point. Both the young men went away immediately after supper. They were pursued by a nervously malicious, but somewhat faint-hearted laugh from Madame Kukshin; her vanity had been deeply wounded by neither of them having paid any attention to her. She stayed later than any one at the ball, and at four o'clock in the morning she was dancing a polka-mazurka with Sitnikov in the Parisian style. This edifying spectacle was the final event of the Governor's ball.

XV

"LET'S SEE what species of mammalia this specimen belongs to," Bazarov said to Arkady the following day, as they mounted the staircase of the hotel in which Madame Odintsov was staying. "I scent out something wrong here."

"I'm surprised at you!" cried Arkady. "What? You, you, Bazarov, clinging to the narrow morality, which . . ."

"What a funny fellow you are!" Bazarov cut him short, carelessly. "Don't you know that 'something wrong' means 'something right' in my dialect and for me? It's an advantage for me, of course. Didn't you tell me yourself this morning that she made a strange marriage, though, to my mind, to marry a rich old man is by no means a strange thing to do, but, on the contrary, very sensible. I don't believe the gossip of the town; but I should like to think, as our cultivated Governor says, that it's well-grounded."

Arkady made no answer, and knocked at the door of the apartments. A young servant in livery conducted the two friends into a large room, badly furnished, like all rooms in Russian hotels, but filled with flowers. Soon Madame Odintsov herself appeared in a simple morning dress. She seemed still younger by the light of the spring sunshine. Arkady presented Bazarov, and noticed with secret amazement that he seemed embarrassed, while Madame Odintsov remained perfectly tranquil, as she had been the previous day. Bazarov himself was conscious of being embarrassed, and was irritated by it. "Here's a go!—frightened of a petticoat!" he thought, and lolling, quite like Sitnikov, in an easy-chair, he began talking with an exaggerated appearance of ease, while Madame Odintsov kept her clear eyes fixed on him.

Anna Sergyevna Odintsov was the daughter of Sergay Nikolaevitch Loktev, notorious for his personal beauty, his speculations, and his gambling propensities, who after cutting a figure and making a sensation for fifteen years in Petersburg and Moscow, finished by ruining himself completely at cards, and was forced to retire to the country, where, however, he soon after died, leaving a very small property to his two daughters—Anna, a girl of twenty, and Katya, a child of twelve. Their mother, who came of an impoverished line of princes—the H—s—had died at Petersburg when her husband was in his heyday. Anna's position after her father's death was very difficult. The brilliant education she had received in Petersburg had not fitted her for putting up with the cares of domestic life and economy,—for an obscure existence in the country. She knew positively no one in the whole neighbourhood, and there was no one she could consult. Her father had tried to avoid all contact with the neighbours; he despised them in his way, and they despised him in theirs. She did not lose her head, however, and promptly sent for a sister of her mother's, Princess Avdotya Stepanovna H——, a spiteful and arrogant old lady, who, on installing herself in her niece's house, appropriated all the best rooms for her own use, scolded and grumbled from morning till night, and would not go for a walk even in the garden unattended by her one serf, a surly footman in a threadbare pea-green livery with light blue trimming and a three-cornered hat. Anna put up patiently with all her aunt's whims, gradually set to work on her sister's education, and was, it seemed, already getting reconciled to the idea of wasting her life in the wilds. . . . But destiny had decreed another fate of her. She chanced to be seen by Odintsov, a very wealthy man of forty-six, an eccentric hypochondriac, stout, heavy, and sour; but not stupid, and not ill-natured; he fell in love with her, and offered her his hand. She consented to become his wife, and he lived six years with her, and on his death settled all his property upon her. Anna Sergyevna remained in the country for nearly a year after his death; then she went abroad with her sister, but only stopped in Germany; she got tired of it and came back to live at her favourite Nikolskoe, which was nearly thirty miles from the town of X——. There she had a magnificent, splendidly furnished house and a beautiful garden, with conservatories; her late husband had spared no expense to gratify his fancies. Anna Sergyevna went very rarely to the town, generally only on business, and even then she did not stay long. She was not liked in the province; there had been a fearful outcry at her marriage with Odintsov, all sorts of fictions were told about her; it was asserted that she had helped her father in his cardsharping tricks, and even that she had gone abroad for excellent reasons, that it had been necessary to conceal the lamentable consequences . . . "You understand?" the indignant gossips would wind up. "She has gone through the fire," was said of her; to which a noted provincial wit usually added: "And through all the other elements?" All this talk reached her; but she turned a deaf ear to it; there was much independence and a good deal of determination in her character.

Madame Odintsov sat leaning back in her easy-chair, and listened with folded hands to Bazarov. He, contrary to his habit, was talking a good deal, and obviously trying to interest her—again a surprise for Arkady. He could not make up his mind whether Bazarov was attaining his object. It was difficult to conjecture from Anna Sergyevna's face what impression was being made on her; it retained the same expression, gracious and refined; her beautiful eyes were lighted up by attention, but by quiet attention. Bazarov's bad manners had impressed her unpleasantly for the first minutes of the visit like a bad smell or a discordant sound; but she saw at once that he was nervous, and that even flattered her. Nothing was repulsive to her but vulgarity, and no one could have accused Bazarov of vulgarity. Arkady was fated to meet with surprises that day. He had expected that Bazarov would talk to a clever woman like Madame Odintsov about his opinions and his views; she had herself expressed a desire to listen to the man "who dares to have no belief in anything"; but, instead of that, Bazarov talked about medicine, about homœopathy, and about botany. It turned out that Madame Odintsov had not wasted her time in solitude; she had read a good many excellent books, and spoke herself in excellent Russian. She turned the conversation upon music; but noticing that Bazarov did not appreciate art, she quietly brought it back to botany, even though Arkady was just launching into a discourse upon the significance of national melodies. Madame Odintsov treated him as though he were a younger brother; she seemed to appreciate his good-nature and youthful simplicity and that was all. For over three hours, a lively conversation was kept up, ranging freely over various subjects.

The friends at last got up and began to take leave. Anna Sergyevna looked cordially at them, held out her beautiful, white hand to both, and, after a moment's thought, said with a doubtful but delightful smile, "If you are not afraid of being dull, gentlemen, come and see me at Nikolskoe."

"Oh, Anna Sergyevna," cried Arkady, "I shall think it the greatest happiness . . ."

"And you, Monsieur Bazarov?"

Bazarov only bowed, and a last surprise was in store for Arkady; he noticed that his friend was blushing.

"Well?" he said to him in the street; "are you still of the same opinion—that she's . . ."

"Who can tell? See how correct she is!" retorted Bazarov; and after a brief pause he added, "She's a perfect grand-duchess, a royal personage. She only needs a train on behind, and a crown on her head."

"Our grand-duchesses don't talk Russian like that," remarked Arkady.

"She's seen ups and downs, my dear boy; she's known what it is to be hard up!"

"Any way, she's charming," observed Arkady.

"What a magnificent body," pursued Bazarov. "Shouldn't I like to see it on the dissecting-table."

"Hush, for mercy's sake, Yevgeny! that's beyond everything."

"Well, don't get angry, you baby. I mean it's first rate. We must go to stay with her."

"When?"

"Well, why not the day after to-morrow. What is there to do here? Drink champagne with Kukshina? Listen to your cousin, the Liberal dignitary? . . . Let's be off the day after to-morrow. By the way, too—my father's little place is not far from there. This Nikolskoe's on the S—— road, isn't it?"

"Yes."

"Optime, why hesitate? Leave that to fools and prigs! I say, what a splendid body!"

Three days later the two friends were driving along the road to Nikolskoe. The day was bright, and not too hot, and the sleek posting-horses trotted smartly along, switching their tied and plaited tails. Arkady looked at the road, and not knowing why, he smiled.

"Congratulate me," cried Bazarov suddenly, "to-day's the 22nd of June, my guardian angel's day. Let's see how he will watch over me. To-day they expect me home," he added, dropping his voice. . . . "Well, they can go on expecting. . . . What does it matter!"

XVI

THE COUNTRY-HOUSE in which Anna Sergyevna lived stood on an exposed hill at no great distance from a yellow stone church with a green roof, white columns, and a fresco over the principal entrance representing the "Resurrection of Christ" in the "Italian" style. Sprawling in the foreground of the picture was a swarthy warrior in a helmet, specially conspicuous for his rotund contours. Behind the church a long village stretched in two rows, with chimneys peeping out here and there above the thatched roofs.

The manor-house was built in the same style as the church, the style known among us as that of Alexander; the house, too, was painted yellow, and had a green roof, and white columns, and a pediment with an escutcheon on it. The architect had designed both buildings with the approval of the deceased Odintsov, who could not endure—as he expressed it—idle and arbitrary innovations. The house was enclosed on both sides by the dark trees of an old garden; an avenue of lopped pines led up to the entrance.

Our friends were met in the hall by two tall footmen in livery; one of them at once ran for the steward. The steward, a stout man in a black dress coat, promptly appeared and led the visitors by a staircase covered with rugs to a special room, in which two bedsteads were already prepared for them with all necessaries for the toilet. It was clear that order reigned supreme in the house; everything was clean, everywhere there was a peculiar delicate fragrance, just as there is in the reception rooms of ministers.

"Anna Sergyevna asks you to come to her in half-an-hour," the steward announced; "will there be orders to give meanwhile?"

"No orders," answered Bazarov; "perhaps you will be so good as to trouble yourself to bring me a glass of vodka."

"Yes, sir," said the steward, looking in some perplexity, and he withdrew, his boots creaking as he walked.

"What *grand genre!*" remarked Bazarov. "That's what it's called in your set, isn't it? She's a grand-duchess, and that's all about it."

"A nice grand-duchess," retorted Arkady, "at the very first meeting she invited such great aristocrats as you and me to stay with her."

"Especially me, a future doctor, and a doctor's son, and a village sexton's grandson. . . . You know, I suppose, I'm the grandson of a sexton? Like the great Speransky," added Bazarov after a brief pause, contracting his lips. "At any rate she likes to be comfortable; oh, doesn't she, this lady! Oughtn't we to put on evening dress?"

Arkady only shrugged his shoulders . . . but he, too, was conscious of a little nervousness.

Half-an-hour later Bazarov and Arkady went together into the drawing-room. It was a large lofty room, furnished rather luxuriously but without particularly good taste. Heavy, expensive furniture stood in the ordinary stiff arrangement along the walls, which were covered with cinnamon-coloured paper with gold flowers on it; Odintsov had ordered the furniture from Moscow through a friend and agent of his, a spirit merchant. Over a sofa in the centre of one wall hung a portrait of a faded light-haired man—and it seemed to look with displeasure at the visitors. "It must be the late lamented," Bazarov whispered to Arkady, and turning up his nose, he added, "Hadn't we better bolt . . . ?" But at that instant the lady of the house entered. She wore a light barège dress; her hair smoothly combed back behind her ears gave a girlish expression to her pure and fresh face.

"Thank you for keeping your promise," she began. "You must stay a little while with me; it's really not bad here. I will introduce you to my sister; she plays the piano well. That is a matter of indifference to you, Monsieur Bazarov; but you, I think, Monsieur Kirsanov, are fond of music. Besides my sister I have an old aunt living with me, and one of our neighbours comes in sometimes to play cards; that makes up all our circle. And now let us sit down."

Madame Odintsov delivered all this little speech with peculiar precision, as though she had learned it by heart; then she turned to Arkady. It appeared that her mother had known Arkady's mother, and had even been her confidante in her love for Nikolai Petrovitch. Arkady began talking with great warmth of his dead mother; while Bazarov fell to turning over albums. "What a tame cat I'm getting!" he was thinking to himself.

A beautiful greyhound with a blue collar on, ran into the drawing-room, tapping on the floor with his paws, and after him entered a girl of eighteen, black-haired and dark-skinned, with a rather round but pleasing face, and small dark eyes. In her hands she held a basket filled with flowers.

"This is my Katya," said Madame Odintsov, indicating her with a motion of her head. Katya made a slight curtsey, placed herself beside her sister, and began picking out flowers. The greyhound, whose name was Fifi, went up to both of the visitors, in turn wagging his tail, and thrusting his cold nose into their hands.

"Did you pick all that yourself?" asked Madame Odintsov.

"Yes," answered Katya.

"Is auntie coming to tea?"

"Yes."

When Katya spoke, she had a very charming smile, sweet, timid, and candid, and looked up from under her eyebrows with a sort of humorous severity. Everything about her was still young and undeveloped; the voice, and the bloom on her whole face, and the rosy hands, with white palms, and the rather narrow shoulders. . . . She was constantly blushing and getting out of breath.

Madame Odintsov turned to Bazarov. "You are looking at pictures from politeness, Yevgeny Vassilyitch," she began. "That does not interest you. You had better come nearer to us, and let us have a discussion about something."

Bazarov went closer. "What subject have you decided upon for discussion?" he said.

"What you like. I warn you, I am dreadfully argumentative."

"You?"

"Yes. That seems to surprise you. Why?"

"Because, as far as I can judge, you have a calm, cool character, and one must be impulsive to be argumentative."

"How can you have had time to understand me so soon? In the first place, I am impatient and obstinate—you should ask Katya; and secondly, I am very easily carried away."

Bazarov looked at Anna Sergyevna. "Perhaps; you must know best. And so you are inclined for a discussion—by all means. I was looking through the views of the Saxon mountains in your album, and you remarked that that couldn't interest me. You said so, because you suppose me to have no feeling for art, and as a fact I haven't any; but these views might be interesting to me from a geological standpoint, for the formation of the mountains, for instance."

"Excuse me; but as a geologist, you would sooner have recourse to a book, to a special work on the subject and not to a drawing."

"The drawing shows me at a glance what would be spread over ten pages in a book."

Anna Sergyevna was silent for a little.

"And so you haven't the least artistic feeling?" she observed, putting her elbow on the table, and by that very action bringing her face nearer to Bazarov. "How can you get on without it?"

"Why, what is it wanted for, may I ask?"

"Well, at least to enable one to study and understand men."

Bazarov smiled. "In the first place, experience of life does that; and in the second, I assure you, studying separate individuals is not worth the trouble. All people are like one another, in soul as in body; each of us has brain, spleen, heart, and lungs made alike; and the so-called moral qualities are the same in all; the slight variations are of no importance. A single human specimen is sufficient to judge of all by. People are like trees in a forest; no botanist would think of studying each individual birch-tree."

Katya, who was arranging the flowers, one at a time in a leisurely fashion, lifted her eyes to Bazarov with a puzzled look, and meeting his rapid and careless glance, she crimsoned up to her ears. Anna Sergyevna shook her head.

"The trees in a forest," she repeated. "Then according to you there is no difference between the stupid and the clever person, between the good-natured and ill-natured?"

"No, there is a difference, just as between the sick and the healthy. The lungs of a consumptive patient are not in the same condition as yours and mine, though they are made on the same plan. We know approximately what physical diseases come from; moral diseases come from bad education, from all the nonsense people's heads are stuffed with from childhood up, from the defective state of society; in short, reform society, and there will be no diseases."

Bazarov said all this with an air, as though he were all the while thinking to himself, "Believe me or not, as you like, it's all one to me!" He slowly passed his fingers over his whiskers, while his eyes strayed about the room.

"And you conclude," observed Anna Sergyevna, "that when society is reformed, there will be no stupid nor wicked people?"

"At any rate, in a proper organization of society, it will be absolutely the same whether a man is stupid or clever, wicked or good."

"Yes, I understand; they will all have the same spleen."

"Precisely so, madam."

Madame Odintsov turned to Arkady. "And what is your opinion, Arkady Nikolaevitch?"

"I agree with Yevgeny," he answered.

Katya looked up at him from under her eyelids.

"You amaze me, gentlemen," commented Madame Odintsov, "but we will have more talk together. But now I hear my aunt coming in to tea; we must spare her."

Anna Sergyevna's aunt, Princess H——, a thin little woman with a pinched-up face, drawn together like a fist, and staring ill-natured-looking eyes under a grey front, came in, and, scarcely bowing to the guests, she dropped into a wide velvet covered arm-chair, upon which no one but herself was privileged to sit. Katya put a footstool under her feet; the old lady did not thank her, did not even look at her, only her hands shook under the yellow shawl, which almost covered her feeble body. The Princess liked yellow; her cap, too, had bright yellow ribbons.

"How have you slept, aunt?" inquired Madame Odintsov, raising her voice.

"That dog in here again," the old lady muttered in reply, and noticing Fifi was making two hesitating steps in her direction, she cried, "Ss—ss!"

Katya called Fifi and opened the door for him.

Fifi rushed out delighted, in the expectation of being taken out for a walk; but when he was left alone outside the door, he began scratching and whining. The princess scowled. Katya was about to go out. . . .

"I expect tea is ready," said Madame Odintsov.

"Come, gentlemen; aunt, will you go in to tea?"

The princess got up from her chair without speaking and led the way out of the drawing-room. They all followed her into the dining-room. A little page in livery drew back, with a scraping sound, from the table, an arm-chair covered with cushions, devoted to the princess's use; she sank into it; Katya in pouring out the tea handed her first a cup emblazoned with a heraldic crest. The old lady put some honey in her cup (she considered it both sinful and extravagant to drink tea with sugar in it, though she never spent a farthing herself on anything), and suddenly asked in a hoarse voice, "And what does Prince Ivan write?"

No one made her any reply. Bazarov and Arkady soon guessed that they paid no attention to her, though they treated her respectfully.

"Because of her grand family," thought Bazarov. . . .

After tea, Anna Sergyevna suggested they should go out for a walk; but it began to rain a little, and the whole party, with the exception of the princess, returned to the drawing-room. The neighbour, the devoted card-player, arrived; his name was Porfiry Platonitch, a stoutish, greyish man with short, spindly legs, very polite and ready to be amused. Anna Sergyevna, who still talked principally with Bazarov, asked him whether he'd like to try a contest with them in the old-fashioned way at preference? Bazarov assented, saying "that he ought to prepare himself beforehand for the duties awaiting him as a country doctor."

"You must be careful," observed Anna Sergyevna; "Porfiry Platonitch and I will beat you. And you, Katya," she added, "play something to Arkady Nikolaevitch; he is fond of music, and we can listen, too."

Katya went unwillingly to the piano; and Arkady, though he certainly was fond of music, unwillingly followed her; it seemed to him that Madame Odintsov was sending him away, and already, like every young man at his age, he felt a vague and oppressive emotion surging up in his heart, like the forebodings of love. Katya raised the top of the piano, and not looking at Arkady, she said in a low voice:

"What am I to play you?"

"What you like," answered Arkady indifferently.

"What sort of music do you like best?" repeated Katya, without changing her attitude.

"Classical," Arkady answered in the same tone of voice.

"Do you like Mozart?"

"Yes, I like Mozart."

Katya pulled out Mozart's Sonata-Fantasia in C minor. She played very well, though rather over correctly and precisely. She sat upright and immovable, her eyes fixed on the notes, and her lips tightly compressed, only at the end of the sonata her face glowed, her hair came loose, and a little lock fell on to her dark brow.

Arkady was particularly struck by the last part of the sonata, the part in which, in the midst of the bewitching gaiety of the careless melody, the pangs of such mournful, almost tragic suffering, suddenly break in. . . . But the ideas stirred in him by Mozart's music had no reference to Katya. Looking at her, he simply thought, "Well, that young lady doesn't play badly, and she's not bad-looking either."

When she had finished the sonata, Katya, without taking her hands from the keys, asked, "Is that enough?" Arkady declared that he could not venture to trouble her again, and began talking to her about Mozart; he asked her whether she had chosen that sonata herself, or some one had recommended it to her. But Katya answered him in monosyllables; she withdrew into herself, went back into her shell. When this happened to her, she did not very quickly come out again; her face even assumed at such times an obstinate, almost stupid expression. She was not exactly shy, but diffident, and rather overawed by her sister, who had educated her, and who had no suspicion of the fact. Arkady was reduced at last to calling Fifi to him, and with an affable smile patting him on the head to give himself an appearance of being at home.

Katya set to work again upon her flowers.

Bazarov meanwhile was losing and losing. Anna Sergyevna played cards in masterly fashion; Porfiry Platonitch, too, could hold his own in the game. Bazarov lost a sum which, though trifling in itself, was not altogether pleasant for him. At supper Anna Sergyevna again turned the conversation on botany.

"We will go for a walk to-morrow morning," she said to him. "I want you to teach me the Latin names of the wild flowers and their species."

"What use are the Latin names to you?" asked Bazarov.

"Order is needed in everything," she answered.

"What an exquisite woman Anna Sergyevna is!" cried Arkady, when he was alone with his friend in the room assigned to them.

"Yes," answered Bazarov, "a female with brains. Yes, and she's seen life too."

"In what sense do you mean that, Yevgeny Vassilitch?"

"In a good sense, a good sense, my dear friend, Arkady Nikolaeitch! I'm convinced she manages her estate capitally too. But what's splendid is not her, but her sister."

"What, that little dark thing?"

"Yes, that little dark thing. She now is fresh and untouched, and shy and silent, and anything you like. She's worth educating and developing. You might make something fine out of her; but the other's—a stale loaf."

Arkady made no reply to Bazarov, and each of them got into bed with rather singular thoughts in his head.

Anna Sergyevna, too, thought of her guests that evening. She liked Bazarov for the absence of gallantry in him, and even for his sharply defined views. She found in him something new, which she had not chanced to meet before, and she was curious.

Anna Sergyevna was a rather strange creature. Having no prejudices of any kind, having no strong convictions even, she never gave way or went out of her way for anything. She had seen many things very clearly; she had been interested in many things, but nothing had completely satisfied her; indeed, she hardly desired complete satisfaction. Her intellect was at the same time inquiring and indifferent; her doubts were never soothed to forgetfulness, and they never grew strong enough to distract her. Had she not been rich and independent, she would perhaps have thrown herself into the struggle, and have known passion. But life was easy for her, though she was bored at times, and she went on passing day after day with deliberation, never in a hurry, placid, and only rarely disturbed. Dreams sometimes danced in rainbow colours before her eyes even, but she breathed more freely when they died away, and did not regret them. Her imagination indeed overstepped the limits of what is reckoned permissible by conventional morality; but even then the blood flowed as quietly as ever in her fascinatingly graceful, tranquil body. Sometimes coming out of her fragrant bath all warm and enervated, she would fall to musing on the nothingness of life, the sorrow, the labour, the malice of it. . . . Her soul would be filled with sudden daring, and would flow with generous ardour, but a draught would blow from a half-closed window, and Anna Sergyevna would shrink into herself, and feel plaintive and almost angry, and there was only one thing she cared for at that instant—to get away from that horrid draught.

Like all women who have not succeeded in loving, she wanted something, without herself knowing what. Strictly speaking, she wanted nothing; but it seemed to her that she wanted everything. She could hardly endure the late Odintsov (she had married him from prudential motives, though probably she would not have consented to become his wife if she had not considered him a good sort of man), and had conceived a secret repugnance for all men, whom she could only figure to herself as slovenly, heavy, drowsy, and feebly importunate creatures. Once, somewhere abroad, she had met a handsome young Swede, with a chivalrous expression, with honest blue eyes under an open brow; he had made a powerful impression on her, but it had not prevented her from going back to Russia.

"A strange man this doctor!" she thought as she lay in her luxurious bed on lace pillows under a light silk coverlet. . . . Anna Sergyevna had inherited from her father a little of his inclination for splendour. She had fondly loved her sinful but good-natured father, and he had idolized her, used to joke with her in a friendly way as though she were an equal, and to confide in her fully, to ask her advice. Her mother she scarcely remembered.

"This doctor is a strange man!" she repeated to herself. She stretched, smiled, clasped her hands behind her head, then ran her eyes over two pages of a stupid French novel, dropped the book—and fell asleep, all pure and cold, in her pure and fragrant linen.

The following morning Anna Sergyevna went off botanizing with Bazarov directly after lunch, and returned just before dinner; Arkady did not go off anywhere, and spent about an hour with Katya. He was not bored with her; she offered of herself to repeat the sonata of the day before; but when Madame Odintsov came back at last, when he caught sight of her, he felt an instantaneous pang at his heart. She came through the garden with a rather tired step; her cheeks were glowing and her eyes shining more brightly than usual under her round straw hat. She was twirling in her fingers the thin stalk of a wildflower, a light mantle had slipped down to her elbows, and the wide gray ribbons of her hat were clinging to her bosom. Bazarov walked behind her, self-confident and careless as usual, but the expression of his face, cheerful and even friendly as it was, did not please Arkady. Muttering between his teeth, "Good-morning!" Bazarov went away to his room, while Madame Odintsov shook Arkady's hand abstractedly, and also walked past him.

"Good-morning!" thought Arkady. . . . "As though we had not seen each other already to-day!"

XVII

Time, it is well known, sometimes flies like a bird, sometimes crawls like a worm; but man is wont to be particularly happy when he does not even notice whether it passes quickly or slowly. It was in that way Arkady and Bazarov spent a fortnight at Madame Odintsov's. The good order she had established in her house and in her life partly contributed to this result. She adhered strictly to this order herself, and forced others to submit to it. Everything during the day was done at a fixed time. In the morning, precisely at eight o'clock, all the party assembled for tea; from morning tea till lunch time every one did what he pleased, the hostess herself was engaged with her bailiff (the estate was on the rent system), her steward, and her head housekeeper. Before dinner the party met again for conversation or reading; the evening was devoted to walking, cards, and music; at half-past ten Anna Sergyevna retired to her own room, gave her orders for the following day, and went to bed. Bazarov did not like this measured, somewhat ostentatious punctuality in daily life, "like moving along rails," he pronounced it to be; the footmen in livery, the decorous stewards, offended his democratic sentiments. He declared that if one went so far, one might as well dine in the English style at once—in tail-coats and white ties. He once spoke plainly upon the subject to Anna Sergyevna. Her attitude was such that no one hesitated to speak his mind freely before her. She heard him out; and then her comment was, "From your point of view, you are right— and perhaps, in that respect, I am too much of a lady; but there's no living in the country without order, one would be devoured by ennui," and she continued to go her own way. Bazarov grumbled, but the very reason life was so easy for him and Arkady at Madame Odintsov's was that everything in the house "moved on rails." For all that, a change had taken place in both the young men since the first days of their stay at Nikolskoe. Bazarov, in whom Anna Sergyevna was obviously interested, though she seldom agreed with him, began to show signs of an unrest, unprecedented in him; he was easily put out of temper, and unwilling to talk, he looked irritated, and could not sit still in one place, just as though he were possessed by some secret longing; while Arkady, who had made up his mind conclusively that he was in love with Madame Odintsov, had begun to yield to a gentle melancholy. This melancholy did not, however, prevent him from becoming friendly with Katya; it even impelled him to get into friendly, affectionate terms with her. "*She* does not appreciate me? So be it. . . . But here is a good creature, who does not repulse me," he thought, and his heart again knew the sweetness of magnanimous emotions. Katya vaguely realized that he was seeking a sort of consolation in her company, and did not deny him or herself the innocent pleasure of a half-shy, half-confidential friendship. They did not talk to each other in Anna Sergyevna's presence; Katya always shrank into herself under her sister's sharp eyes; while Arkady, as befits a man in love, could pay attention to nothing else when near the object of his passion; but he was happy with Katya alone. He was conscious that he did not possess the power to interest Madame Odintsov; he was shy and at a loss when he was left alone with her, and she did not know what to say to him, he was too young for her. With Katya, on the other hand, Arkady felt at home; he treated her condescendingly, encouraged her to express the impressions made on her by music, reading novels, verses, and other such trifles, without noticing or realizing that these trifles were what interested him too. Katya, on her side, did not try to drive away melancholy. Arkady was at his ease with Katya, Madame Odintsov with Bazarov, and thus it usually came to pass that the two couples, after being a little while together, went off on their separate ways, especially during the walks. Katya adored nature, and Arkady loved it, though he did not dare to acknowledge it; Madame Odintsov was, like Bazarov, rather indifferent to the beauties of nature. The almost continual separation of the two friends was not without its consequences; the relations between them began to change. Bazarov gave up talking to Arkady about Madame Odintsov, gave up even abusing her "aristocratic ways"; Katya, it is true, he praised as before, and only advised him to restrain her sentimental tendencies, but his praises were hurried, his advice dry, and in general he talked less to Arkady than before . . . he seemed to avoid him, seemed ill at ease with him.

Arkady observed it all, but he kept his observations to himself.

The real cause of all this "newness" was the feeling inspired in Bazarov by Madame Odintsov, a feeling which tortured and maddened him, and which he would at once have denied, with scornful laughter and cynical abuse, if any one had ever so remotely hinted at the possibility of what was taking place in him. Bazarov had a great love for women and for feminine beauty; but love in the ideal, or, as he expressed it, romantic sense, he called lunacy, unpardonable imbecility; he regarded chivalrous sentiments as something of the nature of deformity or disease, and had more than once expressed his wonder that Toggenburg and all the minnesingers and troubadours had not been put into a lunatic asylum. "If a woman takes your fancy," he used to say, "try and gain your end; but if you can't—well, turn your back on her—there are lots of good fish in the sea." Madame Odintsov had taken his fancy; the rumours about her, the freedom and independence of her ideas, her unmistakable liking for him, all seemed to be in his favour, but he soon saw that with her he would not "gain his ends," and to turn his back on her he found, to his own bewilderment, beyond his power. His blood was on fire directly if he merely thought of her; he could easily have mastered his blood, but something else was taking root in him, something he had never admitted, at which he had always jeered, at which all his pride revolted. In his conversations with Anna Sergyevna he expressed more strongly than ever his calm contempt for everything idealistic; but when he was alone, with indignation he recognized idealism in himself. Then he would set off to the forest and walk with long strides about it, smashing the twigs that came in his way, and cursing under his breath both her and himself; or he would get into the hay-loft in the barn, and, obstinately closing his eyes, try to force himself to sleep, in which, of course, he did not always succeed. Suddenly his fancy would bring before him those chaste hands twining one day about his neck, those proud lips responding to his kisses, those intellectual eyes dwelling with tenderness—yes, with tenderness—on his, and his head went round, and he forgot himself for an instant, till indignation boiled up in him again. He caught himself in all sorts of "shameful" thoughts, as though he were driven on by a devil mocking him. Sometimes he fancied that there was a change taking place in Madame Odintsov too; that there were signs in the expression of her face of something special; that, perhaps . . . but at that point he would stamp, or grind his teeth, and clench his fists.

Meanwhile Bazarov was not altogether mistaken. He had struck Madame Odintsov's imagination; he interested her, she thought a great deal about him. In his absence, she was not dull, she was not impatient for his coming, but she always grew more lively on his appearance; she liked to be left alone with him, and she liked talking to him, even when he irritated her or offended her taste, her refined habits. She was, as it were, eager at once to sound him and to analyze herself.

One day walking in the garden with her, he suddenly announced, in a surly voice, that he intended going to his father's place very soon. . . . She turned white, as though something had given her a pang, and such a pang, that she wondered and pondered long after, what could be the meaning of it. Bazarov had spoken of his departure with no idea of putting her to the test, of seeing what would come of it; he never "fabricated." On the morning of that day he had an interview with his father's bailiff, who had taken care of him when he was a child, Timofeitch. This Timofeitch, a little old man of much experience and astuteness, with faded yellow hair, a weather-beaten red face, and tiny tear-drops in his shrunken eyes, unexpectedly appeared before Bazarov, in his shortish overcoat of stout greyish-blue cloth, girt with a strip of leather, and in tarred boots.

"Hullo, old man; how are you?" cried Bazarov.

"How do you do, Yevgeny Vassilyitch?" began the little old man, and he smiled with delight, so that his whole face was all at once covered with wrinkles.

"What have you come for? They sent for me, eh?"

"Upon my word, sir, how could we?" mumbled Timofeitch. (He remembered the strict injunctions he had received from his master on starting.) "We were sent to the town on business, and we'd heard news of your honour, so here we turned off on our way, that's to say—to have a look at your honour . . . as if we could think of disturbing you!"

"Come, don't tell lies!" Bazarov cut him short. "Is this the road to the town, do you mean to tell me?" Timofeitch hesitated, and made no answer. "Is my father well?"

"Thank God, yes."

"And my mother?"

"Anna Vlasyevna too, glory be to God."

"They are expecting me, I suppose?"

The little old man held his tiny head on one side.

"Ah, Yevgeny Vassilyitch, it makes one's heart ache to see them; it does really."

"Come, all right, all right, shut up! Tell them I'm coming soon."

"Yes, sir," answered Timofeitch, with a sigh.

As he went out of the house, he pulled his cap down on his head with both hands, clambered into a wretched-looking racing droshky, and went off at a trot, but not in the direction of the town.

On the evening of the same day, Madame Odintsov was sitting in her own room with Bazarov, while Arkady walked up and down the hall listening to Katya's playing. The princess had gone upstairs to her own room; she could not bear guests as a rule, and "especially this new riff-raff lot," as she called them. In the common rooms she only sulked; but she made up for it in her own room by breaking out into such abuse before her maid that the cap danced on her head, wig and all. Madame Odintsov was well aware of all this.

"How is it you are proposing to leave us?" she began; "how about your promise?"

Bazarov started. "What promise?"

"Have you forgotten? You meant to give me some lessons in chemistry."

"It can't be helped! My father expects me; I can't loiter any longer. However, you can read Pelouse et Frémy, *Notions générales de Chimie;* it's a good book, and clearly written. You will find everything you need in it."

"But do you remember; you assured me a book cannot take the place of . . . I've forgotten how you put it, but you know what I mean . . . do you remember?"

"It can't be helped!" repeated Bazarov.

"Why go away?" said Madame Odintsov, dropping her voice.

He glanced at her. Her head had fallen on to the back of her easy-chair, and her arms, bare to the elbows, were folded on her bosom. She seemed paler in the light of the single lamp covered with a perforated paper shade. An ample white gown hid her completely in its soft folds; even the tips of her feet, also crossed, were hardly seen.

"And why stay?" answered Bazarov.

Madame Odintsov turned her head slightly. "You ask why? Have you not enjoyed yourself with me? Or do you suppose you will not be missed here?"

"I am sure of it."

Madame Odintsov was silent a minute. "You are wrong in thinking that. But I don't believe you. You could not say that seriously." Bazarov still sat immovable. "Yevgeny Vassilyitch, why don't you speak?"

"Why, what am I to say to you? People are not generally worth being missed, and I less than most."

"Why so?"

"I'm a practical, uninteresting person. I don't know how to talk."

"You are fishing, Yevgeny Vassilyitch."

"That's not a habit of mine. Don't you know yourself that I've nothing in common with the elegant side of life, the side you prize so much?"

Madame Odintsov bit the corner of her handkerchief.

"You may think what you like, but I shall be dull when you go away."

"Arkady will remain," remarked Bazarov. Madame Odintsov shrugged her shoulders slightly. "I shall be dull," she repeated.

"Really? In any case you will not feel dull for long."

"What makes you suppose that?"

"Because you told me yourself that you are only dull when your regular routine is broken in upon. You have ordered your existence with such unimpeachable regularity that there can be no place in it for dulness or sadness . . . for any unpleasant emotions."

"And do you consider I am so unimpeachable . . . that's to say, that I have ordered my life with such regularity?"

"I should think so. Here's an example: in a few minutes it will strike ten, and I know beforehand that you will drive me away."

"No; I'm not going to drive you away, Yevgeny Vassilyitch. You may stay. Open that window. . . . I feel half-stifled."

Bazarov got up and gave a push to the window. It flew up with a loud crash. . . . He had not expected it to open so easily; besides, his hands were shaking. The soft, dark night looked in to the room with its almost black sky, its faintly rustling trees, and the fresh fragrance of the pure open air.

"Draw the blind and sit down," said Madame Odintsov; "I want to have a talk with you before you go away. Tell me something about yourself; you never talk about yourself."

"I try to talk to you upon improving subjects, Anna Sergyevna."

"You are very modest. . . . But I should like to know something about you, about your family, about your father, for whom you are forsaking us."

"Why is she talking like that?" thought Bazarov.

"All that's not in the least interesting," he uttered aloud, "especially for you; we are obscure people. . . ."

"And you regard me as an aristocrat?"

Bazarov lifted his eyes to Madame Odintsov.

"Yes," he said, with exaggerated sharpness.

She smiled. "I see you know me very little, though you do maintain that all people are alike, and it's not worth while to study them. I will tell you my life some time or other . . . but first you tell me yours."

"I know you very little," repeated Bazarov. "Perhaps you are right; perhaps, really, every one is a riddle. You, for instance; you avoid society, you are oppressed by it, and you have invited two students to stay with you. What makes you, with your intellect, with your beauty, live in the country?"

"What? What was it you said?" Madame Odintsov interposed eagerly. "With my . . . beauty?"

Bazarov scowled. "Never mind that," he muttered; "I meant to say that I don't exactly understand why you have settled in the country."

"You don't understand it. . . . But you explain it to yourself in some way?"

"Yes. . . I assume that you remain continually in the same place because you indulge yourself, because you are very fond of comfort and ease, and very indifferent to everything else."

Madame Odintsov smiled again. "You would absolutely refuse to believe that I am capable of being carried away by anything?"

Bazarov glanced at her from under his brows.

"By curiosity, perhaps; but not otherwise."

"Really? Well, now I understand why we are such friends; you are just like me, you see."

"We are such friends . . ." Bazarov articulated in a choked voice.

Bazarov got up. The lamp burnt dimly in the middle of the dark, luxurious, isolated room; from time to time the blind was shaken, and there flowed in the freshness of the insidious night; there was heard its mysterious whisperings. Madame Odintsov did not move in a single limb; but she was gradually possessed by concealed emotion.

It communicated itself to Bazarov. He was suddenly conscious that he was alone with a young and lovely woman. . . .

"Where are you going?" she said slowly.

He answered nothing, and sank into a chair.

"And so you consider me a placid, pampered, spoiled creature," she went on in the same voice, never taking her eyes off the window. "While I know so much about myself, that I am unhappy."

"You unhappy? What for? Surely you can't attach any importance to idle gossip?"

Madame Odintsov frowned. It annoyed her that he had given such a meaning to her words.

"Such gossip does not even affect me, Yevgeny Vassilyitch, and I am too proud to allow it to disturb me. I am unhappy because . . . I have no desires, no passion for life. You look at me incredulously; you think that's said by an 'aristocrat,' who is all in lace, and sitting in a velvet armchair. I don't conceal the fact: I love what you call comfort, and at the same time I have little desire to live. Explain that contradiction as best you can. But all that's romanticism in your eyes."

Bazarov shook his head. "You are in good health, independent, rich; what more would you have? What do you want?"

"What do I want?" echoed Madame Odintsov, and she sighed. "I am very tired, I am old, I feel as if I have had a very long life. Yes, I am old," she added, softly drawing the ends of her lace over her bare arms. Her eyes met Bazarov's eyes, and she faintly blushed. "Behind me I have already so many memories: my life in Petersburg, wealth, then poverty, then my father's death, marriage, then the inevitable tour in due order. . . . So many memories, and nothing to remember, and before me, before me—a long, long road, and no goal. . . . I have no wish to go on."

"Are you disillusioned?" queried Bazarov.

"No, but I am dissatisfied," Madame Odintsov replied, dwelling on each syllable. "I think if I could interest myself strongly in something. . . ."

"You want to fall in love," Bazarov interrupted her, "and you can't love; that's where your unhappiness lies."

Madame Odintsov began to examine the sleeve of her lace.

"Is it true I can't love?" she said.

"I should say not! Only I was wrong in calling that an unhappiness. On the contrary, any one's more to be pitied when such a mischance befalls him."

"Mischance, what?"

"Falling in love."

"And how do you come to know that?"

"By hearsay," answered Bazarov angrily.

"You're flirting," he thought; "you're bored, and teasing me for want of something to do, while I . . ." His heart really seemed as though it were being torn to pieces.

"Besides, you are perhaps too exacting," he said, bending his whole frame forward and playing with the fringe of the chair.

"Perhaps. My idea is everything or nothing. A life for a life. Take mine, give up thine, and that without regret or turning back. Or else better have nothing."

"Well?" observed Bazarov; "that's fair terms, and I'm surprised that so far you . . . have not found what you wanted."

"And do you think it would be easy to give oneself up wholly to anything whatever?"

"Not easy, if you begin reflecting, waiting and attaching value to yourself, prizing yourself, I mean; but to give oneself up without reflection is very easy."

"How can one help prizing oneself? If I am of no value, who could need my devotion?"

"That's not my affair; that's the other's business to discover what is my value. The chief thing is to be able to devote oneself."

Madame Odintsov bent forward from the back of her chair. "You speak," she began, "as though you had experienced all that."

"It happened to come up, Anna Sergyevna; all that, as you know, is not in my line."

"But you could devote yourself?"

"I don't know. I shouldn't like to boast."

Madame Odintsov said nothing, and Bazarov was mute. The sounds of the piano floated up to them from the drawing-room.

"How is it Katya is playing so late?" observed Madame Odintsov.

Bazarov got up. "Yes, it is really late now; it's time for you to go to bed."

"Wait a little; why are you in a hurry? . . . I want to say one word to you."

"What is it?"

"Wait a little," whispered Madame Odintsov. Her eyes rested on Bazarov; it seemed as though she were examining him attentively.

He walked across the room, then suddenly went up to her, hurriedly said, "Good-bye," squeezed her hand so that she almost screamed, and was gone. She raised her crushed fingers to her lips, breathed on them, and suddenly, impulsively getting up from her low chair, she moved with rapid steps towards the door, as though she wished to bring Bazarov back. . . . A maid came into the room with a decanter on a silver tray. Madame Odintsov stood still, told her she could go, and sat down again, and again sank into thought. Her hair slipped loose and fell in a dark coil down her shoulders. Long after the lamp was still burning in Anna Sergyevna's room, and for long she stayed without moving, only from time to time chafing her hands, which ached a little from the cold of the night.

Bazarov went back two hours later to his bedroom with his boots wet with dew, dishevelled and ill-humoured. He found Arkady at the writing table with a book in his hands, his coat buttoned up to the throat.

"You're not in bed yet?" he said, in a tone, it seemed, of annoyance.

"You stopped a long while with Anna Sergyevna this evening," remarked Arkady, not answering him.

"Yes, I stopped with her all the while you were playing the piano with Katya Sergyevna."

"I did not play . . . " Arkady began, and he stopped. He felt the tears were coming into his eyes, and he did not like to cry before his sarcastic friend.

XVIII

THE FOLLOWING MORNING when Madame Odintsov came down to morning tea, Bazarov sat a long while bending over his cup, then suddenly he glanced up at her. . . . She turned to him as though he had struck her a blow, and he fancied that her face was a little paler since the night before. She quickly went off to her own room, and did not appear till lunch. It rained from early morning; there was no possibility of going for a walk. The whole company assembled in the drawing-room. Arkady took up the new number of a journal and began reading it aloud. The princess, as was her habit, tried to express her amazement in her face, as though he were doing something improper, then glared angrily at him; but he paid no attention to her.

"Yevgeny Vassilyitch," said Anna Sergyevna, "come to my room. . . . I want to ask you. . . . You mentioned a text-book yesterday. . . ."

She got up and went to the door. The princess looked round with an expression that seemed to say, "Look at me; see how shocked I am!" and again glared at Arkady; but he raised his voice, and exchanging glances with Katya, near whom he was sitting, he went on reading.

Madame Odintsov went with rapid steps to her study. Bazarov followed her quickly, not raising his eyes, and only with his ears catching the delicate swish and rustle of her silk gown gliding before him. Madame Odintsov sank into the same easy-chair in which she had sat the previous evening, and Bazarov took up the same position as before.

"What was the name of that book?" she began, after a brief silence.

"Pelouse et Frémy, *Notions générales*," answered Bazarov. "I might though recommend you also Ganot, *Traité élémentaire de physique ex-*

périmentale. In that book the illustrations are clearer, and in general it's a text-book."

Madame Odintsov stretched out her hand. "Yevgeny Vassilyitch, I beg your pardon, but I didn't invite you in here to discuss text-books. I wanted to continue our conversation of last night. You went away so suddenly. . . . It will not bore you. . . ."

"I am at your service, Anna Sergyevna. But what were we talking about last night?"

Madame Odintsov flung a sidelong glance at Bazarov.

"We were talking of happiness, I believe. I told you about myself. By the way, I mentioned the word 'happiness.' Tell me why it is that even when we are enjoying music, for instance, or a fine evening, or a conversation with sympathetic people, it all seems an intimation of some measureless happiness existing apart somewhere rather than actual happiness—such, I mean, as we ourselves are in possession of? Why is it? Or perhaps you have no feeling like that?"

"You know the saying, 'Happiness is where we are not,'" replied Bazarov; "besides, you told me yesterday you are discontented. I certainly never have such ideas come into my head."

"Perhaps they seem ridiculous to you?"

"No; but they don't come into my head."

"Really? Do you know, I should very much like to know what you think about?"

"What? I don't understand."

"Listen; I have long wanted to speak openly to you. There's no need to tell you—you are conscious of it yourself—that you are not an ordinary man; you are still young—all life is before you. What are you preparing yourself for? What future is awaiting you? I mean to say—what object do you want to attain? What are you going forward to? What is in your heart? In short, who are you, what are you?"

"You surprise me, Anna Sergyevna. You are aware that I am studying natural science, and who I . . ."

"Well, who are you?"

"I have explained to you already that I am going to be a district doctor."

Anna Sergyevna made a movement of impatience.

"What do you say that for? You don't believe it yourself. Arkady might answer me in that way, but not you."

"Why, in what is Arkady . . ."

"Stop! Is it possible you could content yourself with such a humble career, and aren't you always maintaining yourself that you don't believe in medicine? You—with your ambition—a district doctor! You answer me like that to put me off, because you have no confidence in me. But, do you know, Yevgeny Vassilyitch, that I could understand you; I have been poor myself, and ambitious, like you; I have been perhaps through the same trials as you."

"That is all very well, Anna Sergyevna, but you must pardon me for . . .

I am not the habit of talking freely about myself at any time as a rule, and between you and me there is such a gulf . . ."

"What sort of gulf? You mean to tell me again that I am an aristocrat? No more of that, Yevgeny Vassilyitch; I thought I had proved to you . . ."

"And even apart from that," broke in Bazarov, "what could induce one to talk and think about the future, which for the most part does not depend on us? If a chance turns up of doing something—so much the better; and if it doesn't turn up—at least one will be glad one didn't gossip idly about it beforehand."

"You call a friendly conversation idle gossip? . . . Or perhaps you consider me as a woman unworthy of your confidence? I know you despise us all."

"I don't despise you, Anna Sergyevna, and you know that."

"No, I don't know anything . . . but let us suppose so. I understand your disinclination to talk of your future career; but as to what is taking place within you now . . ."

"Taking place!" repeated Bazarov, "as though I were some sort of government or society! In any case, it is utterly uninteresting; and besides, can a man always speak of everything that 'takes place' in him?"

"Why, I don't see why you can't speak freely of everything you have in your heart."

"Can you?" asked Bazarov.

"Yes," answered Anna Sergyevna, after a brief hesitation.

Bazarov bowed his head. "You are more fortunate than I am."

Anna Sergyevna looked at him questioningly. "As you please," she went on, "but still something tells me that we have not come together for nothing; that we shall be great friends. I am sure this—what should I say, constraint, reticence in you will vanish at last."

"So you have noticed reticence . . . as you expressed it . . . constraint?"

"Yes."

Bazarov got up and went to the window. "And would you like to know the reason of this reticence? Would you like to know what is passing within me?"

"Yes," repeated Madame Odintsov, with a sort of dread she did not at the time understand.

"And you will not be angry?"

"No."

"No?" Bazarov was standing with his back to her. "Let me tell you then that I love you like a fool, like a madman. . . . There, you've forced it out of me."

Madame Odintsov held both her hands out before her; but Bazarov was leaning with his forehead pressed against the window pane. He breathed hard: his whole body was visibly trembling. But it was not the tremor of youthful timidity, not the sweet alarm of the first declaration that possessed him; it was passion struggling in him, strong and painful—passion not unlike hatred, and perhaps akin to it . . . Madame Odintsov felt both afraid and sorry for him.

"Yevgeny Vassilyitch!" she said, and there was the ring of unconscious tenderness in her voice.

He turned quickly, flung a searching look on her, and snatching both her hands, he drew her suddenly to his breast.

She did not at once free herself from his embrace, but an instant later she was standing far away in a corner, and looking from there at Bazarov. He rushed at her. . . .

"You have misunderstood me," she whispered hurriedly, in alarm. It seemed as if he had made another step she would have screamed. . . . Bazarov bit his lips, and went out.

Half an hour after a maid gave Anna Sergyevna a note from Bazarov; it consisted simply of one line: "Am I to go to-day, or can I stop till to-morrow?"

"Why should you go? I did not understand you—you did not understand me," Anna Sergyevna answered him, but to herself she thought: "I did not understand myself either."

She did not show herself till dinner time, and kept walking to and fro in her room, stopping sometimes at the window, sometimes at the looking-glass, and slowly rubbing her handkerchief over her neck, on which she still seemed to feel a burning spot. She asked herself what had induced her to "force" on Bazarov's words, his confidence, and whether she had suspected nothing. . . . "I am to blame," she decided aloud, "but I could not have foreseen this." She fell to musing, and blushed crimson, remembering Bazarov's almost animal face when he had rushed at her. . . .

"Or?" she uttered suddenly aloud, and she stopped short and shook back her curls. . . . She caught sight of herself in the glass; her head thrown back, with a mysterious smile on the half-crossed, half opened eyes and lips, told her, it seemed, in a flash something at which she herself was confused. . . .

"No," she made up her mind at last. "God knows what it would lead to; he couldn't be played with; peace is anyway the best thing in the world."

Her peace of mind was not shaken; but she felt gloomy, and even shed a few tears once, though she could not have said why—certainly not for the insult done her. She did not feel insulted; she was more inclined to feel guilty. Under the influence of various vague emotions, the sense of life passing by, the desire of novelty, she had forced herself to go up to a certain point, forced herself to look behind herself, and had seen behind her not even an abyss, but what was empty . . . or revolting.

XIX

GREAT as was Madame Odintsov's self-control, and superior as she was to every kind of prejudice, she felt awkward when she went into the dining-room to dinner. The meal went off fairly successfully, however. Porfiry Platonovitch made his appearance and told various anecdotes; he had just come back from the town. Among other things, he informed them that the governor had ordered his secretaries on special commissions to wear spurs, in case he might send them off anywhere for greater speed on horseback. Arkady talked in an undertone to Katya, and diplomatically attended to the princess's wants. Bazarov maintained a grim and obstinate silence. Madame Odintsov looked at him twice, not stealthily, but straight in the face, which was bilious and forbidding, with downcast eyes, and contemptuous determination stamped on every feature, and thought: "No . . . no . . . no." . . . After dinner, she went with the whole company into the garden, and seeing that Bazarov wanted to speak to her, she took a few steps to one side and stopped. He went up to her, but even then did not raise his eyes, and said hoarsely:

"I have to apologize to you, Anna Sergyevna. You must be in a fury with me."

"No, I'm not angry with you, Yevgeny Vassilyitch," answered Madame Odintsov; "but I am sorry."

"So much the worse. Anyway, I'm sufficiently punished. My position, you will certainly agree, is most foolish. You wrote to me, 'Why go away?' But I cannot stay, and don't wish to. To-morrow I shall be gone."

"Yevgeny Vassilyitch, why are you . . ."

"Why am I going away?"

"No; I didn't mean to say that."

"There's no recalling the past, Anna Sergyevna . . . and this was bound to come about sooner or later. Consequently I must go. I can only conceive of one condition upon which I could remain; but that condition will never be. Excuse my impertinence, but you don't love me, and you never will love me, I suppose?"

Bazarov's eyes glittered for an instant under their dark brows.

Anna Sergyevna did not answer him. "I'm afraid of this man," flashed through her brain.

"Good-bye, then," said Bazarov, as though he guessed her thought, and he went back into the house.

Anna Sergyevna walked slowly after him, and calling Katya to her, she took her arm. She did not leave her side till quite evening. She did not play cards, and was constantly laughing, which did not at all accord with her pale and perplexed face. Arkady was bewildered, and looked on at her as all young people look on—that's to say, he was constantly asking himself, "What is the meaning of that?" Bazarov shut himself up in his room; he came back to tea, however. Anna Sergyevna longed to say some friendly word to him, but she did not know how to address him. . . .

An unexpected incident relieved her from her embarrassment; a steward announced the arrival of Sitnikov.

It is difficult to do justice in words to the strange figure cut by the young apostle of progress as he fluttered into the room. Though, with his characteristic impudence, he had made up his mind to go into the country to visit a woman whom he hardly knew, who had never invited him; but with whom, according to information he had gathered, such talented and intimate friends were staying, he was nevertheless trembling to the marrow of his bones; and instead of bringing out the apologies and compliments he had learned by heart beforehand, he muttered some absurdity about Evdoksya Kukshin having sent him to inquire after Anna Sergyevna's health, and Arkady Nicolaevitch's too, having always spoken to him in the highest terms. . . . At this point he faltered and lost his presence of mind so completely that he sat down on his own hat. However, since no one turned him out, and Anna Sergyevna even presented him to her aunt and her sister, he soon recovered himself and began to chatter volubly. The introduction of the commonplace is often an advantage in life; it relieves overstrained tension, and sobers too self-confident or self-sacrificing emotions by recalling its close kinship with them. With Sitnikov's appearance everything became somehow duller and simpler; they all even ate a more solid supper, and retired to bed half an hour earlier than usual.

"I might now repeat to you," said Arkady, as he lay down in bed, to Bazarov, who was also undressing, "what you once said to me, 'Why are you so melancholy? One would think you had fulfilled some sacred duty.'" For some time past a sort of pretence of free-and-easy banter had sprung up between the two young men, which is always an unmistakable sign of secret displeasure or unexpressed suspicions.

"I'm going to my father's to-morrow," said Bazarov.

Arkady raised himself and leaned on his elbow. He felt both surprised, and for some reason or other pleased. "Ah!" he commented, "and is that why you're sad?"

Bazarov yawned. "You'll get old if you know too much."

"And Anna Sergyevna?" persisted Arkady.

"What about Anna Sergyevna?"

"I mean, will she let you go?"

"I'm not her paid man."

Arkady grew thoughtful, while Bazarov lay down and turned with his face to the wall.

Some minutes went by in silence. "Yevgeny?" cried Arkady suddenly. "Well?"

"I will leave with you to-morrow, too."

Bazarov made no answer.

"Only I will go home," continued Arkady. "We will go together as far as Hohlovsky, and there you can get horses at Fedot's. I should be delighted to make the acquaintance of your people, but I'm afraid of being in their way and yours. You are coming to us again later, of course?"

"I've left all my things with you," Bazarov said, without turning round.

"Why doesn't he ask me why I am going, and just as suddenly as he?" thought Arkady. "In reality, why am I going, and why is he going?" he pursued his reflections. He could find no satisfactory answer to his own question, though his heart was filled with some bitter feeling. He felt it would be hard to part from this life to which he had grown so accustomed; but for him to remain alone would be rather odd. "Something has passed between them," he reasoned to himself; "what good would it be for me to hang on after he's gone? She's utterly sick of me; I'm losing the last that remained to me." He began to imagine Anna Sergyevna to himself, then other features gradually eclipsed the lovely young image of the young widow.

"I'm sorry to lose Katya too!" Arkady whispered to his pillow, on which a tear had already fallen. . . . All at once he shook back his hair and said aloud:

"What the devil made that fool of a Sitnikov turn up here?"

Bazarov at first stirred a little in his bed, then he uttered the following rejoinder: "You're still a fool, my boy, I see. Sitnikovs are indispensable to us. I—do you understand? I need dolts like him. It's not for the gods to bake bricks, in fact!" . . .

"Oho!" Arkady thought to himself, and then in a flash all the fathomless depths of Bazarov's conceit dawned upon him. "Are you and I gods then? At least, you're a god; am not I a dolt then?"

"Yes," repeated Bazarov; "you're still a fool."

Madame Odintsov expressed no special surprise when Arkady told her the next day that he was going with Bazarov; she seemed tired and absorbed. Katya looked at him silently and seriously; the princess went so far as to cross herself under her shawl so that he could not help noticing it. Sitnikov, on the other hand, was completely disconcerted. He had only just come in to lunch in a new and fashionable get-up, not on this occasion of a Slavophil cut; the evening before he had astonished the man told off to wait on him by the amount of linen he had brought with him, and now all of a sudden his comrades were deserting him! He took a few tiny steps, doubled back like a hunted hare at the edge of a copse, and abruptly, almost with dismay, almost with a wail, announced that he proposed going too. Madame Odintsov did not attempt to detain him.

"I have a very comfortable carriage," added the luckless young man, turning to Arkady; "I can take you, while Yevgeny Vassilyitch can take your coach, so it will be even more convenient."

"But, really, it's not at all in your way, and it's a long way to my place."

"That's nothing, nothing; I've plenty of time; besides, I have business in that direction."

"Gin-selling?" asked Arkady, rather too contemptuously.

But Sitnikov was reduced to such desperation that he did not even laugh as usual. "I assure you, my carriage is exceedingly comfortable," he muttered; "and there will be room for all."

"Don't wound Monsieur Sitnikov by a refusal," commented Anna Sergyevna.

Arkady glanced at her, and bowed his head significantly.

The visitors started off after lunch. As she said good-bye to Bazarov,

Madame Odintsov held out her hand to him, and said, "We shall meet again, shan't we?"

"As you command," answered Bazarov.

"In that case, we shall."

Arkady was the first to descend the steps; he got into Sitnikov's carriage. A steward tucked him in respectfully, but he could have killed him with pleasure, or have burst into tears. Bazarov took his seat in the coach. When they reached Hohlovsky, Arkady waited till Fedot, the keeper of the posting-station, had put in the horses, and going up to the coach he said, with his old smile, to Bazarov, "Yevgeny, take me with you; I want to come to you."

"Get in," Bazarov brought out through his teeth.

Sitnikov, who had been walking to and fro round the wheels of his carriage, whistling briskly, could only gape when he heard these words; while Arkady coolly pulled his luggage out of the carriage, took his seat beside Bazarov, and bowing politely to his former fellow-traveler, he called, "Whip up!" The coach rolled away, and was soon out of sight . . . Sitnikov, utterly confused, looked at his coachman, but the latter was flicking his whip about the tail of the off horse. Then Sitnikov jumped into the carriage, and growling at two passing peasants, "Put on your caps, idiots!" he drove to the town, where he arrived very late, and where, next day, at Madame Kukshin's, he dwelt very severely with two "disgusting stuck-up churls."

When he was seated in the coach by Bazarov, Arkady pressed his hand warmly, and for a long while he said nothing. It seemed as though Bazarov understood and appreciated both the pressure and the silence. He had not slept all the previous night, and had not smoked, and had eaten scarcely anything for several days. His profile, already thinner, stood out darkly and sharply under his cap, which was pulled down to his eyebrows.

"Well, brother," he said at last, "give us a cigarette. But look, I say, is my tongue yellow?"

"Yes, it is," answered Arkady.

"Hm . . . and the cigarette's tasteless. The machine's out of gear."

"You look changed lately certainly," observed Arkady.

"It's nothing! We shall soon be all right. One thing's a bother—my mother's so tender-hearted; if you don't grow as round as a tub, and eat ten times a day, she's quite upset. My father's all right, he's known all sorts of ups and downs himself. No, I can't smoke," he added, and he flung the cigarette into the dust of the road.

"Do you think it's twenty miles?" asked Arkady.

"Yes. But ask this sage here." He indicated the peasant sitting on the box, a labourer of Fedot's.

But the sage only answered, "Who's to know—miles hereabout aren't measured," and went on swearing in an undertone at the shaft horse for "kicking with her head-piece," that is, shaking with her head down.

"Yes, yes," began Bazarov; "it's a lesson to you, my young friend, an instructive example. God knows, what rot it is. Every man hangs on a thread, the abyss may open under his feet any minute, and yet he must go and invent all sorts of discomforts for himself, and spoil his life."

"What are you alluding to?" asked Arkady.

"I'm not alluding to anything; I'm saying straight out that we've both behaved like fools. What's the use of talking about it! Still, I've noticed in hospital practice, the man who's furious at his illness—he's sure to get over it."

"I don't quite understand you," observed Arkady; "I should have thought you had nothing to complain of."

"And since you don't quite understand me, I'll tell you this—to my mind, it's better to break stones on the highroad than to let a woman have the mastery of even the end of one's little finger. That's all . . ." Bazarov was on the point of uttering his favourite word, "romanticism," but he checked himself, and said, "rubbish. You don't believe me now, but I tell you; you and I have been in feminine society, and very nice we found it; but to throw up society like that is for all the world like a dip in cold water on a hot day. A man hasn't time to attend to such trifles; a man ought not to be tame, says an excellent Spanish proverb. Now, you, I suppose, my sage friend," he added, turning to the peasant sitting on the box—"you've a wife?"

The peasant showed both the friends his dull blear-eyed face.

"A wife? Yes. Every man has a wife."

"Do you beat her?"

"My wife? Everything happens sometimes. We don't beat her without good reason!"

"That's excellent. Well, and does she beat you?"

The peasant gave a tug at the reins. "That's a strange thing to say, sir. You like your joke. . . ." He was obviously offended.

"You hear, Arkady Nikolaevitch! But we have taken a beating . . . that's what comes of being educated people."

Arkady gave a forced laugh, while Bazarov turned away, and did not open his mouth again the whole journey.

The twenty miles seemed to Arkady quite forty. But at last, on the slope of some rising ground, appeared the small hamlet where Bazarov's parents lived. Beside it, in a young birch copse, could be seen a small house with a thatched roof. Two peasants stood with their hats on at the first hut, abusing each other. "You're a great sow," said one; "and worse than a little sucking pig."

"And your wife's a witch," retorted the other.

"From their unconstrained behaviour," Bazarov remarked to Arkady, "and the playfulness of their retorts, you can guess that my father's peasants are not too much oppressed. Why, there he is himself coming out on the steps of his house. They must have heard the bells. It's he; it's he—I know his figure. Ay, ay! how grey he's grown though, poor chap!"

XX

Bazarov leaned out of the coach, while Arkady thrust his head out behind his companion's back, and caught sight on the steps of the little manor-house of a tall, thinnish man with dishevelled hair, and thin hawk nose, dressed in an old military coat not buttoned up. He was standing, his legs wide apart, smoking a long pipe and screwing up his eyes to keep the sun out of them.

The horses stopped.

"Arrived at last," said Bazarov's father, still going on smoking though the pipe was fairly dancing up and down between his fingers. "Come, get out; get out; let me hug you."

He began embracing his son. . . . "Enyusha, Enyusha," was heard a trembling woman's voice. The door was flung open, and in the doorway was seen a plump, short, little old woman in a white cap and a short striped jacket. She moaned, staggered, and would certainly have fallen, had not Bazarov supported her. Her plump little hands were instantly twined round his neck, her head was pressed to his breast, and there was a complete hush. The only sound heard was her broken sobs.

Old Bazarov breathed hard and screwed his eyes up more than ever.

"There, that's enough, that's enough, Arisha! give over," he said, exchanging a glance with Arkady, who remained motionless in the coach, while the peasant on the box even turned his head away; "that's not at all necessary, please give over."

"Ah, Vassily Ivanovitch," faltered the old woman, "for what ages, my dear one, my darling, Enyusha," . . . and, not unclasping her hands, she drew her wrinkled face, wet with tears and working with tenderness, a little away from Bazarov, and gazed at him with blissful and comic-looking eyes, and again fell on his neck.

"Well, well, to be sure, that's all in the nature of things," commented Vassily Ivanovitch, "only we'd better come indoors. Here's a visitor come with Yevgeny. You must excuse it," he added, turning to Arkady, and scraping with his foot; "you understand, a woman's weakness; and well, a mother's heart . . ."

His lips and eyebrows, too, were twitching, and his beard was quivering . . . but he was obviously trying to control himself and appear almost indifferent.

"Let's come in, mother, really," said Bazarov, and he led the enfeebled old woman into the house. Putting her into a comfortable armchair, he once more hurriedly embraced his father and introduced Arkady to him.

"Heartily glad to make your acquaintance," said Vassily Ivanovitch, "but you mustn't expect great things; everything here in my house is done in a plain way, on a military footing. Arina Vlasyevna, calm yourself, pray; what weakness! The gentleman our guest will think ill of you."

"My dear sir," said the old lady through her tears, "your name and your father's I haven't the honour of knowing. . . ."

"Arkady Nikolaitch," put in Vassily Ivanovitch solemnly, in a low voice.

"You must excuse a silly old woman like me." The old women blew her nose, and bending her head to right and to left, carefully wiped one eye after the other. "You must excuse me. You see, I thought I should die, that I should not live to see my da . . arling."

"Well, here we have lived to see him, madam," put in Vassily Ivanovitch. "Tanyushka," he turned to a barelegged little girl of thirteen in a bright red cotton dress, who was timidly peeping in at the door, "bring your mistress a glass of water—on a tray, do you hear?—and you, gentlemen," he added, with a kind of old-fashioned playfulness, "let me ask you into the study of a retired old veteran."

"Just once more let me embrace you, Enyusha," moaned Arina Vlasyevna. Bazarov bent down to her. "Why, what a handsome fellow you have grown!"

"Well, I don't know about being handsome," remarked Vassily Ivanovitch, "but he's a man, as the saying is, *ommfay*. And now I hope, Arina Vlasyevna, that having satisfied your maternal heart, you will turn your thoughts to satisfying the appetites of our dear guests, because, as you're aware, even nightingales can't be fed on fairy tales."

The old lady got up from her chair. "This minute, Vassily Ivanovitch, the table shall be laid. I will run myself to the kitchen and order the samovar to be brought in; everything shall be ready, everything. Why, I have not seen him, not given him food or drink these three years; is that nothing?"

"There, mind, good mother, bustle about; don't put us to shame; while you, gentlemen, I beg you to follow me. Here's Timofeitch come to pay his respects to you, Yevgeny. He, too, I daresay, is delighted, the old dog. Eh, aren't you delighted, old dog? Be so good as to follow me."

And Vassily Ivanovitch went bustling forward, scraping and flapping with his slippers trodden down at heel.

His whole house consisted of six tiny rooms. One of them—the one to which he led our friends—was called the study. A thick-legged table, littered over with papers black with the accumulation of ancient dust as though they had been smoked, occupied all the space between the two windows; on the walls hung Turkish firearms, whips, a sabre, two maps, some anatomical diagrams, a portrait of Hoffland, a monogram woven in hair in a blackened frame, and a diploma under glass; a leather sofa, torn and worn into hollows in parts, was placed between two huge cupboards of birchwood; on the shelves books, boxes, stuffed birds, jars, and phials were huddled together in confusion; in one corner stood a broken galvanic battery.

"I warned you, my dear Arkady Nikolaitch," began Vassily Ivanovitch, "that we live, so to say, bivouacking. . . ."

"There, stop that, what are you apologizing for?" Bazarov interrupted.

"Kirsanov knows very well we're not Crœsuses, and that you have no butler. Where are we going to put him, that's the question?"

"To be sure, Yevgeny; I have a capital room there in the little lodge; he will be very comfortable there."

"Have you had a lodge put up then?"

"Why, where the bath-house is," put in Timofeitch.

"That is next to the bathroom," Vassily Ivanovitch added hurriedly. "It's summer now . . . I will run over there at once, and make arrangements; and you, Timofeitch, meanwhile bring in their things. You, Yevgeny, I shall of course offer my study. *Suum cuique*."

"There you have him! A comical old chap, and very good natured," remarked Bazarov, directly Vassily Ivanovitch had gone. "Just such a queer fish as yours, only in another way. He chatters too much."

"And your mother seems an awfully nice woman," observed Arkady.

"Yes, there's no humbug about her. You'll see what a dinner she'll give us."

"They didn't expect you to-day, sir; they've not brought any beef," observed Timofeitch, who was just dragging in Bazarov's box.

"We shall get on very well without beef. It's no use crying for the moon. Poverty, they say, is no vice."

"How many serfs has your father?" Arkady asked suddenly.

"The estate's not his, but mother's; there are fifteen serfs, if I remember."

"Twenty-two in all," Timofeitch added, with an air of displeasure.

The flapping of slippers was heard, and Vassily Ivanovitch reappeared. "In a few minutes your room will be ready to receive you," he cried triumphantly. "Arkady . . . Nikolaitch? I think that is right? And here is your attendant," he added, indicating a short-cropped boy, who had come in with him in a blue full-skirted coat with ragged elbows and a pair of boots which did not belong to him. "His name is Fedka. Again, I repeat, even though my son tells me not to, you mustn't expect great things. He knows how to fill a pipe, though. You smoke, of course?"

"I generally smoke cigars," answered Arkady.

"And you do very sensibly. I myself give the preference to cigars, but in these solitudes it is exceedingly difficult to obtain them."

"There, that's enough humble pie," Bazarov interrupted again. "You'd much better sit here on the sofa and let us have a look at you."

Vassily Ivanovitch laughed and sat down. He was very like his son in face, only his brow was lower and narrower, and his mouth rather wider, and he was forever restless, shrugging up his shoulder as though his coat cut him under the armpits, blinking, clearing his throat, and gesticulating with his fingers, while his son was distinguished by a kind of nonchalant immobility.

"Humble pie!" repeated Vassily Ivanovitch. "You must not imagine, Yevgeny, I want to appeal, so to speak, to our guest's sympathies by making out we live in such a wilderness. Quite the contrary, I maintain that for a thinking man nothing is a wilderness. At least, I try as far as possible not to get rusty, so to speak, not to fall behind the age."

Vassily Ivanovitch drew out of his pocket a new yellow silk handkerchief, which he had had time to snatch up on the way to Arkady's room, and flourishing it in the air, he proceeded: "I am not now alluding to the fact that, for example, at the cost of sacrifices not inconsiderable for me, I have put my peasants on the rent-system and given up my land to them on half profits. I regarded that as my duty; common sense itself enjoins such a proceeding, though other proprietors do not even dream of it; I am alluding to the sciences, to culture."

"Yes; I see you have here *The Friend of Health* for 1855," remarked Bazarov.

"It's sent to me by an old comrade out of friendship," Vassily Ivanovitch made haste to answer; "but we have, for instance, some idea even of phrenology," he added, addressing himself principally, however, to Arkady, and pointing to a small plaster head on the cupboard, divided into numbered squares; "we are not unacquainted even with Schenlein and Rademacher."

"Why do people still believe in Rademacher in this province?" asked Bazarov.

Vassily Ivanovitch cleared his throat. "In this province. . . . Of course, gentlemen, you know best; how could we keep pace with you? You are here to take our places. In my day, too, there was some sort of a Humouralist school, Hoffmann, and Brown too with his vitalism—they seemed very ridiculous to us, but, of course, they too had been great men at one time or other. Some one new has taken the place of Rademacher with you; you bow down to him, but in another twenty years it will be his turn to be laughed at."

"For your consolation I will tell you," observed Bazarov, "that nowadays we laugh at medicine altogether, and don't bow down to any one."

"How's that? Why, you're going to be a doctor, aren't you?"

"Yes, but the one fact doesn't prevent the other."

Vassily Ivanovitch poked his third finger into his pipe, where a little smouldering ash was still left. "Well, perhaps—I am not going to dispute. What am I? A retired army-doctor, *volla-too;* now fate has made me take to farming. I served in your grandfather's brigade," he addressed himself again to Arkady; "yes, yes, I have seen many sights in my day. And I was thrown into all kinds of society, brought into contact with all sorts of people! I myself, the man you see before you now, have felt the pulse of Prince Wittgenstein and of Zhukovsky! They were in the southern army, in the fourteenth, you understand" (and here Vassily Ivanovitch pursed his mouth up significantly). "Well, well, but my business was on one side; stick to your lancet, and let everything else go hang! Your grandfather was a very honourable man, a real soldier."

"Confess, now, he was rather a blockhead," remarked Bazarov, lazily.

"Ah, Yevgeny, how can you use such an expression! Do consider. . . . Of course, General Kirsanov was not one of the . . ."

"Come, drop him," broke in Bazarov; "I was pleased as I was driving along here to see your birch copse; it has shot up capitally."

Vassily Ivanovitch brightened up. "And you must see what a little garden I've got now! I planted every tree myself. I've fruit, and raspberries, and all kinds of medicinal herbs. However clever you young gentlemen may be, old Paracelsus spoke the holy truth: *in herbis, verbis et lapidibus.* . . . I've retired from practice, you know, of course, but two or three times a week it will happen that I'm brought back to my old work. They come for advice—I can't drive them away. Sometimes the poor have recourse to me for help. And indeed there are no doctors here at all. There's one of the neighbours here, a retired major, only fancy, he doctors the people too. I asked the question, 'Has he studied medicine?' And they told me, 'No, he's not studied; he does it more from philanthropy.' . . . Ha! ha! ha! from philanthropy! What do you think of that? Ha! ha! ha!"

"Fedka, fill me a pipe!" said Bazarov rudely.

"And there's another doctor here who just got to a patient," Vassily Ivanovitch persisted in a kind of desperation, "when the patient had gone *ad patres;* the servant didn't let the doctor speak; 'you're no longer wanted,' he told him. He hadn't expected this, got confused, and asked, 'Why, did your master hiccup before his death?' 'Yes.' 'Did he hiccup much?' 'Yes.' 'Ah, well, that's all right,' and off he set back again. Ha! ha! ha!"

The old man was alone in his laughter; Arkady forced a smile on his face. Bazarov simply stretched. The conversation went on in this way for about an hour; Arkady had time to go to his room, which turned out to be the anteroom attached to the bathroom, but was very snug and clean. At last Tanyusha came in and announced that dinner was ready.

Vassily Ivanovitch was the first to get up. "Come, gentlemen. You must be magnanimous and pardon me if I've bored you. I daresay my good wife will give you more satisfaction."

The dinner, though prepared in haste, turned out to be very good, even abundant; only the wine was not quite up to the mark; it was almost black sherry, bought by Timofeitch in the town at a well-known merchant's, and had a faint coppery, resinous taste, and the flies were a great nuisance. On ordinary days a serf-boy used to keep driving them away with a large green branch; but on this occasion Vassily Ivanovitch had sent him away through dread of the criticism of the younger generation. Arina Vlasyevna had had time to dress; she had put on a high cap with silk ribbons and a pale blue flowered shawl. She broke down again directly she caught sight of her Enyusha, but her husband had no need to admonish her; she made haste to wipe away her tears herself, for fear of spotting her shawl. Only the young men ate anything; the master and mistress of the house had dined long ago. Fedka waited at table, obviously encumbered by having boots on for the first time; he was assisted by a woman of a masculine cast of face and one eye, by name Anfisushka, who performed the duties of house-keeper, poultry-woman, and laundress. Vassily Ivanovitch walked up and down during the whole of dinner, and with a perfectly happy, positively beatific countenance, talked about the serious anxiety he felt at Napoleon's policy, and the intricacy of the Italian question. Arina Vlasyevna took no notice of Arkady; leaning her round face, to which the full cherry-coloured lips and the little moles on the cheeks and over the eyebrows gave a very simple, good-natured expression, on her little closed fist, she did not take her eyes off her son, and kept constantly sighing; she was dying to know for how long he had come, but she was afraid to ask him.

"What if he says for two days," she thought, and her heart sank. After the roast Vassily Ivanovitch disappeared for an instant, and returned with an opened half-bottle of champagne. "Here," he cried, "though we do live in the wilds, we have something to make merry with on festive occasions!" He filled three champagne glasses and a little wineglass, proposed the health of "our inestimable guests," and at once tossed off his glass in military fashion; while he made Arina Vlasyevna drink her wineglass to the last drop. When the time came in due course for preserves, Arkady, who could not bear anything sweet, thought it his duty, however, to taste four different kinds which had been freshly made, all the more as Bazarov flatly refused them and began at once smoking a cigarette. Then tea came on the scene with cream, butter, and cracknels; then Vassily Ivanovitch took them all into the garden to admire the beauty of the evening. As they passed a garden seat he whispered to Arkady—

"At this spot I love to meditate, as I watch the sunset; it suits a recluse like me. And there, a little farther off, I have planted some of the trees beloved of Horace."

"What trees?" asked Bazarov, overhearing.

"Oh . . . acacias."

Bazarov began to yawn.

"I imagine it's time our travellers were in the arms of Morpheus," observed Vassily Ivanovitch.

"That is, it's time for bed," Bazarov put in. "That's a correct idea. It is time, certainly."

As he said good-night to his mother, he kissed her on the forehead, while she embraced him, and stealthily behind his back she gave him her blessing three times. Vassily Ivanovitch conducted Arkady to his room, and wished him "as refreshing repose as I enjoyed at your happy years." And Arkady did as a fact sleep excellently in his bath-house; there was a smell of mint in it, and two crickets behind the stove rivalled each other in their drowsy chirping. Vassily Ivanovitch went from Arkady's room to his study, and perching on the sofa at his son's feet, he was looking forward to having a chat with him; but Bazarov at once sent him away, saying he was sleepy, and did not fall asleep till morning. With wide open eyes he stared vindictively into the darkness; the memories of childhood had no power over him; and besides, he had not yet had time to get rid of the impression of his recent bitter emotions. Arina Vlasyevna first prayed to her heart's content, then she had a long, long conversation with Anfisushka, who stood stockstill before her mistress, and fixing her solitary eye upon her, communicated in a mysterious whisper all her observations and conjectures in regard to Yevgeny Vassilyitch. The old lady's head was giddy with happiness and wine and tobacco smoke: her husband tried to talk to her, but with a wave of his hand gave it up in despair.

Arina Vlasyevna was a genuine Russian gentlewoman of the olden times; she ought to have lived two centuries before, in the old Moscow days. She was very devout and emotional; she believed in fortune-telling, charms, dreams, and omens of every possible kind; she believed in the prophecies of crazy people, in house-spirits, in wood-spirits, in unlucky meetings, in the evil eye, in popular remedies, she ate specially prepared salt on Holy Thursday, and believed that the end of the world was at hand; she believed that if on Easter Sunday the lights did not go out at vespers, then there would be a good crop of buckwheat, and that a mushroom will not grow after it has been looked on by the eye of man; she believed that the devil likes to be where there is water, and that every Jew has a blood-stained patch on his breast; she was afraid of mice, of snakes, of frogs, of sparrows, of leeches, of thunder, of cold water, of draughts, of horses, of goats, of red-haired people, and black cats, and she regarded crickets and dogs as unclean beasts; she never ate veal, doves, crayfishes, cheese, asparagus, artichokes, hares, nor water-melons, because a cut water-melon suggested the head of John the Baptist, and of oysters she could not speak without a shudder; she was fond of eating—and fasted rigidly; she slept ten hours out of the twenty-four—and never went to bed at all if Vassily Ivanovitch had so much as a headache; she had never read a single book except *Alexis or the Cottage in the Forest;* she wrote one, or at the most two letters in a year, but was great in housewifery, preserving, and jam-making, though with her own hands she never touched a thing, and was generally disinclined to move from her place. Arina Vlasyevna was very kindhearted, and in her way not at all stupid. She knew that the world is divided into masters whose duty it is to command, and simple folk whose duty it is to serve them—and so she felt no repugnance to servility and prostrations to the ground; but she treated those in subjection to her kindly and gently, never let a single beggar go away empty-handed, and never spoke ill of any one, though she was fond of gossip. In her youth she had been pretty, had played the clavichord, and spoken French a little; but in the course of many years' wanderings with her husband, whom she had married against her will, she had grown stout, and forgotten music and French. Her son she loved and feared unutterably; she had given up the management of the property to Vassily Ivanovitch—and now did not interfere in anything; she used to groan, wave her handkerchief, and raise her eyebrows higher and higher with horror directly her old husband began to discuss the impending government reforms and his own plans. She was apprehensive, and constantly expecting some great misfortune, and began to weep directly she remembered anything sorrowful. . . . Such women are not common nowadays. God knows whether we ought to rejoice!

XXI

ON GETTING UP Arkady opened the window, and the first object that met his view was Vassily Ivanovitch. In an Oriental dressing-gown girt round the waist with a pocket-handkerchief he was industriously digging in his garden. He perceived his young visitor, and leaning on his spade, he called, "The best of health to you! How have you slept?"

"Capitally," answered Arkady.

"Here am I, as you see, like some Cincinnatus, marking out a bed for late turnips. The time has come now—and thank God for it!—when every one ought to obtain his sustenance with his own hands; it's useless to reckon on others; one must labour oneself. And it turns out that Jean Jacques Rousseau is right. Half an hour ago, my dear young gentleman, you might have seen me in a totally different position. One peasant woman, who complained of looseness—that's how they express it, but in our language, dysentery—I . . . how can I express it best? I administered opium; and for another I extracted a tooth. I proposed an anæsthetic to her . . . but she would not consent. All that I do *gratis—anamatyer (en amateur)*. I'm used to it, though; you see, I'm a plebeian, *homo novus*—not one of the old stock, not like my spouse. . . . Wouldn't you like to come this way into the shade, to breathe the morning freshness a little before tea?"

Arkady went out to him.

"Welcome once again," said Vassily Ivanovitch, raising his hand in a military salute to the greasy skull-cap which covered his head. "You, I know, are accustomed to luxury, to amusements, but even the great ones of this world do not disdain to spend a brief space under a cottage roof."

"Good heavens," protested Arkady, "as though I were one of the great ones of this world! And I'm not accustomed to luxury."

"Pardon me, pardon me," rejoined Vassily Ivanovitch with a polite simper. "Though I am laid on the shelf now, I have knocked about the world too—I can tell a bird by its flight. I am something of a psychologist, too, in my own way, and a physiognomist. If I had not, I will venture to say, been endowed with that gift, I should have come to grief long ago; I should have stood no chance, a poor man like me. I tell you without flattery, I am sincerely delighted at the friendship I observe between you and my son. I have just seen him; he got up as he usually does—no doubt you are aware of it—very early, and went a ramble about the neighbourhood. Permit me to inquire—have you known my son long?"

"Since last winter."

"Indeed. And permit me to question you further—but hadn't we better sit down? Permit me, as a father, to ask without reserve, What is your opinion of my Yevgeny?"

"Your son is one of the most remarkable men I have ever met," Arkady answered emphatically.

Vassily Ivanovitch's eyes suddenly grew round, and his cheeks were suffused with a faint flush. The spade fell out of his hand.

"And so you expect," he began . . .

"I'm convinced," Arkady put in, "that your son has a great future before him; that he will do honour to your name. I've been certain of that ever since I first met him."

"How . . . how was that?" Vassily Ivanovitch articulated with an effort. His wide mouth was relaxed in a triumphant smile, which would not leave it.

"Would you like me to tell you how we met?"

"Yes . . . and altogether. . . ."

Arkady began to tell his tale, and to talk of Bazarov with even greater warmth, even greater enthusiasm than he had done on the evening when he danced a mazurka with Madame Odintsov.

Vassily Ivanovitch listened and listened, blinked, and rolled his handkerchief up into a ball in both his hands, cleared his throat, ruffled up his hair, and at last could stand it no longer; he bent down to Arkady and kissed him on his shoulder. "You have made me perfectly happy," he said, never ceasing to smile. "I ought to tell you, I . . . idolise my son; my old wife I won't speak of—we all know what mothers are!—but I dare not show my feelings before him, because he doesn't like it. He is averse to every kind of demonstration of feeling; many people even find fault with him for such firmness of character, and regard it as a proof of pride or lack of feeling, but men like him ought not to be judged by the common standard, ought they? And here, for example, many another fellow in his place would have been a constant drag on his parents; but he, would you believe it, has never from the day he was born taken a farthing more than he could help, that's God's truth!"

"He is a disinterested, honest man," observed Arkady.

"Exactly so; he is disinterested. And I don't only idolise him, Arkady Nikolaitch, I am proud of him, and the height of my ambition is that some day there will be the following lines in his biography: 'The son of a simple army-doctor, who was, however, capable of divining his greatness betimes, and spared nothing for his education . . .'" The old man's voice broke.

Arkady pressed his hand.

"What do you think," inquired Vassily Ivanovitch, after a short silence, "will it be in the career of medicine that he will attain the celebrity you anticipate for him?"

"Of course, not in medicine, though even in that department he will be one of the leading scientific men."

"In what then, Arkady Nikolaitch?"

"It would be hard to say now, but he will be famous."

"He will be famous!" repeated the old man, and he sank into a reverie.

"Arina Vlasyevna sent me to call you in to tea," announced Anfisushka, coming by with an immense dish of ripe raspberries.

Vassily Ivanovitch started. "And will there be cooled cream for the raspberries?"

"Yes."

"Cold now, mind! Don't stand on ceremony, Arkady Nikolaitch; take some more. How is it Yevgeny doesn't come?"

"I'm here," was heard Bazarov's voice from Arkady's room.

Vassily Ivanovitch turned round quickly. "Aha! you wanted to pay a visit to your friend; but you were too late, *amice*, and we have already had a long conversation with him. Now we must go in to tea, mother summons us. By the way, I want to have a little talk with you."

"What about?"

"There's a peasant here; he's suffering from icterus. . . ."

"You mean jaundice?"

"Yes, a chronic and very obstinate case of icterus. I have prescribed him centaury and St. John's wort, ordered him to eat carrots, given him soda; but all that's merely palliative measures; we want some more decided treatment. Though you do laugh at medicine, I am certain you can give me practical advice. But we will talk of that later. Now come in to tea."

Vassily Ivanovitch jumped up briskly from the garden seat, and hummed from *Robert le Diable*—

> *The rule, the rule we set ourselves,*
> *To live, to live for pleasure!*

"Singular vitality!" observed Bazarov, going away from the window.

It was midday. The sun was burning hot behind a thin veil of unbroken whitish clouds. Everything was hushed; there was no sound but the cocks crowing irritably at one another in the village, producing in every one who heard them a strange sense of drowsiness and ennui; and somewhere, high up in a tree-top, the incessant plaintive cheep of a young hawk. Arkady and Bazarov lay in the shade of a small haystack, putting under themselves two armfuls of dry and rustling but still greenish and fragrant grass.

"That aspen-tree," began Bazarov, "reminds me of my childhood; it grows at the edge of the clay-pits where the bricks were dug, and in those days I believed firmly that that clay-pit and aspen-tree possessed a peculiar talismanic power; I never felt dull near them. I did not understand then that I was not dull, because I was a child. Well, now I'm grown up, the talisman's lost its power."

"How long did you live here altogether?" asked Arkady.

"Two years on end; then we travelled about. We led a roving life, wandering from town to town for the most part."

"And has this house been standing long?"

"Yes. My grandfather built it—my mother's father."

"Who was he—your grandfather?"

"Devil knows. Some second-major. He served with Suvorov, and was always telling stories about the crossing of the Alps—inventions probably."

"You have a portrait of Suvorov hanging in the drawing-room. I like these dear little houses like yours; they're so warm and old-fashioned; and there's always a special sort of scent about them."

"A smell of lamp-oil and clover," Bazarov remarked, yawning. "And the flies in those dear little houses. . . . Faugh!"

"Tell me," began Arkady, after a brief pause, "were they strict with you when you were a child?"

"You can see what my parents are like. They're not a severe sort."

"Are you fond of them, Yevgeny?"

"I am, Arkady."

"How fond they are of you!"

Bazarov was silent for a little. "Do you know what I'm thinking about?" he brought out at last, clasping his hands behind his head.

"No. What is it?"

"I'm thinking life is a happy thing for my parents. My father at sixty is fussing around, talking about 'palliative' measures, doctoring people, playing the bountiful master with the peasants—having a festive time, in fact; and my mother's happy too; her day's so chockful of duties of all sorts, and sighs and groans that she's no time even to think of herself; while I . . ."

"While you?"

"I think; here I lie under a haystack. . . . The tiny space I occupy is so infinitely small in comparison with the rest of space, in which I am not, and which has nothing to do with me; and the period of time in which it is my lot to live is so petty beside the eternity in which I have not been, and shall not be. . . . And in this atom, this mathematical point, the blood is circulating, the brain is working and wanting something. . . . Isn't it loathsome? Isn't it petty?"

"Allow me to remark that what you're saying applies to men in general."

"You are right," Bazarov cut in. "I was going to say that they now—my parents, I mean—are absorbed and don't trouble themselves about their own nothingness; it doesn't sicken them . . . while I . . . I feel nothing but weariness and anger."

"Anger? Why anger?"

"Why? How can you ask why? Have you forgotten?"

"I remember everything, but still I don't admit that you have any right to be angry. You're unlucky, I'll allow, but . . ."

"Pooh! then you, Arkady Nikolaevitch, I can see, regard love like all modern young men; cluck, cluck, cluck you call to the hen, but if the hen comes near you, you run away. I'm not like that. But that's enough of that. What can't be helped, it's shameful to talk about." He turned over on his side. "Aha! there goes a valiant ant dragging off a half-dead fly. Take her, brother, take her! Don't pay attention to her resistance; it's your privilege as an animal to be free from the sentiment of pity—make the most of it—not like us conscientious self-destructive animals!"

"You shouldn't say that, Yevgeny! When have you destroyed yourself!"

Bazarov raised his head. "That's the only thing I pride myself on. I haven't crushed myself, so a woman can't crush me. Amen! It's all over! You shall not hear another word from me about it."

Both the friends lay for some time in silence.

"Yes," began Bazarov, "man's a strange animal. When one gets a side view from a distance of the dead-alive life our 'fathers' lead here, one thinks, What could be better? You eat and drink, and know you are acting in the most reasonable, most judicious manner. But if not, you're devoured by ennui. One wants to have to do with people if only to abuse them."

"One ought so to order one's life that every moment in it should be of significance," Arkady affirmed reflectively.

"I dare say! What's of significance is sweet, however mistaken; one could make up one's mind to what's insignificant even. But pettiness, pettiness, that's what's insufferable."

"Pettiness doesn't exist for a man so long as he refuses to recognise it."

"H'm . . . what you've just said is a commonplace reversed."

"What? What do you mean by that term?"

"I'll tell you: saying, for instance, that education is beneficial, that's a commonplace; but to say that education is injurious, that's a commonplace turned upside down. There's more style about it, so to say, but in reality it's one and the same."

"And the truth is—where, which side?"

"Where? Like an echo I answer, 'Where?'"

"You're in a melancholy mood to-day, Yevgeny."

"Really? The sun must have softened my brain, I suppose, and I can't stand so many raspberries either."

"In that case, a nap's not a bad thing," observed Arkady.

"Certainly; only don't look at me; every man's face is stupid when he's asleep."

"But isn't it all the same to you what people think of you?"

"I don't know what to say to you. A real man ought not to care; a real man is one whom it's no use thinking about, whom one must either obey or hate."

"It's funny! I don't hate anybody," observed Arkady, after a moment's thought.

"And I hate so many. You are a soft-hearted, mawkish creature; how could you hate any one? . . . You're timid; you don't rely on yourself much."

"And you," interrupted Arkady, "do you expect much of yourself? Have you a high opinion of yourself?"

Bazarov paused. "When I meet a man who can hold his own beside me," he said, dwelling on every syllable, "then I'll change my opinion of myself. Yes, hatred! You said, for instance, to-day as we passed our bailiff Philip's cottage—it's the one that's so nice and clean—well, you said, Russia will come to perfection when the poorest peasant has a house like that, and every one of us ought to work to bring it about. . . . And I felt such a hatred for this poorest peasant, this Philip or Sidor, for whom I'm to be ready to jump out of my skin, and who won't even thank me for it . . . and why should he thank me? Why, suppose he does live in a clean house, while the nettles are growing out of me,—well what do I gain by it?"

"Hush, Yevgeny . . . if one listened to you to-day one would be driven to agreeing with those who reproach us for want of principles."

"You talk like your uncle. There are no general principles—you've not made out that even yet! There are feelings. Everything depends on them."

"How so?"

"Why, I, for instance, take up a negative attitude, by virtue of my sensations; I like to deny—my brain's made on that plan, and that's all about it! Why do I like chemistry? Why do you like apples?—by virtue of our sensations. It's all the same thing. Deeper than that men will never penetrate. Not every one will tell you that, and, in fact, I shan't tell you so another time."

"What, and is honesty a matter of the senses?"

"I should rather think so."

"Yevgeny!" Arkady was beginning in a dejected voice . . .

"Well? What? Isn't it to your taste?" broke in Bazarov. "No, brother. If you've made up your mind to mow down everything, don't spare your own legs. But we've talked enough metaphysics. 'Nature breathes the silence of sleep,' said Pushkin."

"He never said anything of the sort," protested Arkady.

"Well, if he didn't, as a poet he might have—and ought to have said it. By the way, he must have been a military man."

"Pushkin never was a military man!"

"Why, on every page of him there's, 'To arms! to arms! for Russia's honour!'"

"Why, what stories you invent! I declare, it's positive calumny."

"Calumny? That's a mighty matter! What a word he's found to frighten me with! Whatever charge you make against a man, you may be certain he deserves twenty times worse than that in reality."

"We had better go to sleep," said Arkady, in a tone of vexation.

"With the greatest pleasure," answered Bazarov. But neither of them slept. A feeling almost of hostility had come over both the young men. Five minutes later, they opened their eyes and glanced at one another in silence.

"Look," said Arkady suddenly, "a dry maple leaf has come off and is falling to the earth; its movement is exactly like a butterfly's flight. Isn't it strange? Gloom and decay—like brightness and life."

"Oh, my friend, Arkady Nikolaitch!" cried Bazarov, "one thing I entreat of you; no fine talk."

"I talk as best I can . . . And, I declare, it's perfect despotism. An idea came into my head; why shouldn't I utter it?"

"Yes; and why shouldn't I utter my ideas? I think that fine talk's positively indecent."

"And what is decent? Abuse?"

"Ha! ha! you really do intend, I see, to walk in your uncle's footsteps. How pleased that worthy imbecile would have been if he had heard you!"

"What did you call Pavel Petrovitch?"

"I called him, very justly, an imbecile."

"But this is unbearable!" cried Arkady.

"Aha! family feeling spoke there," Bazarov commented coolly. "I've noticed how obstinately it sticks to people. A man's ready to give up everything and break with every prejudice; but to admit that his brother, for instance, who steals handkerchiefs, is a thief—that's too much for him. And when one comes to think of it: my brother, mine—and no genius . . . that's an idea no one can swallow."

"It was a simple sense of justice spoke in me and not in the least family feeling," retorted Arkady passionately. "But since that's a sense you don't understand, since you haven't that sensation, you can't judge of it."

"In other words, Arkady Kirsanov is too exalted for my comprehension. I bow down before him and say no more."

"Don't, please, Yevgeny; we shall really quarrel at last."

"Ah, Arkady! do me a kindness. I entreat you, let us quarrel for once in earnest. . . ."

"But then perhaps we should end by . . ."

"Fighting?" put in Bazarov. "Well? Here, on the hay, in these idyllic surroundings, far from the world and the eyes of men, it wouldn't matter. But you'd be no match for me. I'd have you by the throat in a minute."

Bazarov spread out his long, cruel fingers. . . . Arkady turned round and prepared, as though in jest, to resist. . . . But his friend's face struck him as so vindictive—there was such menace in grim earnest in the smile that distorted his lips, and in his glittering eyes, that he felt instinctively afraid.

"Ah! so this is where you have got to!" the voice of Vassily Ivanovitch was heard saying at that instant, and the old army-doctor appeared before the young men, garbed in a home-made linen pea-jacket, with a straw hat, also home-made, on his head. "I've been looking everywhere for you. . . . Well, you've picked out a capital place, and you're excellently employed. Lying on the 'earth, gazing up to heaven.' Do you know, there's a special significance in that?"

"I never gaze up to heaven except when I want to sneeze," growled Bazarov, and turning to Arkady he added in an undertone: "Pity he interrupted us."

"I look at you, my youthful friends," Vassily Ivanovitch was saying meantime, shaking his head, and leaning his folded arms on a rather cunningly bent stick of his own carving, with a Turk's figure for a top,—"I look, and I cannot refrain from admiration. You have so much strength, such youth and bloom, such abilities, such talents! Positively, a Castor and Pollux."

"Get along with you—going off into mythology!" commented Bazarov. "You can see at once that he was a great Latinist in his day! Why, I seem to remember, you gained the silver medal for Latin prose—didn't you?"

"The Dioscuri, the Dioscuri!" repeated Vassily Ivanovitch.

"Come, shut up, father; don't show off."

"Once in a way it's surely permissible," murmured the old man. "However, I have not been seeking for you, gentlemen, to pay you compliments; but with the object, in the first place, of announcing to you that we shall soon be dining; and secondly, I wanted to prepare you, Yevgeny. . . . You are a sensible man, you know the world, and you know what women are, and consequently you will excuse. . . . Your mother wished to have a Te Deum sung on the occasion of your arrival. You must not imagine that I am inviting you to attend this thanksgiving—it is over indeed now; but Father Alexey . . ."

"The village priest?"

"Well, yes, the priest; he . . . is to dine . . . with us. . . . I did not anticipate this, and did not even approve of it . . . but it somehow came about . . . he did not understand me. . . . And, well . . . Arina Vlasyevna . . . Besides, he's a worthy, reasonable man."

"He won't eat my share at dinner, I suppose?" queried Bazarov.

Vassily Ivanovitch laughed. "How you talk!"

"Well, that's all I ask. I'm ready to sit down to table with any man."

Vassily Ivanovitch set his hat straight. "I was certain before I spoke," he said, "that you were above any kind of prejudice. Here am I, an old man at sixty-two, and I have none." (Vassily Ivanovitch did not dare to confess that he had himself desired the thanksgiving service. He was no less religious than his wife.) "And Father Alexey very much wanted to make your acquaintance. You will like him, you'll see. He's no objection even to cards, and he sometimes—but this is between ourselves . . . positively smokes a pipe."

"All right. We'll have a round of whist after dinner, and I'll clean him out."

"He! he! he! We shall see! That remains to be seen."

"I know you're an old hand," said Bazarov, with a peculiar emphasis.

Vassily Ivanovitch's bronzed cheeks were suffused with an uneasy flush.

"For shame, Yevgeny . . . Let bygones be bygones. Well, I'm ready to acknowledge before this gentleman I had that passion in my youth; and I have paid for it too! How hot it is, though! Let me sit down with you. I shan't be in your way, I hope?"

"Oh, not at all," answered Arkady.

Vassily Ivanovitch lowered himself, sighing, into the hay. "Your present quarters remind me, my dear sirs," he began, "of my military bivouacking existence, the ambulance halts, somewhere like this under a haystack, and even for that we were thankful." He sighed. "I have had many, many experiences in my life. For example, if you will allow me, I will tell you a curious episode of the plague in Bessarabia."

"For which you got the Vladimir cross?" put in Bazarov. "We know, we know. . . . By the way, why is it you're not wearing it?"

"Why, I told you that I have no prejudices," muttered Vassily Ivanovitch (he had only the evening before had the red ribbon unpicked off his coat), and he proceeded to relate the episode of the plague. "Why, he's fallen asleep," he whispered all at once to Arkady, pointing to Yevgeny, and winking good-naturedly. "Yevgeny! get up," he went on aloud. "Let's go in to dinner."

Father Alexey, a good-looking stout man with thick, carefully combed hair, with an embroidered girdle round his lilac silk cassock, appeared to be a man of much tact and adaptability. He made haste to be the first to offer his hand to Arkady and Bazarov, as though understanding beforehand that they did not want his blessing, and he behaved himself in general without constraint. He neither derogated from his own dignity, nor gave offence to others; he vouchsafed a passing smile at the seminary Latin, and stood up for his bishop; drank two small glasses of wine, but refused a third; accepted a cigar from Arkady, but did not proceed to smoke it, saying he would take it home with him. The only thing not quite agreeable about him was a way he had of constantly raising his hand with care and deliberation to catch the flies on his face, sometimes succeeding in smashing them. He took his seat at the green table, expressing his satisfaction at so doing in measured terms, and ended by winning from Bazarov two rubles and a half in paper money; they had no idea of even reckoning in silver in the house of Arina Vlasyevna. . . . She was sitting, as before, near her son (she did not play cards), her cheek, as before, propped on her little fist; she only got up to order some new dainty to be served. She was afraid to caress Bazarov, and he gave her no encouragement, he did not invite her caresses; and besides, Vassily Ivanovitch had advised her not to "worry" him too much. "Young men are not fond of that sort of thing," he declared to her. (It's needless to say what the dinner was like that day; Timofeitch in person had galloped off at early dawn for beef; the bailiff had gone off in another direction for turbot, gremille, and crayfish; for mushrooms alone forty-two farthings had been paid the peasant women in copper); but Arina Vlasyevna's eyes, bent steadfastly on Bazarov, did not express only devotion and tenderness; in them was to be seen sorrow also, mingled with awe and curiosity; there was to be seen too a sort of humble reproachfulness.

Bazarov, however, was not in a humour to analyse the exact expression of his mother's eyes; he seldom turned to her, and then only with some short question. Once he asked her for her hand "for luck"; she gently laid her soft, little hand on his rough, broad palm.

"Well," she asked, after waiting a little, "has it been any use?"

"Worse luck than ever," he answered, with a careless laugh.

"He plays too rashly," pronounced Father Alexey, as it were compassionately, and he stroked his beard.

"Napoleon's rule, good Father, Napoleon's rule," put in Vassily Ivanovitch, leading an ace.

"It brought him to St. Helena, though," observed Father Alexey, as he trumped the ace.

"Wouldn't you like some currant tea, Enyusha?" inquired Arina Vlasyevna.

Bazarov merely shrugged his shoulders.

"No!" he said to Arkady the next day, "I'm off from here to-morrow. I'm bored; I want to work, but I can't work here. I will come to your place again; I've left all my apparatus there, too. In your house one can at any rate shut oneself up. While here my father repeats to me, 'My study is at your disposal—nobody shall interfere with you,' and all the time he himself is never a yard away. And I'm ashamed somehow to shut myself away from him. It's the same thing, too, with mother. I hear her sighing the other side of the wall, and if one goes in to her, one's nothing to say to her."

"She will be very much grieved," observed Arkady, "and so will he."

"I shall come back again to them."

"When?"

"Why, when on my way to Petersburg."

"I feel sorry for your mother particularly."

"Why's that? Has she won your heart with strawberries, or what?"

Arkady dropped his eyes. "You don't understand your mother, Yevgeny. She's not only a very good woman, she's very clever really. This morning she talked to me for half-an-hour, and so sensibly, interestingly."

"I suppose she was expatiating upon me all the while?"

"We didn't talk only about you."

"Perhaps; lookers-on see most. If a woman can keep up half-an-hour's conversation, it's always a hopeful sign. But I'm going, all the same."

"It won't be very easy for you to break it to them."

"No, it won't be easy. Some demon drove me to tease my father to-day; he had one of his rent-paying peasants flogged the other day, and quite right too—yes, yes, you needn't look at me in such horror—he did quite right, because he's an awful thief and drunkard; only my father had no idea that I, as they say, was cognisant of the facts. He was greatly perturbed, and now I shall have to upset him more than ever. . . . Never mind! Never say die! He'll get over it!"

Bazarov said, "Never mind"; but the whole day passed before he could make up his mind to inform Vassily Ivanovitch of his intentions. At last, when he was just saying good-night to him in the study, he observed, with a feigned yawn—

"Oh . . . I was almost forgetting to tell you. . . . Send to Fedot's for our horses to-morrow."

Vassily Ivanovitch was dumfounded. "Is Mr. Kirsanov leaving us, then?"

"Yes; and I'm going with him."

Vassily Ivanovitch positively reeled. "You are going?"

"Yes . . . I must. Make the arrangements about the horses, please."

"Very good. . . ." faltered the old man; "to Fedot's . . . very good . . . only . . . only. . . . How is it?"

"I must go to stay with him for a little time. I will come back here again later."

"Ah! For a little time . . . very good." Vassily Ivanovitch drew out his handkerchief, and, blowing his nose, doubled up almost to the ground. "Well . . . everything shall be done. I had thought you were to be with us . . . a little longer. Three days. . . . After three years, it's rather little; rather little, Yevgeny!"

"But, I tell you, I'm coming back directly. It's necessary for me to go."

"Necessary. . . . Well! Duty before everything. So the horses shall be in readiness. Very good. Arina and I, of course, did not anticipate this. She has just begged some flowers from a neighbour; she meant to decorate the room for you." (Vassily Ivanovitch did not even mention that every morning almost at dawn he took counsel with Timofeitch, standing with his bare feet in his slippers, and pulling out with trembling fingers one dog's-eared ruble note after another, charged him with various purchases, with special reference to good things to eat, and to red wine, which, as far as he could observe, the young men liked extremely.) "Liberty . . . is the great thing; that's my rule. . . . I don't want to hamper you . . . not . . ."

He suddenly ceased, and made for the door.

"We shall soon see each other again, father, really."

But Vassily Ivanovitch, without turning round, merely waved his hand and was gone. When he got back to his bedroom he found his wife in bed, and began to say his prayers in a whisper, so as not to wake her up. She woke, however. "Is that you, Vassily Ivanovitch?" she asked.

"Yes, mother."

"Have you come from Enyusha? Do you know, I'm afraid of his not being comfortable on that sofa. I told Anfisushka to put him your travelling mattress and the new pillows; I should have given him our feather-bed, but I seem to remember he doesn't like too soft a bed. . . ."

"Never mind, mother; don't worry yourself. He's all right. Lord, have mercy on me, a sinner," he went on with his prayer in a low voice. Vassily Ivanovitch was sorry for his old wife; he did not mean to tell her over night what a sorrow there was in store for her.

Bazarov and Arkady set off the next day. From early morning all was dejection in the house; Anfisushka let the tray slip out of her hands; even Fedka was bewildered, and was reduced to taking off his boots. Vassily Ivanovitch was more fussy than ever; he was obviously trying to put a good face on it, talked loudly, and stamped with his feet, but his face looked haggard, and his eyes were continually avoiding his son. Arina Vlasyevna was crying quietly; she was utterly crushed, and could not have controlled herself at all if her husband had not spent two whole hours early in the morning exhorting her. When Bazarov, after repeated promises to come back certainly not later than in a month's time, tore himself at last from the embraces detaining him, and took his seat in the coach; when the horses had started, the bell was ringing, and the wheels were turning round, and when it was no longer any good to look after them, and the dust had settled, and Timofeitch, all bent and tottering as he walked, had crept back to his little room; when the old people were left alone in their little house, which seemed suddenly to have grown shrunken and decrepit too, Vassily Ivanovitch, after a few more moments of hearty waving of his handkerchief on the steps, sank into a chair, and his head dropped on to his breast. "He has cast us off; he has forsaken us," he faltered; "forsaken us; he was dull with us. Alone, alone!" he repeated several times. Then Arina Vlasyevna went up to him, and, leaning her grey head against his grey head, said, "There's no help for it, Vasya! A son is a separate piece cut off. He's like the falcon that flies home and flies away at his pleasure; while you and I are like funguses in the hollow of a tree, we sit side by side, and don't move from our place. Only I am left you unchanged forever, as you for me."

Vassily Ivanovitch took his hands from his face and clasped his wife, his friend, as firmly as he had never clasped in youth; she comforted him in his grief.

XXII

IN SILENCE, only rarely exchanging a few insignificant words, our friends travelled as far as Fedot's. Bazarov was not altogether pleased with himself. Arkady was displeased with him. He was feeling, too, that causeless melancholy which is only known to very young people. The coachman changed the horses, and getting up on to the box, inquired, "To the right or to the left?"

Arkady started. The road to the right led to the town, and from there home; the road to the left led to Madame Odintsov's.

He looked at Bazarov.

"Yevgeny," he queried; "to the left?"

Bazarov turned away. "What folly is this?" he muttered.

"I know it's folly," answered Arkady. . . . "But what does that matter? It's not the first time."

Bazarov pulled his cap down over his brows. "As you choose," he said at last. "Turn to the left," shouted Arkady.

The coach rolled away in the direction of Nikolskoe. But having resolved on the folly, the friends were even more obstinately silent than before, and seemed positively ill-humoured.

Directly the steward met them on the steps of Madame Odintsov's house, the friends could perceive that they had acted injudiciously in giving way so suddenly to a passing impulse. They were obviously not expected. They sat rather a long while, looking rather foolish, in the drawing-room. Madame Odintsov came in to them at last. She greeted them with her customary politeness, but was surprised at their hasty return; and, so far as could be judged from the deliberation of her gestures and words, she was not over pleased at it. They made haste to announce that they had only called on their road, and must go on farther, to the town, within four hours. She confined herself to a slight exclamation, begged Arkady to remember her to his father, and sent for her aunt. The princess appeared very sleepy, which gave her wrinkled old face an even more ill-natured expression. Katya was not well; she did not leave her room. Arkady suddenly realised that he was at least as anxious to see Katya as Anna Sergyevna herself. The four hours were spent in insignificant discussion of one thing and another; Anna Sergyevna both listened and spoke without a smile. It was only quite at parting that her former friendliness seemed, as it were, to revive.

"I have an attack of spleen just now," she said; "but you must not pay attention to that, and come again—I say this to both of you—before long."

Both Bazarov and Arkady responded with a silent bow, took their seats in the coach, and without stopping again anywhere, went straight home to Maryino, where they arrived safely on the evening of the following day. During the whole course of the journey neither one nor the other even mentioned the name of Madame Odintsov; Bazarov, in particular, scarcely opened his mouth, and kept staring in a side direction away from the road, with a kind of exasperated intensity.

At Maryino every one was exceedingly delighted to see them. The prolonged absence of his son had begun to make Nikolai Petrovitch uneasy; he uttered a cry of joy, and bounced about on the sofa, dangling his legs, when Fenitchka ran to him with sparkling eyes, and informed him of the arrival of the "young gentlemen"; even Pavel Petrovitch was conscious of some degree of agreeable excitement, and smiled condescendingly as he shook hands with the returned wanderers. Talk, questions followed; Arkady talked most, especially at supper, which was prolonged long after midnight. Nikolai Petrovitch ordered up some bottles of porter which had only just been sent from Moscow, and partook of the festive beverage till his cheeks were crimson, and he kept laughing a half-childish, half-nervous little chuckle. Even the servants were infected by the general gaiety. Dunyasha ran up and down like one possessed, and was continually slamming doors; while Piotr was, at three o'clock in the morning, still attempting to strum a Cossack waltz on the guitar. The strings gave forth a sweet and plaintive sound in the still air; but with the exception of a small preliminary flourish, nothing came of the cultured valet's efforts; nature had given him no more musical talent than all the rest of the world.

But meanwhile things were not going over harmoniously at Maryino, and poor Nikolai Petrovitch was having a bad time of it. Difficulties on the farm sprang up every day—hired labourers had become insupportable. Some asked for their wages to be settled, or for an increase of wages, while others made off with the wages they had received in advance; the horses fell sick; the harness fell to pieces as though it were burnt; the work was carelessly done; a threshing machine that had been ordered from Moscow turned out to be useless from its great weight, another was ruined the first time it was used; half the cattle sheds were burnt down through an old blind woman on the farm going in windy weather with a burning brand to fumigate her cow . . . the old woman, it is true, maintained that the whole mischief could be traced to the master's plan of introducing new-fangled cheeses and milk-products. The overseer suddenly turned lazy, and began to grow fat, as every Russian grows fat when he gets a snug berth. When he caught sight of Nikolai Petrovitch in the distance, he would fling a stick at a passing pig, or threaten a half-naked urchin, to show his zeal, but the rest of the time he was generally asleep. The peasants who had been put on the rent system did not bring their money at the time due, and stole the forest-timber; almost every night the keepers caught peasants' horses in the meadows of the "farm," and sometimes forcibly bore them off. Nikolai Petrovitch would fix a money fine for damages, but the matter usually ended after the horses had been kept a day or two on the master's forage by their returning to their owners. To crown all, the peasants began quarrelling among themselves; brothers asked for a division of property, their wives could not get on together in one house; all of a sudden the squabble, as though at a given signal, came to a head, and at once the whole village came running to the counting-house steps, crawling to the master, often drunken and with battered face, demanding justice and judgment; then arose an uproar and clamour, the shrill wailing of the women mixed with the curses of the men. Then one had to examine the contending parties, and shout oneself hoarse, knowing all the while that one could never anyway arrive at a just decision. . . . There were not hands enough for the harvest; a neighbouring small owner, with the most benevolent countenance, contracted to supply him with reapers for a commission of two rubles an acre, and cheated him in the most shameless fashion; his peasant women demanded unheard-of sums, and the corn meanwhile went to waste; and here they were not getting on with the mowing, and there the Council of Guardians threatened and demanded prompt payment, in full, of interest due. . . .

"I can do nothing!" Nikolai Petrovitch cried more than once in despair. "I can't flog them myself; and as for calling in the police captain, my principles don't allow of it, while you can do nothing with them without the fear of punishment!"

"*Du calme, du calme,*" Pavel Petrovitch would remark upon this, but even he hummed to himself, knitted his brows, and tugged at his moustache.

Bazarov held aloof from these matters, and indeed as a guest it was not for him to meddle in other people's business. The day after his arrival at Maryino, he set to work on his frogs, his infusoria, and his chemical experiments, and was forever busy with them. Arkady, on the contrary, thought it his duty, if not to help his father, at least to make a show of being ready to help him. He gave him a patient hearing, and once offered him some advice, not with any idea of its being acted upon, but to show his interest. Farming details did not arouse any aversion in him; he used even to dream with pleasure of work on the land, but at this time his brain was swarming with other ideas. Arkady, to his own astonishment, thought incessantly of Nikolskoe; in former days he would simply have shrugged his shoulders if any one had told him that he could ever feel dull under the same roof as Bazarov—and that roof his father's! But he actually was dull and longed to get away. He tried going long walks till he was tired, but that was no use. In conversation with his father one day, he found out that Nikolai Petrovitch had in his possession rather interesting letters, written by Madame Odintsov's mother to his wife, and he gave him no rest till he got hold of the letters, for which Nikolai Petrovitch had to rummage in twenty drawers and boxes. Having gained possession of these half-crumbling papers, Arkady felt, as it were, soothed, just as though he had caught a glimpse of the goal towards which he ought now to go. "I mean that for both of you," he was constantly whispering—she had added that herself! "I'll go, I'll go, hang it all!" but he recalled the last visit, the cold reception, and his former embarrassment, and timidity got the better of him. The "go-ahead" feeling of youth, the secret desire to try his luck, to prove his worth in solitude, without the protection of any one whatever, gained the day at last. Before ten days had passed after his return to Maryino, on the pretext of studying the working of the Sunday schools, he galloped off to the town again, and from there to Nikolskoe. Urging the driver on without intermission, he flew along, like a young officer riding to battle; and he felt both frightened and light-hearted, and was breathless with impatience. "The great thing is —one mustn't think," he kept repeating to himself. His driver happened to be a lad of spirit; he halted before every public house, saying, "A drink or not a drink" but, to make up for it, when he had drunk he did not spare his horses. At last the lofty roof of the familiar house came in sight. . . . "What am I to do?" flashed through Arkady's head. "Well, there's no turning back now!" The three horses galloped in unison; the driver whooped and whistled at them. And now the bridge was groaning under the hoofs and wheels, and now the avenue of lopped pines seemed running to meet them. . . . There was a glimpse of a woman's pink dress against the dark green, a young face peeped out from under the light fringe of a parasol. . . . He recognised Katya, and she recognised him. Arkady told the driver to stop the galloping horses, leaped out of the carriage, and went up to her. "It's you!" she cried, gradually flushing all over; "let us go to my sister, she's here in the garden; she will be pleased to see you."

Katya led Arkady into the garden. His meeting with her struck him as a particularly happy omen; he was delighted to see her, as though she were of his own kindred. Everything had happened so splendidly; no steward, no formal announcement. At a turn in the path he caught sight of Anna Sergyevna. She was standing with her back to him. Hearing footsteps, she turned slowly round.

Arkady felt confused again, but the first words she uttered soothed him at once. "Welcome back, runaway!" she said in her even, caressing voice, and came to meet him, smiling and frowning to keep the sun and wind out of her eyes. "Where did you pick him up, Katya?"

"I have brought you something, Anna Sergyevna," he began, "which you certainly don't expect."

"You have brought yourself; that's better than anything."

XXIII

HAVING seen Arkady off with ironical compassion, and given him to understand that he was not in the least deceived as to the real object of his journey,

Bazarov shut himself up in complete solitude; he was overtaken by a fever for work. He did not dispute now with Pavel Petrovitch, especially as the latter assumed an excessively aristocratic demeanour in his presence, and expressed his opinions more in inarticulate sounds than in words. Only on one occasion Pavel Petrovitch fell into a controversy with the *nihilist* on the subject of the question then much discussed of the rights of the nobles of the Baltic province; but suddenly he stopped of his own accord, remarking with chilly politeness, "However, we cannot understand one another; I, at least, have not the honour of understanding you."

"I should think not!" cried Bazarov. "A man's capable of understanding anything—how the æther vibrates, and what's going on in the sun—but how any other man can blow his nose differently from him, that he's incapable of understanding."

"What, is that an epigram?" observed Pavel Petrovitch inquiringly, and he walked away.

However, he sometimes asked permission to be present at Bazarov's experiments, and once even placed his perfumed face, washed with the very best soap, near the microscope to see how a transparent infusoria swallowed a green speck, and busily munched it with two very rapid sort of clappers which were in its throat. Nikolai Petrovitch visited Bazarov much oftener than his brother; he would have come every day, as he expressed it, to "study," if his worries on the farm had not taken off his attention. He did not hinder the young man in his scientific researches; he used to sit down somewhere in a corner of the room and look on attentively, occasionally permitting himself a discreet question. During dinner and supper-time he used to try to turn the conversation upon physics, geology, or chemistry, seeing that all other topics, even agriculture, to say nothing of politics, might lead, if not to collisions, at least to mutual unpleasantness. Nikolai Petrovitch surmised that his brother's dislike for Bazarov was no less. An unimportant incident, among many others, confirmed his surmises. The cholera began to make its appearance in some places in the neighbourhood, and even "carried off" two persons from Maryino itself. In the night Pavel Petrovitch happened to have rather severe symptoms. He was in pain till the morning, but did not have recourse to Bazarov's skill. And when he met him the following day, in reply to his question, "Why he had not sent for him?" answered, still quite pale, but scrupulously brushed and shaved, "Why, I seem to recollect you said yourself you didn't believe in medicine." So the days went by. Bazarov went on obstinately and grimly working . . . and meanwhile there was in Nikolai Petrovitch's house one creature to whom, if he did not open his heart, he at least was glad to talk. . . . That creature was Fenitchka.

He used to meet her for the most part early in the morning, in the garden, or the farmyard; he never used to go to her room to see her, and she had only once been to his door to inquire—ought she to let Mitya have his bath or not? It was not only that she confided in him, that she was not afraid of him—she was positively freer and more at her ease in her behaviour with him than with Nikolai Petrovitch himself. It is hard to say how it came about; perhaps it was because she unconsciously felt the absence in Bazarov of all gentility, of all that superiority which at once attracts and overawes. In her eyes he was both an excellent doctor and a simple man. She looked after her baby without constraint in his presence; and once when she was suddenly attacked with giddiness and headache—she took a spoonful of medicine from his hand. Before Nikolai Petrovitch she kept, as it were, at a distance from Bazarov; she acted in this way not from hypocrisy, but from a kind of feeling of propriety. Pavel Petrovitch she was more afraid of than ever; for some time he had begun to watch her, and would suddenly make his appearance, as though he sprang out of the earth behind her back, in his English suit, with his immovable vigilant face, and his hands in his pockets. "It's like a bucket of cold water on one," Fenitchka complained to Dunyasha, and the latter sighed in response, and thought of another "heartless" man. Bazarov, without the least suspicion of the fact, had become the *cruel tyrant* of her heart.

Fenitchka liked Bazarov; but he liked her too. His face was positively transformed when he talked to her; it took a bright, almost kind expression, and his habitual nonchalance was replaced by a sort of jesting attentiveness. Fenitchka was growing prettier every day. There is a time in the life of young women when they suddenly begin to expand and blossom like summer roses; this time had come for Fenitchka. Dressed in a delicate white dress, she seemed herself slighter and whiter; she was not tanned by the sun; but the heat, from which she could not shield herself, spread a slight flush over her cheeks and ears, and, shedding a soft indolence over her whole body, was reflected in a dreamy languor in her pretty eyes. She was almost unable to work; her hands seemed to fall naturally into her lap. She scarcely walked at all, and was constantly sighing and complaining with comic helplessness.

"You should go oftener to bathe," Nikolai Petrovitch told her. He had made a large bath covered in with an awning in one of his ponds which had not yet quite disappeared.

"Oh, Nikolai Petrovitch! But by the time one gets to the pond, one's utterly dead, and, coming back, one's dead again. You see, there's no shade in the garden."

"That's true, there's no shade," replied Nikolai Petrovitch, rubbing his forehead.

One day at seven o'clock in the morning, Bazarov, returning from a walk, came upon Fenitchka in the lilac arbour, which was long past flowering, but was still thick and green. She was sitting on the garden seat, and had as usual thrown a white kerchief over her head; near her lay a whole heap of red and white roses still wet with dew. He said good morning to her.

"Ah! Yevgeny Vassilyitch!" she said, and lifted the edge of her kerchief a little to look at him, in doing which her arm was left bare to the elbow.

"What are you doing here?" said Bazarov, sitting down beside her. "Are you making a nosegay?"

"Yes, for the table at lunch. Nikolai Petrovitch likes it."

"But it's a long while yet to lunch time. What a heap of flowers!"

"I gathered them now, for it will be hot then, and one can't go out. One can only just breathe now. I feel quite weak with the heat. I'm really afraid whether I'm not going to be ill."

"What an idea! Let me feel your pulse." Bazarov took her hand, felt for the evenly-beating pulse, but did not even begin to count its throbs. "You'll live a hundred years!" he said, dropping her hand.

"Ah, God forbid!" she cried.

"Why? Don't you want a long life?"

"Well, but a hundred years! There was an old woman near us eighty-five years old—and what a martyr she was! Dirty and deaf and bent and coughing all the time; nothing but a burden to herself. That's a dreadful life!"

"So it's better to be young?"

"Well, isn't it?"

"But why is it better? Tell me!"

"How can you ask why? Why, here I now, while I'm young, I can do everything—go and come and carry, and needn't ask any one for anything. . . . What can be better?"

"And to me it's all the same whether I'm young or old."

"How do you mean—it's all the same? It's not possible what you say."

"Well, judge for yourself, Fedosya Nikolaevna, what good is my youth to me. I live alone, a poor lonely creature . . ."

"That always depends on you."

"It doesn't at all depend on me! At least, some one ought to take pity on me."

Fenitchka gave a sidelong look at Bazarov, but said nothing. "What's this book you have?" she asked after a short pause.

"That? That's a scientific book, very difficult."

"And are you still studying? And don't you find it dull? You know everything already, I should say."

"It seems not everything. You try to read a little."

"But I don't understand anything here. Is it Russian?" asked Fenitchka, taking the heavily bound book in both hands. "How thick it is!"

"Yes, it's Russian."

"All the same, I shan't understand anything."

"Well, I didn't give it you for you to understand it. I wanted to look at you while you were reading. When you read, the end of your little nose moves so nicely."

Fenitchka, who had set to work to spell out in a low voice the article on "Creosote" she had chanced upon, laughed and threw down the book . . . it slipped from the seat on to the ground.

"I like it, too, when you laugh," observed Bazarov.

"Nonsense!"

"I like it when you talk. It's just like a little brook babbling."

Fenitchka turned her head away. "What a person you are to talk!" she commented, picking the flowers over with her finger. "And how can you care to listen to me? You have talked with such clever ladies."

"Ah, Fedosya Nikolaevna, believe me; all the clever ladies in the world are not worth your little elbow."

"Come, there's another invention!" murmured Fenitchka, clasping her hands.

Bazarov picked the book up from the ground.

"That's a medical book; why do you throw it away?"

"Medical?" repeated Fenitchka, and she turned to him again. "Do you know, ever since you gave me those drops—do you remember?—Mitya has slept so well! I really can't think how to thank you; you are so good, really."

"But you have to pay doctors," observed Bazarov with a smile. "Doctors, you know yourself, are grasping people."

Fenitchka raised her eyes, which seemed still darker from the whitish reflection cast on the upper part of her face, and looked at Bazarov. She did not know whether he was joking or not.

"If you please, we shall be delighted. . . . I must ask Nikolai Petrovitch . . ."

"Why, do you think I want money?" Bazarov interposed. "No; I don't want money from you."

"What then?" asked Fenitchka.

"What?" repeated Bazarov. "Guess!"

"A likely person I am to guess!"

"Well, I will tell you; I want . . . one of those roses."

Fenitchka laughed again, and even clapped her hands, so amusing Bazarov's request seemed to her. She laughed, and at the same time felt flattered. Bazarov was looking intently at her.

"By all means," she said at last; and, bending down to the seat, she began picking over the roses. "Which will you have—a red or a white one?"

"Red—and not too large."

She sat up again. "Here, take it," she said, but at once drew back her outstretched hand, and, biting her lips, looked towards the entrance of the arbour, then listened.

"What is it?" asked Bazarov. "Nikolai Petrovitch?"

"No . . . Mr. Kirsanov has gone to the fields . . . besides, I'm not afraid of him . . . but Pavel Petrovitch . . . I fancied . . ."

"What?"

"I fancied he was coming here. No . . . it was no one. Take it." Fenitchka gave Bazarov the rose.

"On what grounds are you afraid of Pavel Petrovitch?"

"He always scares me. And I know you don't like him. Do you remember, you always used to quarrel with him? I don't know what your quarrel was about, but I can see you turn him about like this and like that."

Fenitchka showed with her hands how in her opinion Bazarov turned Pavel Petrovitch about.

Bazarov smiled. "But if he gave me a beating," he asked, "would you stand up for me?'

"How could I stand up for you? But no, no one will get the better of you."

"Do you think so? But I know a hand which could overcome me if it liked."

"What hand?"

"Why, don't you know, really? Smell, how delicious this rose smells you gave me."

Fenitchka stretched her little neck forward, and put her face close to the flower. . . . The kerchief slipped from her head on to her shoulders; her soft mass of dark, shining, slightly ruffled hair was visible.

"Wait a minute; I want to smell it with you," said Bazarov. He bent down and kissed her vigorously on her parted lips.

She started, pushed him back with both her hands on his breast, but pushed feebly, and he was able to renew and prolong his kiss.

A dry cough was heard behind the lilac bushes. Fenitchka instantly moved away to the other end of the seat. Pavel Petrovitch showed himself, made a slight bow, and saying with a sort of malicious mournfulness, "You are here," he retreated. Fenitchka at once gathered up all her roses and went out of the arbour. "It was wrong of you, Yevgeny Vassilyitch," she whispered as she went. There was a note of genuine reproach in her whisper.

Bazarov remembered another recent scene, and he felt both shame and contemptuous annoyance. But he shook his head directly, ironically congratulated himself "on his final assumption of the part of the gay Lothario," and went off to his own room.

Pavel Petrovitch went out of the garden, and made his way with deliberate steps to the copse. He stayed there rather a long while; and when he returned to lunch, Nikolai Petrovitch inquired anxiously whether he were quite well—his face looked so gloomy.

"You know, I sometimes suffer with my liver," Pavel Petrovitch answered tranquilly.

XXIV

Two hours later he knocked at Bazarov's door.

"I must apologise for hindering you in your scientific pursuits," he began, seating himself on a chair in the window, and leaning with both hands on a handsome walking-stick with an ivory knob (he usually walked without a stick), "But I am constrained to beg you to spare me five minutes of your time . . . no more."

"All my time is at your disposal," answered Bazarov, over whose face there passed a quick change of expression directly Pavel Petrovitch crossed the threshold.

"Five minutes will be enough for me. I have come to put a single question to you."

"A question? What is it about?"

"I will tell you, if you will kindly hear me out. At the commencement of your stay in my brother's house, before I had renounced the pleasure of conversing with you, it was my fortune to hear your opinions on many subjects; but so far as my memory serves, neither between us, nor in my presence, was the subject of single combats and duelling in general broached. Allow me to hear what are your views on that subject?"

Bazarov, who had risen to meet Pavel Petrovitch, sat down on the edge of the table and folded his arms.

"My view is," he said, "that from the theoretical standpoint, duelling is absurd; from the practical standpoint, now—it's quite a different matter."

"That is, you mean to say, if I understand you right, that whatever your theoretical views on duelling, you would not in practice allow yourself to be insulted without demanding satisfaction?"

"You have guessed my meaning absolutely."

"Very good. I am very glad to hear you say so. Your words relieve me from a state of incertitude."

"Of uncertainty, you mean to say."

"That is all the same; I express myself so as to be understood; I . . . am not a seminary rat. Your words save me from a rather deplorable necessity. I have made up my mind to fight you."

Bazarov opened his eyes wide. "Me?"

"Undoubtedly."

"But what for, pray?"

"I could explain the reason to you," began Pavel Petrovitch, "but I prefer to be silent about it. To my idea your presence here is superfluous; I cannot endure you; I despise you; and if that is not enough for you . . ."

Pavel Petrovitch's eyes glittered . . . Bazarov's, too, were flashing.

"Very good," he assented. "No need of further explanations. You've a whim to try your chivalrous spirit upon me. I might refuse you this pleasure, but—so be it!"

"I am sensible of my obligation to you," replied Pavel Petrovitch; "and may reckon then on your accepting my challenge without compelling me to resort to violent measures."

"That means, speaking without metaphor, to that stick?" Bazarov remarked coolly. "That is precisely correct. It's quite unnecessary for you to insult me. Indeed, it would not be a perfectly safe proceeding. You can remain a gentleman. . . . I accept your challenge, too, like a gentleman."

"That is excellent," observed Pavel Petrovitch, putting his stick in the corner. "We will say a few words directly about the conditions of our duel; but I should like first to know whether you think it necessary to resort to the formality of a trifling dispute, which might serve as a pretext for my challenge?"

"No; it's better without formalities."

"I think so myself. I presume it is also out of place to go into the real grounds of our difference. We cannot endure one another. What more is necessary?"

"What more, indeed?" repeated Bazarov ironically.

"As regards the conditions of the meeting itself, seeing that we shall have no seconds—for where could we get them?"

"Exactly so; where could we get them?"

"Then I have the honour to lay the following proposition before you: The combat to take place early to-morrow, at six, let us say, behind the copse, with pistols, at a distance of ten paces . . ."

"At ten paces? That will do; we hate one another at that distance."

"We might have it eight," remarked Pavel Petrovitch.

"We might."

"To fire twice; and, to be ready for any result, let each put a letter in his pocket, in which he accuses himself of his end."

"Now, that I don't approve of at all," observed Bazarov. "There's a slight flavour of the French novel about it, something not very plausible."

"Perhaps. You will agree, however, that it would be unpleasant to incur a suspicion of murder?"

"I agree as to that. But there is a means of avoiding that painful reproach. We shall have no seconds, but we can have a witness."

"And whom, allow me to inquire?"

"Why, Piotr."

"What Piotr?"

"Your brother's valet. He's a man who has attained to the acme of contemporary culture, and he will perform his part with all the *comilfo* (*comme il faut*) necessary in such cases."

"I think you are joking, sir."

"Not at all. If you think over my suggestion, you will be convinced that it's full of common sense and simplicity. You can't hide a candle under a bushel; but I'll undertake to prepare Piotr in a fitting manner, and bring him on to the field of battle."

"You persist in jesting still," Pavel Petrovitch declared, getting up from his chair. "But after the courteous readiness you have shown me, I have no right to pretend to lay down. . . . And so, everything is arranged. . . . By the way, perhaps you have no pistols?"

"How should I have pistols, Pavel Petrovitch? I'm not in the army."

"In that case, I offer you mine. You may rest assured that it's five years now since I shot with them."

"That's a very consoling piece of news."

Pavel Petrovitch took up his stick. . . . "And now, my dear sir, it only remains for me to thank you and to leave you to your studies. I have the honour to take leave of you."

"Till we have the pleasure of meeting again, my dear sir," said Bazarov, conducting his visitor to the door.

Pavel Petrovitch went out, while Bazarov remained standing a minute before the door, and suddenly exclaimed, "Pish, well, I'm dashed! How fine, and how foolish! A pretty farce we've been through! Like trained dogs dancing on their hind-paws. But to decline was out of the question; why, I do believe he'd have struck me, and then . . ." (Bazarov turned white at the very thought; all his pride was up in arms at once)—"then it might have come to my strangling him like a cat." He went back to his microscope, but his heart was beating, and the composure necessary for taking observations had disappeared. "He caught sight of us to-day," he thought; "but would he really act like this on his brother's account? And what a mighty matter is it—a kiss? There must be something else in it. Bah! isn't he perhaps in love with her himself? To be sure, he's in love; it's as clear as day. What a complication! It's a nuisance!" he decided at last; "it's a bad job, look at it which way you will. In the first place, to risk a bullet through one's brains, and in any case to go away; and then Arkady . . . and that dear innocent pussy, Nikolai Petrovitch. It's a bad job, an awfully bad job."

The day passed in a kind of peculiar stillness and languor. Fenitchka gave no sign of her existence; she sat in her little room like a mouse in its hole. Nikolai Petrovitch had a careworn air. He had just heard that blight had begun to appear in his wheat, upon which he had in particular rested his hopes. Pavel Petrovitch overwhelmed every one, even Prokofitch, with his icy courtesy. Bazarov began a letter to his father, but tore it up, and threw it under the table.

"If I die," he thought, "they will find it out; but I'm not going to die. No, I shall struggle along in this world a good while yet." He gave Piotr orders to come to him on important business the next morning directly it was light. Piotr imagined that he wanted to take him to Petersburg with him. Bazarov went late to bed, and all night long he was harassed by disordered dreams . . . Madame Odintsov kept appearing in them, now she was his mother, and she was followed by a kitten with black whiskers, and this kitten seemed to be Fenitchka; then Pavel Petrovitch took the shape of a great wood, with which he had yet to fight. Piotr waked him up at four o'clock; he dressed at once, and went out with him.

It was a lovely, fresh morning; tiny flecked clouds hovered overhead in little curls of foam on the pale clear blue; a fine dew lay in drops on the leaves and grass, and sparkled like silver on the spiders' webs; the damp, dark earth seemed still to keep traces of the rosy dawn; from the whole sky the songs of larks came pouring in showers. Bazarov walked as far as the copse, sat down in the shade at its edge, and only then disclosed to Piotr the nature of the service he expected of him. The refined valet was mortally alarmed; but Bazarov soothed him by the assurance that he would have nothing to do but stand at a distance and look on, and that he would not incur any sort of responsibility. "And meantime," he added, "only think what an important part you have to play!" Piotr threw up his hands, looked down, and leaned against a birch-tree, looking green with terror.

The road from Maryino skirted the copse; a light dust lay on it, untouched by wheel or foot since the previous day. Bazarov unconsciously stared along this road, picked and gnawed a blade of grass, while he kept repeating to himself, "What a piece of foolery!" The chill of the early morning made him shiver twice. . . . Piotr looked at him dejectedly, but Bazarov only smiled; he was not afraid.

The tramp of horses' hoofs was heard along the road. . . . A peasant came into sight from behind the trees. He was driving before him two horses hobbled together, and as he passed Bazarov he looked at him rather strangely, without touching his cap, which it was easy to see disturbed Piotr, as an unlucky omen. "There's some one else up early too," thought Bazarov; "but he at least has got up for work, while we . . ."

"Fancy the gentleman's coming," Piotr faltered suddenly. Bazarov raised his head and saw Pavel Petrovitch. Dressed in a light check jacket and snow-white trousers, he was walking rapidly along the road; under his arm he carried a box wrapped up in green cloth.

"I beg your pardon, I believe I have kept you waiting," he observed, bowing first to Bazarov, then to Piotr, whom he treated respectfully at that instant, as representing something in the nature of a second. "I was unwilling to wake my man."

"It doesn't matter," answered Bazarov; "we've only just arrived ourselves."

"Ah! so much the better!" Pavel Petrovitch took a look round. "There's no one in sight; no one hinders us. We can proceed?"

"Let us proceed."

"You do not, I presume, desire any fresh explanations?"

"No, I don't."

"Would you like to load?" inquired Pavel Petrovitch, taking the pistols out of the box.

"No; you load, and I will measure out the paces. My legs are longer," added Bazarov with a smile. "One, two, three."

"Yevgeny Vassilyitch," Piotr faltered with an effort (he was shaking as though he were in a fever), "say what you like, I am going farther off."

"Four . . . five . . . Good. Move away, my good fellow, move away; you may get behind a tree even, and stop up your ears, only don't shut your eyes; and if any one falls, run and pick him up. Six . . . seven . . . eight . . ." Bazarov stopped. "Is that enough?" he said, turning to Pavel Petrovitch; "or shall I add two paces more?"

"As you like," replied the latter, pressing down the second bullet.

"Well, we'll make it two paces more." Bazarov drew a line on the ground with the toe of his boot. "There's the barrier then. By the way, how many paces may each of us go back from the barrier? That's an important question too. That point was not discussed yesterday."

"I imagine, ten," replied Pavel Petrovitch, handing Bazarov both pistols. "Will you be so good as to choose?"

"I will be so good. But, Pavel Petrovitch, you must admit our combat is singular to the point of absurdity. Only look at the countenance of our second."

"You are disposed to laugh at everything," answered Pavel Petrovitch. "I acknowledge the strangeness of our duel, but I think it my duty to warn you that I intend to fight seriously. *A bon entendeur, salut!*"

"Oh! I don't doubt that we've made up our minds to make away with each other; but why not laugh too and unite *utile dulci?* You talk to me in French, while I talk to you in Latin."

"I am going to fight in earnest," repeated Pavel Petrovitch, and he walked off to his place. Bazarov on his side counted off ten paces from the barrier, and stood still.

"Are you ready?" asked Pavel Petrovitch.

"Perfectly."

"We can approach one another."

Bazarov moved slowly forward, and Pavel Petrovitch, his left hand thrust in his pocket, walked towards him, gradually raising the muzzle of his pistol. . . . "He's aiming straight at my nose," thought Bazarov, "and doesn't he blink down it carefully, the ruffian! Not an agreeable sensation, though. I'm going to look at his watch chain."

Something whizzed sharply by his very ear, and at the same instant there was the sound of a shot. "I heard it, so it must be all right," had time to flash through Bazarov's brain. He took one more step, and without taking aim pressed the spring.

Pavel Petrovitch gave a slight start, and clutched at his thigh. A stream of blood began to trickle down his white trousers.

Bazarov flung aside the pistol, and went up to his antagonist. "Are you wounded?" he said.

"You had the right to call me up to the barrier," said Pavel Petrovitch, "but that's of no consequence. According to our agreement, each of us has the right to one more shot."

"All right, but, excuse me, that'll do another time," answered Bazarov, catching hold of Pavel Petrovitch, who was beginning to turn pale. "Now, I'm not a duellist, but a doctor, and I must have a look at your wound before anything else. Piotr, come here, Piotr! where have you gone to?"

"That's all nonsense . . . I need no one's aid," Pavel Petrovitch declared jerkily, "and . . . we must . . . again . . ." He tried to pull at his moustaches, but his hand failed him, his eyes grew dim, and he lost consciousness.

"Here's a pretty pass! A fainting fit! What next!" Bazarov cried unconsciously, as he laid Pavel Petrovitch on the grass. "Let's have a look what's wrong." He pulled out a handkerchief, wiped away the blood, and began feeling round the wound. . . . "The bone's not touched," he muttered through his teeth; "the ball didn't go deep; one muscle, *vastus externus*, grazed. He'll be dancing about in three weeks! . . . And to faint! Oh, these nervous people, how I hate them! My word, what a delicate skin!"

"Is he killed?" the quaking voice of Piotr came rustling behind his back.

Bazarov looked round. "Go for some water as quick as you can, my good fellow, and he'll outlive us yet."

But the modern servant seemed not to understand his words, and he did not stir. Pavel Petrovitch slowly opened his eyes. "He will die!" whispered Piotr, and he began crossing himself.

"You are right. . . . What an imbecile countenance!" remarked the wounded gentleman with a forced smile.

"Well, go for the water, damn you!" shouted Bazarov.

"No need. . . . It was a momentary *vertigo*. . . . Help me to sit up. . . . there, that's right. . . . I only need something to bind up this scratch, and I can reach home on foot, or else you can send a droshky for me. The duel, if you are willing, shall not be renewed. You have behaved honourably . . . to-day, to-day—observe."

"There's no need to recall the past," rejoined Bazarov; "and as regards the future, it's not worth while for you to trouble your head about that either, for I intend being off without delay. Let me bind up your leg now; your wound's not serious, but it's always best to stop bleeding. But first I must bring this corpse to his senses."

Bazarov shook Piotr by the collar, and sent him for a droshky.

"Mind, you don't frighten my brother," Pavel Petrovitch said to him; "don't dream of informing him."

Piotr flew off; and while he was running for a droshky, the two antagonists sat on the ground and said nothing. Pavel Petrovitch tried not to look at Bazarov; he did not want to be reconciled to him in any case; he was ashamed of his own haughtiness, of his failure; he was ashamed of the whole position he had brought about, even while he felt it could not have ended in a more favourable manner. "At any rate, there will be no scandal," he consoled himself by reflecting, "and for that I am thankful." The silence was prolonged, a silence distressing and awkward. Both of them were ill at ease. Each was conscious that the other understood him. That is pleasant to friends, and always very unpleasant to those who are not friends, especially when it is impossible either to have things out or to separate.

"Haven't I bound up your leg too tight?" inquired Bazarov at last.

"No, not at all; it's capital," answered Pavel Petrovitch; and after a brief pause, he added, "There's no deceiving my brother; we shall have to tell him we quarrelled over politics."

"Very good," assented Bazarov. "You can say I insulted all anglomaniacs."

"That will do capitally. What do you imagine that man thinks of us now?" continued Pavel Petrovitch, pointing to the same peasant, who had driven the hobbled horses past Bazarov a few minutes before the duel, and going back again along the road, took off his cap at the sight of the "gentlefolk."

"Who can tell?" answered Bazarov. "It is quite likely he thinks nothing. The Russian peasant is that mysterious unknown about whom Mrs. Radcliffe used to talk so much. Who is to understand him! He doesn't understand himself!"

"Ah! so that's your idea!" Pavel Petrovitch began; and suddenly he cried, "Look what your fool of a Piotr has done! Here's my brother galloping up to us!"

Bazarov turned round and saw the pale face of Nikolai Petrovitch, who was sitting in the droshky. He jumped out of it before it had stopped, and rushed up to his brother.

"What does this mean?" he said in an agitated voice. "Yevgeny Vassilyitch, pray, what is this?"

"Nothing," answered Pavel Petrovitch; "they have alarmed you for nothing. I had a little dispute with Mr. Bazarov, and I have had to pay for it a little."

"But what was it all about, mercy on us!"

"How can I tell you? Mr. Bazarov alluded disrespectfully to Sir Robert Peel. I must hasten to add that I am the only person to blame in all this, while Mr. Bazarov has behaved most honourably. I called him out."

"But you're covered with blood, good heavens!"

"Well, did you suppose I had water in my veins? But this blood-letting is positively beneficial to me. Isn't that so, doctor? Help me to get into the droshky, and don't give way to melancholy. I shall be quite well to-morrow. That's it; capital. Drive on, coachman."

Nikolai Petrovitch walked after the droshky; Bazarov was remaining where he was. . . .

"I must ask you to look after my brother," Nikolai Petrovitch said to him, "till we get another doctor from the town."

Bazarov nodded his head without speaking. In an hour's time Pavel Petrovitch was already lying in bed with a skilfully bandaged leg. The whole house was alarmed; Fenitchka fainted. Nikolai Petrovitch kept stealthily wringing his hands, while Pavel Petrovitch laughed and joked, especially with Bazarov; he had put on a fine cambric night shirt, an elegant morning wrapper, and a fez, did not allow the blinds to be drawn down, and humourously complained of the necessity of being kept from food.

Towards night, however, he began to be feverish; his head ached. The doctor arrived from the town. (Nikolai Petrovitch would not listen to his brother, and indeed Bazarov himself did not wish him to; he sat the whole day in his room, looking yellow and vindictive, and only went in to the invalid for as brief a time as possible; twice he happened to meet Fenitchka, but she shrank away from him with horror.) The new doctor advised a cooling diet; he confirmed, however, Bazarov's assertion that there was no danger. Nikolai Petrovitch told him his brother had wounded himself by accident, to which the doctor responded, "Hm!" but having twenty-five silver rubles slipped into his hand on the spot, he observed, "You don't say so! Well, it's a thing that often happens, to be sure."

No one in the house went to bed or undressed. Nikolai Petrovitch kept going in to his brother on tiptoe, retreating on tiptoe again; the latter dozed, moaned a little, told him in French, *Couchez-vous*, and asked for drink. Nikolai Petrovitch sent Fenitchka twice to take him a glass of lemonade; Pavel Petrovitch gazed at her intently, and drank off the glass to the last drop. Towards morning the fever had increased a little; there was slight delirium. At first Pavel Petrovitch uttered incoherent words; then suddenly he opened his eyes, and seeing his brother near his bed bending anxiously over him, he said, "Don't you think, Nikolai, Fenitchka has something in common with Nellie?"

"What Nellie, Pavel dear?"

"How can you ask? Princess R——. Especially in the upper part of the face. *C'est de la même famille.*"

Nikolai Petrovitch made no answer, while inwardly he marveled at the persistence of old passions in man. "It's like this when it comes to the surface," he thought.

"Ah, how I love that light-headed creature!" moaned Pavel Petrovitch, clasping his hands mournfully behind his head. "I can't bear any insolent upstart to dare to touch . . ." he whispered a few minutes later.

Nikolai Petrovitch only sighed; he did not even suspect to whom these words referred.

Bazarov presented himself before him at eight o'clock the next day. He had already had time to pack, and to set free all his frogs, insects, and birds.

"You have come to say good-bye to me?" said Nikolai Petrovitch, getting up to meet him.

"Yes."

"I understand you, and approve of you fully. My poor brother, of course, is to blame; and he is punished for it. He told me himself that he made it impossible for you to act otherwise. I believe that you could not avoid this duel, which . . . which to some extent is explained by the almost constant antagonism of your respective views." (Nikolai Petrovitch began to get a little mixed up in his words.) "My brother is a man of the old school, hot-tempered and obstinate. . . . Thank God that it has ended as it has. I have taken every precaution to avoid publicity."

"I'm leaving you my address, in case there's any fuss," Bazarov remarked casually.

"I hope there will be no fuss, Yevgeny Vassilyitch. . . . I am very sorry your stay in my house should have such a . . . such an end. It is the more distressing to me through Arkady's . . ."

"I shall be seeing him, I expect," replied Bazarov, in whom "explanations" and "protestations" of every sort always aroused a feeling of impatience; "in case I don't, I beg you to say good-bye to him for me, and accept the expression of my regret."

"And I beg . . ." answered Nikolai Petrovitch. But Bazarov went off without waiting for the end of his sentence.

When he heard of Bazarov's going, Pavel Petrovitch expressed a desire to see him, and shook his hand. But even then he remained as cold as ice; he realized that Pavel Petrovitch wanted to play the magnanimous. He did not succeed in saying good-bye to Fenitchka; he only exchanged glances with her at the window. Her face struck him as looking dejected. "She'll come to grief, perhaps," he said to himself. . . . "But who knows? she'll pull through somehow, I daresay!" Piotr, however, was so overcome that he wept on his shoulder, till Bazarov damped him by asking if he'd a constant supply laid on in his eyes; while Dunyasha was obliged to run away into the wood to hide her emotion. The originator of all this woe got into a light cart, smoked a cigar, and when at the third mile, at the bend in the road, the Kirsanovs' farm, with its new house, could be seen in a long line, he merely spat, and muttering, "Cursed mobs!" wrapped himself closer in his cloak.

Pavel Petrovitch was soon better; but he had to keep his bed about a week. He bore his captivity, as he called it, pretty patiently, though he took great pains over his toilette, and had everything scented with eau-de-cologne. Nikolai Petrovitch used to read him the journals; Fenitchka waited on him as before, brought him lemonade, soup, boiled eggs, and tea; but she was overcome with secret dread whenever she went into his room. Pavel Petrovitch's unexpected action had alarmed every one in the house, and her more than any one; Prokofitch was the only person not agitated by it; he discoursed upon how gentlemen in his day used to fight, but only with real gentlemen; low curs like that they used to order a horsewhipping in the stable for their insolence.

Fenitchka's conscience scarcely reproached her; but she was tormented at times by the thought of the real cause of the quarrel; and Pavel Petrovitch, too, looked at her so strangely . . . that even when her back was turned she felt his eyes upon her. She grew thinner from constant inward agitation, and, as is always the way, became still more charming.

One day—the incident took place in the morning—Pavel Petrovitch felt better, and moved from his bed to the sofa, while Nikolai Petrovitch, having satisfied himself he was better, went off to the threshing floor. Fenitchka brought him a cup of tea, and setting it down on a little table, was about to withdraw. Pavel Petrovitch detained her.

"Where are you going in such a hurry, Fedosya Nikolaevna?" he began; "are you busy?"

"No . . . I have to pour out tea."

"Dunyasha will do that without you; sit a little while with a poor invalid. By the way, I must have a little talk with you."

Fenitchka sat down on the edge of an easy-chair, without speaking.

"Listen," said Pavel Petrovitch, tugging at his moustaches; "I have long wanted to ask you something; you seem somehow afraid of me?"

"I?"

"Yes, you. You never look at me, as though your conscience were not at rest."

Fenitchka crimsoned, but looked at Pavel Petrovitch. He impressed her as looking strange, and her heart began throbbing slowly.

"Is your conscience at rest?" he questioned her.

"Why should it not be at rest?" she faltered.

"Goodness knows why! Besides, whom can you have wronged? Me? That is not likely. Any other people in the house here? That, too, is something incredible. Can it be my brother? But you love him, don't you?"

"I love him."

"With your whole soul, with your whole heart?"

"I love Nikolai Petrovitch with my whole heart."

"Truly? Look at me, Fenitchka." (It was the first time he had called her that name.) "You know, it's a great sin telling lies!"

"I am not telling lies, Pavel Petrovitch. Not love Nikolai Petrovitch—I shouldn't care to live after that."

"And will you never give him up for any one?"

"For whom could I give him up?"

"For whom indeed! Well, how about that gentleman who has just gone away from here?"

Fenitchka got up. "My God, Pavel Petrovitch, what are you torturing me for? What have I done to you? How can such things be said?" . . .

"Fenitchka," said Pavel Petrovitch, in a sorrowful voice, "you know I saw . . ."

"What did you see?"

"Well, there . . . in the arbour."

Fenitchka crimsoned to her hair and to her ears. "How was I to blame for that?" she articulated with an effort.

Pavel Petrovitch raised himself up. "You were not to blame? No? Not at all?"

"I love Nikolai Petrovitch, and no one else in the world, and I shall always love him!" cried Fenitchka with sudden force, while her throat seemed fairly breaking with sobs. "As for what you saw, at the dreadful day of judgment I will say I'm not to blame, and wasn't to blame for it, and I would rather die at once if people can suspect me of such a thing against my benefactor, Nikolai Petrovitch."

But here her voice broke, and at the same time she felt that Pavel Petrovitch was snatching and pressing her hand. . . . She looked at him, and was fairly petrified. He had turned even paler than before; his eyes were shining, and what was most marvelous of all, one large solitary tear was rolling down his cheek.

"Fenitchka!" he was saying in a strange whisper; "love him, love my brother! Don't give him up for any one in the world; don't listen to any one else! Think what can be more terrible than to love and not be loved! Never leave my poor Nikolai!"

Fenitchka's eyes were dry, and her terror had passed away, so great was her amazement. But what were her feelings when Pavel Petrovitch, Pavel Petrovitch himself, put her hand to his lips and seemed to pierce into it without kissing it, and only heaving convulsive sighs from time to time. . . .

"Goodness," she thought, "isn't it some attack coming on him?" . . .

At that instant his whole ruined life was stirred up within him.

The staircase creaked under rapidly approaching footsteps. . . . He pushed her away from him, and let his head drop back on the pillow. The door opened, and Nikolai Petrovitch entered, cheerful, fresh, and ruddy. Mitya, as fresh and ruddy as his father, in nothing but his little shirt, was frisking on his shoulder, catching the big buttons of his rough country coat with his little bare toes.

Fenitchka simply flung herself upon him, and clasping him and her son together in her arms, dropped her head on his shoulder. Nikolai Petrovitch was surprised; Fenitchka, the reserved and staid Fenitchka, had never given him a caress in the presence of a third person.

"What's the matter?" he said, and, glancing at his brother, he gave her Mitya. "You don't feel worse?" he inquired, going up to Pavel Petrovitch.

He buried his face in a cambric handkerchief. "No . . . not at all . . . on the contrary, I am much better."

"You were in too great a hurry to move on to the sofa. Where are you going?" added Nikolai Petrovitch, turning round to Fenitchka; but she had already closed the door behind her. "I was bringing in my young hero to show you; he's been crying for his uncle. Why has she carried him off? What's wrong with you, though? Has anything passed between you, eh?"

"Brother!" said Pavel Petrovitch solemnly.

Nikolai Petrovitch started. He felt dismayed, he could not have said why himself.

"Brother," repeated Pavel Petrovitch, "give me your word that you will carry out my one request."

"What request? Tell me."

"It is very important; the whole happiness of your life, to my idea, depends on it. I have been thinking a great deal all this time over what I want to say to you now. . . . Brother, do your duty, the duty of an honest and generous man; put an end to the scandal and bad example you are setting— you, the best of men!"

"What do you mean, Pavel?"

"Marry Fenitchka. . . . She loves you; she is the mother of your son."

Nikolai Petrovitch stepped back a pace, and flung up his hands. "Do you say that, Pavel? You whom I have always regarded as the most determined opponent of such marriages! You say that? Don't you know that it has simply been out of respect for you that I have not done what you so rightly call my duty?"

"You were wrong to respect me in that case," Pavel Petrovitch responded, with a weary smile. "I begin to think Bazarov was right in accusing me of snobbishness. No, dear brother, don't let us worry ourselves about appearances and the world's opinion any more; we are old folks and humble now; it's time we laid aside vanity of all kinds. Let us, just as you say, do our duty; and mind, we shall get happiness that way into the bargain."

Nikolai Petrovitch rushed to embrace his brother.

"You have opened my eyes completely!" he cried. "I was right in always declaring you the wisest and kindest-hearted fellow in the world, and now I see you are just as reasonable as you are noble-hearted."

"Quietly, quietly," Pavel Petrovitch interrupted him; "don't hurt the leg of your reasonable brother, who at close upon fifty has been fighting a duel like an ensign. So, then, it's a settled matter; Fenitchka is to be my . . . *belle soeur.*"

"My dearest Pavel! But what will Arkady say?"

"Arkady? He'll be in ecstasies, you may depend upon it! Marriage is against his principles, but then the sentiment of equality in him will be gratified. And, after all, what sense have class distinctions *au dix-neuvième siècle?*"

"Ah, Pavel, Pavel, let me kiss you once more! Don't be afraid, I'll be careful."

The brothers embraced each other.

"What do you think, should you not inform her of your intention now?" queried Pavel Petrovitch.

"Why be in a hurry?" responded Nikolai Petrovitch. "Has there been any conversation between you?"

"Conversation between us? *Quelle idée!*"

"Well, that is all right then. First of all, you must get well, and meanwhile there's plenty of time. We must think it over well, and consider . . ."

"But your mind is made up, I suppose?"

"Of course, my mind is made up, and I thank you from the bottom of my heart. I will leave you now; you must rest; any excitement is bad for you. . . . But we will talk it over again. Sleep well, dear heart, and God bless you!"

"What is he thanking me like that for?" thought Pavel Petrovitch, when he was left alone. "As though it did not depend on him! I will go away directly he is married, somewhere a long way off—to Dresden or Florence, and will live there till——"

Pavel Petrovitch moistened his forehead with eau de cologne, and closed his eyes. His beautiful, emaciated head, the glaring daylight shining full upon it, lay on the white pillow like the head of a dead man. . . . And indeed he was a dead man.

XXV

AT NIKOLSKOE KATYA and Arkady were sitting in the garden on a turf seat in the shade of a tall ash tree; Fifi had placed himself on the ground near them, giving his slender body that graceful curve, which is known among dog fanciers as "the hare bend." Both Arkady and Katya were silent; he was holding a half-open book in his hands, while she was picking out of a basket a few crumbs of bread left in it, and throwing them to a small family of sparrows, who with the frightened impudence peculiar to them were hopping and chirping at her very feet. A faint breeze stirring in the ash leaves kept slowly moving pale-gold flecks of sunlight up and down over the path of Fifi's tawny back; a patch of unbroken shade fell upon Arkady and Katya; only from time to time a bright streak gleamed on her hair. Both were silent, but the very way in which they were silent, in which they were sitting together, was expressive of confidential intimacy; each of them seemed not even to be thinking of his companion, while secretly rejoicing in his presence. Their faces, too, had changed since we saw them last; Arkady looked more tranquil, Katya brighter and more daring.

"Don't you think," began Arkady, "that the ash has been very well named in Russian *yasen*; no other tree is so slightly and brightly transparent (*yasno*) against the air as it is."

Katya raised her eyes to look upward, and assented "Yes", while Arkady thought, "Well, she does not reproach me for *talking finely*."

"I don't like Heine," said Katya, glancing towards the book which Arkady was holding in his hands, "either when he laughs or when he weeps; I like him when he's thoughtful and melancholy."

"And I like him when he laughs," remarked Arkady.

"That's the relics left in you of your old satirical tendencies." ("Relics!" thought Arkady—"if Bazarov had heard that?") "Wait a little; we shall transform you."

"Who will transform me? You?"

"Who?—my sister; Porfiry Platonovitch, whom you've given up quarrelling with; auntie, whom you escorted to church the day before yesterday."

"Well, I couldn't refuse! And as for Anna Sergyevna, she agreed with Yevgeny in a great many things, you remember?"

"My sister was under his influence then, just as you were."

"As I was? Do you discover, may I ask, that I've shaken off his influence now?"

Katya did not speak.

"I know," pursued Arkady, "you never liked him."

"I can have no opinion about him."

"Do you know, Katerina Sergyevna, every time I hear that answer I disbelieve it. . . . There is no man that every one of us could not have an opinion about! That's simply a way of getting out of it."

"Well, I'll say, then, I don't. . . . It's not exactly that I don't like him, but I feel that he's of a different order from me, and I am different from him . . . and you, too, are different from him."

"How's that?"

"How can I tell you? . . . He's a wild animal, and you and I are tame."

"Am I tame too?"

Katya nodded.

Arkady scratched his ear. "Let me tell you, Katerina Sergyevna, do you know, that's really an insult?"

"Why, would you like to be a wild——"

"Not wild, but strong, full of force."

"It's no good wishing for that. . . . Your friend, you see, doesn't wish for it, but he has it."

"Hm! So you imagine he had a great influence on Anna Sergyevna?"

"Yes. But no one can keep the upper hand of her for long," added Katya in a low voice.

"Why do you think that?"

"She's very proud. . . . I didn't mean that . . . she values her independence a great deal."

"Who doesn't value it?" asked Arkady, and the thought flashed through his mind, "What good is it?" "What good is it?" it occurred to Katya to wonder too. When young people are often together on friendly terms, they are constantly stumbling on the same ideas.

Arkady smiled, and coming slightly closer to Katya, he said in a whisper, "Confess that you are a little afraid of her."

"Of whom?"

"Her," repeated Arkady, significantly.

"And how about you?" Katya asked in her turn.

"I am too, observe I said I am, *too.*"

Katya threatened him with her finger. "I wonder at that," she began; "my sister has never felt so friendly to you as just now; much more so than when you first came."

"Really!"

"Why, haven't you noticed it? Aren't you glad of it?" Arkady grew thoughtful.

"How have I succeeded in gaining Anna Sergyevna's good opinion? Wasn't it because I brought her your mother's letters?"

"Both that and other causes, which I shan't tell you."

"Why?"

"I shan't say."

"Oh! I know; you're very obstinate."

"Yes, I am."

"And observant."

Katya gave Arkady a sidelong look. "Perhaps so; does that irritate you? What are you thinking of?"

"I am wondering how you have come to be as observant as in fact you are. You are so shy, so reserved; you keep every one at a distance."

"I have lived a great deal alone; that drives one to reflection. But do I really keep every one at a distance?"

Arkady flung a grateful glance at Katya.

"That's all very well," he pursued; "but people in your position—I mean in your circumstances—don't often have that faculty; it is hard for them, as it is for sovereigns, to get at the truth."

"But, you see, I am not rich."

Arkady was taken aback, and did not at once understand Katya. "Why, of course, the property's all her sister's!" struck him suddenly; the thought was not unpleasing to him. "How nicely you said that!" he commented.

"What?"

"You said it nicely, simply, without being ashamed or making a boast of it. By the way, I imagine there must always be something special, a kind of pride of a sort in the feeling of any man, who knows and says he is poor."

"I have never experienced anything of that sort, thanks to my sister. I only referred to my position just now because it happened to come up."

"Well; but you must own you have a share of that pride I spoke of just now."

"For instance?"

"For instance, you—forgive the question—you wouldn't marry a rich man, I fancy, would you?"

"If I loved him very much. . . . No, I think even then I wouldn't marry him."

"There! you see!" cried Arkady, and after a short pause he added, "And why wouldn't you marry him?"

"Because even in the ballads unequal matches are always unlucky."

"You want to rule, perhaps, or . . ."

"Oh, no! why should I? On the contrary, I am ready to obey; only inequality is intolerable. To respect one's self and obey, that I can understand, that's happiness; but a subordinate existence . . . No, I've had enough of that as it is."

"Enough of that as it is," Arkady repeated after Katya. "Yes, yes," he went on, "you're not Anna Sergyevna's sister for nothing; you're just as independent as she is; but you're more reserved. I'm certain you wouldn't be the first to give expression to your feeling, however strong and holy it might be . . ."

"Well, what would you expect?" asked Katya.

"You're equally clever; and you've as much, if not more, character than she."

"Don't compare me with my sister, please," interposed Katya hurriedly; "that's too much to my disadvantage. You seem to forget my sister's beautiful and clever, and . . . you in particular, Arkady Nikolaevitch, ought not to say such things, and with such a serious face, too."

"What do you mean by 'you in particular'—and what makes you suppose I am joking?"

"Of course, you are joking."

"You think so? But what if I'm persuaded of what I say? If I believe I have not put it strong enough even?"

"I don't understand you."

"Really? Well, now I see; I certainly took you to be more observant than you are."

"How?"

Arkady made no answer, and turned away, while Katya looked for a few more crumbs in the basket, and began throwing them to the sparrows; but she moved her arm too vigorously, and they flew away, without stopping to pick them up.

"Katerina Sergyevna!" began Arkady suddenly; "it's of no consequence to you, probably; but, let me tell you, I put you not only above your sister, but above every one in the world."

He got up and went quickly away, as though he were frightened at the words that had fallen from his lips.

Katya let her two hands drop together with the basket on to her lap, and with bent head she stared a long while after Arkady. Gradually a crimson flush came faintly out upon her cheeks; but her lips did not smile, and her dark eyes had a look of perplexity and some other, as yet undefined, feeling.

"Are you alone?" she heard the voice of Anna Sergyevna near her; "I thought you came into the garden with Arkady."

Katya slowly raised her eyes to her sister (elegantly, even elaborately dressed, she was standing in the path and tickling Fifi's ears with the tip of her open parasol), and slowly replied. "Yes, I'm alone."

"So I see," she answered with a smile; "I suppose he has gone to his room." "Yes."

"Have you been reading together?"
"Yes."

Anna Sergyevna took Katya by the chin and lifted her face up.

"You have not been quarrelling, I hope?"

"No," said Katya, and she quietly removed her sister's hand.

"How solemnly you answer! I expected to find him here, and meant to suggest his coming a walk with me. That's what he is always asking for. They have sent you some shoes from the town; go and try them on; I noticed only yesterday your old ones are quite shabby. You never think enough about it, and you have such charming little feet! Your hands are nice too . . . though they're large; so you must make the most of your little feet. But you're not vain."

Anna Sergyevna went farther along the path with a light rustle of her beautiful gown; Katya got up from the grass, and, taking Heine with her, went away too—but not to try on her shoes.

"Charming little feet!" she thought, as she slowly and lightly mounted the stone steps of the terrace, which were burning with the heat of the sun; "charming little feet you call them. . . . Well, he shall be at them."

But all at once a feeling of shame came upon her, and she ran swiftly upstairs.

Arkady had gone along the corridor to his room; a steward had overtaken him, and announced that Mr. Bazarov was in his room.

"Yevgeny!" murmured Arkady, almost with dismay; "has he been here long?"

"Mr. Bazarov arrived this minute, sir, and gave orders not to announce him to Anna Sergyevna, but to show him straight up to you."

"Can any misfortune have happened at home?" thought Arkady, and running hurriedly up the stairs, he at once opened the door. The sight of Bazarov at once reassured him, though a more experienced eye might very probably have discerned signs of inward agitation in the sunken, though still energetic face of the unexpected visitor. With a dusty cloak over his shoulders, with a cap on his head, he was sitting at the window; he did not even get up when Arkady flung himself with noisy exclamations on his neck.

"This is unexpected! What good luck brought you?" he kept repeating, bustling about the room like one who both imagines himself and wishes to show himself delighted. "I suppose everything's all right at home; every one's well, eh?"

"Everything's all right, but not every one's well," said Bazarov. "Don't be a chatterbox, but send for some kvass for me, sit down, and listen while I tell you all about it in a few, but, I hope, pretty vigorous sentences."

Arkady was quiet while Bazarov described his duel with Pavel Petrovitch. Arkady was very much surprised, and even grieved, but he did not think it necessary to show this; he only asked whether his uncle's wound was really not serious; and on receiving the reply that it was most interesting, but not from a medical point of view, he gave a forced smile, but at heart he felt both wounded and as it were ashamed. Bazarov seemed to understand him.

"Yes, my dear fellow," he commented, "you see what comes of living with feudal personages. You turn a feudal personage yourself, and find yourself taking part in knightly tournaments. Well, so I set off for my father's," Bazarov wound up, "and I've turned in here on the way. . . . to tell you all this, I should say, if I didn't think a useless lie a piece of foolery. No, I turned in here—the devil only knows why. You see, it's sometimes a good thing for a man to take himself by the scruff of the neck and pull himself up, like a radish out of its bed; that's what I've been doing of late. . . . But I wanted to have one more look at what I'm giving up, at the bed where I've been planted."

"I hope those words don't refer to me," responded Arkady with some emotion; "I hope you don't think of giving me up?"

Bazarov turned an intent, almost piercing look upon him.

"Would that be such a grief to you? It strikes me *you* have given me up already, you look so fresh and smart. . . . Your affair with Anna Sergyevna must be getting on successfully."

"What do you mean by my affair with Anna Sergyevna?"

"Why, didn't you come here from the town on her account, chicken? By the way, how are those Sunday schools getting on? Do you mean to tell me you're not in love with her? Or have you already reached the stage of discretion?"

"Yevgeny, you know I have always been open with you; I can assure you, I swear to you, you're making a mistake."

"Hm! That's another story," remarked Bazarov in an undertone. "But you needn't be in a taking, it's a matter of absolute indifference to me. A sentimentalist would say, 'I feel that our paths are beginning to part,' but I will simply say that we're tired of each other."

"Yevgeny . . ."

"My dear soul, there's no great harm in that. One gets tired of much more than that in this life. And now I suppose we'd better say good-bye, hadn't we? Ever since I've been here I've had such a loathsome feeling, just as if I'd been reading Gogol's effusions to the governor of Kalouga's wife. By the way, I didn't tell them to take the horses out."

"Upon my word, this is too much!"

"Why?"

"I'll say nothing of myself; but that would be discourteous to the last degree to Anna Sergyevna, who will certainly wish to see you."

"Oh, you're mistaken there."

"On the contrary, I am certain I'm right," retorted Arkady. "And what are you pretending for? If it comes to that, haven't you come here on her account yourself?"

"That may be so, but you're mistaken any way."

But Arkady was right. Anna Sergyevna desired to see Bazarov, and sent a summons to him by a steward. Bazarov changed his clothes before going to her; it turned out that he had packed his new suit so as to be able to get it out easily.

Madame Odintsov received him not in the room where he had so unexpectedly declared his love to her, but in the drawing-room. She held her finger tips out to him cordially, but her face betrayed an involuntary sense of tension.

"Anna Sergyevna," Bazarov hastened to say, "before everything else I must set your mind at rest. Before you is a poor mortal, who has come to his senses long ago, and hopes other people, too, have forgotten his follies. I am going away for a long while; and though, as you will allow, I'm by no means a very soft creature, it would be anything but cheerful for me to carry away with me the idea that you remember me with repugnance."

Anna Sergyevna gave a deep sigh like one who has just climbed up a high mountain, and her face was lighted up by a smile. She held out her hand a second time to Bazarov, and responded to his pressure.

"Let bygones be bygones," she said. "I am all the readier to do so because, speaking from my conscience, I was to blame then, too, for flirting or something. In a word, let us be friends as before. That was a dream, wasn't it? And who remembers dreams?"

"Who remembers them? And besides, love . . . you know, is a purely imaginary feeling."

"Really? I am very glad to hear that."

So Anna Sergyevna spoke, and so spoke Bazarov; they both supposed they were speaking the truth. Was the truth, the whole truth, to be found in their words? They could not themselves have said, and much less could the author. But a conversation followed between them precisely as though they completely believed one another.

Anna Sergyevna asked Bazarov, among other things, what he had been doing at the Kirsanovs'. He was on the point of telling her about his duel with Pavel Petrovitch, but he checked himself with the thought that she might imagine he was trying to make himself interesting, and answered that he had been at work all the time.

"And I," observed Anna Sergyevna, "had a fit of depression at first, goodness knows why; I even made plans for going abroad, fancy! . . . Then it passed off, your friend Arkady Nikolaitch came, and I fell back into my old routine, and took up my real part again."

"What part is that, may I ask?"

"The character of aunt, guardian, mother—call it what you like. By the way, do you know I used not quite to understand your close friendship with Arkady Nikolaitch; I thought him rather insignificant. But now I have come to know him better, and to see that he is clever. . . . And he's young, he's young . . . that's the great thing . . . not like you and me, Yevgeny Vassilyitch."

"Is he still shy in your company?" queried Bazarov.

"Why, was he?" . . . Anna Sergyevna began, and after a brief pause she went on: "He has grown more confiding now; he talks to me. He used to avoid me before. Though, indeed, I didn't seek his society either. He's more friends with Katya."

Bazarov felt irritated. "A woman can't help humbugging, of course!" he thought. "You say he used to avoid you," he said aloud, with a chilly smile; "but it is probably no secret to you that he was in love with you?"

"What! he too?" fell from Anna Sergyevna's lips.

"He too," repeated Bazarov, with a submissive bow. "Can it be you didn't know it, and I've told you something new?"

Anna Sergyevna dropped her eyes. "You are mistaken, Yevgeny Vassilyitch."

"I don't think so. But perhaps I ought not to have mentioned it." "And don't you try telling me lies again for the future," he added to himself.

"Why not? But I imagine that in this, too, you are attributing too much importance to a passing impression. I begin to suspect you are inclined to exaggeration."

"We had better not talk about it, Anna Sergyevna."

"Oh, why?" she retorted; but she herself led the conversation into another channel. She was still ill at ease with Bazarov, though she had told him, and assured herself that everything was forgotten. While she was exchanging the simplest sentences with him, even while she was jesting with him, she was conscious of a faint spasm of dread. So people on a steamer at sea talk and laugh carelessly, for all the world as though they were on dry land; but let only the slightest hitch occur, let the least sign be seen of anything out of the common, and at once on every face there comes out an expression of peculiar alarm, betraying the constant consciousness of constant danger.

Anna Sergyevna's conversation with Bazarov did not last long. She began to seem absorbed in thought, answered abstractly, and suggested at last that they should go into the hall, where they found the princess and Katya. "But where is Arkady Nikolaitch?" inquired the lady of the house; and on hearing that he had not shown himself for more than an hour, she sent for him. He was not very quickly found; he had hidden himself in the very thickest part of the garden, and with his chin propped on his folded hands, he was sitting lost in meditation. They were deep and serious meditations, but not mournful. He knew Anna Sergyevna was sitting alone with Bazarov, and he felt no jealousy, as once he had; on the contrary, his face slowly brightened; he seemed to be at once wondering and rejoicing, and resolving on something.

XXVI

THE deceased Odintsov had not liked innovations, but he had tolerated "the fine arts within a certain sphere," and had in consequence put up in his garden, between the hothouse and the lake, an erection after the fashion of a Greek temple, made of Russian brick. Along the dark wall at the back of this temple or gallery were placed six niches for statues, which Odintsov had proceeded to order from abroad. These statues were to represent Solitude, Silence, Meditation, Melancholy, Modesty, and Sensibility. One of them, the goddess of Silence, with her finger on her lip, had been sent and put up; but on the very same day some boys on the farm had broken her nose; and though a plasterer of the neighbourhood undertook to make her a new nose "twice as good as the old one," Odintsov ordered her to be taken away, and she was still to be seen in the corner of the threshing barn, where she had stood many long years, a source of superstitious terror to the peasant women. The front part of the temple had long been overgrown with thick bushes; only the pediments of the columns could be seen above the dense green. In the temple itself it was cool even at mid-day. Anna Sergyevna had not liked visiting this place ever since she had seen a snake there; but Katya often came and sat on the wide stone seat under one of the niches. Here, in the midst of the shade and coolness, she used to read and work, or to give herself up to that sensation of perfect peace, known, doubtless, to each of us, the charm of which consists in the half-unconscious, silent listening to the vast current of life that flows forever both around us and within us.

The day after Bazarov's arrival Katya was sitting on her favourite stone seat, and beside her again was sitting Arkady. He had besought her to come with him to the "temple."

There was about an hour still to lunch time; the dewy morning had already given place to a sultry day. Arkady's face retained the expression of the preceding day; Katya had a preoccupied look. Her sister had, directly after their morning tea, called her into her room, and after some preliminary caresses, which always scared Katya a little, she had advised her to be more guarded in her behaviour with Arkady, and especially to avoid solitary talks with him, as likely to attract the notice of her aunt and all the household. Besides this, even the previous evening Anna Sergyevna had not been herself; and Katya herself had felt ill at ease, as though she were conscious of some fault in herself. As she yielded to Arkady's entreaties, she said to herself that it was for the last time.

"Katerina Sergyevna," he began with a sort of bashful easiness, "since I've had the happiness of living in the same house with you, I have discussed a great many things with you; but meanwhile there is one, very important . . . for me . . . one question, which I have not touched upon up till now. You remarked yesterday that I have been changed here," he went on, at once catching and avoiding the questioning glance Katya was turning upon him. "I have changed certainly a great deal, and you know that better than any one else—you to whom I really owe this change."

"I? . . . Me? . . ." said Katya.

"I am not now the conceited boy I was when I came here," Arkady went on. "I've not reached twenty-three for nothing; as before, I want to be useful, I want to devote all my powers to the truth; but I no longer look for my ideals where I did; they present themselves to me . . . much closer to hand. Up till now I did not understand myself; I set myself tasks which were beyond my powers . . . My eyes have been opened lately, thanks to one feeling. . . . I'm not expressing myself quite clearly, but I hope you understand me."

Katya made no reply, but she ceased looking at Arkady.

"I suppose," he began again, this time in a more agitated voice, while above his head a chaffinch sang its song unheeding among the leaves of the birch—"I suppose it's the duty of every one to be open with those . . . with those people who . . . in fact, with those who are near to him, and so I . . . I resolved . . ."

But here Arkady's eloquence deserted him; he lost the thread, stammered, and was forced to be silent for a moment. Katya still did not raise her eyes. She seemed not to understand what he was leading up to in all this, and to be waiting for something.

"I foresee I shall surprise you," began Arkady, pulling himself together again with an effort, "especially since this feeling relates in a way . . . in a way, notice . . . to you. You reproached me, if you remember, yesterday with a want of seriousness," Arkady went on, with the air of a man who has got into a bog, feels that he is sinking further and further in at every step, and yet hurries onwards in the hope of crossing it as soon as possible; "that reproach is often aimed . . . often falls . . . on young men even when they cease to deserve it; and if I had more self-confidence . . ." ("Come, help me, do help me!" Arkady was thinking, in desperation; but, as before, Katya did not turn her head.) "If I could hope . . ."

"If I could feel sure of what you say," was heard at that instant the clear voice of Anna Sergyevna.

Arkady was still at once, while Katya turned pale. Close by the bushes that screened the temple ran a little path. Anna Sergyevna was walking along it escorted by Bazarov. Katya and Arkady could not see them, but they heard every word, the rustle of their clothes, their very breathing. They walked on a few steps, and, as though on purpose, stood still just opposite the temple.

"You see," pursued Anna Sergyevna, "you and I made a mistake; we are both past our first youth, I especially so; we have seen life, we are tired; we are both—why affect not to know it?—clever; at first we interested each other, curiosity was aroused . . . and then . . ."

"And then I grew stale," put in Bazarov.

"You know that was not the cause of our misunderstanding. But, however, it was to be, we had no need of one another, that's the chief point; there was too much . . . what shall I say? . . . that was alike in us. We did not realise it all at once. Now, Arkady . . ."

"Do you need him?" queried Bazarov.

"Hush, Yevgeny Vassilyitch. You tell me he is not indifferent to me, and it always seemed to me he liked me. I know that I might well be his aunt, but I don't wish to conceal from you that I have come to think more often of him. In such youthful, fresh feeling there is a special charm . . ."

"The word *fascination* is most usual in such cases," Bazarov interrupted; the effervescence of his spleen could be heard in his choked though steady voice. "Arkady was mysterious over something with me yesterday, and didn't talk either of you or of your sister. . . . That's a serious symptom."

"He is just like a brother with Katya," commented Anna Sergyevna, "and I like that in him, though, perhaps, I ought not to have allowed such intimacy between them."

"That idea is prompted by . . . your feelings as a sister?" Bazarov brought out, drawling.

"Of course . . . but why are we standing still? Let us go on. What a strange talk we are having, aren't we? I could never have believed I should talk to you like this. You know, I am afraid of you . . . and at the same time I trust you, because in reality you are so good."

"In the first place, I am not in the least good; and in the second place, I have lost all significance for you, and you tell me I am good . . . It's like laying a wreath of flowers on the head of a corpse."

"Yevgeny Vassilyitch, we are not responsible . . ." Anna Sergyevna began; but a gust of wind blew across, set the leaves rustling, and carried away her words. "Of course, you are free . . ." Bazarov declared after a brief pause. Nothing more could be distinguished; the steps retreated . . . everything was still.

Arkady turned to Katya. She was sitting in the same position, but her head was bent still lower. "Katerina Sergyevna," he said with a shaking voice, and clasping his hands tightly together, "I love you forever and irrevocably, and I love no one but you. I wanted to tell you this, to find out your opinion of me, and to ask for your hand, since I am not rich, and I feel ready for any sacrifice. . . . You don't answer me? You don't believe me? Do you think I speak lightly? But remember these last days! Surely for a long time past you must have known that everything—understand me—everything else has vanished long ago and left no trace? Look at me, say one word to me . . . I love . . . I love you . . . believe me!"

Katya glanced at Arkady with a bright and serious look, and after long hesitation, with the faintest smile, she said, "Yes."

Arkady leaped up from the stone seat. "Yes! You said Yes, Katerina Sergyevna! What does that word mean? Only that I do love you, that you believe me . . . or . . . or . . . I daren't go on . . ."

"Yes," repeated Katya, and this time he understood her. He snatched her large beautiful hands, and, breathless with rapture, pressed them to his heart. He could scarcely stand on his feet, and could only repeat, "Katya, Katya . . ." while she began weeping in a guileless way, smiling gently at her own tears. No one who has not seen those tears in the eyes of the beloved, knows yet to what a point, faint with shame and gratitude, a man may be happy on earth.

The next day, early in the morning, Anna Sergyevna sent to summon Bazarov to her boudoir, and with a forced laugh handed him a folded sheet of notepaper. It was a letter from Arkady; in it he asked for her sister's hand. Bazarov quickly scanned the letter, and made an effort to control himself, that he might not show the malignant feeling which was instantaneously aflame in his breast.

"So that's how it is," he commented; "and you, I fancy, only yesterday imagined he loved Katerina Sergyevna as a brother. What are you intending to do now?"

"What do you advise me?" asked Anna Sergyevna, still laughing.

"Well, I suppose," answered Bazarov, also with a laugh, though he felt anything but cheerful, and had no more inclination to laugh than she had; "I suppose you ought to give the young people your blessing. It's a good match in every respect; Kirsanov's position is passable, he's the only son, and his father's a good-natured fellow, he won't try to thwart him."

Madame Odintsov walked up and down the room. By turns her face flushed and grew pale. "You think so," she said. "Well, I see no obstacles . . . I am glad for Katya . . . and for Arkady Nikolaevitch too. Of course, I will wait for his father's answer. I will send him in person to him. But it turns out, you see, that I was right yesterday when I told you we were both old people. . . . How was it I saw nothing? That's what amazes me!" Anna Sergyevna laughed again, and quickly turned her head away.

"The younger generation have grown awfully sly," remarked Bazarov, and he, too, laughed. "Good-bye," he began after a short silence. "I hope you will bring the matter to the most satisfactory conclusion; and I will rejoice from a distance."

Madame Odintsov turned quickly to him. "You are not going away? Why should you not stay *now?* Stay . . . it's exciting talking to you . . . one seems walking on the edge of a precipice. At first one feels timid, but one gains courage as one goes on. Do stay."

"Thanks for the suggestion, Anna Sergyevna, and for your flattering opinion of my conversational talents. But I think I have already been moving too long in a sphere which is not my own. Flying fishes can hold out for a time in the air, but soon they must splash back into the water; allow me, too, to paddle in my own element."

Madame Odintsov looked at Bazarov. His pale face was twitching with a bitter smile. "This man did love me!" she thought, and she felt pity for him, and held out her hand to him with sympathy.

But he, too, understood her. "No!" he said, stepping back a pace. "I'm a poor man, but I've never taken charity so far. Good-bye, and good luck to you."

"I am certain we are not seeing each other for the last time," Anna Sergyevna declared with an unconscious gesture.

"Anything may happen!" answered Bazarov, and he bowed and went away.

"So you are thinking of making yourself a nest?" he said the same day to Arkady, as he packed his box, crouching on the floor. "Well, it's a capital thing. But you needn't have been such a humbug. I expected something from you in quite another quarter. Perhaps, though, it took you by surprise yourself?"

"I certainly didn't expect this when I parted from you," answered Arkady; "but why are you, a humbug yourself, calling it 'a capital thing,' as though I didn't know your opinion of marriage."

"Ah, my dear fellow," said Bazarov, "how you talk! You see what I'm doing; there seems to be an empty space in the box, and I am putting hay in; that's how it is in the box of our life; we would stuff it up with anything rather than have a void. Don't be offended, please; you remember, no doubt, the opinion I have always had of Katerina Sergyevna. Many a young lady's called clever simply because she can sigh cleverly; but yours can hold her own, and, indeed, she'll hold it so well that she'll have you under her thumb—to be sure, though, that's quite as it ought to be." He slammed the lid to, and got up from the floor. "And now, I say again, good-bye, for it's useless to deceive ourselves—we are parting for good, and you know that yourself . . . you have acted sensibly; you're not made for our bitter, rough, lonely existence. There's no dash, no hate in you, but you've the daring of youth and the fire of youth. Your sort, you gentry, can never get beyond refined submission or refined indignation, and that's no good. You won't fight—and yet you fancy yourselves gallant chaps—but we mean to fight. Oh well! Our dust would get into your eyes, our mud would be-spatter you, but yet you're not up to our level, you're admiring yourselves unconsciously, you like to abuse yourselves; but we're sick of that—we want something else! we want to smash other people! You're a capital fellow; but you're a sugary, liberal snob for all that—*ay volla-too*, as my parent is fond of saying."

"You are parting from me for ever, Yevgeny," responded Arkady mournfully; "and have you nothing else to say to me?"

Bazarov scratched the back of his head. "Yes, Arkady, yes, I have other things to say to you, but I'm not going to say them, because that's senti-mentalism—that means, mawkishness. And you get married as soon as you can; and build your nest, and get children to your heart's content. They'll have the wit to be born in a better time than you and me. Aha! I see the horses are ready. Time's up! I've said good-bye to every one. . . . What now? embracing, eh?"

Arkady flung himself on the neck of his former leader and friend, and the tears fairly gushed from his eyes.

"That's what comes of being young!" Bazarov commented calmly. "But I rest my hopes on Katerina Sergyevna. You'll see how quickly she'll console you! Good-bye, brother!" he said to Arkady when he had got into the light cart, and, pointing to a pair of jackdaws sitting side by side on the stable roof, he added, "That's for you! follow that example."

"What does that mean?" asked Arkady.

"What? Are you so weak in natural history, or have you forgotten that the jackdaw is a most respectable family bird? An example to you! . . . Good-bye!"

The cart creaked and rolled away.

Bazarov had spoken truly. In talking that evening with Katya, Arkady completely forgot about his former teacher. He already began to follow her lead, and Katya was conscious of this, and not surprised at it. He was to set off the next day for Maryino, to see Nikolai Petrovitch. Anna Sergyevna was not disposed to put any constraint on the young people, and only on account of the proprieties did not leave them by themselves for too long together. She magnanimously kept the princess out of their way; the latter had been reduced to a state of tearful frenzy by the news of the proposed marriage. At first Anna Sergyevna was afraid the sight of their happiness might prove rather trying to herself, but it turned out quite the other way; this sight not only did not distress her, it interested her, it even softened her at last. Anna Sergyevna felt both glad and sorry at this. "It is clear that Bazarov was right," she thought; "it has been curiosity, nothing but curiosity, and love of ease, and egoism . . ."

"Children," she said aloud, "what do you say, is love a purely imaginary feeling?"

But neither Katya nor Arkady even understood her. They were shy with her; the fragment of conversation they had involuntarily overheard haunted their minds. But Anna Sergyevna soon set their minds at rest; and it was not difficult for her—she had set her own mind at rest.

XXVII

BAZAROV'S OLD PARENTS were all the more overjoyed by their son's arrival, as it was quite unexpected. Arina Vlasyevna was greatly excited, and kept running backwards and forwards in the house, so that Vassily Ivanovitch compared her to a "hen partridge"; the short tail of her abbreviated jacket did, in fact, give her something of a birdlike appearance. He himself merely growled and gnawed the amber mouthpiece of his pipe, or, clutching his neck with his fingers, turned his head round, as though he were trying whether it were properly screwed on, then all at once he opened his wide mouth and went off into a perfectly noiseless chuckle. "I've come to you for six whole weeks, governor," Bazarov said to him. "I want to work, so please don't hinder me now."

"You shall forget my face completely, if you call that hindering you!" answered Vassily Ivanovitch.

He kept his promise. After installing his son as before in his study, he almost hid himself away from him, and kept his wife from all superfluous demonstrations of tenderness. "On Enyusha's first visit, my dear soul," he said to her, "we bothered him a little; we must be wiser this time." Arina Vlasyevna agreed with her husband, but that was small compensation since she saw her son only at meals, and was now absolutely afraid to address him. "Enyushenka," she would say sometimes—and before he had time to look round, she was nervously fingering the tassels of her reticule and faltering, "Never mind, never mind, I only——" and afterwards she would go to Vassily Ivanovitch and, her cheek in her hand, would consult him: "If you could only find out, darling, which Enyusha would like for dinner to-day—cabbage broth or beet-root soup?"—"But why didn't you ask him yourself?"—"Oh, he will get sick of me!" Bazarov, however, soon ceased to shut himself up; the fever of work fell away, and was replaced by dreary boredom or vague restlessness. A strange weariness began to show itself in all his movements; even his walk, firm, bold and strenuous, was changed. He gave up walking in solitude, and began to seek society; he drank tea in the drawing-room, strolled about the kitchen-garden with Vassily Ivanovitch, and smoked with him in silence; once even asked after Father Alexey. Vassily Ivanovitch at first rejoiced at this change, but his joy was not long-lived. "Enyusha's breaking my heart," he complained in secret to his wife: "it's not that he's discontented or angry—that would be nothing; he's sad, he's sorrowful—that's what's so terrible. He's always silent. If he'd only abuse us; he's growing thin, he's lost his colour."—"Mercy on us, mercy on us!" whispered the old woman; "I would put an amulet on his neck, but, of course, he won't allow it." Vassily Ivanovitch several times attempted in the most circumspect manner to question Bazarov about his work, about his health, and about Arkady. . . . But Bazarov's replies were reluctant and casual; and, once noticing that his father was trying gradually to lead up to something in conversation, he said to him in a tone of vexation: "Why do you always seem to be walking round me on tiptoe? That way's worse than the old one."—"There, there, I meant nothing!" poor Vassily Ivanovitch answered hurriedly. So his diplomatic hints remained fruitless. He hoped to awaken his son's sympathy one day by beginning, à propos of the approaching emancipation of the peasantry, to talk about progress; but the latter responded indifferently: "Yesterday I was walking under the fence, and I heard the peasant boys here, instead of some old ballad, bawling a street song. That's what progress is."

Sometimes Bazarov went into the village, and in his usual bantering tone entered into conversation with some peasant: "Come," he would say to him, "expound your views on life to me, brother; you see, they say all the strength and future of Russia lies in your hands, a new epoch in history will be started by you—you give us our real language and our laws."

The peasant either made no reply, or articulated a few words of this sort, "Well, we'll try . . . because, you see, to be sure. . . ."

"You explain to me what your *mir* is," Bazarov interrupted; "and is it the same *mir* that is said to rest on three fishes?"

"That, little father, is the earth that rests on three fishes," the peasant would declare soothingly, in a kind of patriarchal, simple-hearted singsong; "and over against ours, that's to say, the *mir*, we know there's the master's will; wherefore you are our fathers. And the stricter the master's rule, the better for the peasant."

After listening to such a reply one day, Bazarov shrugged his shoulders contemptuously and turned away, while the peasant sauntered slowly homewards.

"What was he talking about?" inquired another peasant of middle age and surly aspect, who at a distance from the door of his hut had been following his conversation with Bazarov.—"Arrears? eh?"

"Arrears, no indeed, mate!" answered the first peasant, and now there was no trace of patriarchal singsong in his voice; on the contrary, there was a certain scornful gruffness to be heard in it: "Oh, he clacked away about something or other; wanted to stretch his tongue a bit. Of course, he's a gentleman; what does he understand?"

"What should he understand!" answered the other peasant, and jerking back their caps and pushing down their belts, they proceeded to deliberate upon their work and their wants. Alas! Bazarov, shrugging his shoulders contemptuously, Bazarov, who knew how to talk to peasants (as he had boasted in his dispute with Pavel Petrovitch), did not in his self-confidence even suspect that in their eyes he was all the while something of the nature of a buffooning clown.

He found employment for himself at last, however. One day Vassily Ivanovitch bound up a peasant's wounded leg before him, but the old man's hands trembled, and he could not manage the bandages; his son helped him, and from time to time began to take a share in his practice, though at the same time he was constantly sneering both at the remedies he himself advised and at his father, who hastened to make use of them. But Bazarov's jeers did not in the least perturb Vassily Ivanovitch; they were positively a comfort to him. Holding his greasy dressing-gown across his stomach with two fingers, and smoking his pipe, he used to listen with enjoyment to Bazarov; and the more malicious his sallies, the more good-humouredly did his delighted father chuckle, showing every one of his black teeth. He used even to repeat these sometimes flat or pointless retorts, and would, for instance, for several days constantly without rhyme or reason, reiterate, "Not a matter of the first importance!" simply because his son, on hearing he was going to matins, had made use of that expression. "Thank God! he has got over his melancholy!" he whispered to his wife; "how he gave it to me to-day, it was splendid!" Moreover, the idea of having such an assistant excited him to ecstasy, filled him with pride. "Yes, yes," he would say to some peasant woman in a man's cloak, and a cap shaped like a horn, as he handed her a bottle of Goulard's extract or box of white ointment, "you ought to be thanking God, my good woman, every minute that my son is staying with me; you will be treated now by the most scientific, most modern method. Do you know what that means? The Emperor of the French, Napoleon, even, has no better doctor." And the peasant woman, who had come to complain that she felt so sort of queer all over (the exact meaning of these words she was not able, however, herself to explain), merely bowed low and rummaged in her bosom, where four eggs lay tied up in the corner of a towel.

Bazarov once even pulled out a tooth for a passing pedlar of cloth; and though this tooth was an average specimen, Vassily Ivanovitch preserved it as a curiosity, and incessantly repeated, as he showed it to Father Alexey, "Just look, what a fang! The force Yevgeny has! The pedlar seemed to leap into the air. If it had been an oak, he'd have rooted it up!"

"Most promising!" Father Alexey would comment at last, not knowing what answer to make, and how to get rid of the ecstatic old man.

One day a peasant from a neighbouring village brought his brother to Vassily Ivanovitch, ill with typhus. The unhappy man, lying flat on a truss of straw, was dying; his body was covered with dark patches, he had long ago lost consciousness. Vassily Ivanovitch expressed his regret that no one had taken steps to procure medical aid sooner, and declared there was no hope. And, in fact, the peasant did not get his brother home again; he died in the cart.

Three days later Bazarov came into his father's room and asked him if he had any caustic.

"Yes; what do you want it for?"

"I must have some . . . to burn a cut."

"For whom?"

"For myself."

"What, yourself? Why is that? What sort of a cut? Where is it?"

"Look here, on my finger. I went to-day to the village, you know, where they brought that peasant with typhus fever. They were just going to open the body for some reason or other, and I've had no practice of that sort for a long while."

"Well?"

"Well, so I asked the district doctor about it; and so I dissected it."

Vassily Ivanovitch all at once turned quite white, and, without uttering a word, rushed to his study, from which he returned at once with a bit of caustic in his hand. Bazarov was about to take it and go away.

"For mercy's sake," said Vassily Ivanovitch, "let me do it myself."

Bazarov smiled. "What a devoted practitioner!"

"Don't laugh, please. Show me your finger. The cut is not a large one. Do I hurt?"

"Press harder; don't be afraid."

Vassily Ivanovitch stopped. "What do you think, Yevgeny; wouldn't it be better to burn it with hot iron?"

"That ought to have been done sooner; the caustic even is useless, really, now. If I've taken the infection, it's too late now."

"How . . . too late. . . ." Vassily Ivanovitch could scarcely articulate the words.

"I should think so! It's more than four hours ago."

Vassily Ivanovitch burnt the cut a little more. "But had the district doctor no caustic?"

"No."

"How was that, good Heavens? A doctor not have such an indispensable thing as that!"

"You should have seen his lancets," observed Bazarov as he walked away.

Up till late that evening, and all the following day, Vassily Ivanovitch kept catching at every possible excuse to go into his son's room; and though far from referring to the cut—he even tried to talk about the most irrelevant subjects—he looked so persistently into his face, and watched him in such trepidation, that Bazarov lost patience and threatened to go away. Vassily Ivanovitch gave him a promise not to bother him, the more readily as Arina Vlasyevna, from whom, of course, he kept it all secret, was beginning to worry him as to why he did not sleep, and what had come over him. For two whole days he held himself in, though he did not at all like the look of his son, whom he kept watching stealthily, . . . but on the third day, at dinner, he could bear it no longer. Bazarov sat with downcast looks, and had not touched a single dish.

"Why don't you eat, Yevgeny?" he inquired, putting on an expression of the most perfect carelessness. "The food, I think, is very nicely cooked."

"I don't want anything, so I don't eat."

"Have you no appetite? And your head," he added timidly; "does it ache?"

"Yes. Of course, it aches."

Arina Vlasyevna sat up and was all alert.

"Don't be angry, please, Yevgeny," continued Vassily Ivanovitch; "won't you let me feel your pulse?"

Bazarov got up. "I can tell you without feeling my pulse; I'm feverish."

"Has there been any shivering?"

"Yes, there has been shivering too. I'll go and lie down, and you can send me some lime-flower tea. I must have caught cold."

"To be sure, I heard you coughing last night," observed Arina Vlasyevna.

"I've caught cold," repeated Bazarov, and he went away.

Arina Vlasyevna busied herself about the preparation of the decoction of lime-flowers, while Vassily Ivanovitch went into the next room and clutched at his hair in silent desperation.

Bazarov did not get up again that day, and passed the whole night in heavy, half-unconscious torpor. At one o'clock in the morning, opening his eyes with an effort, he saw by the light of a lamp his father's pale face bending over him, and told him to go away. The old man begged his pardon, but he quickly came back on tiptoe, and half-hidden by the cupboard door, he gazed persistently at his son. Arina Vlasyevna did not go to bed either, and leaving the study door just open a very little, she kept coming up to it to listen "how Enyusha was breathing," and to look at Vassily Ivanovitch. She could see nothing but his motionless bent back, but even that afforded her some faint consolation. In the morning Bazarov tried to get up; he was seized with giddiness, his nose began to bleed; he lay down again. Vassily Ivanovitch waited on him in silence; Arina Vlasyevna went in to him and asked him how he was feeling. He answered, "Better," and turned to the wall. Vassily Ivanovitch gesticulated at his wife with both hands; she bit her lips so as not to cry, and went away. The whole house seemed suddenly darkened; every one looked gloomy; there was a strange hush; a shrill cock was carried away from the yard to the village, unable to comprehend why he should be treated so. Bazarov still lay, turned to the wall. Vassily Ivanovitch tried to address him with various questions, but they fatigued Bazarov, and the old man sank into his arm-chair, motionless, only cracking his finger-joints now and then. He went for a few minutes into the garden, stood there like a statue, as though overwhelmed with unutterable bewilderment (the expression of amazement never left his face all through), and went back again to his son, trying to avoid his wife's questions. She caught him by the arm at last, and passionately, almost menacingly, said, "What is wrong with him?" Then he came to himself, and forced himself to smile at her in reply; but to his own horror, instead of a smile, he found himself taken somehow by a fit of laughter. He had sent at daybreak for a doctor. He thought it necessary to inform his son of this, for fear he should be angry. Bazarov suddenly turned over on the sofa, bent a fixed dull look on his father, and asked for drink.

Vassily Ivanovitch gave him some water, and as he did so felt his forehead. It seemed on fire.

"Governor," began Bazarov, in a slow, drowsy voice; "I'm in a bad way; I've got the infection, and in a few days you'll have to bury me."

Vassily Ivanovitch staggered back, as though some one had aimed a blow at his legs.

"Yevgeny!" he faltered; "what do you mean! . . . God have mercy on you! You've caught cold!"

"Hush!" Bazarov interposed deliberately. "A doctor can't be allowed to talk like that. There's every symptom of infection; you know yourself."

"Where are the symptoms . . . of infection, Yevgeny? . . . Good Heavens!"

"What's this?" said Bazarov, and, pulling up his shirt-sleeve, he showed his father the ominous red patches coming out on his arm.

Vassily Ivanovitch was shaking and chill with terror.

"Supposing," he said at last, "even supposing . . . if even there's something like . . . infection . . ."

"Pyæmia," put in his son.

"Well, well . . . something of the epidemic . . ."

"Pyæmia," Bazarov repeated sharply and distinctly; "have you forgotten your text-books?"

"Well, well—as you like. . . . Anyway, we will cure you!"

"Come, that's humbug. But that's not the point. I didn't expect to die so soon; it's a most unpleasant incident, to tell the truth. You and mother ought to make the most of your strong religious belief; now's the time to put it to the test." He drank off a little water. "I want to ask you about one thing . . . while my head is still under my control. To-morrow or next day my brain, you know, will send in its resignation. I'm not quite certain even now whether I'm expressing myself clearly. While I've been lying here, I've kept fancying red dogs were running round me, while you were making them point at me, as if I were a woodcock. Just as if I were drunk. Do you understand me all right?"

"I assure you, Yevgeny, you are talking perfectly correctly."

"All the better. You told me you'd sent for the doctor. You did that to comfort yourself . . . comfort me too; send a messenger . . ."

"To Arkady Nikolaitch?" put in the old man.

"Who's Arkady Nikolaitch?" said Bazarov, as though in doubt. . . . "Oh, yes! that chicken! No, let him alone; he's turned jackdaw now. Don't be surprised; that's not delirium yet. You send a messenger to Madame Odintsov, Anna Sergyevna; she's a lady with an estate. . . . Do you know?" (Vassily Ivanovitch nodded.) "Yevgeny Bazarov, say, sends his greetings, and sends word he is dying. Will you do that?"

"Yes, I will do it. . . . But is it a possible thing for you to die, Yevgeny? . . . Think only! Where would divine justice be after that?"

"I know nothing about that; only you send the messenger."

"I'll send this minute, and I'll write a letter myself."

"No, why? Say I send greetings; nothing more is necessary. And now I'll go back to my dogs. Strange! I want to fix my thoughts on death, and nothing comes of it. I see a kind of blur . . . and nothing more."

He turned painfully back to the wall again; while Vassily Ivanovitch went out of the study, and struggling as far as his wife's bedroom, simply dropped down on to his knees before the holy pictures.

"Pray, Arina, pray for us!" he moaned; "our son is dying."

The doctor, the same district doctor who had had no caustic, arrived, and after looking at the patient, advised them to persevere with a cooling treatment, and at that point said a few words of the chance of recovery.

"Have you ever chanced to see people in my state *not* set off for Elysium?" asked Bazarov, and suddenly snatching the leg of a heavy table that stood near his sofa, he swung it round, and pushed it away. "There's strength, there's strength," he murmured; "everything's here still, and I must die! . . . An old man at least has time to be weaned from life, but I . . . Well, go and try to disprove death. Death will disprove you, and that's all! Who's crying there?" he added, after a short pause.—"Mother? Poor thing!

Whom will she feed now with her exquisite beet-root soup? You, Vassily Ivanovitch, whimpering too, I do believe! Why, if Christianity's no help to you, be a philosopher, a Stoic, or what not! Why, didn't you boast you were a philosopher?"

"Me a philosopher!" wailed Vassily Ivanovitch, while the tears fairly streamed down his cheeks.

Bazarov got worse every hour; the progress of the disease was rapid, as is usually the way in cases of surgical poisoning. He still had not lost consciousness, and understood what was said to him; he was still struggling. "I don't want to lose my wits," he muttered, clenching his fists; "what rot it all is!" And at once he would say, "Come, take ten from eight, what remains?" Vassily Ivanovitch wandered about like one possessed, proposed first one remedy, then another, and ended by doing nothing but cover up his son's feet. "Try cold pack . . . emetic . . . mustard plasters on the stomach . . . bleeding," he would murmur with an effort. The doctor, whom he had entreated to remain, agreed with him, ordered the patient lemonade to drink, and for himself asked for a pipe and something "warming and strengthening"—that's to say, brandy. Arina Vlasyevna sat on a low stool near the door, and only went out from time to time to pray. A few days before, a looking-glass had slipped out of her hands and been broken, and this she had always considered an omen of evil; even Anfisushka could say nothing to her. Timofeitch had gone off to Madame Odintsov's.

The night passed badly for Bazarov. . . . He was in the agonies of high fever. Towards morning he was a little easier. He asked for Arina Vlasyevna to comb his hair, kissed her hand, and swallowed two gulps of tea. Vassily Ivanovitch revived a little.

"Thank God!" he kept declaring; "the crisis is coming, the crisis is at hand!"

"There, to think now!" murmured Bazarov; "what a word can do! He's found it; he's said 'crisis,' and is comforted. It's an astounding thing how man believes in words. If he's told he's a fool, for instance, though he's not thrashed, he'll be wretched; call him a clever fellow, and he'll be delighted if you go off without paying him."

This little speech of Bazarov's, recalling his old retorts, moved Vassily Ivanovitch greatly.

"Bravo! well said, very good!" he cried, making as though he were clapping his hands.

Bazarov smiled mournfully.

"So what do you think," he said; "is the crisis over, or coming?"

"You are better, that's what I see, that's what rejoices me," answered Vassily Ivanovitch.

"Well, that's good; rejoicings never come amiss. And to her, do you remember, did you send?"

"To be sure I did."

The change for the better did not last long. The disease resumed its onslaughts. Vassily Ivanovitch was sitting by Bazarov. It seemed as though the old man were tormented by some special anguish. He was several times on the point of speaking—and could not.

"Yevgeny!" he brought out at last; "my son, my one, dear son!"

This unfamiliar mode of address produced an effect on Bazarov. He turned his head a little, and, obviously trying to fight against the load of oblivion weighing upon him, he articulated: "What is it, father?"

"Yevgeny," Vassily Ivanovitch went on, and he fell on his knees before Bazarov, though the latter had closed his eyes and could not see him. "Yevgeny, you are better now; please God, you will get well, but make use of this time, comfort your mother and me, perform the duty of a Christian! What it means for me to say this to you, it's awful; but still more awful . . . for ever and ever, Yevgeny . . . think a little, what . . ."

The old man's voice broke, and a strange look passed over his son's face, though he still lay with closed eyes.

"I won't refuse, if that can be any comfort to you," he brought out at last; "but it seems to me there's no need to be in a hurry. You say yourself I am better."

"Oh, yes, Yevgeny, better certainly; but who knows, it is all in God's hands, and in doing the duty . . ."

"No, I will wait a bit," broke in Bazarov. "I agree with you that the crisis has come. And if we're mistaken, well! they give the sacrament to men who're unconscious, you know."

"Yevgeny, I beg."

"I'll wait a little. And now I want to go to sleep. Don't disturb me." And he laid his head back on the pillow.

The old man rose from his knees, sat down in the arm-chair, and clutching his beard, began biting his own fingers . . .

The sound of a light carriage on springs, that sound which is peculiarly impressive in the wilds of the country, suddenly struck upon his hearing. Nearer and nearer rolled the light wheels; now even the neighing of the horses could be heard. . . . Vassily Ivanovitch jumped up and ran to the little window. There drove into the courtyard of his little house a carriage with seats for two, with four horses harnessed abreast. Without stopping to consider what it could mean, with a rush of a sort of senseless joy, he ran out on to the steps. . . . A groom in livery was opening the carriage doors; a lady in a black veil and a black mantle was getting out of it . . .

"I am Madame Odintsov," she said. "Yevgeny Vassilyitch is still living? You are his father? I have a doctor with me."

"Benefactress!" cried Vassily Ivanovitch, and snatching her hand, he pressed it convulsively to his lips, while the doctor brought by Anna Sergyevna, a little man in spectacles, of German physiognomy, stepped very deliberately out of the carriage. "Still living, my Yevgeny is living, and now he will be saved! Wife! wife! . . . An angel from heaven has come to us. . . ."

"What does it mean, good Lord!" faltered the old woman, running out of the drawing-room; and, comprehending nothing, she fell on the spot in the passage at Anna Sergyevna's feet, and began kissing her garments like a mad woman.

"What are you doing!" protested Anna Sergyevna; but Arina Vlasyevna did not heed her, while Vassily Ivanovitch could only repeat, "An angel! an angel!"

"*Wo ist der Kranke?* and where is the patient?" said the doctor at last, with some impatience.

Vassily Ivanovitch recovered himself. "Here, here, follow me, *würdigster Herr Collega,*" he added through old associations.

"Ah!" articulated the German, grinning sourly.

Vassily Ivanovitch led him into the study. "The doctor from Anna Sergyevna Odintsov," he said, bending down quite to his son's ear, "and she herself is here."

Bazarov suddenly opened his eyes. "What did you say?"

"I say that Anna Sergyevna is here, and has brought this gentleman, a doctor, to you."

Bazarov moved his eyes about him. "She is here. . . . I want to see her."

"You shall see her, Yevgeny; but first we must have a little talk with the doctor. I will tell him the whole history of your illness since Sidor Sidoritch" (this was the name of the district doctor) "has gone, and we will have a little consultation."

Bazarov glanced at the German. "Well, talk away quickly, only not in Latin; you see, I know the meaning of *jam moritur.*

"*Der Herr scheint des Deutschen mächtig zu sein,*" began the new follower of Æsculapius, turning to Vassily Ivanovitch.

"*Ich. . . . gabe . . .* We had better speak Russian," said the old man.

"Ah, ah! so that's how it is. . . . To be sure . . ." And the consultation began.

Half-an-hour later Anna Sergyevna, conducted by Vassily Ivanovitch, came into the study. The doctor had had time to whisper to her that it was hopeless even to think of the patient's recovery.

She looked at Bazarov . . . and stood still in the doorway, so greatly was she impressed by the inflamed, and at the same time deathly face, with its dim eyes fastened upon her. She felt simply dismayed, with a sort of cold and suffocating dismay; the thought that she would not have felt like that if she had really loved him flashed instantaneously through her brain.

"Thanks," he said painfully, "I did not expect this. It's a deed of mercy. So we have seen each other again, as you promised."

"Anna Sergyevna has been so kind," began Vassily Ivanovitch . . .

"Father, leave us alone. Anna Sergyevna, you will allow it, I fancy, now?" With a motion of his head, he indicated his prostrate helpless frame. Vassily Ivanovitch went out.

"Well, thanks," repeated Bazarov. "This is royally done. Monarchs, they say, visit the dying too."

"Yevgeny Vassilyitch, I hope—"

"Ah, Anna Sergyevna, let us speak the truth. It's all over with me. I'm under the wheel. So it turns out that it was useless to think of the future. Death's an old joke, but it comes fresh to every one. So far I'm not afraid . . . but there, senselessness is coming, and then it's all up!——" he waved his hand feebly. "Well, what had I to say to you . . . I loved you! there was no sense in that even before, and less than ever now. Love is a form, and my own form is already breaking up. Better say how lovely you are! And now here you stand, so beautiful . . ."

Anna Sergyevna gave an involuntary shudder.

"Never mind, don't be uneasy. . . . Sit down there . . . Don't come close to me; you know, my illness is catching."

Anna Sergyevna swiftly crossed the room, and sat down in the armchair near the sofa on which Bazarov was lying.

"Noble-hearted!" he whispered. "Oh, how near, and how young, and fresh, and pure . . . in this loathsome room! . . . Well, good-bye! live long, that's the best of all, and make the most of it while there is time. You see what a hideous spectacle; the worm half crushed, but writhing still. And, you see, I thought too: I'd break down so many things, I wouldn't die, why should I, there were problems to solve, and I was a giant! And now all the problem for the giant is how to die decently, though that makes no difference to any one either . . . Never mind; I'm not going to turn tail."

Bazarov was silent, and began feeling with his hand for the glass. Anna Sergyevna gave him some drink, not taking off her glove, and drawing her breath timorously.

"You will forget me," he began again; "the dead's no companion for the living. My father will tell you what a man Russia is losing. . . . That's nonsense, but don't contradict the old man. Whatever toy will comfort the child . . . you know. And be kind to mother. People like them aren't to be found in your great world if you look by daylight with a candle. . . . I was needed by Russia. . . . No, it's clear, I wasn't needed. And who is needed? The shoemaker's needed, the tailor's needed, the butcher . . . gives us meat . . . the butcher . . . wait a little, I'm getting mixed. . . . There's a forest here . . ."

Bazarov put his hand to his brow.

Anna Sergyevna bent down to him. "Yevgeny Vassilyitch, I am here . . ."

He at once took his hand away, and raised himself.

"Good-bye," he said with sudden force, and his eyes gleamed with their last light. "Good-bye. . . . Listen . . . you know I didn't kiss you then. . . . Breathe on the dying lamp, and let it go out . . ."

Anna Sergyevna put her lips to his forehead.

"Enough!" he murmured, and dropped back on to the pillow. "Now . . . darkness . . ."

Anna Sergyevna went softly out. "Well?" Vassily Ivanovitch asked her in a whisper.

"He has fallen asleep," she answered, hardly audibly. Bazarov was not fated to awaken. Towards evening he sank into complete unconsciousness, and the following day he died. Father Alexey performed the last rites of religion over him. When they anointed him with the last unction, when the holy oil touched his breast, one eye opened, and it seemed as though at the sight of the priest in his vestments, the smoking censers, the light before the image, something like a shudder of horror passed over the death-stricken face. When at last he had breathed his last, and there arose a universal lamentation in the house, Vassily Ivanovitch was seized by a sudden frenzy. "I said I should rebel," he shrieked hoarsely, with his face inflamed and distorted, shaking his fist in the air, as though threatening some one; "and I rebel, I rebel!" But Arina Vlasyevna, all in tears, hung upon his neck, and both fell on their faces together. "Side by side," Anfisushka related afterwards in the servants' room, "they drooped their poor heads like lambs at noonday . . ."

But the heat of noonday passes, and evening comes and night, and then, too, the return to the kindly refuge, where sleep is sweet for the weary and heavy laden. . . .

XXVIII

SIX MONTHS HAD PASSED BY. White winter had come with the cruel stillness of unclouded frosts, the thick-lying, crunching snow, the rosy rime on the trees, the pale emerald sky, the wreaths of smoke above the chimneys, the clouds of steam rushing out of the doors when they are opened for an instant, with the fresh faces, that look stung by the cold, and the hurrying trot of the chilled horses. A January day was drawing to its close; the cold of evening was more keen than ever in the motionless air, and a lurid sunset was rapidly dying away. There were lights burning in the windows of the house at Maryino; Prokofitch in a black frock coat and white gloves, with a special solemnity, laid the table for seven. A week before in the small parish church two weddings had taken place quietly, and almost without witnesses—Arkady and Katya's, and Nikolai Petrovitch and Fenitchka's; and on this day Nikolai Petrovitch was giving a farewell dinner to his brother, who was going away to Moscow on business. Anna Sergyevna had gone there also directly after the ceremony was over, after making very handsome presents to the young people.

Precisely at three o'clock they all gathered about the table. Mitya was placed there too; with him appeared a nurse in a cap of glazed brocade. Pavel Petrovitch took his seat between Katya and Fenitchka; the "husbands" took their places beside their wives. Our friends had changed of late; they all seemed to have grown stronger and better looking; only Pavel Petrovitch was thinner, which gave even more of an elegant and "grand seigneur" air to his expressive features. . . . And Fenitchka, too, was different. In a fresh silk gown, with a wide velvet head-dress on her hair, with a gold chain round her neck, she sat with deprecating immobility, respectful towards herself and everything surrounding her, and smiled as though she would say, "I beg your pardon; I'm not to blame." And not she alone—all the others smiled, and also seemed apologetic; they were all a little awkward, a little sorry, and in reality very happy. They all helped one another with humourous attentiveness, as though they had all agreed to rehearse a sort of artless farce. Katya was the most composed of all; she looked confidently about her, and it could be seen that Nikolai Petrovitch was already devotedly fond of her. At the end of dinner he got up, and his glass in his hand, turned to Pavel Petrovitch.

"You are leaving us . . . you are leaving us, dear brother," he began; "not for long, to be sure; but still, I cannot help expressing what I . . . what we . . . how much I . . . how much we. . . . There, the worst of it is, we don't know how to make speeches. Arkady, you speak."

"No, daddy, I've not prepared anything."

"As though I were so well prepared! Well, brother, I will simply say, let us embrace you, wish you all good luck, and come back to us as quick as you can!"

Pavel Petrovitch exchanged kisses with every one, of course not excluding Mitya; in Fenitchka's case, he kissed also her hand, which she had not yet learned to offer properly, and drinking off the glass which had been filled again, he said with a deep sigh, "May you be happy my friends! *Farewell!*" This English finale passed unnoticed; but all were touched.

"To the memory of Bazarov," Katya whispered in her husband's ear, as she clinked glasses with him. Arkady pressed her hand warmly in response, but he did not venture to propose this toast aloud.

The end, would it seem? But perhaps some one of our readers would care to know what each of the characters we have introduced is doing in the present, the actual present. We are ready to satisfy him.

Anna Sergyevna has recently made a marriage, not of love but of good sense, with one of the future leaders of Russia, a very clever man, a lawyer, possessed of vigourous practical sense, a strong will, and remarkable fluency —still young, good-natured, and cold as ice. They live in the greatest harmony together, and will live perhaps to attain complete happiness . . . perhaps love. The Princess K—is dead, forgotten the day of her death. The Kirsanovs, father and son, live at Maryino; their fortunes are beginning to mend. Arkady has become zealous in the management of the estate, and the "farm" now yields a fairly good income. Nikolai Petrovitch has been made one of the mediators appointed to carry out the emancipation reforms, and works with all his energies; he is forever driving about over his district; delivers long speeches (he maintains the opinion that the peasants ought to be "brought to comprehend things," that is to say, they ought to be reduced to a state of quiescence by the constant repetition of the same words); and yet, to tell the truth, he does not give complete satisfaction either to the refined gentry, who talk with *chic*, or depression of the *emancipation* (pronouncing it as though it were French), nor to the uncultivated gentry, who unceremoniously curse "the damned '*mancipation*.'" He is too soft-hearted for both sets. Katerina Sergyevna has a son, little Nikolai, while Mitya runs about merrily and talks fluently. Fenitchka, Fedosya Nikolaevna, after her husband and Mitya, adores no one so much as her daughter-in-law, and when the latter is at the piano, she would gladly spend the whole day at her side. A passing word of Piotr. He has grown perfectly rigid with stupidity and dignity, but he too is married, and received a respectable dowry with his bride, the daughter of a market-gardener of the town, who had refused two excellent suitors, only because they had no watch; while Piotr had not only a watch—he had a pair of kid shoes.

In the Brühl Terrace in Dresden, between two and four o'clock—the most fashionable time for walking—you may meet a man about fifty, quite grey, and looking as though he suffered from gout, but still handsome, elegantly dressed, and with that special stamp, which is only gained by moving a long time in the higher strata of society. That is Pavel Petrovitch. From Moscow he went abroad for the sake of his health, and has settled for good at Dresden, where he associates most with English and Russian visitors. With English people he behaves simply, almost modestly, but with dignity; they find him rather a bore, but respect him for being, as they say, *"a perfect gentleman."* With Russians he is more free and easy, gives vent to his spleen, and makes fun of himself and them, but that is done by him with great amiability, negligence, and propriety. He holds Slavophil views; it is well known that in the highest society this is regarded as *très distingué!* He reads nothing in Russian, but on his writing table there is a silver ashpan in the shape of a peasant's plaited shoe. He is much run after by our tourists. Matvy Ilyitch Kolyazin, happening to be in temporary opposition, paid him a majestic visit; while the natives, with whom, however, he is very little seen, positively grovel before him. No one can so readily and quickly obtain a ticket for the court chapel, for the theatre, and such things as *der Herr Baron von Kirsanoff.* He does everything good-naturedly that he can; he still makes some little noise in the world; it is not for nothing that he was once a great society lion;—but life is a burden to him . . . a heavier burden than he suspects himself. One need but glance at him in the Russian church, when, leaning against the wall on one side, he sinks into thought, and remains long without stirring, bitterly compressing his lips, then suddenly recollects himself, and begins almost imperceptibly crossing himself. . . .

Madame Kushkin, too, went abroad. She is in Heidelberg, and is now studying not natural science, but architecture, in which, according to her own account, she has discovered new laws. She still fraternises with students, especially with the young Russians studying natural science and chemistry, with whom Heidelberg is crowded, and who, astounding the naïve German professors at first by the soundness of their views of things, astound the same professors no less in the sequel by their complete inefficiency and absolute idleness. In company with two or three such young chemists, who don't know oxygen from nitrogen, but are filled with scepticism and self-conceit, and, too, with the great Elisyevitch, Sitnikov roams about Petersburg, also getting ready to be great, and in his own conviction continues the "work" of Bazarov. There is a story that some one recently gave him a beating; but he was avenged upon him; in an obscure little article, hidden in an obscure little journal, he has hinted that the man who beat him was a coward. He calls this irony. His father bullies him as before, while his wife regards him as a fool . . . and a literary man.

There is a small village graveyard in one of the remote corners of Russia. Like almost all our graveyards, it presents a wretched appearance; the ditches surrounding it have long been overgrown; the grey wooden crosses lie fallen and rotting under their once painted gables; the stone slabs are all displaced, as though some one were pushing them up from behind; two or three bare trees give a scanty shade; the sheep wander unchecked among the tombs. . . . But among them is one untouched by man, untrampled by beast, only the birds perch upon it and sing at daybreak. An iron railing runs round it; two young fir-trees have been planted, one at each end. Yevgeny Bazarov is buried in this tomb. Often from the little village not far off, two quite feeble old people come to visit it—a husband and wife. Supporting one another, they move to it with heavy steps; they go up to the railing, fall down, and remain on their knees, and long and bitterly they weep, and yearn, and intently they gaze at the dumb stone, under which their son is lying; they exchange some brief word, wipe away the dust from the stone, set straight a branch of a fir-tree, and pray again, and cannot tear themselves from this place, where they seem to be nearer to their son, to their memories of him. . . . Can it be that their prayers, their tears are fruitless? Can it be that love, sacred, devoted love, is not all-powerful? Oh, no! However passionate, sinning, and rebellious the heart hidden in the tomb, the flowers growing over it peep serenely at us with their innocent eyes; they tell us not of eternal peace alone, of that great peace of "indifferent" nature; they tell us, too, of eternal reconciliation and of life without end.

SMOKE

On the 10th of august 1862, at four o'clock in the afternoon, a great number of people were thronging before the well-known *Konversation* in Baden-Baden. The weather was lovely; everything around—the green trees, the bright houses of the gay city, and the undulating outline of the mountains—everything was in holiday mood, basking in the rays of the kindly sunshine; everything seemed smiling with a sort of blind, confiding delight; and the same glad, vague smile strayed over the human faces too, old and young, ugly and beautiful alike. Even the blackened and whitened visages of the Parisian demi-monde could not destroy the general impression of bright content and elation, while their many-coloured ribbons and feathers and the sparks of gold and steel on their hats and veils involuntarily recalled the intensified brilliance and light fluttering of birds in spring, with their rainbow-tinted wings. But the dry, guttural snapping of the French jargon, heard on all sides could not equal the song of birds, nor be compared with it.

Everything, however, was going on in its accustomed way. The orchestra in the Pavilion played first a medley from the Traviata, then one of Strauss's waltzes, then 'Tell her,' a Russian song, adapted for instruments by an obliging conductor. In the gambling saloons, round the green tables, crowded the same familiar figures, with the same dull, greedy, half-stupefied, half-exasperated, wholly rapacious expression, which the gambling fever lends to all, even the most aristocratic, features. The same well-fed and ultra-fashionably dressed Russian landowner from Tambov with wide staring eyes leaned over the table, and with uncomprehending haste, heedless of the cold smiles of the croupiers themselves, at the very instant of the cry '*rien ne va plus*,' laid with perspiring hand golden rings of *louis d'or* on all the four corners of the roulette, depriving himself by so doing of every possibility of gaining anything, even in case of success. This did not in the least prevent him the same evening from affirming the contrary with disinterested indignation to Prince Kokó, one of the well-known leaders of the aristocratic opposition, the Prince Kokó, who in Paris at the salon of the Princess Mathilde, so happily remarked in the presence of the Emperor: '*Madame, le principe de la propriété est profondément ébranlé en Russie.*' At the Russian tree, *à l'arbre Russe*, our dear fellow-countrymen and countrywomen were assembled after their wont. They approached haughtily and carelessly in fashionable style, greeted each other with dignity and elegant ease, as befits beings who find themselves at the topmost pinnacle of contemporary culture. But when they had met and sat down together, they were absolutely at a loss for anything to say to one another, and had to be content with a pitiful interchange of inanities, or with the exceedingly indecent and exceedingly insipid old jokes of a hopelessly stale French wit, once a journalist, a chattering buffoon with Jewish shoes on his paltry little legs, and a contemptible little beard on his mean little visage. He retailed to them, *à ces princes russes*, all the sweet absurdities from the old comic almanacs *Charivari* and *Tintamarre*, and they, *ces princes russes*, burst into grateful laughter, as though forced in spite of themselves to recognise the crushing superiority of foreign wit, and their own hopeless incapacity to invent anything amusing. Yet here were almost all the '*fine fleur*' of our society, ' all the high-life and mirrors of fashion.' Here was Count X., our incomparable dilettante, a profoundly musical nature, who so divinely recites songs on the piano, but cannot in fact take two notes correctly without fumbling at random on the keys, and sings in a style something between that of a poor gypsy singer and a Parisian hairdresser. Here was our enchanting Baron Q., a master in every line: literature, administration, oratory, and card-sharping. Here, too, was Prince Y., the friend of religion and the people, who in the blissful epoch when the spirit-trade was a monopoly, had made himself betimes a huge fortune by the sale of vodka adulterated with belladonna; and the brilliant General O. O., who had achieved the subjugation of something, and the pacification of something else, and who is nevertheless still a nonentity, and does not know what to do with himself. And R. R. the amusing fat man, who regards himself as a great invalid and a great wit, though he is, in fact, as strong as a bull, and as dull as a post. . . . This R. R. is almost the only man in our day who has preserved the traditions of the dandies of the forties, of the epoch of the ' Hero of our Times,' and the Countess Vorotinsky. He has preserved, too, the special gait with the swing on the heels, and *le culte de la pose* (it cannot even be put into words in Russian), the unnatural deliberation of movement, the sleepy dignity of expression, the immovable, offended-looking countenance, and the habit of interrupting other people's remarks with a yawn, gazing at his own finger-nails, laughing through his nose, suddenly shifting his hat from the back of his head on to his eyebrows, etc. Here, too, were people in government circles, diplomats, big-wigs with European names, men of wisdom and intellect, who imagine that the Golden Bull was an edict of the Pope, and that the English poor-tax is a tax levied on the poor. And here, too, were the hot-blooded, though tongue-tied, devotees of the *dames aux camellias*, young society dandies, with superb partings down the back of their heads, and splendid drooping whiskers, dressed in real London costumes, young bucks whom one would fancy there was nothing to hinder from becoming as vulgar as the illustrious French wit above mentioned. But no! our home products are not in fashion it seems; and Countess S., the celebrated arbitress of fashion and *grand genre*, by spiteful tongues nicknamed ' Queen of the Wasps,' and ' Medusa in a mob-cap,' prefers, in the absence of the French wit, to consort with the Italians, Moldavians, American spiritualists, smart secretaries of foreign embassies, and Germans of effeminate, but prematurely circumspect, physiognomy, of whom the place is full. The example of the Countess is followed by the Princess Babette, she in whose arms Chopin died (the ladies in Europe in whose arms he expired are to be reckoned by thousands); and the Princess Annette, who would have been perfectly captivating, if the simple village washerwoman had not suddenly peeped out in her at times, like a smell of cabbage wafted across the most delicate perfume; and Princess Pachette, to whom the following mischance had occurred: her husband had fallen into a good berth, and all at once, *Dieu sait pourquoi*, he had thrashed the provost and stolen 20,000 roubles of public money; and the laughing Princess Zizi; and the tearful Princess Zozo. They all left their compatriots on one side, and were merciless in their treatment of them. Let us too leave them on one side, these charming ladies, and walk away from the renowned tree near which they sit in such costly but somewhat tasteless costumes, and God grant them relief from the boredom consuming them!

II

A FEW PACES from the 'Russian tree,' at a little table in front of Weber's coffee-house, there was sitting a good-looking man, about thirty, of medium height, thin and dark, with a manly and pleasant face. He sat bending forward with both arms leaning on his stick, with the calm and simple air of a man to whom the idea had not occurred that any one would notice him or pay any attention to him. His large expressive golden-brown eyes were gazing deliberately about him, sometimes screwed up to keep the sunshine out of them, and then watching fixedly some eccentric figure that passed by him while a childlike smile faintly stirred his fine moustache and lips, and his prominent short chin. He wore a roomy coat of German cut, and a soft grey hat hid half of his high forehead. At the first glance he made the impression of an honest, sensible, rather self-confident young man such as there are many in the world. He seemed to be resting from prolonged labours and to be deriving all the more simple-minded amusement from the scene spread out before him because his thoughts were far away, and because they moved too, those thoughts, in a world utterly unlike that which surrounded him at the moment. He was a Russian; his name was Grigory Mihalovitch Litvinov.

We have to make his acquaintance, and so it will be well to relate in a few words his past, which presents little of much interest or complexity.

He was the son of an honest retired official of plebeian extraction, but he was educated, not as one would naturally expect, in the town, but in the country. His mother was of noble family, and had been educated in a government school. She was a good-natured and very enthusiastic creature, not devoid of character, however. Though she was twenty years younger than her husband, she remodelled him, as far as she could, drew him out of the petty official groove into the landowner's way of life, and softened and refined his harsh and stubborn character. Thanks to her, he began to dress with neatness, and to behave with decorum; he came to respect learned men and learning, though, of course, he never took a single book in his hand; he gave up swearing, and tried in every way not to demean himself. He even arrived at walking more quietly and speaking in a subdued voice, mostly of elevated subjects, which cost him no small effort. 'Ah!

they ought to be flogged, and that's all about it! ' he sometimes thought to himself, but aloud he pronounced: 'Yes, yes, that's so . . . of course; it is a great question.' Litvinov's mother set her household too upon a European footing; she addressed the servants by the plural 'you' instead of the familiar 'thou,' and never allowed any one to gorge himself into a state of lethargy at her table. As regards the property belonging to her, neither she nor her husband was capable of looking after it at all. It had been long allowed to run to waste, but there was plenty of land, with all sorts of useful appurtenances, forest-lands and a lake, on which there had once stood a factory, which had been founded by a zealous but unsystematic owner, and had flourished in the hands of a scoundrelly merchant, and gone utterly to ruin under the superintendence of a conscientious German manager. Madame Litvinov was contented so long as she did not dissipate her fortune or contract debts. Unluckily she could not boast of good health, and she died of consumption in the very year that her son entered the Moscow university. He did not complete his course there owing to circumstances of which the reader will hear more later on, and went back to his provincial home, where he idled away some time without work and without ties, almost without acquaintances. Thanks to the disinclination for active service of the local gentry, who were, however, not so much penetrated by the Western theory of the evils of 'absenteeism,' as by the home-grown conviction that 'one's own shirt is the nearest to one's skin,' he was drawn for military service in 1855, and almost died of typhus in the Crimea, where he spent six months in a mud-hut on the shore of the Putrid Sea, without ever seeing a single ally. After that, he served, not of course without unpleasant experiences, on the councils of the nobility, and after being a little time in the country, acquired a passion for farming. He realised that his mother's property, under the indolent and feeble management of his infirm old father, did not yield a tenth of the revenue it might yield, and that in experienced and skilful hands it might be converted into a perfect gold mine. But he realised, too, that experience and skill were just what he lacked —and he went abroad to study agriculture and technology—to learn them from the first rudiments. More than four years he had spent in Mecklenburg, in Silesia, and in Carlsruhe, and he had travelled in Belgium and in England. He had worked conscientiously and accumulated information; he had not acquired it easily; but he had persevered through his difficulties to the end, and now with confidence in himself, in his future, and in his usefulness to his neighbours, perhaps even to the whole countryside, he was preparing to return home, where he was summoned with despairing prayers and entreaties in every letter from his father, now completely bewildered by the emancipation, the re-division of lands, and the terms of redemption—by the new régime in short. But why was he in Baden?

Well, he was in Baden because he was from day to day expecting the arrival there of his cousin and betrothed, Tatyana Petrovna Shestov. He had known her almost from childhood, and had spent the spring and summer with her at Dresden, where she was living with her aunt. He felt sincere love and profound respect for his young kinswoman, and on the conclusion of his dull preparatory labours, when he was preparing to enter on a new field, to begin real, unofficial duties, he proposed to her as a woman dearly loved, a comrade and a friend, to unite her life with his—for happiness and for sorrow, for labour and for rest, 'for better, for worse' as the English say. She had consented, and he had returned to Carlsruhe, where his books, papers and properties had been left. . . . But why was he at Baden, you ask again?

Well, he was at Baden, because Tatyana's aunt, who had brought her up, Kapitolina Markovna Shestov, an old unmarried lady of fifty-five, a most good-natured, honest, eccentric soul, a free thinker, all aglow with the fire of self-sacrifice and abnegation, and *esprit fort* (she read Strauss, it is true she concealed the fact from her niece) and a democrat, sworn opponent of aristocracy and fashionable society, could not resist the temptation of gazing for once on this aristocratic society in such a fashionable place as Baden. . . . Kapitolina Markovna wore no crinoline and had her white hair cut in a round crop, but luxury and splendour had a secret fascination for her, and it was her favourite pastime to rail at them and express her contempt of them. How could one refuse to gratify the good old lady? But Litvinov was so quiet and simple, he gazed so self-confidently about him, because his life lay so clearly mapped out before him, because his career was defined, and because he was proud of this career, and rejoiced in it as the work of his own hands.

III

'HULLO! HULLO! here he is!' he suddenly heard a squeaky voice just above his ear, and a plump hand slapped him on the shoulder. He lifted his head, and perceived one of his few Moscow acquaintances, a certain Bambaev, a good-natured but good-for-nothing fellow. He was no longer young, he had a flabby nose and soft cheeks, that looked as if they had been boiled, dishevelled greasy locks, and a fat squat person. Everlastingly short of cash, and everlastingly in raptures over something, Rostislav Bambaev wandered, aimless but exclamatory, over the face of our long-suffering mother-earth.

'Well, this is something like a meeting!' he repeated, opening wide his sunken eyes, and drawing down his thick lips, over which the straggling dyed moustaches seemed strangely out of place. 'Ah, Baden! All the world runs here like black-beetles! How did you come here, Grisha?'

There was positively no one in the world Bambaev did not address by his Christian name.

'I came here three days ago.'

'From where?'

'Why do you ask?'

'Why indeed? But stop, stop a minute, Grisha. You are, perhaps, not aware who has just arrived here! Gubaryov himself, in person! That's who's here! He came yesterday from Heidelberg. You know him of course?'

'I have heard of him.'

'Is that all? Upon my word! At once, this very minute we will haul you along to him. Not know a man like that! And by the way here's Voroshilov. . . . Stop a minute, Grisha, perhaps you don't know him either? I have the honour to present you to one another. Both learned men! He's a phœnix indeed! Kiss each other!'

And uttering these words, Bambaev turned to a good-looking young man standing near him with a fresh and rosy, but prematurely demure face. Litvinov got up, and, it need hardly be said, did not kiss him, but exchanged a cursory bow with the phœnix, who, to judge from the severity of his demeanour, was not overpleased at this unexpected introduction.

'I said a phœnix, and I will not go back from my word,' continued Bambaev; 'go to Petersburg, to the military school, and look at the golden board; whose name stands first there? The name of Voroshilov, Semyon Yakovlevitch! But, Gubaryov, Gubaryov, my dear fellow! It's to him we must fly! I absolutely worship that man! And I'm not alone, every one's at his feet! Ah, what a work he is writing, O—O—O! . . .'

'What is his work about?' inquired Litvinov.

'About everything, my dear boy, after the style of Buckle, you know . . . but more profound, more profound. . . . Everything will be solved and made clear in it?'

'And have you read this work yourself?'

'No, I have not read it, and indeed it's a secret, which must not be spread about; but from Gubaryov one may expect everything, everything! Yes!' Bambaev sighed and clasped his hands. 'Ah, if we had two or three intellects like that growing up in Russia, ah, what mightn't we see then, my God! I tell you one thing, Grisha; whatever pursuit you may have been engaged in in these latter days—and I don't even know what your pursuits are in general—whatever your convictions may be—I don't know them either—from him, Gubaryov, you will find something to learn. Unluckily, he is not here for long. We must make the most of him, we must go. To him, to him!'

A passing dandy with reddish curls and a blue ribbon on his low hat, turned round and stared through his eyeglass with a sarcastic smile at Bambaev. Litvinov felt irritated.

'What are you shouting for?' he said; 'one would think you were hallooing dogs on at a hunt! I have not had dinner yet.'

'Well, think of that! we can go at once to Weber's . . . the three of us . . . capital! You have the cash to pay for me?' he added in an undertone.

'Yes, yes; only, I really don't know——'

'Leave off, please; you will thank me for it, and he will be delighted. Ah, heavens!' Bambaev interrupted himself. 'It's the finale from Ernani they're playing. How delicious! . . . *A som . . . mo Carlo*. . . . What a fellow I am, though! In tears in a minute. Well, Semyon Yakovlevitch! Voroshilov! shall we go, eh?'

Voroshilov, who had remained all the while standing with immovable propriety, still maintaining his former haughty dignity of demeanour, dropped his eyes expressively, frowned, and muttered something between his teeth . . . But he did not refuse; and Litvinov thought, 'Well, we may as well do it, as I've plenty of time on my hands.' Bambaev took his arm, but before turning towards the café he beckoned to Isabelle the renowned flower-girl of the Jockey Club: he had conceived the idea of buying a bunch of flowers of her. But the aristocratic flower-girl did not stir; and, indeed, what should induce her to approach a gentleman without gloves, in a soiled fustian jacket, streaky cravat, and boots trodden down at heel, whom she had not even seen in Paris? Then Voroshilov in his turn beckoned to her. To him she responded, and he, taking a tiny bunch of violets from her basket, flung her a florin. He thought to astonish her by his munificence, but not an eyelash on her face quivered, and when he had turned away, she pursed up her mouth contemptuously. Voroshilov was dressed very fashionably, even exquisitely, but the experienced eye of the Parisian girl noted at once in his get-up and in his bearing, in his very walk, which showed traces of premature military drill, the absence of genuine, pure-blooded 'chic.'

When they had taken their seats in the principal dining-hall at Weber's, and ordered dinner, our friends fell into conversation. Bambaev discoursed loudly and hotly upon the immense importance of Gubaryov, but soon he ceased speaking, and, gasping and chewing noisily, drained off glass after glass. Voroshilov ate and drank little, and as it were reluctantly, and after questioning Litvinov as to the nature of his interests, fell to giving expression to his own opinions—not so much on those interests, as on questions of various kinds in general. . . . All at once he warmed up, and set off at a gallop like a spirited horse, boldly and decisively assigning to every syllable, every letter, its due weight, like a confident cadet going up for his 'final' examination, with vehement, but inappropriate gestures. At every instant, since no one interrupted him, he became more eloquent, more emphatic; it seemed as though he were reading a dissertation or lecture. The names of the most recent scientific authorities—with the addition of the dates of the birth or death of each of them—the titles of pamphlets that had only just appeared, and names, names, names . . . fell in showers together from his tongue, affording himself intense satisfaction, reflected in his glowing eyes. Voroshilov, seemingly, despised everything old, and attached value only to the cream of culture, the latest, most advanced points of science; to mention, however inappropriately, a book of some Doctor Zauerbengel on Pennsylvanian prisons, or yesterday's articles in the *Asiatic Journal* on the Vedas and Puranas (he pronounced it *Journal* in the English fashion, though he certainly did not know English) was for him a real joy, a felicity. Litvinov listened and listened to him, and could not make out what could be his special line. At one moment his talk was of the part played by the Celtic race in history; then he was carried away to the ancient world, and discoursed upon the Æginetan marbles, harangued with great warmth on the sculptor living earlier than Phidias, Onetas, who was, however, transformed by him into Jonathan, which lent his whole discourse a half-

Biblical, half-American flavour; then he suddenly bounded away to political economy and called Bastiat a fool or a blockhead, 'as bad as Adam Smith and all the physiocrats.' 'Physiocrats,' murmured Bambaev after him . . . 'aristocrats?' Among other things Voroshilov called forth an expression of bewilderment on Bambaev's face by a criticism, dropped casually in passing, of Macaulay, as an old-fashioned writer, superseded by modern historical science; as for Gneist, he declared he need scarcely refer to him, and he shrugged his shoulders. Bambaev shrugged his shoulders too. 'And all this at once, without any inducement, before strangers, in a café' —Litvinov reflected, looking at the fair hair, clear eyes, and white teeth of his new acquaintance (he was specially embarrassed by those large sugar-white teeth, and those hands with their inappropriate gesticulations), 'and he doesn't once smile; and with it all, he would seem to be a nice lad, and absolutely inexperienced.' Voroshilov began to calm down at last, his voice, youthfully resonant and shrill as a young cock's, broke a little . . . Bambaev seized the opportunity to declaim verses and again nearly burst into tears, which scandalised one table near them, round which was seated an English family, and set another tittering; two Parisian *cocottes* were dining at this second table with a creature who resembled an ancient baby in a wig. The waiter brought the bill; the friends paid it.

'Well,' cried Bambaev, getting heavily up from his chair, 'now for a cup of coffee, and quick march. There she is, our Russia,' he added, stopping in the doorway, and pointing almost rapturously with his soft red hand to Voroshilov and Litvinov. . . . 'What do you think of her? . . .'

'Russia, indeed,' thought Litvinov; and Voroshilov, whose face had by now regained its concentrated expression, again smiled condescendingly, and gave a little tap with his heels.

Within five minutes they were all three mounting the stairs of the hotel where Stepan Nikolaitch Gubaryov was staying. . . . A tall slender lady, in a hat with a short black veil, was coming quickly down the same staircase. Catching sight of Litvinov she turned suddenly round to him, and stopped still as though struck by amazement. Her face flushed instantaneously, and then as quickly grew pale under its thick lace veil; but Litvinov did not observe her, and the lady ran down the wide steps more quickly than before.

IV

'GRIGORY LITVINOV, a brick, a true Russian heart. I commend him to you,' cried Bambaev, conducting Litvinov up to a short man of the figure of a country gentleman, with an unbuttoned collar, in a short jacket, grey morning trousers and slippers, standing in the middle of a light, and very well-furnished room; 'and this,' he added, addressing himself to Litvinov, 'is he, the man himself, do you understand? Gubaryov, then, in a word.'

Litvinov stared with curiosity at 'the man himself.' He did not at first sight find in him anything out of the common. He saw before him a gentleman of respectable, somewhat dull exterior, with a broad forehead, large eyes, full lips, a big beard, and a thick neck, with a fixed gaze, bent sidelong and downwards. This gentleman simpered, and said, 'Mmm. . . . ah . . . very pleased, . . .' raised his hand to his own face, and at once turning his back on Litvinov, took a few paces upon the carpet, with a slow and peculiar shuffle, as though he were trying to slink along unseen. Gubaryov had the habit of continually walking up and down, and constantly plucking and combing his beard with the tips of his long hard nails. Besides Gubaryov, there was also in the room a lady of about fifty, in a shabby silk dress, with an excessively mobile face almost as yellow as a lemon, a little black moustache on her upper lip, and eyes which moved so quickly that they seemed as though they were jumping out of her head; there was too a broad-shouldered man sitting bent up in a corner.

'Well, honoured Matrona Semyonovna,' began Gubaryov, turning to the lady, and apparently not considering it necessary to introduce Litvinov to her, 'what was it you were beginning to tell us?'

The lady (her name was Matrona Semyonovna Suhantchikov—she was a widow, childless, and not rich, and had been travelling from country to country for two years past) began with peculiar exasperated vehemence:

'Well, so he appears before the prince and says to him: "Your Excellency," he says, "in such an office and such a position as yours, what will it cost you to alleviate my lot? You," he says, "cannot but respect the purity of my ideas! And is it possible," he says, "in these days to persecute a man for his ideas?" And what do you suppose the prince did, that cultivated dignitary in that exalted position?'

'Why, what did he do?' observed Gubaryov, lighting a cigarette with a meditative air.

The lady drew herself up and held out her bony right hand, with the first finger separated from the rest.

'He called his groom and said to him, "Take off that man's coat at once, and keep it yourself. I make you a present of that coat!"'

'And did the groom take it?' asked Bambaev, throwing up his arms.

'He took it and kept it. And that was done by Prince Barnaulov, the well-known rich grandee, invested with special powers, the representative of the government. What is one to expect after that!'

The whole frail person of Madame Suhantchikov was shaking with indignation, spasms passed over her face, her withered bosom was heaving convulsively under her flat corset; of her eyes it is needless to speak, they were fairly leaping out of her head. But then they were always leaping, whatever she might be talking about.

'A crying shame, a crying shame!' cried Bambaev. 'No punishment could be bad enough!'

'Mmm. . . . Mmm. . . . From top to bottom it's all rotten,' observed Gubaryov, without raising his voice, however. In that case punishment is not . . . that needs . . . other measures.'

'But is it really true?' commented Litvinov.

'Is it true?' broke in Madame Suhantchikov. 'Why, that one can't even dream of doubting . . . can't even d-d-d-ream of it.' She pronounced these words with such energy that she was fairly shaking with the effort. 'I was told of that by a very trustworthy man. And you, Stepan Nikolaitch, know him—Elistratov, Kapiton. He heard it himself from eyewitnesses, spectators of this disgraceful scene.'

'What Elistratov?' inquired Gubaryov. 'The one who was in Kazan?'

'Yes. I know, Stepan Nikolaitch, a rumour was spread about him that he took bribes there from some contractors or distillers. But then who is it says so? Pelikanov! And how can one believe Pelikanov, when every one knows he is simply—a spy!'

'No, with your permission, Matrona Semyonovna,' interposed Bambaev, 'I am friends with Pelikanov, he is not a spy at all.'

'Yes, yes, that's just what he is, a spy!'

'But wait a minute, kindly——'

'A spy, a spy!' shrieked Madame Suhantchikov.

'No, no, one minute, I tell you what,' shrieked Bambaev in his turn.

'A spy, a spy,' persisted Madame Suhantchikov.

'No, no! There's Tentelyev now, that's a different matter,' roared Bambaev with all the force of his lungs.

Madame Suhantchikov was silent for a moment.

'I know for a fact about that gentleman,' he continued in his ordinary voice, 'that when he was summoned before the secret police, he grovelled at the feet of the Countess Blazenkrampff and kept whining, "Save me, intercede for me!" But Pelikanov never demeaned himself to baseness like that.'

'Mm. . . . Tentelyev . . .' muttered Gubaryov, 'that . . . that ought to be noted.'

Madame Suhantchikov shrugged her shoulders contemptuously.

'They're one worse than another,' she said, 'but I know a still better story about Tentelyev. He was, as every one knows, a most horrible despot with his serfs, though he gave himself out for an emancipator. Well, he was once at some friend's house in Paris, and suddenly in comes Madame Beecher Stowe—you know, *Uncle Tom's Cabin*. Tentelyev, who's an awfully pushing fellow, began asking the host to present him; but directly she heard his name. "What?" she said, "he presumes to be introduced to the author of *Uncle Tom?*" And she gave him a slap on the cheek! "Go away!" she says, "at once!" And what do you think? Tentelyev took his hat and slunk away, pretty crestfallen.'

'Come, I think that's exaggerated,' observed Bambaev. '"Go away" she certainly did say, that's a fact, but she didn't give him a smack!'

'She did, she did!' repeated Madame Suhantchikov with convulsive intensity: 'I am not talking idle gossip. And you are friends with men like that!'

'Excuse me, excuse me, Matrona Semyonovna, I never spoke of Tentelyev as a friend of mine; I was speaking of Pelikanov.'

'Well, if it's not Tentelyev, it's another. Mihnyov, for example.'

'What did he do then?' asked Bambaev, already showing signs of alarm.

'What? Is it possible you don't know? He exclaimed on the Poznesensky Prospect in the hearing of all the world that all the liberals ought to be in prison; and what's more, an old schoolfellow came to him, a poor man of course, and said, "Can I come to dinner with you?" And this was his answer. "No, impossible; I have two counts dining with me to-day . . . get along with you!"'

'But that's slander, upon my word!' vociferated Bambaev.

'Slander? . . . slander? In the first place, Prince Vahrushkin, who was also dining at your Mihnyov's——'

'Prince Vahrushkin,' Gubaryov interpolated severely, 'is my cousin; but I don't allow him to enter my house. . . . So there is no need to mention him even.'

'In the second place,' continued Madame Suhantchikov, with a submissive nod in Gubaryov's direction, 'Praskovya Yakovlevna told me so herself.'

'You have hit on a fine authority to quote! Why, she and Sarkizov are the greatest scandal-mongers going.'

'I beg your pardon, Sarkizov is a liar, certainly. He filched the very pall of brocade off his dead father's coffin. I will never dispute that; but Praskovya Yakovlevna—there's no comparison! Remember how magnanimously she parted from her husband! But you, I know, are always ready——'

'Come, enough, enough, Matrona Semyonovna,' said Bambaev, interrupting her, 'let us give up this tittle-tattle, and take a loftier flight. I am not new to the work, you know. Have you read *Mlle. de la Quintinie?* That's something charming now! And quite in accord with your principles at the same time!'

'I never read novels now,' was Madame Suhantchikov's dry and sharp reply.

'Why?'

'Because I have not the time now; I have no thoughts now but for one thing, sewing machines.'

'What machines?' inquired Litvinov.

'Sewing, sewing; all women ought to provide themselves with sewing-machines, and form societies; in that way they will all be enabled to earn their living, and will become independent at once. In no other way can they ever be emancipated. That is an important, most important social question. I had such an argument about it with Boleslav Stadnitsky. Boleslav Stadnitsky is a marvellous nature, but he looks at these things in an awfully frivolous spirit. He does nothing but laugh. Idiot!'

'All will in their due time be called to account, from all it will be exacted,' pronounced Gubaryov deliberately, in a tone half-professorial, half-prophetic.

'Yes, yes,' repeated Bambaev, 'it will be exacted, precisely so, it will be exacted. But, Stepan Nikolaitch,' he added, dropping his voice, ' how goes the great work? '

' I am collecting materials,' replied Gubaryov, knitting his brows; and, turning to Litvinov, whose head began to swim from the medley of unfamiliar names, and the frenzy of backbiting, he asked him what subjects he was interested in.

Litvinov satisfied his curiosity.

' Ah! to be sure, the natural sciences. That is useful, as training; as training, not as an end in itself. The end at present should be . . . mm. . . . should be . . . different. Allow me to ask what views do you hold? '

' What views? '

' Yes, that is, more accurately speaking, what are your political views? '

Litvinov smiled.

' Strictly speaking, I have no political views.'

The broad-shouldered man sitting in the corner raised his head quickly at these words and looked attentively at Litvinov.

' How is that? ' observed Gubaryov with peculiar gentleness. 'Have you not yet reflected on the subject, or have you grown weary of it? '

' How shall I say? It seems to me that for us Russians, it is too early yet to have political views or to imagine that we have them. Observe that I attribute to the word " political " the meaning which belongs to it by right, and that—— '

' Aha! he belongs to the undeveloped,' Gubaryov interrupted him, with the same gentleness, and going up to Voroshilov, he asked him: ' Had he read the pamphlet he had given him? '

Voroshilov, to Litvinov's astonishment, had not uttered a word ever since his entrance, but had only knitted his brows and rolled his eyes (as a rule he was either speechifying or else perfectly dumb). He now expanded his chest in soldierly fashion, and with a tap of his heels, nodded assent.

' Well, and how was it? Did you like it? '

' As regards the fundamental principles, I liked it; but I did not agree with the inferences.'

' Mmm. . . . Andrei Ivanitch praised that pamphlet, however. You must expand your doubts to me later.'

' You desire it in writing?'

Gubaryov was obviously surprised; he had not expected this; however, after a moment's thought, he replied:

' Yes, in writing. By the way, I will ask you to explain to me your views also . . . in regard to . . . in regard to associations.'

' Associations on Lassalle's system, do you desire, or on the system of Schulze-Delitzsch? '

' Mmm. . . . on both. For us Russians, you understand, the financial aspect of the matter is specially important. Yes, and the *artel* . . . as the germ. . . . All that, one must take note of. One must go deeply into it. And the question, too, of the land to be apportioned to the peasants. . . .'

' And you, Stepan Nikolaitch, what is your view as to the number of acres suitable? ' inquired Voroshilov, with reverential delicacy in his voice.

' Mmm. . . . and the commune? ' articulated Gubaryov, deep in thought, and biting a tuft of his beard he stared at the table-leg. ' The commune! . . . Do you understand. That is a grand word! Then what is the significance of these conflagrations? these . . . these government measures against Sunday-schools, reading-rooms, journals? And the refusal of the peasants to sign the charters regulating their position in the future? And finally, what of what is happening in Poland? Don't you see that . . . mmm. . . . that we . . . we have to unite with the people . . . find out . . . find out their views——' Suddenly a heavy, almost a wrathful emotion seemed to take possession of Gubaryov; he even grew black in the face and breathed heavily, but still did not raise his eyes, and continued to gnaw at his beard. ' Can't you see——'

' Yevseyev is a wretch! ' Madame Suhantchikov burst out noisily all of a sudden. Bambaev had been relating something to her in a voice lowered out of respect for their host. Gubaryov turned round swiftly on his heels, and again began limping about the room.

Fresh guests began to arrive; towards the end of the evening a good many people were assembled. Among them came, too, Mr. Yevseyev whom Madame Suhantchikov had vilified so cruelly. She entered into conversation with him very cordially, and asked him to escort her home; there arrived too a certain Pishtchalkin, an ideal mediator, one of those men of precisely whom perhaps Russia stands in need—a man, that is, narrow, of little information, and no great gifts, but conscientious, patient, and honest; the peasants of his district almost worshipped him, and he regarded himself very respectfully as a creature genuinely deserving of esteem. A few officers, too, were there, escaped for a brief furlough to Europe, and rejoicing— though of course warily, and ever mindful of their colonel in the background of their brains—in the opportunity of dallying a little with intellectual—even rather dangerous—people; two lanky students from Heidelberg came hurrying in, one looked about him very contemptuously, the other giggled spasmodically . . . both were very ill at ease; after them a Frenchman—a so-called *petit jeune homme*—poked his nose in; a nasty, silly, pitiful little creature, . . . who enjoyed some repute among his fellow *commis-voyageurs* on the theory that Russian countesses had fallen in love with him; for his own part, his reflections were centred more upon getting a supper gratis; the last to appear was Tit Bindasov, in appearance a rollicking German student, in reality a skinflint, in words a terrorist, by vocation a police-officer, a friend of Russian merchants' wives and Parisian *cocottes;* bald, toothless, and drunken; he arrived very red and sodden, affirming that he had lost his last farthing to that blackguard Benazet; in reality, he had won sixteen guldens. . . . In short, there were a number of people. Remarkable—really remarkable—was the respect with which all these people treated Gubaryov as a preceptor or chief; they laid their ideas before him, and submitted them to his judgment; and he replied by muttering, plucking at his beard, averting his eyes, or by some disconnected, meaning-

less words, which were at once seized upon as the utterances of the loftiest
wisdom. Gubaryov himself seldom interposed in the discussions; but the
others strained their lungs to the utmost to make up for it. It happened more
than once that three or four were shouting for ten minutes together, and
all were content and understood. The conversation lasted till after midnight, and was as usual distinguished by the number and variety of the
subjects discussed. Madame Suhantchikov talked about Garibaldi, about
a certain Karl Ivanovitch, who had been flogged by the serfs of his own
household, about Napoleon III., about women's work, about a merchant,
Pleskatchov, who had designedly caused the death of twelve work-women,
and had received a medal for it with the inscription 'for public services';
about the proletariat, about the Georgian Prince Tchuktcheulidzov, who
had shot his wife with a cannon, and about the future of Russia. Pishtchalkin, too, talked of the future of Russia, and of the spirit monopoly, and
of the significance of nationalities, and of how he hated above everything
what was vulgar. There was an outburst all of a sudden from Voroshilov;
in a single breath, almost choking himself, he mentioned Draper, Virchow,
Shelgunov, Bichat, Helmholtz, Star, St. Raymund, Johann Müller the phys-
iologist, and Johann Müller the historian—obviously confounding them—
Taine, Renan, Shtchapov; and then Thomas Nash, Peele, Greene. . . .
'What sort of queer fish may they be?' Bambaev muttered bewildered,
Shakespeare's predecessors having the same relation to him as the ranges
of the Alps to Mont Blanc. Voroshilov replied cuttingly, and he too
touched on the future of Russia. Bambaev also spoke of the future of
Russia, and even depicted it in glowing colours: but he was thrown into
special raptures over the thought of Russian music, in which he saw something. 'Ah! great indeed!' and in confirmation he began humming a song
of Varlamov's, but was soon interrupted by a general shout, 'He is singing
the *Miserere* from the *Trovatore*, and singing it excruciatingly too.'
One little officer was reviling Russian literature in the midst of the hubbub;
another was quoting verses from *Sparks*; but Tit Bindasov went even
further; he declared that all these swindlers ought to have their teeth
knocked out, . . . and that's all about it, but he did not particularise who
were the swindlers alluded to. The smoke from the cigars became stifling;
all were hot and exhausted, every one was hoarse, all eyes were growing
dim, and the perspiration stood out in drops on every face. Bottles of iced
beer were brought in and drunk off instantaneously. 'What was I saying?'
remarked one; 'and with whom was I disputing, and about what?' inquired
another. And among all the uproar and the smoke, Gubaryov walked inde-
fatigably up and down as before, swaying from side to side and twitching
at his beard; now listening, turning an ear to some controversy, now putting
in a word of his own; and every one was forced to feel that he, Gubaryov,
was the source of it all, that he was the master here, and the most eminent
personality. . . .

Litvinov, towards ten o'clock, began to have a terrible headache, and,
taking advantage of a louder outburst of general excitement, went off

quietly unobserved. Madame Suhantchikov had recollected a fresh act of injustice of Prince Barnaulov; he had all but given orders to have some one's ears bitten off.

The fresh night air enfolded Litvinov's flushed face caressingly, the fragrant breeze breathed on his parched lips. 'What is it,' he thought as he went along the dark avenue, 'that I have been present at? Why were they met together? What were they shouting, scolding, and making such a pother about? What was it all for?' Litvinov shrugged his shoulders, and turning into Weber's, he picked up a newspaper and asked for an ice. The newspaper was taken up with a discussion on the Roman question, and the ice turned out to be very nasty. He was already preparing to go home, when suddenly an unknown person in a wide-brimmed hat drew near, and saying in Russian: 'I hope I am not in your way?' sat down at his table. Only then, after a closer glance at the stranger, Litvinov recognised him as the broad-shouldered gentleman hidden away in a corner at Gubaryov's, who had stared at him with such attention when the conversation had turned on political views. During the whole evening this gentleman had not once opened his mouth, and now, sitting down near Litvinov, and taking off his hat, he looked at him with an expression of friendliness and some embarrassment.

V

'Mr. GUBARYOV, at whose rooms I had the pleasure of meeting you to-day,' he began, 'did not introduce me to you; so that, with your leave, I will now introduce myself—Potugin, retired councillor. I was in the department of finances in St. Petersburg. I hope you do not think it strange. . . . I am not in the habit as a rule of making friends so abruptly . . . but with you. . . .'

Here Potugin grew rather mixed, and he asked the waiter to bring him a little glass of kirsch-wasser. 'To give me courage,' he added with a smile.

Litvinov looked with redoubled interest at the last of all the new persons with whom it had been his lot to be brought into contact that day. His thought was at once, 'He is not the same as those.'

Certainly he was not. There sat before him, drumming with delicate fingers on the edge of the table, a broad-shouldered man, with an ample frame on short legs, a downcast head of curly hair, with very intelligent and very mournful eyes under bushy brows, a thick well-cut mouth, bad teeth, and that purely Russian nose to which is assigned the epithet 'potato'; a man of awkward, even odd exterior; at least, he was certainly not of a common type. He was carelessly dressed; his old-fashioned coat hung on him like a sack, and his cravat was twisted awry. His sudden friendliness, far from striking Litvinov as intrusive, secretly flattered him; it was impossible not to see that it was not a common practice with this man to attach himself to strangers. He made a curious impression on Litvinov; he awakened in him respect and liking, and a kind of involuntary compassion.

' I am not in your way then? ' he repeated in a soft, rather languid and faint voice, which was marvellously in keeping with his whole personality.

' No, indeed,' replied Litvinov; ' quite the contrary, I am very glad.'

' Really? Well, then, I am glad too. I have heard a great deal about you; I know what you are engaged in, and what your plans are. It's a good work. That's why you were silent this evening.'

' Yes; you too said very little, I fancy,' observed Litvinov.

Potugin sighed. ' The others said enough and to spare. I listened. Well,' he added, after a moment's pause, raising his eyebrows with a rather humorous expression, ' did you like our building of the Tower of Babel? '

' That's just what it was. You have expressed it capitally. I kept wanting to ask those gentlemen what they were in such a fuss about.'

Potugin sighed again.

' That's the whole point of it, that they don't know that themselves. In former days the expression used about them would have been: " they are the blind instruments of higher ends "; well, nowadays we make use of sharper epithets. And take note that I am not in the least intending to blame them; I will say more, they are all . . . that is, almost all, excellent people. Of Madame Suhantchikov, for instance, I know for certain much that is good; she gave away the last of her fortune to two poor nieces. Even admitting that the desire of doing something picturesque, of showing herself off, was not without its influence on her, still you will agree that it was a remarkable act of self-sacrifice in a woman not herself well-off! Of Mr. Pishtchalkin there is no need to speak even; the peasants of his district will certainly in time present him with a silver bowl like a pumpkin, and perhaps even a holy picture representing his patron saint, and though he will tell them in his speech of thanks that he does not deserve such an honour, he won't tell the truth there; he does deserve it. Mr. Bambaev, your friend, has a wonderfully good heart; it's true that it's with him as with the poet Yazikov, who they say used to sing the praises of Bacchic revelry, sitting over a book and sipping water; his enthusiasm is completely without a special object, still it is enthusiasm; and Mr. Voroshilov, too, is the most good-natured fellow; like all his sort, all men who've taken the first prizes at school, he's an *aide-de-camp* of the sciences, and he even holds his tongue sententiously, but then he is so young. Yes, yes, they are all excellent people, and when you come to results, there's nothing to show for it; the ingredients are all first-rate, but the dish is not worth eating.'

Litvinov listened to Potugin with growing astonishment: every phrase, every turn of his slow but self-confident speech betrayed both the power of speaking and the desire to speak.

Potugin did, in fact, like speaking, and could speak well; but, as a man in whom life had succeeded in wearing away vanity, he waited with philosophic calm for a good opportunity, a meeting with a kindred spirit.

' Yes, yes,' he began again, with the special dejected but not peevish humour peculiar to him, ' it is all very strange. And there is something else I want you to note. Let a dozen Englishmen, for example, come together, and they will at once begin to talk of the submarine telegraph, or the tax on paper, or a method of tanning rats' skins,—of something, that's to say, practical and definite; a dozen Germans, and of course Schleswig-Holstein and the unity of Germany will be brought on the scene; given a dozen Frenchmen, and the conversation will infallibly turn upon amorous adventures, however much you try to divert them from the subject; but let a dozen Russians meet together, and instantly there springs up the question—you had an opportunity of being convinced of the fact this evening—the question of the significance and the future of Russia, and in terms so general, beginning with creation, without facts or conclusions. They worry and worry away at that unlucky subject, as children chew away at a bit of india-rubber —neither for pleasure nor profit, as the saying is. Well, then, of course the rotten West comes in for its share. It's a curious thing, it beats us at every point, this West—but yet we declare that it's rotten! And if only we had a genuine contempt for it,' pursued Potugin, ' but that's really all cant and humbug. We can do well enough as far as abuse goes, but the opinion of the West is the only thing we value, the opinion, that's to say, of the Parisian loafers. . . . I know a man—a good fellow, I fancy—the father of a family, and no longer young; he was thrown into deep dejection for some days because in a Parisian restaurant he had asked for *une portion de biftek aux pommes de terre*, and a real Frenchman thereupon shouted: *Garçon! biftek pommes!* My friend was ready to die with shame, and after that he shouted everywhere, *Biftek pommes!* and taught others to do the same. The very *cocottes* are surprised at the reverential trepidation with which our young barbarians enter their shameful drawing-rooms. "Good God!" they are thinking, " is this really where I am, with no less a person than Anna Deslions herself! " '

' Tell me, pray,' continued Litvinov, ' to what do you ascribe the influence Gubaryov undoubtedly has over all about him? Is it his talent, his abilities? '

' No, no; there is nothing of that sort about him. . . .'

' His personal character is it, then? '

' Not that either, but he has a strong will. We Slavs, for the most part, as we all know, are badly off for that commodity, and we grovel before it. It is Mr. Gubaryov's will to be a ruler, and every one has recognised him as a ruler. What would you have? The government has freed us from the dependence of serfdom—and many thanks to it! but the habits of slavery are too deeply ingrained in us; we cannot easily be rid of them. We want a master in everything and everywhere; as a rule this master is a living person, sometimes it is some so-called tendency which gains authority over us. . . . At present, for instance, we are all the bondslaves of natural science. . . . Why, owing to what causes, we take this bondage upon us, that is a matter difficult to see into; but such seemingly is our nature. But the great thing is, that we should have a master. Well, here he is amongst us; that means he is ours, and we can afford to despise everything else! Simply slaves! And our pride is slavish, and slavish too is our humility. If a new master arises—it's all over with the old one. Then it was Yakov, and now it is Sidor; we box Yakov's ears and kneel to Sidor! Call to mind how many tricks of that sort have been played amongst us! We talk of scepticism as our special characteristic; but even in our scepticism we are not like a free man fighting with a sword, but like a lackey hitting out with his fist, and very likely he is doing even that at his master's bidding. Then, we are a soft people too; it's not difficult to keep the curb on us. So that's the way Mr. Gubaryov has become a power among us; he has chipped and chipped away at one point, till he has chipped himself into success. People see that he is a man who has a great opinion of himself, who believes in himself, and commands. That's the great thing, that he can command; it follows that he must be right, and we ought to obey him. All our sects, our Onuphrists and Akulinists, were founded exactly in that way. He who holds the rod is the corporal.'

Potugin's cheeks were flushed and his eyes grew dim; but, strange to say, his speech, cruel and even malicious as it was, had no touch of bitterness, but rather of sorrow, genuine and sincere sorrow.

'How did you come to know Gubaryov?' asked Litvinov.

'I have known him a long while. And observe, another peculiarity among us; a certain writer, for example, spent his whole life in inveighing in prose and verse against drunkenness, and attacking the system of the drink monopoly, and lo and behold! he went and bought two spirit distilleries and opened a hundred drink-shops—and it made no difference! Any other man might have been wiped off the face of the earth, but he was not even reproached for it. And here is Mr. Gubaryov; he is a Slavophil and a democrat and a socialist and anything you like, but his property has been and is still managed by his brother, a master of the old style, one of those who were famous for their fists. And the very Madame Suhantchikov, who makes Mrs. Beecher Stowe box Tentelyev's ears, is positively in the dust before Gubaryov's feet. And you know the only thing he has to back him is that he reads clever books, and always gets at the pith of them. You could see for yourself to-day what sort of gift he has for expression; and thank God, too, that he does talk little, and keeps in his shell. For when he is in good spirits, and lets himself go, then it's more than even I, patient as I am, can stand. He begins by coarse joking and telling filthy anecdotes . . . yes, really, our majestic Mr. Gubaryov tells filthy anecdotes, and guffaws so revoltingly over them all the time.'

'Are you so patient?' observed Litvinov. 'I should have supposed the contrary. But let me ask your name and your father's name?'

Potugin sipped a little kirsch-wasser.

'My name is Sozont. . . . Sozont Ivanitch. They gave me that magnificent name in honour of a kinsman, an archimandrite, to whom I am indebted for nothing else. I am, if I may venture so to express myself, of most reverend stock. And as for your doubts about my patience, they are quite groundless: I am very patient. I served for twenty-two years under the authority of my own uncle, an actual councillor of state, Irinarh Potugin. You don't know him? '

' No.'

' I congratulate you. No, I am patient. "But let us return to our first head," as my esteemed colleague, who was burned alive some centuries ago, the protopope Avvakum, used to say. I am amazed, my dear sir, at my fellow-countrymen. They are all depressed, they all walk with downcast heads, and at the same time they are all filled with hope, and on the smallest excuse they lose their heads and fly off into ecstasies. Look at the Slavophils even, among whom Mr. Gubaryov reckons himself: they are most excellent people, but there is the same mixture of despair and exultation, they too live in the future tense. Everything will be, will be, if you please. In reality there is nothing done, and Russia for ten whole centuries has created nothing of its own, either in government, in law, in science, in art, or even in handi-craft. . . . But wait a little, have patience; it is all coming. And why is it coming; give us leave to inquire? Why because we, to be sure, the cultured classes are all worthless; but the people . . . Oh, the great people! You see that peasant's smock? That is the source that everything is to come from. All the other idols have broken down; let us have faith in the smock-frock. Well, but suppose the smock-frock fails us? No, it will not fail. Read Kohanovsky, and cast your eyes up to heaven! Really, if I were a painter, I would paint a picture of this sort: a cultivated man standing before a peasant, doing him homage: heal me, dear master-peasant, I am perishing of disease; and a peasant doing homage in his turn to the cultivated man: teach me, dear master-gentleman, I am perishing from ignorance. Well, and of course, both are standing still. But what we ought to do is to feel really humble for a little—not only in words—and to borrow from our elder brothers what they have invented already before us and better than us! Waiter, *noch ein Gläschen Kirsch!* You mustn't think I'm a drunkard, but alcohol loosens my tongue.'

' After what you have just said,' observed Litvinov with a smile, ' I need not even inquire to which party you belong, and what is your opinion about Europe. But let me make one observation to you. You say that we ought to borrow from our elder brothers: but how can we borrow without consideration of the conditions of climate and of soil, the local and national peculiarities? My father, I recollect, ordered from Butenop a cast-iron thrashing machine highly recommended; the machine was very good, cer-tainly—but what happened? For five long years it remained useless in the barn, till it was replaced by a wooden American one—far more suitable to our ways and habits, as the American machines are as a rule. One cannot borrow at random, Sozont Ivanitch.'

Potugin lifted his head.

' I did not expect such a criticism as that from you, excellent Grigory Mihalovitch,' he began, after a moment's pause. ' Who wants to make you borrow at random? Of course you steal what belongs to another man, not because it is some one else's, but because it suits you; so it follows that you consider, you make a selection. And as for results, pray don't let us be unjust to ourselves; there will be originality enough in them by virtue of those very local, climatic, and other conditions which you mention. Only lay good food before it, and the natural stomach will digest it in its own way; and in time, as the organism gains in vigour, it will give it a sauce of its own. Take our language even as an instance. Peter the Great deluged it with thousands of foreign words, Dutch, French, and German; those words expressed ideas with which the Russian people had to be familiarised; without scruple or ceremony Peter poured them wholesale by bucketsful into us. At first, of course, the result was something of a monstrous product; but later there began precisely that process of digestion to which I have alluded. The ideas had been introduced and assimilated; the foreign forms evaporated gradually, and the language found substitutes for them from within itself; and now your humble servant, the most mediocre stylist, will undertake to translate any page you like out of Hegel—yes, indeed, out of Hegel—without making use of a single word not Slavonic. What has happened with the language, one must hope will happen in other departments. It all turns on the question: is it a nature of strong vitality? and our nature —well, it will stand the test; it has gone through greater trials than that. Only nations in a state of nervous debility, feeble nations, need fear for their health and their independence, just as it is only weak-minded people who are capable of falling into triumphant rhapsodies over the fact that we are Russians. I am very careful over my health, but I don't go into ecstasies over it: I should be ashamed.'

'That is all very true, Sozont Ivanitch,' observed Litvinov in his turn; 'but why inevitably expose ourselves to such tests? You say yourself that at first the result was monstrous! Well, what if that monstrous product had persisted? Indeed it has persisted, as you know yourself.'

'Only not in the language—and that means a great deal! And it is our people, not I, who have done it; I am not to blame because they are destined to go through a discipline of this kind. "The Germans have developed in a normal way," cry the Slavophils, "let us too have a normal development!" But how are you to get it when the very first historical step taken by our race—the summoning of a prince from over the sea to rule over them—is an irregularity, an abnormality, which is repeated in every one of us down to the present day; each of us, at least once in his life, has certainly said to something foreign, not Russian: "Come, rule and reign over me!" I am ready, of course, to agree that when we put a foreign substance into our own body we cannot tell for certain what it is we are putting there, bread or poison; yet it is a well-known thing that you can never get from bad to good through what is better, but always through a worse state of transition, and poison too is useful in medicine. It is only fit for fools or knaves to point with triumph to the poverty of the peasants after the emancipation, and the increase of drunkenness since the abolition of the farming of the spirit-tax. . . . Through worse to better!'

Potugin passed his hand over his face. 'You asked me what was my opinion of Europe,' he began again: ' I admire her, and am devoted to her principles to the last degree, and don't in the least think it necessary to conceal the fact. I have long—no, not long—for some time ceased to be afraid to give full expression to my convictions—and I saw that you too had no hesitation in informing Mr. Gubaryov of your own way of thinking. Thank God I have given up paying attention to the ideas and points of view and habits of the man I am conversing with. Really, I know of nothing worse than that quite superfluous cowardice, that cringing desire to be agreeable, by virtue of which you may see an important dignitary among us trying to ingratiate himself with some little student who is quite insignificant in his eyes, positively playing down to him, with all sorts of tricks and devices. Even if we admit that the dignitary may do it out of desire for popularity, what induces us common folk to shuffle and degrade ourselves. Yes, yes, I am a Westerner, I am devoted to Europe: that's to say, speaking more accurately, I am devoted to culture—the culture at which they make fun so wittily among us just now—and to civilisation—yes, yes, that is a better word—and I love it with my whole heart and believe in it, and I have no other belief, and never shall have. That word, ci-vi-li-sa-tion (Potugin pronounced each syllable with full stress and emphasis), is intelligible, and pure, and holy, and all the other ideals, nationality, glory, or what you like—they smell of blood. . . . Away with them! '

' Well, but Russia, Sozont Ivanitch, your country—you love it? '

Potugin passed his hand over his face. ' I love her passionately and passionately hate her.'

Litvinov shrugged his shoulders.

' That's stale, Sozont Ivanitch, that's a commonplace.'

' And what of it? So that's what you're afraid of! A commonplace! I know many excellent commonplaces. Here, for example, Law and Liberty is a well-known commonplace. Why, do you consider it's better as it is with us, lawlessness and beaureaucratic tyranny? And, besides, all those phrases by which so many young heads are turned: vile bourgeoisie, *souveraineté du peuple*, right to labour, aren't they commonplaces too? And as for love, inseparable from hate . . .'

' Byronism,' interposed Litvinov, ' the romanticism of the thirties.'

' Excuse me, you're mistaken; such a mingling of emotions was first mentioned by Catullus, the Roman poet Catullus,[1] two thousand years ago. I have read that, for I know a little Latin, thanks to my clerical origin, if so I may venture to express myself. Yes, indeed, I both love and hate my Russia, my strange, sweet, nasty, precious country. I have left her just now. I want a little fresh air after sitting for twenty years on a clerk's high stool in a government office; I have left Russia, and I am happy and contented here; but I shall soon go back again: I feel that. It's a beautiful land of gardens—but our wild berries will not grow here.'

[1]Odi et amo. Quare id faciam, fortasse requiris.
Nescio: sed fieri sentio, et excrucior.—CATULL 86.

'You are happy and contented, and I too like the place,' said Litvinov, 'and I came here to study; but that does not prevent me from seeing things like that.'

He pointed to two *cocottes* who passed by, attended by a little group of members of the Jockey Club, grimacing and lisping, and to the gambling saloon, full to overflowing in spite of the lateness of the hour.

'And who told you I am blind to that?' Potugin broke in. 'But pardon my saying it, your remark reminds me of the triumphant allusions made by our unhappy journalists at the time of the Crimean war, to the defects in the English War Department, exposed in the *Times*. I am not an optimist myself, and all humanity, all our life, all this comedy with tragic issues presents itself to me in no roseate colours: but why fasten upon the West what is perhaps ingrained in our very human nature? That gambling hall is disgusting, certainly; but is our home-bred card-sharping any lovelier, think you? No, my dear Grigory Mihalovitch, let us be more humble, more retiring. A good pupil sees his master's faults, but he keeps a respectful silence about them; these very faults are of use to him, and set him on the right path. But if nothing will satisfy you but sharpening your teeth on the unlucky West, there goes Prince Kokó at a gallop, he will most likely lose in a quarter of an hour over the green table the hardly earned rent wrung from a hundred and fifty families; his nerves are upset, for I saw him at Marx's to-day turning over a pamphlet of Vaillot. . . . He will be a capital person for you to talk to!'

'But, please, please,' said Litvinov hurriedly, seeing that Potugin was getting up from his place, 'I know Prince Kokó very little, and besides, of course, I greatly prefer talking to you.'

'Thanks very much,' Potugin interrupted him, getting up and making a bow; 'but I have already had a good deal of conversation with you; that's to say, really, I have talked alone, and you have probably noticed yourself that a man is always as it were ashamed and awkward when he has done all the talking, especially so on a first meeting, as if to show what a fine fellow one is. Good-bye for the present. And I repeat I am very glad to have made your acquaintance.'

'But wait a minute, Sozont Ivanitch, tell me at least where you live, and whether you intend to remain here long.'

Potugin seemed a little put out.

'I shall remain about a week in Baden. We can meet here though, at Weber's or at Marx's, or else I will come to you.'

'Still I must know your address.'

'Yes. But you see I am not alone.'

'You are married?' asked Litvinov suddenly.

'No, good heavens! . . . what an absurd idea! But I have a girl with me.' . . .

'Oh!' articulated Litvinov, with a face of studied politeness, as though he would ask pardon, and he dropped his eyes.

'She is only six years old,' pursued Potugin. 'She's an orphan . . . the daughter of a lady . . . a good friend of mine. So we had better meet here. Good-bye.'

He pulled his hat over his curly head, and disappeared quickly. Twice there was a glimpse of him under the gas-lamps in the rather meanly lighted road that leads into the Lichtenthaler Allee.

VI

'A STRANGE MAN!' thought Litvinov, as he turned into the hotel where he was staying; 'a strange man! I must see more of him!' He went into his room; a letter on the table caught his eye. 'Ah! from Tanya!' he thought, and was overjoyed at once; but the letter was from his country place, from his father. Litvinov broke the thick heraldic seal, and was just setting to work to read it . . . when he was struck by a strong, very agreeable, and familiar fragrance, and saw in the window a great bunch of fresh heliotrope in a glass of water. Litvinov bent over them not without amazement, touched them, and smelt them. . . . Something seemed to stir in his memory, something very remote . . . but what, precisely, he could not discover. He rang for the servant and asked him where these flowers had come from. The man replied that they had been brought by a lady who would not give her name, but said that 'Herr Zlitenhov' would be sure to guess who she was by the flowers. Again something stirred in Litvinov's memory. He asked the man what the lady looked like, and the servant informed him that she was tall and grandly dressed and had a veil over her face. 'A Russian countess most likely,' he added.

'What makes you think that?' asked Litvinov.

'She gave me two guldens,' responded the servant with a grin.

Litvinov dismissed him, and for a long while after he stood in deep thought before the window; at last, however, with a wave of his hand, he began again upon the letter from the country. His father poured out to him his usual complaints, asserting that no one would take their corn, even for nothing, that the people had got quite out of all habits of obedience, and that probably the end of the world was coming soon. 'Fancy,' he wrote, among other things, ' my last coachman, the Kalmuck boy, do you remember him? has been bewitched, and the fellow would certainly have died, and I should have had none to drive me, but, thank goodness, some kind folks suggested and advised to send the sick man to Ryazan, to a priest, well-known as a master against witchcraft: and his cure has actually succeeded as well as possible, in confirmation of which I lay before you the letter of the good father as a document.' Litvinov ran through this document with curiosity. In it was set forth: ' that the serving-man Nicanor Dmitriev was beset with a malady which could not be touched by the medical faculty; and this malady was the work of wicked people; but he himself, Nicanor, was the cause of it, since he had not fulfilled his promise to a certain girl, and therefore by the aid of others she had made him unfit for anything, and if I had not appeared to aid him in these circumstances, he would surely have perished utterly, like a worm; but I, trusting in the All-seeing Eye, have become a stay to him in his life; and how I accomplished it, that is a mystery; I beg your excellency not to countenance a girl who has such wicked arts, and even to chide her would be no harm, or she may again work him a mischief.'

Litvinov fell to musing over this document; it brought him a whiff of the desert, of the steppes, of the blind darkness of the life mouldering there, and it seemed a marvellous thing that he should be reading such a letter in Baden, of all places. Meanwhile it had long struck midnight; Litvinov went to bed and put out his light. But he could not get to sleep; the faces he had seen, the talk he had heard, kept coming back and revolving, strangely interwoven and entangled in his burning head, which ached from the fumes of tobacco. Now he seemed to hear Gubaryov's muttering, and fancied his eyes with their dull, persistent stare fastened on the floor; then suddenly those eyes began to glow and leap, and he recognised Madame Suhantchikov, and listened to her shrill voice, and involuntarily repeated after her in a whisper, 'she did, she did, slap his face.' Then the clumsy figure of Potugin passed before him; and for the tenth, and the twentieth time he went over every word he had uttered; then, like a jack in the box, Voroshilov jumped up in his trim coat, which fitted him like a new uniform; and Pishtchalkin gravely and sagaciously nodded his well-cut and truly well-intentioned head; and then Bindasov bawled and swore, and Bambaev fell into tearful transports. . . . And above all—this scent, this persistent, sweet, heavy scent gave him no rest, and grew more and more powerful in the darkness, and more and more importunately it reminded him of something which still eluded his grasp. . . . The idea occurred to Litvinov that the scent of flowers at night in a bedroom was injurious, and he got up, and groping his way to the nosegay, carried it into the next room; but even from there the oppressive fragrance penetrated to him on his pillow and under the counterpane, and he tossed in misery from side to side. A slight delirium had already begun to creep over him; already the priest, 'the master against witchcraft' had twice run across his road in the guise of a very playful hare with a beard and a pig-tail, and Voroshilov was trilling before him, sitting in a huge general's plumed cock-hat like a nightingale in a bush. . . . When suddenly he jumped up in bed, and clasping his hands, cried, 'Can it be she? it can't be!'

But to explain this exclamation of Litvinov's we must beg the indulgent reader to go back a few years with us.

VII

EARLY IN THE FIFTIES, there was living in Moscow, in very straitened circumstances, almost in poverty, the numerous family of the Princes Osinin. These were real princes—not Tartar-Georgians, but pure-blooded descendants of Rurik. Their name is often to be met with in our chronicles under the first grand princes of Moscow, who created a united Russia. They possessed wide acres and many domains. Many a time they were rewarded for 'service and blood and disablement.' They sat in the Council of Boyars. One of them even rose to a very high position. But they fell under the ban of the empire through the plots of enemies 'on a charge of witchcraft and evil philtres,' and they were ruined ' terribly and beyond recall.' They were deprived of their rank, and banished to remote parts; the Osinins fell and had never risen again, had never attained to power again. The ban was taken off in time, and they were even reinstated in their Moscow house and belongings, but it was of no avail. Their family was impoverished, ' run to seed '; it did not revive under Peter, nor under Catherine; and constantly dwindling and growing humbler, it had by now reckoned private stewards, managers of wine-shops, and ward police-inspectors among its members. The family of Osinins, of whom we have made mention, consisted of a husband and wife and five children. It was living near the Dogs' Place, in a one-storied little wooden house, with a striped portico looking on to the street, green lions on the gates, and all the other pretensions of nobility, though it could hardly make both ends meet, was constantly in debt at the green-grocer's, and often sitting without firewood or candles in the winter. The prince himself was a dull, indolent man, who had once been a handsome dandy, but had gone to seed completely. More from regard for his wife, who had been a maid-of-honour, than from respect for his name, he had been presented with one of those old-fashioned Moscow posts that have a small salary, a queer-sounding name, and absolutely no duties attached. He never meddled in anything, and did nothing but smoke from morning till night, breathing heavily, and always wrapped in a dressing-gown. His wife was a sickly irritable woman, for ever worried over domestic trifles— over getting her children placed in government schools, and keeping up her Petersburg connections; she could never accustom herself to her position and her remoteness from the Court.

Litvinov's father had made acquaintance with the Osinins during his residence at Moscow, had had occasion to do them some services, and had once lent them three hundred roubles; and his son often visited them while he was a student; his lodging happened to be at no great distance from their house. But he was not drawn to them simply as near neighbours, nor tempted by their comfortless way of living. He began to be a frequent visitor at their house after he had fallen in love with their eldest daughter Irina.

She had then completed her seventeenth year; she had only just left school, from which her mother withdrew her through a disagreement with the principal. This disagreement arose from the fact that Irina was to have delivered at a public function some verses in French, complimentary to the curator, and just before the performance her place was filled by another girl, the daughter of a very rich spirit-contractor. The princess could not stomach this affront; and indeed Irina herself never forgave the principal for this act of injustice; she had been dreaming beforehand of how she would rise before the eyes of every one, attracting universal attention, and would deliver her speech, and how Moscow would talk about her afterwards! . . . And, indeed, Moscow would have talked about her afterwards. She was a tall, slim girl, with a somewhat hollow chest and narrow unformed shoulders, with a skin of a dead-white, rare at her age, and pure and smooth as china, with thick fair hair; there were darker tresses mingled in a very original way with the light ones. Her features—exquisitely, almost too perfectly, correct—had not yet quite lost the innocent expression that belongs to childhood; the languid curves of her lovely neck, and her smile —half-indifferent, half-weary—betrayed the nervous temperament of a delicate girl; but in the lines of those fine, faintly-smiling lips, of that small, falcon, slightly-narrow nose, there was something wilful and passionate, something dangerous for herself and others. Astounding, really astounding were her eyes, dark grey with greenish lights, languishing, almond-shaped as an Egyptian goddess's, with shining lashes and bold sweep of eyebrow. There was a strange look in those eyes; they seemed looking out intently and thoughtfully—looking out from some unknown depth and distance. At school, Irina had been reputed one of the best pupils for intelligence and abilities, but of uneven temper, fond of power, and headstrong; one classmistress prophesied that her passions would be her ruin—'*vos passions vous perdront*'; on the other hand, another class-mistress censured her for coldness and want of feeling, and called her '*une jeune fille sans cœur.*' Irina's companions thought her proud and reserved: her brothers and sisters stood a little in awe of her: her mother had no confidence in her: and her father felt ill at ease when she fastened her mysterious eyes upon him. But she inspired a feeling of involuntary respect in both her father and her mother, not so much through her qualities, as from a peculiar, vague sense of expectations which she had, in some undefined way, awakened in them.

'You will see, Praskovya Danilovna,' said the old prince one day, taking his pipe out of his mouth, ' our chit of an Irina will give us all a lift in the world yet.'

The princess got angry, and told her husband that he made use of ' *des expressions insupportables*'; afterwards, however, she fell to musing over his words, and repeated through her teeth:

'Well . . . and it would be a good thing if we did get a lift.'

Irina enjoyed almost unlimited freedom in her parents' house; they did not spoil her, they even avoided her a little, but they did not thwart her, and that was all she wanted. . . . Sometimes—during some too humiliating scene—when some tradesman would come and keep shouting, to be heard over the whole court, that he was sick of coming after his money, or their own servants would begin abusing their masters to their face, with 'fine princes you are, to be sure; you may whistle for your supper, and go hungry to bed'—Irina would not stir a muscle; she would sit unmoved, an evil smile on her dark face; and her smile alone was more bitter to her parents than any reproaches, and they felt themselves guilty—

guilty, though guiltless—towards this being on whom had been bestowed, as it seemed, from her very birth, the right to wealth, to luxury, and to homage.

Litvinov fell in love with Irina from the moment he saw her (he was only three years older than she was), but for a long while he failed to obtain not only a response, but even a hearing. Her manner to him was even overcast with a shade of something like hostility; he did in fact wound her pride, and she concealed the wound, and could never forgive it. He was too young and too modest at that time to understand what might be concealed under this hostile, almost contemptuous severity. Often, forgetful of lectures and exercises, he would sit and sit in the Osinins' cheerless drawing-room, stealthily watching Irina, his heart slowly and painfully throbbing and suffocating him; and she would seem angry or bored, would get up and walk about the room, look coldly at him as though he were a table or chair, shrug her shoulders, and fold her arms. Or for a whole evening, even when talking with Litvinov, she would purposely avoid looking at him, as though denying him even that grace. Or she would at last take up a book and stare at it, not reading, but frowning and biting her lips. Or else she would suddenly ask her father or brother aloud: 'What's the German for patience?' He tried to tear himself away from the enchanted circle in which he suffered and struggled impotently like a bird in a trap; he went away from Moscow for a week. He nearly went out of his mind with misery and dulness; he returned quite thin and ill to the Osinins'. . . . Strange to say, Irina too had grown perceptibly thinner during those days; her face had grown pale, her cheeks were wan. . . . But she met him with still greater coldness, with almost malignant indifference; as though he had intensified that secret wound he had dealt at her pride. . . . She tortured him in this way for two months. Then everything was transformed in one day. It was as though love had broken into flame with the heat, or had dropped down from a storm-cloud. One day—long will he remember that day—he was once more sitting in the Osinins' drawing-room at the window, and was looking mechanically into the street. There was vexation and weariness in his heart, he despised himself, and yet he could not move from his place. . . . He thought that if a river ran there under the window, he would throw himself in, with a shudder of fear, but without a regret. Irina placed herself not far from him, and was somehow strangely silent and motionless. For some days now she had not talked to him at all, or to any one else; she kept sitting, leaning on her elbows, as though she were in perplexity, and only rarely she looked slowly round. This cold torture was at last more than Litvinov could bear; he got up, and without saying good-bye, he began to look for his hat. 'Stay,' sounded suddenly, in a soft whisper. Litvinov's heart throbbed, he did not at once recognise Irina's voice; in that one word, there was a ring of something that had never been in it before. He lifted his head and was stupefied; Irina was looking fondly—yes, fondly at him. 'Stay,' she repeated; 'don't go. I want to be with you.' Her voice sank still lower.

'Don't go. . . . I wish it.' Understanding nothing, not fully conscious
what he was doing, he drew near her, stretched out his hands. . . . She
gave him both of hers at once, then smiling, flushing hotly, she turned
away, and still smiling, went out of the room. She came back a few minutes
later with her youngest sister, looked at him again with the same prolonged tender gaze, and made him sit near her. . . . At first she could
say nothing; she only sighed and blushed; then she began, timidly as it
were, to question him about his pursuits, a thing she had never done before.
In the evening of the same day, she tried several times to beg his forgiveness for not having done him justice before, assured him she had now
become quite different, astonished him by a sudden outburst of republicanism (he had at that time a positive hero-worship for Robespierre, and
did not presume to criticise Marat aloud), and only a week later he
knew that she loved him. Yes; he long remembered that first day . . . but
he did not forget those that came after either—those days, when still forcing
himself to doubt, afraid to believe in it, he saw clearly, with transports of
rapture, almost of dread, bliss unhoped for coming to life, growing, irresistibly carrying everything before it, reaching him at last. Then followed the radiant moments of first love—moments which are not destined
to be, and could not fittingly be, repeated in the same life. Irina became
all at once as docile as a lamb, as soft as silk, and boundlessly kind; she
began giving lessons to her younger sisters—not on the piano, she was no
musician, but in French and English; she read their school-books with
them, and looked after the housekeeping; everything was amusing and
interesting to her; she would sometimes chatter incessantly, and sometimes sink into speechless tenderness; she made all sorts of plans, and was
lost in endless anticipations of what she would do when she was married
to Litvinov (they never doubted that their marriage would come to pass),
and how together they would . . . 'Work?' prompted Litvinov. . . .
'Yes; work,' repeated Irina, 'and read . . . but travel before all things.'
She particularly wanted to leave Moscow as soon as possible, and when
Litvinov reminded her that he had not yet finished his course of study at
the university, she always replied, after a moment's thought, that it was
quite possible to finish his studies at Berlin or . . . somewhere or other.
Irina was very little reserved in the expression of her feelings, and so
her relations with Litvinov did not long remain a secret from the prince
and princess. Rejoice they could not; but, taking all circumstances into
consideration, they saw no necessity for putting a veto on it at once.
Litvinov's fortune was considerable. . . .
    'But his family, his family!' . . . protested the princess. 'Yes, his family,
of course,' replied the prince; 'but at least he's not quite a plebeian; and,
what's the principal point, Irina, you know, will not listen to us. Has there
ever been a time when she did not do what she chose? *Vous connaissez sa
violence!* Besides, there is nothing fixed definitely yet.' So reasoned the
prince, but mentally he added, however: 'Madame Litvinov—is that all?
I had expected something else.' Irina took complete possession of her

future *fiancé*, and indeed he himself eagerly surrendered himself into her hands. It was as if he had fallen into a rapid river, and had lost himself. . . . And bitter and sweet it was to him, and he regretted nothing and heeded nothing. To reflect on the significance and the duties of marriage, or whether he, so hopelessly enslaved, could be a good husband, and what sort of wife Irina would make, and whether their relations to one another were what they should be—was more than he could bring himself to. His blood was on fire, he could think of nothing, only—to follow her, be with her, for the future without end, and then—let come what may!

But in spite of the complete absence of opposition on Litvinov's side, and the wealth of impulsive tenderness on Irina's, they did not get on quite without any misunderstandings and quarrels. One day he ran to her straight from the university in an old coat and ink-stained hands. She rushed to meet him with her accustomed fond welcome; suddenly she stopped short. ' You have no gloves,' she said abruptly, and added directly after: ' Fie! what a student you are! '

' You are too particular, Irina,' remarked Litvinov.

' You are a regular student,' she repeated. '*Vous n'êtes pas distingué*'; and turning her back on him she went out of the room. It is true that an hour later she begged him to forgive her. . . . As a rule she readily censured herself and accused herself to him; but, strange to say, she often almost with tears blamed herself for evil propensities which she had not, and obstinately denied her real defects. Another time he found her in tears, her head in her hands, and her hair in disorder; and when, all in agitation, he asked her the cause of her grief, she pointed with her finger at her own bosom without speaking. Litvinov gave an involuntary shiver. ' Consumption! ' flashed through his brain, and he seized her hand.

' Are you ill, Irina? ' he articulated in a shaking voice. (They had already begun on great occasions to call each other by their first names.) ' Let me go at once for a doctor.'

But Irina did not let him finish; she stamped with her foot in vexation. ' I am perfectly well. . . . but this dress . . . don't you understand? '

' What is it? . . . this dress,' he repeated in bewilderment.

' What is it? Why, that I have no other, and that it is old and disgusting, and I am obliged to put on this dress every day . . . even when you— Grisha—Grigory, come here. . . . You will leave off loving me, at last, seeing me so slovenly! '

' For goodness sake, Irina, what are you saying? That dress is very nice. . . . It is dear to me too because I saw you for the first time in it, darling.' Irina blushed.

' Do not remind me, if you please, Grigory Mihalovitch, that I had no other dress even then.'

' But I assure you, Irina Pavlovna, it suits you so exquisitely.'

' No, it is horrid, horrid,' she persisted, nervously pulling at her long, soft curls. ' Ugh, this poverty, poverty and squalor! How is one to escape from this sordidness! How get out of this squalor! '

Litvinov did not know what to say, and slightly turned away from her.

All at once Irina jumped up from her chair, and laid both her hands on his shoulders.

'But you love me, Grisha? You love me?' she murmured, putting her face close to him, and her eyes, still filled with tears, sparkled with the light of happiness, 'You love me, dear, even in this horrid dress?'

Litvinov flung himself on his knees before her.

'Ah, love me, love me, my sweet, my saviour,' she whispered, bending over him.

So the days flew, the weeks passed, and though as yet there had been no formal declaration, though Litvinov still deferred his demand for her hand, not, certainly, at his own desire, but awaiting directions from Irina (she remarked sometimes that they were both ridiculously young, and they must add at least a few weeks more to their years), still everything was moving to a conclusion, and the future as it came nearer grew more and more clearly defined, when suddenly an event occurred, which scattered all their dreams and plans like light roadside dust.

VIII

THAT WINTER the court visited Moscow. One festivity followed another; in its turn came the customary great ball in the Hall of Nobility. The news of this ball, only, it is true, in the form of an announcement in the *Political Gazette*, reached even the little house in Dogs' Place. The prince was the first to be roused by it; he decided at once that he must not fail to go and take Irina, that it would be unpardonable to let slip the opportunity of seeing their sovereigns, that for the old nobility this constituted indeed a duty in its own way. He defended his opinion with a peculiar warmth, not habitual in him; the princess agreed with him to some extent, and only sighed over the expense; but a resolute opposition was displayed by Irina. 'It is not necessary, I will not go,' she replied to all her parents' arguments. Her obstinacy reached such proportions that the old prince decided at last to beg Litvinov to try to persuade her, by reminding her among other reasons that it was not proper for a young girl to avoid society, that she ought to 'have this experience,' that no one ever saw her anywhere, as it was. Litvinov undertook to lay these 'reasons' before her. Irina looked steadily and scrutinisingly at him, so steadily and scrutinisingly that he was confused, and then, playing with the ends of her sash, she said calmly:

'Do you desire it, you?'

'Yes. . . . I suppose so,' replied Litvinov hesitatingly. 'I agree with your papa. . . . Indeed, why should you not go . . . to see the world, and show yourself,' he added with a short laugh.

'To show myself,' she repeated slowly. 'Very well then, I will go. . . . Only remember, it is you yourself who desired it.'

'That's to say, I——.' Litvinov was beginning.

'You yourself have desired it,' she interposed. 'And here is one condition more; you must promise me that you will not be at this ball.'

'But why?'

'I wish it to be so.'

Litvinov unclasped his hands.

'I submit . . . but I confess I should so have enjoyed seeing you in all your grandeur, witnessing the sensation you are certain to make. . . . How proud I should be of you!' he added with a sigh.

Irina laughed.

'All the grandeur will consist of a white frock, and as for the sensation. . . . Well, any way, I wish it.'

'Irina, darling, you seem to be angry?'

Irina laughed again.

'Oh, no! I am not angry. Only, Grisha . . .' (She fastened her eyes on him, and he thought he had never before seen such an expression in them.) 'Perhaps, it must be,' she added in an undertone.

'But, Irina, you love me, dear?'

'I love you,' she answered with almost solemn gravity, and she clasped his hand firmly like a man.

All the following days Irina was busily occupied over her dress and her coiffure; on the day before the ball she felt unwell, she could not sit still, and twice she burst into tears in solitude; before Litvinov she wore the same uniform smile. . . . She treated him, however, with her old tenderness, but carelessly, and was constantly looking at herself in the glass. On the day of the ball she was silent and pale, but collected. At nine o'clock in the evening Litvinov came to look at her. When she came to meet him in a white tarlatan gown, with a spray of small blue flowers in her slightly raised hair, he almost uttered a cry; she seemed to him so lovely and stately beyond what was natural to her years. 'Yes, she has grown up since this morning!' he thought, 'and how she holds herself! That's what race does!' Irina stood before him, her hands hanging loose, without smiles or affectation, and looked resolutely, almost boldly, not at him, but away into the distance straight before her.

'You are just like a princess in a story book,' said Litvinov at last. 'You are like a warrior before the battle, before victory. . . . You did not allow me to go to this ball,' he went on, while she remained motionless as before, not because she was not listening to him, but because she was following another inner voice, 'but you will not refuse to accept and take with you these flowers?'

He offered her a bunch of heliotrope. She looked quickly at Litvinov, stretched out her hand, and suddenly seizing the end of the spray which decorated her hair, she said:

'Do you wish it, Grisha? Only say the word, and I will tear off all this, and stop at home.'

Litvinov's heart seemed fairly bursting. Irina's hand had already snatched the spray. . . .

'No, no, what for? ' he interposed hurriedly, in a rush of generous and magnanimous feeling, 'I am not an egoist. . . . Why should I restrict your freedom . . . when I know that your heart—'

'Well, don't come near me, you will crush my dress,' she said hastily.

Litvinov was disturbed.

'But you will take the nosegay? ' he asked.

'Of course; it is very pretty, and I love that scent. *Merci*—I shall keep it in memory—'

'Of your first coming out,' observed Litvinov, 'your first triumph. '

Irina looked over her shoulder at herself in the glass, scarcely bending her figure.

'And do I really look so nice? You are not partial? '

Litvinov overflowed in enthusiastic praises. Irina was already not listening to him, and holding the flowers up to her face, she was again looking away into the distance with her strange, as it were, overshadowed, dilated eyes, and the ends of her delicate ribbons stirred by a faint current of air rose slightly behind her shoulders like wings.

The prince made his appearance, his hair well becurled, in a white tie, and a shabby black evening coat, with the medal of nobility on a Vladimir ribbon in his buttonhole. After him came the princess in a china silk dress of antique cut, and with the anxious severity under which mothers try to conceal their agitation, set her daughter to rights behind, that is to say, quite needlessly shook out the folds of her gown. An antiquated hired coach with seats for four, drawn by two shaggy hacks, crawled up to the steps, its wheels grating over the frozen mounds of unswept snow, and a decrepit groom in a most unlikely-looking livery came running out of the passage, and with a sort of desperate courage announced that the carriage was ready. . . . After giving a blessing for the night to the children left at home, and enfolding themselves in their fur wraps, the prince and princess went out to the steps; Irina in a little cloak, too thin and too short—how she hated the little cloak at that moment!—followed them in silence. Litvinov escorted them outside, hoping for a last look from Irina, but she took her seat in the carriage without turning her head.

About midnight he walked under the windows of the Hall of Nobility. Countless lights of huge candelabra shone with brilliant radiance through the red curtains; and the whole square, blocked with carriages, was ringing with the insolent, festive, seductive strains of a waltz of Strauss.

The next day at one o'clock, Litvinov betook himself to the Osinins'. He found no one at home but the prince, who informed him at once that Irina had a headache, that she was in bed, and would not get up till the evening, that such an indisposition was however little to be wondered at after a first ball.

'*C'est très naturel, vous savez, dans les jeunes filles*,' he added in French, somewhat to Litvinov's surprise; the latter observed at the same instant that the prince was not in his dressing-gown as usual, but was wearing a coat.

'And besides,' continued Osinin, 'she may well be a little upset after the events of yesterday!'

'Events?' muttered Litvinov.

'Yes, yes, events, events, *de vrais événements*. You cannot imagine, Grigory Mihalovitch, *quel succès elle a eu!* The whole court noticed her! Prince Alexandr Fedorovitch said that her place was not here, and that she reminded him of Countess Devonshire. You know . . . that . . . celebrated. . . . And old Blazenkrampf declared in the hearing of all, that Irina was *la reine du bal*, and desired to be introduced to her; he was introduced to me too, that's to say, he told me that he remembered me a hussar, and asked me where I was holding office now. Most entertaining man that Count, and such an *adorateur du beau sexe!* But that's not all; my princess . . . they gave her no peace either: Natalya Nikitishna herself conversed with her . . . what more could we have? Irina danced *avec tous les meilleurs cavaliers;* they kept bringing them up to me. . . . I positively lost count of them. Would you believe it, they were all flocking about us in crowds; in the mazurka they did nothing but seek her out. One foreign diplomatist, hearing she was a Moscow girl, said to the Tsar: '*Sire,*' he said, '*décidément c'est Moscou qui est le centre de votre empire!*' and another diplomatist added: '*C'est une vraie révolution, Sire—révélation* or *révolution* . . . something of that sort. Yes, yes, it was. I tell you it was something extraordinary.'

'Well, and Irina Pavlovna herself?' inquired Litvinov, whose hands and feet had grown cold hearing the prince's speech, 'did she enjoy herself, did she seem pleased?'

'Of course she enjoyed herself; how could she fail to be pleased? But, as you know, she's not to be seen through at a glance! Every one was saying to me yesterday: it is really surprising! *jamais on ne dirait que mademoiselle votre fille est à son premier bal*. Count Reisenbach among the rest . . . you know him most likely.'

'No, I don't know him at all, and have never heard of him.'

'My wife's cousin.'

'I don't know him.'

'A rich man, a chamberlain, living in Petersburg, in the swim of things; in Livonia every one is in his hands. Hitherto he has neglected us . . . but there, I don't bear him ill-will for that. *J'ai l'humeur facile, comme vous savez*. Well, that's the kind of man he is. He sat near Irina, conversed with her for a quarter of an hour, not more, and said afterwards to my princess: "*Ma cousine,*" he says, "*votre fille est une perle; c'est une perfection*, every one is congratulating me on such a niece. . . ." And afterwards I look round—and he had gone up to a . . . a very great personage, and was talking, and kept looking at Irina . . . and the personage was looking at her too.' . . .

'And so Irina Pavlovna will not appear all day?' Litvinov asked again.

'Quite so; her head aches very badly. She told me to greet you from her, and thank you for your flowers, *qu'on a trouvé charmant*. She needs rest.

. . . The princess has gone out on a round of visits . . . and I myself . . .
you see. . . .'

The prince cleared his throat, and began to fidget as though he were at a
loss what to add further. Litvinov took his hat, and saying he did not want
to disturb him, and would call again later to inquire after her health, he
went away.

A few steps from the Osinins' house he saw an elegant carriage for two
persons standing before the police sentry-box. A groom in livery, equally
elegant, was bending negligently from the box, and inquiring of the Finnish
police-sergeant whereabouts Prince Pavel Vassilyevitch Osinin lived. Litvinov glanced at the carriage; in it sat a middle-aged man of bloated complexion, with a wrinkled and haughty face, a Greek nose, and an evil mouth,
muffled in a sable wrap, by all outward signs a very great man indeed.

IX

Litvinov did not keep his promise of returning later; he reflected that it
would be better to defer his visit till the following day. When he went
into the too familiar drawing-room at about twelve o'clock, he found there
the two youngest princesses, Viktorinka and Kleopatrinka. He greeted them,
and then inquired, ' Was Irina Pavlovna better, and could he see her? '

' Irinotchka has gone away with mammy,' replied Viktorinka; she lisped
a little, but was more forward than her sister.

' How . . . gone away? ' repeated Litvinov, and there was a sort of still
shudder in the very bottom of his heart. ' Does she not, does she not look
after you about this time, and give you your lessons? '

' Irinotchka will not give us any lessons any more now,' answered Viktorinka. ' Not any more now,' Kleopatrinka repeated after her.

' Is your papa at home? ' asked Litvinov.

' Papa is not at home,' continued Viktorinka, ' and Irinotchka is not well;
all night long she was crying and crying. . . .'

' Crying? '

' Yes, crying . . . Yegorovna told me, and her eyes are so red, they are
quite in-inflamed. . . .'

Litvinov walked twice up and down the room shuddering as though with
cold, and went back to his lodging. He experienced a sensation like that
which gains possession of a man when he looks down from a high tower;
everything failed within him, and his head was swimming slowly with a
sense of nausea. Dull stupefaction, and thoughts scurrying like mice, vague
terror, and the numbness of expectation, and curiosity—strange, almost
malignant—and the weight of crushed tears in his heavy laden breast, on
his lips the forced empty smile, and a meaningless prayer—addressed to
no one. . . . Oh, how bitter it all was, and how hideously degrading!
' Irina does not want to see me,' was the thought that was incessantly
revolving in his brain; ' so much is clear; but why is it? What can have

happened at that ill-fated ball? And how is such a change possible all at once? So suddenly. . . .' People always see death coming suddenly, but they can never get accustomed to its suddenness, they feel it senseless. ' She sends no message for me, does not want to explain herself to me. . . .'

' Grigory Mihalitch,' called a strained voice positively in his ear.

Litvinov started, and saw before him his servant with a note in his hand. He recognised Irina's writing. . . . Before he had broken the seal, he had a foreknowledge of woe, and bent his head on his breast and hunched his shoulders, as though shrinking from the blow.

He plucked up courage at last, and tore open the envelope all at once. On a small sheet of notepaper were the following lines:

' Forgive me, Grigory Mihalitch. All is over between us; I am going away to Petersburg. I am dreadfully unhappy, but the thing is done. It seems my fate . . . but no, I do not want to justify myself. My presentiments have been realised. Forgive me, forget me; I am not worthy of you.—Irina. Be magnanimous: do not try to see me.'

Litvinov read these five lines, and slowly dropped on to the sofa, as though some one had dealt him a blow on the breast. He dropped the note, picked it up, read it again, whispered ' to Petersburg,' and dropped it again; that was all. There even came upon him a sense of peace; he even, with his hands thrown behind him, smoothed the pillow under his head. ' Men wounded to death don't fling themselves about,' he thought, ' as it has come, so it has gone. All this is natural enough: I always expected it. . . .' (He was lying to himself; he had never expected anything like it.) ' Crying? . . . Was she crying? . . . What was she crying for? Why, she did not love me! But all that is easily understood and in accordance with her character. She—she is not worthy of me. . . . That's it! ' (He laughed bitterly.) ' She did not know herself what power was latent in her,—well, convinced of it in her effect at the ball, was it likely she would stay with an insignificant student?—all that's easily understood.'

But then he remembered her tender words, her smile, and those eyes, those never to be forgotten eyes, which he would never see again, which used to shine and melt at simply meeting his eyes; he recalled one swift, timorous, burning kiss—and suddenly he fell to sobbing, sobbing convulsively, furiously, vindictively; turned over on his face, and choking and stifling with frenzied satisfaction as though thirsting to tear himself to pieces with all around him, he turned his hot face in the sofa pillow, and bit it in his teeth.

Alas! the gentleman whom Litvinov had seen the day before in the carriage was no other than the cousin of the Princess Osinin, the rich chamberlain, Count Reisenbach. Noticing the sensation produced by Irina on certain personages of the highest rank, and instantaneously reflecting what advantages might *mit etwas Accuratesse* be derived from the fact, the count made his plan at once like a man of energy and a skilful courtier. He decided to act swiftly, in Napoleonic style. ' I will take that original girl into my house,' was what he meditated, ' in Petersburg; I will make her my heiress, devil take me, of my whole property even; as I have no children. She is my niece, and my countess is dull all alone. . . . It's always more agreeable to have a pretty face in one's drawing-room. . . . Yes, yes; . . . that's it; *es ist eine Idee, es ist eine Idee!* ' He would have to dazzle, bewilder, and impress the parents. ' They've not enough to eat'—the count pursued his reflection when he was in the carriage and on his way to Dogs' Place—' so, I warrant, they won't be obstinate. They're not such oversentimental folks either. I might give them a sum of money down into the bargain. And she? She will consent. Honey is sweet—she had a taste of it last night. It's a whim on my part, granted; let them profit by it, . . . the fools. I shall say to them one thing and another . . . and you must decide—otherwise I shall adopt another—an orphan—which would be still more suitable. Yes or no— twenty-four hours I fix for the term—*und damit Punctum.*'

And with these very words on his lips, the count presented himself before the prince, whom he had forewarned of his visit the evening before at the ball. On the result of this visit it seems hardly worth while to enlarge further. The count was not mistaken in his prognostications: the prince and princess were in fact not obstinate, and accepted the sum of money; and Irina did in fact consent before the allotted term had expired. It was not easy for her to break off her relations with Litvinov; she loved him; and after sending him her note, she almost kept her bed, weeping continually, and grew thin and wan. But for all that, a month later the princess carried her off to Petersburg, and established her at the count's; committing her to the care of the countess, a very kind-hearted woman, but with the brain of a hen, and something of a hen's exterior.

Litvinov threw up the university, and went home to his father in the country. Little by little his wound healed. At first he had no news of Irina, and indeed he avoided all conversation that touched on Petersburg and Petersburg society. Later on, by degrees, rumours—not evil exactly, but curious—began to circulate about her; gossip began to be busy about her. The name of the young Princess Osinin, encircled in splendour, impressed with quite a special stamp, began to be more and more frequently mentioned even in provincial circles. It was pronounced with curiosity, respect, and envy, as men at one time used to mention the name of the Countess Vorotinsky. At last the news came of her marriage. But Litvinov hardly paid attention to these last tidings; he was already betrothed to Tatyana.

Now, the reader can no doubt easily understand exactly what it was Litvinov recalled when he cried, ' Can it be she? ' and therefore we will return to Baden and take up again the broken thread of our story.

X

LITVINOV FELL ASLEEP very late, and did not sleep long; the sun had only just risen when he got out of bed. The summits of dark mountains visible from his windows stood out in misty purple against the clear sky. ' How cool it must be there under the trees! ' he thought; and he dressed in haste, and looked with indifference at the bouquet which had opened more luxuriantly after the night; he took a stick and set off towards the ' Old Castle ' on the famous ' Cliffs.' Invigorating and soothing was the caressing contact of the fresh morning about him. He drew long breaths, and stepped out boldly; the vigorous health of youth was throbbing in every vein; the very earth seemed springy under his light feet. With every step he grew more light-hearted, more happy; he walked in the dewy shade in the thick sand of the little paths, beside the fir-trees that were fringed with the vivid green of the spring shoots at the end of every twig. ' How jolly it is! ' he kept repeating to himself. Suddenly he heard the sound of familiar voices; he looked ahead and saw Voroshilov and Bambaev coming to meet him. The sight of them jarred upon him; he rushed away like a school-boy avoiding his teacher, and hid himself behind a bush. . . . ' My Creator! ' he prayed, ' mercifully remove my countrymen! ' He felt that he would not have grudged any money at the moment if only they did not see him. . . . And they actually did not see him: the Creator was merciful to him. Voroshilov, in his self-confident military voice, was holding forth to Bambaev on the various phases of Gothic architecture, and Bambaev only grunted approvingly; it was obvious that Voroshilov had been dinning his phrases into him a long while, and the good-natured enthusiast was beginning to be bored. Compressing his lips and craning his neck, Litvinov listened a long while to their retreating footsteps; for a long time the accents of instructive discourse—now guttural, now nasal—reached his ears; at last, all was still again. Litvinov breathed freely, came out of his ambush, and walked on.

For three hours he wandered about the mountains. Sometimes he left the path, and jumped from rock to rock, slipping now and then on the smooth moss; then he would sit down on a fragment of the cliff under an oak or a beech, and muse on pleasant fancies to the never-ceasing gurgle of the little rills overgrown with ferns, the soothing rustle of the leaves, and the shrill notes of a solitary blackbird. A light and equally pleasant drowsiness began to steal over him, it seemed to approach him caressingly, and he dropped asleep . . . but suddenly he smiled and looked round; the gold and green of the forest, and the moving foliage beat down softly on his eyes—and again he smiled and again closed them. He began to want breakfast, and he made his way towards the old castle where for a few kreutzers he could get a glass of good milk and coffee. But he had hardly had time to establish himself at one of the little white-painted tables set on the platform before the castle, when the heavy tramping of horses was heard, and three open carriages drove up, out of which stepped a rather numerous company of ladies and gentlemen. . . . Litvinov at once recognised them as Russians, though they were all talking French . . . just because they were all talking French. The ladies' dresses were marked by a studied elegance; the gentlemen wore close-fitting coats with waists—which is not altogether usual nowadays—grey trousers of fancy material, and very glossy town hats. A narrow black cravat closely fettered the neck of each of these gentlemen, and something military was apparent in their whole deportment. They were, in fact, military men; Litvinov had chanced upon a picnic party of young generals—persons of the highest society, of weight and importance. Their importance was clearly expressed in everything: in their discreet nonchalance, in their amiably condescending smiles, in the intense indifference of their expression, the effeminate little movements of their shoulders, the swing of the figure, and the crook of the knees; it was expressed, too, in the sound of their voices, which seemed to be affably and fastidiously thanking a subservient multitude. All these officers were superlatively washed and shaved, and thoroughly saturated with that genuine aroma of nobility and the Guards, compounded of the best cigar smoke, and the most marvellous patchouli. They all had the hands too of noblemen —white and large, with nails firm as ivory; their moustaches seemed positively polished, their teeth shone, and their skin—rosy on their cheeks, bluish on their chins—was most delicate and fine. Some of the young generals were frivolous, others were serious; but the stamp of the best breeding was on all of them. Each of them seemed to be deeply conscious of his own dignity, and the importance of his own future part in the government, and conducted himself with severity and ease, with a faint shade of that carelessness, that 'deuce-take-it' air, which comes out so naturally during foreign travel. The party seated themselves with much noise and ostentation, and called the obsequious waiters. Litvinov made haste to drink off his glass of milk, paid for it, and putting his hat on, was just making off past the party of generals. . . .

'Grigory Mihalitch,' he heard a woman's voice. 'Don't you recognise me?'

He stopped involuntarily. That voice. . . . that voice had too often set his heart beating in the past. . . . He turned round and saw Irina.

She was sitting at a table, her arms folded on the back of a chair drawn up near; with her head bent on one side and a smile on her face, she was looking at him cordially, almost with delight.

Litvinov knew her at once, though she had changed since he saw her that last time ten years ago, though she had been transformed from a girl into a woman. Her slim figure had developed and reached its perfection, the lines of her once narrow shoulders now recalled the goddesses that stand out on the ceilings of ancient Italian palaces. But her eyes remained the same, and it seemed to Litvinov that they were looking at him just as in those days in the little house in Moscow.

'Irina Pavlovna,' he uttered irresolutely.

'You know me? How glad I am! how glad——'

She stopped short, slightly blushing, and drew herself up.

'This is a very pleasant meeting,' she continued now in French. 'Let me introduce you to my husband. *Valérien, Monsieur Litvinov, un ami d'enfance*; Valerian Vladimirovitch Ratmirov, my husband.'

One of the young generals, almost the most elegant of all, got up from his seat, and with excessive courtesy bowed to Litvinov, while the rest of his companions faintly knitted their brows, or rather each of them withdrew for an instant into himself, as though protesting betimes against any contact with an extraneous civilian, and the other ladies taking part in the picnic thought fit to screw up their eyes a little and simper, and even to assume an air of perplexity.

'Have you—er—been long in Baden?' asked General Ratmirov, with a dandified air utterly un-Russian. He obviously did not know what to talk about with the friend of his wife's childhood.

'No, not long!' replied Litvinov.

'And do you intend to stay long?' pursued the polite general.

'I have not made up my mind yet.'

'Ah! that is very delightful . . . very.'

The general paused. Litvinov, too, was speechless. Both held their hats in their hands and bending forward with a grin, gazed at the top of each other's heads.

'*Deux gendarmes un beau dimanche*,' began humming—out of tune of course, we have never come across a Russian nobleman who did not sing out of tune—a dull-eyed and yellow-faced general, with an expression of constant irritability on his face, as though he could not forgive himself for his own appearance. Among all his companions he alone had not the complexion of a rose.

'But why don't you sit down, Grigory Mihalitch,' observed Irina at last. Litvinov obeyed and sat down.

'*I say, Valérien, give me some fire*,' remarked in English another general, also young, but already stout, with fixed eyes which seemed staring into the air, and thick silky whiskers, into which he slowly plunged his snow-white fingers. Ratmirov gave him a silver matchbox.

'*Avez vous des papiros?*' asked one of the ladies, with a lisp.

'*De vrais papelitos, comtesse.*'

'*Deux gendarmes un beau dimanche*,' the dull-eyed general hummed again, with intense exasperation.

'You must be sure to come and see us,' Irina was saying to Litvinov meantime; 'we are staying at the Hôtel de l'Europe. From four to six I am always at home. We have not seen each other for such a long time.'

Litvinov looked at Irina; she did not drop her eyes.

'Yes, Irina Pavlovna, it is a long time—ever since we were at Moscow.'

'At Moscow, yes, at Moscow,' she repeated abruptly. 'Come and see me, we will talk and recall old times. Do you know, Grigory Mihalitch, you have not changed much.'

'Really? But you have changed, Irina Pavlovna.'

'I have grown older.'

'No, I did not mean that.'

'*Irène?*' said a lady in a yellow hat and with yellow hair in an interrogative voice after some preliminary whispering and giggling with the officer sitting near her. '*Irène?*'

'I am older,' pursued Irina, without answering the lady, 'but I am not changed. No, no, I am changed in nothing.'

'*Deux gendarmes un beau dimanche!*' was heard again. The irritable general only remembered the first line of the well-known ditty.

'It still pricks a little, your excellency,' observed the stout general with the whiskers, with a loud and broad intonation, apparently quoting from some amusing story, well-known to the whole *beau monde,* and with a short wooden laugh he again fell to staring into the air. All the rest of the party laughed too.

'What a sad dog you are, Boris!' observed Ratmirov in an undertone. He spoke in English and pronounced even the name 'Boris' as if it were English.

'*Irène?*' the lady in the yellow hat said inquiringly for the third time. Irina turned sharply round to her.

'*Eh bien? quoi? que me voulez-vous?*'

'*Je vous dirai plus tard,*' replied the lady, mincing. With a very unattractive exterior, she was for ever mincing and grimacing. Some wit said of her that she '*minaudait dans le vide,*' 'grimaced upon the desert air.'

Irina frowned and shrugged her shoulders impatiently. '*Mais que fait donc Monsieur Verdier? Pourquoi ne vient-il pas?*' cried one lady with that prolonged drawl which is the peculiarity of the Great Russian accent, and is so insupportable to French ears.

'Ah, voo, ah, voo, mossoo Verdew, mossoo Verdew,' sighed another lady, whose birthplace was Arzamass.

'*Tranquillisez-vous, mesdames,*' interposed Ratmirov. '*Monsieur Verdier m'a promis de venir se mettre à vos pieds.*'

'He, he, he!'—The ladies fluttered their fans.

The waiter brought some glasses of beer.

'*Baierisch-Bier?*' inquired the general with whiskers, assuming a bass voice, and affecting astonishment—'*Guten Morgen.*'

'Well? Is Count Pavel still there?' one young general inquired coldly and listlessly of another.

'Yes,' replied the other equally coldly, '*Mais c'est provisoire. Serge,* they say, will be put in his place.'

'Aha!' filtered the first through his teeth.

'Ah, yes,' filtered the second.

'I can't understand,' began the general who had hummed the song, 'I can't understand what induced Paul to defend himself—to bring forward all sorts of reasons. Certainly, he crushed the merchant pretty well, *il lui a fait rendre gorge* . . . well, and what of it? He may have had his own motives.'

'He was afraid . . . of being shown up in the newspapers,' muttered some one.

The irritable general grew hot.

'Well, it is too much! Newspapers! Shown up! If it depended on me, I would not let anything be printed in those papers but the taxes on meat or bread, and announcements of sales of boots or furs.'

'And gentlemen's properties up for auction,' put in Ratmirov.

'Possibly under present circumstances. . . . What a conversation, though, in Baden *au Vieux-Château*.'

'*Mais pas du tout! pas du tout!*' replied the lady in the yellow hat, '*j'adore les questions politiques*.'

'*Madame a raison*,' interposed another general with an exceedingly pleasant and girlish-looking face. 'Why should we avoid those questions . . . even in Baden?'

As he said these words he looked urbanely at Litvinov and smiled condescendingly. 'A man of honour ought never under any circumstances to disown his convictions. Don't you think so?'

'Of course,' rejoined the irritable general, darting a look at Litvinov, and as it were indirectly attacking him, 'but I don't see the necessity . . .'

'No, no,' the condescending general interposed with the same mildness, 'your friend, Valerian Vladimirovitch, just referred to the sale of gentlemen's estates. Well? Is not that a fact?'

'But it's impossible to sell them nowadays; nobody wants them!' cried the irritable general.

'Perhaps . . . perhaps. For that very reason we ought to proclaim that fact . . . that sad fact at every step. We are ruined . . . very good; we are beggared . . . there's no disputing about that; but we, the great owners, we still represent a principle . . . *un principe*. To preserve that principle is our duty. *Pardon, madame*, I think you dropped your handkerchief. When some, so to say, darkness has come over even the highest minds, we ought submissively to point out (the general held out his finger) with the finger of a citizen the abyss to which everything is tending. We ought to warn, we ought to say with respectful firmness, "turn back, turn back. . . ." That is what we ought to say.'

'There's no turning back altogether, though,' observed Ratmirov moodily.

The condescending general only grinned.

'Yes, altogether, altogether, *mon très cher*. The further back the better.'

The general again looked courteously at Litvinov. The latter could not stand it.

'Are we to return as far as the Seven Boyars your excellency?'

'Why not? I express my opinion without hesitation; we must undo . . . yes . . . undo all that has been done.'

'And the emancipation of the serfs.'

'And the emancipation . . . as far as that is possible. *On est patriote ou on ne l'est pas.* "And freedom?" they say to me. Do you suppose that freedom is prized by the people? Ask them——'

'Just try,' broke in Litvinov, 'taking that freedom away again.'

'*Comment nommez-vous ce monsieur?*' whispered the general to Ratmirov.

'What are you discussing here?' began the stout general suddenly. He obviously played the part of the spoilt child of the party. 'Is it all about the newspapers? About penny-a-liners? Let me tell you a little anecdote of what happened to me with a scribbling fellow—such a lovely thing. I was told he had written a libel on me. Well, of course, I at once had him brought before me. They brought me the penny-a-liner. " How was it," said I, " my dear chap, you came to write this libel? Was your patriotism too much for you? " " Yes, it was too much," says he. " Well," says I, " and do you like money? " " Yes," says he. Then, gentlemen, I gave him the knob of my cane to sniff at. " And do you like that, my angel? " " No," says he, " I don't like that." " But sniff it as you ought," says I, " my hands are clean." " I don't like it," says he, " and that's all." " But I like it very much, my angel," says I, " though not for myself. Do you understand that allegory, my treasure? " " Yes," says he. " Then mind and be a good boy for the future, and now here's a rouble sterling for you; go away and be grateful to me night and day," and so the scribbling chap went off.'

The general burst out laughing and again every one followed his example —every one except Irina, who did not even smile and looked darkly at the speaker.

The condescending general slapped Boris on the shoulder.

' That's all your invention, O friend of my bosom. . . . You threatening any one with a stick. . . . You haven't got a stick. *C'est pour faire rire ces dames.* For the sake of a good story. But that's not the point. I said just now that we must turn back completely. Understand me. I am not hostile to so-called progress, but all these universities and seminaries, and popular schools, these students, priests' sons, and commoners, all these small fry, *tout ce fond du sac, la petite propriété, pire que le prolétariat* (the general uttered this in a languishing, almost faint voice) *voilà ce qui m'effraie* . . . that's where one ought to draw the line, and make other people draw it too.' (Again he gave Litvinov a genial glance.) ' Yes, one must draw the line. Don't forget that among us no one makes any demand, no one is asking for anything. Local government, for instance—who asks for that? Do you ask for it? or you, or you? or you, *mesdames?* You rule not only yourselves but all of us, you know.' (The general's handsome face was lighted up by a smile of amusement.) ' My dear friends, why should we curry favour with the multitude. You like democracy, it flatters you, and serves your ends . . . but you know it's a double weapon. It is better in the old way, as before . . . far more secure. Don't deign to reason with the herd, trust in the aristocracy, in that alone is power. . . . Indeed it will be better. And progress . . . I certainly have nothing against progress. Only don't give us lawyers and sworn juries and elective officials . . . only don't touch discipline, discipline before all things—you may build bridges, and quays, and hospitals, and why not light the streets with gas? '

' Petersburg has been set on fire from one end to the other, so there you have your progress! ' hissed the irritable general.

' Yes, you're a mischievous fellow, I can see,' said the stout general, shaking his head lazily; ' you would do for a chief-prosecutor, but in my opinion *avec Orphée aux enfers le progrès a dit son dernier mot.*'

' *Vous dites toujours des bêtises,*' giggled the lady from Arzamass.

The general looked dignified.

'*Je ne suis jamais plus sérieux, madame, que quand je dis des bêtises.*'

'Monsieur Verdier has uttered that very phrase several times already,' observed Irina in a low voice.

'*De la poigne et des formes,*' cried the stout general, '*de la poigne surtout.* And to translate into Russian: be civil but don't spare your fists.'

'Ah, you're a rascal, an incorrigible rascal,' interposed the condescending general. '*Mesdames,* don't listen to him, please. A barking dog does not bite. He cares for nothing but flirtation.'

'That's not right, though, Boris,' began Ratmirov, after exchanging a glance with his wife, 'it's all very well to be mischievous, but that's going too far. Progress is a phenomenon of social life, and this is what we must not forget; it's a symptom. It's what we must watch.'

'All right, I say,' observed the stout general, wrinkling up his nose; 'we all know you are aiming at the ministry.'

'Not at all . . . the ministry indeed! But really one can't refuse to recognise things.'

Boris plunged his fingers again into his whiskers, and stared into the air.

'Social life is very important, because in the development of the people, in the destinies, so to speak, of the country——'

'*Valérien,*' interrupted Boris reprovingly, *il y a des dames ici.* I did not expect this of you, or do you want to get on to a committee? '

'But they are all closed now, thank God,' put in the irritable general, and he began humming again '*Deux gendarmes un beau dimanche.*'

Ratmirov raised a cambric handkerchief to his nose and gracefully retired from the discussion; the condescending general repeated 'Rascal! rascal! ' but Boris turned to the lady who 'grimaced upon the desert air ' and without lowering his voice, or a change in the expression of his face, began to ply her with questions as to when 'she would reward his devotion,' as though he were desperately in love with her and suffering tortures on her account.

At every moment during this conversation Litvinov felt more and more ill at ease. His pride, his clean plebeian pride, was fairly in revolt.

What had he, the son of a petty official, in common with these military aristocrats of Petersburg? He loved everything they hated; he hated everything they loved; he was only too vividly conscious of it, he felt it in every part of his being. Their jokes he thought dull, their tone intolerable, every gesture false; in the very smoothness of their speeches he detected a note of revolting contemptuousness—and yet he was, as it were, abashed before them, before these creatures, these enemies. 'Ugh! how disgusting! I am in their way, I am ridiculous to them,' was the thought that kept revolving in his head. 'Why am I stopping? Let me escape at once, at once.' Irina's presence could not retain him; she, too, aroused melancholy emotions in him. He got up from his seat and began to take leave.

'You are going already?' said Irina, but after a moment's reflection she did not press him to stay, and only extracted a promise from him that he

would not fail to come and see her. General Ratmirov took leave of him
with the same refined courtesy, shook hands with him and accompanied him
to the end of the platform. . . . But Litvinov had scarcely had time to
turn round the first bend in the road when he heard a general roar
of laughter behind him. This laughter had no reference to him, but was
occasioned by the long-expected Monsieur Verdier, who suddenly made
his appearance on the platform, in a Tyrolese hat, and blue blouse, riding
a donkey, but the blood fairly rushed into Litvinov's cheeks, and he felt
intense bitterness: his tightly compressed lips seemed as though drawn by
wormwood. 'Despicable, vulgar creatures,' he muttered, without reflecting
that the few minutes he had spent in their company had not given him
sufficient ground for such severe criticism. And this was the world into
which Irina had fallen, Irina, once his Irina! In this world she moved, and
lived, and reigned; for it, she had sacrificed her personal dignity, the noblest
feelings of her heart. . . . It was clearly as it should be; it was clear that
she had deserved no better fate! How glad he was that she had not thought
of questioning him about his intentions! He might have opened his heart
before 'them' in 'their' presence. . . . 'For nothing in the world! never!'
murmured Litvinov, inhaling deep draughts of the fresh air and descending
the road towards Baden almost at a run. He thought of his betrothed, his
sweet, good, sacred Tatyana, and how pure, how noble, how true she
seemed to him. With what unmixed tenderness he recalled her features, her
words, her very gestures . . . with what impatience he looked forward to
her return.

The rapid exercise soothed his nerves. Returning home he sat down at
the table and took up a book; suddenly he let it fall, even with a shudder.
. . . What had happened to him? Nothing had happened, but Irina . . .
Irina. . . . All at once his meeting with her seemed something marvellous,
strange, extraordinary. Was it possible? he had met, he had talked with
the same Irina. . . . And why was there no trace in her of that hateful
worldliness which was so sharply stamped upon all these others? Why did
he fancy that she seemed, as it were, weary, or sad, or sick of her position?
She was in their camp, but she was not an enemy. And what could have
impelled her to receive him joyfully, to invite him to see her?

Litvinov started. 'O Tanya, Tanya!' he cried passionately, 'you are my
guardian angel, you only, my good genius. I love you only and will love
you for ever. And I will not go to see *her*. Forget her altogether! Let her
amuse herself with her generals.' Litvinov set to his book again.

XI

LITVINOV took up his book again, but he could not read. He went out of
the house, walked a little, listened to the music, glanced in at the gambling,
returned again to his room, and tried again to read—still without success.
The time seemed to drag by with peculiar dreariness. Pishtchalkin, the well-

intentioned peaceable mediator, came in and sat with him for three hours. He talked, argued, stated questions, and discoursed intermittently, first of elevated, and then of practical topics, and succeeded in diffusing around him such an atmosphere of dulness that poor Litvinov was ready to cry. In raising dulness—agonising, chilling, helpless, hopeless dulness—to a fine art, Pishtchalkin was absolutely unrivalled even among persons of the highest morality, who are notoriously masters in that line. The mere sight of his well-cut and well-brushed head, his clear lifeless eyes, his benevolent nose, produced an involuntary despondency, and his deliberate, drowsy, lazy tone seemed to have been created only to state with conviction and lucidity such sententious truths as that twice two makes four and not five or three, that water is liquid, and benevolence laudable; that to the private individual, no less than to the state, and to the state no less than to the private individual, credit is absolutely indispensable for financial operations. And with all this he was such an excellent man! But such is the sentence the fates have passed on Russia; among us, good men are dull. Pishtchalkin retreated at last; he was replaced by Bindasov, who, without any beating about the bush, asked Litvinov with great effrontery for a loan of a hundred guldens, and the latter gave it him, in spite of the fact that Bindasov was not only unattractive, but even repulsive to him, that he knew for certain that he would never get his money back; and was, besides, himself in need of it. What made him give him the money then, the reader will inquire. Who can tell! That is another Russian weakness. Let the reader lay his hand on his heart and remember how many acts in his own life have had absolutely no other reason. And Bindasov did not even thank Litvinov; he asked for a glass of red Baden wine, and without wiping his lips departed, loudly and offensively tramping with his boots. And how vexed Litvinov was with himself already, as he watched the red nape of the retreating sharper's neck! Before evening he received a letter from Tatyana in which she informed him that as her aunt was not well, she could not come to Baden for five or six days. This news had a depressing influence on Litvinov; it increased his vexation, and he went to bed early in a disagreeable frame of mind. The following day turned out no better, if not worse, than the preceding. From early morning Litvinov's room was filled with his own countrymen; Bambaev, Voroshilov, Pishtchalkin, the two officers, the two Heidelberg students, all crowded in at once, and yet did not go away right up till dinner time, though they had soon said all they had to say and were obviously bored. They simply did not know what to do with themselves, and having got into Litvinov's lodgings they 'stuck' there, as they say. First they discussed the fact that Gubaryov had gone back to Heidelberg, and that they would have to go after him; then they philosophised a little, and touched on the Polish question; then they advanced to reflections on gambling and *cocottes*, and fell to repeating scandalous anecdotes; at last the conversation sank into a discussion of all sorts of 'strong men' and monsters of obesity and gluttony. First, they trotted out all the ancient stories of Lukin, of the deacon who ate no less than thirty-three herrings for a wager, of the Uhlan colonel, Ezyedinov, renowned for his corpulence, and of the soldier who broke the shin-bone on his own forehead; then followed unadulterated lying. Pishtchalkin himself related with a yawn that he knew a peasant woman in Little Russia, who at the time of her death had proved to weigh half a ton and some pounds, and a landowner who had eaten three geese and a sturgeon for luncheon; Bambaev suddenly fell into an ecstatic condition, and declared he himself was able to eat a whole sheep, ‘with seasoning’ of course; and Voroshilov burst out with something about a comrade, an athletic cadet, so grotesque that every one was reduced to silence, and after looking at each other, they took up their hats, and the party broke up. Litvinov, when he was left alone, tried to occupy himself, but he felt just as if his head was full of smouldering soot; he could do nothing that was of any use, and the evening too was wasted. The next morning he was just preparing for lunch, when some one knocked at his door. ‘ Good Lord,’ thought Litvinov, ‘ one of yesterday’s dear friends again,’ and not without some trepidation he pronounced:

‘ Herein! ’

The door opened slowly and in walked Potugin. Litvinov was exceedingly delighted to see him.

‘ This is nice! ’ he began, warmly shaking hands with his unexpected visitor, ‘ this is good of you! I should certainly have looked you up myself, but you would not tell me where you live. Sit down, please, put down your hat. Sit down.’

Potugin made no response to Litvinov’s warm welcome, and remained standing in the middle of the room, shifting from one leg to the other; he only laughed a little and shook his head. Litvinov’s cordial reception obviously touched him, but there was some constraint in the expression of his face.

‘ There’s . . . some little misunderstanding,’ he began, not without hesitation. ‘ Of course, it would always be . . . a pleasure . . . to me . . . but I have been sent . . . especially to you.’

‘ That’s to say, do you mean,’ commented Litvinov in an injured voice, ‘ that you would not have come to me of your own accord? ’

‘ Oh, no, . . . indeed! But I . . . I should, perhaps, not have made up my mind to intrude on you to-day, if I had not been asked to come to you. In fact, I have a message for you.’

‘ From whom, may I ask? ’

‘ From a person you know, from Irina Pavlovna Ratmirov. You promised three days ago to go and see her and you have not been.’

Litvinov stared at Potugin in amazement.

‘ You know Madame Ratmirov? ’

‘ As you see.’

‘ And you know her well? ’

‘ I am to a certain degree a friend of hers.’

Litvinov was silent for a little.

' Allow me to ask you,' he began at last, ' do you know why Irina Pavlovna wants to see me? '

Potugin went up to the window.

' To a certain degree I do. She was, as far as I can judge, very pleased at meeting you,—well,—and she wants to renew your former relations.'

' Renew,' repeated Litvinov. ' Excuse my indiscretion, but allow me to question you a little more. Do you know what was the nature of those relations? '

' Strictly speaking . . . no, I don't know. But I imagine,' added Potugin, turning suddenly to Litvinov and looking affectionately at him, ' I imagine that they were of some value. Irina Pavlovna spoke very highly of you, and I was obliged to promise her I would bring you. Will you come? '

' When? '

' Now . . . at once.'

Litvinov merely made a gesture with his hand.

' Irina Pavlovna,' pursued Potugin, ' supposes that the . . . how can I express it . . . the environment, shall we say, in which you found her the other day, was not likely to be particularly attractive to you; but she told me to tell you, that the devil is not so black as he is fancied.'

' Hm. . . . Does that saying apply strictly to the environment? '

' Yes . . . and in general.'

' Hm. . . . Well, and what is your opinion, Sozont Ivanitch, of the devil? '

' I think, Grigory Mihalitch, that he is in any case not what he is fancied.'

' Is he better? '

' Whether better or worse it's hard to say, but certainly he is not the same as he is fancied. Well, shall we go? '

' Sit here a little first. I must own that it still seems rather strange to me.'

' What seems strange, may I make bold to inquire? '

' In what way can you have become a friend of Irina Pavlovna? '

Potugin scanned himself.

' With my appearance, and my position in society, it certainly does seem rather incredible; but you know—Shakespeare has said already, " There are more things in heaven and earth, Horatio, etc." Life too is not to be trifled with. Here is a simile for you; a tree stands before you when there is no wind; in what way can a leaf on a lower branch touch a leaf on an upper branch? It's impossible. But when the storm rises it is all changed . . . and the two leaves touch.'

' Aha! So there were storms? '

' I should think so! Can one live without them? But enough of philosophy. It's time to go.'

Litvinov was still hesitating.

' O good Lord! ' cried Potugin with a comic face, ' what are young men coming to nowadays! A most charming lady invites them to see her, sends messengers after them on purpose, and they raise difficulties. You ought to be ashamed, my dear sir, you ought to be ashamed. Here's your hat. Take it and "Vorwärts," as our ardent friends the Germans say.'

Litvinov still stood irresolute for a moment, but he ended by taking his hat and going out of the room with Potugin.

XII

THEY WENT to one of the best hotels in Baden and asked for Madame Ratmirov. The porter first inquired their names, and then answered at once that ' *die Frau Fürstin ist zu Hause,*' and went himself to conduct them up the staircase and knock at the door of the apartment and announce them. '*Die Frau Fürstin*' received them promptly: she was alone, her husband had gone off to Carlsruhe for an interview with a great official, an influential personage who was passing through that town.

Irina was sitting at a small table, embroidering on canvas when Potugin and Litvinov crossed the threshold. She quickly flung her embroidery aside, pushed away the little table and got up; an expression of genuine pleasure overspread her face. She wore a morning dress, high at the neck; the superb lines of her shoulders and arms could be seen through the thin stuff; her carelessly-coiled hair had come loose and fell low on her slender neck. Irina flung a swift glance at Potugin, murmured ' *merci,*' and holding out her hand to Litvinov reproached him amicably for forgetfulness.

'And you such an old friend! ' she added.

Litvinov was beginning to apologise. ' *C'est bien, c'est bien,*' she assented hurriedly and, taking his hat from him, with friendly insistence made him sit down. Potugin, too, was sitting down, but got up again directly, and saying that he had an engagement he could not put off, and that he would come in again after dinner, he proceeded to take leave. Irina again flung him a rapid glance, and gave him a friendly nod, but she did not try to keep him, and directly he had vanished behind the portière, she turned with eager impatience to Litvinov.

' Grigory Mihalitch,' she began, speaking Russian in her soft musical voice, ' here we are alone at last, and I can tell you how glad I am at our meeting, because it . . . it gives me a chance . . .' (Irina looked him straight in the face) ' of asking your forgiveness.'

Litvinov gave an involuntary start. He had not expected so swift an attack. He had not expected she would herself turn the conversation upon old times.

'Forgiveness . . . for what? ' . . . he muttered.

Irina flushed.

'For what? . . . you know for what,' she said, and she turned slightly away. ' I wronged you, Grigory Mihalitch . . . though, of course, it was my fate ' (Litvinov was reminded of her letter) ' and I do not regret it . . . it would be in any case too late; but, meeting you so unexpectedly, I said to myself that we absolutely must become friends, absolutely . . . and I should feel it deeply, if it did not come about . . . and it seems to me ₁or that we must have an explanation, without putting it off, and once for all, so that afterwards there should be no . . . *gêne,* no awkwardness, once for all, Grigory Mihalitch; and that you must tell me you forgive me, or else I shall imagine you feel . . . *de la rancune. Voilà!* It is perhaps a great piece of fatuity on my part, for you have probably forgotten everything long, long ago, but no matter, tell me, you have forgiven me.'

Irina uttered this whole speech without taking breath, and Litvinov could see that there were tears shining in her eyes . . . yes, actually tears.

'Really, Irina Pavlovna,' he began hurriedly, 'how can you beg my pardon, ask forgiveness? . . . That is all past and buried, and I can only feel astounded that, in the midst of all the splendour which surrounds you, you have still preserved a recollection of the obscure companions of your youth. . . .'

'Does it astound you? ' said Irina softly.

'It touches me,' Litvinov went on, 'because I could never have imagined——'

'You have not told me you have forgiven me, though,' interposed Irina.

'I sincerely rejoice at your happiness, Irina Pavlovna. With my whole heart I wish you all that is best on earth. . . .'

'And you will not remember evil against me? '

'I will remember nothing but the happy moments for which I was once indebted to you.'

Irina held out both hands to him; Litvinov clasped them warmly, and did not at once let them go. . . . Something that long had not been, secretly stirred in his heart at that soft contact. Irina was again looking straight into his face; but this time she was smiling. . . . And he for the first time gazed directly and intently at her. . . . Again he recognised the features once so precious, and those deep eyes, with their marvellous lashes, and the little mole on her cheek, and the peculiar growth of her hair on her forehead, and her habit of somehow sweetly and humorously curving her lips and faintly twitching her eyebrows, all, all he recognised. . . . But how beautiful she had grown! What fascination, what power in her fresh, woman's body! And no rouge, no touching up, no powder, nothing false on that fresh pure face. . . . Yes, this was a beautiful woman. A mood of musing came upon Litvinov. . . . He was still looking at her, but his thoughts were far away. . . . Irina perceived it.

'Well, that is excellent,' she said aloud; 'now my conscience is at rest then, and I can satisfy my curiosity.'

'Curiosity,' repeated Litvinov, as though puzzled.

'Yes, yes. . . . I want above all things to know what you have been doing all this time, what plans you have; I want to know all, how, what, when . . . all, all. And you will have to tell me the truth, for I must warn you, I have not lost sight of you . . . so far as I could.'

'You did not lose sight of me, you . . . there . . . in Petersburg? '

'In the midst of the splendour which surrounded me, as you expressed it just now. Positively, yes, I did not. As for that splendour we will talk about that again; but now you must tell me, you must tell me so much, at such length, no one will disturb us. Ah, how delightful it will be,' added Irina, gaily sitting down and arranging herself at her ease in an armchair. 'Come, begin.'

'Before telling my story, I have to thank you,' began Litvinov.

'What for?'

'For the bouquet of flowers, which made its appearance in my room.'

'What bouquet? I know nothing about it.'

'What?'

'I tell you I know nothing about it. . . . But I am waiting . . . I am waiting for your story. . . . Ah, what a good fellow that Potugin is to have brought you!'

Litvinov pricked up his ears.

'Have you known this Mr. Potugin long?' he queried.

'Yes, a long while . . . but tell me your story.'

'And do you know him well?'

'Oh, yes!' Irina sighed. 'There are special reasons. . . . You have heard, of course, of Eliza Byelsky. . . . Who died, you know, the year before last, such a dreadful death? . . . Ah, to be sure, I'd forgotten you don't know all our scandals. . . . It is well, it is well indeed, that you don't know them. O *quelle chance!* at last, at last, a man, a live man, who knows nothing of us! And to be able to talk Russian with him, bad Russian of course, but still Russian, not that everlasting mawkish, sickening French patter of Petersburg.'

'And Potugin, you say, was connected with——'

'It's very painful for me even to refer to it,' Irina broke in. 'Eliza was my greatest friend at school, and afterwards in Petersburg we saw each other continually. She confided all her secrets to me, she was very unhappy, she suffered much. Potugin behaved splendidly in the affair, with true chivalry. He sacrificed himself. It was only then I learnt to appreciate him! But we have drifted away again. I am waiting for your story, Grigory Mihalitch.'

'But my story cannot interest you the least, Irina Pavlovna.'

'That's not your affair.'

'Think, Irina Pavlovna, we have not seen each other for ten years, ten whole years. How much water has flowed by since then.'

'Not water only! not water only!' she repeated with a peculiar bitter expression; 'that's just why I want to hear what you are going to tell me.'

'And beside I really don't know where to begin.'

'At the beginning. From the very time when you . . . when I went away to Petersburg. You left Moscow then. . . . Do you know I have never been back to Moscow since!'

'Really?'

'It was impossible at first; and afterwards when I was married——.'

'Have you been married long?'

'Four years.'

'Have you no children? '

'No,' she answered drily.

Litvinov was silent for a little.

'And did you go on living at that, what was his name, Count Reisenbach's, till your marriage? '

Irina looked steadily at him, as though she were trying to make up her mind why he asked that question.

'No,' . . . was her answer at last.

'I suppose your parents. . . . By the way, I haven't asked after them. Are they——'

'They are both well.'

'And living at Moscow as before? '

'At Moscow as before.'

'And your brothers and sisters? '

'They are all right; I have provided for all of them.'

'Ah! ' Litvinov glanced up from under his brows at Irina. 'In reality, Irina Pavlovna, it's not I who ought to tell my story, but you, if only——' He suddenly felt embarrassed and stopped.

Irina raised her hands to her face and turned her wedding-ring round upon her finger.

'Well? I will not refuse,' she assented at last. 'Some day . . . perhaps. . . . But first you . . . because, do you see, though I tried to follow you up, I know scarcely anything of you; while of me . . . well, of me you have heard enough certainly. Haven't you? I suppose you have heard of me, tell me? '

'You, Irina Pavlovna, occupied too conspicuous a place in the world, not to be the subject of talk . . . especially in the provinces, where I have been and where every rumour is believed."

'And do you believe the rumours? And of what kind were the rumours? '

'To tell the truth, Irina Pavlovna, such rumours very seldom reached me. I have led a very solitary life.'

'How so? why, you were in the Crimea, in the militia? '

'You know that too? '

'As you see. I tell you, you have been watched.'

Again Litvinov felt puzzled.

'Why am I to tell you what you know without me? ' said Litvinov in an undertone.

'Why . . . to do what I ask you. You see I ask you, Grigory Mihalitch.'

Litvinov bowed his head and began . . . began in rather a confused fashion to recount in rough outline to Irina his uninteresting adventures. He often stopped and looked inquiringly at Irina, as though to ask whether he had told enough. But she insistently demanded the continuation of his narrative and pushing her hair back behind her ears, her elbows on the arm of her chair, she seemed to be catching every word with strained attention. Looking at her from one side and following the expression on her face, any one might perhaps have imagined she did not hear what Litvinov was saying at all, but was only deep in meditation. . . . But it was not of Litvinov she was meditating, though he grew confused and red under her persistent gaze A whole life was rising up before her, a very different one, not his life, but her own.

Litvinov did not finish his story, but stopped short under the influence of an unpleasant sense of growing inner discomfort. This time Irina said nothing to him, and did not urge him to go on, but pressing her open hand to her eyes, as though she were tired, she leaned slowly back in her chair, and remained motionless. Litvinov waited for a little; then, reflecting that his visit had already lasted more than two hours, he was stretching out his hand for his hat, when suddenly in an adjoining room there was the sound of the rapid creak of thin kid boots, and preceded by the same exquisite aristocratic perfume, there entered Valerian Vladimirovitch Ratmirov.

Latvinov rose and interchanged bows with the good-looking general, while Irina, with no sign of haste, took her hand from her face, and looking coldly at her husband, remarked in French. 'Ah! so you've come back! But what time is it? '

'Nearly four, *ma chère amie*, and you not dressed yet—the princess will be expecting us,' answered the general; and with an elegant bend of his tightly-laced figure in Litvinov's direction, he added with the almost effeminate playfulness of intonation characteristic of him, 'It's clear an agreeable visitor has made you forgetful of time.'

The reader will permit us at this point to give him some information about General Ratmirov. His father was the natural . . . what do you suppose? You are not wrong—but we didn't mean to say that . . . the natural son of an illustrious personage of the reign of Alexander I. and of a pretty little French actress. The illustrious personage brought his son forward in the world, but left him no fortune, and the son himself (the father of our hero) had not time to grow rich; he died before he had risen above the rank of a colonel in the police. A year before his death he had married a handsome young widow who had happened to put herself under his protection. His son by the widow, Valerian Alexandrovitch, having got into the Corps of Pages by favour, attracted the notice of the authorities, not so much by his success in the sciences, as by his fine bearing, his fine manners, and his good behaviour (though he had been exposed to all that pupils in the government military schools were inevitably exposed to in former days) and went into the Guards. His career was a brilliant one, thanks to the discreet gaiety of his disposition, his skill in dancing, his excellent seat on horseback when an orderly at reviews, and lastly, by a kind of special trick of deferential familiarity with his superiors, of tender, attentive almost clinging subservience, with a flavour of vague liberalism, light as air. . . . This liberalism had not, however, prevented him from flogging fifty peasants in a White Russian village, where he had been sent to put down a riot. His personal appearance was most prepossessing and singularly youthful-looking; smooth-faced and rosy-cheeked, pliant and persistent, he made the most of his amazing success with women; ladies of the highest rank and mature age simply went out of their senses over him. Cautious from habit, silent from motives of prudence, General Ratmirov moved constantly in the highest society, like the busy bee gathering honey even from the least attractive flowers—and without morals, without information of any kind, but with the reputation of being good at business; with an insight into men, and a ready comprehension of the exigencies of the moment, and above all, a never-swerving desire for his own advantage, he saw at last all paths lying open before him. . . .

Litvinov smiled constrainedly, while Irina merely shrugged her shoulders.

'Well,' she said in the same cold tone, 'did you see the Count?'

'To be sure I saw him. He told me to remember him to you.'

'Ah! is he as imbecile as ever, that patron of yours?'

General Ratmirov made no reply. He only smiled to himself, as though lenient to the overhastiness of a woman's judgment. With just such a smile kindly-disposed grown-up people respond to the nonsensical whims of children.

'Yes,' Irina went on, 'the stupidity of your friend the Count is too striking, even when one has seen a good deal of the world.'

'You sent me to him yourself,' muttered the general, and turning to Litvinov he asked him in Russian, 'Was he getting any benefit from the Baden waters?'

'I am in perfect health, I'm thankful to say,' answered Litvinov.

'That's the greatest of blessings,' pursued the general, with an affable grimace; 'and indeed one doesn't, as a rule, come to Baden for the waters; but the waters here are very effectual, *je veux dire, efficaces;* and any one who suffers, as I do for instance, from a nervous cough——'

Irina rose quickly. 'We will see each other again, Grigory Mihalitch, and I hope soon,' she said in French, contemptuously cutting short her husband's speech, 'but now I must go and dress. That old princess is insufferable with her everlasting *parties de plaisir,* of which nothing comes but boredom.'

'You're hard on every one to-day,' muttered her husband, and he slipped away into the next room.

Litvinov was turning towards the door. . . . Irina stopped him.

'You have told me everything,' she said, 'but the chief thing you concealed.'

'What's that?'

'You are going to be married, I'm told?'

Litvinov blushed up to his ears. . . . As a fact, he had intentionally not referred to Tanya; but he felt horribly vexed, first, that Irina knew about his marriage, and, secondly, that she had, as it were, convicted him of a desire to conceal it from her. He was completely at a loss what to say, while Irina did not take her eyes off him.

'Yes, I am going to be married,' he said at last, and at once withdrew.

Ratmirov came back into the room.

'Well, why aren't you dressed?' he asked.

'You can go alone; my head aches.'

'But the princess . . .'

Irina scanned her husband from head to foot in one look, turned her back upon him, and went away to her boudoir.

XIII

LITVINOV FELT MUCH ANNOYED with himself, as though he had lost money at roulette, or failed to keep his word. An inward voice told him that he—on the eve of marriage, a man of sober sense, not a boy—ought not to have given way to the promptings of curiosity, nor the allurements of recollection. 'Much need there was to go!' he reflected. 'On her side simply flirtation, whim, caprice. . . . She's bored, she's sick of everything, she clutched at me . . . as some one pampered with dainties will suddenly long for black bread . . . well, that's natural enough. . . . But why did I go? Can I feel anything but contempt for her?' This last phrase he could not utter even in thought without an effort. . . . 'Of course, there's no kind of danger, and never could be,' he pursued his reflections. 'I know whom I have to deal with. But still one ought not to play with fire. . . . I'll never set my foot in her place again.' Litvinov dared not, or could not as yet, confess to himself how beautiful Irina had seemed to him, how powerfully she had worked upon his feelings.

Again the day passed dully and drearily. At dinner, Litvinov chanced to sit beside a majestic *belhomme*, with dyed moustaches, who said nothing, and only panted and rolled his eyes . . . but, being suddenly taken with a hiccup, proved himself to be a fellow-countryman, by at once exclaiming, with feeling, in Russian, 'There, I said I ought not to eat melons!' In the evening, too, nothing happened to compensate for a lost day; Bindasov, before Litvinov's very eyes, won a sum four times what he had borrowed from him, but, far from repaying his debt, he positively glared in his face with a menacing air, as though he were prepared to borrow more from him just because he had been a witness of his winnings. The next morning he was again invaded by a host of his compatriots; Litvinov got rid of them with difficulty, and setting off to the mountains, he first came across Irina—he pretended not to recognise her, and passed quickly by—and then Potugin. He was about to begin a conversation with Potugin, but the latter did not respond to him readily. He was leading by the hand a smartly dressed little girl, with fluffy, almost white curls, large black eyes, and a pale, sickly little face, with that peculiar peremptory and impatient expression characteristic of spoiled children. Litvinov spent two hours in the mountains, and then went back homewards along the Lichtenthaler Allee. . . . A lady, sitting on a bench, with a blue veil over her face, got up quickly, and came up to him. . . . He recognised Irina.

'Why do you avoid me, Grigory Mihalitch?' she said, in the unsteady voice of one who is boiling over within.

Litvinov was taken aback. 'I avoid you, Irina Pavlovna?'

'Yes, you . . . you—"

Irina seemed excited, almost angry.

'You are mistaken, I assure you.'

'No, I am not mistaken. Do you suppose this morning—when we met, I mean—do you suppose I didn't see that you knew me? Do you mean to say you did not know me? Tell me.'

'I really . . . Irina Pavlovna—'

'Grigory Mihalitch, you're a straightforward man, you have always told the truth; tell me, tell me, you knew me, didn't you? you turned away on purpose?'

Litvinov glanced at Irina. Her eyes shone with a strange light, while her cheeks and lips were of a deathly pallor under the thick net of her veil. In the expression of her face, in the very sound of her abruptly jerked-out whisper, there was something so irresistibly mournful, beseeching . . . Litvinov could not pretend any longer.

'Yes . . . I knew you,' he uttered not without effort.

Irina slowly shuddered, and slowly dropped her hands.

'Why did you not come up to me?' she whispered.

'Why . . . why!' Litvinov moved on one side, away from the path, Irina followed him in silence. 'Why?' he repeated once more, and suddenly his face was aflame, and he felt his chest and throat choking with a passion akin to hatred. 'You . . . you ask such a question, after all that has passed between us? Not now, of course, not now; but there . . . there . . . in Moscow.'

'But, you know, we decided; you know, you promised—' Irina was beginning.

'I have promised nothing! Pardon the harshness of my expressions, but you ask for the truth—so think for yourself: to what but a caprice—incomprehensible, I confess, to me—to what but a desire to try how much power you still have over me, can I attribute your . . . I don't know what to call it . . . your persistence? Our paths have lain so far apart! I have forgotten it all, I've lived through all that suffering long ago, I've become a different man completely; you are married—happy, at least, in appearance—you fill an envied position in the world; what's the object, what's the use of our meeting? What am I to you? what are you to me? We cannot even understand each other now; there is absolutely nothing in common between us now, neither in the past nor in the present! Especially . . . especially in the past!'

Litvinov uttered all this speech hurriedly, jerkily, without turning his head. Irina did not stir, except from time to time she faintly stretched her hands out to him. It seemed as though she were beseeching him to stop and listen to her, while, at his last words, she slightly bit her lower lip, as though to master the pain of a sharp, rapid wound.

'Grigory Mihalitch,' she began at last, in a calmer voice, and she moved still further away from the path, along which people from time to time passed.

Litvinov in his turn followed her.

'Grigory Mihalitch, believe me, if I could imagine I had one hair's-breadth of power over you left, I would be the first to avoid you. If I have not done so, if I made up my mind, in spite of my . . . of the wrong I did you in the past, to renew my acquaintance with you, it was because . . . because——'

'Because what?' asked Litvinov, almost rudely.

'Because,' Irina declared with sudden force—'it's too insufferable, too unbearably stifling for me in society, in the envied position you talk about; because meeting you, a live man, after all these dead puppets—you have seen samples of them three days ago, there *au Vieux Château*,—I rejoice over you as an oasis in the desert, while you suspect me of flirting, and despise me and repulse me on the ground that I wronged you—as indeed I did—but far more myself!'

'You chose your lot yourself, Irina Pavlovna, Litvinov rejoined sullenly, as before not turning his head.

'I chose it myself, yes . . . and I don't complain, I have no right to complain,' said Irina hurriedly; she seemed to derive a secret consolation from Litvinov's very harshness. 'I know that you must think ill of me, and I won't justify myself; I only want to explain my feeling to you, I want to convince you I am in no flirting humour now. . . . Me flirting with you! Why, there is no sense in it. . . . When I saw you, all that was good, that was young in me, revived . . . that time when I had not yet chosen my lot, everything that lies behind in that streak of brightness behind those ten years. . . .'

'Come, really, Irina Pavlovna! So far as I am aware, the brightness in your life began precisely with the time we separated. . . .'

Irina put her handkerchief to her lips.

'That's very cruel, what you say, Grigory Mihalitch; but I can't feel angry with you. Oh, no, that was not a bright time, it was not for happiness I left Moscow; I have known not one moment, not one instant of happiness . . . believe me, whatever you have been told. If I were happy, could I talk to you as I am talking now. . . . I repeat to you, you don't know what these people are. . . . Why, they understand nothing, feel for nothing; they've no intelligence even, *ni esprit ni intelligence*, nothing but tact and cunning; why, in reality, music and poetry and art are all equally remote from them. . . . You will say that I was rather indifferent to all that myself; but not to the same degree, Grigory Mihalitch . . . not to the same degree! It's not a woman of the world before you now, you need only look at me—not a society queen. . . . That's what they call us, I believe . . . but a poor, poor creature, really deserving of pity. Don't wonder at my words. . . . I am beyond feeling pride now! I hold out my hand to you as a beggar, will you understand, just as a beggar. . . . I ask for charity,' she added suddenly, in an involuntary, irrepressible outburst, ' I ask for charity, and you——'

Her voice broke. Litvinov raised his head and looked at Irina; her breathing came quickly, her lips were quivering. Suddenly his heart beat fast, and the feeling of hatred vanished.

' You say that our paths have lain apart,' Irina went on, ' I know you are about to marry from inclination, you have a plan laid out for your whole life; yes, that's all so, but we have not become strangers to one another, Grigory Mihalitch; we can still understand each other. Or do you imagine I have grown altogether dull—altogether debased in the mire? Ah, no, don't think that, please! Let me open my heart, I beseech you—there—even for the sake of those old days, if you are not willing to forget them. Do so, that our meeting may not have come to pass in vain; that would be too bitter; it would not last long in any case. . . . I don't know how to say it properly, but you will understand me, because I ask for little, so little . . . only a little sympathy, only that you should not repulse me, that you should let me open my heart——'

Irina ceased speaking, there were tears in her voice. She sighed, and timidly, with a kind of furtive, searching look, gazed at Litvinov, held out her hand to him. . .

Litvinov slowly took the hand and faintly pressed it.

' Let us be friends,' whispered Irina.

' Friends,' repeated Litvinov dreamily.

' Yes, friends . . . or if that is too much to ask, then let us at least be friendly. . . . Let us be simply as though nothing had happened.'

' As though nothing had happened, . . .' repeated Litvinov again. ' You said just now, Irina Pavlovna, that I was unwilling to forget the old days. . . . But what if I can't forget them? '

A blissful smile flashed over Irina's face, and at once disappeared, to be replaced by a harassed, almost scared expression.

' Be like me, Grigory Mihalitch, remember only what was good in them; and most of all, give me your word. . . . Your word of honour. . . .'

' Well? '

' Not to avoid me . . . not to hurt me for nothing. You promise? tell me! '

' Yes.'

' And you will dismiss all evil thoughts of me from your mind.'

' Yes . . . but as for understanding you—I give it up.'

' There's no need of that . . . wait a little, though, you will understand. But will you promise? '

' I have said yes already.'

' Thanks. You see I am used to believe you. I shall expect you to-day, to-morrow, I will not go out of the house. And now I must leave you. The Grand Duchess is coming along the avenue. . . . She's caught sight of me, and I can't avoid going up to speak to her. . . . Good-bye till we meet. . . . Give me your hand, *vite, vite*. Till we meet.'

And warmly pressing Litvinov's hand, Irina walked towards a middle-aged person of dignified appearance, who was coming slowly along the gravel path, escorted by two other ladies, and a strikingly handsome groom in livery.

'*Eh bonjour, chère Madame,*' said the personage, while Irina curtseyed respectfully to her. '*Comment allez-vous aujourd'hui? Venez un peu avec moi.*'

'*Votre Altesse a trop de bonté,*' Irina's insinuating voice was heard in reply.

XIV

LITVINOV let the Grand Duchess and all her suite get out of sight, and then he too went up along the avenue. He could not make up his mind clearly what he was feeling; he was conscious both of shame and dread, while his vanity was flattered. . . . The unexpected explanation with Irina had taken him utterly by surprise; her rapid burning words had passed over him like a thunder-storm. 'Queer creatures these society women,' he thought; 'there's no consistency in them . . . and how perverted they are by the surroundings in which they go on living, while they're conscious of its hideousness themselves!' . . . In reality he was not thinking this at all, but only mechanically repeating these hackneyed phrases, as though he were trying to ward off other more painful thoughts. He felt that he must not think seriously just now, that he would probably have to blame himself, and he moved with lagging steps, almost forcing himself to pay attention to everything that happened to meet him. . . . He suddenly found himself before a seat, caught sight of some one's legs in front of it, and looked upwards from them. . . . The legs belonged to a man, sitting on the seat, and reading a newspaper; this man turned out to be Potugin. Litvinov uttered a faint exclamation. Potugin laid the paper down on his knees, and looked attentively, without a smile, at Litvinov; and Litvinov also attentively, and also without a smile, looked at Potugin.

'May I sit by you?' he asked at last.

'By all means, I shall be delighted. Only I warn you, if you want to have a talk with me, you mustn't be offended with me—I'm in a most misanthropic humour just now, and I see everything in an exaggeratedly repulsive light.'

'That's no matter, Sozont Ivanitch,' responded Litvinov, sinking down on the seat, 'indeed it's particularly appropriate. . . . But why has such a mood come over you?'

'I ought not by rights to be ill-humoured,' began Potugin. 'I've just read in the paper a project for judicial reforms in Russia, and I see with genuine pleasure that we've got some sense at last, and they're not as usual on the pretext of independence, nationalism, or originality, proposing to tack a little home-made tag of our own on to the clear straightforward logic of Europe; but are taking what's good from abroad intact. A single adaptation in its application to the peasants' sphere is enough. . . . There's no doing away with communal ownership! . . . Certainly, certainly, I ought not to be ill-humoured; but to my misfortune I chanced upon a Russian "rough diamond," and had a talk with him, and these rough diamonds, these self-educated geniuses, would make me turn in my grave! '

' What do you mean by a rough diamond? ' asked Litvinov.

' Why, there's a gentleman disporting himself here, who imagines he's a musical genius. " I have done nothing, of course," he'll tell you. " I'm a cipher, because I've had no training, but I've incomparably more melody and more ideas in me than in Meyerbeer." In the first place, I say: why have you had no training? and secondly, that, not to talk of Meyerbeer, the humblest German flute-player, modestly blowing his part in the humblest German orchestra, has twenty times as many ideas as all our untaught geniuses; only the flute-player keeps his ideas to himself, and doesn't trot them out with a flourish in the land of Mozarts and Haydns; while our friend the rough diamond has only to strum some little waltz or song, and at once you see him with his hands in his trouser pocket and a sneer of contempt on his lips: I'm a genius, he says. And in painting it's just the same, and in everything else. Oh, these natural geniuses, how I hate them! As if every one didn't know that it's only where there's no real science fully assimilated, and no real art, that there's this flaunting affectation of them. Surely it's time to have done with this flaunting, this vulgar twaddle, together with all hackneyed phrases such as " no one ever dies of hunger in Russia," " nowhere is there such fast travelling as in Russia," " we Russians could bury all our enemies under our hats." I'm for ever hearing of the richness of the Russian nature, their unerring instinct, and of Kulibin. . . . But what is this richness, after all, gentlemen? Half-awakened mutterings or else half-animal sagacity. Instinct, indeed! A fine boast. Take an ant in a forest and set it down a mile from its ant-hill, it will find its way home; man can do nothing like it; but what of it? do you suppose he's inferior to the ant? Instinct, be it ever so unerring, is unworthy of man; sense, simple, straightforward, common sense—that's our heritage, our pride; sense won't perform any such tricks, but it's that that everything rests upon. As for Kulibin, who without any knowledge of mechanics succeeded in making some very bad watches, why, I'd have those watches set up in the pillory, and say: see, good people, this is the way *not* to do it. Kulibin's not to blame for it, but his work's rubbish. To admire Telushkin's boldness and cleverness because he climbed on to the Admiralty spire is well enough; why not admire him? But there's no need to shout that he's made the German architects look foolish, that they're no good, except at making money. . . . He's not made them look foolish in the least; they had to put a scaffolding round the spire afterwards, and repair it in the usual way. For mercy's sake, never encourage the idea in Russia that anything can be done without training. No; you may have the brain of a Solomon, but you must study, study from the A B C. Or else hold your tongue, and sit still, and be humble! Phoo! it makes one hot all over! '

Potugin took off his hat and began fanning himself with his handkerchief.

'Russian art,' he began again. 'Russian art, indeed! . . . Russian impudence and conceit, I know, and Russian feebleness too, but Russian art, begging your pardon, I've never come across. For twenty years on end they've been doing homage to that bloated nonentity Bryullov, and fancying that we have founded a school of our own, and even that it will be better than all others. . . . Russian art, ha, ha, ha! ho, ho!'

'Excuse me, though, Sozont Ivanitch,' remarked Litvinov, 'would you refuse to recognise Glinka too, then?'

Potugin scratched his head.

'The exception, you know, only proves the rule, but even in that instance we could not dispense with bragging. If we'd said, for example, that Glinka was really a remarkable musician, who was only prevented by circumstances —outer and inner—from becoming the founder of the Russian opera, none would have disputed it; but no, that was too much to expect! They must at once raise him to the dignity of commander-in-chief, of grand-marshal, in the musical world, and disparage other nations while they were about it; they have nothing to compare with him, they declare, then quote you some marvellous home-bred genius whose compositions are nothing but a poor imitation of second-rate foreign composers, yes, second-rate ones, for they're the easiest to imitate. Nothing to compare with him? Oh, poor benighted barbarians, for whom standards in art are non-existent, and artists are something of the same species as the strong man Rappo: there's a foreign prodigy, they say, can lift fifteen stone in one hand, but our man can lift thirty! Nothing to compare with us, indeed! I will venture to tell you some thing I remember, and can't get out of my head. Last spring I visited the Crystal Palace near London; in that Palace, as you're aware, there's a sort of exhibition of everything that has been devised by the ingenuity of man—an encyclopædia of humanity one might call it. Well, I walked to and fro among the machines and implements and statues of great men; and all the while I thought, if it were decreed that some nation or other should disappear from the face of the earth, and with it everything that nation had invented, should disappear from the Crystal Palace, our dear mother, Holy Russia, could go and hide herself in the lower regions, without disarranging a single nail in the place: everything might remain undisturbed where it is; for even the *samovar*, the woven bast shoes, the yoke-bridle, and the knout—these are our famous products—were not invented by us. One could not carry out the same experiment on the Sandwich islanders; those islanders have made some peculiar canoes and javelins of their own; their absence would be noticed by visitors. It's a libel! it's too severe, you say perhaps. . . . But I say, first, I don't know how to roar like any sucking dove; and secondly, it's plain that it's not only the devil no one dares to look straight in the face, for no one dares to look straight at himself, and it's not only children who like being soothed to sleep. Our older inventions came to us from the East, our later ones we've borrowed, and half spoiled, from the West, while we still persist in talking about the independence of Russian art! Some bold spirits have even discovered an original Russian science; twice two makes four with us as elsewhere, but the result's obtained more ingeniously, it appears.'

'But wait a minute, Sozont Ivanitch,' cried Litvinov. 'Do wait a minute! You know we send something to the universal exhibitions, and doesn't Europe import something from us?'

'Yes, raw material, raw products. And note, my dear sir: this raw produce of ours is generally only good by virtue of other exceedingly bad conditions; our bristles, for instance, are large and strong, because our pigs are poor; our hides are stout and thick because our cows are thin; our tallow's rich because it's boiled down with half the flesh. . . . But why am I enlarging on that to you, though; you are a student of technology, to be sure, you must know all that better than I do. They talk to me of our inventive faculty! The inventive faculty of the Russians! Why our worthy farmers complain bitterly and suffer loss because there's no satisfactory machine for drying grain in existence, to save them from the necessity of putting their sheaves in ovens, as they did in the days of Rurik; these ovens are fearfully wasteful—just as our bast shoes and our Russian mats are,—and they are constantly getting on fire. The farmers complain, but still there's no sign of a drying-machine. And why is there none? Because the German farmer doesn't need them; he can thrash his wheat as it is, so he doesn't bother to invent one, and we . . . are not capable of doing it! Not capable—and that's all about it! Try as we may! From this day forward I declare whenever I come across one of those rough diamonds, these self-taught geniuses, I shall say: "Stop a minute, my worthy friend! Where's that drying-machine? let's have it!" But that's beyond them! Picking up some old cast-off shoe, dropped ages ago by St. Simon or Fourier, and sticking it on our heads and treating it as a sacred relic— that's what we're capable of; or scribbling an article on the historical and contemporary significance of the proletariat in the principal towns of France—that we can do too; but I tried once, asking a writer and political economist of that sort—rather like your friend, Mr. Voroshilov—to mention twenty towns in France, and what do you think came of that? Why the economist in despair at last mentioned Mont-Fermeuil as one of the French towns, remembering it probably from some novel of Paul de Kock's. And that reminds me of the following anecdote. I was one day strolling through a wood with a dog and a gun——'

'Are you a sportsman then?' asked Litvinov.

'I shoot a little. I was making my way to a swamp in search of snipe; I'd been told of the swamp by other sportsmen. I saw sitting in a clearing before a hut a timber merchant's clerk, as fresh and smooth as a peeled nut, he was sitting there, smiling away—what at, I can't say. So I asked him: "Whereabouts was the swamp, and were there many snipe in it?" "To be sure, to be sure," he sang out promptly, and with an expression of face as though I'd given him a rouble; "the swamp's first-rate, I'm thankful to say; and as for all kinds of wild fowl,—my goodness, they're to be found there in wonderful plenty." I set off, but not only found no wild fowl, the swamp itself had been dry for a long time. Now tell me, please, why is the Russian a liar? Why does the political economist lie, and why the lie about the wild fowl too?'

Litvinov made no answer, but only sighed sympathetically.

'But turn the conversation with the same political economist,' pursued Potugin, 'on the most abstruse problems of social science, keeping to theory, without facts . . . !—he takes flight like a bird, a perfect eagle. I did once succeed, though, in catching one of those birds. I used a pretty snare, though an obvious one, as you shall see if you please. I was talking with one of our latter-day "new young men" about various questions, as they call them. Well, he got very hot, as they always do. Marriage among other things he attacked with really childish exasperation. I brought forward one argument after another . . . I might as well have talked to a stone wall! I saw I should never get round him like that. And then I had a happy thought! "Allow me to submit to you," I began,—one must always talk very respectfully to these "new young men"—"I am really surprised at you, my dear sir; you are studying natural science, and your attention has never up till now been caught by the fact that all carnivorous and predatory animals— wild beasts and birds—all who have to go out in search of prey, and to exert themselves to obtain animal food for themselves and their young . . . and I suppose you would include man in the category of such animals?" "Of course, I should," said the "new young man," "man is nothing but a carnivorous animal." "And predatory?" I added. "And predatory," he declared. "Well said," I observed. "Well, then I am surprised you've never noticed that such animals live in monogamy." The "new young man" started. "How so?" "Why, it is so. Think of the lion, the wolf, the fox, the vulture, the kite; and, indeed, would you condescend to suggest how they could do otherwise? It's hard work enough for the two together to get a living for their offspring." My "new young man" grew thoughtful. "Well," says he, "in that case the animal is not a rule for man." Thereupon I called him an idealist, and wasn't he hurt at that! He almost cried. I had to comfort him by promising not to tell of him to his friends. To deserve to be called an idealist is no laughing matter! The main point in which our latter-day young people are out in their reckoning is this. They fancy that the time for the old, obscure, underground work is over, that it was all very well for their old-fashioned fathers to burrow like moles, but that's too humiliating a part for us, we will take action in the light of day, we will take action . . . Poor darlings! why your children even won't take action; and don't you care to go back to burrowing, burrowing underground again in the old tracks?'

A brief silence followed.

'I am of opinion, my dear sir,' began Potugin again, 'that we are not only indebted to civilisation for science, art, and law, but that even the very feeling for beauty and poetry is developed and strengthened under the influence of the same civilisation, and that the so-called popular, simple, unconscious creation is twaddling and rubbishy. Even in Homer there are traces of a refined and varied civilisation ; love itself is enriched by it. The Slavophils would cheerfully hang me for such a heresy, if they were not such chicken-hearted creatures ; but I will stick up for my own ideas all the same ; and however much they press Madame Kohanovsky and " The swarm of bees at rest " upon me,—I can't stand the odour of that *triple extrait de mougik Russe*, as I don't belong to the highest society, which finds it absolutely necessary to assure itself from time to time that it has not turned quite French, and for whose exclusive benefit this literature *en cuir de Russie* is manufactured. Try reading the raciest, most " popular " passages from the " Bees " to a common peasant—a real one ; he 'll think you 're repeating him a new spell against fever or drunkenness. I repeat, without civilisation there 's not even poetry. If you want to get a clear idea of the poetic ideal of the uncivilised Russian, you should turn up our ballads, our legends. To say nothing of the fact that love is always presented as the result of witchcraft, of sorcery, and produced by some philtre, to say nothing of our so-called epic literature being the only one among all the European and Asiatic literatures—the only one, observe, which does not present any typical pair of lovers—unless you reckon Vanka-Tanka as such ; and of the Holy Russian knight always beginning his acquaintance with his destined bride by beating her " most pitilessly " on her white body, because " the race of women is puffed up " ! all that I pass over ; but I should like to call your attention to the artistic form of the young hero, the *jeune premier*, as he was depicted by the imagination of the primitive, uncivilised Slav. Just fancy him a minute ; the *jeune premier* enters ; a cloak he has worked himself of sable, back-stitched along every seam, a sash of seven-fold silk girt close about his armpits, his fingers hidden away under his hanging sleevelets, the collar of his coat raised high above his head, from before, his rosy face no man can see, nor, from behind, his little white neck ; his cap is on one ear, while on his feet are boots of morocco, with points as sharp as a cobbler's awl, and the heels peaked like nails. Round the points an egg can be rolled, and a sparrow can fly under the heels. And the young hero advances with that peculiar mincing gait by means of which our Alcibiades, Tchivilo Plenkovitch, produced such a striking, almost medical, effect on old women and young girls, the same gait which we see in our loose-limbed waiters, that cream, that flower of Russian dandyism, that *ne plus ultra* of Russian taste. This I maintain without joking ; a sack-like gracefulness, that 's an artistic ideal. What do you think, is it a fine type ? Does it present many materials for painting, for sculpture ? And the beauty who fascinates the young hero, whose " face is as red as the blood of the hare " ? . . . But I think you're not listening to me ? '

Litvinov started. He had not, in fact, heard what Potugin was saying ; he kept thinking, persistently thinking of Irina, of his last interview with her. . . .

'I beg your pardon, Sozont Ivanitch,' he began, 'but I'm going to attack you again with my former question about . . . about Madame Ratmirov.'

Potugin folded up his newspaper and put it in his pocket.

'You want to know again how I came to know her?'

'No, not exactly. I should like to hear your opinion . . . on the part she played in Petersburg. What was that part, in reality?'

'I really don't know what to say to you, Grigory Mihalitch; I was brought into rather intimate terms with Madame Ratmirov . . . but quite accidentally, and not for long. I never got an insight into her world, and what took place in it remained unknown to me. There was some gossip before me, but as you know, it's not only in democratic circles that slander reigns supreme among us. Besides I was not inquisitive. I see though,' he added, after a short silence, 'she interests you.'

'Yes; we have twice talked together rather openly. I ask myself, though, is she sincere?'

Potugin looked down. 'When she is carried away by feeling, she is sincere, like all women of strong passions. Pride too, sometimes prevents her from lying.'

'Is she proud? I should rather have supposed she was capricious.'

'Proud as the devil; but that's no harm.'

'I fancy she sometimes exaggerates. . . .'

'That's nothing either, she's sincere all the same. Though after all, how can you expect truth? The best of those society women are rotten to the marrow of their bones.'

'But, Sozont Ivanitch, if you remember, you called yourself her friend. Didn't you drag me almost by force to go and see her?'

'What of that? she asked me to get hold of you; and I thought, why not? And I really am her friend. She has her good qualities: she's very kind, that is to say, generous, that's to say she gives others what she has no sort of need of herself. But of course you must know her at least as well as I do.'

'I used to know Irina Pavlovna ten years ago; but since then——'

'Ah, Grigory Mihalitch, why do you say that? Do you suppose any one's character changes? Such as one is in one's cradle, such one is still in one's tomb. Or perhaps it is' (here Potugin bowed his head still lower) 'perhaps, you're afraid of falling into her clutches? that's certainly . . . But of course one is bound to fall into some woman's clutches.'

Litvinov gave a constrained laugh. 'You think so?'

'There's no escape. Man is weak, woman is strong, opportunity is all-powerful, to make up one's mind to a joyless life is hard, to forget oneself utterly is impossible . . . and on one side is beauty and sympathy and warmth and light,—how is one to resist it? Why, one runs like a child to its nurse. Ah, well, afterwards to be sure comes cold and darkness and emptiness . . . in due course. And you end by being strange to everything, by losing comprehension of everything. At first you don't understand how love is possible; afterwards one won't understand how life is possible.'

Litvinov looked at Potugin, and it struck him that he had never yet met a man more lonely, more desolate . . . more unhappy. This time he was not shy, he was not stiff; downcast and pale, his head on his breast, and his hands on his knees, he sat without moving, merely smiling his dejected smile. Litvinov felt sorry for the poor, embittered, eccentric creature.

'Irina Pavlovna mentioned among other things,' he began in a low voice, 'a very intimate friend of hers, whose name if I remember was Byelsky, or Dolsky. . . .'

Potugin raised his mournful eyes and looked at Litvinov.

'Ah!' he commented thickly. . . . 'She mentioned . . . well, what of it? It's time, though,' he added with a rather artificial yawn, 'for me to be getting home—to dinner. Good-bye.'

He jumped up from the seat and made off quickly before Litvinov had time to utter a word. . . . His compassion gave way to annoyance— annoyance with himself, be it understood. Want of consideration of any kind was foreign to his nature; he had wished to express his sympathy for Potugin, and it had resulted in something like a clumsy insinuation. With secret dissatisfaction in his heart, he went back to his hotel.

'Rotten to the marrow of her bones,' he thought a little later. . . . 'but proud as the devil! She, that woman who is almost on her knees to me, proud? proud and not capricious?'

Litvinov tried to drive Irina's image out of his head, but he did not succeed. For this very reason he did not think of his betrothed; he felt to-day this haunting image would not give up its place. He made up his mind to await without further anxiety the solution of all this 'strange business'; the solution could not be long in coming, and Litvinov had not the slightest doubt it would turn out to be most innocent and natural. So he fancied, but meanwhile he was not only haunted by Irina's image—every word she had uttered kept recurring in its turn to his memory.

The waiter brought him a note: it was from the same Irina:

'If you have nothing to do this evening, come to me; I shall not be alone; I shall have guests, and you will get a closer view of our set, our society. I want you very much to see something of them; I fancy they will show themselves in all their brilliance. You ought to know what sort of atmosphere I am breathing. Come; I shall be glad to see you, and you will not be bored. (Irina had spelt the Russian incorrectly here.) Prove to me that our explanation to-day has made any sort of misunderstanding between us impossible for ever.—Yours devotedly,   I.'

Litvinov put on a frock coat and a white tie, and set off to Irina's. 'All this is of no importance,' he repeated mentally on the way, 'as for looking at *them* . . . why shouldn't I have a look at them? It will be curious.' A few days before, these very people had aroused a different sensation in him; they had aroused his indignation.

He walked with quickened steps, his cap pulled down over his eyes, and a constrained smile on his lips, while Bambaev, sitting before Weber's café, and pointing him out from a distance to Voroshilov and Pishtchalkin, cried excitedly : ' Do you see that man ? He 's a stone ! he 's a rock ! he 's a flint ! ! ! '

XV

LITVINOV found rather many guests at Irina's. In a corner at a card-table were sitting three of the generals of the picnic : the stout one, the irascible one, and the condescending one. They were playing whist with dummy, and there is no word in the language of man to express the solemnity with which they dealt, took tricks, led clubs and led diamonds . . . there was no doubt about their being statesmen now ! These gallant generals left to mere commoners, *aux bourgeois*, the little turns and phrases commonly used during play, and uttered only the most indispensable syllables ; the stout general however permitted himself to jerk off between two deals : ' *Ce satané as de pique !* ' Among the visitors Litvinov recognised ladies who had been present at the picnic ; but there were others there also whom he had not seen before. There was one so ancient that it seemed every instant as though she would fall to pieces : she shrugged her bare, gruesome, dingy grey shoulders, and, covering her mouth with her fan, leered languishingly with her absolutely death-like eyes upon Ratmirov ; he paid her much attention ; she was held in great honour in the highest society, as the last of the Maids of Honour of the Empress Catherine. At the window, dressed like a shepherdess, sat Countess S., ' the Queen of the Wasps,' surrounded by young men. Among them the celebrated millionaire and beau Finikov was conspicuous for his supercilious deportment, his absolutely flat skull, and his expression of soulless brutality, worthy of a Khan of Bucharia, or a Roman Heliogabalus. Another lady, also a countess, known by the pet name of *Lise*, was talking to a long-haired, fair, and pale spiritualistic medium. Beside them was standing a gentleman, also pale and long-haired, who kept laughing in a meaning way. This gentleman also believed in spiritualism, but added to that an interest in prophecy, and, on the basis of the Apocalypse and the Talmud, was in the habit of foretelling all kinds of marvellous events. Not a single one of these events had come to pass ; but he was in no wise disturbed by that fact, and went on prophesying as before. At the piano, the musical genius had installed himself, the rough diamond, who had stirred Potugin to such indignation ; he was striking chords with a careless hand, *d'une main distraite*, and kept staring vaguely about him. Irina was sitting on a sofa between Prince Kokó and Madame H., once a celebrated beauty and wit, who had long ago become a repulsive old crone, with the odour of sanctity and evaporated sinfulness about her. On catching sight of Litvinov, Irina blushed and got up, and when he went up to her, she pressed his hand warmly. She was wearing a dress of black crépon, relieved by a few inconspicuous gold ornaments ; her shoulders were a dead white, while her face, pale too, under the momentary flood of crimson overspreading it, was breathing with the triumph of beauty, and not of beauty alone ; a hidden, almost ironical happiness was shining in her half-closed eyes, and quivering about her lips and nostrils. . . .

Ratmirov approached Litvinov and after exchanging with him his customary civilities, unaccompanied however by his customary playfulness, he presented him to two or three ladies : the ancient ruin, the Queen of the Wasps, Countess Liza . . . they gave him a rather gracious reception. Litvinov did not belong to their set ; but he was good-looking, extremely so, indeed, and the expressive features of his youthful face awakened their interest. Only he did not know how to fasten that interest upon himself ; he was unaccustomed to society and was conscious of some embarrassment, added to which the stout general stared at him persistently. ' Aha ! lubberly civilian ! free-thinker ! ' that fixed heavy stare seemed to be saying : ' down on your knees to us ; crawl to kiss our hands ! ' Irina came to Litvinov's aid. She managed so adroitly that he got into a corner near the door, a little behind her. As she addressed him, she had each time to turn round to him, and every time he admired the exquisite curve of her splendid neck, he drank in the subtle fragrance of her hair. An expression of gratitude, deep and calm, never left her face ; he could not help seeing that gratitude and nothing else was what those smiles, those glances expressed, and he too was all aglow with the same emotion, and he felt shame, and delight and dread at once . . . and at the same time she seemed continually as though she would ask, ' Well ? what do you think of them ? ' With special clearness Litvinov heard this unspoken question whenever any one of the party was guilty of some vulgar phrase or act, and that occurred more than once during the evening. Once she did not even conceal her feelings, and laughed aloud.

Countess Liza, a lady of superstitious bent, with an inclination for everything extraordinary, after discoursing to her heart's content with the spiritualist upon Home, turning tables, self-playing concertinas, and so on, wound up by asking him whether there were animals which could be influenced by mesmerism.

' There is one such animal any way,' Prince Kokó declared from some way off. ' You know Melvanovsky, don't you ? They put him to sleep before me, and didn't he snore, he, he ! '

' You are very naughty, *mon prince ;* I am speaking of real animals, *je parle des bêtes.*'

' *Mais moi aussi, madame, je parle d'une bête.* . . .'

' There are such,' put in the spiritualist ; ' for instance—crabs ; they are very nervous, and are easily thrown into a cataleptic state.'

The countess was astounded. ' What ? Crabs ! Really ? Oh, that 's awfully interesting ! Now, that I should like to see, M'sieu Luzhin,' she added to a young man with a face as stony as a new doll's, and a stony collar (he prided himself on the fact that he had bedewed the aforesaid face and collar with the sprays of Niagara and the Nubian Nile, though he remembered nothing of all his travels, and cared for nothing but Russian puns . . .). 'M'sieu Luzhin, if you would be so good, do bring us a crab quick.'

M'sieu Luzhin smirked. 'Quick must it be, or quickly?' he queried.

The countess did not understand him. '*Mais oui*, a crab,' she repeated, *une écrevisse.*'

'Eh? what is it? a crab? a crab?' the Countess S. broke in harshly. The absence of M. Verdier irritated her; she could not imagine why Irina had not invited that most fascinating of Frenchmen. The ancient ruin, who had long since ceased understanding anything—moreover she was completely deaf—only shook her head.

'*Oui, oui, vous allez voir*. M'sieu Luzhin, please. . . .'

The young traveller bowed, went out, and returned quickly. A waiter walked behind him, and grinning from ear to ear, carried in a dish, on which a large black crab was to be seen.

'*Voici, madame*,' cried Luzhin; 'now we can proceed to the operation on cancer. Ha, ha, ha!' (Russians are always the first to laugh at their own witticisms.)

'He, he, he!' Count Kokó did his duty condescendingly as a good patriot, and patron of all national products.

(We beg the reader not to be amazed and indignant; who can say confidently for himself that sitting in the stalls of the Alexander Theatre, and infected by its atmosphere, he has not applauded even worse puns?)

'*Merci, merci*,' said the countess. '*Allons, allons, Monsieur Fox, montrez nous ça.*'

The waiter put the dish down on a little round table. There was a slight movement among the guests; several heads were craned forward; only the generals at the card-table preserved the serene solemnity of their pose. The spiritualist ruffled up his hair, frowned, and, approaching the table, began waving his hands in the air; the crab stretched itself, backed, and raised its claws. The spiritualist repeated and quickened his movements; the crab stretched itself as before.

'*Mais que doit-elle donc faire?*' inquired the countess.

'*Elle doâ rester immobile et se dresser sur sa quiou*,' replied Mr. Fox, with a strong American accent, and he brandished his fingers with convulsive energy over the dish; but the mesmerism had no effect, the crab continued to move. The spiritualist declared that he was not himself, and retired with an air of displeasure from the table. The countess began to console him, by assuring him that similar failures occurred sometimes even with Mr. Home. . . . Prince Kokó confirmed her words. The authority on the Apocalypse and the Talmud stealthily went up to the table, and making rapid but vigorous thrusts with his fingers in the direction of the crab, he too tried his luck, but without success; no symptom of catalepsy showed itself. Then the waiter was called, and told to take away the crab, which he accordingly did, grinning from ear to ear, as before; he could be heard exploding outside the door. . . . There was much laughter afterwards in the kitchen *über diese Russen*. The self-taught genius, who had gone on striking notes during the experiments with the crab, dwelling on melancholy chords, on the ground that there was no knowing what influence music might have—the self-taught genius played his invariable waltz, and, of course, was deemed worthy of the most flattering applause. Pricked on by rivalry, Count H., our incomparable dilettante (see Chapter 1.), gave a little song of his own composition, cribbed wholesale from Offenbach. Its playful refrain to the words : ' *Quel œuf ? quel bœuf ?* ' set almost all the ladies' heads swinging to right and to left ; one went so far as to hum the tune lightly, and the irrepressible, inevitable word, ' *Charmant ! charmant !* ' was fluttering on every one's lips. Irina exchanged a glance with Litvinov, and again the same secret, ironical expression quivered about her lips. . . . But a little later it was still more strongly marked, there was even a shade of malice in it, when Prince Kokó, that representative and champion of the interests of the nobility, thought fit to propound his views to the spiritualist, and, of course, gave utterance before long to his famous phrase about the shock to the principle of property, accompanied naturally by an attack on democrats. The spiritualist's American blood was stirred ; he began to argue. The prince, as his habit was, at once fell to shouting at the top of his voice ; instead of any kind of argument he repeated incessantly : *C'est absurde ! cela n'a pas le sens commun !* ' The millionaire Finikov began saying insulting things, without much heed to whom they referred ; the Talmudist's piping notes and even the Countess S.'s jarring voice could be heard. . . . In fact, almost the same incongruous uproar arose as at Gubaryov's ; the only difference was that here there was no beer nor tobacco-smoke, and every one was better dressed. Ratmirov tried to restore tranquility (the generals manifested their displeasure, Boris's exclamation could be heard, ' *Encore cette satanée politique !* '), but his efforts were not successful, and at that point, a high official of the stealthily inquisitorial type, who was present, and undertook to present *le résumé en peu de mots*, sustained a defeat : in fact he so hummed and hawed, so repeated himself, and was so obviously incapable of listening to or taking in the answers he received, and so unmistakably failed to perceive himself what precisely constituted *la question* that no other result could possibly have been anticipated. And then too Irina was slily provoking the disputants and setting them against one another, constantly exchanging glances and slight signs with Litvinov as she did so. . . . But he was sitting like one spell-bound, he was hearing nothing, and waiting for nothing but for those splendid eyes to sparkle again, that pale, tender, mischievous, exquisite face to flash upon him again. . . . It ended by the ladies growing restive, and requesting that the dispute should cease. . . . Ratmirov entreated the dilettante to sing his song again, and the self-taught genius once more played his waltz. . . .

Litvinov stayed till after midnight, and went away later than all the rest. The conversation had in the course of the evening touched upon a number of subjects, studiously avoiding anything of the faintest interest ; the generals, after finishing their solemn game, solemnly joined in it : the influence of these statesmen was at once apparent. The conversation turned upon notorieties of the Parisian demi-monde, with whose names and talents every one seemed intimately acquainted, on Sardou's latest play, on a novel of About's, on Patti in the *Traviata*. Some one proposed a game of ' secretary,' *au secrétaire ;* but it was not a success. The answers given were pointless, and often not free from grammatical mistakes ; the stout general related that he had once in answer to the question : *Que'est-ce que l'amour ?* replied, *Une colique remontée au cœur,* and promptly went off into his wooden guffaw ; the ancient ruin with a mighty effort struck him with her fan on the arm ; a flake of plaster was shaken off her forehead by this rash action. The old crone was beginning a reference to the Slavonic principalities and the necessity of orthodox propaganda on the Danube, but, meeting with no response, she subsided with a hiss. In reality they talked more about Home than anything else ; even the ' Queen of the Wasps ' described how hands had once crept about her, and how she had seen them, and put her own ring on one of them. It was certainly a triumph for Irina : even if Litvinov had paid more attention to what was being said around him, he still could not have gleaned one single sincere saying, one single clever thought, one single new fact from all their disconnected and lifeless babble. Even in their cries and exclamations, there was no note of real feeling, in their slander no real heat. Only at rare intervals under the mask of assumed patriotic indignation, or of assumed contempt and indifference, the dread of possible losses could be heard in a plaintive whimper, and a few names, which will not be forgotten by posterity, were pronounced with gnashing of teeth . . . And not a drop of living water under all this noise and wrangle ! What stale, what unprofitable nonsense, what wretched trivialities were absorbing all these heads and hearts, and not for that one evening, not in society only, but at home too, every hour and every day, in all the depth and breadth of their existence ! And what ignorance, when all is said ! What lack of understanding of all on which human life is built, all by which life is made beautiful !

On parting from Litvinov, Irina again pressed his hand and whispered significantly, ' Well ? Are you pleased ? Have you seen enough ? Do you like it ? ' He made her no reply, but merely bowed low in silence.

Left alone with her husband, Irina was just going to her bedroom. . . . He stopped her.

' *Je vous ai beaucoup admirée ce soir, madame,*' he observed, smoking a cigarette, and leaning against the mantelpiece, ' *vous vous êtes parfaitement moquée de nous tous.*'

' *Pas plus cette fois-ci que les autres,*' she answered indifferently.

' How do you mean me to understand you ? ' asked Ratmirov.

' As you like.'

' Hm. *C'est clair.*' Ratmirov warily, like a cat, knocked off the ash of the cigarette with the tip of the long nail of his little finger. ' Oh, by the way ! This new friend of yours—what the dickens is his name ?—Mr. Litvinov— doubtless enjoys the reputation of a very clever man.'

At the name of Litvinov, Irina turned quickly round.

'What do you mean to say?'

The general smiled.

'He keeps very quiet . . . one can see he's afraid of compromising himself.'

Irina too smiled; it was a very different smile from her husband's.

'Better keep quiet than talk . . . as some people talk.'

'*Attrapé!*' answered Ratmirov with feigned submissiveness. 'Joking apart, he has a very interesting face. Such a . . . concentrated expression . . . and his whole bearing. . . . Yes. . . .' The general straightened his cravat, and bending his head stared at his own moustache. 'He's a republican, I imagine, of the same sort as your other friend, Mr. Potugin; that's another of your clever fellows who are dumb.'

Irina's brows were slowly raised above her wide open clear eyes, while her lips were tightly pressed together and faintly curved.

'What's your object in saying that, Valerian Vladimiritch,' she remarked, as though sympathetically. 'You are wasting your arrows on the empty air. . . . We are not in Russia, and there is no one to hear you.'

Ratmirov was stung.

'That's not merely my opinion, Irina Pavlovna,' he began in a voice suddenly guttural; 'other people too notice that that gentleman has the air of a conspirator.'

'Really? who are these other people?'

'Well, Boris for instance——'

'What? was it necessary for him too to express his opinion?'

Irina shrugged her shoulders as though shrinking from the cold, and slowly passed the tips of her fingers over them.

'Him . . . yes, him. Allow me to remark, Irina Pavlovna, that you seem angry; and you know if one is angry——'

'Am I angry? Oh, what for?'

'I don't know; possibly you have been disagreeably affected by the observation I permitted myself to make in reference to——'

Ratmirov stammered.

'In reference to?' Irina repeated interrogatively. 'Ah, if you please, no irony, and make haste. I'm tired and sleepy.'

She took a candle from the table. 'In reference to——?'

'Well, in reference to this same Mr. Litvinov; since there's no doubt now that you take a great interest in him.'

Irina lifted the hand in which she was holding the candlestick, till the flame was brought on a level with her husband's face, and attentively, almost with curiosity, looking him straight in the face, she suddenly burst into laughter.

'What is it?' asked Ratmirov scowling.

Irina went on laughing.

'Well, what is it?' he repeated, and he stamped his foot.

He felt insulted, wounded, and at the same time against his will he was impressed by the beauty of this woman, standing so lightly and boldly before him . . . she was tormenting him. He saw everything, all her charms—even the pink reflection of the delicate nails on her slender finger-tips, as they tightly clasped the dark bronze of the heavy candlestick—even that did not escape him . . . while the insult cut deeper and deeper into his heart. And still Irina laughed.

'What? you? you jealous?' she brought out at last, and turning her back on her husband she went out of the room. 'He's jealous!' he heard outside the door, and again came the sound of her laugh.

Ratmirov looked moodily after his wife; he could not even then help noticing the bewitching grace of her figure, her movements, and with a violent blow, crushing the cigarette on the marble slab of the mantelpiece, he flung it to a distance. His cheeks had suddenly turned white, a spasm passed over the lower half of his face, and with a dull animal stare his eyes strayed about the floor, as though in search of something. . . . Every semblance of refinement had vanished from his face. Such an expression it must have worn when he was flogging the White Russian peasants.

Litvinov had gone home to his rooms, and sitting down to the table he had buried his head in both hands, and remained a long while without stirring. He got up at last, opened a box, and taking out a pocket-book, he drew out of an inner pocket a photograph of Tatyana. Her face gazed out mournfully at him, looking ugly and old, as photographs usually do. Litvinov's betrothed was a girl of Great Russian blood, a blonde, rather plump, and with the features of her face rather heavy, but with a wonderful expression of kindness and goodness in her intelligent, clear brown eyes, with a serene, white brow, on which it seemed as though a sunbeam always rested. For a long time Litvinov did not take his eyes from the photograph, then he pushed it gently away and again clutched his head in both hands. 'All is at an end!' he whispered at last, 'Irina! Irina!'

Only now, only at that instant, he realised that he was irrevocably, senselessly, in love with her, that he had loved her since the very day of that first meeting with her at the Old Castle, that he had never ceased to love her. And yet how astounded, how incredulous, how scornful, he would have been, had he been told so a few hours back!

'But Tanya, Tanya, my God! Tanya! Tanya!' he repeated in contrition; while Irina's shape fairly rose before his eyes in her black almost funereal garb, with the radiant calm of victory on her marble white face.

XVI

LITVINOV DID NOT SLEEP all night, and did not undress. He was very miserable. As an honest and straightforward man, he realised the force of obligations, the sacredness of duty, and would have been ashamed of any double dealing with himself, his weakness, his fault. At first he was overcome by apathy; it was long before he could throw off the gloomy burden of a single half-conscious, obscure sensation; then terror took possession of him at the thought that the future, his almost conquered future, had slipped back into the darkness, that his home, the solidly-built home he had only just raised, was suddenly tottering about him. . . .

He began reproaching himself without mercy, but at once checked his own vehemence. 'What feebleness!' he thought. 'It's no time for self-reproach and cowardice; now I must act. Tanya is my betrothed, she has faith in my love, my honour, we are bound together for life, and cannot, must not, be put asunder.' He vividly pictured to himself all Tanya's qualities, mentally he picked them out and reckoned them up; he was trying to call up feeling and tenderness in himself. 'One thing's left for me,' he thought again, 'to run away, to run away directly, without waiting for her arrival, to hasten to meet her; whether I suffer, whether I am wretched with Tanya—that's not likely—but in any case to think of that, to take that into consideration is useless; I must do my duty, if I die for it! But you have no right to deceive her,' whispered another voice within him. 'You have no right to hide from her the change in your feelings; it may be that when she knows you love another woman, she will not be willing to become your wife? Rubbish! rubbish!' he answered, 'that's all sophistry, shameful double-dealing, deceitful conscientiousness; I have no right not to keep my word, that's the thing. Well, so be it. . . . Then I must go away from here, without seeing the other. . . .'

But at that point Litvinov's heart throbbed wih anguish, he turned cold, physically cold, a momentary shiver passed over him, his teeth chattered weakly. He stretched and yawned, as though he were in a fever. Without dwelling longer on his last thought, choking back that thought, turning away from it, he set himself to marvelling and wondering in perplexity how he could again . . . again love that corrupt worldly creature, all of whose surroundings were so hateful, so repulsive to him. He tried to put to himself the question : 'What nonsense, do you really love her?' and could only wring his hands in despair. He was still marvelling and wondering, and suddenly there rose up before his eyes, as though from a soft fragrant mist, a seductive shape, shining eyelashes were lifted, and softly and irresistibly the marvellous eyes pierced him to the heart and a voice was singing with sweetness in his ears, and resplendent shoulders, the shoulders of a young queen, were breathing with voluptuous freshness and warmth. . . .

Towards morning a determination was at last fully formed in Litvinov's mind. He decided to set off that day to meet Tatyana, and seeing Irina for the last time, to tell her, since there was nothing else for it, the whole truth, and to part from her for ever.

He set in order and packed his things, waited till twelve o'clock, and started to go to her. But at the sight of her half-curtained windows Litvinov's heart fairly failed him . . . he could not summon up courage to enter the hotel. He walked once or twice up and down Lichtenthaler Allee. 'A very good day to Mr. Litvinov!' he suddenly heard an ironical voice call from the top of a swiftly-moving 'dogcart.' Litvinov raised his eyes and saw General Ratmirov sitting beside Prince M., a well-known sportsman and fancier of English carriages and horses. The prince was driving, the general was leaning over on one side, grinning, while he lifted his hat high above his head. Litvinov bowed to him, and at the same instant, as though he were obeying a secret command, he set off at a run towards Irina's.

She was at home. He sent up his name; he was at once received. When he went in, she was standing in the middle of the room. She was wearing a morning blouse with wide open sleeves; her face, pale as the day before, but not fresh as it had been then, expressed weariness ; the languid smile with which she welcomed her visitor emphasised that expression even more clearly. She held out her hand to him in a friendly way, but absent-mindedly.

'Thanks for coming,' she began in a plaintive voice, and she sank into a low chair. 'I am not very well this morning ; I spent a bad night. Well, what have you to say about last night ? Wasn't I right ? '

Litvinov sat down.

'I have come to you, Irina Pavlovna,' he began.

She instantly sat up and turned round ; her eyes simply fastened upon Litvinov.

'What is it,' she cried. 'You're pale as death, you're ill. What's the matter with you ? '

Litvinov was confused.

'With me, Irina Pavlovna ? '

'Have you had bad news ? Some misfortune has happened, tell me, tell me——'

Litvinov in his turn looked at Irina.

'I have had no bad news,' he brought out not without effort, 'but a misfortune has certainly happened, a great misfortune . . . and it has brought me to you.'

'A misfortune ? What is it ? '

'Why . . . that——'

Litvinov tried to go on . . . and could not. He only pinched his hands together so that his fingers cracked. Irina was bending forward and seemed turned to stone.

'Oh ! I love you ! ' broke at last with a low groan from Litvinov's breast, and he turned away, as though he would hide his face.

'What, Grigory Mihalitch, you ' . . . Irina too could not finish her sentence, and leaning back in her chair, she put both her hands to her eyes. 'You . . . love me.'

'Yes . . . yes . . . yes,' he repeated with bitterness, turning his head further and further away.

Everything was silent in the room ; a butterfly that had flown in was fluttering its wings and struggling between the curtain and the window.

The first to speak was Litvinov.

'That, Irina Pavlovna,' he began, 'that is the misfortune, which . . . has befallen me, which I ought to have foreseen and avoided, if I had not now just as in the Moscow days been carried off my feet at once. It seems fate is pleased to force me once again through you to suffer tortures, which one would have thought should not be repeated again. . . . It was not without cause I struggled. . . . I tried to struggle; but of course there's no escaping one's fate. And I tell you all this to put an end at once to this . . . this tragic farce,' he added with a fresh outburst of shame and bitterness.

Litvinov was silent again; the butterfly was struggling and fluttering as before. Irina did not take her hands from her face.

'And you are not mistaken?' her whisper sounded from under those white, bloodless-looking hands.

'I am not mistaken,' answered Litvinov in a colourless voice. 'I love you, as I have never loved any one but you. I am not going to reproach you; that would be too foolish; I'm not going to tell you that perhaps nothing of all this would have happened if you yourself had behaved differently with me. . . . Of course, I alone am to blame, my self-confidence has been my ruin; I am deservedly punished, and you could not have anticipated it. Of course you did not consider that it would have been far less dangerous for me if you had not been so keenly alive to your wrong . . . your supposed wrong to me; and had not wished to make up for it . . . but what's done can't be undone. I only wanted to make clear my position to you; it's hard enough as it is. . . . But at least there will be, as you say, no misunderstanding, while the openness of my confession will soften, I hope, the feeling of offence which you cannot but feel.'

Litvinov spoke without raising his eyes, but even if he had glanced at Irina, he could not have seen what was passing in her face, as she still as before kept her hands over her eyes. But what was passing over her face meanwhile would probably have astounded him; both alarm and delight were apparent on it, and a kind of blissful helplessness and agitation; her eyes hardly glimmered under their overhanging lids, and her slow, broken breathing was chill upon her lips, that were parted as though with thirst. . . .

Litvinov was silent, waiting for a response, some sound. . . . Nothing!

'There is one thing left for me,' he began again, 'to go away; I have come to say good-bye to you.'

Irina slowly dropped her hands on to her knees.

'But I remember, Grigory Mihalitch,' she began; 'that . . . that person of whom you spoke to me, she was to have come here? You are expecting her?'

'Yes; but I shall write to her . . . she will stop somewhere on the way . . . at Heidelberg, for instance.'

'Ah! Heidelberg. . . . Yes. . . . It's nice there. . . . But all this must upset your plans. Are you perfectly certain, Grigory Mihalitch, that you are not exaggerating, *et que ce n'est pas une fausse alarme?*'

Irina spoke softly, almost coldly, with short pauses, looking away towards the window. Litvinov made no answer to her last question.

'Only, why did you talk of offence?' she went on. 'I am not offended . . . oh, no! and if one or other of us is to blame, in any case it's not you; not you alone. . . . Remember our last conversations, and you will be convinced that it's not you who are to blame.'

'I have never doubted your magnanimity,' Litvinov muttered between his teeth, 'but I should like to know, do you approve of my intention?'

'To go away?'

'Yes.'

Irina continued to look away.

'At the first moment, your intention struck me as premature. . . . but now I have thought over what you have said . . . and if you are really not mistaken, then I suppose that you ought to go away. It will be better so . . . better for us both.'

Irina's voice had grown lower and lower, and her words too came more and more slowly.

'General Ratmirov, certainly, might notice,' Litvinov was beginning. . . .

Irina's eyes dropped again, and something strange quivered about her lips, quivered and died away.

'No; you did not understand me,' she interrupted him. 'I was not think‑ ing of my husband. Why should I? And there is nothing to notice. But I repeat, separation is necessary for us both.'

Litvinov picked up his hat, which had fallen on the ground.

'Everything is over,' he thought, 'I must go. And so it only remains for me to say good-bye to you, Irina Pavlovna,' he said aloud, and suddenly felt a pang, as though he were preparing to pronounce his own sentence on himself. 'It only remains for me to hope that you will not remember evil against me, and . . . and that if we ever——'

Irina again cut him short.

'Wait a little, Grigory Mihalitch, don't say good-bye to me yet. That would be too hurried.'

Something wavered in Litvinov, but the burning pain broke out again and with redoubled violence in his heart.

'But I can't stay,' he cried. 'What for? Why prolong this torture?'

'Don't say good-bye to me yet,' repeated Irina. 'I must see you once more. . . . Another such dumb parting as in Moscow again—no, I don't want that. You can go now, but you must promise me, give me your word of honour that you won't go away without seeing me once more.'

'You wish that?'

'I insist on it. If you go away without saying good-bye to me, I shall never forgive it, do you hear, never! Strange!' she added as though to herself, 'I cannot persuade myself that I am in Baden. . . . I keep feeling that I am in Moscow. . . . Go now.'

Litvinov got up.

'Irina Pavlovna,' he said, 'give me your hand.'

Irina shook her head.

'I told you that I don't want to say good-bye to you. . . .'

'I don't ask it for that.'

Irina was about to stretch out her hand, but she glanced at Litvinov for the first time since his avowal, and drew it back.

'No, no,' she whispered, 'I will not give you my hand. No . . . no. Go now.'

Litvinov bowed and went away. He could not tell why Irina had refused him that last friendly handshake. . . . He could not know what she feared.

He went away, and Irina again sank into the armchair and again covered her face.

XVII

LITVINOV DID NOT RETURN HOME; he went up to the hills, and getting into a thick copse, he flung himself face downwards on the earth, and lay there about an hour. He did not suffer tortures, did not weep; he sank into a kind of heavy, oppressive stupor. Never had he felt anything like it; it was an insufferably aching and gnawing sensation of emptiness, emptiness in himself, his surroundings, everywhere. . . . He thought neither of Irina nor of Tatyana. He felt one thing only : a blow had fallen and life was sundered like a cord, and all of him was being drawn along in the clutches of something chill and unfamiliar. Sometimes it seemed to him that a whirlwind had swooped down upon him, and he had the sensation of its swift whirling round and the irregular beating of its dark wings. But his resolution did not waver. To remain in Baden . . . that could not even be considered. In thought he had already gone, he was already sitting in the rattling, snorting train, hurrying, hurrying into the dumb, dead distance. He got up at last, and leaning his head against a tree, stayed motionless ; only with one hand, he all unconsciously snatched and swung in rhythm the topmost frond of a fern. The sound of approaching footsteps drew him out of his stupor : two charcoal-burners were making their way down the steep path with large sacks on their shoulders. 'It's time!' whispered Litvinov, and he followed the charcoal-burners to the town, turned into the railway station, and sent off a telegram to Tatyana's aunt, Kapitolina Markovna. In this telegram he informed her of his immediate departure, and appointed as a meeting-place, Schrader's hotel in Heidelberg.

'Make an end, make an end at once,' he thought ; 'it's useless putting it off till tomorrow.' Then he went to the gambling saloon, stared with dull curiosity at the faces of two or three gamblers, got a back view of Bindasov's ugly head in the distance, noticed the irreproachable countenance of Pishtchalkin, and after waiting a little under the colonnade, he set off deliberately to Irina's. He was not going to her through the force of sudden, involuntary temptation ; when he made up his mind to go away, he also made up his mind to keep his word and see her once more. He went into the hotel unobserved by the porter, ascended the staircase, not meeting any one, and without knocking at the door, he mechanically pushed it open and went into the room.

In the room, in the same armchair, in the same dress, in precisely the same attitude as three hours before, was sitting Irina. . . . It was obvious that she had not moved from the place, had not stirred all that time. She slowly raised her head, and seeing Litvinov, she trembled all over and clutched the arm of the chair. 'You frightened me,' she whispered.

Litvinov looked at her with speechless bewilderment. The expression of her face, her lustreless eyes, astounded him.

Irina gave a forced smile and smoothed her ruffled hair. 'Never mind. . . . I really don't know. . . . I think I must have fallen asleep here.'

'I beg your pardon, Irina Pavlovna,' began Litvinov. 'I came in un-announced. . . . I wanted to do what you thought fit to require of me. So as I am going away to-day——'

'To-day? But I thought you told me that you meant first to write a letter——'

'I have sent a telegram.'

'Ah! you found it necessary to make haste. And when are you going? What time, I mean?'

'At seven o'clock this evening.'

'Ah! at seven o'clock! And you have come to say good-bye?'

'Yes, Irina Pavlovna, to say good-bye.'

Irina was silent for a little.

'I ought to thank you, Grigory Mihalitch, it was probably not easy for you to come here.'

'No, Irina Pavlovna, it was anything but easy.'

'Life is not generally easy, Grigory Mihalitch; what do you think about it?'

'It depends, Irina Pavlovna.'

Irina was silent again for a little; she seemed sunk in thought.

'You have proved your affection for me by coming,' she said at last, 'I thank you. And I fully approve of your decision to put an end to every-thing as soon as possible . . . because any delay . . . because . . . because I, even I whom you have reproached as a flirt, called an actress . . . that, I think, was what you called me? . . .'

Irina got up swiftly, and, sitting down in another chair, stooped down and pressed her face and arms on the edge of the table.

'Because I love you . . .' she whispered between her clasped fingers.

Litvinov staggered, as though some one had dealt him a blow in the chest. Irina turned her head dejectedly away from him, as though she in her turn wanted to hide her face from him, and laid it down on the table.

'Yes, I love you . . . I love you . . . and you know it.'

'I? I know it?' Litvinov said at last; 'I?'

'Well, now you see,' Irina went on, 'that you certainly must go, that delay's impossible . . . both for you, and for me delay's impossible.

It's dangerous, it's terrible . . . good-bye!' she added, rising impulsively from her chair, 'good-bye!'

She took a few steps in the direction of the door of her boudoir, and putting her hand behind her back, made a hurried movement in the air, as though she would find and press the hand of Litvinov; but he stood like a block of wood, at a distance . . . Once more she said, 'Good-bye, forget me,' and without looking round she rushed away.

Litvinov remained alone, and yet still could not come to himself. He recovered himself at last, went quickly to the boudoir door, uttered Irina's name once, twice, three times . . . He had already his hand on the lock . . . From the hotel stairs rose the sound of Ratmirov's sonorous voice.

Litvinov pulled down his hat over his eyes, and went out on to the staircase. The elegant general was standing before the Swiss porter's box and explaining to him in bad German that he wanted a hired carriage for the whole of the next day. On catching sight of Litvinov, he again lifted his hat unnaturally high, and again wished him 'a very good-day'; he was obviously jeering at him, but Litvinov had no thoughts for that. He hardly responded to Ratmirov's bow, and, making his way to his lodging, he stood still before his already packed and closed trunk. His head was turning round and his heart vibrating like a harp-string. What was to be done now? And could he have foreseen this?

Yes, he had foreseen it, however unlikely it seemed. It had stunned him like a clap of thunder, yet he had foreseen it, though he had not courage even to acknowledge it. Besides he knew nothing now for certain. Everything was confusion and turmoil within him; he had lost the thread of his own thoughts. He remembered Moscow, he remembered how then too 'it' had come upon him like a sudden tempest. He was breathless; rapture, but a rapture comfortless and hopeless, oppressed and tore his heart. For nothing in the world would he have consented that the words uttered by Irina should not have actually been uttered by her. . . . But then? those words could not for all that change the resolution he had taken. As before, it did not waver; it stood firm like an anchor. Litvinov had lost the thread of his own thoughts . . . yes; but his will still remained to him, and he disposed of himself as of another man dependent on him. He rang for the waiter, asked him for the bill, bespoke a place in the evening omnibus; designedly he cut himself off all paths of retreat. 'If I die for it after!' he declared, as he had in the previous sleepless night; that phrase seemed especially to his taste. 'Then even if I die for it!' he repeated, walking slowly up and down the room, and only at rare intervals, unconsciously, he shut his eyes and held his breath, while those words, those words of Irina's forced their way into his soul, and set it aflame. 'It seems you won't love twice,' he thought; 'another life came to you, you let it come into yours—never to be rid of that poison to the end, you will never break those bonds! Yes; but what does that prove? Happiness? . . . Is it possible? You love her, granted . . . and she . . . she loves you . . .'

But at this point again he had to pull himself up. As a traveller on a dark

night, seeing before him a light, and afraid of losing the path, never for an
instant takes his eyes off it, so Litvinov continually bent all the force of
his attention on a single point, a single aim. To reach his betrothed, and not
precisely even his betrothed (he was trying not to think of her) but to
reach a room in the Heidelberg hotel, that was what stood immovably
before him, a guiding light. What would be later, he did not know, nor did
he want to know . . . One thing was beyond doubt, he would not come
back. 'If I die first!' he repeated for the tenth time, and he glanced at his
watch.

A quarter-past six! How long still to wait! He paced once more up and
down. The sun was nearly setting, the sky was crimson above the trees,
and the pink flush of twilight lay on the narrow windows of his darkening
room. Suddenly Litvinov fancied the door had been opened quickly and
softly behind him and as quickly closed again . . . He turned round; at
the door, muffled in a dark cloak, was standing a woman . . .

'Irina,' he cried, and clapped his hands together in amazement . . . She
raised her head and fell upon his breast.

Two hours later he was sitting in his room on the sofa. His box stood in
the corner, open and empty, and on the table in the midst of things flung
about in disorder, lay a letter from Tatyana, just received by him. She
wrote to him that she had decided to hasten her departure from Dresden,
since her aunt's health was completely restored, and that if nothing happened to delay them, they would both be in Baden the following day at
twelve o'clock, and hoped that he would come to meet them at the station. Apartments had already been taken for them by Litvinov in the
same hotel in which he was staying.

The same evening he sent a note to Irina, and the following morning
he received a reply from her. 'Sooner or later,' she wrote, 'it must have
been. I tell you again what I said yesterday: my life is in your hands, do
with me what you will. I do not want to hamper your freedom, but let
me say, that if necessary, I will throw up everything, and follow you to the
ends of the earth. We shall see each other to-morrow, of course.—Your
Irina.'

The last two words were written in a large, bold, resolute hand.

XVIII

AMONG THE PERSONS assembled on the 18th of August at twelve o'clock on
the platform at the railway station was Litvinov. Not long before, he had
seen Irina: she was sitting in an open carriage with her husband and another gentleman, somewhat elderly. She caught sight of Litvinov, and he
perceived that some obscure emotion flitted over her eyes; but at once she
hid herself from him with her parasol.

A strange transformation had taken place in him since the previous day—
in his whole appearance, his movements, the expression of his face; and in-

deed he felt himself a different man. His self-confidence had vanished, and his peace of mind had vanished too, and his respect for himself; of his former spiritual condition nothing was left. Recent ineffaceable impressions obscured all the rest from him. Some sensation unknown before had come, strong, sweet—and evil; the mysterious guest had made its way to the innermost shrine and taken possession and lain down in it, in silence, but in all its magnitude, like the owner in a new house. Litvinov was no longer ashamed, he was afraid; at the same time a desperate hardihood had sprung up in him; the captured, the vanquished know well this mixture of opposing feelings; the thief too knows something of it after his first robbery. Litvinov had been vanquished, vanquished suddenly . . . and what had become of his honesty?

The train was a few minutes late. Litvinov's suspense passed into agonising torture; he could not stop still in one place, and, pale all over, moved about jostling in the crowd. 'My God,' he thought, 'if I only had another twenty-four hours' . . . The first look at Tanya, the first look of Tanya . . . that was what filled him with terror . . . that was what he had to live through directly . . . And afterwards? Afterwards . . . come, what may come! . . . He now made no more resolutions, he could not answer for himself now. His phrase of yesterday flashed painfully through his head . . . And this was how he was meeting Tanya. . . .

A prolonged whistle sounded at last, a heavy momentarily increasing rumble was heard, and, slowly rolling round a bend in the line, the train came into sight. The crowd hurried to meet it, and Litvinov followed it, dragging his feet like a condemned man. Faces, ladies' hats began to appear out of the carriages, at one window a white handkerchief gleamed. . . . Kapitolina Markovna was waving to him. . . . It was over; she had caught sight of Litvinov and he recognised her. The train stood still; Litvinov rushed to the carriage door, and opened it; Tatyana was standing near her aunt, smiling brightly and holding out her hand.

He helped them both to get out, uttered a few words of welcome, unfinished and confused, and at once bustled about, began taking their tickets, their travelling bags, and rugs, ran to find a porter, called a fly; other people were bustling around them. He was glad of their presence, their fuss, and loud talk. Tatyana moved a little aside, and, still smiling, waited calmly for his hurried arrangements to be concluded. Kapitolina Markovna, on the other hand, could not keep still; she could not believe that she was at last at Baden.

She suddenly cried, 'But the parasols? Tanya, where are our parasols?' all unconscious that she was holding them fast under her arm; then she began taking a loud and prolonged farewell of another lady with whom she had made friends on the journey from Heidelberg to Baden. This lady was no other than our old friend Madame Suhantchikov. She had gone away to Heidelberg to do obeisance to Gubaryov, and was returning with 'instructions.' Kapitolina Markovna wore a rather peculiar striped mantle and a round travelling hat of a mushroom-shape, from under which her short white hair fell in disorder; short and thin, she was flushed with travelling and kept talking Russian in a shrill and penetrating voice. . . . She was an object of attention at once.

Litvinov at last put her and Tatyana into a fly, and placed himself opposite them. The horses started. Then followed questionings, renewed hand-shaking, interchanging of smiles and welcomes. . . . Litvinov breathed freely; the first moment had passed off satisfactorily. Nothing in him, apparently, had struck or bewildered Tanya; she was smiling just as brightly and confidently, she was blushing as charmingly, and laughing as good-naturedly. He brought himself at last to take a look at her; not a stealthy cursory glance, but a direct steady look at her, hitherto his own eyes had refused to obey him. His heart throbbed with involuntary emotion: the serene expression of that honest, candid face gave him a pang of bitter reproach. 'So you are here, poor girl,' he thought, 'you whom I have so longed for, so urged to come, with whom I had hoped to spend my life to the end, you have come, you believed in me . . . while I . . . while I.' . . . Litvinov's head sank; but Kapitolina Markovna gave him no time for musing; she was pelting him with questions.

'What is that building with columns? Where is it the gambling's done? Who is that coming along? Tanya, Tanya, look, what crinolines! And who can that be? I suppose they are mostly French creatures from Paris here? Mercy, what a hat! Can you get everything here just as in Paris? But, I expect, everything's awfully dear, eh? Ah, I've made the acquaintance of such a splendid, intellectual woman! You know her, Grigory Mihalitch; she told me she had met you at some Russian's, who's a wonderfully intellectual person too. She promised to come and see us. How she does abuse all these aristocrats—it's simply superb! What is that gentleman with grey moustaches? The Prussian king? Tanya, Tanya, look, that's the Prussian king. No? not the Prussian king, the Dutch ambassador, did you say? I can't hear, the wheels rattle so. Ah, what exquisite trees!'

'Yes, exquisite, aunt,' Tanya assented, 'and how green everything is here, how bright and gay! Isn't it, Grigory Mihalitch?'

'Oh, very bright and gay' . . . he answered through his teeth.

The carriage stopped at last before the hotel. Litvinov conducted the two travellers to the room taken for them, promised to come back within an hour, and went to his own room. Directly he entered it, he fell again under the spell which had been lulled for a while. Here, in that room, since the day before, Irina reigned supreme; everything was eloquent of her, the very air seemed to have kept secret traces of her visit. . . . Again Litvinov felt himself her slave. He drew out her handkerchief, hidden in his bosom, pressed it to his lips, and burning memories flowed in subtle poison through his veins. He realized that there was no turning back, no choosing now; the sorrowful emotion aroused in him by Tatyana melted away like snow in the fire, and remorse died down . . . died down so completely that his uneasiness even was soothed, and the possibility—present to his intellect— of hypocrisy no longer revolted him. . . . Love, Irina's love, that was now his truth, his bond, his conscience. . . . The sensible Litvinov did not even ponder how to get out of a position, the horror and hideousness of which he bore lightly, as if it did not concern him.

The hour had not yet passed when a waiter came to Litvinov from the newly arrived ladies; they begged him to come to them in the public drawing-room. He followed the messenger and found them already dressed and in their hats. They both expressed a desire to go out at once to see Baden, as the weather was so fine. Kapitolina Markovna especially seemed burning with impatience; she was quite cast down when she heard that the hour of the fashionable promenade before the Konversation Hall had not yet arrived. Litvinov gave her his arm, and the ceremony of sight-seeing began. Tatyana walked beside her aunt, looking about her with quiet interest; Kapitolina Markovna pursued her inquiries. The sight of the roulette, the dignified croupiers, whom—had she met them in any other place—she would certainly have taken for ministers, the quickly moving scoops, the heaps of gold and silver on the green cloth, the old women gambling, and the painted *cocottes* reduced Kapitolina Markovna to a sort of speechless stupor; she altogether forgot that she ought to feel moral indignation, and could only gaze and gaze, giving a start of surprise at every new sight. . . . The whiz of the ivory ball into the bottom of the roulette thrilled her to the marrow of her bones, and it was only when she was again in the open air that, drawing a long breath, she recovered energy enough to denounce games of chance as an immoral invention of aristocracy. A fixed, unpleasant smile had made its appearance on Litvinov's lips; he had spoken abruptly and lazily, as though he were annoyed or bored. . . . But now he turned round towards Tatyana, and was thrown into secret confusion; she was looking attentively at him, with an expression as though she were asking herself what sort of an impression was being made on her. He made haste to nod his head to her, she responded with the same gesture, and again looked at him questioningly, with a sort of strained effort, as though he were standing much further off than he really was. Litvinov led his ladies away from the Konversation Hall, and passing the 'Russian tree,' under which two Russian ladies were already sitting, he went towards Lichtenthaler Allee. He had hardly entered the avenue when he saw Irina in the distance.

She was walking towards him with her husband and Potugin. Litvinov turned white as a sheet; he did not slacken his pace, however, and when he was on a level with her, he made a bow without speaking. She too bowed to him, politely, but coldly, and taking in Tatyana in a rapid glance, she glided by. . . . Ratmirov lifted his hat high, Potugin muttered something.

'Who is that lady?' Tatyana asked suddenly. Till that instant she had hardly opened her lips.

'That lady?' repeated Litvinov, 'that lady? That is a Madame Ratmirov.'

'Is she Russian?'

'Yes.'

'Did you make her acquaintance here ? '

'No ; I have known her a long while.'

'How beautiful she is ! '

'Did you notice her dress ? ' put in Kapitolina Markovna. ' Ten families might live for a whole year on the cost of her lace alone. Was that her husband with her ? ' she inquired turning to Litvinov.

'Yes.'

'He must be awfully rich, I suppose ? '

'Really I don't know ; I don't think so.'

'What is his rank ? '

'He's a general.'

'What eyes she has ! ' said Tatyana, 'and what a strange expression in them : pensive and penetrating at the same time. . . . I have never seen such eyes.'

Litvinov made no answer ; he fancied that he felt again Tatyana's questioning glance bent on his face, but he was wrong, she was looking at her own feet, at the sand of the path.

'Mercy on us ! Who is that fright ? ' cried Kapitolina Markovna suddenly, pointing to a low jaunting-car in which a red-haired pug-nosed woman lay lolling impudently, in an extraordinarily gorgeous costume and lilac stockings.

'That fright ! why, that's the celebrated Ma'mselle Cora.'

'Who ? '

'Ma'mselle Cora . . . a Parisian . . . notoriety.'

'What? That pug? Why, but she's hideous ! '

'It seems that's no hindrance.'

Kapitolina Markovna could only lift her hands in astonishment.

'Well, this Baden of yours ! ' she brought out at last. ' Can one sit down on a seat here ? I'm rather tired.'

'Of course you can, Kapitolina Markovna. . . . That's what the seats are put here for.'

'Well, really, there's no knowing ! But there in Paris, I'm told, there are seats, too, along the boulevards ; but it's not proper to sit on them.'

Litvinov made no reply to Kapitolina Markovna ; only at that moment he realized that two paces away was the very spot where he had had that explanation with Irina, which had decided everything. Then he recalled that he had noticed a small rosy spot on her cheek to-day. . . .

Kapitolina Markovna sank down on to the seat, Tatyana sat down beside her. Litvinov remained on the path ; between Tatyana and him—or was it only his fancy ?—something seemed to have happened . . . unconsciously and gradually.

'Ah, she's a wretch, a perfect wretch ! ' Kapitolina Markovna declared, shaking her head commiseratingly ; 'why, with the price of *her* get-up, you could keep not ten, but a hundred families. Did you see under her hat, on her red hair, there were diamonds ? Upon my word, diamonds in the day-time ! '

'Her hair's not red,' remarked Litvinov; 'she dyes it red—that's the fashion now.'

Again Kapitolina Markovna could only lift her hands; she was positively dumbfounded.

'Well,' she said at last, 'where we were, in Dresden, things had not got to such a scandalous pitch yet. It's a little further from Paris, anyway, that's why. Don't you think that's it, Grigory Mihalitch, eh?'

'Don't I think so?' answered Litvinov. While he thought to himself, 'What on earth is she talking of?' 'I? Of course . . . of course. . . .'

But at this point the sound of slow footsteps was heard, and Potugin approached the seat.

'Good-morning, Grigory Mihalitch,' he began, smiling and nodding.

Litvinov grasped him by the hand at once.

'Good-morning, good-morning, Sozont Ivanitch. I fancy I passed you just now with . . . just now in the avenue?'

'Yes, it was me.'

Potugin bowed respectfully to the ladies sitting on the seat.

'Let me introduce you, Sozont Ivanitch. Old friends and relatives of mine, who have only just arrived in Baden. Potugin, Sozont Ivanitch, a countryman of ours, also staying in Baden.'

Both ladies rose a little. Potugin renewed his bows.

'It's quite a levée here,' Kapitolina Markovna began in a delicate voice; the kind-hearted old lady was easily intimidated, but she tried before all to keep up her dignity. 'Every one regards it as an agreeable duty to stay here.'

'Baden is an agreeable place, certainly,' answered Potugin, with a sidelong look at Tatyana; 'a very agreeable place, Baden.'

'Yes; but it's really too aristocratic, so far as I can form an opinion. You see we have been staying all this time in Dresden . . . a very interesting town; but here there's positively a levée.'

'She's pleased with the word,' thought Potugin. 'You are perfectly right in that observation,' he said aloud; 'but then the scenery here is exquisite, and the site of the place is something one cannot often find. Your fellow-traveller especially is sure to appreciate that. Are you not, madam?' he added, addressing himself this time directly to Tatyana.

Tatyana raised her large, clear eyes to Potugin. It seemed as though she were perplexed. What was wanted of her, and why had Litvinov introduced her, on the first day of her arrival, to this unknown man, who had, though, a kind and clever face, and was looking at her with cordial and friendly eyes.

'Yes,' she said at last, 'it's very nice here.'

'You ought to visit the old castle,' Potugin went on; 'I especially advise a drive to——'

'The Saxon Switzerland——' Kapitolina Markovna was beginning.

The blare of wind instruments floated up the avenue; it was the Prussian military band from Rastadt (in 1862 Rastadt was still an allied fortress), beginning its weekly concert in the pavilion. Kapitolina Markovna got up.

'The music!' she said; 'the music *à la Conversation!* . . . We must go there. It's four o'clock now . . . isn't it? Will the fashionable world be there now?'

'Yes,' answered Potugin: 'this is the most fashionable time, and the music is excellent.'

'Well, then, don't let us linger. Tanya, come along.'

'You allow me to accompany you?' asked Potugin, to Litvinov's considerable astonishment; it was not possible for it even to enter his head that Irina had sent Potugin.

Kapitolina Markovna simpered.

'With the greatest pleasure—M'sieu . . . M'sieu——'

'Potugin,' he murmured, and he offered her his arm.

Litvinov gave his to Tatyana, and both couples walked towards the Konversation Hall.

Potugin went on talking with Kapitolina Markovna. But Litvinov walked without uttering a word; yet twice, without any cause, he smiled, and faintly pressed Tatyana's arm against his. There was a falsehood in those demonstrations, to which she made no response, and Litvinov was conscious of the lie. They did not express a mutual confidence in the close union of two souls given up to one another; they were a temporary substitute—for words which he could not find. That unspoken something which was beginning between them grew and gained strength. Once more Tatyana looked attentively, almost intently, at him.

It was the same before the Konversation Hall at the little table round which they all four seated themselves, with this sole difference, that, in the noisy bustle of the crowd, the clash and roar of the music, Litvinov's silence seemed more comprehensible. Kapitolina Markovna became quite excited; Potugin hardly had time to answer her questions, to satisfy her curiosity. Luckily for him, there suddenly appeared in the mass of moving figures the lank person and everlastingly leaping eyes of Madame Suhantchikov. Kapitolina Markovna at once recognised her, invited her to their table, made her sit down, and a hurricane of words arose.

Potugin turned to Tatyana, and began a conversation with her in a soft, subdued voice, his face bent slightly down towards her with a very friendly expression; and she, to her own surprise, answered him easily and freely; she was glad to talk with this stranger, this outsider, while Litvinov sat immovable as before, with the same fixed and unpleasant smile on his lips.

Dinner-time came at last. The music ceased, the crowd thinned. Kapitolina Markovna parted from Madame Suhantchikov on the warmest terms. She had conceived an immense respect for her, though she did say afterwards to her niece, that 'this person is really too severe; but then she does know everything and everybody; and we must really get sewing-machines directly the wedding festivities are over.' Potugin took leave of them; Litvinov conducted his ladies home. As they were going into the hotel, he was handed a note ; he moved aside and hurriedly tore open the envelope. On a tiny scrap of vellum paper were the following words, scribbled in pencil : ' Come to me this evening at seven, for one minute, I entreat you.—Irina.' Litvinov thrust the note into his pocket, and, turning round, put on his smile again . . . to whom ? why ? Tatyana was standing with her back to him. They dined at the common table of the hotel. Litvinov was sitting between Kapitolina Markovna and Tatyana, and he began talking, telling anecdotes and pouring out wine for himself and the ladies, with a strange, sudden joviality. He conducted himself in such a free and easy manner, that a French infantry officer from Strasbourg, sitting opposite, with a beard and moustaches à la Napoleon III., thought it admissible to join in the conversation, and even wound up by a toast à la santé des belles Moscovites! After dinner, Litvinov escorted the two ladies to their room, and after standing a little while at the window with a scowl on his face, he suddenly announced that he had to go out for a short time on business, but would be back without fail by the evening. Tatyana said nothing ; she turned pale and dropped her eyes. Kapitolina Markovna was in the habit of taking a nap after dinner ; Tatyana was well aware that Litvinov knew of this habit of her aunt's ; she had expected him to take advantage of it, to remain with her, for he had not been alone with her, nor spoken frankly to her, since her arrival. And now he was going out ! What was she to make of it ? And, indeed, his whole behaviour all along. . . .

Litvinov withdrew hurriedly, not waiting for remonstrances ; Kapitolina Markovna lay down on the sofa, and with one or two sighs and groans, fell into a serene sleep ; while Tatyana moved away into a corner, and sat down in a low chair, folding her arms tightly across her bosom.

XIX

LITVINOV WENT QUICKLY up the staircase of the *Hôtel de l'Europe;* a little girl of thirteen, with a sly little face of Kalmuck cast, who had apparently been on the look-out for him, stopped him, saying in Russian : ' Come this way, please ; Irina Pavlovna will be here directly.' He looked at her in perplexity. She smiled, repeated : ' Come along, come along,' and led him to a small room, facing Irina's bedroom, and filled with travelling trunks and portmanteaus, then at once disappeared, closing the door very softly. Litvinov had not time to look about him, before the door was quickly opened, and before him in a pink ball-dress, with pearls in her hair and on her neck, stood Irina. She simply rushed at him, clutched him by both hands, and for a few instants was speechless; her eyes were shining, and her bosom heaving as though she had run up to a height.

' I could not receive . . . you there,' she began in a hurried whisper : ' we are just going to a dinner party, but I wanted above everything to see you. . . . That is your betrothed, I suppose, with whom I met you to-day ? '

'Yes, that was my betrothed,' said Litvinov, with emphasis on the word 'was.'

'And so I wanted to see you for one minute, to tell you that you must consider yourself absolutely free, that everything that happened yesterday ought not to affect your plans. . . .'

'Irina!' cried Litvinov, 'why are you saying this?' He uttered these words in a loud voice. There was a note in them of unbounded passion. Irina involuntarily closed her eyes for a minute.

'Oh, my sweet one!' she went on in a whisper still more subdued, but with unrestrained emotion, 'you don't know how I love you, but yesterday I only paid my debt, I made up for the past. . . . Ah! I could not give you back my youth, as I would, but I have laid no obligations on you, I have exacted no promise of any sort of you, my sweet! Do what you will, you are free as air, you are bound in no way, understand that, understand that!'

'But I can't live without you, Irina,' Litvinov interrupted, in a whisper now; 'I am yours for ever and always, since yesterday. . . . I can only breathe at your feet. . . .'

He stooped down all in a tremble to kiss her hands. Irina gazed at his bent head.

'Then let me say,' she said, 'that I too am ready for anything, that I too will consider no one, and nothing. As you decide, so it shall be. I, too, am for ever yours . . . yours.'

Some one tapped warily at the door. Irina stooped, whispered once more, 'Yours . . . good-bye!' Litvinov felt her breath on his hair, the touch of her lips. When he stood up, she was no longer in the room, but her dress was rustling in the corridor, and from the distance came the voice of Ratmirov: '*Eh bien? Vous ne venez pas?*'

Litvinov sat down on a high chest, and hid his face. A feminine fragrance, fresh and delicate, clung about him. . . . Irina had held his hand in her hands. 'It's too much, too much,' was his thought. The little girl came into the room, and smiling again in response to his agitated glance, said:

'Kindly come, now——'

He got up, and went out of the hotel. It was no good even to think of returning home: he had to regain his balance first. His heart was beating heavily and unevenly; the earth seemed faintly reeling under his feet. Litvinov turned again along the Lichtenthaler Allee. He realised that the decisive moment had come, that to put it off longer, to dissemble, to turn away, had become impossible, that an explanation with Tatyana had become inevitable; he could imagine how she was sitting there, never stirring, waiting for him . . . he could foresee what he would say to her; but how was he to act, how was he to begin? He had turned his back on his upright, well-organised, orderly future; he knew that he was flinging himself headlong into a gulf . . . but that did not confound him. The thing was done, but how was he to face his judge? And if only his judge would come to meet him—an angel with a flaming sword; that would be easier for a sinning heart . . . instead of which he had himself to plunge the knife in. . . . Infamous ! But to turn back, to abandon that other, to take advantage of the freedom offered him, recognised as his. . . . No ! better to die ! No, he would have none of such loathsome freedom . . . but would humble himself in the dust, and might those eyes look down on him with love. . . .

'Grigory Mihalitch,' said a melancholy voice, and some one's hand was laid heavily upon Litvinov.

He looked round in some alarm and recognised Potugin.

'I beg your pardon, Grigory Mihalitch,' began the latter with his customary humility, 'I am disturbing you perhaps, but, seeing you in the distance, I thought. . . . However if you're not in the humour. . . .'

'On the contrary I'm delighted,' Litvinov muttered between his teeth.

Potugin walked beside him.

'What a lovely evening ! ' he began, 'so warm ! Have you been walking long ? '

'No, not long.'

'Why do I ask though ; I 've just seen you come out of the *Hôtel de l'Europe.*'

'Then you 've been following me ? '

'Yes.'

'You have something to say to me ? '

'Yes,' Potugin repeated, hardly audibly.

Litvinov stopped and looked at his uninvited companion. His face was pale, his eyes moved restlessly ; his contorted features seemed overshadowed by old, long-standing grief.

'What do you specially want to say to me ? ' Litvinov said slowly, and he moved forward.

'Ah, with your permission . . . directly. If it 's all the same to you, let us sit down here on this seat. It will be most convenient.'

'Why, this is something mysterious,' Litvinov declared, seating himself near him. 'You don't seem quite yourself, Sozont Ivanitch.'

'No ; I 'm all right ; and it 's nothing mysterious either. I specially wanted to tell you . . . the impression made on me by your betrothed . . . she is betrothed to you, I think ? . . . well, anyway, by the girl to whom you introduced me to-day. I must say that in the course of my whole existence I have never met a more attractive creature. A heart of gold, a really angelic nature.'

Potugin uttered all these words with the same bitter and mournful air, so that even Litvinov could not help noticing the incongruity between his expression of face and his speech.

'You have formed a perfectly correct estimate of Tatyana Petrovna,' Litvinov began, 'though I can't help being surprised, first that you should be aware of the relation in which I stand to her ; and secondly, that you should have understood her so quickly. She really has an angelic nature ; but allow me to ask, did you want to talk to me about this ? '

'It 's impossible not to understand her at once,' Potugin replied quickly, as though evading the last question. 'One need only take one look into her eyes. She deserves every possible happiness on earth, and enviable is the fate of the man whose lot it is to give her that happiness! One must hope he may prove worthy of such a fate.'

Litvinov frowned slightly.

'Excuse me, Sozont Ivanitch,' he said, 'I must confess our conversation strikes me as altogether rather original. . . . I should like to know, does the hint contained in your words refer to me?'

Potugin did not at once answer Litvinov; he was visibly struggling with himself.

'Grigory Mihalitch,' he began at last, 'either I am completely mistaken in you, or you are capable of hearing the truth, from whomsoever it may come, and in however unattractive a form it may present itself. I told you just now, that I saw where you came from.'

'Why, from the *Hôtel de l'Europe*. What of that?'

'I know, of course, whom you have been to see there.'

'What?'

'You have been to see Madame Ratmirov.'

'Well, I have been to see her. What next?'

'What next? . . . You, betrothed to Tatyana Petrovna, have been to see Madame Ratmirov, whom you love . . . and who loves you.'

Litvinov instantly got up from the seat; the blood rushed to his head.

'What's this?' he cried at last, in a voice of concentrated exasperation: 'stupid jesting, spying? Kindly explain yourself.'

Potugin turned a weary look upon him.

'Ah! don't be offended at my words. Grigory Mihalitch, me you cannot offend. I did not begin to talk to you for that, and I'm in no joking humour now.'

'Perhaps, perhaps. I'm ready to believe in the excellence of your intentions; but still I may be allowed to ask you by what right you meddle in the private affairs, in the inner life, of another man, a man who is nothing to you; and what grounds you have for so confidently giving out your own . . . invention for the truth?'

'My invention! If I had imagined it, it should not have made you angry; and as for my right, well I never heard before that a man ought to ask himself whether he had the right to hold out a hand to a drowning man.'

'I am humbly grateful for your tender solicitude,' cried Litvinov passionately, 'but I am not in the least in need of it, and all the phrases about the ruin of inexperienced young men wrought by society women, about the immorality of fashionable society, and so on, I look upon merely as stock phrases, and indeed in a sense I positively despise them; and so I beg you to spare your rescuing arm, and to let me drown in peace.'

Potugin again raised his eyes to Litvinov. He was breathing hard, his lips were twitching.

'But look at me, young man,' broke from him at last, and he clapped himself on the breast : 'can you suppose I have anything in common with the ordinary, self-satisfied moralist, a preacher? Don't you understand that simply from interest in you, however strong it might be, I would never have let fall a word, I would never have given you grounds for reproaching me with what I hate above all things—indiscretion, intrusiveness? Don't you see that this is something of a different kind altogether, that before you is a man crushed, utterly obliterated by the very passion, from the results of which he would save you, and . . . and for the same woman !'

Litvinov stepped back a pace.

'Is it possible? What did you say? . . . You . . . you . . . Sozont Ivanitch? But Madame Byelsky . . . that child?'

'Ah, don't cross-examine me . . . Believe me! That is a dark terrible story, and I'm not going to tell you it. Madame Byelsky I hardly knew, that child is not mine, but I took it all upon myself . . . because . . . *she* wished it, because it was necessary for *her*. Why am I here in your hateful Baden? And, in fact, could you suppose, could you for one instant imagine, that I'd have brought myself to caution you out of sympathy for you? I'm sorry for that sweet, good girl, your *fiancée*, but what have I to do with your future, with you both? . . . But I am afraid for her . . . for her.'

'You do me great honour, Mr. Potugin,' began Litvinov, 'but since, according to you, we are both in the same position, why is it you don't apply such exhortations to yourself, and ought I not to ascribe your apprehensions to another feeling?'

'That is to jealousy, you mean? Ah, young man, young man, it's shameful of you to shuffle and make pretences, it's shameful of you not to realise what a bitter sorrow is speaking to you now by my lips! No, I am not in the same position as you! I, I am old, ridiculous, an utterly harmless old fool—but you! But there's no need to talk about it! You would not for one second agree to accept the position I fill, and fill with gratitude! Jealousy? A man is not jealous who has never had even a drop of hope, and this is not the first time it has been my lot to endure this feeling. I am only afraid . . . afraid for her, understand that. And could I have guessed when she sent me to you that the feeling of having wronged you—she owned to feeling that—would carry her so far?'

'But excuse me, Sozont Ivanitch, you seem to know . . .'

'I know nothing, and I know everything! I know,' he added, turning away, 'I know where she was yesterday. But there's no holding her back now ; like a stone set rolling, she must roll on to the bottom. I should be a great idiot indeed, if I imagined my words could hold you back at once . . . you, when a woman like that . . . But that's enough of this. I couldn't restrain myself, that's my whole excuse. And after all how can one know, and why not try? Perhaps, you will think again ; perhaps, some word of mine will go to your heart, you will not care to ruin her and yourself, and that innocent sweet creature . . . Ah! don't be angry, don't stamp about! What have I to fear? Why should I mince matters? It's not jealousy speaking in me, not anger . . . I'm ready to fall at your feet, to beseech you . . . Good-bye, though. You needn't be afraid, all this will be kept secret. I wished for your good.'

Potugin strode off along the avenue and quickly vanished in the now falling darkness. Litvinov did not detain him.

'A terrible dark story . . .' Potugin had said to Litvinov, and would not tell it . . . Let us pass it over with a few words only.

Eight years before, it had happened to him to be sent by his department to Count Reisenbach as a temporary clerk. It was in the summer. Potugin used to drive to his country villa with papers, and be whole days there at a time. Irina was then living at the count's. She was never haughty with people in a humbler station, at least she never treated them superciliously, and the countess more than once reproved her for her excessive Moscow familiarity. Irina soon detected a man of intelligence in the humble clerk, attired in the stiffly buttoned frockcoat that was his uniform. She used often and eagerly to talk to him . . . while he . . . he fell in love with her passionately, profoundly, secretly . . . Secretly! So *he* thought. The summer passed; the count no longer needed any outside assistance. Potugin lost sight of Irina but could not forget her. Three years after, he utterly unexpectedly received an invitation, through a third person, to go to see a lady slightly known to him. This lady at first was reluctant to speak out, but after exacting an oath from him to keep everything he was going to hear absolutely secret, she proposed to him . . . to marry a girl, who occupied a conspicuous position in society, and for whom marriage had become a necessity. The lady scarcely ventured to hint at the principal personage, and then promised Potugin money . . . a large sum of money. Potugin was not offended, astonishment stifled all feeling of anger in him; but, of course, he point-blank declined. Then the lady handed him a note—from Irina. 'You are a generous, noble man,' she wrote, 'and I know you would do anything for me; I beg of you this sacrifice. You will save one who is very dear to me. In saving her, you will save me too . . . Do not ask me how. I could never have brought myself to any one with such an entreaty, but to you, I hold out my hands and say to you, do it for my sake.' Potugin pondered, and said that for Irina Pavlovna, certainly he was ready to do a great deal; but he should like to hear her wishes from her own lips. The interview took place the same evening; it did not last long, and no one knew of it, except the same lady. Irina was no longer living at Count Reisenbach's.

'What made you think of me, of all people?' Potugin asked her.

She was beginning to expatiate on his noble qualities, but suddenly she stopped . . .

'No,' she said, 'you must be told the truth. I know, I know that you love me; so that was why I made up my mind . . .' and then she told him everything.

Eliza Byelsky was an orphan; her relations did not like her, and reckoned on her inheritance . . . ruin was facing her. In saving her, Irina was really doing a service to him who was responsible for it all, and who was himself now standing in a very close relation to Irina . . . Potugin, without speaking, looked long at Irina, and consented. She wept, and flung herself all in tears on his neck. And he too wept . . . but very different were their tears. Everything had already been made ready for the secret marriage, a powerful hand removed all obstacles. . . . But illness came . . . and then a daughter was born, and then the mother . . . poisoned herself. What was to be done with the child ? Potugin received it into his charge, received it from the same hands, from the hands of Irina.

A terrible dark story . . . Let us pass on, readers, pass on !

Over an hour more passed before Litvinov could bring himself to go back to his hotel. He had almost reached it when he suddenly heard steps behind him. It seemed as though they were following him persistently, and walking faster when he quickened his pace. When he moved under a lamp-post Litvinov turned round and recognised General Ratmirov. In a white tie, in a fashionable overcoat, flung open, with a row of stars and crosses on a golden chain in the buttonhole of his dresscoat, the general was returning from dinner, alone. His eyes, fastened with insolent persistence on Litvinov, expressed such contempt and such hatred, his whole deportment was suggestive of such intense defiance, that Litvinov thought it his duty, stifling his wrath, to go to meet him, to face a ' scandal.' But when he was on a level with Litvinov, the general's face suddenly changed, his habitual playful refinement reappeared upon it, and his hand in its pale lavender glove flourished his glossy hat high in the air. Litvinov took off his in silence, and each went on his way.

' He has noticed something, for certain ! ' thought Litvinov.

' If only it were . . . any one else ! ' thought the general.

Tatyana was playing picquet with her aunt when Litvinov entered their room.

' Well, I must say, you 're a pretty fellow ! ' cried Kapitolina Markovna, and she threw down her cards. ' Our first day, and he 's lost for the whole evening ! Here we 've been waiting and waiting, and scolding and scolding . . .'

' I said nothing, aunt,' observed Tatyana.

' Well, you 're meekness itself, we all know ! You ought to be ashamed, sir ! and you betrothed too ! '

Litvinov made some sort of excuse and sat down to the table.

' Why have you left off your game ? ' he asked after a brief silence.

' Well, that 's a nice question ! We 've been playing cards from sheer dulness, not knowing what to do with ourselves . . . but now you 've come.'

' If you would care to hear the evening music,' observed Litvinov, ' I should be delighted to take you.'

Kapitolina Markovna looked at her niece.

' Let us go, aunt, I am ready,' she said, ' but wouldn't it be better to stay at home ? '

'To be sure! Let us have tea in our own old Moscow way, with the samovar, and have a good chat. We've not had a proper gossip yet.'

Litvinov ordered tea to be sent up, but the good chat did not come off. He felt a continual gnawing of conscience; whatever he said, it always seemed to him that he was telling lies and Tatyana was seeing through it. Meanwhile there was no change to be observed in her; she behaved just as unconstrainedly . . . only her look never once rested upon Litvinov, but with a kind of indulgent timorousness glided over him, and she was paler than usual.

Kapitolina Markovna asked her whether she had not a headache.

Tatyana was at first about to say no, but after a moment's thought, she said, 'Yes, a little.'

'It's the journey,' suggested Litvinov, and he positively blushed with shame.

'Yes, the journey,' repeated Tatyana, and her eyes again glided over him.

'You ought to rest, Tanya darling.'

'Yes, I will go to bed soon, aunt.'

On the table lay a *Guide des Voyageurs*; Litvinov fell to reading aloud the description of the environs of Baden.

'Quite so,' Kapitolina Markovna interrupted, 'but there's something we mustn't forget. I'm told linen is very cheap here, so we must be sure to buy some for the trousseau.'

Tatyana dropped her eyes.

'We have plenty of time, aunt. You never think of yourself, but you really ought to get yourself some clothes. You see how smart every one is here.'

'Eh, my love! what would be the good of that? I'm not a fine lady! It would be another thing if I were such a beauty as your friend, Grigory Mihalitch, what was her name?'

'What friend?'

'Why, that we met to-day.'

'Oh, she!' said Litvinov, with feigned indifference, and again he felt disgust and shame. 'No!' he thought, 'to go on like this is impossible.'

He was sitting by his betrothed, while a few inches from her in his side pocket, was Irina's handkerchief.

Kapitolina Markovna went for a minute into the other room.

'Tanya . . .' said Litvinov, with an effort. It was the first time that day he had called her by that name.

She turned towards him.

'I . . . I have something very important to say to you.'

'Oh! really? when? directly?'

'No, to-morrow.'

'Oh! to-morrow. Very well.'

Litvinov's soul was suddenly filled with boundless pity. He took Tatyana's hand and kissed it humbly, like a sinner; her heart throbbed faintly and she felt no happiness.

In the night, at two o'clock, Kapitolina Markovna, who was sleeping in the same room with her niece, suddenly lifted up her head and listened.

'Tanya,' she said, 'you are crying?'

Tatyana did not at once answer.

'No, aunt,' sounded her gentle voice, 'I've caught a cold.'

XX

'WHY DID I SAY that to her?' Litvinov thought the next morning as he sat in his room at the window. He shrugged his shoulders in vexation: he had said that to Tatyana simply to cut himself off all way of retreat. In the window lay a note from Irina: she asked him to see her at twelve. Potugin's words incessantly recurred to his mind, they seemed to reach him with a faint ill-omened sound as of a rumbling underground. He was angry with himself, but could not get rid of them anyhow. Some one knocked at the door.

'*Wer da?*' asked Litvinov.

'Ah! you're at home! open!' he heard Bindasov's hoarse bass.

The door handle creaked.

Litvinov turned white with exasperation.

'I'm not at home,' he declared sharply.

'Not at home? That's a good joke!'

'I tell you—not at home, get along.'

'That's civil! And I came to ask you for a little loan,' grumbled Bindasov. He walked off, however, tramping on his heels as usual.

Litvinov was all but dashing out after him, he felt such a longing to throttle the hateful ruffian. The events of the last few days had unstrung his nerves; a little more, and he would have burst into tears. He drank off a glass of cold water, locked up all the drawers in the furniture, he could not have said why, and went to Tatyana's.

He found her alone. Kapitolina Markovna had gone out shopping. Tatyana was sitting on the sofa, holding a book in both hands. She was not reading it, and scarcely knew what book it was. She did not stir, but her heart was beating quickly in her bosom, and the little white collar round her neck quivered visibly and evenly.

Litvinov was confused. . . . However, he sat down by her, said good-morning, smiled at her; she too smiled at him without speaking. She had bowed to him when he came in, bowed courteously, not affectionately, and she did not glance at him. He held out his hand to her; she gave him her chill fingers, but at once freed them again, and took up the book. Litvinov felt that to begin the conversation with unimportant subjects would be insulting Tatyana; she after her custom made no demands, but everything in her said plainly, 'I am waiting, I am waiting.' . . . He must fulfil his promise. But though almost the whole night he had thought of nothing else, he had not prepared even the first introductory words, and absolutely did not know in what way to break this cruel silence.

'Tanya,' he began at last, 'I told you yesterday that I have something important to say to you. I am ready, only I beg you beforehand not to be angry against me, and to rest assured that my feelings for you . . .'

He stopped. He caught his breath. Tatyana still did not stir, and did not look at him; she only clutched the book tighter than ever.

'There has always been,' Litvinov went on, without finishing the sentence he had begun, 'there has always been perfect openness between us; I respect you too much to be a hypocrite with you; I want to prove to you that I know how to value the nobleness and independence of your nature, even though . . . though of course . . .'

'Grigory Mihalitch,' began Tatyana in a measured voice while a deathly pallor overspread her whole face, 'I will come to your assistance, you no longer love me, and you don't know how to tell me so.'

Litvinov involuntarily shuddered.

'Why?' . . . he said, hardly intelligibly, 'why could you suppose? . . . I really don't understand . . .'

'What! isn't it the truth? Isn't it the truth?—tell me, tell me.'

Tatyana turned quite round to Litvinov; her face, with her hair brushed back from it, approached his face, and her eyes, which for so long had not looked at him, seemed to penetrate into his eyes.

'Isn't it the truth?' she repeated.

He said nothing, did not utter a single sound. He could not have lied at that instant, even if he had known she would believe him, and that his lie would save her; he was not even able to bear her eyes upon him. Litvinov said nothing, but she needed no answer, she read the answer in his very silence, in those guilty downcast eyes—and she turned away again and dropped the book. . . . She had been still uncertain till that instant, and Litvinov understood that; he understood that she had been still uncertain—and how hideous, actually hideous was all that he was doing.

He flung himself on his knees before her.

'Tanya,' he cried, 'if only you knew how hard it is for me to see you in this position, how awful to me to think that it's I . . . I! My heart is torn to pieces, I don't know myself, I have lost myself, and you, and everything . . . Everything is shattered, Tanya, everything! Could I dream that I . . . I should bring such a blow upon you, my best friend, my guardian angel? . . . Could I dream that we should meet like this, should spend such a day as yesterday! . . .'

Tatyana was trying to get up and go away. He held her back by the border of her dress.

'No, listen to me a minute longer. You see I am on my knees before you, but I have not come to beg your forgiveness; you cannot, you ought not to forgive me. I have come to tell you that your friend is ruined, that he is falling into the pit, and would not drag you down with him. . . . But save me . . . no! even you cannot save me. I should push you away, I am ruined, Tanya, I am ruined past all help.'

Tatyana looked at Litvinov.

'You are ruined?' she said, as though not fully understanding him. 'You are ruined?'

'Yes, Tanya, I am ruined. All the past, all that was precious, everything I have lived for up till now, is ruined for me; everything is wretched, everything is shattered, and I don't know what awaits me in the future. You said just now that I no longer loved you. . . . No, Tanya, I have not ceased to love you, but a different, terrible, irresistible passion has come upon me, has overborne me. I fought against it while I could. . . .'

Tatyana got up, her brows twitched, her pale face darkened. Litvinov too rose to his feet.

'You love another woman,' she began, 'and I guess who she is. . . . We met her yesterday, didn't we? . . . Well, I see what is left for me to do now. Since you say yourself this passion is unalterable' . . . (Tatyana paused an instant, possibly she had still hoped Litvinov would not let this last word pass unchallenged, but he said nothing), 'it only remains for me to give you back . . . your word.'

Litvinov bent his head, as though submissively receiving a well-deserved blow.

'You have every right to be angry with me,' he said. 'You have every right to reproach me for feebleness . . . for deceit.'

Tatyana looked at him again.

'I have not reproached you, Litvinov, I don't blame you. I agree with you: the bitterest truth is better than what went on yesterday. What sort of a life could ours have been now!'

'What sort of a life will mine be now!' echoed mournfully in Litvinov's soul.

Tatyana went towards the door of the bedroom.

'I will ask you to leave me alone for a little time, Grigory Mihalitch—we will see each other again, we will talk again. All this has been so unexpected I want to collect myself a little . . . leave me alone . . . spare my pride. We shall see each other again.'

And uttering these words, Tatyana hurriedly withdrew and locked the door after her.

Litvinov went out into the street like a man dazed and stunned; in the very depths of his heart something dark and bitter lay hid, such a sensation must a man feel who has murdered another; and at the same time he felt easier as though he had at last flung off a hated load. Tatyana's magnanimity had crushed him, he felt vividly all that he had lost . . . and yet? with his regret was mingled irritation; he yearned towards Irina as to the sole refuge left him, and felt bitter against her. For some time Litvinov's feelings had been every day growing more violent and more complex; this complexity tortured him, exasperated him, he was lost in this chaos. He thirsted for one thing; to get out at last on to the path, whatever it might be, if only not to wander longer in this incomprehensible half-darkness. Practical people of Litvinov's sort ought never to be carried away by passion, it destroys the very meaning of their lives. . . . But nature cares nothing for logic, our human logic ; she has her own, which we do not recognise and do not acknowledge till we are crushed under its wheel.

On parting from Tatyana, Litvinov held one thought in his mind, to see Irina ; he set off indeed to see her. But the general was at home, so at least the porter told him, and he did not care to go in, he did not feel himself capable of hypocrisy, and he moved slowly off towards the Konversation Hall. Litvinov's incapacity for hypocrisy was evident that day to both Voroshilov and Pishtchalkin, who happened to meet him ; he simply blurted out to the former that he was empty as a drum ; to the latter that he bored every one to extinction ; it was lucky indeed that Bindasov did come across him ; there would certainly have been a ' *grosser Scandal.*' Both the young men were stupefied ; Voroshilov went so far as to ask himself whether his honour as an officer did not demand satisfaction? But like Gogol's lieutenant, Pirogov, he calmed himself with bread and butter in a café. Litvinov caught sight in the distance of Kapitolina Markovna running busily from shop to shop in her striped mantle. . . . He felt ashamed to face the good, absurd, generous old lady. Then he recalled Potugin, their conversation yesterday. . . . Then something was wafted to him, something intangible and unmistakable : if a falling shadow shed a fragrance, it could not be more elusive, but he felt at once that it was Irina near him, and in fact she appeared a few paces from him, arm-in-arm with another lady ; their eyes met at once. Irina probably noticed something peculiar in the expression of Litvinov's face ; she stopped before a shop, in which a number of tiny wooden clocks of Black Forest make were exhibited, and summoning him by a motion of her head, she pointed to one of these clocks, and calling upon him to admire a charming clock-face with a painted cuckoo above it, she said, not in a whisper, but as though finishing a phrase begun, in her ordinary tone of voice, much less likely to attract the attention of outsiders, ' Come in an hour's time, I shall be alone.'

But at this moment the renowned lady-killer Monsieur Verdier swooped down upon her, and began to fall into ecstasies over the colour, *feuille morte,* of her gown and the low-crowned Spanish hat she wore tilted almost down to her eyebrows . . . Litvinov vanished in the crowd.

XXI

' GRIGORY,' Irina was saying to him two hours later, as she sat beside him on the sofa, and laid both hands on his shoulder, ' what is the matter with you ? Tell me now quickly, while we 're alone.'

' The matter with me ? ' said Litvinov. ' I am happy, happy, that's what 's the matter with me.'

Irina looked down, smiled, sighed.

'That's not an answer to my question, my dear one.'

Litvinov grew thoughtful.

'Well, let me tell you then . . . since you insist positively on it' (Irina opened her eyes wide and trembled slightly), 'I have told everything to-day to my betrothed.'

'What, everything? You mentioned me?'

Litvinov fairly threw up his arms.

'Irina, for God's sake, how could such an idea enter your head! that I——'

'There, forgive me . . . forgive me. What did you say?'

'I told her that I no longer loved her.'

'She asked why?'

'I did not disguise the fact that I loved another woman, and that we must part.'

'Ah . . . and what did she do? Agreed?'

'O Irina! what a girl she is! She was all self-sacrifice, all generosity!'

'I've no doubt, I've no doubt . . . there was nothing else for her to do, though.'

'And not one reproach, not one hard word to me, who have spoiled her whole life, deceived her, pitilessly flung her over. . . .'

Irina scrutinised her finger nails.

'Tell me, Grigory . . . did she love you?'

'Yes, Irina, she loved me.'

Irina was silent a minute, she straightened her dress.

'I must confess,' she began, 'I don't quite understand what induced you to explain matters to her.'

'What induced me, Irina! Would you have liked me to lie, to be a hypocrite to her, that pure soul? or did you suppose——'

'I supposed nothing,' Irina interrupted. 'I must admit I have thought very little about her. I don't know how to think of two people at once.'

'That is, you mean——'

'Well, and so what then? Is she going away, that pure soul?' Irina interrupted a second time.

'I know nothing,' answered Litvinov. 'I am to see her again. But she will not stay.'

'Ah! *bon voyage!*'

'No, she will not stay. But I'm not thinking of her either now, I am thinking of what you said to me, what you have promised me.'

Irina looked up at him from under her eyelids.

'Ungrateful one! aren't you content yet?'

'No, Irina, I'm not content. You have made me happy, but I'm not content, and you understand me.'

'That is, I——'

'Yes, you understand me. Remember your words, remember what you wrote to me. I can't share you with others; no, no, I can't consent to the pitiful rôle of secret lover; not my life alone, this other life too I have flung at your feet, I have renounced everything, I have crushed it all to dust, without compunction and beyond recall; but in return I trust, I firmly believe, that you too will keep your promise, and unite your lot with mine for ever.'

'You want me to run away with you? I am ready. . . .' (Litvinov bent down to her hands in ecstasy.) 'I am ready. I will not go back from my word. But have you yourself thought over all the difficulties—have you made preparations?'

'I? I have not had time yet to think over or prepare anything, but only say yes, let me act, and before a month is over . . .'

'A month! we start for Italy in a fortnight.'

'A fortnight, then, is enough for me. O Irina, you seem to take my proposition coldly; perhaps it seems unpractical to you, but I am not a boy, I am not used to comforting myself with dreams, I know what a tremendous step this is, I know what a responsibility I am taking on myself; but I can see no other course. Think of it, I must break every tie with the past, if only not to be a contemptible liar in the eyes of the girl I have sacrificed for you!'

Irina drew herself up suddenly and her eyes flashed.

'Oh, I beg your pardon, Grigory Mihalitch! If I decide, if I run away, then it will at least be with a man who does it for my sake, for my sake simply, and not in order that he may not degrade himself in the good opinion of a phlegmatic young person, with milk and water, *du lait coupé* instead of blood, in her veins! And I must tell you too, it's the first time, I confess, that it's been my lot to hear that the man I honour with my regard is deserving of commiseration, playing a pitiful part! I know a far more pitiful part, the part of a man who doesn't know what is going on in his own heart!'

Litvinov drew himself up in his turn.

'Irina,' he was beginning——

But all at once she clapped both hands to her forehead, and with a convulsive motion, flinging herself on his breast, she embraced him with force beyond a woman's.

'Forgive me, forgive me,' she began, with a shaking voice, 'forgive me, Grigory! You see how corrupted I am, how horrid I am, how jealous and wicked! You see how I need your aid, your indulgence! Yes, save me, drag me out of this mire, before I am quite ruined! Yes, let us run away, let us run away from these people, from this society to some far off, fair, free country! Perhaps your Irina will at last be worthier of the sacrifices you are making for her! Don't be angry with me, forgive me, my sweet, and know that I will do everything you command, I will go anywhere you will take me!'

Litvinov's heart was in a turmoil. Irina clung closer than before to him with all her youthful supple body. He bent over her fragrant, disordered tresses, and in an intoxication of gratitude and ecstasy, he hardly dared to caress them with his hand, he hardly touched them with his lips.

'Irina, Irina,' he repeated,—'my angel. . . .'

She suddenly raised her head, listened. . . .

'It's my husband's step, . . . he has gone into his room,' she whispered, and, moving hurriedly away, she crossed over to another armchair. Litvinov was getting up. . . . 'What are you doing?' she went on in the same whisper; 'you must stay, he suspects you as it is. Or are you afraid of him?' She did not take her eyes off the door. 'Yes, it's he; he will come in here directly. Tell me something, talk to me.' Litvinov could not at once recover himself and was silent. 'Aren't you going to the theatre to-morrow?' she uttered aloud. 'They're giving *Le Verre d'Eau,* an old-fashioned piece, and Plessy is awfully affected. . . . We're as though we were in a perfect fever,' she added, dropping her voice. 'We can't do anything like this; we must think things over well. I ought to warn you that all my money is in his hands; *mais j'ai mes bijoux.* We'll go to Spain, would you like that?' She raised her voice again. 'Why is it all actresses get so fat? Madeleine Brohan for instance. . . . Do talk, don't sit so silent. My head is going round. But you, you must not doubt me. . . . I will let you know where to come to-morrow. Only it was a mistake to have told that young lady. . . . *Ah, mais c'est charmant!*' she cried suddenly and with a nervous laugh, she tore the lace edge of her handkerchief.

'May I come in?' asked Ratmirov from the other room.

'Yes . . . yes.'

The door opened, and in the doorway appeared the general. He scowled on seeing Litvinov; however, he bowed to them, that is to say, he bent the upper portion of his person.

'I did not know you had a visitor,' he said: '*je vous demande pardon de mon indiscrétion.* So you still find Baden entertaining, M'sieu—Litvinov?'

Ratmirov always uttered Litvinov's surname with hesitation, every time, as though he had forgotten it, and could not at once recall it. . . . In this way, as well as by the lofty flourish of his hat in saluting him, he meant to insult his pride.

'I am not bored here, *m'sieu le général.*'

'Really? Well, I find Baden fearfully boring. We are soon going away, are we not, Irina Pavlovna? *Assez de Bade comme ça.* By the way, I've won you five hundred francs to-day.'

Irina stretched out her hand coquettishly.

'Where are they? Please let me have them for pin-money.'

'You shall have them, you shall have them. . . . You are going, M'sieu—Litvinov?'

'Yes, I am going, as you see.'

Ratmirov again bent his body.

'Till we meet again!'

'Good-bye, Grigory Mihalitch,' said Irina. 'I will keep my promise.'

'What is that? May I be inquisitive?' her husband queried.

Irina smiled.

'No, it was only . . . something we've been talking of. *C'est à propos du voyage . . . où il vous plaira.* You know—Stael's book?'

' Ah ! ah ! to be sure, I know. Charming illustrations.'

Ratmirov seemed on the best of terms with his wife ; he called her by her pet name in addressing her.

XXII

' BETTER NOT THINK now, really,' Litvinov repeated, as he strode along the street, feeling that the inward riot was rising up again in him. ' The thing's decided. She will keep her promise, and it only remains for me to take all necessary steps. . . . Yet she hesitates, it seems.' . . . He shook his head. His own designs struck even his own imagination in a strange light ; there was a smack of artificiality, of unreality about them. One cannot dwell long upon the same thoughts ; they gradually shift like the bits of glass in a kaleidoscope . . . one peeps in, and already the shapes before one's eyes are utterly different. A sensation of intense weariness overcame Litvinov. . . . If he could for one short hour but rest ! . . . But Tanya ? He started, and, without reflecting even, turned submissively homewards, merely struck by the idea, that this day was tossing him like a ball from one to the other. . . . No matter ; he must make an end. He went back to his hotel, and with the same submissiveness, insensibility, numbness, without hesitation or delay, he went to see Tatyana.

He was met by Kapitolina Markovna. From the first glance at her, he knew that she knew about it all ; the poor maiden lady's eyes were swollen with weeping, and her flushed face, fringed with her dishevelled white locks, expressed dismay and an agony of indignation, sorrow, and boundless amazement. She was on the point of rushing up to Litvinov, but she stopped short, and, biting her quivering lip, she looked at him as though she would supplicate him, and kill him, and assure herself that it was a dream, a senseless, impossible thing, wasn't it ?

' Here you . . . you are come,' she began. . . . The door from the next room opened instantaneously, and with a light tread Tatyana came in ; she was of a transparent pallor, but she was quite calm.

She gently put one arm round her aunt and made her sit down beside her.

' You sit down too, Grigory Mihalitch,' she said to Litvinov, who was standing like one distraught at the door. ' I am very glad to see you once more. I have informed auntie of your decision, our common decision ; she fully shares it and approves of it. . . . Without mutual love there can be no happiness, mutual esteem alone is not enough ' (at the word ' esteem ' Litvinov involuntarily looked down) ' and better to separate now, than to repent later. Isn't it, aunt ? '

' Yes, of course,' began Kapitolina Markovna, ' of course, Tanya darling, the man who does not know how to appreciate you . . . who could bring himself——'

' Aunt, aunt,' Tatyana interrupted, ' remember what you promised me. You always told me yourself : truth, Tatyana, truth before everything—

and independence. Well, truth's not always sweet, nor independence either; or else where would be the virtue of it?'

She kissed Kapitolina Markovna on her white hair, and turning to Litvinov, she went on:

'We propose, aunt and I, leaving Baden. . . . I think it will be more comfortable so for all of us.'

'When do you think of going?' Litvinov said thickly. He remembered that Irina had said the very same words to him not long before.

Kapitolina Markovna was darting forward, but Tatyana held her back, with a caressing touch on her shoulder.

'Probably soon, very soon.'

'And will you allow me to ask where you intend going?' Litvinov said in the same voice.

'First to Dresden, then probably to Russia.'

'But what can you want to know that for now, Grigory Mihalitch?' . . . cried Kapitolina Markovna.

'Aunt, aunt,' Tatyana interposed again. A brief silence followed.

'Tatyana Petrovna,' began Litvinov, 'you know how agonisingly painful and bitter my feelings must be at this instant.'

Tatyana got up.

'Grigory Mihalitch,' she said, 'we will not talk about that . . . if you please, I beg you for my sake, if not for your own. I have known you long enough, and I can very well imagine what you must be feeling now. But what's the use of talking, of touching a sore' (she stopped; it was clear she wanted to stem the emotion rushing upon her, to swallow the rising tears; she succeeded)—'why fret a sore we cannot heal? Leave that to time. And now I have to ask a service of you, Grigory Mihalitch; if you will be so good, I will give you a letter directly: take it to the post yourself, it is rather important, but aunt and I have no time now. . . . I shall be much obliged to you. Wait a minute. . . . I will bring it directly. . . .'

In the doorway Tatyana glanced uneasily at Kapitolina Markovna; but she was sitting with such dignity and decorum, with such a severe expression on her knitted brows and tightly compressed lips, that Tatyana merely gave her a significant nod and went out.

But scarcely had the door closed behind her, when every trace of dignity and severity instantaneously vanished from Kapitolina Markovna's face; she got up, ran on tiptoe up to Litvinov, and all hunched together and trying to look him in the face, she began in a quaking tearful whisper:

'Good God,' she said, 'Grigory Mihalitch, what does it mean? is it a dream or what? *You* give up Tanya, you tired of her, you breaking your word! You doing this, Grigory Mihalitch, you on whom we all counted as if you were a stone wall! You? you? you, Grisha?' . . . Kapitolina Markovna stopped. 'Why, you will kill her, Grigory Mihalitch,' she went on, without waiting for an answer, while her tears fairly coursed in fine drops over her cheeks. 'You mustn't judge by her bearing up now, you know her character! She never complains; she does not think of herself, so others must think of her! She keeps saying to me, "Aunt, we must save our dignity!" but what's dignity, when I foresee death, death before us?' . . . Tatyana's chair creaked in the next room. 'Yes, I foresee death,' the old lady went on still more softly. 'And how can such a thing have come about? Is it witchcraft, or what? It's not long since you were writing her the tenderest letters. And in fact can an honest man act like this? I'm a woman, free, as you know, from prejudice of any sort, *esprit fort,* and I have given Tanya too the same sort of education, she too has a free mind. . . .'

'Aunt!' came Tatyana's voice from the next room.

'But one's word of honour is a duty, Grigory Mihalitch, especially for people of your, of my principles! If we're not going to recognise duty, what is left us? This cannot be broken off in this way, at your whim, without regard to what may happen to another! It's unprincipled . . . yes, it's a crime; a strange sort of freedom!'

'Aunt, come here please,' was heard again.

'I'm coming, my love, I'm coming . . .' Kapitolina Markovna clutched at Litvinov's hand.—'I see you are angry, Grigory Mihalitch.' . . . ('Me! me angry?' he wanted to exclaim, but his tongue was dumb.) 'I don't want to make you angry—oh, really, quite the contrary! I've come even to entreat you; think again while there is time; don't destroy her, don't destroy your own happiness, she will still trust you, Grisha, she will believe in you, nothing is lost yet; why, she loves you as no one will ever love you! Leave this hateful Baden-Baden, let us go away together, only throw off this enchantment, and, above all, have pity, have pity——'

'Aunt!' called Tatyana, with a shade of impatience in her voice.

But Kapitolina Markovna did not hear her.

'Only say "yes,"' she repeated to Litvinov; 'and I will still make everything smooth. . . . You need only nod your head to me, just one little nod like this.'

Litvinov would gladly, he felt, have died at that instant; but the word 'yes' he did not utter, and he did not nod his head.

Tatyana reappeared with a letter in her hand. Kapitolina Markovna at once darted away from Litvinov, and, averting her face, bent low over the table, as though she were looking over the bills and papers that lay on it.

Tatyana went up to Litvinov.

'Here,' she said, 'is the letter I spoke of. . . . You will go to the post at once with it, won't you?'

Litvinov raised his eyes. . . . Before him, really, stood his judge. Tatyana struck him as taller, slenderer; her face, shining with unwonted beauty, had the stony grandeur of a statue's; her bosom did not heave, and her gown, of one colour and straight as a Greek chiton, fell in the long, unbroken folds of marble drapery to her feet, which were hidden by it. Tatyana was looking straight before her, only at Litvinov; her cold, calm gaze, too, was the gaze of a statue. He read his sentence in it; he bowed, took a letter from the hand held out so immovably to him, and silently withdrew.

Kapitolina Markovna ran to Tatyana; but the latter turned off her embraces and dropped her eyes; a flush of colour spread over her face, and with the words, ' and now, the sooner the better,' she went into the bedroom. Kapitolina Markovna followed her with hanging head.

The letter, entrusted to Litvinov by Tatyana, was addressed to one of her Dresden friends—a German lady—who let small furnished apartments. Litvinov dropped the letter into the post-box, and it seemed to him as though with that tiny scrap of paper he was dropping all his past, all his life into the tomb. He went out of the town, and strolled a long time by narrow paths between vineyards; he could not shake off the persistent sensation of contempt for himself, like the importunate buzzing of flies in summer: an unenviable part, indeed, he had played in the last interview. . . . And when he went back to his hotel, and after a little time inquired about the ladies, he was told that immediately after he had gone out, they had given orders to be driven to the railway station, and had departed by the mail train—to what destination was not known. Their things had been packed and their bills paid ever since the morning. Tatyana had asked Litvinov to take her letter to the post, obviously with the object of getting him out of the way. He ventured to ask the hall-porter whether the ladies had left any letters for him, but the porter replied in the negative, and looked amazed even; it was clear that this sudden exit from rooms taken for a week struck him too as strange and dubious. Litvinov turned his back on him, and locked himself up in his room.

He did not leave it till the following day: the greater part of the night he was sitting at the table, writing, and tearing what he had written. . . . The dawn was already beginning when he finished his task—it was a letter to Irina.

XXIII

THIS WAS WHAT was in this letter to Irina:

' My betrothed went away yesterday; we shall never see each other again. . . . I do not know even for certain where she is going to live. With her, she takes all that till now seemed precious and desirable to me; all my previous ideas, my plans, my intentions, have gone with her; my labours even are wasted, my work of years ends in nothing, all my pursuits have no meaning, no applicability; all that is dead; myself, my old self, is dead and buried since yesterday. I feel, I see, I know this clearly . . . far am I from regretting this. Not to lament of it, have I begun upon this to you. . . . As though I could complain when you love me, Irina! I wanted only to tell you that, of all this dead past, all those hopes and efforts, turned to smoke and ashes, there is only one thing left living, invincible, my love for you. Except that love, nothing is left for me; to say it is the sole thing precious to me, would be too little; I live wholly in that love; that love is my whole being; in it are my future, my career, my vocation, my country! You know me, Irina; you know that fine talk of any sort is foreign to my nature, hateful to me,

and however strong the words in which I try to express my feelings, you
will have no doubts of their sincerity, you will not suppose them exaggerated. I'm not a boy, in the impulse of momentary ecstasy, lisping unre-
flecting vows to you, but a man of matured age—simply and plainly, almost
with terror, telling you what he has recognised for unmistakable truth. Yes,
your love has replaced everything for me—everything, everything ! Judge
for yourself: can I leave this my *all* in the hands of another ? can I let him
dispose of you ? You—you will belong to him, my whole being, my heart's
blood will belong to him—while I myself . . . where am I ? what am I ?
An outsider—an onlooker . . . looking on at my own life ! No, that's
impossible, impossible ! To share, to share in secret that without which it's
useless, impossible to live . . . that's deceit and death. I know how great a
sacrifice I am asking of you, without any sort of right to it ; indeed, what
can give one a right to sacrifice ? But I am not acting thus from egoism :
an egoist would find it easier and smoother not to raise this question at all.
Yes, my demands are difficult, and I am not surprised that they alarm you.
The people among whom you have to live are hateful to you, you are sick
of society, but are you strong enough to throw up that society ? to trample
on the success it has crowned you with ? to rouse public opinion against
you—the opinion of these hateful people ? Ask yourself, Irina, don't take
a burden upon you greater than you can bear. I don't want to reproach you;
but remember : once already you could not hold out against temptation. I
can give you so little in return for all you are losing. Hear my last word :
if you don't feel capable to-morrow, to-day even, of leaving all and following me—you see how boldly I speak, how little I spare myself,—if you are
frightened at the uncertainty of the future, and estrangement and solitude
and the censure of men, if you cannot rely on yourself, in fact, tell me so
openly and without delay, and I will go away ; I shall go with a broken
heart, but I shall bless you for your truthfulness. But if you really, my
beautiful, radiant queen, love a man so petty, so obscure as I, and are really
ready to share his fate,—well, then, give me your hand, and let us set off
together on our difficult way ! Only understand, my decision is unchanging ;
either all or nothing. It's unreasonable . . . but I could not do otherwise—
I cannot, Irina ! I love you too much.—Yours,   G. L.'

Litvinov did not much like this letter himself ; it did not quite truly and
exactly express what he wanted to say ; it was full of awkward expressions,
high flown or bookish, and doubtless it was not better than many of the
other letters he had torn up ; but it was the last, the chief point was thoroughly stated anyway, and harassed, and worn out, Litvinov did not feel
capable of dragging anything else out of his head. Besides he did not possess
the faculty of putting his thought into literary form, and like all people with
whom it is not habitual, he took great trouble over the style. His first letter
was probably the best ; it came warmer from the heart. However that might
be, Litvinov despatched his missive to Irina.

She replied in a brief note :

'Come to me to-day,' she wrote to him : '*he* has gone away for the whole day. Your letter has greatly disturbed me. I keep thinking, thinking . . . and my head is in a whirl. I am very wretched, but you love me, and I am happy. Come. Yours,   I.'

She was sitting in her boudoir when Litvinov went in. He was conducted there by the same little girl of thirteen who on the previous day had watched for him on the stairs. On the table before Irina was standing an open, semi-circular, cardboard box of lace: she was carelessly turning over the lace with one hand, in the other she was holding Litvinov's letter. She had only just left off crying ; her eyelashes were wet, and her eyelids swollen ; on her cheeks could be seen the traces of undried tears not wiped away. Litvinov stood still in the doorway ; she did not notice his entrance.

'You are crying? ' he said wonderingly.

She started, passed her hand over her hair and smiled.

'Why are you crying ? ' repeated Litvinov. She pointed in silence to the letter. 'So you were . . . over that,' he articulated haltingly.

'Come here, sit down,' she said, 'give me your hand. Well, yes, I was crying . . . what are you surprised at ? Is that nothing ? ' she pointed again to the letter.

Litvinov sat down.

'I know it 's not easy, Irina, I tell you so indeed in my letter . . . I under-stand your position. But if you believe in the value of your love for me, if my words have convinced you, you ought, too, to understand what I feel now at the sight of your tears. I have come here, like a man on his trial, and I await what is to be my sentence ? Death or life ? Your answer decides everything. Only don't look at me with those eyes. . . . They remind me of the eyes I saw in old days in Moscow.'

Irina flushed at once, and turned away, as though herself conscious of something evil in her gaze.

'Why do you say that, Grigory ? For shame ! You want to know my answer . . . do you mean to say you can doubt it ? You are troubled by my tears . . . but you don't understand them. Your letter, dearest, has set me thinking. Here you write that my love has replaced everything for you, that even your former studies can never now be put into practice ; but I ask myself, can a man live for love alone ? Won't it weary him at last, won't he want an active career, and won't he cast the blame on what drew him away from active life ? That 's the thought that dismays me, that 's what I am afraid of, and not what you imagine.'

Litvinov looked intently at Irina, and Irina intently looked at him, as though each would penetrate deeper and further into the soul of the other, deeper and further than word can reach, or word betray.

'You are wrong in being afraid of that,' began Litvinov. 'I must have expressed myself badly. Weariness ? Inactivity ? With the new impetus your love will give me ? O Irina, in your love there 's a whole world for me, and I can't yet foresee myself what may develop from it.'

Irina grew thoughtful.

'Where are we going?' she whispered.

'Where? We will talk of that later. But, of course, then . . . then you agree? you agree, Irina?'

She looked at him. 'And you will be happy?'

'O Irina!'

'You will regret nothing? Never?'

She bent over the cardboard box, and again began looking over the lace in it.

'Don't be angry with me, dear one, for attending to this trash at such a moment. . . . I am obliged to go to a ball at a certain lady's, these bits of finery have been sent me, and I must choose to-day. Ah! I am awfully wretched!' she cried suddenly, and she laid her face down on the edge of the box. Tears began falling again from her eyes. . . . She turned away; the tears might spoil the lace.

'Irina, you are crying again,' Litvinov began uneasily.

'Ah, yes, again,' Irina interposed hurriedly. 'O Grigory, don't torture me, don't torture yourself! . . . Let us be free people! What does it matter if I do cry! And indeed do I know myself why my tears are flowing? You know, you have heard my decision, you believe it will not be changed. That I agree to . . . What was it you said? . . . to all or nothing . . . what more would you have? Let us be free! Why these mutual chains? We are alone together now, you love me. I love you; is it possible we have nothing to do but wringing our thoughts out of each other? Look at me, I don't want to talk about myself, I have never by one word hinted that for me perhaps it was not so easy to set at nought my duty as a wife . . . and, of course, I don't deceive myself, I know I am a criminal, and that *he* has a right to kill me. Well, what of it? Let us be free, I say. To-day is ours— a life-time's ours.'

She got up from the armchair and looked at Litvinov with her head thrown back, faintly smiling and moving her eyebrows, while with one arm bare to the elbow she pushed back from her face a long tress on which a few tears glistened. A rich scarf slipped from the table and fell on the floor at Irina's feet. She trampled contemptuously on it. 'Or don't you like me, to-day? Have I grown ugly since yesterday? Tell me, have you often seen a prettier hand? And this hair? Tell me, do you love me?'

She clasped him in both arms, held his head close to her bosom, her comb fell out with a ringing sound, and her falling hair wrapped him in a soft flood of fragrance.

XXIV

LITVINOV WALKED up and down his room in the hotel, his head bowed in thought. He had now to pass from theory to practice, to devise ways and means for flight, for moving to unknown countries. . . . But, strange to say, he was not pondering so much upon ways and means as upon whether actually, beyond doubt, the decision had been reached on which he had so obstinately insisted ? Had the ultimate, irrevocable word been uttered ? But Irina to be sure had said to him at parting, ' Act, act, and when every thing is ready, only let me know.' That was final ! Away with all doubts. . . . He must proceed to action. And Litvinov proceeded—in the meantime—to calculation. Money first of all. Litvinov had, he found, in ready money one thousand three hundred and twenty-eight guldens, in French money, two thousand eight hundred and fifty-five francs ; the sum was trifling, but it was enough for the first necessities, and then he must at once write to his father to send him all he could ; he would have to sell the forest part of the land. But on what pretext ? . . . Well, a pretext would be found. Irina had spoken, it's true, of her *bijoux,* but that must not be taken into his reckoning ; that, who knows, might come in for a rainy day. He had besides a good Geneva watch, for which he might get . . . well, say, four hundred francs. Litvinov went to a banker's, and with much circumlocution introduced the question whether it was possible, in case of need, to borrow money; but bankers at Baden are wary old foxes, and in response to such circumlocutions they promptly assume a drooping and blighted air, for all the world like a wild flower whose stalk has been severed by the scythe ; some indeed laugh outright in your face, as though appreciating an innocent joke on your part. Litvinov, to his shame, even tried his luck at roulette, even, oh ignominy ! put a thaler on the number thirty, corresponding with his own age. He did this with a view to augmenting and rounding off his capital ; and if he did not augment it, he certainly did round off his capital by losing the odd twenty-eight guldens. There was a second question, also not an unimportant one ; that was the passport. But for a woman a passport is not quite so obligatory, and there are countries where it is not required at all, Belgium, for instance, and England; besides, one might even get some other passport, not Russian. Litvinov pondered very seriously on all this; his decision was firm, absolutely unwavering, and yet all the time against his will, overriding his will, something not serious, almost humorous came in, filtered through his musings, as though the very enterprise were a comic business, and no one ever did elope with any one in reality, but only in plays and novels, and perhaps somewhere in the provinces, in some of those remote districts, where, according to the statements of travellers, people are literally sick continually from *ennui.* At that point Litvinov recalled how an acquaintance of his, a retired cornet, Batsov, had eloped with a merchant's daughter in a staging sledge with bells and three horses, having as a preliminary measure made the parents drunk, and adopted the same precaution as well with the bride, and how, as it afterwards turned out, he was outwitted and within an ace of a thrashing into the bargain. Litvinov felt exceedingly irritated with himself for such inappropriate reminiscences, and then with the recollection of Tatyana, her sudden departure, all that grief and suffering and shame, he felt only too acutely that the affair he was arranging was deadly earnest, and how right he had been when he had told Irina that his honour

even left no other course open. . . . And again at the mere name something
of flame turned with sweet ache about his heart and died away again.

The tramp of horses' hoofs sounded behind him. . . . He moved aside.
. . . Irina overtook him on horseback ; beside her rode the stout general.
She recognised Litvinov, nodded to him, and lashing her horse with a
sidestroke of her whip, she put him into a gallop, and suddenly dashed away
at headlong speed. Her dark veil fluttered in the wind. . . .

'*Pas si vite ! Nom de Dieu ! pas si vite !*' cried the general, and he too
galloped after her.

XXV

THE NEXT MORNING Litvinov had only just come home from seeing the
banker, with whom he had had another conversation on the playful in-
stability of our exchange, and the best means of sending money abroad,
when the hotel porter handed him a letter. He recognised Irina's handwriting, and without breaking the seal—a presentiment of evil, Heaven
knows why, was astir in him—he went into his room. This was what he
read (the letter was in French) :

' My dear one, I have been thinking all night of your plan. . . . I am not
going to shuffle with you. You have been open with me, and I will be open
with you ; I *cannot* run away with you, I *have not the strength* to do it.
I feel how I am wronging you ; my second sin is greater than the first,
I despise myself, my cowardice, I cover myself with reproaches, but I cannot change myself. In vain I tell myself that I have destroyed your happiness, that you have the right now to regard me as a frivolous flirt, that I
myself drew you on, that I have given you solemn promises. . . . I am
full of horror, of hatred for myself, but I can't do otherwise, I can't, I can't.
I don't want to justify myself, I won't tell you I was carried away myself
. . . all that's of no importance ; but I want to tell you, and to say it again
and yet again, I am yours, yours for ever, do with me as you will when
you will, free from all obligation, from all responsibility ! I am yours. . . .
But run away, throw up everything . . . no ! no ! no ! I besought you to
save me, I hoped to wipe out everything, to burn up the past as in a fire
. . . but I see there is no salvation for me ; I see the poison has gone too
deeply into me ; I see one cannot breathe this atmosphere for years with
impunity. I have long hesitated whether to write you this letter, I dread
to think what decision you may come to, I trust only to your love for me.
Bu I felt it would be dishonest on my part to hide the truth from you—
especially as perhaps you have already begun to take the first steps for
carrying out our project. Ah ! it was lovely but impracticable. O my dear
one, think me a weak, worthless woman, despise, but don't abandon me,
don't abandon your Irina ! . . . To leave this life I have not the courage,
but live it without you I cannot either. We soon go back to Petersburg,
come there, live there, we will find occupation for you, your labours in

the past shall not be thrown away, you shall find good use for them . . . only live near me, only love me ; such as I am, with all my weaknesses and my vices, and believe me, no heart will ever be so tenderly devoted to you as the heart of your Irina. Come soon to me, I shall not have an instant's peace until I see you.—Yours, yours, yours,   I.'

The blood beat like a sledge-hammer in Litvinov's head, then slowly and painfully sank to his heart, and was chill as a stone in it. He read through Irina's letter, and just as on that day at Moscow he fell in exhaustion on the sofa, and stayed there motionless. A dark abyss seemed suddenly to have opened on all sides of him, and he stared into this darkness in senseless despair. And so again, again deceit, no, worse than deceit, lying and base-ness. . . . And life shattered, everything torn up by its roots utterly, and the sole thing which he could cling to—the last prop in fragments too ! ' Come after us to Petersburg,' he repeated with a bitter inward laugh, ' we will find you occupation. . . . Find me a place as a head clerk, eh ? and who are *we*? Here there's a hint of her past. Here we have the secret, hideous something I know nothing of, but which she has been trying to wipe out, to burn as in a fire. Here we have that world of intrigues, of secret relations, of shameful stories of Byelskys and Dolskys. . . . And what a future, what a lovely part awaiting me! To live close to her, visit her, share with her the morbid melancholy of the lady of fashion who is sick and weary of the world, but can't live outside its circle, be the friend of the house of course, of his Excellency . . . until . . . until the whim changes and the plebeian lover loses his piquancy, and is replaced by that fat general or Mr. Finikov—that's possible and pleasant, and I dare say use-ful. . . . She talks of a good use for my talents ? . . . but the other proj-ect's impracticable, impracticable. . . . In Litvinov's soul rose, like sudden gusts of wind before a storm, momentary impulses of fury. . . . Every expression in Irina's letter roused his indignation, her very assertions of her unchanging feelings affronted him. ' She can't let it go like that,' he cried at last, ' I won't allow her to play with my life so mercilessly.'

Litvinov jumped up, snatched his hat. But what was he to do ? Run to her ? Answer her letter ? He stopped short, and his hands fell.

' Yes; what was to be done ?'

Had he not himself put this fatal choice to her ? It had not turned out as he had wished . . . there was that risk about every choice. She had changed her mind, it was true ; she herself had declared at first that she would throw up everything and follow him ; that was true too ; but she did not deny her guilt, she called herself a weak woman; she did not want to deceive him, she had been deceived in herself. . . . What answer could be made to that ? At any rate she was not hypocritical, she was not deceiving him . . . she was open, remorselessly open. There was nothing forced her to speak out, nothing to prevent her from soothing him with promises, putting things off, and keeping it all in uncertainty till her departure . . .

till her departure with her husband for Italy? But she had ruined his life, ruined two lives. . . . What of that?

But as regards Tatyana, she was not guilty; the guilt was his, his, Litvinov's alone, and he had no right to shake off the responsibility his own sin had laid with iron yoke upon him. . . . All this was so; but what was left him to do now?

Again he flung himself on the sofa and again in gloom, darkly, dimly, without trace, with devouring swiftness, the minutes raced past. . . .

'And why not obey her?' flashed through his brain. 'She loves me, she is mine, and in our very yearning towards each other, in this passion, which after so many years has burst upon us, and forced its way out with such violence, is there not something inevitable, irresistible, like a law of nature? Live in Petersburg . . . and shall I be the first to be put in such a position? And how could we be in safety together? . . .'

And he fell to musing, and Irina's shape, in the guise in which it was imprinted for ever in his late memories, softly rose before him. . . . But not for long. . . . He mastered himself, and with a fresh outburst of indignation drove away from him both those memories and that seductive image.

'You give me to drink from that golden cup,' he cried, 'but there is poison in the draught, and your white wings are besmirched with mire. . . . Away! Remain here with you after the way I . . . I drove away my betrothed . . . a deed of infamy, of infamy!' He wrung his hands with anguish, and another face with the stamp of suffering on its still features, with dumb reproach in its farewell eyes, rose from the depths. . . .

And for a long time Litvinov was in this agony still; for a long time, his tortured thought, like a man fever-stricken, tossed from side to side. . . . He grew calm at last; at last he came to a decision. From the very first instant he had a presentiment of this decision; . . . it had appeared to him at first like a distant, hardly perceptible point in the midst of the darkness and turmoil of his inward conflict; then it had begun to move nearer and nearer, till it ended by cutting with icy edge into his heart.

Litvinov once more dragged his box out of the corner, once more he packed all his things, without haste, even with a kind of stupid carefulness, rang for the waiter, paid his bill, and despatched to Irina a note in Russian to the following purport:

'I don't know whether you are doing me a greater wrong now than then; but I know this present blow is infinitely heavier. . . . It is the end. You tell me, "I cannot"; and I repeat to you, "I cannot . . ." do what you want. I cannot and I don't want to. Don't answer me. You are not capable of giving me the only answer I would accept. I am going away to-morrow early by the first train. Good-bye, may you be happy! We shall in all probability not see each other again.'

Till night-time Litvinov did not leave his room; God knows whether he was expecting anything. About seven o'clock in the evening a lady in a black mantle with a veil on her face twice approached the steps of his hotel. Moving a little aside and gazing far away into the distance, she suddenly made a resolute gesture with her hand, and for the third time went towards the steps. . . .

'Where are you going, Irina Pavlovna?' she heard a voice utter with effort behind her.

She turned with nervous swiftness. . . . Potugin ran up to her.

She stopped short, thought a moment, and fairly flung herself towards him, took his arm, and drew him away.

'Take me away, take me away,' she repeated breathlessly.

'What is it, Irina Pavlovna?' he muttered in bewilderment.

'Take me away,' she reiterated with redoubled force, 'if you don't want me to remain for ever . . . there.'

Potugin bent his head submissively, and hurriedly they went away together.

The following morning early Litvinov was perfectly ready for his journey —into his room walked . . . Potugin.

He went up to him in silence, and in silence shook his hand. Litvinov, too, said nothing. Both of them wore long faces, and both vainly tried to smile.

'I came to wish you a good journey,' Potugin brought out at last.

'And how did you know I was going to-day?' asked Litvinov.

Potugin looked on the floor around him . . . 'I became aware of it . . . as you see. Our last conversation took in the end such a strange turn . . . I did not want to part from you without expressing my sincere good feeling for you.'

'You have good feeling for me now . . . when I am going away?'

Potugin looked mournfully at Litvinov. 'Ah, Grigory Mihalitch, Grigory Mihalitch,' he began with a short sigh, 'it's no time for that with us now, no time for delicacy or fencing. You don't, so far as I have been able to perceive, take much interest in our national literature, and so, perhaps, you have no clear conception of Vaska Buslaev?'

'Of whom?'

'Of Vaska Buslaev, the hero of Novgorod . . . in Kirsch-Danilov's collection.'

'What Buslaev?' said Litvinov, somewhat puzzled by the unexpected turn of the conversation. 'I don't know.'

'Well, never mind. I only wanted to draw your attention to something. Vaska Buslaev, after he had taken away his Novgorodians on a pilgrimage to Jerusalem, and there, to their horror, bathed all naked in the holy river Jordan, for he believed not "in omen nor in dream, nor in the flight of birds," this logical Vaska Buslaev climbed up Mount Tabor, and on the top of this mountain there lies a great stone, over which men of every kind have tried in vain to jump. . . . Vaska too ventured to try his luck. And he chanced upon a dead head, a human skull in his road; he kicked it away with his foot. So the skull said to him; "Why do you kick me? I knew how to live, and I know how to roll in the dust—and it will be the same with you." And in fact, Vaska jumps over the stone, and he did quite clear it, but he caught his heel and broke his skull. And in this place, I must by the way observe that it wouldn't be amiss for our friends, the Slavophils, who are so fond of kicking dead heads and decaying nationalities underfoot to ponder over that legend.'

'But what does all that mean?' Litvinov interposed impatiently at last. 'Excuse me, it's time for me . . .'

'Why, this,' answered Potugin, and his eyes beamed with such affectionate warmth as Litvinov had not even expected of him, 'this, that you do not spurn a dead human head, and for your goodness, perhaps you may succeed in leaping over the fatal stone. I won't keep you any longer, only let me embrace you at parting.'

'I'm not going to try to leap over it even,' Litvinov declared, kissing Potugin three times, and the bitter sensations filling his soul were replaced for an instant by pity for the poor lonely creature.

'But I must go, I must go. . . .' he moved about the room.

'Can I carry anything for you?' Potugin proffered his services.

'No, thank you, don't trouble, I can manage. . . .'

He put on his cap, took up his bag. 'So you say,' he queried, stopping in the doorway, 'you have seen her?'

'Yes, I've seen her.'

'Well . . . tell me about her.'

Potugin was silent a moment. 'She expected you yesterday . . . and to-day she will expect you.'

'Ah! Well, tell her . . . No, there's no need, no need of anything. Good-bye . . . Good-bye!'

'Good-bye, Grigory Mihalitch. . . . Let me say one word more to you. You still have time to listen to me; there's more than half an hour before the train starts. You are returning to Russia . . . There you will . . . in time . . . get to work . . . Allow an old chatterbox—for, alas, I am a chatterbox, and nothing more—to give you advice for your journey. Every time it is your lot to undertake any piece of work, ask yourself: Are you serving the cause of civilisation, in the true and strict sense of the word; are you promoting one of the ideals of civilisation; have your labours that educating, Europeanising character which alone is beneficial and profitable in our day among us? If it is so, go boldly forward, you are on the right path, and your work is a blessing! Thank God for it! You are not alone now. You will not be a "sower in the desert"; there are plenty of workers . . . pioneers . . . even among us now . . . But you have no ears for this now. Good-bye, don't forget me!'

Litvinov descended the staircase at a run, flung himself into a carriage, and drove to the station, not once looking round at the town where so much of his personal life was left behind. He abandoned himself, as it were, to the tide; it snatched him up and bore him along, and he firmly resolved not to struggle against it . . . all other exercise of independent will he renounced

He was just taking his seat in the railway carriage.

'Grigory Mihalitch . . . Grigory . . .' he heard a supplicating whisper behind him.

He started . . . Could it be Irina? Yes; it was she. Wrapped in her maid's shawl, a travelling hat on her dishevelled hair, she was standing on the platform, and gazing at him with worn and weary eyes.

'Come back, come back, I have come for you,' those eyes were saying. And what, what were they not promising? She did not move, she had not power to add a word; everything about her, even the disorder of her dress, everything seemed entreating forgiveness . . .

Litvinov was almost beaten, scarcely could he keep from rushing to her . . . But the tide to which he had surrendered himself reasserted itself. . . . He jumped into the carriage, and turning round, he motioned Irina to a place beside him. She understood him. There was still time. One step, one movement, and two lives made one for ever would have been hurried away into the uncertain distance. . . . While she wavered, a loud whistle sounded and the train moved off.

Litvinov sank back, while Irina moved staggering to a seat, and fell on it, to the immense astonishment of a supernumerary diplomatic official who chanced to be lounging about the railway station. He was slightly acquainted with Irina, and greatly admired her, and seeing that she lay as though overcome by faintness, he imagined that she had '*une attaque de nerfs*,' and therefore deemed it his duty, the duty *d'un galant chevalier*, to go to her assistance. But his astonishment assumed far greater proportions when, at the first word addressed to her, she suddenly got up, repulsed his proffered arm, and hurrying out into the street, had in a few instants vanished in the milky vapour of fog, so characteristic of the climate of the Black Forest in the early days of autumn.

XXVI

WE HAPPENED once to go into the hut of a peasant-woman who had just lost her only, passionately loved son, and to our considerable astonishment we found her perfectly calm, almost cheerful. 'Let her be,' said her husband, to whom probably our astonishment was apparent, 'she is gone numb now.' And Litvinov had in the same way 'gone numb.' The same sort of calm came over him during the first few hours of the journey. Utterly crushed, hopelessly wretched as he was, still he was at rest, at rest after the agonies and sufferings of the last few weeks, after all the blows which had fallen one after another upon his head. They had been the more shattering for him that he was little fitted by nature for such tempests. Now he really hoped for nothing, and tried not to remember, above all not to remember. He was going to Russia . . . he had to go somewhere; but he was making no kind of plans regarding his own personality. He did not recognise himself, he did not comprehend his own actions, he had positively lost his real identity, and, in fact, he took very little interest in his own identity. Sometimes it seemed to him that he was taking his own corpse home, and only the bitter spasms of irremediable spiritual pain passing over him from time to time brought him back to a sense of still being alive. At times it struck him as incomprehensible that a man—a man!—could let a woman, let love, have such power over him . . . 'Ignominious weakness!' he muttered, and shook back his cloak, and sat up more squarely; as though to say, the past is over, let's begin fresh . . . a moment, and he could only smile bitterly and wonder at himself. He fell to looking out of the window. It was grey and damp; there was no rain, but the fog still hung about; and low clouds trailed across the sky. The wind blew facing the train; whitish clouds of steam, some singly, others mingled with other darker clouds of smoke, whirled in endless file past the window at which Litvinov was sitting. He began to watch this steam, this smoke. Incessantly mounting, rising and falling, twisting and hooking on to the grass, to the bushes as though in sportive antics, lengthening out, and hiding away, clouds upon clouds flew by . . . they were for ever changing and stayed still the same in their monotonous, hurrying, wearisome sport! Sometimes the wind changed, the line bent to right or left, and suddenly the whole mass vanished, and at once reappeared at the opposite window; then again the huge tail was flung out, and again it veiled Litvinov's view of the vast plain of the Rhine. He gazed and gazed, and a strange reverie came over him . . . He was alone in the compartment; there was no one to disturb him. 'Smoke, smoke,' he repeated several times; and suddenly it all seemed as smoke to him, everything, his own life, Russian life—everything human, especially everything Russian. All smoke and steam, he thought; all seems for ever changing, on all sides new forms, phantoms flying after phantoms, while in reality it is all the same and the same again; everything hurrying, flying towards something, and everything vanishing without a trace, attaining to nothing; another wind blows, and all is dashing in the opposite direction, and there again the same untiring, restless—and useless gambols! He remembered much that had taken place with clamour and flourish before his eyes in the last few years . . . 'Smoke,' he whispered, 'smoke'; he remembered the hot disputes, the wrangling, the clamour at Gubaryov's, and in other sets of men, of high and low degree, advanced and reactionist, old and young . . . 'Smoke,' he repeated, 'smoke and steam'; he remembered, too, the fashionable picnic, and he remembered various opinions and speeches of other political personages—even all Potugin's sermonising . . . 'Smoke, smoke, nothing but smoke.' And what of his own struggles and passions and agonies and dreams? He could only reply with a gesture of despair.

And meanwhile the train dashed on and on; by now Rastadt, Carlsruhe, and Bruchsal had long been left far behind; the mountains on the right side of the line swerved aside, retreated into the distance, then moved up again, but not so high, and more thinly covered with trees. . . . The train made a sharp turn . . . and there was Heidelberg. The carriage rolled in under the cover of the station; there was the shouting of newspaper-boys, selling papers of all sorts, even Russian; passengers began bustling in their seats, getting out on to the platform, but Litvinov did not leave his corner, and still sat on with downcast head. Suddenly some one called him by name; he raised his eyes; Bindasov's ugly phiz was thrust in at the window; and behind him—or was he dreaming, no, it was really so—all the familiar Baden faces; there was Madame Suhantchikov, there was Voroshilov, and Bambaev too; they all rushed up to him, while Bindasov bellowed:

'But where's Pishtchalkin? We were expecting him; but it's all the same, hop out, and we'll be off to Gubaryov's.'

'Yes, my boy, yes, Gubaryov's expecting us,' Bambaev confirmed, making way for him, 'hop out.'

Litvinov would have flown into a rage, but for a dead load lying on his heart. He glanced at Bindasov and turned away without speaking.

'I tell you Gubaryov's here,' shrieked Madame Suhantchikov, her eyes fairly starting out of her head.

Litvinov did not stir a muscle.

'Come, do listen, Litvinov,' Bambaev began at last, 'there's not only Gubaryov here, there's a whole phalanx here of the most splendid, most intellectual young fellows, Russians—and all studying the natural sciences, all of the noblest convictions! Really you must stop here, if it's only for them. Here, for instance, there's a certain . . . there, I've forgotten his surname, but he's a genius! simply!'

'Oh, let him be, let him be, Rostislav Ardalionovitch,' interposed Madame Suhantchikov, 'let him be! You see what sort of a fellow he is; and all his family are the same. He has an aunt; at first she struck me as a sensible woman, but the day before yesterday I went to see her here—she had only just before gone to Baden and was back here again before you could look round—well, I went to see her; began questioning her . . . Would you believe me, I couldn't get a word out of the stuck-up thing. Horrid aristocrat!'

Poor Kapitolina Markovna an aristocrat! Could she ever have anticipated such a humiliation?

But Litvinov still held his peace, turned away, and pulled his cap over his eyes. The train started at last.

'Well, say something at parting at least, you stonyhearted man!' shouted Bambaev, 'this is really too much!'

'Rotten milksop!' yelled Bindasov. The carriages were moving more and more rapidly, and he could vent his abuse with impunity. 'Niggardly stick-in-the-mud.'

Whether Bindasov invented this last appellation on the spot, or whether it had come to him second-hand, it apparently gave great satisfaction to two of the noble young fellows studying natural science, who happened to be standing by, for only a few days later it appeared in the Russian periodical sheet, published at that time at Heidelberg under the title: *A tout venant je crache!* [1] or, 'We don't care a hang for anybody!'

[1] A historical fact.

But Litvinov repeated again, 'Smoke, smoke, smoke! Here,' he thought, 'in Heidelberg now are over a hundred Russian students; they're all studying chemistry, physics, physiology—they won't even hear of anything else . . . but in five or six years' time there won't be fifteen at the lectures by the same celebrated professors; the wind will change, the smoke will be blowing . . . in another quarter . . . smoke . . . smoke . . . !'[1]

Towards nightfall he passed by Cassel. With the darkness intolerable anguish pounced like a hawk upon him, and he wept, burying himself in the corner of the carriage. For a long time his tears flowed, not easing his heart, but torturing him with a sort of gnawing bitterness; while at the same time, in one of the hotels of Cassel, Tatyana was lying in bed feverishly ill.

Kapitolina Markovna was sitting beside her. 'Tanya,' she was saying, 'for God's sake, let me send a telegram to Grigory Mihalitch, do let me, Tanya!'

'No, aunt,' she answered; 'you mustn't; don't be frightened, give me some water; it will soon pass.'

And a week later she did, in fact, recover, and the two friends continued their journey.

XXVII

STOPPING neither at Petersburg nor at Moscow, Litvinov went back to his estate. He was dismayed when he saw his father; the latter was so weak and failing. The old man rejoiced to have his son, as far as a man can rejoice who is just at the close of life; he at once gave over to him the management of everything, which was in great disorder, and lingering on a few weeks longer, he departed from this earthly sphere. Litvinov was left alone in his ancient little manor-house, and with a heavy heart, without hope, without zeal, and without money, he began to work the land. Working the land is a cheerless business, as many know too well; we will not enlarge on how distasteful it seemed to Litvinov. As for reforms and innovations, there was, of course, no question even of them; the practical application of the information he had gathered abroad was put off for an indefinite period; poverty forced him to make shift from day to day, to consent to all sorts of compromises—both material and moral. The new had 'begun ill,' the old had lost all power; ignorance jostled up against dishonesty; the whole agrarian organisation was shaken and unstable as quagmire bog, and only one great word, 'freedom,' was wafted like the breath of God over the waters. Patience was needed before all things, and a patience not passive, but active, persistent, not without tact and cunning at times. . . . For Litvinov, in his frame of mind, it was doubly hard. He had but little will to live left in him. . . . Where was he to get the will to labour and take trouble?

[1] Litvinov's presentiments came true. In 1866 there were in Heidelberg thirteen Russian students entered for the summer, and twelve for the winter session.

But a year passed, after it another passed, the third was beginning. The mighty idea was being realised by degrees, was passing into flesh and blood, the young shoot had sprung up from the scattered seed, and its foes, both open and secret, could not stamp it out now. Litvinov himself, though he had ended by giving up the greater part of his land to the peasants on the half-profit system, that's to say, by returning to the wretched primitive methods, had yet succeeded in doing something; he had restored the factory, set up a tiny farm with five free hired labourers—he had had at different times fully forty—and had paid his principal private debts. . . . And his spirit had gained strength; he had begun to be like the old Litvinov again. It's true, a deeply buried melancholy never left him, and he was too quiet for his years; he shut himself up in a narrow circle and broke off all his old connections . . . but the deadly indifference had passed, and among the living he moved and acted as a living man again. The last traces, too, had vanished of the enchantment in which he had been held; all that had passed at Baden appeared to him dimly as in a dream. . . . And Irina? even she had paled and vanished too, and Litvinov only had a faint sense of something dangerous behind the mist that gradually enfolded her image. Of Tatyana news reached him from time to time; he knew that she was living with her aunt on her estate, a hundred and sixty miles from him, leading a quiet life, going out little, and scarcely receiving any guests— cheerful and well, however. It happened on one fine May day, that he was sitting in his study, listlessly turning over the last number of a Petersburg paper; a servant came to announce the arrival of an old uncle. This uncle happened to be a cousin of Kapitolina Markovna and had been recently staying with her. He had bought an estate in Litvinov's vicinity and was on his way thither. He stayed twenty-four hours with his nephew and told him a great deal about Tatyana's manner of life. The next day after his departure Litvinov sent her a letter, the first since their separation. He begged for permission to renew her acquaintance, at least by correspondence, and also desired to learn whether he must for ever give up all idea of some day seeing her again? Not without emotion he awaited the answer . . . the answer came at last. Tatyana responded cordially to his overture. 'If you are disposed to pay us a visit,' she finished up, 'we hope you will come; you know the saying, "even the sick are easier together than apart."' Kapitolina Markovna joined in sending her regards. Litvinov was as happy as a child; it was long since his heart had beaten with such delight over anything. He felt suddenly light and bright. . . . Just as when the sun rises and drives away the darkness of night, a light breeze flutters with the sun's rays over the face of the reviving earth. All that day Litvinov kept smiling, even while he went about his farm and gave his orders. He at once began making arrangements for the journey, and a fortnight later he was on his way to Tatyana.

XXVIII

HE DROVE RATHER SLOWLY by cross tracks, without any special adventures; only once the tire of a hind wheel broke; a blacksmith hammered and welded it, swearing both at the tire and at himself, and positively flung up the job; luckily it turned out that among us one can travel capitally even with a tire broken, especially on the 'soft,' that's to say on the mud. On the other hand, Litvinov did come upon some rather curious chance-meetings. At one place he found a Board of Mediators sitting, and at the head of it Pishtchalkin, who made on him the impression of a Solon or a Solomon, such lofty wisdom characterised his remarks, and such boundless respect was shown him both by landowners and peasants. . . . In exterior, too, he had begun to resemble a sage of antiquity; his hair had fallen off the crown of his head, and his full face had completely set in a sort of solemn jelly of positively blatant virtue. He expressed his pleasure at Litvinov's arrival in—'if I may make bold to use so ambitious an expression, my own district,' and altogether seemed fairly overcome by an excess of excellent intentions. One piece of news he did, however, succeed in communicating, and that was about Voroshilov; the hero of the Golden Board had re-entered military service, and had already had time to deliver a lecture to the officers of his regiment on Buddhism or Dynamism, or something of the sort—Pishtchalkin could not quite remember. At the next station it was a long while before the horses were in readiness for Litvinov; it was early dawn, and he was dozing as he sat in his coach. A voice, that struck him as familiar, waked him up; he opened his eyes. . . . Heavens! wasn't it Gubaryov in a grey pea-jacket and full flapping pyjamas standing on the steps of the posting hut, swearing? . . . No, it wasn't Mr. Gubaryov. . . . But what a striking resemblance! . . . Only this worthy had a mouth even wider, teeth even bigger, the expression of his dull eyes was more savage and his nose coarser, and his beard thicker, and the whole countenance heavier and more repulsive.

'Scou-oundrels, scou-oundrels!' he vociferated slowly and viciously, his wolfish mouth gaping wide. 'Filthy louts. . . . Here you have . . . vaunted freedom indeed . . . and can't get horses . . . scou-oundrels!'

'Scou-oundrels, scou-oundrels!' thereupon came the sound of another voice from within, and at the same moment there appeared on the steps— also in a grey smoking pea-jacket and pyjamas—actually, unmistakably, the real Gubaryov himself, Stepan Nikolaevitch Gubaryov. 'Filthy louts!' he went on in imitation of his brother (it turned out that the first gentleman was his elder brother, the man of the old school, famous for his fists, who had managed his estate). 'Flogging's what they want, that's it; a tap or two on the snout, that's the sort of freedom for them. . . . Self-government indeed. . . . I'd let them know it. . . . But where is that M'sieu

Roston ? . . . What is he thinking about ? . . . It's his business, the lazy scamp . . . to see we're not put to inconvenience.'

'Well, I told you, brother,' began the elder Gubaryov, 'that he was a lazy scamp, no good in fact ! But there, for the sake of old times, you . . . M'sieu Roston, M'sieu Roston ! . . . Where have you got to ? '

'Roston ! Roston ! ' bawled the younger, the great Gubaryov. 'Give a good call for him, do brother Dorimedont Nikolaitch ! '

'Well, I am shouting for him, Stepan Nikolaitch ! M'sieu Roston ! '

'Here I am, here I am, here I am ! ' was heard a hurried voice, and round the corner of the hut skipped Bambaev.

Litvinov fairly gasped. On the unlucky enthusiast a shabby braided coat, with holes in the elbows, dangled ruefully ; his features had not exactly changed, but they looked pinched and drawn together ; his over-anxious little eyes expressed a cringing timorousness and hungry servility ; but his dyed whiskers stood out as of old above his swollen lips. The Gubaryov brothers with one accord promptly set to scolding him from the top of the steps ; he stopped, facing them below, in the mud, and with his spine curved deprecatingly, he tried to propitiate them with a little nervous smile, kneading his cap in his red fingers, shifting from one foot to the other, and muttering that the horses would be here directly. . . . But the brothers did not cease, till the younger at last cast his eyes upon Litvinov. Whether he recognised Litvinov, or whether he felt ashamed before a stranger, any-way he turned abruptly on his heels like a bear, and gnawing his beard, went into the station hut ; his brother held his tongue at once, and he too, turning like a bear, followed him in. The great Gubaryov, evidently, had not lost his influence even in his own country.

Bambaev was slowly moving after the brothers. . . . Litvinov called him by his name. He looked round, lifted up his head, and recognising Litvinov, positively flew at him with outstretched arms ; but when he had run up to the carriage, he clutched at the carriage door, leaned over it, and began sobbing violently.

'There, there, Bambaev,' protested Litvinov, bending over him and pat-ting him on the shoulder.

But he went on sobbing. 'You see . . . you see . . . to what . . .' he muttered brokenly.

'Bambaev ! ' thundered the brothers from the hut.

Bambaev raised his head and hurriedly wiped his tears.

'Welcome, dear heart,' he whispered, 'welcome and farewell ! . . . You hear, they are calling me.'

'But what chance brought you here ? ' inquired Litvinov, 'and what does it all mean ? I thought they were calling a Frenchman. . . .'

'I am their . . . house-steward, butler,' answered Bambaev, and he pointed in the direction of the hut. 'And I'm turned Frenchman for a joke. What could I do, brother ? You see, I'd nothing to eat, I'd lost my last farthing, and so one's forced to put one's head under the yoke. One can't afford to be proud.'

'But has he been long in Russia? and how did he part from his comrades?'

'Ah, my boy, that's all on the shelf now. . . . The wind's changed, you see. . . . Madame Suhantchikov, Matrona Semyonovna, he simply kicked out. She went to Portugal in her grief.'

'To Portugal? How absurd!'

'Yes, brother, to Portugal, with two Matronovtsys.'

'With whom?'

'The Matronovtsys; that's what the members of her party are called.'

'Matrona Semyonovna has a party of her own? And is it a numerous one?'

'Well, it consists of precisely those two. And he will soon have been back here six months. Others have got into difficulties, but he was all right. He lives in the country with his brother, and you should just hear him now. . . .'

'Bambaev!'

'Coming, Stepan Nikolaitch, coming. And you, dear old chap, are flourishing, enjoying yourself! Well, thank God for that! Where are you off to now? . . . There, I never thought, I never guessed. . . . You remember Baden? Ah, that was a place to live in! By the way, you remember Bindasov too? Only fancy, he's dead. He turned exciseman, and was in a row in a public-house; he got his head broken with a billiard-cue. Yes, yes, hard times have come now! But still I say, Russia . . . ah, our Russia! Only look at those two geese; why, in the whole of Europe there's nothing like them! The genuine Arzamass breed!'

And with this last tribute to his irrepressible desire for enthusiasm, Bambaev ran off to the station hut, where again, seasoned with approbrious epithets, his name was shouted.

Towards the close of the same day, Litvinov was nearly reaching Tatyana's village. The little house where his former betrothed lived stood on the slope of a hill, above a small river, in the midst of a garden recently planted. The house, too, was new, lately built, and could be seen a long way off across the river and the open country. Litvinov caught sight of it more than a mile and a half off, with its sharp gable, and its row of little windows, gleaming red in the evening sun. At starting from the last station he was conscious of a secret agitation; now he was in a tremor simply—a happy tremor, not unmixed with dread. 'How will they meet me?' he thought, 'how shall I present myself?' . . . To turn off his thoughts with something, he began talking with his driver, a steady peasant with a grey beard, who charged him, however, for twenty-five miles, when the distance was not twenty. He asked him, did he know the Shestov ladies?

'The Shestov ladies? To be sure! Kind-hearted ladies, and no doubt about it! They doctor us too. It's the truth I'm telling you. Doctors they are! People go to them from all about. Yes, indeed. They fairly crawl to them. If any one, take an example, falls sick, or cuts himself or anything, he goes straight to them and they'll give him a lotion directly, or powders, or a plaster, and it'll be all right, it'll do good. But one can't show one's gratitude, we won't consent to that, they say; it's not for money. They've set up a school too. . . . Not but what that's a foolish business ! '

While the driver talked, Litvinov never took his eyes off the house. . . . Out came a woman in white on to the balcony, stood a little, stood and then disappeared. . . . 'Wasn't it she ? ' His heart was fairly bounding within him. 'Quicker, quicker ! ' he shouted to the driver ; the latter urged on the horses. A few instants more . . . and the carriage rolled in through the opened gates. . . . And on the steps Kapitolina Markovna was already standing, and beside herself with joy, was clapping her hands crying, 'I heard him, I knew him first ! It's he ! it's he ! . . . I knew him ! '

Litvinov jumped out of the carriage, without giving the page who ran up time to open the door, and hurriedly embracing Kapitolina Markovna, dashed into the house, through the hall, into the dining-room. . . . Before him, all shamefaced, stood Tatyana. She glanced at him with her kind caressing eyes (she was a little thinner, but it suited her), and gave him her hand. But he did not take her hand, he fell on his knees before her. She had not at all expected this and did not know what to say, what to do. . . . The tears started into her eyes. She was frightened, but her whole face beamed with delight. . . . 'Grigory Mihalitch, what is this, Grigory Mihalitch ? ' she said . . . while he still kissed the hem of her dress . . . and with a thrill of tenderness he recalled that at Baden he had been in the same way on his knees before her. . . . But then—and now !

'Tanya ! ' he repeated, 'Tanya ! you have forgiven me, Tanya ! '

'Aunt, aunt, what is this ? ' cried Tatyana turning to Kapitolina Markovna as she came in.

'Don't hinder him, Tanya,' answered the kind old lady. 'You see the sinner has repented.'

But it is time to make an end ; and indeed there is nothing to add ; the reader can guess the rest by himself. . . . But what of Irina ?

She is still as charming, in spite of her thirty years; young men out of number fall in love with her, and would fall in love with her even more, if . . . if . . .

Reader, would you care to pass with us for a few instants to Petersburg into one of the first houses there ? Look ; before you is a spacious apartment, we will not say richly—that is too low an expression—but grandly, imposingly, inspiringly decorated. Are you conscious of a certain flutter of servility ? Know that you have entered a temple, a temple consecrated to the highest propriety, to the loftiest philanthropy, in a word, to things unearthly. . . . A kind of mystic, truly mystic, hush enfolds you. The velvet hangings on the doors, the velvet curtains on the window, the bloated, spongy rug on the floor, everything as it were destined and fitted before-hand for subduing, for softening all coarse sounds and violent sensations. The carefully hung lamps inspire well-regulated emotions ; a discreet fra-grance is diffused in the close air ; even the samovar on the table hisses in a restrained and modest manner. The lady of the house, an important per-

sonage in the Petersburg world, speaks hardly audibly ; she always speaks
as though there were some one dangerously ill, almost dying in the room ;
the other ladies, following her example, faintly whisper ; while her sister,
pouring out tea, moves her lips so absolutely without sound that a young
man sitting before her, who has been thrown by chance into the temple
of decorum, is positively at a loss to know what she wants of him, while
she for the sixth time breathes to him, ' *Voulez-vous une tasse de thé ?* ' In
the corners are to be seen young, good-looking men ; their glances are
brightly, gently ingratiating ; unruffled gentleness, tinged with obsequious-
ness, is apparent in their faces ; a number of the stars and crosses of distinction gleam softly on their breasts. The conversation is always gentle ; it
turns on religious and patriotic topics, the Mystic Drop, F. N. Glinka,
the missions in the East, the monasteries and brotherhoods in White Russia.
At times, with muffled tread over the soft carpets, move footmen in livery ;
their huge calves, cased in tight silk stockings, shake noiselessly at every
step ; the respectful motion of the solid muscles only augments the general
impression of decorum, of solemnity, of sanctity.

It is a temple, a temple !

' Have you seen Madame Ratmirov to-day ? ' one great lady queries softly.

' I met her to-day at Lise's,' the hostess answers with her Æolian note.
' I feel so sorry for her. . . . She has a satirical intellect . . . *elle n'a pas
la foi.*'

' Yes, yes,' repeats the great lady . . . ' that I remember, Piotr Ivanitch
said about her, and very true it is, *qu'elle a . . . qu'elle a* an ironical intellect.'

' *Elle n'a pas la foi,*' the hostess's voice exhaled like the smoke of incense,—
' *C'est une âme égarée.* She has an ironical mind.'

And that is why the young men are not all without exception in love with
Irina. . . . They are afraid of her . . . afraid of her ' ironical intellect.'
That is the current phrase about her ; in it, as in every phrase, there is a
grain of truth. And not only the young men are afraid of her ; she is feared
by grown men too, and by men in high places, and even by the grandest
personages. No one can so truly and artfully scent out the ridiculous or
petty side of a character, no one else has the gift of stamping it mercilessly
with the never-forgotten word. . . . And the sting of that word is all the
sharper that it comes from lovely, sweetly fragrant lips. . . . It's hard to
say what passes in that soul ; but in the crowd of her adorers rumour does
not recognise in any one the position of a favoured suitor.

Irina's husband is moving rapidly along the path which among the French
is called the path of distinction. The stout general has shot past him ; the
condescending one is left behind. And in the same town in which Irina lives,
lives also our friend Sozont Potugin ; he rarely sees her, and she has no
special necessity to keep up any connection with him. . . . The little girl
who was committed to his care died not long ago.

A DESPERATE CHARACTER

. . . WE WERE A PARTY of eight in the room, and we were talking of contemporary affairs and men.

' I don't understand these men ! ' observed A. : ' they 're such desperate fellows. . . . Really desperate. . . . There has never been anything like it before.'

Yes, there has, put in P., a man getting on in years, with grey hair, born some time in the twenties of this century: there were desperate characters in former days too, only they were not like the desperate fellows of to-day. Of the poet Yazikov some one has said that he had enthusiasm, but not applied to anything—an enthusiasm without an object. So it was with those people—their desperateness was without an object. But there, if you 'll allow me, I 'll tell you the story of my nephew, or rather cousin, Misha Poltyev. It may serve as an example of the desperate characters of those days.

He came into God's world, I remember, in 1828, at his father's native place and property, in one of the sleepiest corners of a sleepy province of the steppes. Misha's father, Andrei Nikolaevitch Poltyev, I remember well to this day. He was a genuine old-world landowner, a God-fearing, sedate man, fairly—for those days—well educated, just a little cracked, to tell the truth—and, moreover, he suffered from epilepsy. . . . That too is an old-world, gentlemanly complaint. . . . Andrei Nikolaevitch's fits were, however, slight, and generally ended in sleep and depression. He was good-hearted, and of an affable demeanour, not without a certain stateliness : I always pictured to myself the tsar Mihail Fedorovitch as like him. The whole life of Andrei Nikolaevitch was passed in the punctual fulfilment of every observance established from old days, in strict conformity with all the usages of the old orthodox holy Russian mode of life. He got up and went to bed, ate his meals, and went to his bath, rejoiced or was wroth (both very rarely, it is true), even smoked his pipe and played cards (two great innovations !), not after his own fancy, not in a way of his own, but according to the custom and ordinance of his fathers—with due decorum and formality. He was tall, well built, and stout ; his voice was soft and rather husky, as is so often the case with virtuous people in Russia ; he was scrupulously neat in his dress and linen, and wore white cravats and full-skirted snuff-coloured coats, but his noble blood was nevertheless evident ; no one could have taken him for a priest's son or a merchant ! At all times, on all possible occasions, and in all possible contingencies, Andrei Nikolaevitch knew without fail what ought to be done, what was to be said, and precisely what expressions were to be used ; he knew when he ought to take medicine, and just what he ought to take; what omens were to be believed and what might be disregarded . . . in fact, he knew everything that ought to be done. . . . For as everything had been provided for and laid down by one's elders, one had only to be sure not to imagine anything of one's self. . . . And above all, without God's blessing not a step to be taken!—It must be confessed that a deadly dulness reigned supreme in his house, in those low-pitched, warm, dark rooms, that so often resounded with the singing of liturgies and all-night services, and had the smell of incense and Lenten dishes almost always hanging about them!

Andrei Nikolaevitch—no longer in his first youth—married a young lady of a neighbouring family, without fortune, a very nervous and sickly person, who had had a boarding-school education. She played the piano fairly, spoke boarding-school French, was easily moved to enthusiasm, and still more easily to melancholy and even tears. . . . She was of unbalanced character, in fact. She regarded her life as wasted, could not care for her husband, who, 'of course,' did not understand her; but she respected him, . . . she put up with him; and being perfectly honest and perfectly cold, she never dreamed of another 'affection.' Besides, she was always completely engrossed in the care, first, of her own really delicate health, secondly, of the health of her husband, whose fits always inspired in her something like superstitious horror, and lastly, of her only son, Misha, whom she brought up herself with great zeal. Andrei Nikolaevitch did not oppose his wife's looking after Misha, on the one condition of his education never overstepping the lines laid down, once and for all, within which everything must move in his house! Thus, for instance, at Christmas-time, and at New Year, and St. Vassily's eve, it was permissible for Misha to dress up and masquerade with the servant boys—and not only permissible, but even a binding duty. . . . But, at any other time, God forbid! and so on, and so on.

II

I REMEMBER MISHA at thirteen. He was a very pretty boy, with rosy little cheeks and soft lips (indeed he was soft and plump-looking all over), with prominent liquid eyes, carefully brushed and combed, caressing and modest —a regular little girl! There was only one thing about him I did not like: he rarely laughed; but when he did laugh, his teeth—large white teeth, pointed like an animal's—showed disagreeably, and the laugh itself had an abrupt, even savage, almost animal sound, and there were unpleasant gleams in his eyes. His mother was always praising him for being so obedient and well behaved, and not caring to make friends with rude boys, but always preferring feminine society. 'A mother's darling, a milksop,' his father, Andrei Nikolaevitch, would call him; 'but he's always ready to go into the house of God. . . . And that I am glad to see.' Only one old neighbour, who had been a police captain, once said before me, speaking of Misha, 'Mark my words, he'll be a rebel.' And this saying, I remember, surprised me very much at the time. The old police captain, it is true, used to see rebels on all sides.

Just such an exemplary youth Misha continued to be till the eighteenth year of his age, up to the death of his parents, both of whom he lost almost on the same day. As I was all the while living constantly at Moscow, I heard nothing of my young kinsman. An acquaintance coming from his province did, it is true, inform me that Misha had sold the paternal estate for a trifling sum ; but this piece of news struck me as too wildly improbable ! And behold, all of a sudden, one autumn morning there flew into the yard of my house a carriage, with a pair of splendid trotting horses, and a coachman of monstrous size on the box; and in the carriage, wrapped in a cloak of military cut, with a beaver collar two yards deep, and with a foraging cap cocked on one side, *à la diable m'emporte*, sat . . . Misha! On catching sight of me (I was standing at the drawing-room window, gazing in astonishment at the flying equipage), he laughed his abrupt laugh, and jauntily flinging back his cloak, he jumped out of the carriage and ran into the house.

'Misha ! Mihail Andreevitch ! ' I was beginning, . . . 'Is it you ? '

'Call me Misha,'—he interrupted me. 'Yes, it's I, . . . I, in my own person. . . . I have come to Moscow . . . to see the world . . . and show myself. And here I am, come to see you. What do you say to my horses ? . . . Eh? ' he laughed again.

Though it was seven years since I had seen Misha last, I recognised him at once. His face had remained just as youthful and as pretty as ever—there was no moustache even visible ; only his cheeks looked a little swollen under his eyes, and a smell of spirits came from his lips.

'Have you been long in Moscow ? ' I inquired. 'I supposed you were at home in the country, looking after the place.' . . .

'Eh! The country I threw up at once! As soon as my parents died—may their souls rest in peace—(Misha crossed himself scrupulously, without a shade of mockery) at once, without a moment's delay, . . . *ein, zwei, drei!* ha, ha! I let it go cheap, damn it! A rascally fellow turned up. But it's no matter! Anyway, I am living as I fancy, and amusing other people. But why are you staring at me like that? Was I, really, to go dragging on in the same old round, do you suppose? . . . My dear fellow, couldn't I have a glass of something? '

Misha spoke fearfully quick and hurriedly, and, at the same time, as though he were only just waked up from sleep.

'Misha, upon my word ! ' I wailed ; 'have you no fear of God ? What do you look like? What an attire! And you ask for a glass too! And to sell such a fine estate for next to nothing. . . .'

'God I fear always, and do not forget,' he broke in. . . . 'But He is good, you know—God is. . . . He will forgive! And I am good too. . . . I have never yet hurt any one in my life. And drink is good too ; and as for hurting, . . . it never hurt any one either. And my get-up is quite the most correct thing. . . . Uncle, would you like me to show you I can walk straight ? Or to do a little dance ? '

'Oh, spare me, please ! A dance, indeed ! You 'd better sit down.'

'As to that, I 'll sit down with pleasure. . . . But why do you say nothing of my greys ? Just look at them, they 're perfect lions ! I 've got them on hire for the time, but I shall buy them for certain, . . . and the coachman too. . . . It 's ever so much cheaper to have one's own horses. And I had the money, but I lost it yesterday at faro. It 's no matter, I 'll make it up to-morrow. Uncle, . . . how about that little glass? '

I was still unable to get over my amazement. 'Really, Misha, how old are you? You ought not to be thinking about horses or cards, . . . but going into the university or the service.'

Misha first laughed again, then gave vent to a prolonged whistle.

'Well, uncle, I see you're in a melancholy humour to-day. I'll come back another time. But I tell you what: you come in the evening to Sokolniki. I've a tent pitched there. The gypsies sing, . . . such goings-on. . . . And there 's a streamer on the tent, and on the streamer, written in large letters: "The Troupe of Poltyev's Gypsies." The streamer coils like a snake, the letters are of gold, attractive for every one to read. A free entertainment—whoever likes to come! . . . No refusal! I'm making the dust fly in Moscow . . . to my glory! . . . Eh? will you come? Ah, I 've one girl there . . . a serpent! Black as your boot, spiteful as a dog, and eyes . . . like living coals! One can never tell what she 's going to do—kiss or bite! . . . Will you come, uncle? . . . Well, good-bye, till we meet! '

And with a sudden embrace, and a smacking kiss on my shoulder, Misha darted away into the courtyard, and into the carriage, waved his cap over his head, hallooed,—the monstrous coachman leered at him over his beard, the greys dashed off, and all vanished!

The next day I—like a sinner—set off to Sokolniki, and did actually see the tent with the streamer and the inscription. The drapery of the tent was raised; from it came clamour, creaking, and shouting. Crowds of people were thronging round it. On a carpet spread on the ground sat gypsies, men and women, singing and beating drums, and in the midst of them, in a red silk shirt and velvet breeches, was Misha, holding a guitar, dancing a jig. 'Gentlemen! honoured friends! walk in, please! the performance is just beginning! Free to all! ' he was shouting in a high, cracked voice. 'Hey! champagne! pop! a pop on the head! pop up to the ceiling! Ha! you rogue there, Paul de Kock! '

Luckily he did not see me, and I hastily made off.

I won't enlarge on my astonishment at the spectacle of this transformation. But, how was it actually possible for that quiet and modest boy to change all at once into a drunken buffoon? Could it all have been latent in him from childhood, and have come to the surface directly the yoke of his parents' control was removed? But that he had made the dust fly in Moscow, as he expressed it—of that, certainly, there could be no doubt. I have seen something of riotous living in my day; but in this there was a sort of violence, a sort of frenzy of self-destruction, a sort of desperation!

III

FOR TWO MONTHS these diversions continued. . . . And once more I was standing at my drawing-room window, looking into the courtyard. . . .

All of a sudden—what could it mean? . . . there came slowly stepping in at the gate a pilgrim . . . a squash hat pulled down on his forehead, his hair combed out straight to right and left below it, a long gown, a leather belt. . . . Could it be Misha? He it was!

I went to meet him on the steps. . . . 'What's this masquerade for?' I demanded.

'It's not a masquerade, uncle,' Misha answered with a deep sigh: since all I had I've squandered to the last farthing—and a great repentance too has come upon me—so I have resolved to go to the Sergiev monastery of the Holy Trinity to expiate my sins in prayer. For what refuge was left me? . . . And so I have come to you to say good-bye, uncle, like a prodigal son.'

I looked intently at Misha. His face was just the same, rosy and fresh (indeed it remained almost unchanged to the end), and the eyes, liquid, affectionate, and languishing—and the hands, as small and white. . . . But he smelt of spirits.

'Well,' I pronounced at last, 'it's a good thing to do—since there's nothing else to be done. But why is it you smell of spirits?'

'A relic of the past,' answered Misha, and he suddenly laughed, but immediately pulled himself up, and, making a straight, low bow—a monk's bow—he added: 'Won't you help me on my way? I'm going, see, on foot to the monastery. . . .'

'When?'

'To-day . . . at once.'

'Why be in such a hurry?'

'Uncle, my motto always was, "Make haste, make haste!"'

'But what is your motto now?'

'It's the same now. . . . Only, make haste towards *good!*'

And so Misha went off, leaving me to ponder on the vicissitudes of human destiny.

But he soon reminded me of his existence. Two months after his visit, I got a letter from him, the first of those letters, of which later on he furnished me with so abundant a supply. And note a peculiar fact: I have seldom seen a neater, more legible handwriting than that unbalanced fellow's. And the wording of his letters was exceedingly correct, just a little flowery. Invariable entreaties for assistance, always attended with resolutions to reform, vows, and promises on his honour. . . . All of it seemed—and perhaps was—sincere. Misha's signature to his letters was always accompanied by peculiar strokes, flourishes, and stops, and he made great use of marks of exclamation. In his first letter Misha informed me of a new 'turn in his fortune.' (Later on he used to refer to these turns as plunges, . . . and frequent were the plunges he took.) He was starting for the Caucasus on active service for his tsar and his country in the capacity of a cadet! And, though a certain benevolent aunt had entered into his impecunious position, and had sent him an inconsiderable sum, still he begged me to assist him in getting his equipment. I did what he asked, and for two years I heard nothing more of him.

I must own I had the gravest doubts as to his having gone to the Caucasus. But it turned out that he really had gone there, had, by favour, got into the T—— regiment as a cadet, and had been serving in it for those two years. A perfect series of legends had sprung up there about him. An officer of his regiment related them to me.

IV

I LEARNED a great deal which I should never have expected of him.—I was, of course, hardly surprised that as a military man, as an officer, he was not a success, that he was in fact worse than useless; but what I had not anticipated was that he was by no means conspicuous for much bravery; that in battle he had a downcast, woebegone air, seemed half-depressed, half-bewildered. Discipline of every sort worried him, and made him miserable; he was daring to the point of insanity when only his *own personal* safety was in question; no bet was too mad for him to accept; but do harm to others, kill, fight, he could not, possibly because his heart was too good—or possibly because his 'cottonwool' education (so he expressed it), had made him too soft. Himself he was quite ready to murder in any way at any moment. . . . But others—no. 'There's no making him out,' his comrades said of him; 'he's a flabby creature, a poor stick—and yet such a desperate fellow—a perfect madman!' I chanced in later days to ask Misha what evil spirit drove him, forced him, to drink to excess, risk his life, and so on. He always had one answer—'wretchedness.'

'But why are you wretched?'

'Why! how can you ask? If one comes, anyway, to one's self, begins to feel, to think of the poverty, of the injustice, of Russia. . . . Well, it's all over with me! . . . one's so wretched at once—one wants to put a bullet through one's head! One's forced to start drinking.'

'Why ever do you drag Russia in?'

'How can I help it? Can't be helped! That's why I'm afraid to think.'

'It all comes, and your wretchedness too, from having nothing to do.'

'But I don't know how to do anything, uncle! dear fellow! Take one's life, and stake it on a card—that I can do! Come, you tell me what I ought to do, what to risk my life for? This instant . . . I'll . . .'

'But you must simply live. . . . Why risk your life?'

'I can't! You say I act thoughtlessly. . . . But what else can I do? . . . If one starts thinking—good God, all that comes into one's head! It's only Germans who can think! . . .'

What use was it talking to him? He was a desperate man, and that's all one can say.

Of the Caucasus legends I have spoken about, I will tell you two or three.

One day, in a party of officers, Misha began boasting of a sabre he had got by exchange—'a genuine Persian blade!' The officers expressed doubts as to its genuineness. Misha began disputing. 'Here then,' he cried at last; 'they say the man that knows most about sabres is Abdulka the one-eyed. I'll go to him, and ask.' The officers wondered. 'What Abdulka? Do you mean that lives in the mountains? The rebel never subdued? Abdul-khan?' ' Yes, that's him.' 'Why, but he'll take you for a spy, will put you in a hole full of bugs, or else cut your head off with your own sabre. And, besides, how are you going to get to him? They'll catch you directly.' 'I'll go to him, though, all the same.' 'Bet you won't!' 'Taken!' And Misha promptly saddled his horse and rode off to Abdulka. He disappeared for three days. All felt certain that the crazy fellow had come by his end. But, behold! he came back—drunk, and with a sabre, not the one he had taken, but another. They began questioning him. 'It was all right,' said he; 'Abdulka's a nice fellow. At first, it's true, he ordered them to put irons on my legs, and was even on the point of having me impaled. Only, I explained why I had come, and showed him the sabre. "And you'd better not keep me," said I; "don't expect a ransom for me; I've not a farthing to bless myself with—and I've no relations." Abdulka was surprised; he looked at me with his solitary eye. "Well," said he, "you are a bold one, you Russian; am I to believe you?" "You may believe me," said I; "I never tell a lie." (And this was true; Misha never lied.) Abdulka looked at me again. "And do you know how to drink wine?" "I do," said I; "give me as much as you will, I'll drink it." Abdulka was surprised again; he called on Allah. And he told his—daughter, I suppose—such a pretty creature, only with an eye like a jackal's—to bring a wine-skin. And I began to get to work on it. "But your sabre," said he, "isn't genuine; here, take the real thing. And now we are pledged friends." But you've lost your bet, gentlemen; pay up.'

The second legend of Misha is of this nature. He was passionately fond of cards; but as he had no money, and could never pay his debts at cards (though he was never a card-sharper), no one at last would sit down to a game with him. So one day he began urgently begging one of his comrades among the officers to play with him! 'But if you lose, you don't pay.' 'The money certainly I can't pay, but I'll put a shot through my left hand, see, with this pistol here!' 'But whatever use will that be to me?' 'No use, but still it will be curious.' This conversation took place after a drinking bout in the presence of witnesses. Whether it was that Misha's proposition struck the officer as really curious—anyway he agreed. Cards were brought, the game began. Misha was in luck; he won a hundred roubles. And there-upon his opponent struck his forehead with vexation. 'What an ass I am!' he cried, 'to be taken in like this! As if you'd have shot your hand if you had lost!—a likely story! hold out your purse!' 'That's a lie,' retorted Misha: 'I've won—but I'll shoot my hand.' He snatched up his pistol—and bang, fired at his own hand. The bullet passed right through it . . . and in a week the wound had completely healed.

Another time, Misha was riding with his comrades along a road at night

. . . and they saw close to the roadside a narrow ravine like a deep cleft, dark—so dark you couldn't see the bottom. ' Look,' said one of the officers, ' Misha may be a desperate fellow, but he wouldn't leap into that ravine.' ' Yes, I'd leap in! ' ' No, you wouldn't, for I dare say it's seventy feet deep, and you might break your neck.' His friend knew his weak point—vanity. . . . There was a great deal of it in Misha. ' But I'll leap in anyway! Would you like to bet on it? Ten roubles.' ' Good! ' And the officer had hardly uttered the word, when Misha and his horse were off—into the ravine—and crashing down over the stones. All were simply petrified. . . . A full minute passed, and they heard Misha's voice, dimly, as it were rising up out of the bowels of the earth: ' All right! fell on the sand . . . but it was a long flight! Ten roubles you've lost! ' ' Climb out! ' shouted his comrades. ' Climb out, I dare say! ' echoed Misha. ' A likely story! I should like to see you climb out. You'll have to go for torches and ropes now. And, meanwhile, to keep up my spirits while I wait, fling down a flask. . . .'

And so Misha had to stay five hours at the bottom of the ravine; and when they dragged him out, it turned out that his shoulder was dislocated. But that in no way troubled him. The next day a bone-setter, one of the blacksmiths, set his shoulder, and he used it as though nothing had been the matter.

His health in general was marvellous, incredible. I have already mentioned that up to the time of his death he kept his almost childishly fresh complexion. Illness was a thing unknown to him, in spite of his excesses; the strength of his constitution never once showed signs of giving way. When any other man would infallibly have been seriously ill, or even have died, he merely shook himself, like a duck in the water, and was more blooming than ever. Once, also in the Caucasus . . . *this* legend is really incredible, but one may judge from it what Misha was thought to be capable of. . . . Well, once, in the Caucasus, in a state of drunkenness, he fell down with the lower half of his body in a stream of water; his head and arms were on the bank, out of water. It was winter-time, there was a hard frost, and when he was found next morning, his legs and body were pulled out from under a thick layer of ice, which had formed over them in the night—and he didn't even catch cold! Another time—this was in Russia (near Orel, and also in a time of severe frost)—he was in a tavern outside the town in company with seven young seminarists (or theological students), and these seminarists were celebrating their final examination, but had invited Misha, as a delightful person, a man of ' inspiration,' as the phrase was then. A very great deal was drunk, and when at last the festive party got ready to depart, Misha, dead drunk, was in an unconscious condition. All the seven seminarists together had but one three-horse sledge with a high back; where were they to stow the unresisting body? Then one of the young men, inspired by classical reminiscences, proposed tying Misha by his feet to the back of the sledge, as Hector was tied to the chariot of Achilles! The proposal met with approval . . . and jolting up and down over the holes, sliding sideways down the slopes, with his legs torn and flayed, and his head rolling in the snow, poor Misha travelled on his back for the mile and a half from the tavern to the town, and hadn't as much as a cough afterwards, hadn't turned a hair! Such heroic health had nature bestowed upon him!

V

FROM THE CAUCASUS he came again to Moscow, in a Circassian dress, a dagger in his sash, a high-peaked cap on his head. This costume he retained to the end, though he was no longer in the army, from which he had been discharged for outstaying his leave. He stayed with me, borrowed a little money . . . and forthwith began his 'plunges,' his wanderings, or, as he expressed it, 'his peregrinations from pillar to post,' then came the sudden disappearances and returns, and the showers of beautifully written letters addressed to people of every possible description, from an archbishop down to stable-boys and midwives! Then came calls upon persons known and unknown! And this is worth noticing: when he made these calls, he was never abject and cringing, he never worried people by begging, but on the contrary behaved with propriety, and had positively a cheerful and pleasant air, though the inveterate smell of spirits accompanied him everywhere, and his Oriental costume gradually changed into rags. 'Give, and God will reward you, though I don't deserve it,' he would say, with a bright smile and a candid blush; 'if you don't give, you'll be perfectly right, and I shan't blame you for it. I shall find food to eat, God will provide! And there are people poorer than I, and much more deserving of help—plenty, plenty!' Misha was particularly successful with women: he knew how to appeal to their sympathy. But don't suppose that he was or fancied himself a Lovelace. . . . Oh, no! in that way he was very modest. Whether it was that he had inherited a cool temperament from his parents, or whether indeed this too is to be set down to his dislike for doing any one harm—as, according to his notions, relations with a woman meant inevitably doing a woman harm—I won't undertake to decide; only in all his behaviour with the fair sex he was extremely delicate. Women felt this, and were the more ready to sympathise with him and help him, until at last he revolted them by his drunkenness and debauchery, by the desperateness of which I have spoken already. . . . I can think of no other word for it.

But in other relations he had by that time lost every sort of delicacy, and was gradually sinking to the lowest depths of degradation. He once, in the public assembly at T——, got as far as setting on the table a jug with a notice: 'Any one, to whom it may seem agreeable to give the high-born nobleman Poltyev (authentic documents in proof of his pedigree are herewith exposed) a flip on the nose, may satisfy this inclination on putting a rouble into this jug.' And I am told there were persons found willing to pay for the privilege of flipping a nobleman's nose! It is true that one such person, who put in only one rouble and gave him *two* flips, he first almost strangled, and then forced to apologise; it is true, too, that part of the money gained in this fashion he promptly distributed among other poor devils . . . but still, think what a disgrace!

In the course of his ' peregrinations from pillar to post,' he made his way, too, to his ancestral home, which he had sold for next to nothing to a speculator and money-lender well known in those days. The money-lender was at home, and hearing of the presence in the neighbourhood of the former owner, now reduced to vagrancy, he gave orders not to admit him into the house, and even, in case of necessity, to drive him away. Misha announced that he would not for his part consent to enter the house, polluted by the presence of so repulsive a person; that he would permit no one to drive him away, but was going to the churchyard to pay his devotions at the grave of his parents. So in fact he did.

In the churchyard he was joined by an old house-serf, who had once been his nurse. The money-lender had deprived this old man of his monthly allowance, and driven him off the estate; since then his refuge had been a corner in a peasant's hut. Misha had been too short a time in possession of his estate to have left behind him a particularly favourable memory; still the old servant could not resist running to the churchyard as soon as he heard of his young master's being there. He found Misha sitting on the ground between the tombstones, asked for his hand to kiss, as in old times, and even shed tears on seeing the rags which clothed the limbs of his once pampered young charge.

Misha gazed long and silently at the old man. ' Timofay! ' he said at last; Timofay started.

' What do you desire? '

' Have you a spade? '

' I can get one. . . . But what do you want with a spade, Mihailo Andreitch, sir? '

' I want to dig myself a grave, Timofay, and to lie here for time everlasting between my father and mother. There's only this spot left me in the world. Get a spade! '

' Yes, sir,' said Timofay; he went and got it. And Misha began at once digging in the ground, while Timofay stood by, his chin propped in his hand, repeating: ' It's all that's left for you and me, master! '

Misha dug and dug, from time to time observing: ' Life's not worth living, is it, Timofay? '

' It's not indeed, master.'

The hole was already of a good depth. People saw what Misha was about, and ran to tell the new owner about it. The money-lender was at first very angry, wanted to send for the police: ' This is sacrilege,' said he. But afterwards, probably reflecting that it was inconvenient anyway to have to do with such a madman, and that it might lead to a scandal,—he went in his own person to the churchyard, and approaching Misha, still toiling, made him a polite bow. He went on with his digging as though he had not noticed his successor. ' Mihail Andreitch,' began the money-lender, ' allow me to ask what you are doing here? '

' You can see—I am digging myself a grave.'

' Why are you doing so? '

' Because I don't want to live any longer.'

The money-lender fairly threw up his hands in amazement. 'You don't want to live?'

Misha glanced menacingly at the money-lender. 'That surprises you? Aren't you the cause of it all? . . . You? . . . You? . . . Wasn't it you, Judas, who robbed me, taking advantage of my childishness? Aren't you flaying the peasants' skins off their backs? Haven't you taken from this poor old man his crust of dry bread? Wasn't it you? . . . O God! everywhere nothing but injustice, and oppression, and evil-doing. . . . Everything must go to ruin then, and me too! I don't care for life, I don't care for life in Russia! ' And the spade moved faster than ever in Misha's hands.

' Here's a devil of a business! ' thought the money-lender; ' he's positively burying himself alive.' 'Mihail Andreevitch,' he began again: ' listen. I've been behaving badly to you, indeed; they told me falsely of you.'

Misha went on digging.

' But why be desperate? '

Misha still went on digging, and kept throwing the earth at the money-lender's feet, as though to say, ' Here you are, land-grabber.'

' Really, you're wrong in this. Won't you be pleased to come in to have some lunch, and rest a bit? '

Misha raised his head. 'So that's it now! And anything to drink? '

The money-lender was delighted. 'Why, of course . . . I should think so.'

' You invite Timofay too? '

' Well, . . . yes, him too.'

Misha pondered. 'Only, mind . . . you made me a beggar, you know. . . . Don't think you can get off with one bottle! '

' Set your mind at rest . . . there shall be all you can want.'

Misha got up and flung down the spade. . . . ' Well, Timosha,' said he to his old nurse; ' let's do honour to our host. . . . Come along.'

' Yes, sir,' answered the old man.

And all three started off to the house together. The money-lender knew the man he had to deal with. At the first start Misha, it is true, exacted a promise from him to ' grant all sorts of immunities ' to the peasants; but an hour later, this same Misha, together with Timofay, both drunk, were dancing a galop in the big apartments, which still seemed pervaded by the God-fearing shade of Andrei Nikolaevitch; and an hour later still, Misha in a dead sleep (he had a very weak head for spirits), laid in a cart with his high cap and dagger, was being driven off to the town, more than twenty miles away, and there was flung under a hedge. . . . As for Timofay, who could still keep on his legs, and only hiccupped—him, of course, they kicked out of the house; since they couldn't get at the master, they had to be content with the old servant.

VI

SOME TIME PASSED again, and I heard nothing of Misha. . . . God knows what he was doing. But one day, as I sat over the samovar at a posting-station on the T—— highroad, waiting for horses, I suddenly heard under the open window of the station room a hoarse voice, uttering in French the words: 'Monsieur . . . monsieur . . . prenez pitié d'un pauvre gentil-homme ruiné.' . . . I lifted my head, glanced. . . . The mangy-looking fur cap, the broken ornaments on the ragged Circassian dress, the dagger in the cracked sheath, the swollen, but still rosy face, the dishevelled, but still thick crop of hair. . . . Mercy on us! Misha! He had come then to begging alms on the highroads. I could not help crying out. He recognised me, started, turned away, and was about to move away from the window. I stopped him . . . but what could I say to him? Give him a lecture? . . . In silence I held out a five-rouble note; he, also in silence, took it in his still white and plump, though shaking and dirty hand, and vanished round the corner of the house.

It was a good while before they gave me horses, and I had time to give myself up to gloomy reflections on my unexpected meeting with Misha; I felt ashamed of having let him go so unsympathetically.

At last I set off on my way, and half a mile from the station I observed ahead of me, in the road, a crowd of people moving along with a curious, as it seemed rhythmic, step. I overtook this crowd—and what did I see?

Some dozen or so beggars, with sacks over their shoulders, were walking two by two, singing and leaping about, while in front of them danced Misha, stamping time with his feet, and shouting, ' Natchiki-tchikaldy, tchuk, tchuk, tchuk! . . . Natchiki-tchikaldy, tchuk, tchuk, tchuk! ' Directly my carriage caught them up, and he saw me, he began at once shouting, ' Hur-rah! Stand in position! right about face, guard of the roadside! '

The beggars took up his shout, and halted; while he, with his peculiar laugh, jumped on to the carriage step, and again yelled: Hurrah!

'What's the meaning of this? ' I asked with involuntary astonishment.

'This? This is my company, my army—all beggars, God's people, friends of my heart. Every one of them, thanks to you, has had a glass; and now we are all rejoicing and making merry! . . . Uncle! Do you know it's only with beggars, God's people, that one can live in the world . . . By God, it is! '

I made him no answer . . . but at that moment he struck me as such a kind good creature, his face expressed such childlike simple-heartedness. . . . A light seemed suddenly as it were to dawn upon me, and I felt a pang in my heart. . . . 'Get into the carriage,' I said to him. He was taken aback. . . .

'What? Into the carriage? '

'Yes, get in, get in,' I repeated; 'I want to make you a suggestion. Sit down. . . . Come along with me.'

'Well, as you will.' He sat down. 'Well, and you, my honoured friends, my dear comrades,' he added, addressing the beggars, 'farewell, till we meet again.' Misha took off his high cap, and bowed low. The beggars all seemed overawed. . . . I told the coachman to whip up the horses, and the carriage rolled off.

The suggestion I wanted to make Misha was this: the idea suddenly occurred to me to take him with me to my home in the country, about five-and-twenty miles from that station, to rescue him, or at least to make an effort to rescue him. 'Listen, Misha,' I said; 'will you come along and live with me? . . . You shall have everything provided you; you shall have clothes and linen made you; you shall be properly fitted out, and you shall have money to spend on tobacco, and so on, only on one condition, that you give up drink. . . . Do you agree? '

Misha was positively aghast with delight; he opened his eyes wide, flushed crimson, and suddenly falling on my shoulder, began kissing me, and repeating in a broken voice, 'Uncle . . . benefactor . . . God reward you.' . . . He burst into tears at last, and taking off his cap fell to wiping his eyes, his nose, his lips with it.

'Mind,' I observed; 'remember the condition, not to touch strong drink.'

'Damnation to it! ' he cried, with a wave of both arms, and with this impetuous movement, I was more than ever conscious of the strong smell of spirits with which he seemed always saturated. . . . 'Uncle, if you knew what my life has been. . . . If it hadn't been for sorrow, a cruel fate. . . . But now I swear, I swear, I will mend my ways, I will show you. . . . Uncle, I've never told a lie—you can ask whom you like. . . . I'm honest, but I'm an unlucky fellow, uncle; I've known no kindness from any one. . . .'

Here he broke down finally into sobs. I tried to soothe him, and succeeded so far that when we reached home Misha had long been lost in a heavy sleep, with his head on my knees.

VII

HE WAS at once assigned a room for himself, and at once, first thing, taken to the bath, which was absolutely essential. All his clothes, and his dagger and cap and torn boots, were carefully put away in a loft; he was dressed in clean linen, slippers, and some clothes of mine, which, as is always the way with poor relations, at once seemed to adapt themselves to his size and figure. When he came to table, washed, clean, and fresh, he seemed so touched and happy, he beamed all over with such joyful gratitude, that I too felt moved and joyful. . . . His face was completely transformed. . . . Boys of twelve have faces like that on Easter Sundays, after the communion, when, thickly pomaded, in new jacket and starched collars, they come to exchange Easter greetings with their parents. Misha was continually—with a sort of cautious incredulity—feeling himself and repeating: 'What does

it mean? . . . Am I in heaven?' The next day he announced that he had
not slept all night, he had been in such ecstasy.

I had living in my house at that time an old aunt with her niece; both
of them were extremely disturbed when they heard of Misha's presence;
they could not comprehend how I could have asked him into my house!
There were very ugly rumours about him. But in the first place, I knew
he was always very courteous with ladies; and, secondly, I counted on his
promises of amendment. And, in fact, for the first two days of his stay
under my roof Misha not merely justified my expectations but surpassed
them, while the ladies of the household were simply enchanted with him.
He played piquet with the old lady, helped her to wind her worsted, showed
her two new games of patience; for the niece, who had a small voice, he
played accompaniments on the piano, and read Russian and French poetry.
He told both the ladies lively but discreet anecdotes; in fact, he showed
them every attention, so that they repeatedly expressed their surprise to me,
and the old lady even observed how unjust people sometimes were. . . . The
things—the things they had said of him . . . and he such a quiet fellow, and
so polite . . . poor Misha! It is true that at table 'poor Misha' licked his
lips in a rather peculiar, hurried way, if he simply glanced at the bottle. But
I had only to shake my finger at him, and he would turn his eyes upwards,
and lay his hand on his heart . . . as if to say, I have sworn. . . . 'I am
regenerated now,' he assured me. . . . 'Well, God grant it be so,' was my
thought. . . . But this regeneration did not last long.

The first two days he was very talkative and cheerful. But even on the
third day he seemed somehow subdued, though he remained, as before, with
the ladies and tried to entertain them. A half mournful, half dreamy expression flitted now and then over his face, and the face itself was paler and
looked thinner. 'Are you unwell?' I asked him.

'Yes,' he answered; 'my head aches a little.' On the fourth day he was
completely silent; for the most part he sat in a corner, hanging his head dis-
consolately, and his dejected appearance worked upon the compassionate
sympathies of the two ladies, who now, in their turn, tried to amuse him.
At table he ate nothing, stared at his plate, and rolled up pellets of bread.
On the fifth day the feeling of compassion in the ladies began to be replaced
by other emotions—uneasiness and even alarm. Misha was so strange, he held
aloof from people, and kept moving along close to the walls, as though
trying to steal by unnoticed, and suddenly looking round as though some
one had called him. And what had become of his rosy colour? It seemed
covered over by a layer of earth. 'Are you still unwell?' I asked him.

'No, I'm all right,' he answered abruptly.

'Are you dull?'

'Why should I be dull?' But he turned away and would not look me
in the face.

'Or is it that wretchedness come over you again?' To this he made no
reply. So passed another twenty-four hours.

Next day my aunt ran into my room in a state of great excitement, declaring that she would leave the house with her niece, if Misha was to remain in it.

'Why so?'

'Why, we are dreadfully scared with him. . . . He's not a man, he's a wolf,—nothing better than a wolf. He keeps moving and moving about, and doesn't speak—and looks so wild. . . . He almost gnashes his teeth at me. My Katia, you know is so nervous. . . . She was so struck with him the first day. . . . I'm in terror for her, and indeed for myself too.' . . . I didn't know what to say to my aunt. I couldn't, anyway, turn Misha out, after inviting him.

He relieved me himself from my difficult position. The same day,—I was still sitting in my own room,—suddenly I heard behind me a husky and angry voice: 'Nikolai Nikolaitch, Nikolai Nikolaitch!' I looked round; Misha was standing in the doorway with a face that was fearful, black-looking and distorted. 'Nikolai Nikolaitch!' he repeated . . . (not 'uncle' now).

'What do you want?'

'Let me go . . . at once!'

'Why?'

'Let me go, or I shall do mischief, I shall set the house on fire or cut some one's throat.' Misha suddenly began trembling. 'Tell them to give me back my clothes, and let a cart take me to the highroad, and let me have some money, however little!'

'Are you displeased, then, at anything?'

'I can't live like this!' he shrieked at the top of his voice. 'I can't live in your respectable, thrice-accursed house! It makes me sick, and ashamed to live so quietly! . . . How *you* manage to endure it!'

'That is,' I interrupted in my turn, 'you mean—you can't live without drink. . . .'

'Well, yes! yes!' he shrieked again: 'only let me go to my brethren, my friends, to the beggars! . . . Away from your respectable, loathsome species!'

I was about to remind him of his sworn promises, but Misha's frenzied look, his breaking voice, the convulsive tremor in his limbs,—it was all so awful, that I made haste to get rid of him; I said that his clothes should be given him at once, and a cart got ready; and taking a note for twenty-five roubles out of a drawer, I laid it on the table. Misha had begun to advance in a menacing way towards me,—but on this, suddenly he stopped, his face worked, flushed, he struck himself on the breast, the tears rushed from his eyes, and muttering, 'Uncle! angel! I know I'm a ruined man! thanks! thanks!' he snatched up the note and ran away.

An hour later he was sitting in the cart dressed once more in his Circassian costume, again rosy and cheerful; and when the horses started, he yelled, tore off the peaked cap, and, waving it over his head, made bow after bow. Just as he was going off, he had given me a long and warm embrace, and whispered, 'Benefactor, benefactor . . . there's no saving me! ' He even ran to the ladies and kissed their hands, fell on his knees, called upon God, and begged their forgiveness! Katia I found afterwards in tears.

The coachman, with whom Misha had set off, on coming home informed me that he had driven him to the first tavern on the highroad—and that there ' his honour had stuck,' had begun treating every one indiscriminately —and had quickly sunk into unconsciousness.

From that day I never came across Misha again, but his ultimate fate I learned in the following manner.

VIII

THREE YEARS LATER, I was again at home in the country; all of a sudden a servant came in and announced that Madame Poltyev was asking to see me. I knew no Madame Poltyev, and the servant, who made this announcement, for some unknown reason smiled sarcastically. To my glance of inquiry, he responded that the lady asking for me was young, poorly dressed, and had come in a peasant's cart with one horse, which she was driving herself! I told him to ask Madame Poltyev up to my room.

I saw a woman of five-and-twenty, in the dress of the small tradesman class, with a large kerchief on her head. Her face was simple, roundish, not without charm; she looked dejected and gloomy, and was shy and awkward in her movements.

' You are Madame Poltyev? ' I inquired, and I asked her to sit down.

' Yes,' she answered in a subdued voice, and she did not sit down. ' I am the widow of your nephew, Mihail Andreevitch Poltyev.'

' Is Mihail Andreevitch dead? Has he been dead long? But sit down, I beg.'

She sank into a chair.

' It's two months.'

' And had you been married to him long? '

' I had been a year with him.'

' Where have you come from now? '

' From out Tula way. . . . There's a village there, Znamenskoe-Glush-kovo—perhaps you may know it. I am the daughter of the deacon there. Mihail Andreitch and I lived there. . . . He lived in my father's house. We were a whole year together.'

The young woman's lips twitched a little, and she put her hand up to them. She seemed to be on the point of tears, but she controlled herself, and cleared her throat.

' Mihail Andreitch,' she went on: ' before his death enjoined upon me to go to you; "You must be sure to go," said he! And he told me to thank you for all your goodness, and to give you . . . this . . . see, this little thing (she took a small packet out of her pocket) which he always had about him. . . . And Mihail Andreitch said, if you would be pleased to accept it in memory of him, if you would not disdain it. . . . " There's nothing else," said he, " I can give him " . . . that is, you. . . .'

In the packet there was a little silver cup with the monogram of Misha's mother. This cup I had often seen in Misha's hands, and once he had even said to me, speaking of some poor fellow, that he really was destitute, since he had neither cup nor bowl, ' while I, see, have this, anyway.'

I thanked her, took the cup, and asked: ' Of what complaint had Misha died? No doubt . . .'

Then I bit my tongue . . . but the young woman understood my unuttered hint. . . . She took a swift glance at me, then looked down again, smiled mournfully, and said at once: ' Oh no! he had quite given that up, ever since he got to know me . . . But he had no health at all! . . . It was shattered quite. As soon as he gave up drink, he fell into ill health directly. He became so steady; he always wanted to help father in his land or in the garden, . . . or any other work there might be . . . in spite of his being of noble birth. But how could he get the strength? . . . At writing, too, he tried to work; as you know, he could do that work capitally, but his hands shook, and he couldn't hold the pen properly. . . . He was always finding fault with himself; " I'm a white-handed poor creature," he would say; " I've never done any good to anybody, never helped, never laboured! " He worried himself very much about that. . . . He used to say that our people labour,—but what use are we? . . . Ah, Nikolai Nikolaitch, he was a good man—and he was fond of me . . . and I . . . Ah, pardon me. . . .'

Here the young woman wept outright. I would have consoled her, but I did not know how.

' Have you a child left you? ' I asked at last.

She sighed. ' No, no child. . . . Is it likely? ' And her tears flowed faster than ever.

' And so that was how Misha's troubled wanderings had ended,' the old man P. wound up his narrative. ' You will agree with me, I am sure, that I'm right in calling him a desperate character; but you will most likely agree too that he was not like the desperate characters of to-day; still, a philosopher, you must admit, would find a family likeness between him and them. In him and in them there's the thirst for self-destruction, the wretchedness, the dissatisfaction. . . . And what it all comes from, I leave the philosopher to decide.'

BOUGIVALLE, *November* 1881.

A STRANGE STORY

FIFTEEN YEARS AGO—began H.—official duties compelled me to spend a few days in the principal town of the province of T——. I stopped at a very fair hotel, which had been established six months before my arrival by a Jewish tailor, who had grown rich. I am told that it did not flourish long, which is often the case with us; but I found it still in its full splendour: the new furniture emitted cracks like pistol-shots at night; the bed-linen, table-cloths, and napkins smelt of soap, and the painted floors reeked of olive oil, which, however, in the opinion of the waiter, an exceedingly elegant but not very clean individual, tended to prevent the spread of insects. This waiter, a former valet of Prince G.'s, was conspicuous for his free-and-easy manners and his self-assurance. He invariably wore a second-hand frock-coat and slippers trodden down at heel, carried a table-napkin under his arm, and had a multitude of pimples on his cheeks. With a free sweeping movement of his moist hands he gave utterance to brief but pregnant obser-vations. He showed a patronising interest in me, as a person capable of appreciating his culture and knowledge of the world; but he regarded his own lot in life with a rather disillusioned eye. 'No doubt about it,' he said to me one day; 'ours is a poor sort of position nowadays. May be sent flying any day!' His name was Ardalion.

I had to make a few visits to official persons in the town. Ardalion pro-cured me a coach and groom, both alike shabby and loose in the joints; but the groom wore livery, the carriage was adorned with an heraldic crest. After making all my official calls, I drove to see a country gentleman, an old friend of my father's, who had been a long time settled in the town. . . . I had not met him for twenty years; he had had time to get married, to bring up a good-sized family, to be left a widower and to make his fortune. His business was with government monopolies, that is to say, he lent contractors for monopolies loans at heavy interest. . . . 'There is always honour in risk,' they say, though indeed the risk was small.

In the course of our conversation there came into the room with hesitat-ing steps, but as lightly as though on tiptoe, a young girl of about seven-teen, delicate-looking and thin. 'Here,' said my acquaintance, 'is my eldest daughter Sophia; let me introduce you. She takes my poor wife's place, looks after the house, and takes care of her brothers and sisters.' I bowed a second time to the girl who had come in (she meanwhile dropped into a chair without speaking), and thought to myself that she did not look much like housekeeping or looking after children. Her face was quite childish, round, with small, pleasing, but immobile features; the blue eyes, under high, also immobile and irregular eyebrows, had an intent, almost astonished look, as though they had just observed something unexpected; the full little mouth with the lifted upper lip, not only did not smile, but seemed as though altogether innocent of such a practice; the rosy flush under the tender skin stood in soft, diffused patches on the cheeks, and neither paled nor deepened. The fluffy, fair hair hung in light clusters each side of the little head. Her bosom breathed softly, and her arms were pressed somehow awkwardly and severely against her narrow waist. Her blue gown fell without folds—like a child's—to her little feet. The general impression this girl made upon me was not one of morbidity, but of something enigmatical. I saw before me not simply a shy, provincial miss, but a creature of a special type—that I could not make out. This type neither attracted nor repelled me; I did not fully understand it, and only felt that I had never come across a nature more sincere. Pity . . . yes! pity was the feeling that rose up within me at the sight of this young, serious, keenly alert life—God knows why! 'Not of this earth,' was my thought, though there was nothing exactly 'ideal' in the expression of the face, and though Mademoiselle Sophia had obviously come into the drawing-room in fulfilment of those duties of lady of the house to which her father had referred.

He began to talk of life in the town of T——, of the social amusements and advantages it offered. 'We're very quiet here,' he observed; 'the governor's a melancholy fellow; the marshal of the province is a bachelor. But there'll be a big ball in the Hall of the Nobility the day after to-morrow. I advise you to go; there are some pretty girls here. And you'll see all our *intelligentsi* too.'

My acquaintance, as a man of university education, was fond of using learned expressions. He pronounced them with irony, but also with respect. Besides, we all know that moneylending, together with respectability, develops a certain thoughtfulness in men.

'Allow me to ask, will you be at the ball?' I said, turning to my friend's daughter. I wanted to hear the sound of her voice.

'Papa intends to go,' she answered, 'and I with him.'

Her voice turned out to be soft and deliberate, and she articulated every syllable fully, as though she were puzzled.

'In that case, allow me to ask you for the first quadrille.'

She bent her head in token of assent, and even then did not smile.

I soon withdrew, and I remember the expression in her eyes, fixed steadily upon me, struck me as so strange that I involuntarily looked over my shoulder to see whether there were not some one or some thing she was looking at behind my back.

I returned to the hotel, and after dining on the never-varied 'soupe-julienne,' cutlets, and green peas, and grouse cooked to a dry, black chip, I sat down on the sofa and gave myself up to reflection. The subject of my meditations was Sophia, this enigmatical daughter of my old acquaintance; but Ardalion, who was clearing the table, explained my thoughtfulness in his own way; he set it down to boredom.

'There is very little in the way of entertainment for visitors in our town,' he began with his usual easy condescension, while he went on at the same time flapping the backs of the chairs with a dirty dinner-napkin—a practice peculiar, as you're doubtless aware, to servants of superior education. 'Very little! ' He paused, and the huge clock on the wall, with a lilac rose on its white face, seemed in its monotonous, sleepy tick, to repeat his words: 'Ve-ry! ve-ry! ' it ticked. 'No concerts, nor theatres,' pursued Ardalion (he had travelled abroad with his master, and had all but stayed in Paris; he knew much better than to mispronounce this last word, as the peasants do)—'nor dances, for example; nor evening receptions among the nobility and gentry—there is nothing of the kind whatever.' (He paused a moment, probably to allow me to observe the choiceness of his diction.) 'They positively visit each other but seldom. Every one sits like a pigeon on its perch. And so it comes to pass that visitors have simply nowhere to go.'

Ardalion stole a sidelong glance at me.

'But there is one thing,' he went on, speaking with a drawl, 'in case you should feel that way inclined. . . .'

He glanced at me a second time and positively leered, but I suppose did not observe signs of the requisite inclination in me.

The polished waiter moved towards the door, pondered a moment, came back, and after fidgeting about uneasily a little, bent down to my ear, and with a playful smile said:

'Would you not like to behold the dead? '

I stared at him in perplexity.

'Yes,' he went on, speaking in a whisper; 'there is a man like that here. He's a simple artisan, and can't even read and write, but he does marvellous things. If you, for example, go to him and desire to see any one of your departed friends, he will be sure to show him you.'

'How does he do it? '

'That's his secret. For though he's an uneducated man—to speak bluntly, illiterate—he's very great in godliness! Greatly respected he is among the merchant gentry! '

'And does every one in the town know about this? '

'Those who need to know; but, there, of course—there's danger from the police to be guarded against. Because, say what you will, such doings are forbidden anyway, and for the common people are a temptation; the common people—the mob, we all know, quickly come to blows.'

'Has he shown you the dead? ' I asked Ardalion.

Ardalion nodded. 'He has; my father he brought before me as if living.'

I stared at Ardalion. He laughed and played with his dinner-napkin, and condescendingly, but unflinchingly, looked at me.

'But this is very curious! ' I cried at last. 'Couldn't I make the acquaintance of this artisan? '

'You can't go straight to him; but one can act through his mother. She's a respectable old woman; she sells pickled apples on the bridge. If you wish it, I will ask her.'

'Please do.'

Ardalion coughed behind his hand. 'And a gratuity, whatever you think fit, nothing much, of course, should also be handed to her—the old lady. And I on my side will make her understand that she has nothing to fear from you, as you are a visitor here, a gentleman—and of course you can understand that this is a secret, and will not in any case get her into any unpleasantness.'

Ardalion took the tray in one hand, and with a graceful swing of the tray and his own person, turned towards the door.

'So I may reckon upon you!' I shouted after him.

'You may trust me!' I heard his self-satisfied voice say: 'We'll talk to the old woman and transmit you her answer exactly.'

I will not enlarge on the train of thought aroused in me by the extraordinary fact Ardalion had related; but I am prepared to admit that I awaited the promised reply with impatience. Late in the evening Ardalion came to me and announced that to his annoyance he could not find the old woman. I handed him, however, by way of encouragement, a three-rouble note. The next morning he appeared again in my room with a beaming countenance; the old woman had consented to see me.

'Hi! boy!' shouted Ardalion in the corridor; 'hi! apprentice! Come here!' A boy of six came up, grimed all over with soot like a kitten, with a shaved head, perfectly bald in places, in a torn, striped smock, and huge goloshes on his bare feet. 'You take the gentleman, you know where,' said Ardalion, addressing the 'apprentice,' and pointing to me. 'And you, sir, when you arrive, ask for Mastridia Karpovna.'

The boy uttered a hoarse grunt, and we set off.

We walked rather a long while about the unpaved streets of the town of T——; at last in one of them, almost the most deserted and desolate of all, my guide stopped before an old two-story wooden house, and wiping his nose all over his smock-sleeve, said: 'Here; go to the right.' I passed through the porch into the outer passage, stumbled towards my right, a low door creaked on rusty hinges, and I saw before me a stout old woman in a brown jacket lined with hare-skin, with a parti-coloured kerchief on her head.

'Mastridia Karpovna?' I inquired.

'The same, at your service,' the old woman replied in a piping voice. 'Please walk in. Won't you take a chair?'

The room into which the old woman conducted me was so littered up with every sort of rubbish, rags, pillows, feather-beds, sacks, that one could hardly turn round in it. The sunlight barely struggled in through two dusty little windows; in one corner, from behind a heap of boxes piled on one another, there came a feeble whimpering and wailing. . . . I could not tell from what; perhaps a sick baby, or perhaps a puppy. I sat down on a chair, and the old woman stood up directly facing me. Her face was yellow, half-transparent like wax; her lips were so fallen in that they formed a single straight line in the midst of a multitude of wrinkles; a tuft of white hair stuck out from below the kerchief on her head, but the sunken grey eyes peered out alertly and cleverly from under the bony over-hanging brow; and the sharp nose fairly stuck out like a spindle, fairly sniffed the air as if it would say: I'm a smart one! 'Well, you're no fool!' was my thought. At the same time she smelt of spirits.

I explained to her the object of my visit, of which, however, as I ob-served, she must be aware. She listened to me, blinked her eyes rapidly, and only lifted her nose till it stuck out still more sharply, as though she were making ready to peck.

'To be sure, to be sure,' she said at last; 'Ardalion Matveitch did say something, certainly; my son Vassinka's art you were wanting. . . . But we can't be sure, my dear sir. . . .'

'Oh, why so?' I interposed. 'As far as I'm concerned, you may feel perfectly easy. . . . I'm not an informer.'

'Oh, mercy on us,' the old woman caught me up hurriedly, 'what do you mean? Could we dare to suppose such a thing of your honour! And on what ground could one inform against us? Do you suppose it's some sin-ful contrivance of ours? No, sir, my son's not the one to lend himself to anything wicked . . . or give way to any sort of witchcraft. . . . God forbid indeed, holy Mother of Heaven! (The old woman crossed herself three times.) He's the foremost in prayer and fasting in the whole province; the foremost, your honour, he is! And that's just it: great grace has been vouchsafed to him. Yes, indeed. It's not the work of his hands. It's from on high, my dear; so it is.'

'So you agree?' I asked: 'when can I see your son?'

The old woman blinked again and shifted her rolled up handkerchief from one sleeve to the other.

'Oh, well, sir—well, sir, I can't say.'

'Allow me, Mastridia Karpovna, to hand you this,' I interrupted, and I gave her a ten-rouble note.

The old woman clutched it at once in her fat, crooked fingers, which recalled the fleshy claws of an owl, quickly slipped it into her sleeve, pon-dered a little, and as though she had suddenly reached a decision, slapped her thighs with her open hand.

'Come here this evening a little after seven,' she said, not in her pre-vious voice, but in quite a different one, more solemn and subdued; 'only not to this room, but kindly go straight up to the floor above, and you'll find a door to your left, and you open that door; and you'll go, your honour, into an empty room, and in that room you'll see a chair. Sit you down on that chair and wait; and whatever you see, don't utter a word and don't do anything; and please don't speak to my son either; for he's but young yet, and he suffers from fits. He's very easily scared; he'll tremble and shake like any chicken . . . a sad thing it is!'

I looked at Mastridia. 'You say he's young, but since he's your son . . .'

'In the spirit, sir, in the spirit. Many's the orphan I have under my care!' she added, wagging her head in the direction of the corner, from which came the plaintive whimper. 'O—O God Almighty, holy Mother of God! And do you, your honour, before you come here, think well which of your deceased relations or friends—the kingdom of Heaven to them!—you're desirous of seeing. Go over your deceased friends, and whichever you select, keep him in your mind, keep him all the while till my son comes!'

'Why, mustn't I tell your son whom . . .'

'Nay, nay, sir, not one word. He will find out what he needs in your thoughts himself. You've only to keep your friend thoroughly in mind; and at your dinner drink a drop of wine—just two or three glasses; wine never comes amiss.' The old woman laughed, licked her lips, passed her hand over her mouth, and sighed.

'So at half-past seven?' I queried, getting up from my chair.

'At half-past seven, your honour, at half-past seven,' Mastridia Karpovna replied reassuringly.

I took leave of the old woman and went back to the hotel. I did not doubt that they were going to make a fool of me, but in what way?—that was what excited my curiosity. With Ardalion I did not exchange more than two or three words. 'Did she see you?' he asked me, knitting his brow, and on my affirmative reply, he exclaimed: 'The old woman's as good as any statesman!' I set to work, in accordance with the 'statesman's' counsel, to run over my deceased friends. After rather prolonged hesitation I fixed, at last, on an old man who had long been dead, a Frenchman, once my tutor. I selected him not because he had any special attraction for me; but his whole figure was so original, so unlike any figure of to-day, that it would be utterly impossible to imitate it. He had an enormous head, fluffy white hair combed straight back, thick black eyebrows, a hawk nose, and two large warts of a pinkish hue in the middle of the forehead; he used to wear a green frockcoat with smooth brass buttons, a striped waistcoat with a stand-up collar, a jabot and lace cuffs. 'If he shows me my old Dessaire,' I thought, 'well, I shall have to admit that he's a sorcerer!'

At dinner I followed the old dame's behest and drank a bottle of Lafitte, of the first quality, so Ardalion averred, though it had a very strong flavour of burnt cork, and a thick sediment at the bottom of each glass.

Exactly at half-past seven I stood in front of the house where I had conversed with the worthy Mastridia Karpovna. All the shutters of the windows were closed, but the door was open. I went into the house, mounted the shaky staircase to the first story, and opening a door on the left, found myself, as the old woman had said, in a perfectly empty, rather large room; a tallow candle set in the window-sill threw a dim light over the room; against the wall opposite the door stood a wicker-bottomed chair. I snuffed the candle, which had already burnt down enough to form a long smouldering wick, sat down on the chair and began to wait.

The first ten minutes passed rather quickly; in the room itself there was absolutely nothing which could distract my attention, but I listened intently to every rustle, looked intently at the closed door. . . . My heart was throbbing. After the first ten minutes followed another ten minutes, then half an hour, three-quarters of an hour, and not a stir of any kind around! I coughed several times to make my presence known; I began to feel bored and out of temper; to be made a fool of in just that way had not entered into my calculations. I was on the point of getting up from my seat, taking the candle from the window, and going downstairs. . . . I looked at it; the wick again wanted snuffing; but as I turned my eyes from the window to the door, I could not help starting; with his back leaning against the door stood a man. He had entered so quickly and noiselessly that I had heard nothing.

He wore a simple blue smock; he was of middle height and rather thickset. With his hands behind his back and his head bent, he was staring at me. In the dim light of the candle I could not distinctly make out his features. I saw nothing but a shaggy mane of matted hair falling on his forehead, and thick, rather drawn lips and whitish eyes. I was nearly speaking to him, but I recollected Mastridia's injunction, and bit my lips. The man, who had come in, continued to gaze at me, and, strange to say, at the same time I felt something like fear, and, as though at the word of command, promptly started thinking of my old tutor. He still stood at the door and breathed heavily, as though he had been climbing a mountain or lifting a weight, while his eyes seemed to expand, seemed to come closer to me—and I felt uncomfortable under their obstinate, heavy, menacing stare; at times those eyes glowed with a malignant inward fire, a fire such as I have seen in the eyes of a pointer dog when it 'points' at a hare; and, like a pointer dog, he kept his eyes intently following mine when I 'tried to double,' that is, tried to turn my eyes away.

So passed I do not know how long—perhaps a minute, perhaps a quarter of an hour. He still gazed at me; I still experienced a certain discomfort and alarm and still thought of the Frenchman. Twice I tried to say to myself, 'What nonsense! what a farce!' I tried to smile, to shrug my shoulders. . . . It was no use! All initiative had all at once 'frozen up' within me—I can find no other word for it. I was overcome by a sort of numbness. Suddenly I noticed that he had left the door, and was standing a step or two nearer to me; then he gave a slight bound, both feet together, and stood closer still. . . . Then again . . . and again; while the menacing eyes were simply fastened on my whole face, and the hands remained behind, and the broad chest heaved painfully. These leaps struck me as ridiculous, but I felt dread too, and what I could not understand at all, a drowsiness began suddenly to come upon me. My eyelids clung together . . . the shaggy figure with the whitish eyes in the blue smock seemed double before me, and suddenly vanished altogether! . . . I shook myself; he was again standing between the door and me, but now much nearer. . . . Then he vanished again—a sort of mist seemed to fall upon him; again he appeared . . . vanished again . . . appeared again, and always closer, closer . . . his hard, almost gasping breathing floated across to me now. . . . Again the mist fell, and all of a sudden out of this mist the head of old Dessaire began to take distinct shape, beginning with the white, brushed-back hair! Yes: there were his warts, his black eyebrows, his hook nose! There too his green coat with the brass buttons, the striped waistcoat and jabot. . . . I shrieked, I got up. . . . The old man vanished, and in his place I saw again the man in the blue smock. He moved staggering to the wall, leaned his head and both arms against it, and heaving like an over-loaded horse, in a husky voice said, ' Tea! ' Mastridia Karpovna—how she came there I can't say—flew to him and saying: ' Vassinka! Vassinka! ' began anxiously wiping away the sweat, which simply trickled from his face and hair. I was on the point of approaching her, but she, so insistently, in such a heart-rending voice cried: ' Your honour! merciful sir! have pity on us, go away, for Christ's sake! ' that I obeyed, while she turned again to her son. ' Bread-winner, darling,' she murmured soothingly: ' you shall have tea directly, directly. And you too, sir, had better take a cup of tea at home! ' she shouted after me.

When I got home I obeyed Mastridia and ordered some tea; I felt tired —even weak. ' Well? ' Ardalion questioned me, ' have you been? did you see something? '

' He did, certainly, show me something . . . which, I'll own, I had not anticipated,' I replied.

' He's a man of marvellous power,' observed Ardalion, carrying off the samovar; ' he is held in high esteem among the merchant gentry.'

As I went to bed, and reflected on the incident that had occurred to me, I fancied at last that I had reached some explanation of it. The man doubtless possessed a considerable magnetic power; acting by some means, which I did not understand of course, upon my nerves, he had evoked within me so vividly, so definitely, the image of the old man of whom I was thinking, that at last I fancied that I saw him before my eyes. . . . Such ' metastases,' such transferences of sensation, are recognised by science. It was all very well; but the force capable of producing such effects still remained, something marvellous and mysterious. ' Say what you will,' I thought, ' I've seen, seen with my own eyes, my dead tutor! '

The next day the ball in the Hall of Nobility took place. Sophia's father called on me and reminded me of the engagement I had made with his daughter. At ten o'clock I was standing by her side in the middle of a ballroom lighted up by a number of copper lamps, and was preparing to execute the not very complicated steps of the French quadrille to the re-sounding blare of the military band. Crowds of people were there; the ladies were especially numerous and very pretty; but the first place among them would certainly have been given to my partner, if it had not been for the rather strange, even rather wild look in her eyes. I noticed that she hardly ever blinked; the unmistakable expression of sincerity in her eyes did not make up for what was extraordinary in them. But she had a charming figure, and moved gracefully, though with constraint. When she waltzed, and, throwing herself a little back, bent her slender neck towards her right shoulder, as though she wanted to get away from her partner, nothing more touchingly youthful and pure could be imagined. She was all in white, with a turquoise cross on a black ribbon.

I asked her for a mazurka, and tried to talk to her. But her answers were few and reluctant, though she listened attentively, with the same expression of dreamy absorption which had struck me when I first met her. Not the slightest trace of desire to please, at her age, with her appearance, and the absence of a smile, and those eyes, continually fixed directly upon the eyes of the person speaking to her, though they seemed at the same time to see something else, to be absorbed with something different. . . . What a strange creature! Not knowing, at last, how to thaw her, I bethought me of telling her of my adventure of the previous day.

She heard me to the end with evident interest, but was not, as I had expected, surprised at what I told her, and merely asked whether *he* was not called Vassily. I recollected that the old woman had called him 'Vassinka.' 'Yes, his name is Vassily,' I answered; 'do you know him?'

'There is a saintly man living here called Vassily,' she observed; 'I wondered whether it was he.'

'Saintliness has nothing to do with this,' I remarked; 'it's simply the action of magnetism—a fact of interest for doctors and students of science.'

I proceeded to expound my views on the peculiar force called magnetism, on the possibility of one man's will being brought under the influence of another's will, and so on; but my explanations—which were, it is true, somewhat confused—seemed to make no impression on her. Sophie listened, dropping her clasped hands on her knees with a fan lying motionless in them; she did not play with it, she did not move her fingers at all, and I felt that all my words rebounded from her as from a statue of stone. She heard them, but clearly she had her own convictions, which nothing could shake or uproot.

'You can hardly admit miracles!' I cried.

'Of course I admit them,' she answered calmly. 'And how can one help admitting them? Are not we told in the gospel that who has but a grain of faith as big as a mustard seed, he can remove mountains? One need only have faith—there will be miracles!'

'It seems there is very little faith nowadays,' I observed; 'anyway, one doesn't hear of miracles.'

'But yet there are miracles; you have seen one yourself. No; faith is not dead nowadays; and the beginning of faith . . .'

'The fear of God is the beginning of wisdom,' I interrupted.

'The beginning of faith,' pursued Sophie, nothing daunted, 'is self-abasement . . . humiliation.'

'Humiliation even? ' I queried.

'Yes. The pride of man, haughtiness, presumption—that is what must be utterly rooted up. You spoke of the will—that's what must be broken.'

I scanned the whole figure of the young girl who was uttering such sentences. . . . 'My word, the child's in earnest, too,' was my thought. I glanced at our neighbours in the mazurka; they, too, glanced at me, and I fancied that my astonishment amused them; one of them even smiled at me sympathetically, as though he would say: 'Well, what do you think of our queer young lady? every one here knows what she's like.'

'Have you tried to break your will? ' I said, turning to Sophie again.

'Every one is bound to do what he thinks right,' she answered in a dogmatic tone.

'Let me ask you,' I began, after a brief silence, 'do you believe in the possibility of calling up the dead? '

Sophie softly shook her head.

'There are no dead.'

'What? '

'There are no dead souls; they are undying and can always appear, when they like. . . . They are always about us.'

'What? Do you suppose, for instance, that an immortal soul may be at this moment hovering about that garrison major with the red nose? '

'Why not? The sunlight falls on him and his nose, and is not the sunlight, all light, from God? And what does external appearance matter? To the pure all things are pure! Only to find a teacher, to find a leader! '

'But excuse me, excuse me,' I put in, not, I must own, without malicious intent. 'You want a leader . . . but what is your priest for? '

Sophie looked coldly at me.

'You mean to laugh at me, I suppose. My priestly father tells me what I ought to do; but what I want is a leader who would show me himself in action how to sacrifice one's self! '

She raised her eyes towards the ceiling. With her childlike face, and that expression of immobile absorption, of secret, continual perplexity, she reminded me of the pre-raphaelite Madonnas. . . .

'I have read somewhere,' she went on, not turning to me, and hardly moving her lips, 'of a grand person who directed that he should be buried under a church porch so that all the people who came in should tread him under foot and trample on him. . . . That is what one ought to do in life.'

Boom! boom! tra-ra-ra! thundered the drums from the band. . . . I must own such a conversation at a ball struck me as eccentric in the extreme; the ideas involuntarily kindled within me were of a nature anything but religious. I took advantage of my partner's being invited to one of the figures of the mazurka to avoid renewing our quasi-theological discussion.

A quarter of an hour later I conducted Mademoiselle Sophie to her father, and two days after I left the town of T——, and the image of the girl with the childlike face and the soul impenetrable as stone slipped quickly out of my memory.

Two years passed, and it chanced that that image was recalled again to me. It was like this: I was talking to a colleague who had just returned from a tour in South Russia. He had spent some time in the town of T——, and told me various items of news about the neighbourhood. 'By the way!' he exclaimed, 'you knew V. G. B. very well, I fancy, didn't you?'

'Of course I know him.'

'And his daughter Sophia, do you know her?'

'I've seen her twice.'

'Only fancy, she's run away!'

'How's that?'

'Well, I don't know. Three months ago she disappeared, and nothing's been heard of her. And the astonishing thing is no one can make out whom she's run off with. Fancy, they've not the slightest idea, not the smallest suspicion! She'd refused all the offers made her, and she was most proper in her behaviour. Ah, these quiet, religious girls are the ones! It's made an awful scandal all over the province! B.'s in despair. . . . And whatever need had she to run away? Her father carried out her wishes in everything. And what's so unaccountable, all the Lovelaces of the province are there all right, not one's missing.'

'And they've not found her up till now?'

'I tell you she might as well be at the bottom of the sea! It's one rich heiress less in the world, that's the worst of it.'

This piece of news greatly astonished me. It did not seem at all in keeping with the recollection I had of Sophia B. But there! anything may happen.

In the autumn of the same year fate brought me—again on official business—into the S—— province, which is, as every one knows, next to the province of T——. It was cold and rainy weather; the worn-out posting-horses could scarcely drag my light trap through the black slush of the highroad. One day, I remember, was particularly unlucky: three times we got 'stuck' in the mud up to the axles of the wheels; my driver was continually giving up one rut and with moans and grunts trudging across to the other, and finding things no better with that. In fact, towards evening I was so exhausted that on reaching the posting-station I decided to spend the night at the inn. I was given a room with a broken-down wooden sofa, a sloping floor, and torn paper on the walls; there was a smell in it of kvas, bast-mats, onions, and even turpentine, and swarms of flies were on everything; but at any rate I could find shelter there from the weather, and the rain had set in, as they say, for the whole day. I ordered a samovar to be brought, and, sitting on the sofa, settled down to those cheerless wayside reflections so familiar to travellers in Russia.

They were broken in upon by a heavy knocking that came from the common room, from which my room was separated by a deal partition. This sound was accompanied by an intermittent metallic jingle, like the clank of chains, and a coarse male voice boomed out suddenly: 'The blessing of God on all within this house. The blessing of God! the blessing of God! Amen, amen! Scatter His enemies! ' repeated the voice, with a sort of incongruous and savage drawl on the last syllable of each word. . . . A noisy sigh was heard, and a ponderous body sank on to the bench with the same jingling sound. ' Akulina! servant of God, come here! ' the voice began again: ' Behold! Clothed in rags and blessed! . . . Ha-ha-ha! Tfoo! Merciful God, merciful God, merciful God! ' the voice droned like a deacon in the choir. ' Merciful God, Creator of my body, behold my iniquity. . . . O-ho-ho! Ha-ha! . . . Tfoo! And all abundance be to this house in the seventh hour! '

' Who's that? ' I asked the hospitable landlady, who came in with the samovar.

' That, your honour,' she answered me in a hurried whisper, ' is a blessed, holy man. He's not long come into our parts; and here he's graciously pleased to visit us. In such weather! The wet's simply trickling from him, poor dear man, in streams! And you should see the chains on him—such a lot! '

' The blessing of God! the blessing of God! ' the voice was heard again. ' Akulina! Hey, Akulina! Akulinushka—friend! where is our paradise? Our fair paradise of bliss? In the wilderness is our paradise, . . . para-dise. . . . And to this house, from beginning of time, great happiness, . . . o . . . o . . . o . . .' The voice muttered something inarticulate, and again, after a protracted yawn, there came the hoarse laugh. This laugh broke out every time, as it were, involuntarily, and every time it was followed by vigorous spitting.

' Ah, me! Stepanitch isn't here! That's the worst of it! ' the landlady said, as it were to herself, as she stood with every sign of the profoundest attention at the door. ' He will say some word of salvation, and I, foolish woman, may not catch it! '

She went out quickly.

In the partition there was a chink; I applied my eye to it. The crazy pilgrim was sitting on a bench with his back to me; I saw nothing but his shaggy head, as huge as a beer-can, and a broad bent back in a patched and soaking shirt. Before him, on the earth floor, knelt a frail-looking woman in a jacket, such as are worn by women of the artisan class—old and wet through—and with a dark kerchief pulled down almost over her eyes. She was trying to pull the holy man's boots off; her fingers slid off the greasy, slippery leather. The landlady was standing near her, with her arms folded across her bosom, gazing reverently at the ' man of God.' He was, as before, mumbling some inarticulate words.

At last the woman succeeded in tugging off the boots. She almost fell backwards, but recovered herself, and began unwinding the strips of rag which were wrapped round the vagrant's legs. On the sole of his foot there was a wound. . . . I turned away.

'A cup of tea wouldn't you bid me get you, my dear?' I heard the hostess saying in an obsequious voice.

'What a notion!' responded the holy man. 'To indulge the sinful body. . . . O-ho-ho! Break all the bones in it . . . but she talks of tea! Oh, oh, worthy old woman, Satan is strong within us. . . . Fight him with hunger, fight him with cold, with the sluice-gates of heaven, the pouring, penetrating rain, and he takes no harm—he is alive still! Remember the day of the Intercession of the Mother of God! You will receive, you will receive in abundance!'

The landlady could not resist uttering a faint groan of admiration.

'Only listen to me! Give all thou hast, give thy head, give thy shirt! If they ask not of thee, yet give! For God is all-seeing! Is it hard for Him to destroy your roof? He has given thee bread in His mercy, and do thou bake it in the oven! He seeth all! Se . . . e . . . eth! Whose eye is in the triangle? Say, whose?'

The landlady stealthily crossed herself under her neckerchief.

'The old enemy is adamant! A . . . da . . . mant! A . . . da . . . mant!' the religious maniac repeated several times, gnashing his teeth. 'The old serpent! But God will arise! Yes, God will arise and scatter His enemies! I will call up all the dead! I will go against His enemy. . . . Ha-ha-ha! Tfoo!'

'Have you any oil?' said another voice, hardly audible; 'let me put some on the wound. . . . I have got a clean rag.'

I peeped through the chink again; the woman in the jacket was still busied with the vagrant's sore foot. . . . 'A Magdalen!' I thought.

'I'll get it directly, my dear,' said the woman, and, coming into my room, she took a spoonful of oil from the lamp burning before the holy picture.

'Who's that waiting on him?' I asked.

'We don't know, sir, who it is; she too, I suppose, is seeking salvation, atoning for her sins. But what a saintly man he is!'

'Akulinushka, my sweet child, my dear daughter,' the crazy pilgrim was repeating meanwhile, and he suddenly burst into tears.

The woman kneeling before him lifted her eyes to him. . . . Heavens! where had I seen those eyes?

The landlady went up to her with the spoonful of oil. She finished her operation, and, getting up from the floor, asked if there were a clean loft and a little hay. . . . 'Vassily Nikititch likes to sleep on hay,' she added.

'To be sure there is, come this way,' answered the woman; 'come this way, my dear,' she turned to the holy man, 'and dry yourself and rest.' The man coughed, slowly got up from the bench—his chains clanked again— and turning round with his face to me, looked for the holy pictures, and began crossing himself with a wide movement.

I recognised him instantly: it was the very artisan Vassily, who had once shown me my dead tutor!

His features were little changed; only their expression had become still more unusual, still more terrible. . . . The lower part of his swollen face was overgrown with unkempt beard. Tattered, filthy, wild-looking, he inspired in me more repugnance than horror. He left off crossing himself, but still his eyes wandered senselessly about the corners of the room, about the floor, as though he were waiting for something. . . .

'Vassily Nikititch, please come,' said the woman in the jacket with a bow. He suddenly threw up his head and turned round, but stumbled and tottered. . . . His companion flew to him at once, and supported him under the arm. Judging by her voice and figure, she seemed still young; her face it was almost impossible to see.

'Akulinushka, friend!' the vagrant repeated once more in a shaking voice, and opening his mouth wide, and smiting himself on the breast with his fist, he uttered a deep groan, that seemed to come from the bottom of his heart. Both followed the landlady out of the room.

I lay down on my hard sofa and mused a long while on what I had seen. My mesmeriser had become a regular religious maniac. This was what he had been brought to by the power which one could not but recognise in him!

The next morning I was preparing to go on my way. The rain was falling as fast as the day before, but I could not delay any longer. My servant, as he gave me water to wash, wore a special smile on his face, a smile of restrained irony. I knew that smile well; it indicated that my servant had heard something discreditable or even shocking about gentle-folks. He was obviously burning with impatience to communicate it to me.

'Well, what is it?' I asked at last.

'Did your honour see the crazy pilgrim yesterday?' my man began at once.

'Yes; what then?'

'And did you see his companion too?'

'Yes, I saw her.'

'She's a young lady, of noble family.'

'What?'

'It's the truth I'm telling you; some merchants arrived here this morning from T——; they recognised her. They did tell me her name, but I've forgotten it.'

It was like a flash of enlightenment. 'Is the pilgrim still here?' I asked.

'I fancy he's not gone yet. He's been ever so long at the gate, and making such a wonderful wise to-do, that there's no getting by. He's amusing himself with this tomfoolery; he finds it pays, no doubt.'

My man belonged to the same class of educated servants as Ardalion.

'And is the lady with him?'

'Yes. She's in attendance on him.'

I went out on to the steps, and got a view of the crazy pilgrim. He was sitting on a bench at the gate, and, bent down with both his open hands pressed on it, he was shaking his drooping head from right to left, for all

the world like a wild beast in a cage. The thick mane of curly hair covered his eyes, and shook from side to side, and so did his pendulous lips. . . .
A strange, almost unhuman muttering came from them. His companion had only just finished washing from a pitcher that was hanging on a pole, and without having yet replaced her kerchief on her head, was making her way back to the gate along a narrow plank laid across the dark puddles of the filthy yard. I glanced at her head, which was now entirely uncovered, and positively threw up my hands with astonishment: before me stood Sophia B.!

She turned quickly round and fixed upon me her blue eyes, immovable as ever. She was much thinner, her skin looked coarser and had the yellowish-ruddy tinge of sunburn, her nose was sharper, and her lips were harder in their lines. But she was not less good-looking; only besides her old expression of dreamy amazement there was now a different look—resolute, almost bold, intense and exalted. There was not a trace of childishness left in the face now.

I went up to her. 'Sophia Vladimirovna,' I cried, 'can it be you? In such a dress . . . in such company. . . .'

She started, looked still more intently at me, as though anxious to find out who was speaking to her, and, without saying a word to me, fairly rushed to her companion.

'Akulinushka,' he faltered, with a heavy sigh, 'our sins, sins . . .'

'Vassily Nikititch, let us go at once! Do you hear, at once, at once,' she said, pulling her kerchief on to her forehead with one hand, while with the other she supported the pilgrim under the elbow; 'let us go, Vassily Nikititch: there is danger here.'

'I'm coming, my good girl, I'm coming,' the crazy pilgrim responded obediently, and, bending his whole body forward, he got up from the seat. 'Here's only this chain to fasten. . . .'

I once more approached Sophia, and told her my name. I began beseeching her to listen to me, to say one word to me. I pointed to the rain, which was coming down in bucketfuls. I begged her to have some care for her health, the health of her companion. I mentioned her father. . . . But she seemed possessed by a sort of wrathful, a sort of vindictive excitement: without paying the slightest attention to me, setting her teeth and breathing hard, she urged on the distracted vagrant in an undertone, in soft insistent words, girt him up, fastened on his chains, pulled on to his hair a child's cloth cap with a broken peak, stuck his staff in his hand, slung a wallet on her own shoulder, and went with him out at the gate into the street. . . . To stop her actually I had not the right, and it would have been of no use; and at my last despairing call she did not even turn round. Supporting the 'man of God' under his arm, she stepped rapidly over the black mud of the street; and in a few moments, across the dim dusk of the foggy morning, through the thick network of falling raindrops, I saw the last glimpse of the two figures, the crazy pilgrim and Sophia. . . . They turned the corner of a projecting hut, and vanished for ever.

I went back to my room. I fell to pondering. I could not understand it; I could not understand how such a girl, well brought up, young, and wealthy, could throw up everything and every one, her own home, her family, her friends, break with all her habits, with all the comforts of life, and for what? To follow a half-insane vagrant, to become his servant! I could not for an instant entertain the idea that the explanation of such a step was to be found in any prompting, however depraved, of the heart, in love or passion. . . . One had but to glance at the repulsive figure of the 'man of God' to dismiss such a notion entirely! No, Sophia had remained pure; and to her all things were pure. I could not understand what Sophia had done; but I did not blame her, as, later on, I have not blamed other girls who too have sacrificed everything for what they thought the truth, for what they held to be their vocation. I could not help regretting that Sophia had chosen just *that* path; but also I could not refuse her admiration, respect even. In good earnest she had talked of self-sacrifice, of abasement . . . in *her*, words were not opposed to acts. She had sought a leader, a guide, and had found him, . . . and, my God, what a guide!

Yes, she had lain down to be trampled, trodden under foot. . . . In the process of time, a rumour reached me that her family had succeeded at last in finding out the lost sheep, and bringing her home. But at home she did not live long, and died, like a "Sister of Silence,' without having spoken a word to any one.

Peace to your heart, poor, enigmatic creature! Vassily Nikititch is probably on his crazy wanderings still; the iron health of such people is truly marvellous. Perhaps, though, his epilepsy may have done for him.

PUNIN AND BABURIN

PIOTR PETROVITCH'S STORY

. . . I AM old and ill now, and my thoughts brood oftenest upon death, every day coming nearer; rarely I think of the past, rarely I turn the eyes of my soul behind me. Only from time to time—in winter, as I sit motionless before the glowing fire, in summer, as I pace with slow tread along the shady avenue—I recall past years, events, faces; but it is not on my mature years nor on my youth that my thoughts rest at such times. They either carry me back to my earliest childhood, or to the first years of boyhood. Now, for instance, I see myself in the country with my stern and wrathful grandmother—I was only twelve—and two figures rise up before my imagination. . . .

But I will begin my story consecutively, and in proper order.

I

1830

THE old footman Filippitch came in, on tiptoe, as usual, with a cravat tied up in a rosette, with tightly compressed lips, ' lest his breath should be smelt,' with a grey tuft of hair standing up in the very middle of his forehead. He came in, bowed, and handed my grandmother on an iron tray a large letter with an heraldic seal. My grandmother put on her spectacles, read the letter through. . . .

' Is he here? ' she asked.

' What is my lady pleased . . .' Filippitch began timidly.

' Imbecile! The man who brought the letter—is he here? '

' He is here, to be sure he is. . . . He is sitting in the counting-house.'

My grandmother rattled her amber rosary beads. . . .

' Tell him to come to me. . . . And you, sir,' she turned to me, ' sit still.'

As it was, I was sitting perfectly still in my corner, on the stool assigned to me.

My grandmother kept me well in hand!

Five minutes later there came into the room a man of five-and-thirty, black-haired and swarthy, with broad cheek-bones, a face marked with smallpox, a hook nose, and thick eyebrows, from under which the small grey eyes looked out with mournful composure. The colour of the eyes and their expression were out of keeping with the Oriental cast of the rest of the face. The man was dressed in a decent, long-skirted coat. He stopped in the doorway, and bowed—only with his head.

' So your name's Baburin? ' queried my grandmother, and she added to herself: ' *Il a l'air d'un arménien.*'

' Yes, it is,' the man answered in a deep and even voice. At the first brusque sound of my grandmother's voice his eyebrows faintly quivered. Surely he had not expected her to address him as an equal?

'Are you a Russian? orthodox?'

'Yes.'

My grandmother took off her spectacles, and scanned Baburin from head to foot deliberately. He did not drop his eyes, he merely folded his hands behind his back. What particularly struck my fancy was his beard; it was very smoothly shaven, but such blue cheeks and chin I had never seen in my life!

'Yakov Petrovitch,' began my grandmother, 'recommends you strongly in his letter as sober and industrious; why, then, did you leave his service?'

'He needs a different sort of person to manage his estate, madam.'

'A different . . . sort? That I don't quite understand.'

My grandmother rattled her beads again. 'Yakov Petrovitch writes to me that there are two peculiarities about you. What peculiarities?'

Baburin shrugged his shoulders slightly.

'I can't tell what he sees fit to call peculiarities. Possibly that I . . . don't allow corporal punishment.'

My grandmother was surprised. 'Do you mean to say Yakov Petrovitch wanted to flog you?'

Baburin's swarthy face grew red to the roots of his hair.

'You have not understood me right, madam. I make it a rule not to employ corporal punishment . . . with the peasants.'

My grandmother was more surprised than ever; she positively threw up her hands.

'Ah!' she pronounced at last, and putting her head a little on one side, once more she scrutinised Baburin attentively. 'So that's your rule, is it? Well, that's of no consequence whatever to me; I don't want an overseer, but a counting-house clerk, a secretary. What sort of a hand do you write?'

'I write well, without mistakes in spelling.'

'That too is of no consequence to me. The great thing for me is for it to be clear, and without any of those new copybook letters with tails, that I don't like. And what's your other peculiarity?'

Baburin moved uneasily, coughed. . . .

'Perhaps . . . the gentleman has referred to the fact that I am not alone.'

'You are married?'

'Oh no . . . but . . .'

My grandmother knit her brows.

'There is a person living with me . . . of the male sex . . . a comrade, a poor friend, from whom I have never parted . . . for . . . let me see . . . ten years now.'

'A relation of yours?'

'No, not a relation—a friend. As to work, there can be no possible hindrance occasioned by him,' Baburin made haste to add, as though foreseeing objections. 'He lives at my cost, occupies the same room with me;

he is more likely to be of use, as he is well educated—speaking without
flattery, extremely so, in fact—and his morals are exemplary.'

My grandmother heard Baburin out, chewing her lips and half closing
her eyes.

'He lives at your expense?'

'Yes.'

'You keep him out of charity?'

'As an act of justice . . . as it's the duty of one poor man to help another
poor man.'

'Indeed! It's the first time I've heard that. I had supposed till now that
that was rather the duty of rich people.'

'For the rich, if I may venture to say so, it is an entertainment . . . but
for such as we . . .'

'Well, well, that's enough, that's enough,' my grandmother cut him short;
and after a moment's thought she queried, speaking through her nose, which
was always a bad sign, 'And what age is he, your protégé?'

'About my own age.'

'Really, I imagined that you were bringing him up.'

'Not so; he is my comrade—and besides . . .'

'That's enough,' my grandmother cut him short a second time. 'You're
a philanthropist, it seems. Yakov Petrovitch is right; for a man in your
position it's something very peculiar. But now let's get to business. I'll
explain to you what your duties will be. And as regards wages. . . . *Que
faites vous ici?*' added my grandmother suddenly, turning her dry, yellow
face to me:—'*Allez étudier votre devoir de mythologie.*'

I jumped up, went up to kiss my grandmother's hand, and went out,—
not to study mythology, but simply into the garden.

The garden on my grandmother's estate was very old and large, and was
bounded on one side by a flowing pond, in which there were not only
plenty of carp and eels, but even loach were caught, those renowned
loach, that have nowadays disappeared almost everywhere. At the head
of this pond was a thick clump of willows; further and higher, on both
sides of a rising slope, were dense bushes of hazel, elder, honeysuckle,
and sloe-thorn, with an undergrowth of heather and clover flowers. Here
and there between the bushes were tiny clearings, covered with emerald-
green, silky, fine grass, in the midst of which squat funguses peeped out with
their comical, variegated pink, lilac, and straw-coloured caps, and golden
balls of 'hen-dazzle' blazed in light patches. Here in spring-time the
nightingales sang, the blackbirds whistled, the cuckoos called; here in the
heat of summer it was always cool—and I loved to make my way into the
wilderness and thicket, where I had favourite secret spots, known—so, at
least, I imagined—only to me.

On coming out of my grandmother's room I made straight for one
of these spots, which I had named 'Switzerland.' But what was my astonishment when, before I had reached 'Switzerland,' I perceived through the

delicate network of half-dry twigs and green branches that some one beside me had found it out! A long, long figure in a long, loose coat of yellow frieze and a tall cap was standing in the very spot I loved best of all! I stole up a little nearer, and made out the face, which was utterly unknown to me, also very long and soft, with small reddish eyes, and a very funny nose; drawn out as long as a pod of peas, it positively overhung the full lips; and these lips, quivering and forming a round O, were giving vent to a shrill little whistle, while the long fingers of the bony hands, placed facing one another on the upper part of the chest, were rapidly moving with a rotatory action. From time to time the motion of the hands subsided, the lips ceased whistling and quivering, the head was bent forward as though listening. I came still nearer, examined him still more closely. . . . The stranger held in each hand a small flat cup, such as people use to tease canaries and make them sing. A twig snapped under my feet; the stranger started, turned his dim little eyes towards the copse, and was staggering away . . . but he stumbled against a tree, uttered an exclamation, and stood still.

I came out into the open space. The stranger smiled.

' Good morning,' said I.

' Good morning, little master! '

I did not like his calling me little master. Such familiarity!

' What are you doing here? ' I asked sternly.

' Why, look here,' he responded, never leaving off smiling, ' I'm calling the little birds to sing.' He showed me his little cups. ' The chaffinches answer splendidly! You, at your tender years, take delight, no doubt, in the feathered songsters' notes! Listen, I beg; I will begin chirping, and they'll answer me directly—it's so delightful! '

He began rubbing his little cups. A chaffinch actually did chirp in response from a mountain ash near. The stranger laughed without a sound, and winked at me.

The laugh and the wink—every gesture of the stranger, his weak, lisping voice, his bent knees and thin hands, his very cap and long frieze coat—everything about him suggested good-nature, something innocent and droll.

' Have you been here long? ' I asked.

' I came to-day.'

' Why, aren't you the person of whom . . .'

' Mr. Baburin spoke to the lady here. The same, the same.'

' Your friend's name's Baburin, and what's yours? '

' I'm Punin. Punin's my name; Punin. He's Baburin and I'm Punin.' He set the little cups humming again. ' Listen, listen to the chaffinch. . . . How it carols! '

This queer creature took my fancy ' awfully ' all at once. Like almost all boys, I was either timid or consequential with strangers, but I felt with this man as if I had known him for ages.

' Come along with me,' I said to him; ' I know a place better than this; there's a seat there; we can sit down, and we can see the dam from there.'

' By all means let us go,' my new friend responded in his singing voice.

I let him pass before me. As he walked he rolled from side to side, tripped over his own feet, and his head fell back.

I noticed on the back of his coat, under the collar, there hung a small tassel. 'What's that you've got hanging there?' I asked.

'Where?' he questioned, and he put his hand up to the collar to feel. 'Ah, the tassel? Let it be! I suppose it was sewn there for ornament! It's not in the way.'

I led him to the seat, and sat down; he settled himself beside me. 'It's lovely here!' he commented, and he drew a deep, deep sigh. 'Oh, how lovely! You have a most splendid garden! Oh, o–oh!'

I looked at him from one side. 'What a queer cap you've got!' I couldn't help exclaiming. 'Show it me here!'

'By all means, little master, by all means.' He took off the cap; I was holding out my hand, but I raised my eyes, and—simply burst out laughing. Punin was completely bald; not a single hair was to be seen on the high conical skull, covered with smooth white skin.

He passed his open hand over it, and he too laughed. When he laughed he seemed, as it were, to gulp, he opened his mouth wide, closed his eyes—and vertical wrinkles flitted across his forehead in three rows, like waves. 'Eh,' said he at last, 'isn't it quite like an egg?'

'Yes, yes, exactly like an egg!' I agreed with enthusiasm. 'And have you been like that long?'

'Yes, a long while; but what hair I used to have!—A golden fleece like that for which the Argonauts sailed over the watery deeps.'

Though I was only twelve, yet, thanks to my mythological studies, I knew who the Argonauts were; I was the more surprised at hearing the name on the lips of a man dressed almost in rags.

'You must have learned mythology, then?' I queried, as I twisted his cap over and over in my hands. It turned out to be wadded, with a mangy-looking fur trimming, and a broken cardboard peak.

'I have studied that subject, my dear little master; I've had time enough for everything in my life! But now restore to me my covering, it is a protection to the nakedness of my head.'

He put on the cap, and, with a downward slope of his whitish eye-brows, asked me who I was, and who were my parents.

'I'm the grandson of the lady who owns this place,' I answered. 'I live alone with her. Papa and mamma are dead.'

Punin crossed himself. 'May the kingdom of heaven be theirs! So then, you're an orphan; and the heir, too. The noble blood in you is visible at once; it fairly sparkles in your eyes, and plays like this . . . sh . . . sh . . . sh . . .' He represented with his fingers the play of the blood. 'Well, and do you know, your noble honour, whether my friend has come to terms with your grandmamma, whether he has obtained the situation he was promised?'

'I don't know.'

Punin cleared his throat. 'Ah! if one could be settled here, if only for a while! Or else one may wander and wander far, and find not a place to rest one's head; the disquieting alarms of life are unceasing, the soul is confounded. . . .'

'Tell me,' I interrupted: 'are you of the clerical profession?'

Punin turned to me and half closed his eyelids. 'And what may be the cause of that question, gentle youth?'

'Why, you talk so—well, as they read in church.'

'Because I use the old scriptural forms of expression? But that ought not to surprise you. Admitting that in ordinary conversation such forms of expression are not always in place; but when one soars on the wings of inspiration, at once the language too grows more exalted. Surely your teacher—the professor of Russian literature—you do have lessons in that, I suppose?—surely he teaches you that, doesn't he?'

'No, he doesn't,' I responded. 'When we stay in the country I have no teacher. In Moscow I have a great many teachers.'

'And will you be staying long in the country?'

'Two months, not longer; grandmother says that I'm spoilt in the country, though I have a governess even here.'

'A French governess?'

'Yes.'

Punin scratched behind his ear. 'A mamselle, that's to say?'

'Yes; she's called Mademoiselle Friquet.' I suddenly felt it disgraceful for me, a boy of twelve, to have not a tutor, but a governess, like a little girl! 'But I don't mind her,' I added contemptuously. 'What do I care!'

Punin shook his head. 'Ah, you gentlefolk, you gentlefolk! you're too fond of foreigners! You have turned away from what is Russian,—towards all that's strange. You've turned your hearts to those that come from foreign parts. . . .'

'Hullo! Are you talking in verse?' I asked.

'Well, and why not? I can do that always, as much as you please; for it comes natural to me. . . .'

But at that very instant there sounded in the garden behind us a loud and shrill whistle. My new acquaintance hurriedly got up from the bench.

'Good-bye, little sir; that's my friend calling me, looking for me. . . . What has he to tell me? Good-bye—excuse me. . . .'

He plunged into the bushes and vanished, while I sat on some time longer on the seat. I felt perplexity and another feeling, rather an agreeable one . . . I had never met nor spoken to any one like this before. Gradually I fell to dreaming, but recollected my mythology and sauntered towards the house.

At home, I learned that my grandmother had arranged to take Baburin; he had been assigned a small room in the servants' quarters, overlooking the stable-yard. He had at once settled in there with his friend.

When I had drunk my tea, next morning, without asking leave of Mademoiselle Friquet, I set off to the servants' quarters. I wanted to have another chat with the queer fellow I had seen the day before. Without knocking at the door—the very idea of doing so would never have occurred to us—I walked straight into the room. I found in it not the man I was looking for, not Punin, but his protector—the philanthropist, Baburin. He was standing before the window, without his outer garment, his legs wide apart. He was busily engaged in rubbing his head and neck with a long towel.

'What do you want?' he observed, keeping his hands still raised, and knitting his brows.

'Punin's not at home, then?' I queried in the most free-and-easy manner, without taking off my cap.

'Mr. Punin, Nikander Vavilitch, at this moment, is not at home, truly,' Baburin responded deliberately; 'but allow me to make an observation, young man: it's not the proper thing to come into another person's room like this, without asking leave.'

I! . . . young man! . . . how dared he! . . . I grew crimson with fury.

'You cannot be aware who I am,' I rejoined, in a manner no longer free-and-easy, but haughty. 'I am the grandson of the mistress here.'

'That's all the same to me,' retorted Baburin, setting to work with his towel again. 'Though you are the seignorial grandson, you have no right to come into other people's rooms.'

'Other people's? What do you mean? I'm—at home here—everywhere.'

'No, excuse me: here—I'm at home; since this room has been assigned to me, by agreement, in exchange for my work.'

'Don't teach me, if you please,' I interrupted: 'I know better than you what . . .'

'You must be taught,' he interrupted in his turn, 'for you're at an age when you . . . I know my duties, but I know my rights too very well, and if you continue to speak to me in that way, I shall have to ask you to go out of the room. . . .'

There is no knowing how our dispute would have ended if Punin had not at that instant entered, shuffling and shambling from side to side. He most likely guessed from the expression of our faces that some unpleasantness had passed between us, and at once turned to me with the warmest expressions of delight.

'Ah! little master! little master!' he cried, waving his hands wildly, and going off into his noiseless laugh: 'the little dear! come to pay me a visit! here he's come, the little dear!' (What's the meaning of it? I thought: can he be speaking in this familiar way to me?) 'There, come along, come with me into the garden. I've found something there. . . . Why stay in this stuffiness here! let's go!'

I followed Punin, but in the doorway I thought it as well to turn round and fling a glance of defiance at Baburin, as though to say, I'm not afraid of you!

He responded in the same way, and positively snorted into the towel— probably to make me thoroughly aware how utterly he despised me!

'What an insolent fellow your friend is!' I said to Punin, directly the door had closed behind me.

Almost with horror, Punin turned his plump face to me.

'To whom did you apply that expression?' he asked me, with round eyes.

'Why, to him, of course. . . . What's his name? that . . . Baburin.'

'Paramon Semyonitch?'

'Why, yes; that . . . blackfaced fellow.'

'Eh . . . eh . . . eh . . . !' Punin protested, with caressing reproachfulness. 'How can you talk like that, little master! Paramon Semyonitch is the most estimable man, of the strictest principles, an extraordinary person! To be sure, he won't allow any disrespect to him, because—he knows his own value. That man possesses a vast amount of knowledge—and it's not a place like this he ought to be filling! You must, my dear, behave very courteously to him; do you know, he's . . .' here Punin bent down quite to my ear,—'a republican!'

I stared at Punin. This I had not at all expected. From Keidanov's manual and other historical works I had gathered the fact that at some period or other, in ancient times, there had existed republicans, Greeks and Romans. For some unknown reason I had always pictured them all in helmets, with round shields on their arms, and big bare legs; but that in real life, in the actual present, above all, in Russia, in the province of X——, one could come across republicans—that upset all my notions, and utterly confounded them!

'Yes, my dear, yes; Paramon Semyonitch is a republican,' repeated Punin; 'there, so you'll know for the future how one should speak of a man like that! But now let's go into the garden. Fancy what I've found there! A cuckoo's egg in a redstart's nest! a lovely thing!'

I went into the garden with Punin; but mentally I kept repeating: 'republican! re . . . pub . . . lican!'

'So,' I decided at last—'that's why he has such a blue chin!'

My attitude to these two persons—Punin and Baburin—took definite shape from that very day. Baburin aroused in me a feeling of hostility with which there was, however, in a short time, mingled something akin to respect. And wasn't I afraid of him! I never got over being afraid of him even when the sharp severity of his manner with me at first had quite disappeared. It is needless to say that of Punin I had no fear; I did not even respect him; I looked upon him—not to put too fine a point on it—as a buffoon; but I loved him with my whole soul! To spend hours at a time in his company, to be alone with him, to listen to his stories, became a genuine delight to me. My grandmother was anything but pleased at this *intimité* with a person of the 'lower classes'—*du commun;* but, whenever I could break away, I flew at once to my queer, amusing, beloved friend. Our meetings became more frequent after the departure of Mademoiselle Friquet, whom my grandmother sent back to Moscow in disgrace because, in conversation with a military staff captain, visiting in the neighbourhood, she had had the insolence to complain of the dulness which reigned in our household. And Punin, for his part, was not bored by long conversations with a boy of twelve; he seemed to seek them of himself. How often have I listened to his stories, sitting with him in the fragrant shade, on the dry, smooth grass, under the canopy of the silver poplars, or among the reeds above the pond, on the coarse, damp sand of the hollow bank, from which the knotted roots protruded, queerly interlaced, like great black veins, like snakes, like creatures emerging from some subterranean region! Punin told me the whole story of his life in minute detail, describing all his happy adventures, and all his misfortunes, with which I always felt the sincerest sympathy! His father had been a deacon;—'a splendid man—but, under the influence of drink, stern to the last extreme.'

Punin himself had received his education in a seminary; but, unable to stand the severe thrashings, and feeling no inclination for the priestly calling, he had become a layman, and in consequence had experienced all sorts of hardships; and, finally, had become a vagrant. 'And had I not met with my benefactor, Paramon Semyonitch,' Punin commonly added (he never spoke of Baburin except in this way), 'I should have sunk into the miry abysses of poverty and vice.' Punin was fond of high-sounding expressions, and had a great propensity, if not for lying, for romancing and exaggeration; he admired everything, fell into ecstasies over everything. . . . And I, in imitation of him, began to exaggerate and be ecstatic, too. 'What a crazy fellow you've grown! God have mercy on you!' my old nurse used to say to me. Punin's narratives used to interest me extremely; but even better than his stories I loved the readings we used to have together.

It is impossible to describe the feeling I experienced when, snatching a favourable moment, suddenly, like a hermit in a tale or a good fairy, he appeared before me with a ponderous volume under his arm, and stealthily beckoning with his long crooked finger, and winking mysteriously, he pointed with his head, his eyebrows, his shoulders, his whole person, toward the deepest recesses of the garden, whither no one could penetrate after us, and where it was impossible to find us out. And when we had succeeded in getting away unnoticed; when we had satisfactorily reached one of our secret nooks, and were sitting side by side, and, at last, the book was slowly opened, emitting a pungent odour, inexpressibly sweet to me then, of mildew and age;—with what a thrill, with what a wave of dumb expectancy, I gazed at the face, at the lips of Punin, those lips from which in a moment a stream of such delicious eloquence was to flow! At last the first sounds of the reading were heard. Everything around me vanished . . . no, not vanished, but grew far away, passed into clouds of mist, leaving behind only an impression of something friendly and protecting. Those trees, those green leaves, those high grasses screen us, hide us from all the rest of the world; no one knows where we are, what we are about—while with us is poetry, we are saturated in it, intoxicated with it, something solemn, grand, mysterious is happening to us. . . . Punin, by preference, kept to poetry, musical, sonorous poetry; he was ready to lay down his life for

poetry. He did not read, he declaimed the verse majestically, in a torrent
of rhythm, in a rolling outpour through his nose, like a man intoxicated,
lifted out of himself, like the Pythian priestess. And another habit he had:
first he would lisp the verses through softly, in a whisper, as it were
mumbling them to himself. . . . This he used to call the rough sketch
of the reading; then he would thunder out the same verse in its 'fair copy,'
and would all at once leap up, throw up his hand, with a half-supplicating,
half-imperious gesture. . . . In this way we went through not only Lomonosov, Sumarokov, and Kantemir (the older the poems, the more they were
to Punin's taste), but even Heraskov's *Rossiad*. And, to tell the truth, it was
this same *Rossiad* which aroused my enthusiasm most. There is in it,
among others, a mighty Tatar woman, a gigantic heroine; I have forgotten
even her name now; but in those days my hands and feet turned cold as
soon as it was mentioned. 'Yes,' Punin would say, nodding his head with
great significance, 'Heraskov, he doesn't let one off easily. At times one
comes upon a line, simply heart-breaking. . . . One can only stick to it,
and do one's best. . . . One tries to master it, but he breaks away again
and trumpets, trumpets, with the crash of cymbals. His name's been well
bestowed on him—the very word, Herrraskov!' Lomonosov Punin found
fault with for too simple and free a style; while to Derzhavin he maintained
an attitude almost of hostility, saying that he was more of a courtier
than a poet. In our house it was not merely that no attention was given to
literature, to poetry; but poetry, especially Russian poetry, was looked
upon as something quite undignified and vulgar; my grandmother did not
even call it poetry, but 'doggrel verses'; every author of such doggrel was,
in her opinion, either a confirmed toper or a perfect idiot. Brought up among
such ideas, it was inevitable that I should either turn from Punin with disgust
—he was untidy and shabby into the bargain, which was an offence to my
seignorial habits—or that, attracted and captivated by him, I should follow
his example, and be infected by his passion for poetry. . . . And so it turned
out. I, too, began reading poetry, or, as my grandmother expressed it,
poring over doggrel trash. . . . I even tried my hand at versifying, and
composed a poem, descriptive of a barrel-organ, in which occurred the
following two lines:

> '*Lo, the barrel turns around,*
> *And the cogs within resound.*'

Punin commended in this effort a certain imitative melody, but disapproved
of the subject itself as low and unworthy of lyrical treatment.

Alas! all those efforts and emotions and transports, our solitary readings,
our life together, our poetry, all came to an end at once. Trouble broke
upon us suddenly, like a clap of thunder.

My grandmother in everything liked cleanliness and order, quite in the
spirit of the active generals of those days; cleanliness and order were to be
maintained too in our garden. And so from time to time they 'drove' into

it poor peasants, who had no families, no land, no beasts of their own, and those among the house serfs who were out of favour or superannuated, and set them to clearing the paths, weeding the borders, breaking up and sifting the earth in the beds, and so on. Well, one day, in the very heat of these operations, my grandmother went into the garden, and took me with her. On all sides, among the trees and about the lawns, we caught glimpses of white, red, and blue smocks; on all sides we heard the scraping and clanging of spades, the dull thud of clods of earth on the slanting sieves. As she passed by the labourers, my grandmother with her eagle eye noticed at once that one of them was working with less energy than the rest, and that he took off his cap, too, with no show of eagerness. This was a youth, still quite young, with a wasted face, and sunken, lustreless eyes. His cotton smock, all torn and patched, scarcely held together over his narrow shoulders.

' Who's that? ' my grandmother inquired of Filippitch, who was walking on tiptoe behind her.

' Of whom . . . you are pleased . . .' Filippitch stammered.

' Oh, fool! I mean the one that looked so sullenly at me. There, standing yonder, not working.'

' Oh, him! Yes . . . th . . . th . . . that's Yermil, son of Pavel Afanasiitch, now deceased.'

Pavel Afanasiitch had been, ten years before, head butler in my grandmother's house, and stood particularly high in her favour. But suddenly falling into disgrace, he was as suddenly degraded to being herdsman, and did not long keep even that position. He sank lower still, and struggled on for a while on a monthly pittance of flour in a little hut far away. At last he had died of paralysis, leaving his family in the most utter destitution.

' Aha! ' commented my grandmother; ' it's clear the apple's not fallen far from the tree. Well, we shall have to make arrangements about this fellow too. I've no need of people like that, with scowling faces.'

My grandmother went back to the house—and made arrangements. Three hours later Yermil, completely ' equipped,' was brought under the window of her room. The unfortunate boy was being transported to a settlement; the other side of the fence, a few steps from him, was a little cart loaded with his poor belongings. Such were the times then. Yermil stood without his cap, with downcast head, barefoot, with his boots tied up with a string behind his back; his face, turned towards the seignorial mansion, expressed not despair nor grief, nor even bewilderment; a stupid smile was frozen on his colourless lips; his eyes, dry and half-closed, looked stubbornly on the ground. My grandmother was apprised of his presence. She got up from the sofa, went, with a faint rustle of her silken skirts, to the window of the study, and, holding her golden-rimmed double eyeglass on the bridge of her nose, looked at the new exile. In her room there happened to be at the moment four other persons, the butler, Baburin, the page who waited on my grandmother in the daytime, and I.

My grandmother nodded her head up and down. . . .

'Madam,' a hoarse almost stifled voice was heard suddenly. I looked round. Baburin's face was red . . . dark red; under his overhanging brows could be seen little sharp points of light. . . . There was no doubt about it; it was he, it was Baburin, who had uttered the word 'Madam.'

My grandmother too looked round, and turned her eyeglass from Yermil to Baburin.

'Who is that . . . speaking?' she articulated slowly . . . through her nose. Baburin moved slightly forward.

'Madam,' he began, 'it is I. . . . I venture . . . I imagine . . . I make bold to submit to your honour that you are making a mistake in acting as . . . as you are pleased to act at this moment.'

'That is?' my grandmother said, in the same voice, not removing her eyeglass.

'I take the liberty . . .' Baburin went on distinctly, uttering every word though with obvious effort—'I am referring to the case of this lad who is being sent away to a settlement . . . for no fault of his. Such arrangements, I venture to submit, lead to dissatisfaction, and to other—which God forbid! —consequences, and are nothing else than a transgression of the powers allowed to seignorial proprietors.'

'And where have you studied, pray?' my grandmother asked after a short silence, and she dropped her eyeglass.

Baburin was disconcerted. 'What are you pleased to wish?' he muttered.

'I ask you: where have you studied? You use such learned words.'

'I . . . my education . . .' Baburin was beginning.

My grandmother shrugged her shoulders contemptuously. 'It seems,' she interrupted, 'that my arrangements are not to your liking. That is of absolutely no consequence to me—among my subjects I am sovereign, and answerable to no one for them, only I am not accustomed to having people criticising me in my presence, and meddling in what is not their business. I have no need of learned philanthropists of nondescript position; I want servants to do my will without question. So I always lived till you came, and so I shall live after you've gone. You do not suit me; you are discharged. Nikolai Antonov,' my grandmother turned to the steward, 'pay this man off; and let him be gone before dinner-time to-day! D'you hear? Don't put me into a passion. And the other too . . . the fool that lives with him—to be sent off too. What's Yermilka waiting for?' she added, looking out of the window, 'I have seen him. What more does he want?' My grandmother shook her handkerchief in the direction of the window, as though to drive away an importunate fly. Then she sat down in a low chair, and turning towards us, gave the order grimly: 'Everybody present to leave the room!'

We all withdrew—all, except the day page, to whom my grandmother's words did not apply, because he was nobody.

My grandmother's decree was carried out to the letter. Before dinner, both Baburin and my friend Punin were driving away from the place.

I will not undertake to describe my grief, my genuine, truly childish despair. It was so strong that it stifled even the feeling of awe-stricken admiration inspired by the bold action of the republican Baburin. After the conversation with my grandmother, he went at once to his room and began packing up. He did not vouchsafe me one word, one look, though I was the whole time hanging about him, or rather, in reality, about Punin. The latter was utterly distraught, and he too said nothing; but he was continually glancing at me, and tears stood in his eyes . . . always the same tears; they neither fell nor dried up. He did not venture to criticise his 'benefactor'—Paramon Semyonitch could not make a mistake,—but great was his distress and dejection. Punin and I made an effort to read something out of the *Rossiad* for the last time; we even locked ourselves up in the lumber-room—it was useless to dream of going into the garden—but at the very first line we both broke down, and I fairly bellowed like a calf, in spite of my twelve years, and my claims to be grown-up.

When he had taken his seat in the carriage Baburin at last turned to me, and with a slight softening of the accustomed sternness of his face, observed: 'It's a lesson for you, young gentleman; remember this incident, and when you grow up, try to put an end to such acts of injustice. Your heart is good, your nature is not yet corrupted. . . . Mind, be careful; things can't go on like this!' Through my tears, which streamed copiously over my nose, my lips, and my chin, I faltered out that I would . . . I would remember, that I promised . . . I would do . . . I would be sure . . . quite sure . . .

But at this point, Punin, whom I had before this embraced twenty times (my cheeks were burning from the contact with his unshaven beard, and I was odiferous of the smell that always clung to him)—at this point a sudden frenzy came over Punin. He jumped up on the seat of the cart, flung both hands up in the air, and began in a voice of thunder (where he got it from!) to declaim the well-known paraphrase of the Psalm of David by Derzhavin, —a poet for this occasion—not a courtier.

> '*God the All-powerful doth arise*
> *And judgeth in the congregation of the mighty!* . . .
> *How long, how long, saith the Lord,*
> *Will ye have mercy on the wicked?*
> "*Ye have to keep the laws.* . . ."'

'Sit down!' Baburin said to him.
Punin sat down, but continued:

> '*To save the guiltless and needy,*
> *To give shelter to the afflicted,*
> *To defend the weak from the oppressors.*'

Punin at the word 'oppressors' pointed to the seignorial abode, and then poked the driver in the back.

> '*To deliver the poor out of bondage!*
> *They know not! neither will they understand!* . . .'

Nikolai Antonov running out of the seignorial abode, shouted at the top of his voice to the coachman: 'Get away with you! owl! go along! don't stay lingering here!' and the cart rolled away. Only in the distance could still be heard:

> 'Arise, O Lord God of righteousness! . . .
> Come forth to judge the unjust—
> And be Thou the only Ruler of the nations!'

'What a clown!' remarked Nikolai Antonov.

'He didn't get enough of the rod in his young days,' observed the deacon, appearing on the steps. He had come to inquire what hour it would please the mistress to fix for the night service.

The same day, learning that Yermil was still in the village, and would not till early next morning be despatched to the town for the execution of certain legal formalities, which were intended to check the arbitrary proceedings of the landowners, but served only as a source of additional revenue to the functionaries in superintendence of them, I sought him out, and, for lack of money of my own, handed him a bundle, in which I had tied up two pocket-handkerchiefs, a shabby pair of slippers, a comb, an old night-gown, and a perfectly new silk cravat. Yermil, whom I had to wake up—he was lying on a heap of straw in the back yard, near the cart—Yermil took my present rather indifferently, with some hesitation in fact, did not thank me, promptly poked his head into the straw and fell asleep again. I went home somewhat disappointed. I had imagined that he would be astonished and overjoyed at my visit, would see in it a pledge of my magnanimous intentions for the future—and instead of that . . .

'You may say what you like—these people have no feeling,' was my reflection on my homeward way.

My grandmother, who had for some reason left me in peace the whole of that memorable day, looked at me suspiciously when I came after supper to say good-night to her.

'Your eyes are red,' she observed to me in French; 'and there's a smell of the peasant's hut about you. I am not going to enter into an examination of what you've been feeling and doing—I should not like to be obliged to punish you—but I hope you will get over all your foolishness, and begin to conduct yourself once more in a manner befitting a well-bred boy. However, we are soon going back to Moscow, and I shall get you a tutor—as I see you need a man's hand to manage you. You can go.'

We did, as a fact, go back soon after to Moscow.

II

1837

SEVEN years had passed by. We were living as before at Moscow—but I was by now a student in my second year—and the authority of my grandmother, who had aged very perceptibly in the last years, no longer weighed upon me. Of all my fellow-students the one with whom I was on the friendliest terms was a light-hearted and good-natured youth called Tarhov. Our habits and our tastes were similar. Tarhov was a great lover of poetry, and himself wrote verses; while in me the seeds sown by Punin had not been without fruit. As is often the case with young people who are very close friends, we had no secrets from one another. But behold, for several days together I noticed a certain excitement and agitation in Tarhov. . . . He disappeared for hours at a time, and I did not know where he had got to—a thing which had never happened before. I was on the point of demanding, in the name of friendship, a full explanation. . . . He anticipated me.

One day I was sitting in his room. . . . 'Petya,' he said suddenly, blushing gaily, and looking me straight in the face, 'I must introduce you to my muse.'

'Your muse! how queerly you talk! Like a classicist. (Romanticism was at that time, in 1837, at its full height.) As if I had not known it ever so long—your muse! Have you written a new poem, or what? '

'You don't understand what I mean,' rejoined Tarhov, still laughing and blushing. 'I will introduce you to a living muse.'

'Aha! so that's it! But how is she—yours? '

'Why, because . . . But hush, I believe it's she coming here.'

There was the light click of hurrying heels, the door opened, and in the doorway appeared a girl of eighteen, in a chintz cotton gown, with a black cloth cape on her shoulders, and a black straw hat on her fair, rather curly hair. On seeing me she was frightened and disconcerted, and was beating a retreat . . . but Tarhov at once rushed to meet her.

'Please, please, Musa Pavlovna, come in! This is my great friend, a splendid fellow—and the soul of discretion. You've no need to be afraid of him. Petya,' he turned to me, 'let me introduce my Musa—Musa Pavlovna Vinogradov, a great friend of mine.'

I bowed.

'How is that . . . Musa? ' I was beginning. . . . Tarhov laughed. 'Ah, you didn't know there was such a name in the calendar? I didn't know it either, my boy, till I met this dear young lady. Musa! such a charming name! And suits her so well! '

I bowed again to my comrade's great friend. She left the door, took two steps forward and stood still. She was very attractive, but I could not agree with Tarhov's opinion, and inwardly said to myself: 'Well, she's a strange sort of muse! '

The features of her curved, rosy face were small and delicate; there was an air of fresh, buoyant youth about all her slender, miniature figure; but of the muse, of the personification of the muse, I—and not only I—all the young people of that time had a very different conception! First of all the muse had infallibly to be dark-haired and pale. An expression of scornful pride, a bitter smile, a glance of inspiration, and that ' something '—mysterious, demonic, fateful—that was essential to our conception of the muse, the muse of Byron, who at that time held sovereign sway over men's fancies. There was nothing of that kind to be discerned in the face of the girl who came in. Had I been a little older and more experienced I should probably have paid more attention to her eyes, which were small and deep-set, with full lids, but dark as agate, alert and bright, a thing rare in fair-haired people. Poetical tendencies I should not have detected in their rapid, as it were elusive, glance, but hints of a passionate soul, passionate to self-forgetfulness. But I was very young then.

I held out my hand to Musa Pavlovna—she did not give me hers—she did not notice my movement; she sat down on the chair Tarhov placed for her, but did not take off her hat and cape.

She was, obviously, ill at ease; my presence embarrassed her. She drew deep breaths, at irregular intervals, as though she were gasping for air.

'I've only come to you for one minute, Vladimir Nikolaitch,' she began—her voice was very soft and deep; from her crimson, almost childish lips, it seemed rather strange;—'but our madame would not let me out for more than half an hour. You weren't well the day before yesterday . . . and so, I thought . . .'

She stammered and hung her head. Under the shade of her thick, low brows her dark eyes darted—to and fro—elusively. There are dark, swift, flashing beetles that flit so in the heat of summer among the blades of dry grass.

'How good you are, Musa, Musotchka!' cried Tarhov. 'But you must stay, you must stay a little. . . . We'll have the samovar in directly.'

'Oh, no, Vladimir Nikolaevitch! it's impossible! I must go away this minute.'

'You must rest a little, anyway. You're out of breath. . . . You're tired.'

'I'm not tired. It's . . . not that . . . only . . . give me another book; I've finished this one.' She took out of her pocket a tattered grey volume of a Moscow edition.

'Of course, of course. Well, did you like it? *Roslavlev*,' added Tarhov, addressing me.

'Yes. Only I think *Yury Miloslavsky* is much better. Our madame is very strict about books. She says they hinder our working. For, to her thinking . . .'

'But, I say, *Yury Miloslavsky's* not equal to Pushkin's *Gipsies*? Eh? Musa Pavlovna?' Tarhov broke in with a smile.

'No, indeed! The *Gipsies* . . .' she murmured slowly. 'Oh yes, another thing, Vladimir Nikolaitch; don't come to-morrow . . . you know where.'

'Why not?'

'It's impossible.'

'But why?'

The girl shrugged her shoulders, and all at once, as though she had received a sudden shove, got up from her chair.

'Why, Musa, Musotchka,' Tarhov expostulated plaintively. 'Stay a little!'

'No, no, I can't.' She went quickly to the door, took hold of the handle. . . .

'Well, at least, take the book!'

'Another time.'

Tarhov rushed towards the girl, but at that instant she darted out of the room. He almost knocked his nose against the door. 'What a girl! She's a regular little viper!' he declared with some vexation, and then sank into thought.

I stayed at Tarhov's. I wanted to find out what was the meaning of it all. Tarhov was not disposed to be reserved. He told me that the girl was a milliner; that he had seen her for the first time three weeks before in a fashionable shop, where he had gone on a commission for his sister, who lived in the provinces, to buy a hat; that he had fallen in love with her at first sight, and that next day he had succeeded in speaking to her in the street; that she had herself, it seemed, taken rather a fancy to him.

'Only, please, don't you suppose,' he added with warmth,—'don't you imagine any harm of her. So far, at any rate, there's been nothing of that sort between us.'

'Harm!' I caught him up; 'I've no doubt of that; and I've no doubt either that you sincerely deplore the fact, my dear fellow! Have patience—everything will come right.'

'I hope so,' Tarhov muttered through his teeth, though with a laugh. 'But really, my boy, that girl . . . I tell you—it's a new type, you know. You hadn't time to get a good look at her. She's a shy thing!—oo! such a shy thing! and what a will of her own! But that very shyness is what I like in her. It's a sign of independence! I'm simply over head and ears, my boy!'

Tarhov fell to talking of his 'charmer,' and even read me the beginning of a poem entitled: 'My Muse.' His emotional outpourings were not quite to my taste. I felt secretly jealous of him. I soon left him.

A few days after I happened to be passing through one of the arcades of the Gostinny Dvor. It was Saturday; there were crowds of people shopping; on all sides, in the midst of the pushing and crushing, the shopmen kept shouting to people to buy. Having bought what I wanted, I was thinking of nothing but getting away from their teasing importunity as soon as possible —when all at once I halted involuntarily: in a fruit shop I caught sight of my comrade's charmer—Musa, Musa Pavlovna! She was standing, profile to me, and seemed to be waiting for something. After a moment's hesitation I made up my mind to go up to her and speak. But I had hardly passed through the doorway of the shop and taken off my cap, when she tottered back dismayed, turned quickly to an old man in a frieze cloak, for whom the shopman was weighing out a pound of raisins, and clutched at his arm, as though fleeing to put herself under his protection. The latter, in his turn, wheeled round facing her—and, imagine my amazement, I recognised him as Punin!

Yes, it was he; there were his inflamed eyes, his full lips, his soft, overhanging nose. He had, in fact, changed little during the last seven years; his face was a little flabbier, perhaps.

'Nikander Vavilitch!' I cried. 'Don't you know me?' Punin started, opened his mouth, stared at me. . . .

'I haven't the honour,' he was beginning—and all at once he piped out shrilly: 'The little master of Troïtsky (my grandmother's property was called Troïtsky)! Can it be the little master of Troïtsky?'

The pound of raisins tumbled out of his hands.

'It really is,' I answered, and, picking up Punin's purchase from the ground, I kissed him.

He was breathless with delight and excitement; he almost cried, removed his cap—which enabled me to satisfy myself that the last traces of hair had vanished from his 'egg'—took a handkerchief out of it, blew his nose, poked the cap into his bosom with the raisins, put it on again, again dropped the raisins. . . . I don't know how Musa was behaving all this time, I tried not to look at her. I don't imagine Punin's agitation proceeded from any extreme attachment to my person; it was simply that his nature could not stand the slightest unexpected shock. The nervous excitability of these poor devils!

'Come and see us, my dear boy,' he faltered at last; 'you won't be too proud to visit our humble nest? You're a student, I see . . .'

'On the contrary, I shall be delighted, really.'

'Are you independent now?'

'Perfectly independent.'

'That's capital! How pleased Paramon Semyonitch will be! To-day he'll be home earlier than usual, and madame lets her, too, off for Saturdays. But, stop, excuse me, I am quite forgetting myself. Of course, you don't know our niece!'

I hastened to slip in that I had not yet had the pleasure.

'Of course, of course! How could you know her! Musotchka . . . Take note, my dear sir, this girl's name is Musa—and it's not a nick-name, but her real name. . . . Isn't that a predestination? Musotchka, I want to introduce you to Mr. . . . Mr. . . .'

'B.,' I prompted.

'B.,' he repeated. 'Musotchka, listen! You see before you the most excellent, most delightful of young men. Fate threw us together when he was still in years of boyhood! I beg you to look on him as a friend!'

I swung off a low bow. Musa, red as a poppy, flashed a look on me from under her eyelids, and dropped them immediately.

'Ah!' thought I, 'you're one of those who in difficult moments don't turn pale, but red; that must be made a note of.'

'You must be indulgent, she's not a fine lady,' observed Punin, and he went out of the shop into the street; Musa and I followed him.

The house in which Punin lodged was a considerable distance from the Gostinny Dvor, being, in fact, in Sadovoy Street. On the way my former preceptor in poetry had time to communicate a good many details of his mode of existence. Since the time of our parting, both he and Baburin had been tossed about holy Russia pretty thoroughly, and had not long—only a year and a half before—found a permanent home in Moscow. Baburin had succeeded in becoming head-clerk in the office of a rich merchant and manufacturer. 'Not a lucrative berth,' Punin observed with a sigh,—'a lot of work, and not much profit . . . but what's one to do? One must be thankful to get that! I, too, am trying to earn something by copying and lessons; only my efforts have so far not been crowned with success. My writing, you perhaps recollect, is old-fashioned, not in accordance with the tastes of the day; and as regards lessons—what has been a great obstacle is the absence of befitting attire; moreover, I greatly fear that in the matter of instruction—in the subject of Russian literature—I am also not in harmony with the tastes of the day; and so it comes about that I am turned away.' (Punin laughed his sleepy, subdued laugh. He had retained his old, somewhat high-flown manner of speech, and his old weakness for falling into rhyme.) 'All run after novelties, nothing but innovations! I dare say you, too, do not honour the old divinities, and fall down before new idols?'

'And you, Nikander Vavilitch, do you really still esteem Heraskov?'

Punin stood still and waved both hands at once. 'In the highest degree, sir! in the high . . . est de . . . gree, I do!'

'And you don't read Pushkin? You don't like Pushkin?'

Punin again flung his hands up higher than his head.

'Pushkin? Pushkin is the snake, lying hid in the grass, who is endowed with the note of the nightingale!'

While Punin and I talked like this, cautiously picking our way over the unevenly laid brick pavement of so-called 'white-stoned' Moscow—in which there is not one stone, and which is not white at all—Musa walked silently beside us on the side further from me. In speaking of her, I called her 'your niece.' Punin was silent for a little, scratched his head, and informed me in an undertone that he had called her so . . . merely as a manner of speaking; that she was really no relation; that she was an orphan picked up and cared for by Baburin in the town of Voronezh; but that he, Punin, might well call her daughter, as he loved her no less than a real daughter. I had no doubt that, though Punin intentionally dropped his voice, Musa could hear all he said very well; and she was at once angry, and shy, and embarrassed; and the lights and shades chased each other over her face, and every thing in it was slightly quivering, the eyelids and brows and lips and narrow nostrils. All this was very charming, and amusing, and queer.

But at last we reached the 'modest nest.' And modest it certainly was, the nest. It consisted of a small, one-storied house, that seemed almost sunk into the ground, with a slanting wooden roof, and four dingy windows in the front. The furniture of the rooms was of the poorest, and not over tidy, indeed. Between the windows and on the walls hung about a dozen tiny wooden cages containing larks, canaries, and siskins. 'My subjects!' Punin pronounced triumphantly, pointing his finger at them. We had hardly time to get in and look about us, Punin had hardly sent Musa for the samovar, when Baburin himself came in. He seemed to me to have aged much more than Punin, though his step was as firm as ever, and the expression of his face altogether was unchanged; but he had grown thin and bent, his cheeks were sunken, and his thick black shock of hair was sprinkled with grey. He did not recognise me, and showed no particular pleasure when Punin mentioned my name; he did not even smile with his eyes, he barely nodded; he asked—very carelessly and drily—whether my *granny* were living—and that was all. 'I'm not over-delighted at a visit from a nobleman,' he seemed to say; 'I don't feel flattered by it.' The republican was a republican still.

Musa came back; a decrepit little old woman followed her, bringing in a tarnished samovar. Punin began fussing about, and pressing me to take things; Baburin sat down to the table, leaned his head on his hands, and looked with weary eyes about him. At tea, however, he began to talk. He was dissatisfied with his position. 'A screw—not a man,' so he spoke of his employer; 'people in a subordinate position are so much dirt to him, of no consequence whatever; and yet it's not so long since he was under the yoke himself. Nothing but cruelty and covetousness. It's a bondage worse than the government's! And all the trade here rests on swindling and flourishes on nothing else!'

Hearing such dispiriting utterances, Punin sighed expressively, assented, shook his head up and down, and from side to side; Musa maintained a stubborn silence. . . . She was obviously fretted by the doubt, what I was, whether I was a discreet person or a gossip. And if I were discreet, whether it was not with some afterthought in my mind. Her dark, swift, restless eyes fairly flashed to and fro under their half-drooping lids. Only once she glanced at me, but so inquisitively, so searchingly, almost viciously . . . I positively started. Baburin scarcely talked to her at all; but whenever he did address her, there was a note of austere, hardly fatherly, tenderness in his voice.

Punin, on the contrary, was continually joking with Musa; she responded unwillingly, however. He called her little snow-maiden, little snowflake.

'Why do you give Musa Pavlovna such names?' I asked.

Punin laughed. 'Because she's such a chilly little thing.'

'Sensible,' put in Baburin: 'as befits a young girl.'

'We may call her the mistress of the house,' cried Punin. 'Hey? Paramon Semyonitch?' Baburin frowned; Musa turned away. . . . I did not understand the hint at the time.

So passed two hours . . . in no very lively fashion, though Punin did his best to 'entertain the honourable company.' For instance, he squatted down in front of the cage of one of the canaries, opened the door, and commanded: 'On the cupola! Begin the concert!' The canary fluttered out at once, perched on the *cupola,* that is to say, on Punin's bald pate, and turning from side to side, and shaking its little wings, carolled with all its might. During the whole time the concert lasted, Punin kept perfectly still, only conducting with his finger, and half closing his eyes. I could not help roaring with laughter . . . but neither Baburin nor Musa laughed.

Just as I was leaving, Baburin surprised me by an unexpected question. He wished to ask me, as a man studying at the university, what sort of person Zeno was, and what were my ideas about him.

'What Zeno?' I asked, somewhat puzzled.

'Zeno, the sage of antiquity. Surely he cannot be unknown to you?'

I vaguely recalled the name of Zeno, as the founder of the school of Stoics; but I knew absolutely nothing more about him.

'Yes, he was a philosopher,' I pronounced, at last.

'Zeno,' Baburin resumed in deliberate tones, 'was that wise man, who declared that suffering was not an evil, since fortitude overcomes all things, and that the good in this world is one: justice; and virtue itself is nothing else than justice.'

Punin turned a reverent ear.

'A man living here who has picked up a lot of old books, told me that saying,' continued Baburin; 'it pleased me much. But I see you are not interested in such subjects.'

Baburin was right. In such subjects I certainly was not interested. Since I had entered the university, I had become as much of a republican as Baburin himself. Of Mirabeau, of Robespierre, I would have talked with zest. Robespierre, indeed . . . why, I had hanging over my writing-table the lithographed portraits of Fouquier-Tinville and Chalier! But Zeno! Why drag in Zeno?

As he said good-bye to me, Punin insisted very warmly on my visiting them next day, Sunday; Baburin did not invite me at all, and even remarked between his teeth, that talking to plain people of nondescript position could not give me any great pleasure, and would most likely be disagreeable to my *granny.* At that word I interrupted him, however, and gave him to understand that my grandmother had no longer any authority over me.

'Why, you've not come into possession of the property, have you?' queried Baburin.

'No, I haven't,' I answered.

'Well, then, it follows . . .' Baburin did not finish his sentence; but I mentally finished it for him: 'it follows that I'm a boy.'

'Good-bye,' I said aloud, and I retired.

I was just going out of the courtyard into the street . . . Musa suddenly ran out of the house, and slipping a piece of crumpled paper into my hand, disappeared at once. At the first lamp-post I unfolded the paper. It turned out to be a note. With difficulty I deciphered the pale pencil-marks. 'For God's sake,' Musa had written, 'come to-morrow after matins to the Alex-androvsky garden near the Kutafia tower I shall wait for you don't refuse me don't make me miserable I simply must see you.' There were no mistakes in spelling in this note, but neither was there any punctuation. I returned home in perplexity.

When, a quarter of an hour before the appointed time, next day, I began to get near the Kutafia tower (it was early in April, the buds were swelling, the grass was growing greener, and the sparrows were noisily chirrupping and quarrelling in the bare lilac bushes), considerably to my surprise, I caught sight of Musa a little to one side, not far from the fence. She was there before me. I was going towards her; but she herself came to meet me.

' Let's go to the Kreml wall,' she whispered in a hurried voice, running her downcast eyes over the ground; ' there are people here.'

We went along the path up the hill.

' Musa Pavlovna,' I was beginning. . . . But she cut me short at once.

' Please,' she began, speaking in the same jerky and subdued voice, ' don't criticise me, don't think any harm of me. I wrote a letter to you, I made an appointment to meet you, because . . . I was afraid. . . . It seemed to me yesterday,—you seemed to be laughing all the time. Listen,' she added, with sudden energy, and she stopped short and turned towards me: ' listen; if you tell with whom . . . if you mention at whose room you met me, I'll throw myself in the water, I'll drown myself, I'll make an end of myself! '

At this point, for the first time, she glanced at me with the inquisitive, piercing look I had seen before.

' Why, she, perhaps, really . . . would do it,' was my thought.

' Really, Musa Pavlovna,' I protested, hurriedly: ' how can you have such a bad opinion of me? Do you suppose I am capable of betraying my friend and injuring you? Besides, come to that, there's nothing in your relations, as far as I'm aware, deserving of censure. . . . For goodness' sake, be calm.'

Musa heard me out, without stirring from the spot, or looking at me again.

' There's something else I ought to tell you,' she began, moving forward again along the path, ' or else you may think I'm quite mad! I ought to tell you, that old man wants to marry me! '

'What old man? The bald one? Punin? '

' No—not he! The other . . . Paramon Semyonitch.'

' Baburin? '

' Yes.'

' Is it possible? Has he made you an offer? '

' Yes.'

' But you didn't consent, of course? '

' Yes, I did consent . . . because I didn't understand what I was about then. Now it's a different matter.'

I flung up my hands. ' Baburin—and you! Why, he must be fifty! '

' He says forty-three. But that makes no difference. If he were five-and-twenty I wouldn't marry him. Much happiness I should find in it! A whole week will go by without his smiling once! Paramon Semyonitch is my benefactor, I am deeply indebted to him; he took care of me, educated me;

I should have been utterly lost but for him; I'm bound to look on him as a father. . . . But be his wife! I'd rather die! I'd rather be in my coffin! '

'Why do you keep talking about death, Musa Pavlovna? '

Musa stopped again.

'Why, is life so sweet, then? Even your friend Vladimir Nikolaitch, I may say, I've come to love from being wretched and dull: and then Paramon Semyonitch with his offers of marriage. . . . Punin, though he bores me with his verses, he doesn't scare me, anyway; he doesn't make me read Karamzin in the evenings, when my head's ready to drop off my shoulders for weariness! And what are these old men to me? They call me cold, too. With them, is it likely I should be warm? If they try to make me—I shall go. Paramon Semyonitch himself's always saying: Freedom! freedom! All right, I want freedom too. Or else it comes to this! Freedom for every one else, and keeping me in a cage! I'll tell him so myself. But if you betray me, or drop a hint—remember; they'll never set eyes on me again! '

Musa stood in the middle of the path.

'They'll never set eyes on me again! ' she repeated sharply. This time, too, she did not raise her eyes to me; she seemed to be aware that she would infallibly betray herself, would show what was in her heart, if any one looked her straight in the face. . . . And that was just why she did not lift her eyes, except when she was angry or annoyed, and then she stared straight at the person she was speaking to. . . . But her small pretty face was aglow with indomitable resolution.

'Why, Tarhov was right,' flashed through my head; 'this girl is a new type.'

'You've no need to be afraid of me,' I declared, at last.

'Truly? Even, if . . . You said something about our relations. . . . But even if there were . . .' she broke off.

'Even in that case, you would have no need to be afraid, Musa Pavlovna. I am not your judge. Your secret is buried here.' I pointed to my bosom. 'Believe me, I know how to appreciate. . .'

'Have you got my letter? ' Musa asked suddenly.

'Yes.'

'Where? '

'In my pocket.'

'Give it here . . . quick, quick! '

I got out the scrap of paper. Musa snatched it in her rough little hand, stood still a moment facing me, as though she were going to thank me; but suddenly started, looked round, and without even a word at parting, ran quickly down the hill.

I looked in the direction she had taken. At no great distance from the tower I discerned, wrapped in an ' Almaviva ' (' Almavivas ' were then in the height of fashion), a figure which I recognised at once as Tarhov.

'Aha, my boy,' thought I, ' you must have had notice, then, since you're on the look-out.'

And whistling to myself, I started homewards.

Next morning I had only just drunk my morning tea, when Punin made his appearance. He came into my room with rather an embarrassed face, and began making bows, looking about him, and apologising for his intrusion, as he called it. I made haste to reassure him. I, sinful man, imagined that Punin had come with the intention of borrowing money. But he confined himself to asking for a glass of tea with rum in it, as, luckily, the samovar had not been cleared away. 'It's with some trepidation and sinking of heart that I have come to see you,' he said, as he nibbled a lump of sugar. 'You I do not fear; but I stand in awe of your honoured grandmother! I am abashed too by my attire, as I have already communicated to you.' Punin passed his finger along the frayed edge of his ancient coat. 'At home it's no matter, and in the street, too, it's no harm; but when one finds one's self in gilded palaces, one's poverty stares one in the face, and one feels confused!' I occupied two small rooms on the ground floor, and certainly it would never have entered any one's head to call them palaces, still less gilded; but Punin apparently was referring to the whole of my grandmother's house, though that too was by no means conspicuously sumptuous. He reproached me for not having been to see them the previous day; 'Paramon Semyonitch,' said he, 'expected you, though he did declare that you would be sure not to come. And Musotchka, too, expected you.'

'What? Musa Pavlovna too?' I queried.

'She too. She's a charming girl we have got with us, isn't she? What do you say?'

'Very charming,' I assented.

Punin rubbed his bare head with extraordinary rapidity.

'She's a beauty, sir, a pearl or even a diamond—it's the truth I am telling you.' He bent down quite to my ear. 'Noble blood, too,' he whispered to me, 'only—you understand—left-handed; the forbidden fruit was eaten. Well, the parents died, the relations would do nothing for her, and flung her to the hazards of destiny, that's to say, despair, dying of hunger! But at that point Paramon Semyonitch steps forward, known as a deliverer from of old! He took her, clothed her and cared for her, brought up the poor nestling; and she has blossomed into our darling! I tell you, a man of the rarest qualities!'

Punin subsided against the back of the armchair, lifted his hands, and again bending forward, began whispering again, but still more mysteriously: 'You see Paramon Semyonitch himself too. . . . Didn't you know? he too is of exalted extraction—and on the left side, too. They do say—his father was a powerful Georgian prince, of the line of King David. . . . What do you make of that? A few words—but how much is said? The blood of King David! What do you think of that? And according to other accounts, the founder of the family of Paramon Semyonitch was an Indian Shah, Babur. Blue blood! That's fine too, isn't it? Eh?'

'Well?' I queried, 'and was he too, Baburin, flung to the hazards of destiny?'

Punin rubbed his pate again. 'To be sure he was! And with even greater cruelty than our little lady! From his earliest childhood nothing but struggling! And, in fact, I will confess that, inspired by Ruban, I composed in allusion to this fact a stanza for the portrait of Paramon Semyonitch. Wait a bit . . . how was it? Yes!

> '*E'en from the cradle fate's remorseless blows*
> *Baburin drove towards the abyss of woes!*
> *But as in darkness gleams the light, so now*
> *The conqueror's laurel wreathes his noble brow!*'

Punin delivered these lines in a rhythmic, sing-song voice, with full rounded vowels, as verses should be read.

'So that's how it is he's a republican!' I exclaimed.

'No, that's not why,' Punin answered simply. 'He forgave his father long ago; but he cannot endure injustice of any sort; it's the sorrows of others that trouble him!'

I wanted to turn the conversation on what I had learned from Musa the day before, that is to say, on Baburin's matrimonial project,—but I did not know how to proceed. Punin himself got me out of the difficulty.

'Did you notice nothing?' he asked me suddenly, slily screwing up his eyes, 'while you were with us? nothing special?'

'Why, was there anything to notice?' I asked in my turn.

Punin looked over his shoulder, as though anxious to satisfy himself that no one was listening. 'Our little beauty, Musotchka, is shortly to be a married lady!'

'How so?'

'Madame Baburin,' Punin announced with an effort, and slapping his knees several times with his open hands, he nodded his head, like a china mandarin.

'Impossible!' I cried, with assumed astonishment.

Punin's head slowly came to rest, and his hands dropped down. 'Why impossible, allow me to ask?'

'Because Paramon Semyonitch is more fit to be your young lady's father; because such a difference in age excludes all likelihood of love—on the girl's side.'

'Excludes?' Punin repeated excitedly. 'But what about gratitude? and pure affection? and tenderness of feeling? Excludes! You must consider this: admitting that Musa's a splendid girl; but then to gain Paramon Semyonitch's affection, to be his comfort, his prop—his spouse, in short! is that not the loftiest possible happiness even for such a girl? And she realises it! You should look, turn an attentive eye! In Paramon Semyonitch's presence Musotchka is all veneration, all tremor and enthusiasm!'

'That's just what's wrong, Nikander Vavilitch, that she is, as you say, all tremor. If you love any one you don't feel tremors in their presence.'

'But with that I can't agree! Here am I, for instance; no one, I suppose, could love Paramon Semyonitch more than I, but I . . . tremble before him.'

' Oh, you—that's a different matter.'

' How is it a different matter? how? how? ' interrupted Punin. I simply did not know him; he got hot, and serious, almost angry, and quite dropped his rhythmic sing-song in speaking. ' No,' he declared; ' I notice that you have not a good eye for character! No; you can't read people's hearts! ' I gave up contradicting him . . . and to give another turn to the conversation, proposed, for the sake of old times, that we should read something together.

Punin was silent for a while.

' One of the old poets? The real ones? ' he asked at last.

' No; a new one.'

' A new one? ' Punin repeated mistrustfully.

' Pushkin,' I answered. I suddenly thought of the *Gipsies,* which Tarhov had mentioned not long before. There, by the way, is the ballad about the old husband. Punin grumbled a little, but I sat him down on the sofa, so that he could listen more comfortably, and began to read Pushkin's poem. The passage came at last, ' old husband, cruel husband'; Punin heard the ballad through to the end, and all at once he got up impulsively.

' I can't,' he pronounced, with an intense emotion, which impressed even me;—' excuse me; I cannot hear more of that author. He is an immoral slanderer; he is a liar . . . he upsets me. I cannot! Permit me to cut short my visit to-day.'

I began trying to persuade Punin to remain; but he insisted on having his own way with a sort of stupid, scared obstinacy: he repeated several times that he felt upset, and wished to get a breath of fresh air—and all the while his lips were faintly quivering and his eyes avoided mine, as though I had wounded him. So he went away. A little while after, I too went out of the house and set off to see Tarhov.

Without inquiring of any one, with a student's usual lack of ceremony, I walked straight into his lodgings. In the first room there was no one. I called Tarhov by name, and receiving no answer, was just going to retreat; but the door of the adjoining room opened, and my friend appeared. He looked at me rather queerly, and shook hands without speaking. I had come to him to repeat all I had heard from Punin; and though I felt at once that I had called on Tarhov at the wrong moment, still, after talking a little about extraneous matters, I ended by informing him of Baburin's intentions in regard to Musa. This piece of news did not, apparently, surprise him much; he quietly sat down at the table, and fixing his eyes intently upon me, and keeping silent as before, gave to his features an expression . . . an expression, as though he would say: ' Well, what more have you to tell? Come, out with your ideas! ' I looked more attentively into his face. . . . It struck me as eager, a little ironical, a little arrogant even. But that did not hinder me from bringing out my ideas. On the contrary. ' You're show-ing off,' was my thought; ' so I am not going to spare you! ' And there and then I proceeded straightway to enlarge upon the mischief of yielding to impulsive feelings, upon the duty of every man to respect the freedom and personal life of another man—in short, I proceeded to enunciate useful and appropriate counsel. Holding forth in this manner, I walked up and down the room, to be more at ease. Tarhov did not interrupt me, and did not stir from his seat; he only played with his fingers on his chin.

' I know,' said I . . . (Exactly what was my motive in speaking so, I have no clear idea myself—envy, most likely; it was not devotion to morality, anyway!) ' I know,' said I, ' that it's no easy matter, no joking matter; I am sure you love Musa, and that Musa loves you—that it is not a passing fancy on your part. . . . But, see, let us suppose! (Here I folded my arms on my breast.) . . . Let us suppose you gratify your passion—what is to follow? You won't marry her, you know. And at the same time you are wrecking the happiness of an excellent, honest man, her benefactor—and—who knows? (here my face expressed at the same time penetration and sorrow)—possibly her own happiness too. . . .'

And so on, and so on!

For about a quarter of an hour my discourse flowed on. Tarhov was still silent. I began to be disconcerted by this silence. I glanced at him from time to time, not so much to satisfy myself as to the impression my words were making on him, as to find out why he neither objected nor agreed, but sat like a deaf mute. At last I fancied that there was . . . yes, there certainly was a change in his face. It began to show signs of uneasiness, agitation, painful agitation. . . . Yet, strange to say, the eager, bright, laughing something, which had struck me at my first glance at Tarhov, still did not leave that agitated, that troubled face! I could not make up my mind whether or no to congratulate myself on the success of my sermon, when Tarhov suddenly got up, and pressing both my hands, said, speaking very quickly, ' Thank you, thank you. You're right, of course, . . . though, on the other side, one might observe . . . What is your Baburin you make so much of, after all? An honest fool—and nothing more! You call him a republican —and he's simply a fool! Oo! That's what he is! All his republicanism simply means that he can never get on anywhere! '

' Ah! so that's your idea! A fool! can never get on!—but let me tell you,' I pursued, with sudden heat, ' let me tell you, my dear Vladimir Nikolaitch, that in these days to get on nowhere is a sign of a fine, a noble nature! None but worthless people—bad people—get on anywhere and accommodate themselves to everything. You say Baburin is an honest fool! Why, is it better, then, to your mind, to be dishonest and clever? '

' You distort my words! ' cried Tarhov. ' I only wanted to explain how I understand that person. Do you think he's such a rare specimen? Not a bit of it! I've met other people like him in my time. A man sits with an air of importance, silent, obstinate, angular. . . . O-ho-ho! say you. It shows that there's a great deal in him! But there's nothing in him, not one idea in his head—nothing but a sense of his own dignity.'

' Even if there is nothing else, that's an honourable thing,' I broke in. ' But let me ask where you have managed to study him like this? You don't know him, do you? Or are you describing him . . . from what Musa tells you?'

Tarhov shrugged his shoulders. 'Musa and I . . . have other things to talk of. I tell you what,' he added, his whole body quivering with impatience,—'I tell you what: if Baburin has such a noble and honest nature, how is it he doesn't see that Musa is not a fit match for him? It's one of two things: either he knows that what he's doing to her is something of the nature of an outrage, all in the name of gratitude . . . and if so, what about his honesty?—or he doesn't realise it . . . and in that case, what can one call him but a fool?'

I was about to reply, but Tarhov again clutched my hands, and again began talking in a hurried voice. 'Though . . . of course . . . I confess you are right, a thousand times right. . . . You are a true friend . . . but now leave me alone, please.'

I was puzzled. 'Leave you alone?'

'Yes. I must, don't you see, think over all you've just said, thoroughly. . . . I have no doubt you are right . . . but now leave me alone!'

'You're in such a state of excitement . . .' I was beginning.

'Excitement? I?' Tarhov laughed, but instantly pulled himself up. 'Yes, of course I am. How could I help being? You say yourself it's no joking matter. Yes; I must think about it . . . alone.' He was still squeezing my hands. 'Good-bye, my dear fellow, good-bye!'

'Good-bye,' I repeated. 'Good-bye, old boy!' As I was going away I flung a last glance at Tarhov. He seemed pleased. At what? At the fact that I, like a true friend and comrade, had pointed out the danger of the way upon which he had set his foot—or that I was going? Ideas of the most diverse kind were floating in my head the whole day till evening—till the very instant when I entered the house occupied by Punin and Baburin, for I went to see them the same day. I am bound to confess that some of Tarhov's phrases had sunk deep into my soul . . . and were ringing in my ears. . . . In truth, was it possible Baburin . . . was it possible he did not see she was not a fit match for him?

But could this possibly be: Baburin, the self-sacrificing Baburin—an honest fool!

Punin had said, when he came to see me, that I had been expected there the day before. That may have been so, but on this day, it is certain, no one expected me. . . . I found every one at home, and every one was surprised at my visit. Baburin and Punin were both unwell: Punin had a headache, and he was lying curled up on the sofa, with his head tied up in a spotted handkerchief, and strips of cucumber applied to his temples. Baburin was suffering from a bilious attack; all yellow, almost dusky, with dark rings round his eyes, with scowling brow and unshaven chin—he did not look much like a bridegroom! I tried to go away. . . . But they would not let me go, and even made tea. I spent anything but a cheerful evening. Musa, it is true, had no ailment, and was less shy than usual too, but she was obviously vexed, angry. . . . At last she could not restrain herself, and, as she handed me a cup of tea, she whispered hurriedly: 'You can say what you like, you may try your utmost, you won't make any difference. . . . So there! ' I looked at her in astonishment, and, seizing a favourable moment, asked her, also in a whisper, 'What's the meaning of your words? ' 'I'll tell you,' she answered, and her black eyes, gleaming angrily under her frowning brows, were fastened for an instant on my face, and turned away at once: 'the meaning is that I heard all you said there to-day, and thank you for nothing, and things won't be as you'd have them, anyway.' 'You were there,' broke from me unconsciously. . . . But at this point Baburin's attention was caught, and he glanced in our direction. Musa walked away from me.

Ten minutes later she managed to come near me again. She seemed to enjoy saying bold and dangerous things to me, and saying them in the presence of her protector, under his vigilant eye, only exercising barely enough caution not to arouse his suspicions. It is well known that walking on the brink, on the very edge, of the precipice is woman's favourite pastime. 'Yes, I was there,' whispered Musa, without any change of countenance, except that her nostrils were faintly quivering and her lips twitching. 'Yes, and if Paramon Semyonitch asks me what I am whispering about with you, I'd tell him this minute. What do I care? '

'Be more careful,' I besought her. 'I really believe they are noticing.'

'I tell you, I'm quite ready to tell them everything. And who's noticing? One's stretching his neck off the pillow, like a sick duck, and hears nothing; and the other's deep in philosophy. Don't you be afraid! ' Musa's voice rose a little, and her cheeks gradually flushed a sort of malignant, dusky red; and this suited her marvellously, and never had she been so pretty. As she cleared the table, and set the cups and saucers in their places, she moved swiftly about the room; there was something challenging about her light, free and easy movement. 'You may criticise me as you like,' she seemed to say; 'but I'm going my own way, and I'm not afraid of you.'

I cannot disguise the fact that I found Musa bewitching just that evening. 'Yes,' I mused; 'she's a little spitfire—she's a new type. . . . She's—exquisite. Those hands know how to deal a blow, I dare say. . . . What of it! No matter! '

'Paramon Semyonitch,' she cried suddenly, 'isn't a republic an empire in which every one does as he chooses? '

'A republic is not an empire,' answered Baburin, raising his head, and contracting his brows; 'it is a . . . form of society in which everything rests on law and justice.'

'Then,' Musa pursued, 'in a republic no one can oppress any one else? '

'No.'

'And every one is free to dispose of himself? '

'Quite free.'

'Ah! that's all I wanted to know.'

'Why do you want to know? '

'Oh, I wanted to—I wanted *you* to tell me that.'

'Our young lady is anxious to learn,' Punin observed from the sofa.

When I went out into the passage Musa accompanied me, not, of course, from politeness, but with the same malicious intent. I asked her, as I took leave, 'Can you really love him so much?'

'Whether I love him, or whether I don't, that's·*my* affair,' she answered. 'What is to be, will be.'

'Mind what you're about; don't play with fire . . . you'll get burnt.'

'Better be burnt than frozen. You . . . with your good advice! And how can you tell he won't marry me? How do you know I so particularly want to get married? If I am ruined . . . what business is it of yours?'

She slammed the door after me.

I remember that on the way home I reflected with some pleasure that my friend Vladimir Tarhov might find things rather hot for him with his new type. . . . He ought to have to pay something for his happiness!

That he would be happy, I was—regretfully—unable to doubt.

Three days passed by. I was sitting in my room at my writing-table, and not so much working as getting myself ready for lunch. . . . I heard a rustle, lifted my head, and I was stupefied. Before me—rigid, terrible, white as chalk, stood an apparition . . . Punin. His half-closed eyes were looking at me, blinking slowly; they expressed a senseless terror, the terror of a frightened hare, and his arms hung at his sides like sticks.

'Nikander Vavilitch! what is the matter with you? How did you come here? Did no one see you? What has happened? Do speak!'

'She has run away,' Punin articulated in a hoarse, hardly audible voice.

'What do you say?'

'She has run away,' he repeated.

'Who?'

'Musa. She went away in the night, and left a note.'

'A note?'

'Yes. "I thank you," she said, "but I am not coming back again. Don't look for me." We ran up and down; we questioned the cook; she knew nothing. I can't speak loud; you must excuse me. I've lost my voice.'

'Musa Pavlovna has left you!' I exclaimed. 'Nonsense! Mr. Baburin must be in despair. What does he intend to do now?'

'He has no intention of doing anything. I wanted to run to the Governor-general: he forbade it. I wanted to give information to the police; he forbade that too, and got very angry. He says, "She's free." He says, "I don't want to constrain her." He has even gone to work, to his office. But he looks more dead than alive. He loved her terribly. . . . Oh, oh, we both loved her!'

Here Punin for the first time showed that he was not a wooden image, but a live man; he lifted both his fists in the air, and brought them down on his pate, which shone like ivory.

'Ungrateful girl!' he groaned; 'who was it gave you food and drink, clothed you, and brought you up? who cared for you, would have given all his life, all his soul . . . And you have forgotten it all! To cast me off, truly, were no great matter, but Paramon Semyonitch, Paramon . . .'

I begged him to sit down, to rest.

Punin shook his head. 'No, I won't. I have come to you . . . I don't know what for. I'm like one distraught; to stay at home alone is fearful; what am I to do with myself? I stand in the middle of the room, shut my eyes, and call, " Musa! Musotchka! " That's the way to go out of one's mind. But no, why am I talking nonsense? I know why I have come to you. You know, the other day you read me that thrice-accursed poem . . . you remember, where there is talk of an old husband. What did you do that for? Did you know something then . . . or guessed something? ' Punin glanced at me. 'Piotr Petrovitch,' he cried suddenly, and he began trembling all over, 'you know, perhaps, where she is. Kind friend, tell me whom she has gone to! '

I was disconcerted, and could not help dropping my eyes. . . .

'Perhaps she said something in her letter,' I began. . . .

'She said she was leaving us because she loved some one else! Dear, good friend, you know, surely, where she is? Save her, let us go to her; we will persuade her. Only think what a man she's bringing to ruin.'

Punin all at once flushed crimson, the blood seemed to rush to his head, he plumped heavily down on his knees. 'Save us, friend, let us go to her.'

My servant appeared in the doorway, and stood still in amazement.

I had no little trouble to get Punin on to his feet again, to convince him that, even if I did suspect something, still it would not do to act like that, on the spur of the moment, especially both together—that would only spoil all our efforts—that I was ready to do my best, but would not answer for anything. Punin did not oppose me, nor did he indeed hear me; he only repeated from time to time in his broken voice, ' Save her, save her and Paramon Semyonitch.' At last he began to cry. 'Tell me at least one thing,' he asked . . . ' is *he* handsome, young? '

' Yes, he is young,' I answered.

' He is young,' repeated Punin, smearing the tears over his cheeks; ' and she is young. . . . It's from that that all the trouble's sprung! '

This rhyme came by chance; poor Punin was in no mood for versifying. I would have given a good deal to hear his rhapsodical eloquence again, or even his almost noiseless laugh. . . . Alas! his eloquence was quenched for ever, and I never heard his laugh again.

I promised to let him know, as soon as I should find out anything positive. . . . Tarhov's name I did not, however, mention. Punin suddenly collapsed completely. ' Very good, very good, sir, thank you,' he said with a pitiful face, using the word ' sir,' which he had never done before; ' only mind, sir, do not say anything to Paramon Semyonitch . . . or he'll be angry. In one word, he has forbidden it. Good-bye, sir.'

As he got up and turned his back to me, Punin struck me as such a poor feeble creature, that I positively marvelled; he limped with both legs, and doubled up at each step. . . .

' It's a bad look-out. It's the end of him, that's what it means,' I thought.

Though I had promised Punin to trace Musa, yet as I set off the same day to Tarhov's, I had not the slightest expectation of learning anything, as I considered it certain that either I should not find him at home, or that he would refuse to see me. My supposition turned out to be a mistaken one. I found Tarhov at home; he received me, and I found out indeed all I wanted to know; but there was nothing gained by that. Directly I crossed the threshold of his door, Tarhov came resolutely, rapidly, to meet me, and his eyes sparkling and glowing, his face grown handsomer and radiant, he said firmly and briskly: 'Listen, Petya, my boy; I guess what you've come for, and what you want to talk about; but I give you warning, if you say a single word about her, or about her action, or about what, according to you, is the course dictated to me by common sense, we're friends no longer, we're not even acquainted, and I shall beg you to treat me as a stranger.'

I looked at Tarhov; he was quivering all over inwardly, like a tightly drawn harpstring; he was tingling all over, hardly could he hold back the tide of brimming youth and passion; violent, ecstatic happiness had burst into his soul, and had taken full possession of him—and he of it.

'Is that your final decision?' I pronounced mournfully.

'Yes, Petya, my boy, it's final.'

'In that case, there's nothing for me but to say good-bye.'

Tarhov faintly dropped his eyelids. . . . He was too happy at that moment.

'Good-bye, Petya, old boy,' he said, a little through his nose, with a candid smile and a gay flash of all his white teeth.

What was I to do? I left him to his 'happiness.' As I slammed the door after me the other door of the room slammed also—I heard it.

It was with a heavy heart that I trudged off next day to see my luckless acquaintances. I secretly hoped—such is human weakness—that I should not find them at home, and again I was mistaken. Both were at home. The change that had taken place in them during the last three days must have struck any one. Punin looked ghastly white and flabby. His talkativeness had completely vanished. He spoke listlessly, feebly, still in the same husky voice, and looked somehow lost and bewildered. Baburin, on the contrary, seemed shrunk into himself, and blacker than ever; taciturn at the best of times, he uttered nothing now but a few abrupt sounds; an expression of stony severity seemed to have frozen on his countenance.

I felt it impossible to be silent; but what was there to say? I confined myself to whispering to Punin, 'I have discovered nothing, and my advice to you is to give up all hope.' Punin glanced at me with his swollen, red little eyes—the only red left in his face—muttered something inaudible, and hobbled away. Baburin most likely guessed what I had been speaking about to Punin, and opening his lips, which were tightly compressed, as though glued together, he pronounced, in a deliberate voice, 'My dear sir, since your last visit to us, something disagreeable has happened to us; our young friend, Musa Pavlovna Vinogradov, finding it no longer convenient to live with us, has decided to leave us, and has given us a written communication to that effect. Not considering that we have any right to hinder her doing so, we have left her to act according to her own views of what is best. We trust that she may be happy,' he added, with some effort; ' and I humbly beg you not to allude to the subject, as any such references are useless, and even painful.'

' So he too, like Tarhov, forbids my speaking of Musa,' was the thought that struck me, and I could not help wondering inwardly. He might well prize Zeno so highly. I wished to impart to him some facts about that sage, but my tongue would not form the words, and it did well.

I soon went about my business. At parting neither Punin nor Baburin said, ' Till we meet! ' both with once voice pronounced, ' Good-bye.'

Punin even returned me a volume of the *Telegraph* I had brought him, as much to say, ' he had no need of anything of that kind now.'

A week later I had a curious encounter. An early spring had set in abruptly; at midday the heat rose to eighteen degrees Réaumur. Everything was turning green, and shooting up out of the spongy, damp earth. I hired a horse at the riding-school, and went out for a ride into the outskirts of the town, towards the Vorobyov hills. On the road I was met by a little cart, drawn by a pair of spirited ponies, splashed with mud up to their ears, with plaited tails, and red ribbons in their manes and forelocks. Their harness was such as sportsmen affect, with copper discs and tassels; they were being driven by a smart young driver, in a blue tunic without sleeves, a yellow striped silk shirt, and a low felt hat with peacock's feathers round the crown. Beside him sat a girl of the artisan or merchant class, in a flowered silk jacket, with a big blue handkerchief on her head—and she was simply bubbling over with mirth. The driver was laughing too. I drew my horse on one side, but did not, however, take particular notice of the swiftly passing, merry couple, when, all at once, the young man shouted to his ponies. . . . Why, that was Tarhov's voice! I looked round. . . . Yes, it was he; unmistakably he, dressed up as a peasant, and beside him—wasn't it Musa?

But at that instant their ponies quickened their pace, and they were out of my sight in a minute. I tried to put my horse into a gallop in pursuit of them, but it was an old riding-school hack, that shambled from side to side as it moved; it went more slowly galloping than trotting.

' Enjoy yourselves, my dear friends! ' I muttered through my teeth.

I ought to observe that I had not seen Tarhov during the whole week, though I had been three times to his rooms. He was never at home. Baburin and Punin I had not seen either. . . . I had not been to see them.

I caught cold on my ride; though it was very warm, there was a piercing wind. I was dangerously ill, and when I recovered I went with my grandmother into the country ' to feed up,' by the doctor's advice. I did not get to Moscow again; in the autumn I was transferred to the Petersburg university.

III

1849

NOT SEVEN, but fully twelve years had passed by, and I was in my thirty-second year. My grandmother had long been dead; I was living in Petersburg, with a host in the Department of Home Affairs. Tarhov I had lost sight of; he had gone into the army, and lived almost always in the provinces. We had met twice, as old friends, glad to see each other; but we had not touched on the past in our talk. At the time of our last meeting he was, if I remember right, already a married man.

One sultry summer day I was sauntering along Gorohov Street, cursing my official duties for keeping me in Petersburg, and the heat and stench and dust of the city. A funeral barred my way. It consisted of a solitary car, that is, to be accurate, of a decrepit hearse, on which a poor-looking wooden coffin, half-covered with a threadbare black cloth, was shaking up and down as it was jolted violently over the uneven pavement. An old man with a white head was walking alone after the hearse.

I looked at him. . . . His face seemed familiar. . . . He too turned his eyes upon me. . . . Merciful heavens! it was Baburin!

I took off my hat, went up to him, mentioned my name, and walked along beside him.

' Whom are you burying? ' I asked.

' Nikander Vavilitch Punin,' he answered.

I felt, I knew beforehand, that he would utter that name, and yet it set my heart aching. I felt melancholy, and yet I was glad that chance had enabled me to pay my last respects to my old friend. . . .

' May I go with you, Paramon Semyonitch? '

' You may. . . . I was following him alone; now there'll be two of us.'

Our walk lasted more than an hour. My companion moved forward, without lifting his eyes or opening his lips. He had become quite an old man since I had seen him last; his deeply furrowed, copper-coloured face stood out sharply against his white hair. Signs of a life of toil and suffering, of continual struggle, could be seen in Baburin's whole figure; want and poverty had worked cruel havoc with him. When everything was over, when what was Punin had disappeared for ever in the damp . . . yes, undoubtedly damp earth of the Smolensky cemetery, Baburin, after standing a couple of minutes with bowed, uncovered head before the newly risen mound of sandy clay, turned to me his emaciated, as it were embittered, face, his dry, sunken eyes, thanked me grimly, and was about to move away; but I detained him.

' Where do you live, Paramon Semyonitch? Let me come and see you. I had no idea you were living in Petersburg. We could recall old days, and talk of our dead friend.'

Baburin did not answer me at once.

'It's two years since I found my way to Petersburg,' he observed at last; 'I live at the very end of the town. However, if you really care to visit me, come.' He gave me his address. 'Come in the evening; in the evening we are always at home . . . both of us.'

'Both of you?'

'I am married. My wife is not very well to-day, and that's why she did not come too. Though, indeed, it's quite enough for one person to go through this empty formality, this ceremony. As if anybody believed in it all!'

I was a little surprised at Baburin's last words, but I said nothing, called a cab, and proposed to Baburin to take him home; but he refused.

The same day I went in the evening to see him. All the way there I was thinking of Punin. I recalled how I had met him the first time, and how ecstatic and amusing he was in those days; and afterwards in Moscow how subdued he had grown—especially the last time I saw him; and now he had made his last reckoning with life;—life is in grim earnest, it seems! Baburin was living in the Viborgsky quarter, in a little house which reminded me of the Moscow 'nest': the Petersburg abode was almost shabbier in appearance. When I went into his room he was sitting on a chair in a corner with his hands on his knees; a tallow candle, burning low, dimly lighted up his bowed, white head. He heard the sound of my footsteps, started up, and welcomed me more warmly than I had expected. A few moments later his wife came in; I recognized her at once as Musa—and only then understood why Baburin had invited me to come; he wanted to show me that he had after all come by his own.

Musa was greatly changed—in face, in voice, and in manners; but her eyes were changed most of all. In old times they had darted about like live creatures, those malicious, beautiful eyes; they had gleamed stealthily, but brilliantly; their glance had pierced, like a pin-prick. . . . Now they looked at one directly, calmly, steadily; their black centres had lost their lustre. 'I am broken in, I am tame, I am good,' her soft and dull gaze seemed to say. Her continued, submissive smile told the same story. And her dress, too, was subdued; brown, with little spots on it. She came up to me, asked me whether I knew her. She obviously felt no embarrassment, and not because she had lost a sense of shame or memory of the past, but simply because all petty self-consciousness had left her.

Musa talked a great deal about Punin, talked in an even voice, which too had lost its fire. I learned that of late years he had become very feeble, had almost sunk into childishness, so much so that he was miserable if he had not toys to play with; they persuaded him, it is true, that he made them out of waste stuff for sale . . . but he really played with them himself. His passion for poetry, however, never died out, and he kept his memory for nothing but verses; a few days before his death he recited a passage from the *Rossiad;* but Pushkin he feared, as children fear bogies. His devotion to

Baburin had also remained undiminished; he worshipped him as much as ever, and even at the last, wrapped about by the chill and dark of the end, he had faltered with halting tongue, ' benefactor! ' I learned also from Musa that soon after the Moscow episode, it had been Baburin's fate once more to wander all over Russia, continually tossed from one private situation to another; that in Petersburg, too, he had been again in a situation, in a private business, which situation he had, however, been obliged to leave a few days before, owing to some unpleasantness with his employer: Baburin had ventured to stand up for the workpeople. . . . The invariable smile, with which Musa accompanied her words, set me musing mournfully; it put the finishing touch to the impression made on me by her husband's appearance. They had hard work, the two of them, to make a bare living— there was no doubt of it. He took very little part in our conversation; he seemed more preoccupied than grieved. . . . Something was worrying him.

' Paramon Semyonitch, come here,' said the cook, suddenly appearing in the doorway.

' What is it? what's wanted? ' he asked in alarm.

' Come here,' the cook repeated insistently and meaningly. Baburin buttoned up his coat and went out.

When I was left alone with Musa, she looked at me with a somewhat changed glance, and observed in a voice which was also changed, and with no smile: ' I don't know, Piotr Petrovitch, what you think of me now, but I dare say you remember what I used to be. . . . I was self-confident, light-hearted . . . and not good; I wanted to live for my own pleasure. But I want to tell you this: when I was abandoned, and was like one lost, and was only waiting for God to take me, or to pluck up spirit to make an end of myself,—once more, just as in Voronezh, I met with Paramon Semyonitch —and he saved me once again. . . . Not a word that could wound me did I hear from him, not a word of reproach; he asked nothing of me—I was not worthy of that; but he loved me . . . and I became his wife. What was I to do? I had failed of dying; and I could not live either after my own choice. . . . What was I to do with myself? Even so—it was a mercy to be thankful for. That is all.'

She ceased, turned away for an instant . . . the same submissive smile came back to her lips. ' Whether life's easy for me, you needn't ask,' was the meaning I fancied now in that smile.

The conversation passed to ordinary subjects. Musa told me that Punin had left a cat that he had been very fond of, and that ever since his death she had gone up to the attic and stayed there, mewing incessantly, as though she were calling some one . . . the neighbours were very much scared, and fancied that it was Punin's soul that had passed into the cat.

' Paramon Semyonitch is worried about something,' I said at last.

' Oh, you noticed it? '—Musa sighed. ' He cannot help being worried. I need hardly tell you that Paramon Semyonitch has remained faithful to his principles. . . . The present condition of affairs can but strengthen them.' (Musa expressed herself quite differently now from in the old days in

Moscow; there was a literary, bookish flavour in her phrases.) ' I don't know, though, whether I can rely upon you, and how you will receive . . .'

' Why should you imagine you cannot rely upon me? '

' Well, you are in the government service—you are an official.'

' Well, what of that? '

' You are, consequently, loyal to the government.'

I marvelled inwardly . . . at Musa's innocence. ' As to my attitude to the government, which is not even aware of my existence, I won't enlarge upon that,' I observed; 'but you may set your mind at rest. I will make no bad use of your confidence. I sympathise with your husband's ideas . . . more than you suppose.'

Musa shook her head.

' Yes; that's all so,' she began, not without hesitation; ' but you see it's like this. Paramon Semyonitch's ideas will shortly, it may be, find expression in action. They can no longer be hidden under a bushel. There are comrades whom we cannot now abandon . . .'

Musa suddenly ceased speaking, as though she had bitten her tongue. Her last words had amazed and a little alarmed me. Most likely my face showed what I was feeling—and Musa noticed it.

As I have said already, our interview took place in the year 1849. Many people still remember what a disturbed and difficult time that was, and by what incidents it was signalised in St. Petersburg. I had been struck myself by certain peculiarities in Baburin's behaviour, in his whole demeanour. Twice he had referred to governmental action, to personages in high authority, with such intense bitterness and hatred, with such loathing, that I had been dumbfounded. . . .

'Well? ' he asked me suddenly: ' did you set your peasants free? '

I was obliged to confess I had not.

' Why, I suppose your granny's dead, isn't she? '

I was obliged to admit that she was.

'To be sure, you noble gentlemen,' Baburin muttered between his teeth, '. . . use other men's hands . . . to poke up your fire . . . that's what you like.'

In the most conspicuous place in his room hung the well-known lithograph portrait of Belinsky; on the table lay a volume of the old *Polar Star*, edited by Bestuzhev.

A long time passed, and Baburin did not come back after the cook had called him away. Musa looked several times uneasily towards the door by which he had gone out. At last she could bear it no longer; she got up, and with an apology she too went out by the same door. A quarter of an hour later she came back with her husband; the faces of both, so at least I thought, looked troubled. But all of a sudden Baburin's face assumed a different, an intensely bitter, almost frenzied expression.

' What will be the end of it? ' he began all at once in a jerky, sobbing voice, utterly unlike him, while his wild eyes shifted restlessly about him. ' One goes on living and living, and hoping that maybe it'll be better, that one will breathe more freely; but it's quite the other way—everything gets worse and worse! They have *squeezed* us right up to the wall! In my youth I bore all with patience; they . . . maybe . . . beat me . . . even . . . yes! ' he added, turning sharply round on his heels and swooping down as it were, upon me: ' I, a man of full age, was subjected to corporal punishment . . . yes;—of other wrongs I will not speak. . . . But is there really nothing before us but to go back to those old times again? The way they are treating the young people now! . . . Yes, it breaks down all endurance at last. . . . It breaks it down! Yes! Wait a bit! '

I had never seen Baburin in such a condition. Musa turned positively white. . . . Baburin suddenly cleared his throat, and sank down into a seat. Not wishing to constrain either him or Musa by my presence, I decided to go, and was just saying good-bye to them, when the door into the next room suddenly opened, and a head appeared. . . . It was not the cook's head, but the dishevelled and terrified-looking head of a young man.

' Something's wrong, Baburin, something's wrong! ' he faltered hurriedly, then vanished at once on perceiving my unfamiliar figure.

Baburin rushed after the young man. I pressed Musa's hand warmly, and withdrew, with presentiments of evil in my heart.

' Come to-morrow,' she whispered anxiously.

' I certainly will come,' I answered.

I was still in bed next morning, when my man handed me a letter from Musa.

' *Dear Piotr Petrovitch!* ' she wrote: ' *Paramon Semyonitch has been this night arrested by the police and carried off to the fortress, or I don't know where; they did not tell me. They ransacked all our papers, sealed up a great many, and took them away with them. It has been the same with our books and letters. They say a mass of people have been arrested in the town. You can fancy how I feel. It is well Nikander Vavilitch did not live to see it! He was taken just in time. Advise me what I am to do. For myself I am not afraid—I shall not die of starvation—but the thought of Paramon Semyonitch gives me no rest. Come, please, if only you are not afraid to visit people in our position.—Yours faithfully,*

MUSA BABURIN.'

Half an hour later I was with Musa. On seeing me she held out her hand, and, though she did not utter a word, a look of gratitude flitted over her face. She was wearing the same clothes as on the previous day; there was every sign that she had not been to bed or slept all night. Her eyes were red, but from sleeplessness, not from tears. She had not been crying. She was in no mood for weeping. She wanted to act, wanted to struggle with the calamity that had fallen upon them: the old, energetic, self-willed Musa had risen up in her again. She had no time even to be indignant, though she was choking with indignation. How to assist Baburin, to whom to appeal so as to soften his lot—she could think of nothing else. She wanted to go instantly,

... to petition, ... demand. ... But where to go, whom to petition, what to demand—this was what she wanted to hear from me, this was what she wanted to consult me about.

I began by counselling her ... to have patience. For the first moment there was nothing left to be done but to wait, and, as far as might be, to make inquiries; and to take any decisive step now when the affair had scarcely begun, and hardly yet taken shape, would be simply senseless, irrational. To hope for any success was irrational, even if I had been a person of much more importance and influence, ... but what could I, a petty official, do? As for her, she was absolutely without any powerful friends. ...

It was no easy matter to make all this plain to her ... but at last she understood my arguments; she understood, too, that I was not prompted by egoistic feeling, when I showed her the uselessness of all efforts.

'But tell me, Musa Pavlovna,' I began, when she sank at last into a chair (till then she had been standing up, as though on the point of setting off at once to the aid of Baburin), 'how Paramon Semyonitch, at his age, comes to be mixed up in such an affair? I feel sure that there are none but young people implicated in it, like the one who came in yesterday to warn you. ...'

'Those young people are our friends!' cried Musa, and her eyes flashed and darted as of old. Something strong, irrepressible, seemed, as it were, to rise up from the bottom of her soul, ... and I suddenly recalled the expression 'a new type,' which Tarhov had once used of her. 'Years are of no consequence when it is a matter of political principles!' Musa laid a special stress on these last two words. One might fancy that in all her sorrow it was not unpleasing to her to show herself before me in this new, unlooked-for character—in the character of a cultivated and mature woman, fit wife of a republican! ... 'Some old men are younger than some young ones,' she pursued, 'more capable of sacrifice. ... But that's not the point.'

'I think, Musa Pavlovna,' I observed, 'that you are exaggerating a little. Knowing the character of Paramon Semyonitch, I should have felt sure beforehand that he would sympathise with every ... sincere impulse; but, on the other hand, I have always regarded him as a man of sense. ... Surely he cannot fail to realise all the impracticability, all the absurdity of conspiracies in Russia? In his position, in his calling ...'

'Oh, of course,' Musa interrupted, with bitterness in her voice, 'he is a working man; and in Russia it is only permissible for noblemen to take part in conspiracies, ... as, for instance, in that of the fourteenth of December, ... that's what you meant to say.'

'In that case, what do you complain of now?' almost broke from my lips, ... but I restrained myself. 'Do you consider that the result of the fourteenth of December was such as to encourage other such attempts?' I said aloud.

Musa frowned. 'It is no good talking to you about it,' was what I read in her downcast face.

'Is Paramon Semyonitch very seriously compromised?' I ventured to ask her. Musa made no reply. . . . A hungry, savage mewing was heard from the attic.

Musa started. 'Ah, it is a good thing Nikander Vavilitch did not see all this!' she moaned almost despairingly. 'He did not see how violently in the night they seized his benefactor, our benefactor—maybe, the best and truest man in the whole world,—he did not see how they treated that noble man at his age, how rudely they addressed him, . . . how they threatened him, and the threats they used to him!—only because he was a working man! That young officer, too, was no doubt just such an unprincipled, heartless wretch as I have known in my life. . . .'

Musa's voice broke. She was quivering all over like a leaf.

Her long-suppressed indignation broke out at last; old memories stirred up, brought to the surface by the general tumult of her soul, showed themselves alive within her. . . . But the conviction I carried off at that moment was that the 'new type' was still the same, still the same passionate, impulsive nature. . . . Only the impulses by which Musa was carried away were not the same as in the days of her youth. What on my first visit I had taken for resignation, for meekness, and what really was so—the subdued, lustreless glance, the cold voice, the quietness and simplicity—all that had significance only in relation to the past, to what would never return. . . .

Now it was the present asserted itself.

I tried to soothe Musa, tried to put our conversation on a more practical level. Some steps must be taken that could not be postponed; we must find out exactly where Baburin was; and then secure both for him and for Musa the means of subsistence. All this presented no inconsiderable difficulty; what was needed was not to find money, but work, which is, as we all know, a far more complicated problem. . . .

I left Musa with a perfect swarm of reflections in my head.

I soon learned that Baburin was in the fortress.

The proceedings began, . . . dragged on. I saw Musa several times every week. She had several interviews with her husband. But just at the moment of the decision of the whole melancholy affair, I was not in Petersburg. Unforeseen business had obliged me to set off to the south of Russia. During my absence I heard that Baburin had been acquitted at the trial; it appeared that all that could be proved against him was, that young people regarding him as a person unlikely to awaken suspicion, had sometimes held meetings at his house, and he had been present at their meetings; he was, however, by administrative order sent into exile in one of the western provinces of Siberia. Musa went with him.

'Paramon Semyonitch did not wish it,' she wrote to me; 'as, according to his ideas, no one ought to sacrifice self for another person, and not for a cause; but I told him there was no question of sacrifice at all. When I said to him in Moscow that I would be his wife, I thought to myself—for ever, indissolubly! So indissoluble it must be till the end of our days. . . .'

IV
1861

TWELVE MORE YEARS passed by. . . . Every one in Russia knows, and will ever remember, what passed between the years 1849 and 1861. In my personal life, too, many changes took place, on which, however, there is no need to enlarge. New interests came into it, new cares. . . . The Baburin couple first fell into the background, then passed out of my mind altogether. Yet I kept up a correspondence with Musa—at very long intervals, however. Sometimes more than a year passed without any tidings of her or of her husband. I heard that soon after 1855 he received permission to return to Russia; but that he preferred to remain in the little Siberian town, where he had been flung by destiny, and where he had apparently made himself a home, and found a haven and a sphere of activity. . . .

And, lo and behold! towards the end of March in 1861, I received the following letter from Musa:—

'It is so long since I have written to you, most honoured Piotr Petrovitch, that I do not even know whether you are still living; and if you are living, have you not forgotten our existence? But no matter; I cannot resist writing to you to-day. Everything till now has gone on with us in the same old way: Paramon Semyonitch and I have been always busy with our schools, which are gradually making good progress; besides that, Paramon Semyonitch was taken up with reading and correspondence and his usual discussions with the Old-believers, members of the clergy, and Polish exiles; his health has been fairly good. . . . So has mine. But yesterday! the manifesto of the 19th of February reached us! We had long been on the look-out for it. Rumours had reached us long before of what was being done among you in Petersburg, . . . but yet I can't describe what it was! You know my husband well; he was not in the least changed by his misfortune; on the contrary, he has grown even stronger and more energetic, and has a will as strong as iron, but at this he could not restrain himself! His hands shook as he read it; then he embraced me three times, and three times he kissed me, tried to say something—but no! he could not! and ended by bursting into tears, which was very astounding to see, and suddenly he shouted, " Hurrah! hurrah! God save the Tsar! " Yes, Piotr Petrovitch, those were his very words! Then he went on: " Now lettest Thou Thy servant depart " . . . and again: " This is the first step, others are bound to follow it "; and, just as he was, bareheaded, ran to tell the great news to our friends. There was a bitter frost, and even a snowstorm coming on. I tried to prevent him, but he would not listen to me. And when he came home, he was all covered with snow, his hair, his face, and his beard—he has a beard right down to his chest now—and the tears were positively frozen on his cheeks! But he was very lively and cheerful, and told me to uncork a bottle of home-made champagne, and he drank with our friends that he had brought back with him, to the health of the Tsar and of Russia, and all free Russians; and taking the glass, and fixing his eyes on the ground, he said: "Nikander, Nikander, do you hear? There are no slaves in Russia any more! Rejoice in the grave, old comrade!" And much more he said; to the effect that his "expectations were fulfilled!" He said, too, that now there could be no turning back; that this was in its way a pledge or promise. . . . I don't remember everything, but it is long since I have seen him so happy. And so I made up my mind to write to you, so that you might know how we have been rejoicing and exulting in the remote Siberian wilds, so that you might rejoice with us. . . .'

This letter I received at the end of March. At the beginning of May another very brief letter arrived from Musa. She informed me that her husband, Paramon Semyonitch Baburin, had taken cold on the very day of the arrival of the manifesto, and died on the 12th of April of inflammation of the lungs, in the 67th year of his age. She added that she intended to remain where his body lay at rest, and to go on with the work he had bequeathed her, since such was the last wish of Paramon Semyonitch, and that was her only law.

Since then I have heard no more of Musa.

PARIS, 1874.

OLD PORTRAITS

About thirty miles from our village there lived, many years ago, a distant cousin of my mother's, a retired officer of the Guards, and rather wealthy landowner, Alexey Sergeitch Teliegin. He lived on his estate and birthplace, Suhodol, did not go out anywhere, and so did not visit us; but I used to be sent, twice a year, to pay him my respects—at first with my tutor, but later on alone. Alexey Sergeitch always gave me a very cordial reception, and I used to stay three or four days at a time with him. He was an old man even when I first made his acquaintance; I was twelve, I remember, on my first visit, and he was then over seventy. He was born in the days of the Empress Elisabeth—in the last year of her reign. He lived alone with his wife, Malania Pavlovna; she was ten years younger than he. They had two daughters; but their daughters had been long married, and rarely visited Suhodol; they were not on the best of terms with their parents, and Alexey Sergeitch hardly ever mentioned their names.

I see, even now, the old-fashioned house, a typical manor-house of the steppes. One story in height, with immense attics, it was built at the beginning of this century, of amazingly thick beams of pine,—such beams came in plenty in those days from the Zhizdrinsky pine-forests; they have passed out of memory now! It was very spacious, and contained a great number of rooms, rather low-pitched and dark, it is true; the windows in the walls had been made small for the sake of greater warmth. In the usual fashion (I ought rather to say, in what was then the usual fashion), the offices and house-serfs' huts surrounded the manorial house on all sides, and the garden was close to it—a small garden, but containing fine fruit-trees, juicy apples, and pipless pears. The flat steppe of rich, black earth stretched for ten miles round. No lofty object for the eye; not a tree, nor even a belfry; somewhere, maybe, jutting up, a windmill, with rents in its sails; truly, well-named Suhodol, or Dry-flat! Inside the house the rooms were filled with ordinary, simple furniture; somewhat unusual was the milestone-post that stood in the window of the drawing-room, with the following inscription:—' If you walk sixty-eight times round this drawing-room you will have gone a mile; if you walk eighty-seven times from the furthest corner of the parlour to the right-hand corner of the billiard-room, you will have gone a mile,' and so on. But what most of all impressed a guest at the house for the first time was the immense collection of pictures hanging on the walls, for the most part works of the so-called Italian masters: all old-fashioned landscapes of a sort, or mythological and religious subjects. But all these pictures were very dark, and even cracked with age;—in one, all that met the eye was some patches of flesh-colour; in another, undulating red draperies on an unseen body; or an arch which seemed to be suspended in the air; or a dishevelled tree with blue foliage; or the bosom of a nymph with an immense breast, like the lid of a soup-tureen; a cut water-melon, with black seeds; a turban, with a feather in it, above a horse's head; or the

343

gigantic brown leg of an apostle, suddenly thrust out, with a muscular calf, and toes turned upwards. In the drawing-room in the place of honour hung a portrait of the Empress Catherine II., full length; a copy of the famous portrait by Lampi—an object of the special reverence, one might say the adoration, of the master of the house. From the ceiling hung glass lustres in bronze settings, very small and very dusty.

Alexey Sergeitch himself was a stumpy, paunchy little old man, with a chubby face of one uniform tint, yet pleasant, with drawn-in lips, and very lively little eyes under high eyebrows. He wore his scanty locks combed to the back of his head; it was only since 1812 that he had given up wearing powder. Alexey Sergeitch invariably wore a grey 'redingote,' with three capes falling over his shoulders, a striped waistcoat, chamois-leather breeches, and high boots of dark red morocco, with heart-shaped scallops and tassels at the tops; he wore a white muslin cravat, a jabot, lace cuffs, and two gold English 'turnip watches,' one in each pocket of his waistcoat. In his right hand he usually carried an enamelled snuff-box full of 'Spanish' snuff, and his left hand leaned on a cane with a silver-chased knob, worn smooth by long use. Alexey Sergeitch had a little nasal, piping voice, and an invariable smile—kindly, but, as it were, condescending, and not without a certain self-complacent dignity. His laugh, too, was kindly—a shrill little laugh that tinkled like glass beads. Courteous and affable he was to the last degree—in the old-fashioned manner of the days of Catherine—and he moved his hands with slow, rounded gestures, also in the old style. His legs were so weak that he could not walk, but ran with hurried little steps from one armchair to another, in which he would suddenly sit down, or rather fall softly, like a cushion.

As I have said already, Alexey Sergeitch went out nowhere, and saw very little of his neighbours, though he liked society, for he was very fond of talking! It is true that he had society in plenty in his own house; various Nikanor Nikanoritchs, Sevastiey Sevastietchs, Fedulitchs, Miheitchs, all poor gentlemen in shabby cossack coats and camisoles, often from the master's wardrobe, lived under his roof, to say nothing of the poor gentlewomen in chintz gowns, black kerchiefs thrown over their shoulders, and worsted reticules in their tightly clenched fingers—all sorts of Avdotia Savishnas, Pelagea Mironovnas, and plain Feklushkas and Arinkas, who found a home in the women's quarters. Never less than fifteen persons sat down to Alexey Sergeitch's table. . . . He was such a hospitable man! Among all those dependents two were particularly conspicuous: a dwarf, nicknamed Janus, or the Double-faced, of Danish—or, as some maintained, Jewish—extraction, and the mad Prince L. Contrary to what was customary in those days, the dwarf did nothing to amuse the master or mistress, and was not a jester— quite the opposite; he was always silent, had an ill-tempered and sullen appearance, and scowled and gnashed his teeth directly a question was addressed to him. Alexey Sergeitch called him a philosopher, and positively respected him; at table the dishes were handed to him first, after the guests and master and mistress. 'God has afflicted him,' Alexey Sergeitch used to

say; 'such is His Divine will; but it's not for me to afflict him further.'
'How is he a philosopher?' I asked him once. (Janus didn't take to me;
if I went near him he would fly into a rage, and mutter thickly, 'Stranger!
keep off!') 'Eh, God bless me! isn't he a philosopher?' answered Alexey
Sergeitch. 'Look ye, little sir, how wisely he holds his tongue!' 'But why
is he double-faced?' 'Because, little sir, he has one face on the outside—and
so you, surface-gazers, judge him. . . . But the other, the real face he hides.
And that face I know, and no one else—and I love him for it . . . because
that face is good. You, for instance, look and see nothing . . . but I see
without a word: he is blaming me for something; for he's a severe critic!
And it's always with good reason. That, little sir, you can't understand;
but you may believe an old man like me!' The real history of the two-
faced Janus—where he came from, and how he came into Alexey Sergeitch's
hands—no one knew; but the story of Prince L. was well known to every
one. He went, a lad of twenty, of a wealthy and distinguished family, to
Petersburg, to serve in a regiment of the Guards. At the first levee the
Empress Catherine noticed him, stood still before him, and, pointing at
him with her fan, she said aloud, addressing one of her courtiers, who happened to be near, 'Look, Adam Vassilievitch, what a pretty fellow! a perfect doll!' The poor boy's head was completely turned; when he got home
he ordered his coach out, and, putting on a ribbon of St. Anne, proceeded
to drive all over the town, as though he had reached the pinnacle of fortune. 'Drive over every one,' he shouted to his coachman, 'who does not
move out of the way!' All this was promptly reported to the empress: the
decree went forth that he should be declared insane, and put under the
guardianship of two of his brothers; and they, without a moment's delay,
carried him off to the country, and flung him into a stone cell in chains.
As they wanted to get the benefit of his property, they did not let the
poor wretch out, even when he had completely recovered his balance, and
positively kept him locked up till he really did go out of his mind. But their
evil doings did not prosper; Prince L. outlived his brothers, and, after long
years of adversity, he came into the charge of Alexey Sergeitch, whose
kinsman he was. He was a stout, completely bald man, with a long, thin
nose and prominent blue eyes. He had quite forgotten how to talk—he
simply uttered a sort of inarticulate grumbling; but he sang old-fashioned
Russian ballads beautifully, preserving the silvery freshness of his voice to
extreme old age; and, while he was singing, he pronounced each word
clearly and distinctly. He had attacks at times of a sort of fury, and then
he became terrible: he would stand in the corner, with his face to the wall,
and all perspiring and red—red all down his bald head and down his neck
—he used to go off into vicious chuckles, and, stamping with his feet, order
some one—his brothers probably—to be punished. 'Beat 'em!' he growled
hoarsely, coughing and choking with laughter; 'flog 'em, don't spare 'em!
beat, beat, beat the monsters, my oppressors! That's it! That's it!' On the
day before his death he greatly alarmed and astonished Alexey Sergeitch.
He came, pale and subdued, into his room, and, making him a low obei-

sance, first thanked him for his care and kindness, and then asked him to send for a priest, for death had come to him—he had seen death, and he must forgive every one and purify his soul. 'How did you see death?' muttered Alexey Sergeitch in bewilderment at hearing connected speech from him for the first time. 'In what shape? with a scythe?' 'No,' answered Prince L.; 'a simple old woman in a jacket, but with only one eye in her forehead, and that eye without an eyelid.' And the next day Prince L. actually did die, duly performing everything, and taking leave of every one in a rational and affecting manner. 'That's just how I shall die,' Alexey Sergeitch would sometimes observe. And, as a fact, something of the same sort did happen with him—but of that later.

But now let us go back to our story. Of the neighbours, as I have stated already, Alexey Sergeitch saw little; and they did not care much for him, called him a queer fish, stuck up, and a scoffer, and even a 'martiniste' who recognised no authorities, though they had no clear idea of the meaning of this term. To a certain extent the neighbours were right: Alexey Serge-itch had lived in his Suhodol for almost seventy years on end, and had had hardly anything whatever to do with the existing authorities, with the police or the law-courts. 'Police-courts are for the robber, and discipline for the soldier,' he used to say; 'but I, thank God, am neither robber nor soldier!' Rather queer Alexey Sergeitch certainly was, but the soul within him was by no means a petty one. I will tell you something about him.

To tell the truth, I never knew what were his political opinions, if an expression so modern can be used in reference to him; but, in his own way, he was an aristocrat—more an aristocrat than a typical Russian country gentleman. More than once he expressed his regret that God had not given him a son and heir, 'for the honour of our name, to keep up the family.' In his own room there hung on the wall the family-tree of the Teliegins, with many branches, and a multitude of little circles like apples in a golden frame. 'We Teliegins,' he used to say, 'are an ancient line, from long, long ago: however many there've been of us Teliegins, we have never hung about great men's ante-rooms; we've never bent our backs, or stood about in waiting, nor picked up a living in the courts, nor run after decorations; we've never gone trailing off to Moscow, nor intriguing in Petersburg; we've sat at home, each in his hole, his own man on his own land . . . home-keeping birds, sir!—I myself, though I did serve in the Guards—but not for long, thank you.' Alexey Sergeitch preferred the old days. 'There was more freedom in those days, more decorum; on my honour, I assure you! but since the year eighteen hundred' (why from that year, precisely, he did not explain), 'militarism, the soldiery, have got the upper hand. Our soldier gentlemen stuck some sort of turbans of cocks' feathers on their heads then, and turned like cocks themselves; began binding their necks up as stiff as could be . . . they croak, and roll their eyes—how could they help it, indeed? The other day a police corporal came to me; "I've come to you," says he, "honourable sir," . . . (fancy his thinking to surprise me with that! . . . I know I'm honourable without his telling me!) " I have business with you." And I said to him, " My good sir, you'd better first unfasten the hooks on your collar. Or else, God have mercy on us—you'll sneeze. Ah, what would happen to you! what would happen to you! You'd break off, like a mushroom . . . and I should have to answer for it! " And they do drink, these military gentlemen—oh, oh, oh! I generally order home-made champagne to be given them, because to them, good wine or poor, it's all the same; it runs so smoothly, so quickly, down their throats —how can they distinguish it? And, another thing, they've started sucking at a pap-bottle, smoking a tobacco-pipe. Your military gentleman thrusts his pap-bottle under his moustaches, between his lips, and puffs the smoke out of his nose, his mouth, and even his ears—and fancies himself a hero! There are my sons-in-law—though one of them's a senator, and the other some sort of an administrator over there—they suck the pap-bottle, and they reckon themselves clever fellows too! '

Alexey Sergeitch could not endure smoking; and moreover, he could not endure dogs, especially little dogs. 'If you're a Frenchman, to be sure, you may well keep a lapdog: you run and you skip about here and there, and it runs after you with its tail up . . . but what's the use of it to people like us? ' He was exceedingly neat and particular. Of the Empress Catherine he never spoke but with enthusiasm, and in exalted, rather bookish phraseology: 'Half divine she was, not human! Only look, little sir, at that smile,' he would add, pointing reverentially to Lampi's portrait, 'and you will agree: half divine! I was so fortunate in my life as to be deemed worthy to behold that smile close, and never will it be effaced from my heart! ' And thereupon he would relate anecdotes of the life of Catherine, such as I have never happened to read or hear elsewhere. Here is one of them. Alexey Sergeitch did not permit the slightest allusion to the weaknesses of the great Tsaritsa. 'And, besides,' he exclaimed, 'can one judge of her as of other people? '

One day while she was sitting in her peignoir during her morning toilette, she commanded her hair to be combed. . . . And what do you think? The lady-in-waiting passed the comb through, and sparks of electricity simply showered out! Then she summoned to her presence the court physician Rogerson, who happened to be in waiting at the court, and said to him: 'I am, I know, censured for certain actions; but do you see this electricity? Consequently, as such is my nature and constitution, you can judge for yourself, as you are a doctor, that it is unjust for them to censure me, and they ought to comprehend me! ' The following incident remained indelible in Alexey Sergeitch's memory. He was standing one day on guard indoors, in the palace—he was only sixteen at the time—and behold the empress comes walking past him; he salutes . . . 'and she,' Alexey Sergeitch would exclaim at this point with much feeling, 'smiling at my youth and my zeal, deigned to give me her hand to kiss and patted my cheek, and asked me " who I was? where I came from? of what family? " and then ' . . . here the old man's voice usually broke . . . 'then she bade me greet my mother in her name and thank her for having brought up her children so well. And whether I was on earth or in heaven, and how and where she deigned to vanish, whether she floated away into the heights or went her way into the other apartments . . . to this day I do not know!'

More than once I tried to question Alexey Sergeitch about those far-away times, about the people who made up the empress's circle. . . . But for the most part he edged off the subject. 'What's the use of talking about old times?' he used to say . . . 'it's only making one's self miserable, remembering that then one was a fine young fellow, and now one hasn't a tooth left in one's head. And what is there to say? They were good old times . . . but there, enough of them! And as for those folks—you were asking, you troublesome boy, about the lucky ones!—haven't you seen how a bubble comes up on the water? As long as it lasts and is whole, what colours play upon it! Red, and blue, and yellow—a perfect rainbow or diamond you'd say it was! Only it soon bursts, and there's no trace of it left. And so it was with those folks.'

'But how about Potiomkin?' I once inquired.

Alexey Sergeitch looked grave. 'Potiomkin, Grigory Alexandrovitch, was a statesman, a theologian, a pupil of Catherine's, her cherished creation, one must say. . . . But enough of that, little sir!'

Alexey Sergeitch was a very devout man, and, though it was a great effort, he attended church regularly. Superstition was not noticeable in him; he laughed at omens, the evil eye, and such 'nonsense,' but he did not like a hare to run across his path, and to meet a priest was not altogether agreeable to him. For all that, he was very respectful to clerical persons, and went up to receive their blessing, and even kissed the priest's hand every time, but he was not willing to enter into conversation with them. 'Such an extremely strong odour comes from them,' he explained: 'and I, poor sinner, am fastidious beyond reason; they've such long hair, and all oily, and they comb it out on all sides—they think they show me respect by so doing, and they clear their throats so loudly when they talk—from shyness may be, or I dare say they want to show respect in that way too. And besides, they make one think of one's last hour. And, I don't know how it is, but I still want to go on living. Only, my little sir, don't you repeat my words; we must respect the clergy—it's only fools that don't respect them; and I'm to blame to babble nonsense in my old age.'

Alexey Sergeitch, like most of the noblemen of his day, had received a very slight education; but he had, to some extent, made good the deficiency himself by reading. He read none but Russian books of the end of last century; the more modern authors he thought insipid and deficient in style. . . . While he read, he had placed at his side on a round, one-legged table, a silver tankard of frothing spiced kvas of a special sort, which sent an agreeable fragrance all over the house. He used to put on the end of his nose a pair of big, round spectacles, but in latter years he did not so much read as gaze dreamily over the rims of his spectacles, lifting his eyebrows, chewing his lips, and sighing. Once I caught him weeping with a book on his knees, greatly, I own, to my surprise.

He had recalled these lines:

> '*O pitiful race of man!*
> *Peace is unknown to thee!*
> *Thou canst not find it save*
> *In the dust of the grave. . . .*
> *Bitter, bitter is that sleep!*
> *Rest, rest in death . . . but living weep!*'

These lines were the composition of a certain Gormitch-Gormitsky, a wandering poet, to whom Alexey Sergeitch had given a home in his house, as he struck him as a man of delicate feeling and even of subtlety; he wore slippers adorned with ribbons, spoke with a broad accent, and frequently sighed, turning his eyes to heaven; in addition to all these qualifications, Gormitch-Gormitsky spoke French decently, having been educated in a Jesuit college, while Alexey Sergeitch only 'followed conversation.' But having once got terribly drunk at the tavern, that same subtle Gormitsky showed a turbulence beyond all bounds; he gave a fearful thrashing to Alexey Sergeitch's valet, the man cook, two laundry-maids who chanced to get in his way, and a carpenter from another village, and he broke several panes in the windows, screaming furiously all the while: 'There, I'll show them, these Russian loafers, rough-hewn billy-goats!'

And the strength the frail-looking creature put forth! It was hard work for eight men to master him! For this violent proceeding Alexey Sergeitch ordered the poet to be turned out of the house, after being put, as a preliminary measure, in the snow—it was winter-time—to sober him.

'Yes,' Alexey Sergeitch used to say, 'my day is over; I was a spirited steed, but I've run my last race now. Then, I used to keep poets at my expense, and I used to buy pictures and books of the Jews, geese of the best breeds, and pouter-pigeons of pure blood. . . . I used to go in for everything! Though dogs I never did care for keeping, because it goes with drinking, foulness, and buffoonery! I was a young man of spirit, not to be outdone. That there should be anything of Teliegin's and not first-rate . . . why, it was not to be thought of! And I had a splendid stud of horses. And my horses came—from what stock do you think, young sir? Why, from none other than the celebrated stables of the Tsar, Ivan Alexeitch, brother of Peter the Great . . . it's the truth I'm telling you! All fawn-coloured stallions, sleek—their manes to their knees, their tails to their hoofs. . . . Lions! And all that was—and is buried in the past. Vanity of vanities—and every kind of vanity! But still—why regret it? Every man has his limits set him. There's no flying above the sky, no living in the water, no getting away from the earth. . . . We'll live a bit longer, anyway!'

And the old man would smile again and sniff his Spanish snuff.

The peasants liked him; he was, in their words, a kind master, not easily angered. Only they, too, repeated that he was a worn-out steed. In former days Alexey Sergeitch used to go into everything himself—he used to drive out to the fields, and to the mill, and to the dairy, and peep into the granaries and the peasants' huts; every one knew his racing droshky, upholstered in crimson plush, and drawn by a tall mare, with a broad white star all over her forehead, called 'Beacon,' of the same famous breed. Alexey Sergeitch used to drive her himself, the ends of the reins crushed up in his fists. But when his seventieth year came, the old man let everything go, and handed over the management of the estate to the bailiff Antip, of whom he was secretly afraid, and whom he called Micromegas (a reminiscence of Voltaire!), or simply, plunderer. 'Well, plunderer, what have you to say? Have you stacked a great deal in the barn?' he would ask with a smile, looking straight into the plunderer's eyes. 'All, by your good favour, please your honour,' Antip would respond cheerfully. 'Favour's all very well, only you mind what I say, Micromegas! don't you dare touch the peasants, my subjects, out of my sight! If they come to complain . . . I've a cane, you see, not far off!' 'Your cane, your honour, Alexey Sergeitch, I always keep well in mind,' Antip Micromegas would respond, stroking his beard. 'All right, don't forget it.' And the master and the bailiff would laugh in each other's faces. With the servants, and with the serfs in general, his 'subjects' (Alexey Sergeitch liked that word) he was gentle in his behaviour. 'Because, think a little, nephew; nothing of their own, but the cross on their neck—and that copper—and daren't hanker after other people's goods . . . how can one expect sense of them?' It is needless to state that of the so-called 'serf question' no one even dreamed in those days; it could not disturb the peace of mind of Alexey Sergeitch: he was quite happy in the possession of his 'subjects'; but he was severe in his censure of bad masters, and used to call them the enemies of their order. He divided the nobles generally into three classes: the prudent, 'of whom there are too few'; the prodigal, 'of whom there are quite enough'; and the senseless, 'of whom there are shoals and shoals.'

'And if any one of them is harsh and oppressive with his subjects'—he would say—'then he sins against God, and is guilty before men!'

Yes, the house-serfs had an easy life of it with the old man; the 'subjects out of sight' no doubt fared worse, in spite of the cane with which he threatened Micromegas. And what a lot there were of them, those house-serfs, in his house! And for the most part sinewy, hairy, grumbling old fellows, with stooping shoulders, in long-skirted nankeen coats, belted round the waist, with a strong, sour smell always clinging to them. And on the women's side, one could hear nothing but the patter of bare feet, the swish of petticoats. The chief valet was called Irinarh, and Alexey Sergeitch always called him in a long-drawn-out call: 'I-ri-na-a-arh!' The others he called: 'Boy! Lad! Whoever's there of the men!' Bells he could not endure: 'It's not an eating-house, God forbid!' And what used to surprise me was that whatever time Alexey Sergeitch called his valet, he always promptly made his appearance, as though he had sprung out of the earth, and with a scrape of his heels, his hands behind his back, would stand before his master, a surly, as it were angry, but devoted servant!

Alexey Sergeitch was liberal beyond his means; but he did not like to be called 'benefactor.' 'Benefactor to you, indeed, sir! . . . I'm doing myself a benefit, and not you, sir!' (when he was angry or indignant, he always addressed people with greater formality). 'Give to a beggar once,' he used to say, 'and give him twice, and three times. . . . And—if he should come a fourth time, give to him still—only then you might say too: "It's time, my good man, you found work for something else, not only for your mouth."' 'But, uncle,' one asked, sometimes, 'suppose even after that the beggar came again, a fifth time?' 'Oh, well, give again the fifth time.' He used to have the sick, who came to him for aid, treated at his expense, though he had no faith in doctors himself, and never sent for them. 'My mother,' he declared, 'used to cure illnesses of all sorts with oil and salt— she gave it internally, and rubbed it on too—it always answered splendidly. And who was my mother? She was born in the days of Peter the Great— only fancy that!'

Alexey Sergeitch was a Russian in everything; he liked none but Russian dishes, he was fond of Russian songs, but the harmonica—a 'manufactured contrivance'—he hated; he liked looking at the serf-girls' dances and the peasant-women's jigs; in his youth, I was told, he had been an enthusiastic singer and a dashing dancer; he liked steaming himself in the bath, and steamed himself so vigorously that Irinarh, who, serving him as bathman, used to beat him with a bundle of birch-twigs steeped in beer, to rub him with a handful of tow, and then with a woollen cloth—the truly devoted Irinarh used to say every time, as he crept off his shelf red as a 'new copper image': 'Well, this time I, the servant of God, Irinarh Tolobiev, have come out alive. How will it be next time?'

And Alexey Sergeitch spoke excellent Russian, a little old-fashioned, but choice and pure as spring water, continually interspersing his remarks with favourite expressions: ''Pon my honour, please God, howsoever that may be, sir, and young sir. . . .'

But enough of him. Let us talk a little about Alexey Sergeitch's wife, Malania Pavlovna.

Malania Pavlovna was born at Moscow. She had been famous as the greatest beauty in Moscow—la Vénus de Moscou. I knew her as a thin old woman with delicate but insignificant features, with crooked teeth, like a hare's, in a tiny little mouth, with a multitude of finely crimped little yellow curls on her forehead, and painted eyebrows. She invariably wore a pyramidal cap with pink ribbons, a high ruff round her neck, a short white dress, and prunella slippers with red heels; and over her dress she wore a jacket of blue satin, with a sleeve hanging loose from her right shoulder. This was precisely the costume in which she was arrayed on St. Peter's Day in the year 1789! On that day she went, being still a girl, with her relations to the Hodinskoe field to see the famous boxing-match arranged by Orlov. 'And Count Alexey Grigorievitch' (oh, how often I used to hear this story!)

'noticing me, approached, bowed very low, taking his hat in both hands, and said: "Peerless beauty," said he, "why have you hung that sleeve from your shoulder? Do you, too, wish to try a tussle with me? ... By all means; only I will tell you beforehand you have vanquished me—I give in! And I am your captive." And every one was looking at us and wondering.' And that very costume she had worn continually ever since. 'Only I didn't wear a cap, but a hat *à la bergère de Trianon;* and though I was powdered, yet my hair shone through it, positively shone through it like gold!' Malania Pavlovna was foolish to the point of 'holy innocence,' as it is called; she chattered quite at random, as though she were hardly aware herself of what dropped from her lips—and mostly about Orlov. Orlov had become, one might say, the principal interest of her life. She usually walked ... or rather swam, into the room with a rhythmic movement of the head, like a peacock, stood still in the middle, with one foot strangely turned out, and two fingers holding the tip of the loose sleeve (I suppose this pose, too, must once have charmed Orlov); she would glance about her with haughty nonchalance, as befits a beauty—and with a positive sniff, and a murmur of 'What next!' as though some importunate gallant were besieging her with compliments, she would go out again, tapping her heels and shrugging her shoulders. She used, too, to take Spanish snuff out of a tiny bonbonnière, picking it up with a tiny golden spoon; and from time to time, especially when any one unknown to her was present, she would hold up—not to her eye she had splendid sight, but to her nose—a double eyeglass in the shape of a half-moon, with a coquettish turn of her little white hand, one finger held out separate from the rest. How often has Malania Pavlovna described to me her wedding in the church of the Ascension, in Arbaty—such a fine church!—and how all Moscow was there ... 'and the crush there was!—awful! Carriages with teams, golden coaches, outriders ... one outrider of Count Zavadovsky got run over! and we were married by the archbishop himself—and what a sermon he gave us! every one was crying—wherever I looked I saw tears ... and the governor-general's horses were tawny, like tigers. And the flowers, the flowers that were brought! ... Simply loads of flowers!' And how on that day a foreigner, a wealthy, tremendously wealthy person, had shot himself from love—and how Orlov too had been there. ... And going up to Alexey Sergeitch, he had congratulated him and called him a lucky man ... 'A lucky man you are, you silly fellow!' said he. And how in answer to these words Alexey Sergeitch had made a wonderful bow, and had swept the floor from left to right with the plumes of his hat, as if he would say: 'Your Excellency, there is a line now between you and my spouse, which you will not overstep!' And Orlov, Alexey Grigorievitch understood at once, and commended him. 'Oh! that was a man! such a man!' And how, 'One day, Alexis and I were at his house at a ball—I was married then—and he had the most marvellous diamond buttons! And I could not resist it, I admired them. "What marvellous diamonds you have, Count!" said I. And he, taking up a knife from the table, at once cut off a button and presented it to me and said: " In your eyes, my charmer, the diamonds are a hundred times brighter; stand before the looking-glass and compare them." And I stood so, and he stood beside me. " Well, who's right? " said he, while he simply rolled his eyes, looking me up and down. And Alexey Sergeitch was very much put out about it, but I said to him: " Alexis," said I, " please don't you be put out; you ought to know me better! " And he answered me: " Don't disturb yourself, Melanie! " And these very diamonds are now round my medallion of Alexey Grigorievitch—you've seen it, I dare say, my dear;—I wear it on feast-days on a St. George ribbon, because he was a brave hero, a knight of St. George: he burned the Turks.'

For all that, Malania Pavlovna was a very kind-hearted woman; she was easily pleased. ' She's not one to snarl, nor to sneer,' the maids used to say of her. Malania Pavlovna was passionately fond of sweet things—and a special old woman who looked after nothing but the jam, and so was called the jam-maid, would bring her, ten times a day, a china dish with rose-leaves crystallised in sugar, or barberries in honey, or sherbet of bananas. Malania Pavlovna was afraid of solitude—dreadful thoughts are apt to come over one, she would say—and was almost always surrounded by companions, whom she would urgently implore: ' Talk, talk! why do you sit like that, simply keeping your seats warm! ' and they would begin twittering like canaries. She was no less devout than Alexey Sergeitch, and was very fond of praying; but as, in her own words, she had never learned to repeat prayers well, she kept for the purpose a poor deacon's widow who prayed with such relish! Never stumbled over a word in her life! And this deacon's widow certainly could utter the words of prayer in a sort of unbroken flow, not interrupting the stream to breathe out or draw breath in, while Malania Pavlovna listened and was much moved. She had another widow in attendance on her—it was her duty to tell her stories in the night. ' But only the old ones,' Malania Pavlovna would beg—' those I know already; the new ones are all so far-fetched.' Malania Pavlovna was flighty in the extreme, and at times she was fanciful too; some ridiculous notion would suddenly come into her head. She did not like the dwarf, Janus, for instance; she was always fancying he would suddenly get up and shout, ' Don't you know who I am? The prince of the Buriats. Mind, you are to obey me! ' Or else that he would set fire to the house in a fit of spleen. Malania Pavlovna was as liberal as Alexey Sergeitch; but she never gave money—she did not like to soil her hands—but kerchiefs, bracelets, dresses, ribbons; or she would send pies from the table, or a piece of roast meat, or a bottle of wine. She liked feasting the peasant-women, too, on holidays; they would dance, and she would tap with her heels and throw herself into attitudes.

Alexey Sergeitch was well aware that his wife was a fool; but almost from the first year of his marriage he had schooled himself to keep up the fiction that she was very witty and fond of saying cutting things. Sometimes when her chatter began to get beyond all bounds, he would threaten her with his finger, and say as he did so: ' Ah, the tongue, the tongue! what it will have to answer for in the other world! It will be pierced with a redhot pin!'

Malania Pavlovna was not offended, however, at this; on the contrary, she seemed to feel flattered at hearing a reproof of that sort, as though she would say, 'Well! is it my fault if I'm naturally witty?'

Malania Pavlovna adored her husband, and had been all her life an exemplarily faithful wife; but there had been a romance even in her life—a young cousin, an hussar, killed, as she supposed, in a duel on her account; but, according to more trustworthy reports, killed by a blow on the head from a billiard-cue in a tavern brawl. A water-colour portrait of this object of her affections was kept by her in a secret drawer. Malania Pavlovna always blushed up to her ears when she mentioned Kapiton—such was the name of the young hero—and Alexey Sergeitch would designedly scowl, shake his finger at his wife again, and say: 'No trusting a horse in the field nor a woman in the house. Don't talk to me of Kapiton, he's Cupidon!' Then Malania Pavlovna would be all of a flutter and say: 'Alexis, Alexis, it's too bad of you! In your young days you flirted, I've no doubt, with all sorts of misses and madams—and so now you imagine . . .' 'Come, that's enough, that's enough, my dear Malania,' Alexey Sergeitch interrupted with a smile. 'Your gown is white—but whiter still your soul!' 'Yes, Alexis, it is whiter!' 'Ah, what a tongue, what a tongue!' Alexis would repeat, patting her hand.

To speak of 'views' in the case of Malania Pavlovna would be even more inappropriate than in the case of Alexey Sergeitch; yet I once chanced to witness a strange manifestation of my aunt's secret feelings. In the course of conversation I once somehow mentioned the famous chief of police, Sheshkovsky; Malania Pavlovna turned suddenly livid—positively livid, green, in spite of her rouge and paint—and in a thick and perfectly unaffected voice (a very rare thing with her—she usually minced a little, intoned, and lisped) she said: 'Oh, what a name to utter! And towards nightfall, too! Don't utter that name!' I was astonished; what kind of significance could his name have for such a harmless and inoffensive creature, incapable —not merely of doing—even of thinking of anything not permissible? Anything but cheerful reflections were aroused in me by this terror, manifesting itself after almost half a century.

Alexey Sergeitch died in his eighty-eighth year—in the year 1848, which apparently disturbed even him. His death, too, was rather strange. He had felt well the same morning, though by that time he never left his easy-chair. And all of a sudden he called his wife: 'Malania, my dear, come here.' 'What is it, Alexis?' 'It's time for me to die, my dear, that's what it is.' 'Mercy on you, Alexey Sergeitch! What for?' 'Because, first of all, one must know when to take leave; and, besides, I was looking the other day at my feet. . . . Look at my feet . . . they are not mine . . . say what you like . . . look at my hands, look at my stomach . . . that stomach's not mine—so really I'm using up another man's life. Send for the priest; and meanwhile, put me to bed—from which I shall not get up again.' Malania Pavlovna was terribly upset; however, she put the old man to bed and sent for the priest. Alexey Sergeitch confessed, took the sacrament, said good-bye to his household, and fell asleep. Malania Pavlovna was sitting by his bedside. 'Alexis!' she cried suddenly, 'don't frighten me, don't shut your eyes! Are you in pain?' The old man looked at his wife: 'No, no pain . . . but it's difficult . . . difficult to breathe.' Then after a brief silence: 'Malania,' he said, 'so life has slipped by—and do you remember when we were married . . . what a couple we were?' 'Yes, we were, my handsome, charming Alexis!' The old man was silent again. 'Malania, my dear, shall we meet again in the next world?' 'I will pray God for it, Alexis,' and the old woman burst into tears. 'Come, don't cry, silly; maybe the Lord God will make us young again then—and again we shall be a fine pair!' 'He will make us young, Alexis!' 'With the Lord all things are possible,' observed Alexey Sergeitch. 'He worketh great marvels!—maybe He will make you sensible. . . . There, my love, I was joking; come, let me kiss your hand.' 'And I yours.' And the two old people kissed each other's hands simultaneously.

Alexey Sergeitch began to grow quieter and to sink into forgetfulness. Malania Pavlovna watched him tenderly, brushing the tears off her eyelashes with her finger-tips. For two hours she continued sitting there. 'Is he asleep?' the old woman with the talent for praying inquired in a whisper, peeping in behind Irinarh, who, immovable as a post, stood in the doorway, gazing intently at his expiring master. 'He is asleep,' answered Malania Pavlovna, also in a whisper. And suddenly Alexey Sergeitch opened his eyes. 'My faithful companion,' he faltered, 'my honoured wife, I would bow down at your little feet for all your love and faithfulness—but how to get up? Let me sign you with the cross.' Malania Pavlovna moved closer, bent down. . . . But the hand he had raised fell back powerless on the quilt, and a few moments later Alexey Sergeitch was no more.

His daughters arrived only on the day of the funeral with their husbands; they had no children either of them. Alexey Sergeitch showed them no animosity in his will, though he never even mentioned them on his deathbed. 'My heart has grown hard to them,' he once said to me. Knowing his kindly nature, I was surprised at his words. It is hard to judge between parents and children. 'A great ravine starts from a little rift,' Alexey Sergeitch said to me once in this connection: 'a wound a yard wide may heal; but once cut off even a finger nail, it will not grow again.'

I fancy the daughters were ashamed of their eccentric old parents.

A month later and Malania Pavlovna too passed away. From the very day of Alexey Sergeitch's death she had hardly risen from her bed, and had not put on her usual attire; but they buried her in the blue jacket, and with Orlov's medallion on her shoulder, only without the diamonds. Those her daughters divided, on the pretext that the diamonds should be used in the setting of some holy pictures; in reality, they used them to adorn their own persons.

And so I can see my old friends as though they were alive and before my eyes, and pleasant is the memory I preserve of them. And yet on my very last visit to them (I was a student by then) an incident occurred which jarred upon the impression of patriarchal harmony always produced in me by the Teliegin household.

Among the house-serfs there was one Ivan, called "Suhys' Ivan,' a coachman or coach-boy, as they called him on account of his small size, in spite of his being no longer young. He was a tiny little man, brisk, snub-nosed, curly-headed, with an everlastingly smiling, childish face, and little eyes, like a mouse's. He was a great joker, a most comic fellow; he was great at all sorts of tricks—he used to fly kites, let off fireworks and rockets, to play all sorts of games, gallop standing up on the horse's back, fly higher than all the rest in the swing, and could even make Chinese shadows. No one could amuse children better; and he would gladly spend the whole day looking after them. When he started laughing, the whole house would seem to liven up; they would answer him—one would say one thing, one another, but he always made them all merry. . . . And even if they abused him, they could not but laugh. Ivan danced marvellously, especially the so-called ' fish dance.' When the chorus struck up a dance tune, the fellow would come into the middle of the ring, and then there would begin such a turning and skipping and stamping, and then he would fall flat on the ground, and imitate the movement of a fish brought out of the water on to dry land; such turning and wriggling, the heels positively clapped up to the head; and then he would get up and shriek—the earth seemed simply quivering under him. At times Alexey Sergeitch, who was, as I have said already, exceedingly fond of watching dancing, could not resist shouting, ' Little Vania, here! coach-boy! Dance us the fish, smartly now '; and a minute later he would whisper enthusiastically: ' Ah, what a fellow it is! '

Well, on my last visit, this Ivan Suhih came into my room, and, without saying a word, fell on his knees. ' Ivan, what's the matter? ' ' Save me, sir.' ' Why, what is it? ' And thereupon Ivan told me his trouble.

He was exchanged, twenty years ago, by the Suhy family for a serf of the Teliegins';—simply exchanged without any kind of formality or written deed: the man given in exchange for him had died, but the Suhys had forgotten about Ivan, and he had stayed on in Alexey Sergeitch's house as his own serf; only his nickname had served to recall his origin. But now his former masters were dead; the estate had passed into other hands; and the new owner, who was reported to be a cruel and oppressive man, having learned that one of his serfs was detained without cause or reason at Alexey Sergeitch's, began to demand him back; in case of refusal he threatened legal proceedings, and the threat was not an empty one, as he was himself of the rank of privy councillor, and had great weight in the province. Ivan had rushed in terror to Alexey Sergeitch. The old man was sorry for his dancer, and he offered the privy councillor to buy Ivan for a considerable sum. But the privy councillor would not hear of it; he was a Little Russian, and obstinate as the devil. The poor fellow would have to be given up. ' I have spent my life here, and I'm at home here; I have served here, here I have eaten my bread, and here I want to die,' Ivan said to me—and there was no smile on his face now; on the contrary, it looked turned to stone.

. . . 'And now I am to go to this wretch. . . . Am I a dog to be flung from one kennel to another with a noose round my neck? . . . to be told: "There, get along with you!" Save me, master; beg your uncle, remember how I always amused you. . . . Or else there'll be harm come of it; it won't end without sin.'

'What sort of sin, Ivan?'

'I shall kill that gentleman. I shall simply go and say to him, "Master, let me go back; or else, mind, be careful of yourself. . . . I shall kill you."'

If a siskin or a chaffinch could have spoken, and had begun declaring that it would peck another bird to death, it would not have reduced me to greater amazement than did Ivan at that moment. What! Suhys' Vania, that dancing, jesting, comic fellow, the favourite playfellow of children, and a child himself, that kindest-hearted of creatures, a murderer! What ridiculous nonsense! Not for an instant did I believe him; what astonished me to such a degree was that he was capable of saying such a thing. Anyway I appealed to Alexey Sergeitch. I did not repeat what Ivan had said to me, but began asking him whether something couldn't be done. 'My young sir,' the old man answered, 'I should be only too happy—but what's to be done? I offered this Little Russian an immense compensation—I offered him three hundred roubles, 'pon my honour, I tell you! but he—there's no moving him! what's one to do? The transaction was not legal, it was done on trust, in the old-fashioned way . . . and now see what mischief's come of it! This Little Russian fellow, you see, will take Ivan by force, do what we will: his arm is powerful, the governor eats cabbage-soup at his table; he'll be sending along soldiers. And I'm afraid of those soldiers! In old days, to be sure, I would have stood up for Ivan, come what might; but now, look at me, what a feeble creature I have grown! How can I make a fight for it?' It was true; on my last visit I found Alexey Sergeitch greatly aged; even the centres of his eyes had that milky colour that babies' eyes have, and his lips wore not his old conscious smile, but that unnatural, mawkish, unconscious grin, which never, even in sleep, leaves the faces of very decrepit old people.

I told Ivan of Alexey Sergeitch's decision. He stood still, was silent for a little, shook his head. 'Well,' said he at last, 'what is to be there's no escaping. Only my mind's made up. There's nothing left, then, but to play the fool to the end. Something for drink, please!' I gave him something; he drank himself drunk, and that day danced the 'fish dance' so that the serf-girls and peasant-women positively shrieked with delight—he surpassed himself in his antics so wonderfully.

Next day I went home, and three months later, in Petersburg, I heard that Ivan had kept his word. He had been sent to his new master; his master had called him into his room, and explained to him that he would be made coachman, that a team of three ponies would be put in his charge, and that he would be severely dealt with if he did not look after them well, and were not punctual in discharging his duties generally. 'I'm not fond of joking.' Ivan heard the master out, first bowed down to his feet, and then announced it was as his honour pleased, but he could not be his servant. 'Let me off for a yearly quit-money, your honour,' said he, 'or send me for a soldier; or else there'll be mischief come of it!'

The master flew into a rage. 'Ah, what a fellow you are! How dare you speak to me like that? In the first place, I'm to be called your excellency, and not your honour; and, secondly, you're beyond the age, and not of a size to be sent for a soldier; and, lastly, what mischief do you threaten me with? Do you mean to set the house on fire, eh?'

'No, your excellency, not the house on fire.'

'Murder me, then, eh?'

Ivan was silent. 'I'm not your servant,' he said at last.

'Oh well, I'll show you,' roared the master, 'whether you're my servant or not.' And he had Ivan cruelly punished, but yet had the three ponies put into his charge, and made him coachman in the stables.

Ivan apparently submitted; he began driving about as coachman. As he drove well, he soon gained favour with the master, especially as Ivan was very quiet and steady in his behaviour, and the ponies improved so much in his hands; he turned them out as sound and sleek as cucumbers—it was quite a sight to see. The master took to driving out with him oftener than with the other coachmen. Sometimes he would ask him, 'I say, Ivan, do you remember how badly we got on when we met? You've got over all that nonsense, eh?' But Ivan never made any response to such remarks. So one day the master was driving with Ivan to the town in his three-horse sledge with bells and a highback covered with carpet. The horses began to walk up the hill, and Ivan got off the box-seat and went behind the back of the sledge as though he had dropped something. It was a sharp frost; the master sat wrapped up, with a beaver cap pulled down on to his ears. Then Ivan took an axe from under his skirt, came up to the master from behind, knocked off his cap, and saying, 'I warned you, Pietr Petrovitch—you've yourself to blame now!' he struck off his head at one blow. Then he stopped the ponies, put the cap on his dead master, and, getting on the box-seat again, drove him to the town, straight to the courts of justice.

'Here's the Suhinsky general for you, dead; I have killed him. As I told him, so I did to him. Put me in fetters.'

They took Ivan, tried him, sentenced him to the knout, and then to hard labour. The light-hearted, bird-like dancer was sent to the mines, and there passed out of sight for ever. . . .

Yes; one can but repeat, in another sense, Alexey Sergeitch's words: 'They were good old times . . . but enough of them!'

THE BRIGADIER

READER, do you know those little homesteads of country gentlefolks, which were plentiful in our Great Russian Oukraïne twenty-five or thirty years ago? Now one rarely comes across them, and in another ten years the last of them will, I suppose, have disappeared for ever. The running pond overgrown with reeds and rushes, the favourite haunt of fussy ducks, among whom one may now and then come across a wary 'teal'; beyond the pond a garden with avenues of lime-trees, the chief beauty and glory of our black-earth plains, with smothered rows of 'Spanish' strawberries, with dense thickets of gooseberries, currants, and raspberries, in the midst of which, in the languid hour of the stagnant noonday heat, one would be sure to catch glimpses of a serf-girl's striped kerchief, and to hear the shrill ring of her voice. Close by would be a summer-house standing on four legs, a conservatory, a neglected kitchen garden, with flocks of sparrows hung on stakes, and a cat curled up on the tumble-down well; a little further, leafy apple-trees in the high grass, which is green below and grey above, straggling cherry-trees, pear-trees, on which there is never any fruit; then flower-beds, poppies, peonies, pansies, milkwort, 'maids in green,' bushes of Tartar honeysuckle, wild jasmine, lilac and acacia, with the continual hum of bees and wasps among their thick, fragrant, sticky branches. At last comes the manor-house, a one-storied building on a brick foundation, with greenish window-panes in narrow frames, a sloping, once painted roof, a little balcony from which the vases of the balustrade are always jutting out, a crooked gable, and a husky old dog in the recess under the steps at the door. Behind the house a wide yard with nettles, wormwood, and burdocks in the corners, outbuildings with doors that stick, doves and rooks on the thatched roofs, a little storehouse with a rusty weathercock, two or three birch-trees with rooks' nests in their bare top branches, and beyond—the road with cushions of soft dust in the ruts and a field and the long hurdles of the hemp patches, and the grey little huts of the village, and the cackle of geese in the far-away rich meadows. . . . Is all this familiar to you, reader? In the house itself everything is a little awry, a little rickety—but no matter. It stands firm and keeps warm; the stoves are like elephants, the furniture is of all sorts, home-made. Little paths of white footmarks run from the doors over the painted floors. In the hall siskins and larks in tiny cages; in the corner of the dining-room an immense English clock in the form of a tower, with the inscription, 'Strike—silent'; in the drawing-room portraits of the family, painted in oils, with an expression of ill-tempered alarm on the brick-coloured faces, and sometimes too an old warped picture of flowers and fruit or a mythological subject. Everywhere there is the smell of kvas, of apples, of linseed-oil and of leather. Flies buzz and hum about the ceiling and the windows. A daring cockroach suddenly shows his countenance from behind the looking-glass frame. . . . No matter, one can live here—and live very well too.

II

JUST such a homestead it was my lot to visit thirty years ago . . . it was in days long past, as you perceive. The little estate in which this house stood belonged to a friend of mine at the university; it had only recently come to him on the death of a bachelor cousin, and he was not living in it himself. . . . But at no great distance from it there were wide tracts of steppe bog, in which at the time of summer migration, when they are on the wing, there are great numbers of snipe; my friend and I, both enthusiastic sportsmen, agreed therefore to go on St. Peter's Day, he from Moscow, I from my own village, to his little house. My friend lingered in Moscow, and was two days late; I did not care to start shooting without him. I was received by an old servant, Narkiz Semyonov, who had had notice of my coming. This old servant was not in the least like 'Savelitch' or 'Caleb'; my friend used to call him in joke 'Marquis.' There was something of conceit, even of affectation, about him; he looked down on us young men with a certain dignity, but cherished no particularly respectful sentiments for other landowners either; of his old master he spoke slightingly, while his own class he simply scorned for their ignorance. He could read and write, expressed himself correctly and with judgment, and did not drink. He seldom went to church, and so was looked upon as a dissenter. In appearance he was thin and tall, had a long and good-looking face, a sharp nose, and overhanging eyebrows, which he was continually either knitting or lifting; he wore a neat, roomy coat, and boots to his knees with heart-shaped scallops at the tops.

III

ON THE DAY of my arrival, Narkiz, having given me lunch and cleared the table, stood in the doorway, looked intently at me, and with some play of the eyebrows observed:

'What are you going to do now, sir?'

'Well, really, I don't know. If Nikolai Petrovitch had kept his word and come, we should have gone shooting together.'

'So you really expected, sir, that he would come at the time he promised?'

'Of course I did.'

'H'm.' Narkiz looked at me again and shook his head as it were with commiseration. 'If you'd care to amuse yourself with reading,' he continued: 'there are some books left of my old master's; I'll get them you, if you like; only you won't read them, I expect.'

'Why?'

'They're books of no value; not written for the gentlemen of these days.'

'Have you read them?'

'If I hadn't read them, I wouldn't have spoken about them. A dream-book, for instance . . . that's not much of a book, is it? There are others too, of course . . . only you won't read them either.'

'Why?'

'They are religious books.'

I was silent for a space. . . . Narkiz was silent too.

'What vexes me most,' I began, 'is staying in the house in such weather.'

'Take a walk in the garden; or go into the copse. We've a copse here beyond the threshing-floor. Are you fond of fishing?'

'Are there fish here?'

'Yes, in the pond. Loaches, sand-eels, and perches are caught there. Now, to be sure, the best time is over; July's here. But anyway, you might try. . . . Shall I get the tackle ready?'

'Yes, do please.'

'I'll send a boy with you . . . to put on the worms. Or maybe I'd better come myself?' Narkiz obviously doubted whether I knew how to set about things properly by myself.

'Come, please, come along.'

Narkiz, without a word, grinned from ear to ear, then suddenly knitted his brows . . . and went out of the room.

IV

HALF AN HOUR later we set off to catch fish. Narkiz had put on an extraordinary sort of cap with ears, and was more dignified than ever. He walked in front with a steady, even step; two rods swayed regularly up and down on his shoulders; a bare-legged boy followed him carrying a can and a pot of worms.

'Here, near the dike, there's a seat, put up on the floating platform on purpose,' Narkiz was beginning to explain to me, but he glanced ahead, and suddenly exclaimed: 'Aha! but our poor folk are here already . . . they keep it up, it seems.'

I craned my head to look from behind him, and saw on the floating platform, on the very seat of which he had been speaking, two persons sitting with their backs to us; they were placidly fishing.

'Who are they?' I asked.

'Neighbours,' Narkiz responded, with displeasure. 'They've nothing to eat at home, and so here they come to us.'

'Are they allowed to?'

'The old master allowed them. . . . Nikolai Petrovitch maybe won't give them permission. . . . The long one is a superannuated deacon—quite a silly creature; and as for the other, that's a little stouter—he's a brigadier.'

'A brigadier?' I repeated, wondering. This 'brigadier's' attire was almost worse than the deacon's.

'I assure you he's a brigadier. And he did have a fine property once. But now he has only a corner given him out of charity, and he lives . . . on what God sends him. But, by the way, what are we to do? They've taken the best place. . . . We shall have to disturb our precious visitors.'

'No, Narkiz, please don't disturb them. We'll sit here a little aside; they won't interfere with us. I should like to make acquaintance with the brigadier.'

'As you like. Only, as far as acquaintance goes . . . you needn't expect much satisfaction from it, sir; he's grown very weak in his head, and in conversation he's silly as a little child. As well he may be; he's past his eightieth year.'

'What's his name?'

'Vassily Fomitch. Guskov's his surname.'

'And the deacon?'

'The deacon? . . . his nickname's Cucumber. Every one about here calls him so; but what his real name is—God knows! A foolish creature! A regular ne'er-do-weel.'

'Do they live together?'

'No; but there—the devil has tied them together, it seems.'

V

WE APPROACHED the platform. The brigadier cast one glance upon us . . . and promptly fixed his eyes on the float; Cucumber jumped up, pulled back his rod, took off his worn-out clerical hat, passed a trembling hand over his rough yellow hair, made a sweeping bow, and gave vent to a feeble little laugh. His bloated face betrayed him an inveterate drunkard; his staring little eyes blinked humbly. He gave his neighbour a poke in the ribs, as though to let him know that they must clear out. . . . The brigadier began to move on the seat.

'Sit still, I beg; don't disturb yourselves,' I hastened to say. 'You won't interfere with us in the least. We'll take up our position here; sit still.'

Cucumber wrapped his ragged smock round him, twitched his shoulders, his lips, his beard. . . . Obviously he felt our presence oppressive and he would have been glad to slink away, . . . but the brigadier was again lost in the contemplation of his float. . . . The 'ne'er-do-weel' coughed twice, sat down on the very edge of the seat, put his hat on his knees, and, tucking his bare legs up under him, he discreetly dropped in his line.

'Any bites?' Narkiz inquired haughtily, as in leisurely fashion he unwound his reel.

'We've caught a matter of five loaches,' answered Cucumber in a cracked and husky voice: 'and he took a good-sized perch.'

'Yes, a perch,' repeated the brigadier in a shrill pipe.

VI

I FELL to watching closely—not him, but his reflection in the pond. It was as clearly reflected as in a looking-glass—a little darker, a little more silvery. The wide stretch of pond wafted a refreshing coolness upon us; a cool breath of air seemed to rise, too, from the steep, damp bank; and it was the sweeter, as in the dark blue, flooded with gold, above the tree tops, the stagnant sultry heat hung, a burden that could be felt, over our heads. There was no stir in the water near the dike; in the shade cast by the drooping bushes on the bank, water spiders gleamed, like tiny bright buttons, as they described their everlasting circles; at long intervals there was a faint ripple just perceptible round the floats, when a fish was 'playing' with the worm. Very few fish were taken; during a whole hour we drew up only two loaches and an eel. I could not say why the brigadier aroused my curiosity; his rank could not have any influence on me; ruined noblemen were not even at that time looked upon as a rarity, and his appearance presented nothing remarkable. Under the warm cap, which covered the whole upper part of his head down to his ears and his eyebrows, could be seen a smooth, red, clean-shaven, round face, with a little nose, little lips, and small, clear grey eyes. Simplicity and weakness of character, and a sort of long-standing, helpless sorrow, were visible in that meek, almost childish face; the plump, white little hands with short fingers had something helpless, incapable about them too. . . . I could not conceive how this forlorn old man could once have been an officer, could have maintained discipline, have given his commands—and that, too, in the stern days of Catherine! I watched him; now and then he puffed out his cheeks and uttered a feeble whistle, like a little child; sometimes he screwed up his eyes painfully, with effort, as all decrepit people will. Once he opened his eyes wide and lifted them. . . . They stared at me from out of the depths of the water—and strangely touching and even full of meaning their dejected glance seemed to me.

VII

I TRIED to begin a conversation with the brigadier . . . but Narkiz had not misinformed me; the poor old man certainly had become weak in his intellect. He asked me my surname, and after repeating his inquiry twice, pondered and pondered, and at last brought out: 'Yes, I fancy there was a judge of that name here. Cucumber, wasn't there a judge about here of that name, hey?' 'To be sure there was, Vassily Fomitch, your honour,' responded Cucumber, who treated him altogether as a child. 'There was, certainly. But let me have your hook; your worm must have been eaten off. . . . Yes, so it is.'

'Did you know the Lomov family? ' the brigadier suddenly asked me in a cracked voice.

'What Lomov family is that? '

'Why, Fiodor Ivanitch, Yevstigney Ivanitch, Alexey Ivanitch the Jew, and Fedulia Ivanovna the plunderer, . . . and then, too . . .'

The brigadier suddenly broke off and looked down confused.

'They were the people he was most intimate with,' Narkiz whispered, bending towards me; ' it was through them, through that same Alexey Ivanitch, that he called a Jew, and through a sister of Alexey Ivanitch's, Agrafena Ivanovna, as you may say, that he lost all his property.'

'What are you saying there about Agrafena Ivanovna? ' the brigadier called out suddenly, and his head was raised, his white eyebrows were frowning. . . . 'You'd better mind! And why Agrafena, pray? Agrippina Ivanovna—that's what you should call her.'

'There—there—there, sir,' Cucumber was beginning to falter.

'Don't you know the verses the poet Milonov wrote about her? ' the old man went on, suddenly getting into a state of excitement, which was a complete surprise to me. 'No hymeneal lights were kindled,' he began chanting, pronouncing all the vowels through his nose, giving the syllables ' an,' ' en,' the nasal sound they have in French; and it was strange to hear this connected speech from his lips: ' No torches . . . No, that's not it:

> *"Not vain Corruption's idols frail*
> *Not amaranth nor porphyry*
> *Rejoiced their hearts . . .*
> *One thing in them . . ."*

That was about us. Do you hear?

> *"One thing in them unquenchable,*
> *Subduing, sweet, desirable,*
> *To nurse their mutual flame in love! "*

And you talk about Agrafena! '

Narkiz chuckled half-contemptuously, half-indifferently. 'What a queer fish it is! ' he said to himself. But the brigadier had again relapsed into dejection, the rod had dropped from his hands and slipped into the water.

VIII

'Well, to my thinking, our fishing is a poor business,' observed Cucumber; ' the fish, see, don't bite at all. It's got fearfully hot, and there's a fit of " mencholy " come over our gentleman. It's clear we must be going home; that will be best.' He cautiously drew out of his pocket a tin bottle with a wooden stopper, uncorked it, scattered snuff on his wrist, and sniffed it up in both nostrils at once. . . .'Ah, what good snuff! ' he moaned, as he

recovered himself. 'It almost made my tooth ache! Now, my dear Vassily
Fomitch, get up—it's time to be off!'

The brigadier got up from the bench.

'Do you live far from here?' I asked Cucumber.

'No, our gentleman lives not far . . . it won't be as much as a mile.'

'Will you allow me to accompany you?' I said, addressing the brigadier.
I felt disinclined to let him go.

He looked at me, and with that peculiar, stately, courteous, and rather
affected smile, which—I don't know how it is with others—to me always
suggests powder, French full-skirted coats with paste buttons—the eighteenth century, in fact—he replied, with the old-fashioned drawl, that he
would be 'high-ly de-lighted' . . . and at once sank back into his former
condition again. The grand gentleman of the old Catherine days flickered
up in him for an instant and vanished.

Narkiz was surprised at my intention; but I paid no attention to the dis-
approving shake of his long-eared cap, and walked out of the garden with
the brigadier, who was supported by Cucumber. The old man moved fairly
quickly, with a motion as though he were on stilts.

IX

WE WALKED ALONG a scarcely trodden path, through a grassy glade between two birch copses. The sun was blazing; the orioles called to each
other in the green thicket; corn-crakes chattered close to the path; blue
butterflies fluttered in crowds about the white and red flowers of the low-
growing clover; in the perfectly still grass bees hung, as though asleep,
languidly buzzing. Cucumber seemed to pull himself together, and brightened up; he was afraid of Narkiz—he lived always under his eye; I was
a stranger—a new comer—with me he was soon quite at home.

'Here's our gentleman,' he said in a rapid flow; 'he's a small eater and
no mistake! but only one perch, is that enough for him? Unless, your
honour, you would like to contribute something? Close here round the
corner, at the little inn, there are first-rate white wheaten rolls. And if so,
please your honour, this poor sinner, too, will gladly drink on this occasion
to your health, and may it be of long years and long days.' I gave him a
little silver, and was only just in time to pull away my hand, which he was
falling upon to kiss. He learned that I was a sportsman, and fell to talking
of a very good friend of his, an officer, who had a 'Mindindenger' Swedish
gun, with a copper stock, just like a cannon, so that when you fire it off
you are almost knocked senseless—it had been left behind by the French—
and a dog—simply one of Nature's marvels! that he himself had always
had a great passion for the chase, and his priest would have made no trouble
about it—he used in fact to catch quails with him—but the ecclesiastical
superior had pursued him with endless persecution; 'and as for Narkiz
Semyonitch,' he observed in a sing-song tone, 'if according to his notions

I'm not a trustworthy person—well, what I say is: he's let his eyebrows grow till he's like a woodcock, and he fancies all the sciences are known to him.' By this time we had reached the inn, a solitary tumble-down, one-roomed little hut without backyard or outbuildings; an emaciated dog lay curled up under the window; a hen was scratching in the dust under his very nose. Cucumber sat the brigadier down on the bank, and darted instantly into the hut. While he was buying the rolls and emptying a glass, I never took my eyes off the brigadier, who, God knows why, struck me as something of an enigma. In the life of this man—so I mused—there must certainly have been something out of the ordinary. But he, it seemed, did not notice me at all. He was sitting huddled up on the bank, and twisting in his fingers some pinks which he had gathered in my friend's garden. Cucumber made his appearance, at last, with a bundle of rolls in his hand; he made his appearance, all red and perspiring, with an expression of gleeful surprise on his face, as though he had just seen something exceedingly agreeable and unexpected. He at once offered the brigadier a roll to eat, and the latter at once ate it. We proceeded on our way.

X

ON THE STRENGTH of the spirits he had drunk, Cucumber quite 'unbent,' as it is called. He began trying to cheer up the brigadier, who was still hurrying forward with a tottering motion as though he were on stilts. 'Why are you so downcast, sir, and hanging your head? Let me sing you a song. That'll cheer you up in a minute.' He turned to me: 'Our gentleman is very fond of a joke, mercy on us, yes! Yesterday, what did I see?— a peasant-woman washing a pair of breeches on the platform, and a great fat woman she was, and he stood behind her, simply all of a shake with laughter—yes, indeed! . . . In a minute, allow me: do you know the song of the hare? You mustn't judge me by my looks; there's a gypsy woman living here in the town, a perfect fright, but sings—'pon my soul! one's ready to lie down and die.' He opened wide his moist red lips and began singing, his head on one side, his eyes shut, and his beard quivering:

> ' The hare beneath the bush lies still,
> The hunters vainly scour the hill;
> The hare lies hid and holds his breath,
> His ears pricked up, he lies there still
> 　　Waiting for death.
> O hunters! what harm have I done,
> To vex or injure you? Although
> Among the cabbages I run,
> One leaf I nibble—only one,
> 　　And that's not yours!
> 　　　Oh, no! '

Cucumber went on with ever-increasing energy:

> '*Into the forest dark he fled,*
> *His tail he let the hunters see;*
> "*Excuse me, gentlemen,*" *says he,*
> "*That so I turn my back on you—*
> *I am not yours!*"'

Cucumber was not singing now . . . he was bellowing:

> '*The hunters hunted day and night,*
> *And still the hare was out of sight.*
> *So, talking over his misdeeds,*
> *They ended by disputing quite—*
> *Alas, the hare is not for us!*
> *The squint-eye is too sharp for us!*'

The first two lines of each stanza Cucumber sang with each syllable drawn out; the other three, on the contrary, very briskly, and accompanied them with little hops and shuffles of his feet; at the conclusion of each verse he cut a caper, in which he kicked himself with his own heels. As he shouted at the top of his voice: 'The squint-eye is too sharp for us!' he turned a somersault. . . . His expectations were fulfilled. The brigadier suddenly went off into a thin, tearful little chuckle, and laughed so heartily that he could not go on, and stayed still in a half-sitting posture, helplessly slapping his knees with his hands. I looked at his face, flushed crimson, and convulsively working, and felt very sorry for him at that instant especially. Encouraged by his success, Cucumber fell to capering about in a squatting position, singing the refrain of: 'Shildi-budildi!' and 'Natchiki-tchikaldi!' He stumbled at last with his nose in the dust. . . . The brigadier suddenly ceased laughing and hobbled on.

XI

WE WENT on another quarter of a mile. A little village came into sight on the edge of a not very deep ravine; on one side stood the 'lodge,' with a half-ruined roof and a solitary chimney; in one of the two rooms of this lodge lived the brigadier. The owner of the village, who always resided in Petersburg, the widow of the civil councillor Lomov, had—so I learned later—bestowed this little nook upon the brigadier. She had given orders that he should receive a monthly pension, and had also assigned for his service a half-witted serf-girl living in the same village, who, though she barely understood human speech, was yet capable, in the lady's opinion, of sweeping a floor and cooking cabbage-soup. At the door of the lodge the brigadier again addressed me with the same eighteenth-century smile: would I be pleased to walk into his ' apartement '? We went into this ' apartement.' Everything in it was exceedingly filthy and poor, so filthy and so poor that the brigadier, noticing, probably, by the expression of my face, the impression it made on me, observed, shrugging his shoulders, and half closing his eyelids: ' Ce n'est pas . . . œil de perdrix.' . . . What precisely he meant by this remained a mystery to me. . . . When I addressed him in French, I got no reply from him in that language. Two objects struck me especially in the brigadier's abode: a large officer's cross of St. George in a black frame, under glass, with an inscription in an old-fashioned handwriting: ' Received by the Colonel of the Tchernigov regiment, Vassily Guskov, for the storming of Prague in the year 1794 '; and secondly, a half-length portrait in oils of a handsome, black-eyed woman with a long, dark face, hair turned up high and powdered, with postiches on the temple and chin, in a flowered, low-cut bodice, with blue frills, the style of 1780. The portrait was badly painted, but was probably a good likeness; there was a wonderful look of life and will, something extraordinarily living and resolute, about the face. It was not looking at the spectator; it was, as it were, turning away and not smiling; the curve of the thin nose, the regular but flat lips, the almost unbroken straight line of the thick eyebrows, all showed an imperious, haughty, fiery temper. No great effort was needed to picture that face glowing with passion or with rage. Just below the portrait on a little pedestal stood a half-withered bunch of simple wild flowers in a thick glass jar. The brigadier went up to the pedestal, stuck the pinks he was carrying into the jar, and turning to me, and lifting his hand in the direction of the portrait, he observed: ' Agrippina Ivanovna Teliegin, by birth Lomov.' The words of Narkiz came back to my mind; and I looked with redoubled interest at the expressive and evil face of the woman for whose sake the brigadier had lost all his fortune.

' You took part, I see, sir, in the storming of Prague,' I began, pointing to the St. George cross, ' and won a sign of distinction, rare at any time, but particularly so then; you must remember Suvorov? '

' Alexander Vassilitch? ' the brigadier answered, after a brief silence, in which he seemed to be pulling his thoughts together; ' to be sure, I remember him; he was a little, brisk old man. Before one could stir a finger, he'd be here and there and everywhere (the brigadier chuckled). He rode into Warsaw on a Cossack horse; he was all in diamonds, and he says to the Poles: " I've no watch, I forgot it in Petersburg—no watch! " and they shouted and huzzaed for him. Queer chaps! Hey! Cucumber! lad! ' he added suddenly, changing and raising his voice (the deacon-buffoon had remained standing at the door), ' where's the rolls, eh? And tell Grunka . . . to bring some kvas! '

' Directly, your honour,' I heard Cucumber's voice reply. He handed the brigadier the bundle of rolls, and, going out of the lodge, approached a dishevelled creature in rags—the half-witted girl, Grunka, I suppose—and as far as I could make out through the dusty little window, proceeded to demand kvas from her—at least, he several times raised one hand like a funnel to his mouth, and waved the other in our direction.

XII

I MADE another attempt to get into conversation with the brigadier; but he was evidently tired: he sank, sighing and groaning, on the little couch, and moaning, ' Oy, oy, my poor bones, my poor bones,' untied his garters. I remember I wondered at the time how a man came to be wearing garters. I did not realise that in former days every one wore them. The brigadier began yawning with prolonged, unconcealed yawns, not taking his drowsy eyes off me all the time; so very little children yawn. The poor old man did not even seem quite to understand my question. . . . And he had taken Prague! He, sword in hand, in the smoke and dust—at the head of Suvorov's soldiers, the bullet-pierced flag waving above him, the hideous corpses under his feet. . . . He . . . he! Wasn't it wonderful! But yet I could not help fancying that there had been events more extraordinary in the brigadier's life. Cucumber brought white kvas in an iron jug; the brigadier drank greedily—his hands shook. Cucumber supported the bottom of the jug. The old man carefully wiped his toothless mouth with both hands—and again staring at me, fell to chewing and munching his lips. I saw how it was, bowed, and went out of the room.

' Now he'll have a nap,' observed Cucumber, coming out behind me. ' He's terribly knocked up to-day—he went to the grave early this morning.'

' To whose grave? '

'To Agrafena Ivanovna's, to pay his devotions . . . She is buried in our parish cemetery here; it'll be four miles from here. Vassily Fomitch visits it every week without fail. Indeed, it was he who buried her and put the fence up at his own expense.'

' Has she been dead long? '

' Well, let's think—twenty years about.'

' Was she a friend of his, or what? '

' Her whole life, you may say, she passed with him . . . really. I myself, I must own never knew the lady, but they do say . . . what there was between them . . . well, well, well! Sir,' the deacon added hurriedly, seeing I had turned away, ' wouldn't you like to give me something for another drop, for it's time I was home in my hut and rolled up in my blanket? '

I thought it useless to question Cucumber further, so gave him a few coppers, and set off homewards.

XIII

AT HOME I betook myself for further information to Narkiz. He, as I might have anticipated, was somewhat unapproachable, stood a little on his dignity, expressed his surprise that such paltry matters could ' interest ' me, and, finally, told me what he knew. I heard the following details.

Vassily Fomitch Guskov had become acquainted with Agrafena Ivan-ovna Teliegin at Moscow soon after the suppression of the Polish insurrection; her husband had had a post under the governor-general, and Vassily Fomitch was on furlough. He fell in love with her there and then, but did not leave the army at once; he was a man of forty with no family, with a fortune. Her husband soon after died. She was left without children, poor, and in debt. . . . Vassily Fomitch heard of her position, threw up the service (he received the rank of brigadier on his retirement) and sought out his charming widow, who was not more than five-and-twenty, paid all her debts, redeemed her estate. . . . From that time he had never parted from her, and finished by living altogether in her house. She, too, seems to have cared for him, but would not marry him. 'She was froward, the deceased lady,' was Narkiz's comment on this: 'My liberty,' she would say, 'is dearer to me than anything.' But as for making use of him—she made use of him 'in every possible way,' and whatever money he had, he dragged to her like an ant. But the frowardness of Agrafena Ivanovna at times assumed extreme proportions; she was not of a mild temper, and somewhat too ready with her hands. . . . Once she pushed her pageboy down the stairs, and he went and broke two of his ribs and one leg. . . . Agrafena Ivanovna was frightened . . . she promptly ordered the page to be shut up in the lumber-room, and she did not leave the house nor give up the key of the room to any one, till the moans within had ceased. . . . The page was secretly buried. . . . 'And had it been in the Empress Catherine's time,' Narkiz added in a whisper, bending down, 'maybe the affair would have ended there—many such deeds were hidden under a bushel in those days, but as . . .' here Narkiz drew himself up and raised his voice: 'as our righteous Tsar Alexander the Blessed was reigning then . . . well, a fuss was made. . . . A trial followed, the body was dug up . . . signs of violence were found on it . . . and a great to-do there was. And what do you think? Vassily Fomitch took it all on himself. "I," said he, "am responsible for it all; it was I pushed him down, and I too shut him up." Well, of course, all the judges then, and the lawyers and the police . . . fell on him directly . . . fell on him and never let him go . . . I can assure you . . . till the last farthing was out of his purse. They'd leave him in peace for a while, and then attack him again. Down to the very time when the French came into Russia they were worrying at him, and only dropped him then. Well, he managed to provide for Agrafena Ivanovna—to be sure, he saved her—that one must say. Well, and afterwards, up to her death, indeed, he lived with her, and they do say she led him a pretty dance—the brigadier, that is; sent him on foot from Moscow into the country—by God, she did—to get her rents in, I suppose. It was on her account, on account of this same Agrafena Ivanovna—he fought a duel with the English milord Hugh Hughes; and the English milord was forced to make a formal apology too. But later on the brigadier went down hill more and more. . . . Well, and now he can't be reckoned a man at all.'

'Who was that Alexey Ivanitch the Jew,' I asked, 'through whom he was brought to ruin?'

'Oh, the brother of Agrafena Ivanovna. A grasping creature, Jewish indeed. He lent his sister money at interest, and Vassily Fomitch was her security. He had to pay for it too . . . pretty heavily!'

'And Fedulia Ivanovna the plunderer—who was she?'

'Her sister too . . . and a sharp one too, as sharp as a lance. A terrible woman!'

XIV

'WHAT a place to find a Werter!' I thought next day, as I set off again towards the brigadier's dwelling. I was at that time very young, and that was possibly why I thought it my duty not to believe in the lasting nature of love. Still, I was impressed and somewhat puzzled by the story I had heard, and felt an intense desire to stir up the old man, to make him talk freely. 'I'll first refer to Suvorov again,' so I resolved within myself; 'there must be some spark of his former fire hidden within him still . . . and then, when he's warmed up, I'll turn the conversation on that . . . what's her name? . . . Agrafena Ivanovna. A queer name for a " Charlotte " —Agrafena!'

I found my Werter-Guskov in the middle of a tiny kitchen-garden, a few steps from the lodge, near the old framework of a never-finished hut, overgrown with nettles. On the mildewed upper beams of this skeleton hut some miserable-looking turkey poults were scrambling, incessantly slipping and flapping their wings and cackling. There was some poor sort of green stuff growing in two or three borders. The brigadier had just pulled a young carrot out of the ground, and rubbing it under his arm 'to clean it,' proceeded to chew its thin tail. . . . I bowed to him, and inquired after his health.

He obviously did not recognise me, though he returned my greeting— that is to say, touched his cap with his hand, though without leaving off munching the carrot.

'You didn't go fishing to-day?' I began, in the hope of recalling myself to his memory by this question.

'To-day?' he repeated and pondered . . . while the carrot, stuck into his mouth, grew shorter and shorter. 'Why, I suppose it's Cucumber fishing! . . . But I'm allowed to, too.'

'Of course, of course, most honoured Vassily Fomitch. . . . I didn't mean that. . . . But aren't you hot . . . like this in the sun?'

The brigadier was wearing a thick wadded dressing-gown.

'Eh? Hot?' he repeated again, as though puzzled over the question, and, having finally swallowed the carrot, he gazed absently upwards.

'Would you care to step into my apartement?' he said suddenly. The poor old man had, it seemed, only this phrase still left him always at his disposal.

We went out of the kitchen-garden . . . but there involuntarily I stopped short. Between us and the lodge stood a huge bull. With his head down to the ground, and a malignant gleam in his eyes, he was snorting heavily and furiously, and with a rapid movement of one fore-leg, he tossed the dust up in the air with his broad cleft hoof, lashed his sides with his tail, and suddenly backing a little, shook his shaggy neck stubbornly, and bellowed—not loud, but plaintively, and at the same time menacingly. I was, I confess, alarmed; but Vassily Fomitch stepped forward with perfect composure, and saying in a stern voice, 'Now then, country bumpkin,' shook his handkerchief at him. The bull backed again, bowed his horns . . . suddenly rushed to one side and ran away, wagging his head from side to side.

'There's no doubt he took Prague,' I thought.

We went into the room. The brigadier pulled his cap off his hair, which was soaked with perspiration, ejaculated, 'Fa!' . . . squatted down on the edge of a chair . . . bowed his head gloomily. . . .

'I have come to you, Vassily Fomitch,' I began my diplomatic approaches, 'because, as you have served under the leadership of the great Suvorov—have taken part altogether in such important events—it would be very interesting for me to hear some particulars of your past.'

The brigadier stared at me. . . . His face kindled strangely—I began to expect, if not a story, at least some word of approval, of sympathy. . . .

'But I, sir, must be going to die soon,' he said in an undertone.

I was utterly nonplussed.

'Why, Vassily Fomitch,' I brought out at last, 'what makes you . . . suppose that?'

The brigadier suddenly flung his arms violently up and down.

'Because, sir . . . I, as maybe you know . . . often in my dreams see Agrippina Ivanovna—Heaven's peace be with her!—and never can I catch her; I am always running after her—but cannot catch her. But last night—I dreamed—she was standing, as it were, before me, half-turned away, and laughing. . . . I ran up to her at once and caught her . . . and she seemed to turn round quite and said to me: "Well, Vassinka, now you have caught me."'

'What do you conclude from that, Vassily Fomitch?'

'Why, sir, I conclude: it has come, that we shall be together. And glory to God for it, I tell you; glory be to God Almighty, the Father, the Son, and the Holy Ghost (the brigadier fell into a chant): as it was in the beginning, is now and ever shall be, Amen!'

The brigadier began crossing himself. I could get nothing more out of him, so I went away.

XV

THE NEXT day my friend arrived. . . . I mentioned the brigadier, and my visits to him. . . . 'Oh yes! of course! I know his story,' answered my friend; 'I know Madame Lomov very well, the privy councillor's widow, by whose favour he obtained a home here. Oh, wait a minute; I believe there must be preserved here his letter to the privy councillor's widow; it was on the strength of that letter that she assigned him his little cot.' My friend rummaged among his papers and actually found the brigadier's letter. Here it is word for word, with the omission of the mistakes in spelling. The brigadier, like every one of his epoch, was a little hazy in that respect. But to preserve these errors seemed unnecessary; his letter bears the stamp of his age without them.

'HONOURED MADAM, RAÏSSA PAVLOVNA!—On the decease of my friend, and your aunt, I had the happiness of addressing to you two letters, the first on the first of June, the second on the sixth of July, of the year 1815, while she expired on the sixth of May in that year; in them I discovered to you the feelings of my soul and of my heart, which were crushed under deadly wrongs, and they reflected in full my bitter despair, in truth deserving of commiseration; both letters were despatched by the imperial mail registered, and hence I cannot conceive that they have not been perused by your eye. By the genuine candour of my letters, I had counted upon winning your benevolent attention; but the compassionate feelings of your heart were far removed from me in my woe! Left on the loss of my one only friend, Agrippina Ivanovna, in the most distressed and poverty-stricken circumstances, I rested, by her instructions, all my hopes on your bounty; she, aware of her end approaching, said to me in these words, as it were from the grave, and never can I forget them: "My friend, I have been your serpent, and am guilty of all your unhappiness. I feel how much you have sacrificed for me, and in return I leave you in a disastrous and truly destitute situation; on my death have recourse to Raïssa Pavlovna"— that is, to you—" and implore her aid, invite her succour! She has a feeling heart, and I have confidence in her, that she will not leave you forlorn." Honoured madam, let me call to witness the all-high Creator of the world that those were her words, and I am speaking with her tongue; and, therefore, trusting firmly in your goodness, to you first of all I addressed myself with my open-hearted and candid letters; but after protracted expectation, receiving no reply to them, I could not conceive otherwise than that your benevolent heart had left me without attention! Such your unfavourable disposition towards me, reduced me to the depths of despair—whither, and to whom, was I to turn in my misfortune I knew not; my soul was troubled, my intellect went astray; at last, for the completion of my ruin, it pleased Providence to chastise me in a still more cruel manner, and to turn my thoughts to your deceased aunt, Fedulia Ivanovna, sister of Agrippina Ivan-ovna, one in blood, but not one in heart! Having present to myself, before my mind's eye, that I had been for twenty years devoted to the whole family of your kindred, the Lomovs, especially to Fedulia Ivanovna, who never called Agrippina Ivanovna otherwise than " my heart's precious treasure," and me " the most honoured and zealous friend of our family ";

picturing all the above, among abundant tears and sighs in the stillness of sorrowful night watches, I thought: " Come, brigadier! so, it seems, it is to be! " and, addressing myself by letter to the said Fedulia Ivanovna, I received a positive assurance that she would share her last crumb with me! The presents sent on by me, more than five hundred roubles' worth in value, were accepted with supreme satisfaction; and afterwards the money too which I brought with me for my maintenance, Fedulia Ivanovna was pleased, on the pretext of guarding it, to take into her care, to the which, to gratify her, I offered no opposition. If you ask me whence, and on what ground I conceived such confidence—to the above, madam, there is but one reply: she was sister of Agrippina Ivanovna, and a member of the Lomov family! But alas and alas! all the money aforesaid I was very soon deprived of, and the hopes which I had rested on Fedulia Ivanovna—that she would share her last crumb with me—turned out to be empty and vain; on the contrary, the said Fedulia Ivanovna enriched herself with my property. To wit, on her saint's day, the fifth of February, I brought her fifty roubles' worth of green French material, at five roubles the yard; I myself received of all that was promised five roubles' worth of white piqué for a waistcoat and a muslin handkerchief for my neck, which gifts were purchased in my presence, as I was aware, with my own money—and that was all that I profited by Fedulia Ivanovna's bounty! So much for the last crumb! And I could further, in all sincerity, disclose the malignant doings of Fedulia Ivanovna to me; and also my expenses, exceeding all reason, as, among the rest, for sweetmeats and fruits, of which Fedulia Ivanovna was exceedingly fond;—but upon all this I am silent, that you may not take such disclosures against the dead in bad part; and also, seeing that God has called her before His judgment seat—and all that I suffered at her hands is blotted out from my heart—and I, as a Christian, forgave her long ago, and pray to God to forgive her!

' But, honoured madam, Raïssa Pavlovna! Surely you will not blame me for that I was a true and loyal friend of your family, and that I loved Agrippina Ivanovna with a love so great and so insurmountable that I sacrificed to her my life, my honour, and all my fortune! that I was utterly in her hands, and hence could not dispose of myself nor of my property, and she disposed at her will of me and also of my estate! It is known to you also that, owing to her action with her servant, I suffer, though innocent, a deadly wrong—this affair I brought after her death before the senate, before the sixth department—it is still unsettled now—in consequence of which I was made an accomplice with her, my estate put under guardianship, and I am still lying under a criminal charge! In my position, at my age, such disgrace is intolerable to me; and it is only left me to console my heart with the mournful reflection that thus, even after Agrippina Ivanovna's death, I suffer for her sake, and so prove my immutable love and loyal gratitude to her!

' In my letters, above mentioned, to you, I gave you an account with every detail of Agrippina Ivanovna's funeral, and what masses were read for her—my affection and love for her spared not outlay! For all the aforesaid, and for the forty days' requiems, and the reading of the psalter six weeks after for her (in addition to above, fifty roubles of mine were lost, which were given as security for payment for the stone, of which I sent you a description)—on all the aforesaid was spent of my money seven hundred and fifty roubles, in which is included, by way of donation to the church, a hundred and fifty roubles.

'In the goodness of your heart, hear the cry of a desperate man, crushed beneath a load of the cruelest calamities! Only your commiseration and humanity can restore the life of a ruined man! Though living—in the suffering of my heart and soul I am as one dead; dead when I think what I was, and what I am; I was a soldier, and served my country in all fidelity and uprightness, as is the bounden duty of a loyal Russian and faithful subject, and was rewarded with the highest honours, and had a fortune befitting my birth and station; and now I must cringe and beg for a morsel of dry bread; dead above all I am when I think what a friend I have lost . . . and what is life to me after that? But there is no hastening one's end, and the earth will not open, but rather seems turned to stone! And so I call upon you, in the benevolence of your heart, hush the talk of the people, do not expose yourself to universal censure, that for all my unbounded devotion I have not where to lay my head; confound them by your bounty to me, turn the tongues of the evil speakers and slanderers to glorifying your good works—and I make bold in all humility to add, comfort in the grave your most precious aunt, Agrippina Ivanovna, who can never be forgotten, and who for your speedy succour, in answer to my sinful prayers, will spread her protecting wings about your head, and comfort in his declining days a lonely old man, who had every reason to expect a different fate! . . . And, with the most profound respect, I have the honour to be, dear madam, your most devoted servant,

VASSILY GUSKOV,
Brigadier and cavalier.'

Several years later I paid another visit to my friend's little place. . . . Vassily Fomitch had long been dead; he died soon after I made his acquaintance. Cucumber was still flourishing. He conducted me to the tomb of Agrafena Ivanovna. An iron railing enclosed a large slab with a detailed and enthusiastically laudatory epitaph on the deceased woman; and there, beside it, as it were at her feet, could be seen a little mound with a slanting cross on it; the servant of God, the brigadier and cavalier, Vassily Guskov, lay under this mound. . . . His ashes found rest at last beside the ashes of the creature he had loved with such unbounded, almost undying, love.

1867.

PYETUSHKOV

In the year 182– . . . there was living in the town of O—— the lieutenant Ivan Afanasiitch Pyetushkov. He was born of poor parents, was left an orphan at five years old, and came into the charge of a guardian. Thanks to this guardian, he found himself with no property whatever; he had a hard struggle to make both ends meet. He was of medium height, and stooped a little; he had a thin face, covered with freckles, but rather pleasing; light brown hair, grey eyes, and a timid expression; his low forehead was furrowed with fine wrinkles. Pyetushkov's whole life had been uneventful in the extreme; at close upon forty he was still youthful and inexperienced as a child. He was shy with acquaintances, and exceedingly mild in his manner with persons over whose lot he could have exerted control. . . .

People condemned by fate to a monotonous and cheerless existence often acquire all sorts of little habits and preferences. Pyetushkov liked to have a new white roll with his tea every morning. He could not do without this dainty. But behold one morning his servant, Onisim, handed him, on a blue-sprigged plate, instead of a roll, three dark red rusks.

Pyetushkov at once asked his servant, with some indignation, what he meant by it.

'The rolls have all been sold out,' answered Onisim, a native of Petersburg, who had been flung by some queer freak of destiny into the very wilds of south Russia.

'Impossible!' exclaimed Ivan Afanasiitch.

'Sold out,' repeated Onisim; 'there's a breakfast at the Marshal's, so they've all gone there, you know.'

Onisim waved his hand in the air, and thrust his right foot forward.

Ivan Afanasiitch walked up and down the room, dressed, and set off himself to the baker's shop. This establishment, the only one of the kind in the town of O——, had been opened ten years before by a German immigrant, had in a short time begun to flourish, and was still flourishing under the guidance of his widow, a fat woman.

Pyetushkov tapped at the window. The fat woman stuck her unhealthy, flabby, sleepy countenance out of the pane that opened.

'A roll, if you please,' Pyetushkov said amiably.

'The rolls are all gone,' piped the fat woman.

'Haven't you any rolls?'

'No.'

'How's that?—really! I take rolls from you every day, and pay for them regularly.'

The woman stared at him in silence. 'Take twists,' she said at last, yawning; 'or a scone.'

'I don't like them,' said Pyetushkov, and he felt positively hurt.

'As you please,' muttered the fat woman, and she slammed to the window-pane.

Ivan Afanasiitch was quite unhinged by his intense vexation. In his perturbation he crossed to the other hide of the street, and gave himself up entirely, like a child, to his displeasure.

'Sir!' . . . he heard a rather agreeable female voice; 'sir!'

Ivan Afanasiitch raised his eyes. From the open pane of the bakehouse window peeped a girl of about seventeen, holding a white roll in her hand. She had a full round face, rosy cheeks, small hazel eyes, rather a turn-up nose, fair hair, and magnificent shoulders. Her features suggested good-nature, laziness, and carelessness.

'Here's a roll for you, sir,' she said, laughing, 'I'd taken for myself; but take it, please, I'll give it up to you.'

'I thank you most sincerely. Allow me . . .'

Pyetushkov began fumbling in his pocket.

'No, no! you are welcome to it.'

She closed the window-pane.

Pyetushkov arrived home in a perfectly agreeable frame of mind.

'You couldn't get any rolls,' he said to his Onisim; 'but here, I've got one, do you see?'

Onisim gave a bitter laugh.

The same day, in the evening, as Ivan Afanasiitch was undressing, he asked his servant, 'Tell me, please, my lad, what's the girl like at the baker's, hey?'

Onisim looked away rather gloomily, and responded, 'What do you want to know for?'

'Oh, nothing,' said Pyetushkov, taking off his boots with his own hands.

'Well, she's a fine girl!' Onisim observed condescendingly.

'Yes, . . . she's not bad-looking,' said Ivan Afanasiitch, also looking away. 'And what's her name, do you know?'

'Vassilissa.'

'And do you know her?'

Onisim did not answer for a minute or two.

'We know her.'

Pyetushkov was on the point of opening his mouth again, but he turned over on the other side and fell asleep.

Onisim went out into the passage, took a pinch of snuff, and gave his head a violent shake.

The next day, early in the morning, Pyetushkov called for his clothes. Onisim brought him his everyday coat—an old grass-coloured coat, with huge striped epaulettes. Pyetushkov gazed a long while at Onisim without speaking, then told him to bring him his new coat. Onisim, with some surprise, obeyed. Pyetushkov dressed, and carefully drew on his chamois-leather gloves.

'You needn't go to the baker's to-day,' said he with some hesitation; 'I'm going myself, . . . it's on my way.'

'Yes, sir,' responded Onisim, as abruptly as if some one had just given him a shove from behind.

Pyetushkov set off, reached the baker's shop, tapped at the window. The fat woman opened the pane.

'Give me a roll, please,' Ivan Afanasiitch articulated slowly.

The fat woman stuck out an arm, bare to the shoulder—a huge arm, more like a leg than an arm—and thrust the hot bread just under his nose.

Ivan Afanasiitch stood some time under the window, walked once or twice up and down the street, glanced into the courtyard, and at last, ashamed of his childishness, returned home with the roll in his hand. He felt ill at ease the whole day, and even in the evening, contrary to his habit, did not drop into conversation with Onisim.

The next morning it was Onisim who went for the roll.

II

SOME weeks went by. Ivan Afanasiitch had completely forgotten Vassilissa, and chatted in a friendly way with his servant as before. One fine morning there came to see him a certain Bublitsyn, an easy-mannered and very agreeable young man. It is true he sometimes hardly knew himself what he was talking about, and was always, as they say, a little wild; but all the same he had the reputation of being an exceedingly agreeable person to talk to. He smoked a great deal with feverish eagerness, with lifted eye-brows and contracted chest—smoked with an expression of intense anxiety, or, one might rather say, with an expression as though, let him have this one more puff at his pipe, and in a minute he would tell you some quite unexpected piece of news; at times he would even give a grunt and a wave of the hand, while himself sucking at his pipe, as though he had suddenly recollected something extraordinarily amusing or important, then he would open his mouth, let off a few rings of smoke, and utter the most common-place remarks, or even keep silence altogether. After gossiping a little with Ivan Afanasiitch about the neighbours, about horses, the daughters of the gentry around, and other such edifying topics, Mr. Bublitsyn suddenly winked, pulled up his shock of hair, and, with a sly smile, approached the remarkably dim looking-glass which was the solitary ornament of Ivan Afanasiitch's room.

'There's no denying the fact,' he pronounced, stroking his light brown whiskers, 'we've got girls here that beat any of your Venus of Medicis hollow. . . . Have you seen Vassilissa, the baker girl, for instance?' . . . Mr. Bublitsyn sucked at his pipe.

Pyetushkov started.

'But why do I ask you?' pursued Bublitsyn, disappearing in a cloud of smoke,—'you're not the man to notice, don't you know, Ivan Afanasiitch! Goodness knows what you do to occupy yourself, Ivan Afanasiitch!'

'The same as you do,' Pyetushkov replied with some vexation, in a drawling voice.

'Oh no, Ivan Afanasiitch, not a bit of it. . . . How can you say so?'

'Well, why not?'

'Nonsense, nonsense.'

'Why so, why so?'

Bublitsyn stuck his pipe in the corner of his mouth, and began scrutinising his not very handsome boots. Pyetushkov felt embarrassed.

'Ah, Ivan Afanasiitch, Ivan Afanasiitch!' pursued Bublitsyn, as though sparing his feelings. 'But as to Vassilissa, the baker girl, I can assure you: a very, ve-ry fine girl, . . . ve-ry.'

Mr. Bublitsyn dilated his nostrils, and slowly plunged his hands into his pockets.

Strange to relate, Ivan Afanasiitch felt something of the nature of jealousy. He began moving restlessly in his chair, burst into explosive laughter at nothing at all, suddenly blushed, yawned, and, as he yawned, his lower jaw twitched a little. Bublitsyn smoked three more pipes, and withdrew. Ivan Afanasiitch went to the window, sighed, and called for something to drink.

Onisim set a glass of kvas on the table, glanced severely at his master, leaned back against the door, and hung his head dejectedly.

'What are you so thoughtful about?' his master asked him genially, but with some inward trepidation.

'What am I thinking about?' retorted Onisim; 'what am I thinking about? . . . it's always about you.'

'About me!'

'Of course it's about you.'

'Why, what is it you are thinking?'

'Why, this is what I'm thinking.' (Here Onisim took a pinch of snuff.) 'You ought to be ashamed, sir—you ought to be ashamed of yourself.'

'Ashamed?'

'Yes, ashamed. . . . Look at Mr. Bublitsyn, Ivan Afanasiitch. . . . Tell me if he's not a fine fellow, now.'

'I don't understand you.'

'You don't understand me. . . . Oh yes, you do understand me.'

Onisim paused.

'Mr. Bublitsyn's a real gentleman—what a gentleman ought to be. But what are you, Ivan Afanasiitch, what are you? Tell me that.'

'Why, I'm a gentleman too.'

'A gentleman, indeed!' . . . retorted Onisim, growing indignant. 'A pretty gentleman you are! You're no better, sir, than a hen in a shower of rain, Ivan Afanasiitch, let me tell you. Here you sit sticking at home the whole blessed day . . . much good it does you, sitting at home like that! You don't play cards, you don't go and see the gentry, and as for . . . well . . .'

Onisim waved his hand expressively.

'Now, come . . . you really go . . . too far . . .' Ivan Afanasiitch said hesitatingly, clutching his pipe.

'Too far, indeed, Ivan Afanasiitch, too far, you say! Judge for yourself. Here again, with Vassilissa . . . why couldn't you . . .'

'But what are you thinking about, Onisim?' Pyetushkov interrupted miserably.

'I know what I'm thinking about. But there—I'd better let you alone! What can you do? Only fancy . . . there you . . .'

Ivan Afanasiitch got up.

'There, there, if you please, you hold your tongue,' he said quickly, seeming to be searching for Onisim with his eyes; 'I shall really, you know . . . I . . . what do you mean by it, really? You'd better help me dress.'

Onisim slowly drew off Ivan Afanasiitch's greasy Tartar dressing-gown, gazed with fatherly commiseration at his master, shook his head, put him on his coat, and fell to beating him about the back with a brush.

Pyetushkov went out, and after a not very protracted stroll about the crooked streets of the town, found himself facing the baker's shop. A queer smile was playing about his lips.

He had hardly time to look twice at the too well-known 'establishment,' when suddenly the little gate opened, and Vassilissa ran out with a yellow kerchief on her head and a jacket flung after the Russian fashion on her shoulders. Ivan Afanasiitch at once overtook her.

'Where are you going, my dear?'

Vassilissa glanced swiftly at him, laughed, turned away, and put her hand over her lips.

'Going shopping, I suppose?' queried Ivan Afanasiitch, fidgeting with his feet.

'How inquisitive we are!' retorted Vassilissa.

'Why inquisitive?' said Pyetushkov, hurriedly gesticulating with his hands. 'Quite the contrary. . . . Oh yes, you know,' he added hastily, as though these last words completely conveyed his meaning.

'Did you eat my roll?'

'To be sure I did,' replied Pyetushkov: 'with special enjoyment.'

Vassilissa continued to walk on and to laugh.

'It's pleasant weather to-day,' pursued Ivan Afanasiitch: 'do you often go out walking?'

'Yes.'

'Ah, how I should like . . .'

'What say?'

The girls in our district utter those words in a very queer way, with a peculiar sharpness and rapidity. . . . Partridges call at sunset with just that sound.

'To go out walking, don't you know, with you . . . into the country, or . . .'

'How can you?'

'Why not?'

'Ah, upon my word, how you do go on!'

'But allow me . . .'

At this point they were overtaken by a dapper little shopman, with a little goat's beard, and with his fingers held apart like antlers, so as to keep his sleeves from slipping over his hands, in a long-skirted bluish coat, and a warm cap that resembled a bloated water-melon. Pyetushkov, for propriety's sake, fell back a little behind Vassilissa, but quickly came up with her again.

'Well, then, what about our walk?'

Vassilissa looked slily at him and giggled again.

'Do you belong to these parts?'

'Yes.'

Vassilissa passed her hand over her hair and walked a little more slowly. Ivan Afanasiitch smiled, and, his heart inwardly sinking with timidity, he stooped a little on one side and put a trembling arm about the beauty's waist.

Vassilissa uttered a shriek.

'Give over, do, for shame, in the street.'

'Come now, there, there,' muttered Ivan Afanasiitch.

'Give over, I tell you, in the street. . . . Don't be rude.'

'A . . . a . . . ah, what a girl you are!' said Pyetushkov reproachfully, while he blushed up to his ears.

Vassilissa stood still.

'Now go along with you, sir—go along, do.'

Pyetushkov obeyed. He got home, and sat for a whole hour without moving from his chair, without even smoking his pipe. At last he took out a sheet of greyish paper, mended a pen, and after long deliberation wrote the following letter.

'DEAR MADAM, VASSILISSA TIMOFYEVNA!—Being naturally a most inoffensive person, how could I have occasioned you annoyance? If I have really been to blame in my conduct to you, then I must tell you: the hints of Mr. Bublitsyn were responsible for this, which was what I never expected. Anyway, I must humbly beg you not to be angry with me. I am a sensitive man, and any kindness I am most sensible of and grateful for. Do not be angry with me, Vassilissa Timofyevna, I beg you most humbly.—I remain respectfully your obedient servant,   IVAN PYETUSHKOV.'

Onisim carried this letter to its address.

III

A FORTNIGHT PASSED. Onisim went every morning as usual to the baker's shop. One day Vassilissa ran out to meet him.

'Good morning, Onisim Sergeitch.'

Onisim put on a gloomy expression, and responded crossly, ' 'Morning.'

'How is it you never come to see us, Onisim Sergeitch?'

Onisim glanced morosely at her.

'What should I come for? you wouldn't give me a cup of tea, no fear.'

'Yes, I would, Onisim Sergeitch, I would. You come and see. Rum in it, too.'

Onisim slowly relaxed into a smile.

'Well, I don't mind if I do, then.'

'When, then—when?'

'When . . . well, you are . . .'

'To-day—this evening, if you like. Drop in.'

'All right, I'll come along,' replied Onisim, and he sauntered home with his slow, rolling step.

The same evening in a little room, beside a bed covered with a striped eider-down, Onisim was sitting at a clumsy little table, facing Vassilissa. A huge, dingy yellow samovar was hissing and bubbling on the table; a pot of geranium stood in the window; in the other corner near the door there stood aslant an ugly chest with a tiny hanging lock; on the chest lay a shapeless heap of all sorts of old rags; on the walls were black, greasy prints. Onisim and Vassilissa drank their tea in silence, looking straight at each other, turning the lumps of sugar over and over in their hands, as it were reluctantly nibbling them, blinking, screwing up their eyes, and with a hissing sound sucking in the yellowish boiling liquid through their teeth. At last they had emptied the whole samovar, turned upside down the round cups—one with the inscription, 'Take your fill'; the other with the words, 'Cupid's dart hath pierced my heart'—then they cleared their throats, wiped their perspiring brows, and gradually dropped into conversation.

'Onisim Sergeitch, how about your master . . .' began Vassilissa, and did not finish her sentence.

'What about my master?' replied Onisim, and he leaned on his hand. 'He's all right. But why do you ask?'

'Oh, I only asked,' answered Vassilissa.

'But I say'—(here Onisim grinned)—'I say, he wrote you a letter, didn't he?'

'Yes, he did.'

Onisim shook his head with an extraordinarily self-satisfied air.

'So he did, did he?' he said huskily, with a smile. 'Well, and what did he say in his letter to you?'

'Oh, all sorts of things. "I didn't mean anything, Madam Vassilissa Timofyevna," says he, "don't you think anything of it; don't you be offended, madam," and a lot more like that he wrote. . . . But I say,' she added after a brief silence: 'what's he like?'

'He's all right,' Onisim responded indifferently.

'Does he get angry?'

'He get angry! Not he. Why, do you like him?'

Vassilissa looked down and giggled in her sleeve.

'Come,' grumbled Onisim.

'Oh, what's that to you, Onisim Sergeitch?'

'Oh, come, I tell you.'

'Well,' Vassilissa brought out at last, 'he's . . . a gentleman. Of course . . . I . . . and besides; he . . . you know yourself . . .'

'Of course I do,' Onisim observed solemnly.

'Of course you're aware, to be sure, Onisim Sergeitch.' . . . Vassilissa was obviously becoming agitated.

'You tell him, your master, that I'm . . . ; say, not angry with him, but that . . .'

She stammered.

'We understand,' responded Onisim, and he got up from his seat. 'We understand. Thanks for the entertainment.'

'Come in again some day.'

'All right, all right.'

Onisim approached the door. The fat woman came into the room.

'Good evening to you, Onisim Sergeitch,' she said in a peculiar chant.

'Good evening to you, Praskovia Ivanovna,' he said in the same sing-song. Both stood still for a little while facing each other.

'Well, good day to you, Praskovia Ivanovna,' Onisim chanted out again.

'Well, good day to you, Onisim Sergeitch,' she responded in the same sing-song.

Onisim arrived home. His master was lying on his bed, gazing at the ceiling.

'Where have you been?'

'Where have I been?' . . . (Onisim had the habit of repeating reproachfully the last words of every question.) 'I've been about your business.'

'What business?'

'Why, don't you know? . . . I've been to see Vassilissa.'

Pyetushkov blinked and turned over on his bed.

'So that's how it is,' observed Onisim, and he coolly took a pinch of snuff. 'So that's how it is. You're always like that. Vassilissa sends you her duty.'

'Really?'

'Really? So that's all about it. Really! . . . She told me to say, Why is it, says she, one never sees him? Why is it, says she, he never comes?'

'Well, and what did you say?'

'What did I say? I told her: You're a silly girl—I told her—as if folks like that are coming to see you! No, you come yourself, I told her.'

'Well, and what did she say?'

'What did she say? . . . She said nothing.'

'That is, how do you mean, nothing?'

'Why nothing, to be sure.'

Pyetushkov said nothing for a little while.

'Well, and is she coming?'

Onisim shook his head.

'She coming! You're in too great a hurry, sir. She coming, indeed! No, you go too fast.' . . .

'But you said yourself that . . .'

'Oh, well, it's easy to talk.'

Pyetushkov was silent again.

'Well, but how's it to be, then, my lad?'

'How? . . . You ought to know best; you're a gentleman.'

'Oh, nonsense! come now!'

Onisim swayed complacently backwards and forwards.

'Do you know Praskovia Ivanovna?' he asked at last.

'No. What Praskovia Ivanovna?'

'Why, the baker woman!'

'Oh yes, the baker woman. I've seen her; she's very fat.'

'She's a worthy woman. She's own aunt to the other, to your girl.'

'Aunt?'

'Why, didn't you know?'

'No, I didn't know.'

'Well . . .'

Onisim was restrained by respect for his master from giving full expression to his feelings.

'That's whom it is you should make friends with.'

'Well, I've no objection.'

Onisim looked approvingly at Ivan Afanasiitch.

'But with what object precisely am I to make friends with her?' inquired Pyetushkov.

'What for, indeed!' answered Onisim serenely.

Ivan Afanasiitch got up, paced up and down the room, stood still before the window, and without turning his head, with some hesitation he articulated:

'Onisim!'

'What say?'

'Won't it be, you know, a little awkward for me with the old woman, eh?'

'Oh, that's as you like.'

'Oh, well, I only thought it might, perhaps. My comrades might notice it; it's a little . . . But I'll think it over. Give me my pipe. . . . So she,' he went on after a short silence—'Vassilissa, I mean, says then . . .'

But Onisim had no desire to continue the conversation, and he assumed his habitual morose expression.

IV

Ivan afanasiitch's acquaintance with Praskovia Ivanovna began in the following manner. Five days after his conversation with Onisim, Pyetushkov set off in the evening to the baker's shop. 'Well,' thought he, as he unlatched the creaking gate, 'I don't know how it's to be.' . . .

He mounted the steps, opened the door. A huge, crested hen rushed, with a deafening cackle, straight under his feet, and long after was still running about the yard in wild excitement. From a room close by peeped the astonished countenance of the fat woman. Ivan Afanasiitch smiled and nodded. The fat woman bowed to him. Tightly grasping his hat, Pyetushkov approached her. Praskovia Ivanovna was apparently anticipating an honoured guest; her dress was fastened up at every hook. Pyetushkov sat down on a chair; Praskovia Ivanovna seated herself opposite him.

'I have come to you, Praskovia Ivanovna, more on account of . . .' Ivan Afanasiitch began at last—and then ceased. His lips were twitching spasmodically.

'You are kindly welcome, sir,' responded Praskovia Ivanovna in the proper sing-song, and with a bow. 'Always delighted to see a guest.'

Pyetushkov took courage a little.

'I have long wished, you know, to have the pleasure of making your acquaintance, Praskovia Ivanovna.'

'Much obliged to you, Ivan Afanasiitch.'

Followed a silence. Praskovia Ivanovna wiped her face with a particoloured handkerchief; Ivan Afanasiitch continued with intense attention to gaze away to one side. Both were rather uncomfortable. But in merchant and petty shopkeeper society, where even old friends never step outside special angular forms of etiquette, a certain constraint in the behaviour of guests and host to one another not only strikes no one as strange, but, on the contrary, is regarded as perfectly correct and indispensable, particularly on a first visit. Praskovia Ivanovna was agreeably impressed by Pyetushkov. He was formal and decorous in his manners, and moreover, wasn't he a man of some rank, too?

'Praskovia Ivanovna, ma'am, I like your rolls very much,' he said to her.

'Really now, really now.'

'Very good they are, you know, very, indeed.'

'May they do you good, sir, may they do you good. Delighted, to be sure.'

'I've never eaten any like them in Moscow.'

'You don't say so now, you don't say so.'

Again a silence followed.

'Tell me, Praskovia Ivanovna,' began Ivan Afanasiitch; 'that's your niece, I fancy, isn't it, living with you?'

'My own niece, sir.'

'How comes it . . . she's with you?' . . .

'She's an orphan, so I keep her.'

'And is she a good worker?'

'Such a girl to work . . . such a girl, sir . . . ay . . . ay . . . to be sure she is.'

Ivan Afanasiitch thought it discreet not to pursue the subject of the niece further.

'What bird is that you have in the cage, Praskovia Ivanovna?'

'God knows. A bird of some sort.'

'H'm! Well, so, good day to you, Praskovia Ivanovna.'

'A very good day to your honour. Pray walk in another time, and take a cup of tea.'

'With the greatest pleasure, Praskovia Ivanovna.'

Pyetushkov walked out. On the steps he met Vassilissa. She giggled.

'Where are you going, my darling?' said Pyetushkov with reckless daring.

'Come, give over, do, you are a one for joking.'

'He, he! And did you get my letter?'

Vassilissa hid the lower part of her face in her sleeve and made no answer.

'And you're not angry with me?'

'Vassilissa!' came the jarring voice of the aunt; 'hey, Vassilissa!'

Vassilissa ran into the house. Pyetushkov returned home. But from that day he began going often to the baker's shop, and his visits were not for nothing. Ivan Afanasiitch's hopes, to use the lofty phraseology suitable, were crowned with success. Usually, the attainment of the goal has a cooling effect on people, but Pyetushkov, on the contrary, grew every day more and more ardent. Love is a thing of accident, it exists in itself, like art, and, like nature, needs no reasons to justify it, as some clever man has said who never loved, himself, but made excellent observations upon love.

Pyetushkov became passionately attached to Vassilissa. He was completely happy. His soul was aglow with bliss. Little by little he carried all his belongings, at any rate all his pipes, to Praskovia Ivanovna's, and for whole days together he sat in her back room. Praskovia Ivanovna charged him something for his dinner and drank his tea, consequently she did not complain of his presence. Vassilissa had grown used to him. She would work, sing, or spin before him, sometimes exchanging a couple of words with him; Pyetushkov watched her, smoked his pipe, swayed to and fro in his chair, laughed, and in leisure hours played 'Fools' with her and Praskovia Ivanovna. Ivan Afanasiitch was happy. . . .

But in this world nothing is perfect, and, small as a man's requirements may be, destiny never quite fulfils them, and positively spoils the whole thing, if possible. . . . The spoonful of pitch is sure to find its way into the barrel of honey! Ivan Afanasiitch experienced this in his case.

In the first place, from the time of his establishing himself at Vassilissa's, Pyetushkov dropped more than ever out of all intercourse with his comrades. He saw them only when absolutely necessary, and then, to avoid allusions and jeers (in which, however, he was not always successful), he put on the desperately sullen and intensely scared look of a hare in a display of fireworks.

Secondly, Onisim gave him no peace; he had lost every trace of respect for him, he mercilessly persecuted him, put him to shame.

And . . . thirdly. . . . Alas! read further, kindly reader.

V

ONE DAY Pyetushkov (who for the reasons given above found little comfort outside Praskovia Ivanovna's doors) was sitting in Vassilissa's room at the back, and was busying himself over some home-brewed concoction, something in the way of jam or syrup. The mistress of the house was not at home. Vassilissa was sitting in the shop singing.

There came a knock at the little pane. Vassilissa got up, went to the window, uttered a little shriek, giggled, and began whispering with some one. On going back to her place, she sighed, and then fell to singing louder than ever.

'Who was that you were talking to?' Pyetushkov asked her.

Vassilissa went on singing carelessly.

'Vassilissa, do you hear? Vassilissa!'

'What do you want?'

'Whom were you talking to?'

'What's that to you?'

'I only asked.'

Pyetushkov came out of the back room in a parti-coloured smoking-jacket with tucked-up sleeves, and a strainer in his hand.

'Oh, a friend of mine,' answered Vassilissa.

'What friend?'

'Oh, Piotr Petrovitch.'

'Piotr Petrovitch? . . . what Piotr Petrovitch?'

'He's one of your lot. He's got such a difficult name.'

'Bublitsyn?'

'Yes, yes . . . Piotr Petrovitch.'

'And do you know him?'

'Rather!' responded Vassilissa, with a wag of her head.

Pyetushkov, without a word, paced ten times up and down the room.

'I say, Vassilissa,' he said at last, 'that is, how do you know him?'

'How do I know him? . . . I know him . . . He's such a nice gentleman.'

'How do you mean nice, though? how nice? how nice?'

Vassilissa gazed at Ivan Afanasiitch.

'Nice,' she said slowly and in perplexity. 'You know what I mean.'

Pyetushkov bit his lips and began again pacing the room.

'What were you talking about with him, eh?'

Vassilissa smiled and looked down.

'Speak, speak, speak, I tell you, speak!'

'How cross you are to-day!' observed Vassilissa.

Pyetushkov was silent.

'Come now, Vassilissa,' he began at last; 'no, I won't be cross. . . . Come, tell me, what were you talking about?'

Vassilissa laughed.

'He is a one to joke, really, that Piotr Petrovitch!'

'Well, what did he say?'

'He is a fellow!'

Pyetushkov was silent again for a little.

'Vassilissa, you love me, don't you?' he asked her.

'Oh, so that's what you're after, too!'

Poor Pyetushkov felt a pang at his heart. Praskovia Ivanovna came in. They sat down to dinner. After dinner Praskovia Ivanovna betook herself to the shelf bed. Ivan Afanasiitch himself lay down on the stove, turned over and dropped asleep. A cautious creak waked him. Ivan Afanasiitch sat up, leaned on his elbow, looked: the door was open. He jumped up—no Vassilissa. He ran into the yard—she was not in the yard; into the street, looked up and down—Vassilissa was nowhere to be seen. He ran without his cap as far as the market—no, Vassilissa was not in sight. Slowly he returned to the baker's shop, clambered on to the stove, and turned with his face to the wall. He felt miserable. Bublitsyn . . . Bublitsyn . . . the name was positively ringing in his ears.

'What's the matter, my good sir?' Praskovia Ivanovna asked him in a drowsy voice. 'Why are you groaning?'

'Oh, nothing, ma'am. Nothing. I feel a weight oppressing me.'

'It's the mushrooms,' murmured Praskovia Ivanovna—'it's all those mushrooms.'

O Lord, have mercy on us sinners!

An hour passed, a second—still no Vassilissa. Twenty times Pyetushkov was on the point of getting up, and twenty times he huddled miserably under the sheepskin. . . . At last he really did get down from the stove and determined to go home, and positively went out into the yard, but came back. Praskovia Ivanovna got up. The hired man, Luka, black as a beetle, though he was a baker, put the bread into the oven. Pyetushkov went again out on to the steps and pondered. The goat that lived in the yard went up to him, and gave him a little friendly poke with his horns. Pyetushkov looked at him, and for some unknown reason said 'Kss, Kss.' Suddenly the low wicket-gate slowly opened and Vassilissa appeared. Ivan Afanasiitch went straight to meet her, took her by the hand, and rather coolly, but resolutely, said to her:

'Come along with me.'

'But, excuse me, Ivan Afanasiitch . . . I . . .'

'Come with me,' he repeated.

She obeyed.

Pyetushkov led her to his lodgings. Onisim, as usual, was lying at full length asleep. Ivan Afanasiitch waked him, told him to light a candle. Vassilissa went to the window and sat down in silence. While Onisim was busy getting a light in the anteroom, Pyetushkov stood motionless at the other window, staring into the street. Onisim came in, with the candle in his hands, was beginning to grumble . . . Ivan Afanasiitch turned quickly round: 'Go along,' he said to him.

Onisim stood still in the middle of the room.

'Go away at once,' Pyetushkov repeated threateningly.

Onisim looked at his master and went out.

Ivan Afanasiitch shouted after him:

'Away, quite away. Out of the house. You can come back in two hours' time.'

Onisim slouched off.

Pyetushkov waited till he heard the gate bang, and at once went up to Vassilissa.

'Where have you been?'

Vassilissa was confused.

'Where have you been? I tell you,' he repeated.

Vassilissa looked round . . .

'I am speaking to you . . . where have you been?' And Pyetushkov raised his arm . . .

'Don't beat me, Ivan Afanasiitch, don't beat me,' Vassilissa whispered in terror.

Pyetushkov turned away.

'Beat you. . . . No! I'm not going to beat you. Beat you? I beg your pardon, my darling. God bless you! While I supposed you loved me, while I . . . I . . .'

Ivan Afanasiitch broke off. He gasped for breath.

'Listen, Vassilissa,' he said at last. 'You know I'm a kind-hearted man, you know it, don't you, Vassilissa, don't you?'

'Yes, I do,' she said faltering.

'I do nobody any harm, nobody, nobody in the world. And I deceive nobody. Why are you deceiving me?'

'But I'm not deceiving you, Ivan Afanasiitch.'

'You aren't deceiving me? Oh, very well! Oh, very well! Then tell me where you've been.'

'I went to see Matrona.'

'That's a lie!'

'Really, I've been at Matrona's. You ask her, if you don't believe me.'

'And Bub—— what's his name . . . have you seen that devil?'

'Yes, I did see him.'

'You did see him! you did see him! Oh, you did see him!'

Pyetushkov turned pale.

'So you were making an appointment with him in the morning at the window—eh? eh?'

'He asked me to come.'

'And so you went. . . . Thanks very much, my girl, thanks very much!' Pyetushkov made Vassilissa a low bow.

'But, Ivan Afanasiitch, you're maybe fancying . . .'

'You'd better not talk to me! And a pretty fool I am! There's nothing to make an outcry for! You may make friends with any one you like. I've nothing to do with you. So there! I don't want to know you even.'

Vassilissa got up.

'That's for you to say, Ivan Afanasiitch.'

'Where are you going?'

'Why, you yourself . . .'

'I'm not sending you away,' Pyetushkov interrupted her.

'Oh no, Ivan Afanasiitch. . . . What's the use of my stopping here?'

Pyetushkov let her get as far as the door.

'So you're going, Vassilissa?'

'You keep on abusing me.'

'I abuse you! You've no fear of God, Vassilissa! When have I abused you? Come, come, say when?'

'Why! Just this minute weren't you all but beating me?'

'Vassilissa, it's wicked of you. Really, it's downright wicked.'

'And then you threw it in my face, that you don't want to know me. "I'm a gentleman," say you.'

Ivan Afanasiitch began wringing his hands speechlessly. Vassilissa got back as far as the middle of the room.

'Well, God be with you, Ivan Afanasiitch. I'll keep myself to myself, and you keep yourself to yourself.'

'Nonsense, Vassilissa, nonsense,' Pyetushkov cut her short. 'You think again; look at me. You see I'm not myself. You see I don't know what I'm saying. . . . You might have some feeling for me.'

'You keep on abusing me, Ivan Afanasiitch.'

'Ah, Vassilissa! Let bygones be bygones. Isn't that right? Come, you're not angry with me, are you?'

'You keep abusing me,' Vassilissa repeated.

'I won't, my love, I won't. Forgive an old man like me. I'll never do it in future. Come, you've forgiven me, eh?'

'God be with you, Ivan Afanasiitch.'

'Come, laugh then, laugh.'

Vassilissa turned away.

'You laughed, you laughed, my love!' cried Pyetushkov, and he capered about like a child.

VI

THE NEXT DAY Pyetushkov went to the baker's shop as usual. Everything went on as before. But there was a settled ache at his heart. He did not laugh now as often, and sometimes he fell to musing. Sunday came. Praskovia Ivanovna had an attack of lumbago; she did not get down from the shelf bed, except with much difficulty to go to mass. After mass Pyetushkov called Vassilissa into the back room. She had been complaining all the morning of feeling dull. To judge by the expression of Ivan Afanasiitch's countenance, he was revolving in his brain some extraordinary idea, unforeseen even by him.

'You sit down here, Vassilissa,' he said to her, 'and I'll sit here. I want to have a little talk with you.'

Vassilissa sat down.

'Tell me, Vassilissa, can you write?'

'Write?'

'Yes, write?'

'No, I can't.'

'What about reading?'

'I can't read either.'

'Then who read you my letter?'

'The deacon.'

Pyetushkov paused.

'But would you like to learn to read and write?'

'Why, what use would reading and writing be to us, Ivan Afanasiitch?'

'What use? You could read books.'

'But what good is there in books?'

'All sorts of good. . . . I tell you what, if you like, I'll bring you a book.'

'But I can't read, you see, Ivan Afanasiitch.'

'I'll read to you.'

'But, I say, won't it be dull?'

'Nonsense! dull! On the contrary, it's the best thing to get rid of dulness.'

'Maybe you'll read stories, then.'

'You shall see to-morrow.'

In the evening Pyetushkov returned home, and began rummaging in his boxes. He found several odd numbers of the Library of Good Reading, five grey Moscow novels, Nazarov's arithmetic, a child's geography with a globe on the title-page, the second part of Keydanov's history, two dream-books, an almanack for the year 1819, two numbers of Galatea, Kozlov's *Natalia Dolgorukaia,* and the first part of *Roslavlev.* He pondered a long while which to choose, and finally made up his mind to take Kozlov's poem, and *Roslavlev.*

Next day Pyetushkov dressed in haste, put both the books under the lapel of his coat, went to the baker's shop, and began reading aloud Zagoskin's novel. Vassilissa sat without moving; at first she smiled, then seemed to become absorbed in thought . . . then she bent a little forward; her eyes closed, her mouth slightly opened, her hands fell on her knees; she was dozing. Pyetushkov read quickly, inarticulately, in a thick voice; he raised his eyes . . .

'Vassilissa, are you asleep?'

She started, rubbed her face, and stretched. Pyetushkov felt angry with her and with himself . . .

'It's dull,' said Vassilissa lazily.

'I tell you what, would you like me to read you poetry?'

'What say?'

'Poetry . . . good poetry.'

'No, that's enough, really.'

Pyetushkov hurriedly picked up Kozlov's poem, jumped up, crossed the room, ran impulsively up to Vassilissa, and began reading. Vassilissa let her head drop backwards, spread out her hands, stared into Ivan Afanasiitch's face, and suddenly went off into a loud harsh guffaw . . . she fairly rolled about with laughing.

Ivan Afanasiitch flung the book on the floor in his annoyance. Vassilissa went on laughing.

'Why, what are you laughing at, silly?'

Vassilissa roared more than ever.

'Laugh away, laugh away,' Pyetushkov muttered between his teeth.

Vassilissa held her sides, gasping.

'But what is it, idiot?'

But Vassilissa could only wave her hands.

Ivan Afanasiitch snatched up his cap, and ran out of the house. With rapid, unsteady steps, he walked about the town, walked on and on, and found himself at the city gates. Suddenly there was the rattle of wheels, the tramp of horses along the street. . . . Some one called him by name. He raised his head and saw a big, old-fashioned wagonette. In the wagonette facing him sat Mr. Bublitsyn between two young ladies, the daughters of Mr. Tiutiurov. Both the girls were dressed exactly alike, as though in outward sign of their immutable affection; both smiled pensively, and carried their heads on one side with a languid grace. On the other side of the carriage appeared the wide straw hat of their excellent papa; and from time to time his round, plump neck presented itself to the gaze of spectators. Beside his straw hat rose the mob-cap of his spouse. The very attitude of both the parents was a sufficient proof of their sincere goodwill towards the young man and their confidence in him. And Bublitsyn obviously was aware of their flattering confidence and appreciated it. He was, of course, sitting in an unconstrained position, and talking and laughing without constraint; but in the very freedom of his manner there could be discerned a shade of tender, touching respectfulness. And the Tiutiurov girls? It is hard to convey in words all that an attentive observer could trace in the faces of the two sisters. Goodwill and gentleness, and discreet gaiety, a melancholy comprehension of life, and a faith, not to be shaken, in themselves, in the lofty and noble destiny of man on earth, courteous attention to their young companion, in intellectual endowments perhaps not fully their equal, but still by the qualities of his heart quite deserving of their indulgence . . . such were the characteristics and the feelings reflected at that moment on the faces of the young ladies. Bublitsyn called to Ivan Afanasiitch for no special reason, simply in the fulness of his inner satisfaction; he bowed to him with excessive friendliness and cordiality. The young ladies even looked at him with gentle amiability, as at a man whose acquaintance they would not object to. . . . The good, sleek, quiet horses went by Ivan Afanasiitch at a gentle trot; the carriage rolled smoothly along the broad road, carrying with it good-humoured, girlish laughter; he caught a final glimpse of Mr. Tiutiurov's hat; the two outer horses turned their heads on each side, jauntily stepping over the short, green grass . . . the coachman gave a whistle of approbation and warning, the carriage disappeared behind some willows.

A long while poor Pyetushkov remained standing still.

'I'm a poor lonely creature,' he whispered at last . . . 'alone in the world.'

A little boy in tatters stopped before him, looked timidly at him, held out his hand . . .

'For Christ's sake, good gentleman.'

Pyetushkov pulled out a copper.

'For your loneliness, poor orphan,' he said with effort, and he walked back to the baker's shop. On the threshold of Vassilissa's room Ivan Afanasiitch stopped.

'Yes,' he thought, 'these are my friends. Here is my family, this is it. . . . And here Bublitsyn and there Bublitsyn.'

Vassilissa was sitting with her back to him, winding worsted, and carelessly singing to herself; she was wearing a striped cotton gown; her hair was done up anyhow. . . . The room, insufferably hot, smelt of feather beds and old rags; jaunty, reddish-brown 'Prussians' scurried rapidly here and there across the walls; on the decrepit chest of drawers, with holes in it where the locks should have been, beside a broken jar, lay a woman's shabby slipper. . . . Kozlov's poem was still where it had fallen on the floor. . . . Pyetushkov shook his head, folded his arms, and went away. He was hurt.

At home he called for his things to dress. Onisim slouched off after his better coat. Pyetushkov had a great desire to draw Onisim into conversation, but Onisim preserved a sullen silence. At last Ivan Afanasiitch could hold out no longer.

'Why don't you ask me where I'm going?'

'Why, what do I want to know where you're going for?'

'What for? Why, suppose some one comes on urgent business, and asks, "Where's Ivan Afanasiitch?" And then you can tell him, "Ivan Afanasiitch has gone here or there."'

'Urgent business. . . . But who ever does come to you on urgent business?'

'Why, are you beginning to be rude again? Again, hey?'

Onisim turned away, and fell to brushing the coat.

'Really, Onisim, you are a most disagreeable person.'

Onisim looked up from under his brows at his master.

'And you're always like this. Yes, positively always.'

Onisim smiled.

'But what's the good of my asking you where you're going, Ivan Afanasiitch? As though I didn't know! To the girl at the baker's shop!'

'There, that's just where you're wrong! that's just where you're mistaken! Not to her at all. I don't intend going to see the girl at the baker's shop any more.'

Onisim dropped his eyelids and brandished the brush. Pyetushkov waited for his approbation; but his servant remained speechless.

'It's not the proper thing,' Pyetushkov went on in a severe voice—'it's unseemly. . . . Come, tell me what you think?'

'What am I to think? It's for you to say. What business have I to think?'

Pyetushkov put on his coat. 'He doesn't believe me, the beast,' he thought to himself.

He went out of the house, but he did not go to see any one. He walked about the streets. He directed his attention to the sunset. At last a little after eight o'clock he returned home. He wore a smile; he repeatedly shrugged his shoulders, as though marvelling at his own folly. 'Yes,' thought he, 'this is what comes of a strong will. . . .'

Next day Pyetushkov got up rather late. He had not passed a very good night, did not go out all day, and was fearfully bored. Pyetushkov read through all his poor books, and praised aloud one story in the Library of Good Reading. As he went to bed, he told Onisim to give him his pipe. Onisim handed him a wretched pipe. Pyetushkov began smoking; the pipe wheezed like a broken-winded horse.

'How disgusting!' cried Ivan Afanasiitch; 'where's my cherrywood pipe?'

'At the baker's shop,' Onisim responded tranquilly.

Pyetushkov blinked spasmodically.

'Well, you wish me to go for it?'

'No, you needn't; don't go . . . no need, don't go, do you hear?'

'Yes, sir.'

The night passed somehow. In the morning Onisim, as usual, gave Pyetushkov on the blue sprigged plate a new white roll. Ivan Afanasiitch looked out of window and asked Onisim: 'You've been to the baker's shop?'

'Who's to go, if I don't?'

'Ah!'

Pyetushkov became plunged in meditation.

'Tell me, please, did you see any one there?'

'Of course I did.'

'Whom did you see there, now, for instance?'

'Why, of course, Vassilissa.'

Ivan Afanasiitch was silent. Onisim cleared the table, and was just going out of the room . . .

'Onisim,' Pyetushkov cried faintly.

'What is it?'

'Er . . . did she ask after me?'

'Of course she didn't.'

Pyetushkov set his teeth. 'Yes,' he thought, 'that's all it's worth, her love, indeed. . . .' His head dropped. 'Absurd I was, to be sure,' he thought again. 'A fine idea to read her poetry. A girl like that! Why, she's a fool! Why, she's good for nothing but to lie on the stove and eat pancakes. Why, she's a post, a perfect post; an uneducated workgirl.'

'She's never come,' he whispered, two hours later, still sitting in the same place, 'she's never come. To think of it; why, she could see that I left her out of temper; why, she might know that I was hurt. There's love for you! And she did not even ask if I were well. Never even said, "Is Ivan Afanasiitch quite well?" She hasn't seen me for two whole days—and not a sign. . . . She's even again, maybe, thought fit to meet that Bub—— Lucky fellow. Ouf, devil take it, what a fool I am!'

Pyetushkov got up, paced up and down the room in silence, stood still, knitted his brows slightly and scratched his neck. 'However,' he said aloud, 'I'll go to see her. I must see what she's about there. I must make her feel ashamed. Most certainly . . . I'll go. Onisim! my clothes.'

'Well,' he mused as he dressed, 'we shall see what comes of it. She may, I dare say, be angry with me. And after all, a man keeps coming and coming, and all of a sudden, for no rhyme or reason, goes and gives up coming. Well, we shall see.'

Ivan Afanasiitch went out of the house, and made his way to the baker's shop. He stopped at the little gate, he wanted to straighten himself out and set himself to rights. . . . Pyetushkov clutched at the folds of his coat with both hands, and almost pulled them out altogether. . . . Convulsively he twisted his tightly compressed neck, fastened the top hook of his collar, drew a deep breath. . . .

'Why are you standing there?' Praskovia Ivanovna bawled to him from the little window. 'Come in.'

Pyetushkov started, and went in. Praskovia Ivanovna met him in the doorway.

'Why didn't you come to see us yesterday, my good sir? Was it, maybe, some ailment prevented you?'

'Yes, I had something of a headache yesterday. . . .'

'Ah, you should have put cucumber on your temples, my good sir. It would have taken it away in a twinkling. Is your head aching now?'

'No, it's not.'

'Ah well, and thank Thee, O Lord, for it.'

Ivan Afanasiitch went off into the back room. Vassilissa saw him.

'Ah! good day, Ivan Afanasiitch.'

'Good day, Vassilissa Ivanovna.'

'Where have you put the tap, Ivan Afanasiitch?'

'Tap? what tap?'

'The wine-tap . . . our tap. You must have taken it home with you. You are such a one . . . Lord, forgive us. . . .'

Pyetushkov put on a dignified and chilly air.

'I will direct my man to look. Seeing that I was not here yesterday,' he pronounced significantly. . . .

'Ah, why, to be sure, you weren't here yesterday.' Vassilissa squatted down on her heels, and began rummaging in the chest. . . .

'Aunt, hi! aunt!'

'What sa-ay?'

'Have you taken my neckerchief?'

'What neckerchief?'

'Why, the yellow one.'

'The yellow one?'

'Yes, the yellow, figured one.'

'No, I've not taken it.'

Pyetushkov bent down to Vassilissa.

'Listen to me, Vassilissa; listen to what I am saying to you. It is not a matter of taps or of neckerchiefs just now; you can attend to such trifles another time.'

Vassilissa did not budge from her position; she only lifted her head.

'You just tell me, on your conscience, do you love me or not? That's what I want to know, once for all.'

'Ah, what a one you are, Ivan Afanasiitch. . . . Well, then, of course.'

'If you love me, how was it you didn't come to see me yesterday? Had you no time? Well, you might have sent to find out if I were ill, as I didn't turn up. But it's little you cared. I might die, I dare say, you wouldn't grieve.'

'Ah, Ivan Afanasiitch, one can't be always thinking of one thing, one's got one's work to do.'

'To be sure,' responded Pyetushkov; 'but all the same . . . And it's improper to laugh at your elders. . . . It's not right. Moreover, it's as well in certain cases . . . But where's my pipe?'

'Here's your pipe.'

Pyetushkov began smoking.

VII

SEVERAL DAYS slipped by again, apparently rather tranquilly. But a storm was getting nearer. Pyetushkov suffered tortures, was jealous, never took his eyes off Vassilissa, kept an alarmed watch over her, annoyed her horribly. Behold, one evening, Vassilissa dressed herself with more care than usual, and, seizing a favourable instant, sallied off to make a visit somewhere. Night came on, she had not returned. Pyetushkov at sunset went home to his lodgings, and at eight o'clock in the morning ran to the baker's shop. . . . Vassilissa had not come in. With an inexpressible sinking at his heart, he waited for her right up to dinner-time. . . . They sat down to the table without her. . . .

'Whatever can have become of her?' Praskovia Ivanovna observed serenely. . . .

'You spoil her, you simply spoil her utterly!' Pyetushkov repeated, in despair.

'Eh! my good sir, there's no looking after a girl!' responded Praskovia Ivanovna. 'Let her go her way! So long as she does her work. . . . Why shouldn't folks enjoy themselves? . . .'

A cold shudder ran over Pyetushkov. At last, towards evening, Vassilissa made her appearance. This was all he was waiting for. Majestically Pyetushkov rose from his seat, folded his arms, scowled menacingly. . . . But Vassilissa looked him boldly in the face, laughed impudently, and before he could utter a single word she went quickly into her own room, and locked herself in. Ivan Afanasiitch opened his mouth, looked in amazement at Praskovia Ivanovna. . . . Praskovia Ivanovna cast down her eyes. Ivan

Afanasiitch stood still a moment, groped after his cap, put it on askew, and went out without closing his mouth.

He reached home, took up a leather cushion, and with it flung himself on the sofa, with his face to the wall. Onisim looked in out of the passage, went into the room, leaned his back against the door, took a pinch of snuff, and crossed his legs.

'Are you unwell, Ivan Afanasiitch?' he asked Pyetushkov.

Pyetushkov made no answer.

'Shall I go for the doctor?' Onisim continued, after a brief pause.

'I'm quite well. . . . Go away,' Ivan Afanasiitch articulated huskily.

'Well? . . . no, you're not well, Ivan Afanasiitch. . . . Is this what you call being well?'

Pyetushkov did not speak.

'Just look at yourself. You've grown so thin, that you're simply not like yourself. And what's it all about? It's enough to turn one's brain to think of it. And you a gentleman born, too!'

Onisim paused. Pyetushkov did not stir.

'Is that the way gentlemen go on? They'd amuse themselves a bit, to be sure . . . why shouldn't they . . . they'd amuse themselves, and then drop it. . . . They may well say, Fall in love with Old Nick, and you'll think him a beauty.'

Ivan Afanasiitch merely writhed.

'Well, it's really like this, Ivan Afanasiitch. If any one had said this and that of you, and your goings on, why, I would have said, "Get along with you, you fool, what do you take me for?" Do you suppose I'd have believed it? Why, as it is, I see it with my own eyes, and I can't believe it. Worse than this nothing can be. Has she put some spell over you or what? Why, what is there in her? If you come to consider, she's below contempt, really. She can't even speak as she ought. . . . She's simply a baggage! Worse, even!'

'Go away,' Ivan Afanasiitch moaned into the cushion.

'No, I'm not going away, Ivan Afanasiitch. Who's to speak, if I don't? Why, upon my word! Here, you're breaking your heart now . . . and over what? Eh, over what? tell me that!'

'Oh, go away, Onisim,' Pyetushkov moaned again. Onisim, for propriety's sake, was silent for a little while.

'And another thing,' he began again, 'she's no feeling of gratitude whatever. Any other girl wouldn't know how to do enough to please you; while she! . . . she doesn't even think of you. Why, it's simply a disgrace. Why, the things people are saying about you, one cannot repeat them, they positively cry shame on me. If I could have known beforehand, I'd have. . . .'

'Oh, go away, do, devil!' shrieked Pyetushkov, not stirring from his place, however, nor raising his head.

'Ivan Afanasiitch, for mercy's sake,' pursued the ruthless Onisim. 'I'm speaking for your good. Despise her, Ivan Afanasiitch; you simply break it off. Listen to me, or else I'll fetch a wise woman; she'll break the spell in no time. You'll laugh at it yourself, later on; you'll say to me, " Onisim, why, it's marvellous how such things happen sometimes! " You just consider yourself: girls like her, they're like dogs . . . you've only to whistle to them. . . .'

Like one frantic, Pyetushkov jumped up from the sofa . . . but, to the amazement of Onisim, who was already lifting both hands to the level of his cheeks, he sat down again, as though some one had cut away his legs from under him. . . . Tears were rolling down his pale face, a tuft of hair stood up straight on the top of his head, his eyes looked dimmed . . . his drawn lips were quivering . . . his head sank on his breast.

Onisim looked at Pyetushkov and plumped heavily down on his knees.

'Dear master, Ivan Afanasiitch,' he cried, 'your honour! Be pleased to punish me. I'm a fool. I've troubled you, Ivan Afanasiitch. . . . How did I dare! Be pleased to punish me, your honour. . . . It's not worth your while to weep over my silly words . . . dear master. Ivan Afanasiitch . . .'

But Pyetushkov did not even look at his servant; he turned away and buried himself in the corner of the sofa again.

Onisim got up, went up to his master, stood over him, and twice he tugged at his own hair.

'Wouldn't you like to undress, sir . . . you should go to bed . . . you should take some raspberry tea . . . don't grieve, please your honour. . . . It's only half a trouble, it's all nothing . . . it'll be all right in the end,' he said to him every two minutes. . . .

But Pyetushkov did not get up from the sofa, and only twitched his shoulders now and then, and drew up his knees to his stomach. . . .

Onisim did not leave his side all night. Towards morning Pyetushkov fell asleep, but he did not sleep long. At seven o'clock he got up from the sofa, pale, dishevelled, and exhausted, and asked for tea.

Onisim with amazing eagerness and speed brought the samovar.

'Ivan Afanasiitch,' he began at last, in a timid voice, 'your honour is not angry with me? '

'Why should I be angry with you, Onisim? ' answered poor Pyetushkov. 'You were perfectly right yesterday, and I quite agreed with you in everything.'

'I only spoke through my devotion to you, Ivan Afanasiitch.'

'I know that.'

Pyetushkov was silent and hung his head.

Onisim saw that things were in a bad way.

'Ivan Afanasiitch,' he said suddenly.

'Well? '

'Would you like me to fetch Vassilissa here? '

Pyetushkov flushed red.

'No, Onisim, I don't wish it. ('Yes, indeed! as if she would come! ' he thought to himself.) One must be firm. It is all nonsense. Yesterday, I . . . It's a disgrace. You are right. One must cut it all short, once for all, as they say. Isn't that true? '

'It's the gospel truth your honour speaks, Ivan Afanasiitch.'

Pyetushkov sank again into reverie. He wondered at himself, he did not seem to know himself. He sat without stirring and stared at the floor. Thoughts whirled round within him, like smoke or fog, while his heart felt empty and heavy at once.

'But what's the meaning of it, after all,' he thought sometimes, and again he grew calmer. 'It's nonsense, silliness! ' he said aloud, and passed his hand over his face, shook himself, and his hand dropped again on his knee, his eyes again rested on the floor.

Intently and mournfully Onisim kept watch on his master.

Pyetushkov lifted his head.

'Tell me, Onisim,' he began, 'is it true, are there really such witches' spells? '

'There are, to be sure there are,' answered Onisim, as he thrust one foot forward. 'Does your honour know the non-commissioned officer, Krupovaty? . . . His brother was ruined by witchcraft. He was bewitched to love an old woman, a cook, if your honour only can explain that! They gave him nothing but a morsel of rye bread, with a muttered spell, of course. And Krupovaty's brother simply lost his heart to the cook, he fairly ran after the cook, he positively adored her—couldn't keep his eyes off her. She might tell him to do anything, he'd obey her on the spot. She'd even make a joke of him before other people, before strangers. Well, she drove him into a decline, at last. And so it was Krupovaty's brother died. And you know, she was a cook, and an old woman too, very old. (Onisim took a pinch of snuff.) Confound the lot of them, these girls and women-folk! '

'She doesn't care for me a bit, that's clear, at last; that's beyond all doubt, at last,' Pyetushkov muttered in an undertone, gesticulating with his head and hands as though he were explaining to a perfectly extraneous person some perfectly extraneous fact.

'Yes,' Onisim resumed, 'there are women like that.'

'There are,' listlessly repeated Pyetushkov, in a tone half questioning, half perplexed.

Onisim looked intently at his master.

'Ivan Afanasiitch,' he began, 'wouldn't you have a snack of something? '

'Wouldn't I have a snack of something? ' repeated Pyetushkov.

'Or may be you'd like to have a pipe? '

'To have a pipe? ' repeated Pyetushkov.

'So this is what it's coming to,' muttered Onisim. 'It's gone deep, it seems.'

VIII

THE creak of boots resounded in the passage, and then there was heard the usual suppressed cough which announces the presence of a person of subordinate position. Onisim went out and promptly came back, accompanied by a diminutive soldier with a little, old woman's face, in a patched cloak yellow with age, and wearing neither breeches nor cravat. Pyetushkov was startled; while the soldier drew himself up, wished him good day, and handed him a large envelope bearing the government seal. In this envelope was a note from the major in command of the garrison: he called upon Pyetushkov to come to him without fail or delay.

Pyetushkov turned the note over in his hands, and could not refrain from asking the messenger, did he know why the major desired his presence, though he was very well aware of the utter futility of his question.

'We cannot tell!' the soldier cried, with great effort, yet hardly audibly, as though he were half asleep.

'Isn't he summoning the other officers?' Pyetushkov pursued.

'We cannot tell,' the soldier cried a second time, in just the same voice.

'All right, you can go,' pronounced Pyetushkov.

The soldier wheeled round to the left, scraping his foot as he did so, and slapping himself below the spine (this was considered smart in the twenties), withdrew.

Pyetushkov exchanged glances with Onisim, who at once assumed a look of anxiety. Without a word Ivan Afanasiitch set off to the major's.

The major was a man of sixty, corpulent and clumsily built, with a red and bloated face, a short neck, and a continual trembling in his fingers, resulting from excessive indulgence in strong drink. He belonged to the class of so-called 'bourbons,' that's to say, soldiers risen from the ranks; had learned to read at thirty, and spoke with difficulty, partly from short-ness of breath, partly from inability to follow his own thought. His temperament exhibited all the varieties known to science: in the morning, before drinking, he was melancholy; in the middle of the day, choleric; and in the evening, phlegmatic, that is to say, he did nothing at that time but snore and grunt till he was put to bed. Ivan Afanasiitch appeared before him during the choleric period. He found him sitting on a sofa, in an open dressing-gown, with a pipe between his teeth. A fat, crop-eared cat had taken up her position beside him.

'Aha! he's come!' growled the major, casting a sidelong glance out of his pewtery eyes upon Pyetushkov, and not stirring from his place. 'Sit down. Well, I'm going to give you a talking to. I've wanted to get hold of you this long while.'

Pyetushkov sank into a chair.

'For,' the major began, with an unexpected lurch of his whole body, 'you're an officer, d'ye see, and so you've got to behave yourself according to rule. If you'd been a soldier, I'd have flogged you, and that's all about it, but, as 'tis, you're an officer. Did any one ever see the like of it? Dis-gracing yourself—is that a nice thing?'

'Allow me to know to what these remarks may refer?' Pyetushkov was beginning. . . .

'I'll have no arguing! I dislike that beyond everything. I've said: I dislike it; and that's all about it! Ugh—why, your hooks are not in good form even;—what a disgrace! He sits, day in and day out, at the baker's shop; and he a gentleman born! There's a petticoat to be found there—and so there he sits. Let her go to the devil, the petticoat! Why, they do say he puts the bread in the oven. It's a stain on the uniform . . . so it is!'

'Allow me to submit,' articulated Pyetushkov with a cold chill at his heart, 'that all this, as far as I can make out, refers to my private life, so to say. . . .'

'No arguing with me, I tell you! Private life, he protests, too! If it had been a matter of the service I'd have sent you straight to the guard-room! Alley, marsheer! Because of the oath. Why, there was a whole birch copse, maybe, used upon my back, so I should think I know the service; every rule of discipline I'm very well up in. And I'd have you to understand, I say this just for the honour of the uniform. You're disgracing the uniform . . . so you are. I say this like a father . . . yes. Because all that's put in my charge. I've to answer for it. And you dare to argue too!' the major shrieked with sudden fury, and his face turned purple, and he foamed at the mouth, while the cat put its tail in the air and jumped down to the ground. 'Why, do you know . . . why, do you know what I can do? . . . I can do anything, anything, anything! Why, do you know whom you're talking to? Your superior officer gives you orders and you argue! Your superior officer . . . your superior officer. . . .'

Here the major positively choked and spluttered, while poor Pyetushkov could only draw himself up and turn pale, sitting on the very edge of his chair.

'I must have' . . . the major continued, with an imperious wave of his trembling hand, 'I must have everything . . . up to the mark! Conduct first-class! I'm not going to put up with any irregularities! You can make friends with whom you like, that makes no odds to me! But if you are a gentleman, why, act as such . . . behave like one! No putting bread in the oven for me! No calling a draggletail old woman auntie! No disgracing the uniform! Silence! No arguing!'

The major's voice broke. He took breath, and turning towards the door into the passage, bawled, 'Frolka, you scoundrel! The herrings!'

Pyetushkov rose hurriedly and darted away, almost upsetting the page-boy, who ran to meet him, carrying some sliced herring and a stout decanter of spirits on an iron tray.

'Silence! No arguing!' sounded after Pyetushkov the disjointed exclamations of his exasperated superior officer.

IX

A QUEER sensation overmastered Ivan Afanasiitch when, at last, he found himself in the street.

'Why am I walking as it were in a dream?' he thought to himself. 'Am

I out of my mind, or what? Why, it passes all belief, at last. Come, damn it, she's tired of me, come, and I've grown tired of her, come, and . . . What is there out of the way in that? '

Pyetushkov frowned.

' I must put an end to it, once for all,' he said almost aloud. ' I'll go and speak out decisively for the last time, so that it may never come up again.'

Pyetushkov made his way with rapid step to the baker's shop. The nephew of the hired man, Luka, a little boy, friend and confidant of the goat that lived in the yard, darted swiftly to the little gate, directly he caught sight of Ivan Afanasiitch in the distance.

Praskovia Ivanovna came out to meet Pyetushkov.

' Is your niece at home? ' asked Pyetushkov.

' No, sir.'

Pyetushkov was inwardly relieved at Vassilissa's absence.

' I came to have a few words with you, Praskovia Ivanovna.'

' What about, my good sir? '

' I'll tell you. You comprehend that after all . . . that has passed . . . after such, so to say, behaviour (Pyetushkov was a little confused) . . . in a word . . . But, pray, don't be angry with me, though.'

' Certainly not, sir.'

' On the contrary, enter into my position, Praskovia Ivanovna.'

' Certainly, sir.'

' You're a reasonable woman, you'll understand of yourself, that . . . that I can't go on coming to see you any more.'

' Certainly, sir,' Praskovia Ivanovna repeated slowly.

' I assure you I greatly regret it; I confess it is positively painful to me, genuinely painful . . .'

' You know best, sir,' Praskovia Ivanovna rejoined serenely. ' It's for you to decide, sir. And, oh, if you'll allow me, I'll give you your little account, sir.'

Pyetushkov had not at all anticipated such a prompt acquiescence. He had not desired acquiescence at all; he had only wanted to frighten Praskovia Ivanovna, and above all Vassilissa. He felt wretched.

' I know,' he began, ' this will not be disagreeable to Vassilissa; on the contrary, I believe she will be glad.'

Praskovia Ivanovna got out her reckoning beads, and began rattling the counters.

' On the other hand,' continued Pyetushkov, growing more and more agitated, ' if Vassilissa were, for instance, to give an explanation of her behaviour . . . possibly. . . . Though, of course . . . I don't know, possibly, I might perceive that after all there was no great matter for blame in it.'

' There's thirty-seven roubles and forty kopecks in notes to your account, sir,' observed Praskovia Ivanovna. ' Here, would you be pleased to go through it? '

Ivan Afanasiitch made no reply.

'Eighteen dinners at seventy kopecks each; twelve roubles sixty kopecks.'

'And so we are to part, Praskovia Ivanovna.'

'If so it must be, sir. Things do turn out so. Twelve samovars at ten kopecks each . . .'

'But you might just tell me, Praskovia Ivanovna, where it was Vassilissa went, and what it was she . . .'

'Oh, I never asked her, sir. . . . One rouble twenty kopecks in silver.'

Ivan Afanasiitch sank into meditation.

'Kvas and effervescing drinks,' pursued Praskovia Ivanovna, holding the counters apart on the frame not with her first, but her third finger, 'half a rouble in silver. Sugar and rolls for tea, half a rouble. Four packets of tobacco bought by your orders, eighty kopecks in silver. To the tailor Kuprian Apollonov . . .'

Ivan Afanasiitch suddenly raised his head, put out his hand and mixed up the counters.

'What are you about, my good man?' cried Praskovia Ivanovna. 'Don't you trust me?'

'Praskovia Ivanovna,' replied Pyetushkov, with a hurried smile, 'I've thought better of it. I was only, you know . . . joking. We'd better remain friends and go on in the old way. What nonsense it is! How can we separate—tell me that, please?'

Praskovia Ivanovna looked down and made him no reply.

'Come, we've been talking nonsense, and there's an end of it,' pursued Ivan Afanasiitch, walking up and down the room, rubbing his hands, and, as it were, resuming his ancient rights. 'Amen! and now I'd better have a pipe.'

Praskovia Ivanovna still did not move from her place. . . .

'I see you are angry with me,' said Pyetushkov. 'I've offended you, perhaps. Well! well! forgive me generously.'

'How could you offend me, my good sir? No offence about it. . . . Only, please, sir,' added Praskovia Ivanovna, bowing, 'be so good as not to go on coming to us.'

'What?'

'It's not for you, sir, to be friends with us, your honour. So, please, do us the favour . . .'

Praskovia Ivanovna went on bowing.

'What ever for?' muttered the astounded Pyetushkov.

'Oh, nothing, sir. For mercy's sake . . .'

'No, Praskovia Ivanovna, you must explain this! . . .'

'Vassilissa asks you. She says, "I thank you, thank you very much, and from my heart; only for the future, your honour, give us up."'

Praskovia Ivanovna bowed down almost to Pyetushkov's feet.

'Vassilissa, you say, begs me not to come?'

'Just so, your honour. When your honour came in to-day, and said what you did, that you didn't wish, you said, to visit us any more, I felt relieved, sir, that I did; thinks I, Well, thank God, how nicely it's all come about! But for that, I should have had hard work to bring my tongue to say it. . . . Be so good, sir.'

Pyetushkov turned red and pale almost at the same instant. Praskovia Ivanovna still went on bowing. . . .

'Very good,' Ivan Afanasiitch cried sharply. 'Good-bye.'

He turned abruptly and put on his cap.

'But the little bill, sir. . . .'

'Send it . . . my orderly shall pay you.'

Pyetushkov went with resolute steps out of the baker's shop, and did not even look round.

X

A FORTNIGHT PASSED. At first Pyetushkov bore up in an extraordinary way. He went out, and visited his comrades, with the exception, of course, of Bublitsyn; but in spite of the exaggerated approbation of Onisim, he almost went out of his mind at last from wretchedness, jealousy, and ennui. Conversations with Onisim about Vassilissa were the only thing that afforded him some consolation. The conversation was always begun, 'scratched up,' by Pyetushkov; Onisim responded unwillingly.

'It's a strange thing, you know,' Ivan Afanasiitch would say, for instance, as he lay on the sofa, while Onisim stood in his usual attitude, leaning against the door, with his hands folded behind his back, 'when you come to think of it, what it was I saw in that girl. One would say that there was nothing unusual in her. It's true she has a good heart. That one can't deny her.'

'Good heart, indeed! ' Onisim would answer with displeasure.

'Come, now, Onisim,' Pyetushkov went on, 'one must tell the truth. It's a thing of the past now; it's no matter to me now, but justice is justice. You don't know her. She's very good-hearted. Not a single beggar does she let pass by; she'll always give, if it's only a crust of bread. Oh! And she's of a cheerful temper, that one must allow, too.'

'What a notion! I don't know where you see the cheerful temper! '

'I tell you . . . you don't know her. And she's not mercenary either . . . that's another thing. She's not grasping, there's no doubt of it. Why I never gave her anything, as you know.'

'That's why she's flung you over.'

'No, that's not why! ' responded Pyetushkov with a sigh.

'Why, you're in love with her to this day,' Onisim retorted malignantly. 'You'd be glad to go back there as before.'

'That's nonsense you're talking. No, my lad, you don't know me either, I can see. Be sent away, and then go dancing attendance—no, thank you, I'd rather be excused. No, I tell you. You may believe me, it's all a thing of the past now.'

'Pray God it be so! '

' But why ever shouldn't I be fair to her, now after all? If now I say she's not good-looking—why, who'd believe me? '

' A queer sort of good looks! '

' Well, find me,—well, mention anybody better-looking . . .'

' Oh, you'd better go back to her, then! . . .'

' Stupid! Do you suppose that's why I say so? Understand me . . .'

' Oh! I understand you,' Onisim answered with a heavy sigh.

Another week passed by. Pyetushkov had positively given up talking with his Onisim, and had given up going out. From morning till night he lay on the sofa, his hands behind his head. He began to get thin and pale, eat unwillingly and hurriedly, and did not smoke at all. Onisim could only shake his head, as he looked at him.

' You're not well, Ivan Afanasiitch,' he said to him more than once.

' No, I'm all right,' replied Pyetushkov.

At last, one fine day (Onisim was not at home) Pyetushkov got up, rummaged in his chest of drawers, put on his cloak, though the sun was rather hot, went stealthily out into the street, and came back a quarter of an hour later. . . . He carried something under his cloak. . . .

Onisim was not at home. The whole morning he had been sitting in his little room, deliberating with himself, grumbling and swearing between his teeth, and, at last, he sallied off to Vassilissa. He found her in the shop. Praskovia Ivanovna was asleep on the stove, rhythmically and soothingly snoring.

' Ah, how d'ye do, Onisim Sergeitch,' began Vassilissa, with a smile; ' why haven't we seen anything of you for so long? '

' Good day.'

' Why are you so depressed? Would you like a cup of tea? '

' It's not me we're talking about now,' rejoined Onisim, in a tone of vexation.

' Why, what then? '

' What! Don't you understand me? What! What have you done to my master, come, you tell me that.'

' What I've done to him? '

' What have you done to him? . . . You go and look at him. Why, before we can look round, he'll be in a decline, or dying outright, maybe.'

' It's not my fault, Onisim Sergeitch.'

' Not your fault! God knows. Why, he's lost his heart to you. And you, God forgive you, treated him as if he were one of yourselves. Don't come, says you, I'm sick of you. Why, though he's not much to boast of, he's a gentleman anyway. He's a gentleman born, you know. . . . Do you realise that? '

' But he's such a dull person, Onisim Sergeitch . . .'

' Dull! So you must have merry fellows about you! '

' And it's not so much that he's dull: he's so cross, so jealous.'

' Ah, you, you're as haughty as a princess! He was in your way, I dare say! '

'But you yourself, Onisim Sergeitch, if you remember, were put out with him about it; "Why is he such friends?" you said; "what's he always coming for?"'

'Well, was I to be pleased with him for it, do you suppose?'

'Well, then, why are you angry with me now? Here, he's given up coming.'

Onisim positively stamped.

'But what am I to do with him, if he's such a madman?' he added, dropping his voice.

'But how am I in fault? What can I do?'

'I'll tell you what: come with me to him.'

'God forbid!'

'Why won't you come?'

'But why should I go to see him? Upon my word!'

'Why? Why, because he says you've a good heart; let me see if you've a good heart.'

'But what good can I do him?'

'Oh, that's my business. You may be sure things are in a bad way, since I've come to you. It's certain I could think of nothing else to do.'

Onisim paused for a while.

'Well, come along, Vassilissa, please, come along.'

'Oh, Onisim Sergeitch, I don't want to be friendly with him again . . .'

'Well, and you needn't—who's talking of it? You've only to say a couple of words; to say, Why does your honour grieve? . . . give over. . . . That's all.'

'Really, Onisim Sergeitch . . .'

'Why, am I to go down on my knees to you, eh? All right—there, I'm on my knees . . .'

'But really . . .'

'Why, what a girl it is! Even that doesn't touch her! . . .'

Vassilissa at last consented, put a kerchief on her head, and went out with Onisim.

'You wait here a little, in the passage,' he said to her, when they reached Pyetushkov's abode, 'and I'll go and let the master know . . .'

He went in to Ivan Afanasiitch. Pyetushkov was standing in the middle of the room, both hands in his pockets, his legs excessively wide apart; he was slightly swaying backwards and forwards. His face was hot, and his eyes were sparkling.

'Hullo, Onisim,' he faltered amiably, articulating the consonants very indistinctly and thickly: 'hullo, my lad. Ah, my lad, when you weren't here . . . he, he, he . . .' Pyetushkov laughed and made a sudden duck forward with his nose. 'Yes, it's an accomplished fact, he, he, he. . . . However,' he added, trying to assume a dignified air, 'I'm all right.' He tried to lift his foot, but almost fell over, and to preserve his dignity pronounced in a deep bass, 'Boy, bring my pipe!'

Onisim gazed in astonishment at his master, glanced round. . . . In the window stood an empty dark-green bottle, with the inscription: 'Best Jamaica rum.'

'I've been drinking, my lad, that's all,' Pyetushkov went on. 'I've been and taken it. I've been drinking, and that's all about it. And where've you been? Tell us . . . don't be shy . . . tell us. You're a good hand at a tale.'

'Ivan Afanasiitch, mercy on us!' wailed Onisim.

'To be sure. To be sure I will,' replied Pyetushkov with a vague wave of his hand. 'I'll have mercy on you, and forgive you. I forgive every one, I forgive you, and Vassilissa I forgive, and every one, every one. Yes, my lad, I've been drinking. . . . Dri-ink-ing, lad. . . . Who's that?' he cried suddenly, pointing to the door into the passage; 'who's there?'

'Nobody's there,' Onisim answered hastily: 'who should be there? . . . where are you going?'

'No, no,' repeated Pyetushkov, breaking away from Onisim, 'let me go, I saw—don't you talk to me,—I saw there, let me go. . . . Vassilissa!' he shrieked all at once.

Pyetushkov turned pale.

'Well . . . well, why don't you come in?' he said at last. 'Come in, Vassilissa, come in. I'm very glad to see you, Vassilissa.'

Vassilissa glanced at Onisim and came into the room. Pyetushkov went nearer to her. . . . He heaved deep, irregular breaths. Onisim watched him. Vassilissa stole timid glances at both of them.

'Sit down, Vassilissa,' Ivan Afanasiitch began again: 'thanks for coming. Excuse my being . . . what shall I say? . . . not quite fit to be seen. I couldn't foresee, couldn't really, you'll own that yourself. Come, sit down, see here, on the sofa . . . So . . . I'm expressing myself all right, I think.'

Vassilissa sat down.

'Well, good day to you,' Ivan Afanasiitch pursued. 'Come, how are you? what have you been doing?'

'I'm well, thank God, Ivan Afanasiitch. And you?'

'I? as you see! A ruined man. And ruined by whom? By you, Vassilissa. But I'm not angry with you. Only I'm a ruined man. You ask him. (He pointed to Onisim.) Don't you mind my being drunk. I'm drunk, certainly; only I'm a ruined man. That's why I'm drunk, because I'm a ruined man.'

'Lord have mercy on us, Ivan Afanasiitch!'

'A ruined man, Vassilissa, I tell you. You may believe me. I've never deceived you. Oh, and how's your aunt?'

'Very well, Ivan Afanasiitch. Thank you.'

Pyetushkov began swaying violently.

'But you're not quite well to-day, Ivan Afanasiitch. You ought to lie down.'

'No, I'm quite well, Vassilissa. No, don't say I'm not well; you'd better say I've fallen into evil ways, lost my morals. That's what would be just. I won't dispute that.'

Ivan Afanasiitch gave a lurch backwards. Onisim ran forward and held his master up.

'And who's to blame for it? I'll tell you, if you like, who's to blame. I'm to blame, in the first place. What ought I to have said? I ought to have said to you: Vassilissa, I love you. Good—well, will you marry me? Will you? It's true you're a working girl, granted; but that's all right. It's done sometimes. Why, there, I knew a fellow, he got married like that. Married a Finnish servant-girl. Took and married her. And you'd have been happy with me. I'm a good-natured chap, I am! Never you mind my being drunk, you look at my heart. There, you ask this . . . fellow. So, you see, I turn out to be in fault. And now, of course, I'm a ruined man.'

Ivan Afanasiitch was more and more in need of Onisim's support.

'All the same, you did wrong, very wrong. I loved you, I respected you . . . what's more, I'm ready to go to church with you this minute. Will you? You've only to say the word, and we'll start at once. Only you wounded me cruelly . . . cruelly. You might at least have turned me away yourself—but through your aunt, through that fat female! Why, the only joy I had in life was you. I'm a homeless man, you know, a poor lonely creature! Who is there now to be kind to me? who says a kind word to me? I'm utterly alone. Stript bare as a crow. You ask this . . .' Ivan Afanasiitch began to cry. 'Vassilissa, listen what I say to you,' he went on: 'let me come and see you as before. Don't be afraid. . . . I'll be . . . quiet as a mouse. You can go and see whom you like, I'll—be all right: not a word, no protests, you know. Eh? do you agree? If you like, I'll go down on my knees.' (And Ivan Afanasiitch bent his knees, but Onisim held him up under the arms.) 'Let me go! It's not your business! It's a matter of the happiness of a whole life, don't you understand, and you hinder . . .'

Vassilissa did not know what to say.

'You won't . . . Well, as you will! God be with you. In that case, good-bye! Good-bye, Vassilissa. I wish you all happiness and prosperity . . . but I . . . but I . . . but I . . .'

And Pyetushkov sobbed violently. Onisim with all his might held him up from behind . . . first his face worked, then he burst out crying. And Vassilissa cried too.

XI

TEN YEARS LATER, one might have met in the streets of the little town of O—— a thinnish man with a reddish nose, dressed in an old green coat with a greasy plush collar. He occupied a small garret in the baker's shop, with which we are familiar. Praskovia Ivanovna was no longer of this world. The business was carried on by her niece, Vassilissa, and her husband, the red-haired, dim-eyed baker, Demofont. The man in the green coat had one weakness: he was over fond of drink. He was, however, always quiet when he was tipsy. The reader has probably recognised him as Ivan Afanasiitch.

1847.

THE JEW

. . . 'TELL US A STORY, colonel,' we said at last to Nikolai Ilyitch.

The colonel smiled, puffed out a coil of tobacco smoke between his moustaches, passed his hand over his grey hair, looked at us and considered. We all had the greatest liking and respect for Nikolai Ilyitch, for his good-heartedness, common sense, and kindly indulgence to us young fellows. He was a tall, broad-shouldered, stoutly-built man; his dark face, 'one of the splendid Russian faces,'[1] straight-forward, clever glance, gentle smile, manly and mellow voice—everything about him pleased and attracted one.

'All right, listen then,' he began.

It happened in 1813, before Dantzig. I was then in the E—— regiment of cuirassiers, and had just, I recollect, been promoted to be a cornet. It is an exhilarating occupation—fighting; and marching too is good enough in its way, but it is fearfully slow in a besieging army. There one sits the whole blessed day within some sort of entrenchment, under a tent, on mud or straw, playing cards from morning till night. Perhaps, from simple boredom, one goes out to watch the bombs and redhot bullets flying.

At first the French kept us amused with sorties, but they quickly subsided. We soon got sick of foraging expeditions too; we were overcome, in fact, by such deadly dulness that we were ready to howl for sheer *ennui*. I was not more than nineteen then; I was a healthy young fellow, fresh as a daisy, thought of nothing but getting all the fun I could out of the French . . . and in other ways too . . . you understand what I mean . . . and this is what happened. Having nothing to do, I fell to gambling. All of a sudden, after dreadful losses, my luck turned, and towards morning (we used to play at night) I had won an immense amount. Exhausted and sleepy, I came out into the fresh air, and sat down on a mound. It was a splendid, calm morning; the long lines of our fortifications were lost in the mist; I gazed till I was weary, and then began to doze where I was sitting.

A discreet cough waked me: I opened my eyes, and saw standing before me a Jew, a man of forty, wearing a long-skirted grey wrapper, slippers, and a black smoking-cap. This Jew, whose name was Girshel, was continually hanging about our camp, offering his services as an agent, getting us wine, provisions, and other such trifles. He was a thinnish, red-haired, little man, marked with smallpox; he blinked incessantly with his diminutive little eyes, which were reddish too; he had a long crooked nose, and was always coughing.

He began fidgeting about me, bowing obsequiously.

'Well, what do you want?' I asked him at last.

'Oh, I only—I've only come, sir, to know if I can't be of use to your honour in some way . . .'

'I don't want you; you can go.'

[1] Lermontov in the *Treasurer's Wife*.—AUTHOR'S NOTE.

'At your honour's service, as you desire. . . . I thought there might be, sir, something . . .'

'You bother me; go along, I tell you.'

'Certainly, sir, certainly. But your honour must permit me to congratulate you on your success. . . .'

'Why, how did you know? '

'Oh, I know, to be sure I do. . . . An immense sum . . . immense. . . . Oh! how immense . . .'

Girshel spread out his fingers and wagged his head.

'But what's the use of talking,' I said peevishly; 'what the devil's the good of money here? '

'Oh! don't say that, your honour; ay, ay, don't say so. Money's a capital thing; always of use; you can get anything for money, your honour; any-thing! anything! Only say the word to the agent, he'll get you anything, your honour, anything! anything! '

'Don't tell lies, Jew.'

'Ay! ay! ' repeated Girshel, shaking his sidelocks. 'Your honour doesn't believe me. . . . Ay . . . ay. . . .' The Jew closed his eyes and slowly wagged his head to right and to left. . . . 'Oh, I know what his honour the officer would like. . . . I know, . . . to be sure I do! '

The Jew assumed an exceedingly knowing leer.

'Really! '

The Jew glanced round timorously, then bent over to me.

'Such a lovely creature, your honour, lovely! . . .' Girshel again closed his eyes and shot out his lips.

'Your honour, you've only to say the word . . . you shall see for yourself . . . whatever I say now, you'll hear . . . but you won't believe . . . better tell me to show you . . . that's the thing, that's the thing! '

I did not speak; I gazed at the Jew.

'Well, all right then; well then, very good; so I'll show you then . . .'

Thereupon Girshel laughed and slapped me lightly on the shoulder, but skipped back at once as though he had been scalded.

'But, your honour, how about a trifle in advance? '

'But you're taking me in, and will show me some scarecrow? '

'Ay, ay, what a thing to say! ' the Jew pronounced with unusual warmth, waving his hands about. 'How can you! Why . . . if so, your honour, you order me to be given five hundred . . . four hundred and fifty lashes,' he added hurriedly. . . . 'You give orders——'

At that moment one of my comrades lifted the edge of his tent and called me by name. I got up hurriedly and flung the Jew a gold coin.

'This evening, this evening,' he muttered after me.

I must confess, my friends, I looked forward to the evening with some impatience. That very day the French made a sortie; our regiment marched to the attack. The evening came on; we sat round the fires . . . the soldiers cooked porridge. My comrades talked. I lay on my cloak, drank tea, and listened to my comrades' stories. They suggested a game of cards—I refused to take part in it. I felt excited. Gradually the officers dispersed to their tents; the fires began to die down; the soldiers too dispersed, or went to sleep on the spot; everything was still. I did not get up. My orderly squatted on his heels before the fire, and was beginning to nod. I sent him away. Soon the whole camp was hushed. The sentries were relieved. I still lay there, as it were waiting for something. The stars peeped out. The night came on. A long while I watched the dying flame. . . . The last fire went out. 'The damned Jew was taking me in,' I thought angrily, and was just going to get up.

'Your honour,' . . . a trembling voice whispered close to my ear.

I looked round: Girshel. He was very pale, he stammered, and whispered something.

'Let's go to your tent, sir.'

I got up and followed him. The Jew shrank into himself, and stepped warily over the short, damp grass. I observed on one side a motionless, muffled-up figure. The Jew beckoned to her—she went up to him. He whispered to her, turned to me, nodded his head several times, and we all three went into the tent. Ridiculous to relate, I was breathless.

'You see, your honour,' the Jew whispered with an effort, 'you see. She's a little frightened at the moment, she's frightened; but I've told her his honour the officer's a good man, a splendid man. . . . Don't be frightened, don't be frightened,' he went on—'don't be frightened. . . .'

The muffled-up figure did not stir. I was myself in a state of dreadful confusion, and didn't know what to say. Girshel too was fidgeting restlessly, and gesticulating in a strange way. . . .

'Any way,' I said to him, 'you get out. . . .' Unwillingly, as it seemed, Girshel obeyed.

I went up to the muffled-up figure, and gently took the dark hood off her head. There was a conflagration in Dantzig: by the faint, reddish, flickering glow of the distant fire I saw the pale face of a young Jewess. Her beauty astounded me. I stood facing her, and gazed at her in silence. She did not raise her eyes. A slight rustle made me look round. Girshel was cautiously poking his head in under the edge of the tent. I waved my hand at him angrily, . . . he vanished.

'What's your name?' I said at last.

'Sara,' she answered, and for one instant I caught in the darkness the gleam of the whites of her large, long-shaped eyes and little, even, flashing teeth.

I snatched up two leather cushions, flung them on the ground, and asked her to sit down. She slipped off her shawl, and sat down. She was wearing a short Cossack jacket, open in front, with round, chased silver buttons, and full sleeves. Her thick black hair was coiled twice round her little head. I sat down beside her and took her dark, slender hand. She resisted a little, but seemed afraid to look at me, and there was a catch in her breath. I admired her Oriental profile, and timidly pressed her cold, shaking fingers.

'Do you know Russian?'

'Yes . . . a little.'

'And do you like Russians?'

'Yes, I like them.'

'Then, you like me too?'

'Yes, I like you.'

I tried to put my arm round her, but she moved away quickly . . .

'No, no, please, sir, please . . .'

'Oh, all right; look at me, any way.'

She let her black, piercing eyes rest upon me, and at once turned away with a smile, and blushed.

I kissed her hand ardently. She peeped at me from under her eyelids and softly laughed.

'What is it?'

She hid her face in her sleeve and laughed more than before.

Girshel showed himself at the entrance of the tent and shook his finger at her. She ceased laughing.

'Go away!' I whispered to him through my teeth; 'you make me sick!' Girshel did not go away.

I took a handful of gold pieces out of my trunk, stuffed them in his hand and pushed him out.

'Your honour, me too . . .' she said.

I dropped several gold coins on her lap; she pounced on them like a cat.

'Well, now I must have a kiss.'

'No, please, please,' she faltered in a frightened and beseeching voice.

'What are you frightened of?'

'I'm afraid.'

'Oh, nonsense. . . .'

'No, please.'

She looked timidly at me, put her head a little on one side and clasped her hands. I let her alone.

'If you like . . . here,' she said after a brief silence, and she raised her hand to my lips. With no great eagerness, I kissed it. Sara laughed again.

My blood was boiling. I was annoyed with myself and did not know what to do. Really, I thought at last, what a fool I am.

I turned to her again.

'Sara, listen, I'm in love with you.'

'I know.'

'You know? And you're not angry? And do you like me too?'

Sara shook her head.

'No, answer me properly.'

'Well, show yourself,' she said.

I bent down to her. Sara laid her hands on my shoulders, began scrutinising my face, frowned, smiled. . . . I could not contain myself, and gave her a rapid kiss on her cheek. She jumped up and in one bound was at the entrance of the tent.

'Come, what a shy thing you are!'

She did not speak and did not stir.

'Come here to me. . . .'

'No, sir, good-bye. Another time.'

Girshel again thrust in his curly head, and said a couple of words to her; she bent down and glided away, like a snake.

I ran out of the tent in pursuit of her, but could not get another glimpse of her nor of Girshel.

The whole night long I could not sleep a wink.

The next night we were sitting in the tent of our captain; I was playing, but with no great zest. My orderly came in.

'Some one's asking for you, your honour.'

'Who is it?'

'A Jew.'

'Can it be Girshel?' I wondered. I waited till the end of the rubber, got up and went out. Yes, it was so; I saw Girshel.

'Well,' he questioned me with an ingratiating smile, 'your honour, are you satisfied?'

'Ah, you——!' (Here the colonel glanced round. 'No ladies present, I believe. . . . Well, never mind, any way.') 'Ah, bless you!' I responded, 'so you're making fun of me, are you?'

'How so?'

'How so, indeed! What a question!'

'Ay, ay, your honour, you're too bad,' Girshel said reproachfully, but never ceasing smiling. 'The girl is young and modest. . . . You frightened her, indeed, you did.'

'Queer sort of modesty! why did she take money, then?'

'Why, what then? If one's given money, why not take it, sir?'

'I say, Girshel, let her come again, and I'll let you off . . . only, please, don't show your stupid phiz inside my tent, and leave us in peace; do you hear?'

Girshel's eyes sparkled.

'What do you say? You like her?'

'Well, yes.'

'She's a lovely creature! there's not another such anywhere. And have you something for me now?'

'Yes, here, only listen; fair play is better than gold. Bring her and then go to the devil. I'll escort her home myself.'

'Oh, no, sir, no, that's impossible, sir,' the Jew rejoined hurriedly. 'Ay, ay, that's impossible. I'll walk about near the tent, your honour, if you like; I'll . . . I'll go away, your honour, if you like, a little. . . . I'm ready to do your honour a service. . . . I'll move away . . . to be sure, I will.'

'Well, mind you do. . . . And bring her, do you hear?'

'Eh, but she's a beauty, your honour, eh? your honour, a beauty, eh?'

Girshel bent down and peeped into my eyes.

'She's good-looking.'

'Well, then, give me another gold piece.'

I threw him a coin; we parted.

The day passed at last. The night came on. I had been sitting for a long while alone in my tent. It was dark outside. It struck two in the town. I was beginning to curse the Jew. . . . Suddenly Sara came in, alone. I jumped up, took her in my arms . . . put my lips to her face. . . . It was cold as ice. I could scarcely distinguish her features. . . . I made her sit down, knelt down before her, took her hands, touched her waist. . . . She did not speak, did not stir, and suddenly she broke into loud, convulsive sobbing. I tried in vain to soothe her, to persuade her. . . . She wept in torrents. . . . I caressed her, wiped her tears; as before, she did not resist, made no answer to my questions and wept—wept, like a waterfall. I felt a pang at my heart; I got up and went out of the tent.

Girshel seemed to pop up out of the earth before me.

'Girshel,' I said to him, 'here's the money I promised you. Take Sara away.'

The Jew at once rushed up to her. She left off weeping, and clutched hold of him.

'Good-bye, Sara,' I said to her. 'God bless you, good-bye. We'll see each other again some other time.'

Girshel was silent and bowed humbly. Sara bent down, took my hand and pressed it to her lips; I turned away. . . .

For five or six days, my friends, I kept thinking of my Jewess. Girshel did not make his appearance, and no one had seen him in the camp. I slept rather badly at nights; I was continually haunted by wet, black eyes, and long eyelashes; my lips could not forget the touch of her cheek, smooth and fresh as a downy plum. I was sent out with a foraging party to a village some distance away. While my soldiers were ransacking the houses, I remained in the street, and did not dismount from my horse. Suddenly some one caught hold of my foot. . . .

'Mercy on us, Sara!'

She was pale and excited.

'Your honour . . . help us, save us, your soldiers are insulting us. . . . Your honour. . . .'

She recognised me and flushed red.

'Why, do you live here?'

'Yes.'

'Where?'

Sara pointed to a little, old house. I set spurs to my horse and galloped up. In the yard of the little house an ugly and tattered Jewess was trying to tear out of the hands of my long sergeant, Siliavka, three hens and a duck. He was holding his booty above his head, laughing; the hens clucked and the duck quacked. . . . Two other cuirassiers were loading their horses with hay, straw, and sacks of flour. Inside the house I heard shouts and oaths in Little-Russian. . . . I called to my men and told them to leave the Jews alone, not to take anything from them. The soldiers obeyed, the sergeant

got on his grey mare, Proserpina, or, as he called her, 'Prozherpila,' and
rode after me into the street.

'Well,' I said to Sara, 'are you pleased with me? '

She looked at me with a smile.

'What has become of you all this time? '

She dropped her eyes.

'I will come to you to-morrow.'

'In the evening? '

'No, sir, in the morning.'

'Mind you do, don't deceive me.'

'No . . . no, I won't.'

I looked greedily at her. By daylight she seemed to me handsomer than
ever. I remember I was particularly struck by the even, amber tint of her
face and the bluish lights in her black hair. . . . I bent down from my
horse and warmly pressed her little hand.

'Good-bye, Sara . . . mind you come.'

'Yes.'

She went home; I told the sergeant to follow me with the party, and
galloped off.

The next day I got up very early, dressed, and went out of the tent. It
was a glorious morning; the sun had just risen and every blade of grass was
sparkling in the dew and the crimson glow. I clambered on to a high breast-
work, and sat down on the edge of an embrasure. Below me a stout, cast-
iron cannon stuck out its black muzzle towards the open country. I looked
carelessly about me . . . and all at once caught sight of a bent figure in a
grey wrapper, a hundred paces from me. I recognised Girshel. He stood
without moving for a long while in one place, then suddenly ran a little
on one side, looked hurriedly and furtively round . . . uttered a cry,
squatted down, cautiously craned his neck and began looking round again
and listening. I could see all his actions very clearly. He put his hand into
his bosom, took out a scrap of paper and a pencil, and began writing or
drawing something. Girshel continually stopped, started like a hare, attentively scrutinised everything around him, and seemed to be sketching
our camp. More than once he hid his scrap of paper, half closed his eyes,
sniffed at the air, and again set to work. At last, the Jew squatted down on
the grass, took off his slipper, and stuffed the paper in it; but he had not
time to regain his legs, when suddenly, ten steps from him, there appeared
from behind the slope of an earthwork the whiskered countenance of the
sergeant Siliavka, and gradually the whole of his long clumsy figure rose up
from the ground. The Jew stood with his back to him. Siliavka went quickly
up to him and laid his heavy paw on his shoulder. Girshel seemed to shrink
into himself. He shook like a leaf and uttered a feeble cry, like a hare's.
Siliavka addressed him threateningly, and seized him by the collar. I could
not hear their conversation, but from the despairing gestures of the Jew,
and his supplicating appearance, I began to guess what it was. The Jew
twice flung himself at the sergeant's feet, put his hand in his pocket, pulled

out a torn check handkerchief, untied a knot, and took out gold coins. . . .
Siliavka took his offering with great dignity, but did not leave off dragging
the Jew by the collar. Girshel made a sudden bound and rushed away; the
sergeant sped after him in pursuit. The Jew ran exceedingly well; his legs,
clad in blue stockings, flashed by, really very rapidly; but Siliavka after
a short run caught the crouching Jew, made him stand up, and carried him
in his arms straight to the camp. I got up and went to meet him.

' Ah! your honour! ' bawled Siliavka,—' it's a spy I'm bringing you—a spy!
. . . ' The sturdy Little-Russian was streaming with perspiration. ' Stop
that wriggling, devilish Jew—now then . . . you wretch! you'd better look
out, I'll throttle you! '

The luckless Girshel was feebly prodding his elbows into Siliavka's chest,
and feebly kicking. . . . His eyes were rolling convulsively . . .

' What's the matter? ' I questioned Siliavka.

' If your honour'll be so good as to take the slipper off his right foot,—
I can't get at it.' He was still holding the Jew in his arms.

I took off the slipper, took out of it a carefully folded piece of paper,
unfolded it, and found an accurate map of our camp. On the margin were
a number of notes written in a fine hand in the Jews' language.

Meanwhile Siliavka had set Girshel on his legs. The Jew opened his eyes,
saw me, and flung himself on his knees before me.

Without speaking, I showed him the paper.

' What's this? '

' It's—nothing, your honour. I was only . . .' His voice broke.

' Are you a spy? '

He did not understand me, muttered disconnected words, pressed my
knees in terror . . .

' Are you a spy? '

' I! ' he cried faintly, and shook his head. ' How could I? I never did; I'm
not at all. It's not possible; utterly impossible. I'm ready—I'll—this minute—
I've money to give . . . I'll pay for it,' he whispered, and closed his eyes.

The smoking-cap had slipped back on to his neck; his reddish hair was
soaked with cold sweat, and hung in tails; his lips were blue, and working
convulsively; his brows were contracted painfully; his face was drawn . . .

Soldiers came up round us. I had at first meant to give Girshel a good
fright, and to tell Siliavka to hold his tongue, but now the affair had
become public, and could not escape ' the cognisance of the authorities.'

' Take him to the general,' I said to the sergeant.

' Your honour, your honour! ' the Jew shrieked in a voice of despair.
' I am not guilty . . . not guilty. . . . Tell him to let me go, tell him . . .'

' His Excellency will decide about that,' said Siliavka. ' Come along.'

' Your honour! ' the Jew shrieked after me—' tell him! have mercy! '

His shriek tortured me; I hastened my pace. Our general was a man of
German extraction, honest and good-hearted, but strict in his adherence to
military discipline. I went into the little house that had been hastily put up
for him, and in a few words explained the reason of my visit. I knew the

severity of the military regulations, and so I did not even pronounce the word 'spy,' but tried to put the whole affair before him as something quite trifling and not worth attention. But, unhappily for Girshel, the general put doing his duty higher than pity.

'You, young man,' he said to me in his broken Russian, 'inexperienced are. You in military matters yet inexperienced are. The matter, of which you to me reported have, is important, very important. . . . And where is this man who taken was? this Jew? where is he? '

I went out and told them to bring in the Jew. They brought in the Jew The wretched creature could scarcely stand up.

'Yes,' pronounced the general, turning to me; ' and where's the plan which on this man found was? '

I handed him the paper. The general opened it, turned away again, screwed up his eyes, frowned . . .

'This is most as-ton-ish-ing . . .' he said slowly. 'Who arrested him? '

'I, your Excellency! ' Siliavka jerked out sharply.

'Ah! good! good! . . . Well, my good man, what do you say in your defence? '

'Your . . . your . . . your Excellency,' stammered Girshel, 'I . . . indeed, . . . your Excellency . . . I'm not guilty . . . your Excellency; ask his honour the officer . . . I'm an agent, your Excellency, an honest agent.'

'He ought to be cross-examined,' the general murmured in an undertone, wagging his head gravely. 'Come, how do you explain this, my friend? '

'I'm not guilty, your Excellency, I'm not guilty.'

'That is not probable, however. You were—how is it said in Russian?— taken on the fact, that is, in the very facts! '

'Hear me, your Excellency; I am not guilty.'

'You drew the plan? you are a spy of the enemy? '

'It wasn't me! ' Girshel shrieked suddenly; 'not I, your Excellency! '

The general looked at Siliavka.

'Why, he's raving, your Excellency. His honour the officer here took the plan out of his slipper.'

The general looked at me. I was obliged to nod assent.

'You are a spy from the enemy, my good man . . .'

'Not I . . . not I . . .' whispered the distracted Jew.

'You have the enemy with similar information before provided? Confess . . .'

'How could I? '

'You will not deceive me, my good man. Are you a spy? '

The Jew closed his eyes, shook his head, and lifted the skirts of his gown.

'Hang him,' the general pronounced expressively after a brief silence, ' according to the law. Where is Mr. Fiodor Schliekelmann? '

They ran to fetch Schliekelmann, the general's adjutant. Girshel began to turn greenish, his mouth fell open, his eyes seemed starting out of his head. The adjutant came in. The general gave him the requisite instructions. The secretary showed his sickly, pock-marked face for an instant. Two or three officers peeped into the room inquisitively.

'Have pity, your Excellency,' I said to the general in German as best I could; 'let him off . . .'

'You, young man,' he answered me in Russian, 'I was saying to you, are inexperienced, and therefore I beg you silent to be, and me no more to trouble.'

Girshel with a shriek dropped at the general's feet.

'Your Excellency, have mercy; I will never again, I will not, your Excellency; I have a wife . . . your Excellency, a daughter . . . have mercy . . .'

'It's no use!'

'Truly, your Excellency, I am guilty . . . it's the first time, your Excellency, the first time, believe me!'

'You furnished no other documents?'

'The first time, your Excellency, . . . my wife . . . my children . . . have mercy . . .'

'But you are a spy.'

'My wife . . . your Excellency . . . my children . . .'

The general felt a twinge, but there was no getting out of it.

'According to the law, hang the Hebrew,' he said constrainedly, with the air of a man forced to do violence to his heart, and sacrifice his better feelings to inexorable duty—'hang him! Fiodor Karlitch, I beg you to draw up a report of the occurrence . . .'

A horrible change suddenly came over Girshel. Instead of the ordinary timorous alarm peculiar to the Jewish nature, in his face was reflected the horrible agony that comes before death. He writhed like a wild beast trapped, his mouth stood open, there was a hoarse rattle in his throat, he positively leapt up and down, convulsively moving his elbows. He had on only one slipper; they had forgotten to put the other on again . . . his gown fell open . . . his cap had fallen off . . .

We all shuddered; the general stopped speaking.

'Your Excellency,' I began again, 'pardon this wretched creature.'

'Impossible! It is the law,' the general replied abruptly, and not without emotion, 'for a warning to others.'

'For pity's sake . . .'

'Mr. Cornet, be so good as to return to your post,' said the general, and he motioned me imperiously to the door.

I bowed and went out. But seeing that in reality I had no post anywhere, I remained at no great distance from the general's house.

Two minutes later Girshel made his appearance, conducted by Siliavka and three soldiers. The poor Jew was in a state of stupefaction, and could hardly move his legs. Siliavka went by me to the camp, and soon returned with a rope in his hands. His coarse but not ill-natured face wore a look of strange, exasperated commiseration. At the sight of the rope the Jew flung up his arms, sat down, and burst into sobs. The soldiers stood silently about him, and stared grimly at the earth. I went up to Girshel, addressed him; he sobbed like a baby, and did not even look at me. With a hopeless gesture I went to my tent, flung myself on a rug, and closed my eyes. . . .

Suddenly some one ran hastily and noisily into my tent. I raised my head and saw Sara; she looked beside herself. She rushed up to me, and clutched at my hands.

'Come along, come along,' she insisted breathlessly.

'Where? what for? let us stop here.'

'To father, to father, quick . . . save him . . . save him!'

'To what father?'

'My father; they are going to hang him . . .'

'What! is Girshel . . . ?'

'My father . . . I'll tell you all about it later,' she added, wringing her hands in despair: 'only come . . . come . . .'

We ran out of the tent. In the open ground, on the way to a solitary birch-tree, we could see a group of soldiers. . . . Sara pointed to them without speaking. . . .

'Stop,' I said to her suddenly: 'where are we running to? The soldiers won't obey me.'

Sara still pulled me after her. . . . I must confess, my head was going round.

'But listen, Sara,' I said to her; 'what sense is there in running here? It would be better for me to go to the general again; let's go together; who knows, we may persuade him.'

Sara suddenly stood still and gazed at me, as though she were crazy.

'Understand me, Sara, for God's sake. I can't do anything for your father, but the general can. Let's go to him.'

'But meanwhile they'll hang him,' she moaned. . . .

I looked round. The secretary was standing not far off.

'Ivanov,' I called to him; 'run, please, over there to them, tell them to wait a little, say I've gone to petition the general.'

'Yes, sir.'

Ivanov ran off.

We were not admitted to the general's presence. In vain I begged, persuaded, swore even, at last . . . in vain, poor Sara tore her hair and rushed at the sentinels; they would not let us pass.

Sara looked wildly round, clutched her head in both hands, and ran at breakneck pace towards the open country, to her father. I followed her. Every one stared at us, wondering.

We ran up to the soldiers. They were standing in a ring, and picture it, gentlemen! they were laughing, laughing at poor Girshel. I flew into a rage and shouted at them. The Jew saw us and fell on his daughter's neck. Sara clung to him passionately.

The poor wretch imagined he was pardoned . . . He was just beginning to thank me . . . I turned away.

'Your honour,' he shrieked and wrung his hands; 'I'm not pardoned?'

I did not speak.

'No?'

'No.'

'Your honour,' he began muttering; 'look, your honour, look. . . she, this girl, see—you know—she's my daughter.'

'I know,' I answered, and turned away again.

'Your honour,' he shrieked, 'I never went away from the tent! I wouldn't for anything . . .'

He stopped, and closed his eyes for an instant. . . . 'I wanted your money, your honour, I must own . . . but not for anything . . .'

I was silent. Girshel was loathsome to me, and she too, his accomplice. . . .

'But now, if you save me,' the Jew articulated in a whisper, 'I'll command her . . . I . . . do you understand? . . . everything . . . I'll go to every length. . . .'

He was trembling like a leaf, and looking about him hurriedly. Sara silently and passionately embraced him.

The adjutant came up to us.

'Cornet,' he said to me; 'his Excellency has given me orders to place you under arrest. And you . . .' he motioned the soldiers to the Jew . . . 'quickly.'

Siliavka went up to the Jew.

'Fiodor Karlitch,' I said to the adjutant (five soldiers had come with him); 'tell them, at least, to take away that poor girl. . . .'

'Of course. Certainly.'

The unhappy girl was scarcely conscious. Girshel was muttering something to her in Yiddish. . . .

The soldiers with difficulty freed Sara from her father's arms, and carefully carried her twenty steps away. But all at once she broke from their arms and rushed towards Girshel. . . . Siliavka stopped her. Sara pushed him away; her face was covered with a faint flush, her eyes flashed, she stretched out her arms.

'So may you be accursed,' she screamed in German; 'accursed, thrice accursed, you and all the hateful breed of you, with the curse of Dathan and Abiram, the curse of poverty and sterility and violent, shameful death! May the earth open under your feet, godless, pitiless, bloodthirsty dogs. . . .'

Her head dropped back . . . she fell to the ground. . . . They lifted her up and carried her away.

The soldiers took Girshel under his arms. I saw then why it was they had been laughing at the Jew when I ran up from the camp with Sara. He was really ludicrous, in spite of all the horror of his position. The intense anguish of parting with life, his daughter, his family, showed itself in the Jew in such strange and grotesque gesticulations, shrieks, and wriggles that we all could not help smiling, though it was horrible—intensely horrible to us too. The poor wretch was half dead with terror. . . .

'Oy! oy! oy!' he shrieked: 'oy . . . wait! I've something to tell you . . . a lot to tell you. Mr. Under-sergeant, you know me. I'm an agent, an honest agent. Don't hold me; wait a minute, a little minute, a tiny minute—wait!

Let me go; I'm a poor Hebrew. Sara . . . where is Sara? Oh, I know, she's at his honour the quarter-lieutenant's.' (God knows why he bestowed such an unheard-of grade upon me.) 'Your honour the quarter-lieutenant, I'm not going away from the tent.' (The soldiers were taking hold of Girshel . . . he uttered a deafening shriek, and wriggled out of their hands.) 'Your Excellency, have pity on the unhappy father of a family. I'll give you ten golden pieces, fifteen I'll give, your Excellency! . . .' (They dragged him to the birch-tree.) 'Spare me! have mercy! your honour the quarter-lieutenant! your Excellency, the general and commander-in-chief!'

They put the noose on the Jew. . . . I shut my eyes and rushed away.

I remained for a fortnight under arrest. I was told that the widow of the luckless Girshel came to fetch away the clothes of the deceased. The general ordered a hundred roubles to be given to her. Sara I never saw again. I was wounded; I was taken to the hospital, and by the time I was well again, Dantzig had surrendered, and I joined my regiment on the banks of the Rhine.

1846.

AN UNHAPPY GIRL

YES, YES, began Piotr Gavrilovitch; those were painful days . . . and I would rather not recall them. . . . But I have made you a promise; I shall have to tell you the whole story. Listen.

I

I WAS living at that time (the winter of 1835) in Moscow, in the house of my aunt, the sister of my dead mother. I was eighteen; I had only just passed from the second into the third course in the faculty 'of Language' (that was what it was called in those days) in the Moscow University. My aunt was a gentle, quiet woman—a widow. She lived in a big, wooden house in Ostozhonka, one of those warm, cosy houses such as, I fancy, one can find nowhere else but in Moscow. She saw hardly any one, sat from morning till night in the drawing-room with two companions, drank the choicest tea, played patience, and was continually requesting that the room should be fumigated. Thereupon her companions ran into the hall; a few minutes later an old servant in livery would bring in a copper pan with a bunch of mint on a hot brick, and stepping hurriedly upon the narrow strips of carpet, he would sprinkle the mint with vinegar. White fumes always puffed up about his wrinkled face, and he frowned and turned away, while the canaries in the dining-room chirped their hardest, exasperated by the hissing of the smouldering mint.

I was fatherless and motherless, and my aunt spoiled me. She placed the whole of the ground floor at my complete disposal. My rooms were furnished very elegantly, not at all like a student's rooms in fact: there were pink curtains in the bedroom, and a muslin canopy, adorned with blue rosettes, towered over my bed. Those rosettes were, I'll own, rather an annoyance to me; to my thinking, such 'effeminacies' were calculated to lower me in the eyes of my companions. As it was, they nicknamed me 'the boarding-school miss.' I could never succeed in forcing myself to smoke. I studied—why conceal my shortcomings?—very lazily, especially at the beginning of the course. I went out a great deal. My aunt had bestowed on me a wide sledge, fit for a general, with a pair of sleek horses. At the houses of 'the gentry' my visits were rare, but at the theatre I was quite at home, and I consumed masses of tarts at the restaurants. For all that, I permitted myself no breach of decorum, and behaved very discreetly, *en jeune homme de bonne maison*. I would not for anything in the world have pained my kind aunt; and besides I was naturally of a rather cool temperament.

II

FROM my earliest years I had been fond of chess; I had no idea of the science of the game, but I didn't play badly. One day in a café, I was the spectator of a prolonged contest at chess, between two players, of whom one, a fair-haired young man of about five-and-twenty, struck me as playing well. The game ended in his favour; I offered to play a match with him. He agreed, . . . and in the course of an hour, beat me easily, three times running.

'You have a natural gift for the game,' he pronounced in a courteous tone, noticing probably that my vanity was suffering; 'but you don't know the openings. You ought to study a chess-book—Allgacir or Petrov.'

'Do you think so? But where can I get such a book? '

'Come to me; I will give you one.'

He gave me his name, and told me where he was living. Next day I went to see him, and a week later we were almost inseparable.

III

MY NEW ACQUAINTANCE was called Alexander Davidovitch Fustov. He lived with his mother, a rather wealthy woman, the widow of a privy councillor, but he occupied a little lodge apart and lived quite independently, just as I did at my aunt's. He had a post in the department of Court affairs. I became genuinely attached to him. I had never in my life met a young man more 'sympathetic.' Everything about him was charming and attractive: his graceful figure, his bearing, his voice, and especially his small, delicate face with the golden-blue eyes, the elegant, as it were coquettishly moulded little nose, the unchanging amiable smile on the crimson lips, the light curls of soft hair over the rather narrow, snow-white brow. Fustov's character was remarkable for exceptional serenity, and a sort of amiable, restrained affability; he was never pre-occupied, and was always satisfied with everything; but on the other hand he was never ecstatic over anything. Every excess, even in a good feeling, jarred upon him; 'that's savage, savage,' he would say with a faint shrug, half closing his golden eyes. Marvellous were those eyes of Fustov's! They invariably expressed sympathy, good-will, even devotion. It was only at a later period that I noticed that the expression of his eyes resulted solely from their setting, that it never changed, even when he was sipping his soup or smoking a cigar. His preciseness became a byword between us. His grandmother, indeed, had been a German. Nature had endowed him with all sorts of talents. He danced capitally, was a dashing horseman, and a first-rate swimmer; did carpentering, carving and joinery, bound books and cut out silhouettes, painted in watercolours nosegays of flowers or Napoleon in profile in a blue uniform; played the zither with feeling; knew a number of tricks, with cards and without; and had a fair knowledge of mechanics, physics, and chemistry; but everything only up to a certain point. Only for languages he had no great facility: even French he spoke rather badly. He spoke in general little, and his share in our students' discussions was mostly limited to the bright sympathy of his glance and smile. To the fair sex Fustov was attractive, undoubtedly, but on this subject, of such importance among young people, he did not care to enlarge, and fully deserved the nickname given him by his comrades, 'the discreet Don Juan.' I was not dazzled by Fustov; there was nothing in him to dazzle, but I prized his affection, though in reality it was only manifested by his never refusing to see me when I called. To my mind Fustov was the happiest man in the world. His life ran so very smoothly. His mother, brothers, sisters, aunts, and uncles all adored him, he was on exceptionally good terms with all of them, and enjoyed the reputation of a paragon in his family.

IV

ONE DAY I went round to him rather early and did not find him in his study. He called to me from the next room; sounds of panting and splashing reached me from there. Every morning Fustov took a cold shower-bath and afterwards for a quarter of an hour practised gymnastic exercises, in which he had attained remarkable proficiency. Excessive anxiety about one's physical health he did not approve of, but he did not neglect necessary care. ('Don't neglect yourself, don't over-excite yourself, work in moderation,' was his precept.) Fustov had not yet made his appearance, when the outer door of the room where I was waiting flew wide open, and there walked in a man about fifty, wearing a bluish uniform. He was a stout, squarely-built man with milky-whitish eyes in a dark-red face and a perfect cap of thick, grey, curly hair. This person stopped short, looked at me, opened his mouth wide, and with a metallic chuckle, he gave himself a smart slap on his haunch, kicking his leg up in front as he did so.

'Ivan Demianitch?' my friend inquired through the door.

'The same, at your service,' the new comer responded. 'What are you up to? At your toilette? That's right! that's right!' (The voice of the man addressed as Ivan Demianitch had the same harsh, metallic note as his laugh.) 'I've trudged all this way to give your little brother his lesson; and he's got a cold, you know, and does nothing but sneeze. He can't do his work. So I've looked in on you for a bit to warm myself.'

Ivan Demianitch laughed again the same strange guffaw, again dealt himself a sounding smack on the leg, and pulling a check handkerchief out of his pocket, blew his nose noisily, ferociously rolling his eyes, spat into the handkerchief, and ejaculated with the whole force of his lungs: 'Tfoo-o-o!'

Fustov came into the room, and shaking hands with both of us, asked us if we were acquainted.

'Not a bit of it!' Ivan Demianitch boomed at once: 'the veteran of the year twelve has not that honour!'

Fustov mentioned my name first, then, indicating the 'veteran of the year twelve,' he pronounced: 'Ivan Demianitch Ratsch, professor of . . . various subjects.'

'Precisely so, various they are, precisely,' Mr. Ratsch chimed in. 'Come to think of it, what is there I haven't taught, and that I'm not teaching now, for that matter! Mathematics and geography and statistics and Italian book-keeping, ha-ha ha-ha! and music! You doubt it, my dear sir? '—he pounced suddenly upon me—'ask Alexander Daviditch if I'm not first-rate on the bassoon. I should be a poor sort of Bohemian—Czech, I should say—if I weren't! Yes, sir, I'm a Czech, and my native place is ancient Prague! By the way, Alexander Daviditch, why haven't we seen you for so long! We ought to have a little duet . . . ha-ha! Really! '

'I was at your place the day before yesterday, Ivan Demianitch,' replied Fustov.

'But I call that a long while, ha-ha! '

When Mr. Ratsch laughed, his white eyes shifted from side to side in a strange, restless way.

'You're surprised, young man, I see, at my behaviour,' he addressed me again. 'But that's because you don't understand my temperament. You must just ask our good friend here, Alexander Daviditch, to tell you about me. What'll he tell you? He'll tell you old Ratsch is a simple, good-hearted chap, a regular Russian, in heart, if not in origin, ha-ha! At his christening named Johann Dietrich, but always called Ivan Demianitch! What's in my mind pops out on my tongue; I wear my heart, as they say, on my sleeve. Cere-mony of all sorts I know naught about and don't want to neither! Can't bear it! You drop in on me one day of an evening, and you'll see for yourself. My good woman—my wife, that is—has no nonsense about her either; she'll cook and bake you . . . something wonderful! Alexander Daviditch, isn't it the truth I'm telling? '

Fustov only smiled, and I remained silent.

'Don't look down on the old fellow, but come round,' pursued Mr. Ratsch. 'But now . . .' (he pulled a fat silver watch out of his pocket and put it up to one of his goggle eyes) 'I'd better be toddling on, I suppose. I've another chick expecting me. . . . Devil knows what I'm teaching him, . . . mythology, by God! And he lives a long way off, the rascal, at the Red Gate! No matter; I'll toddle off on foot. Thanks to your brother's cutting his lesson, I shall be the fifteen kopecks for sledge hire to the good! Ha-ha! A very good day to you, gentlemen, till we meet again! . . . Eh? . . . We must have a little duet! ' Mr. Ratsch bawled from the passage putting on his goloshes noisily, and for the last time we heard his metallic laugh.

V

'WHAT a strange man! ' I said, turning to Fustov, who had already set to work at his turning-lathe. 'Can he be a foreigner? He speaks Russian so fluently.'

'He is a foreigner; only he's been thirty years in Russia. As long ago as 1802, some prince or other brought him from abroad . . . in the capacity of secretary . . . more likely, valet, one would suppose. He does speak Russian fluently, certainly.'

' With such go, such far-fetched turns and phrases,' I put in.

' Well, yes. Only very unnaturally too. They're all like that, these Russian-ised Germans.'

' But he's a Czech, isn't he? '

' I don't know; may be. He talks German with his wife.'

' And why does he call himself a veteran of the year twelve? Was he in the militia, or what? '

' In the militia! indeed! At the time of the fire he remained in Moscow and lost all his property. . . . That was all he did.'

' But what did he stay in Moscow for? '

Fustov still went on with his turning.

' The Lord knows. I have heard that he was a spy on our side; but that must be nonsense. But it's a fact that he received compensation from the treasury for his losses.'

' He wears some sort of uniform. . . . I suppose he's in government serv-ice then? '

' Yes. Professor in the cadet's corps. He has the rank of a petty councillor.'

' What's his wife like? '

' A German settled here, daughter of a sausage maker . . . or butcher . . .'

' And do you often go to see him? '

' Yes.'

' What, is it pleasant there? '

' Rather pleasant.'

' Has he any children? '

' Yes. Three by the German, and a son and daughter by his first wife.'

' And how old is the eldest daughter? '

' About five-and-twenty.'

I fancied Fustov bent lower over his lathe, and the wheel turned more rapidly, and hummed under the even strokes of his feet.

' Is she good-looking? '

' That's a matter of taste. She has a remarkable face, and she's altogether . . . a remarkable person.'

' Aha! ' thought I. Fustov continued his work with special earnestness, and to my next question he only responded by a grunt.

' I must make her acquaintance,' I decided.

VI

A FEW DAYS LATER, Fustov and I set off to Mr. Ratsch's to spend the evening. He lived in a wooden house with a big yard and garden, in Krivoy Place near the Pretchistensky boulevard. He came out into the passage, and meet-ing us with his characteristic jarring guffaw and noise, let us at once into the drawing-room, where he presented me to a stout lady in a skimpy canvas gown, Eleonora Karpovna, his wife. Eleonora Karpovna had most likely in her first youth been possessed of what the French for some unknown reason call *beauté du diable*, that is to say, freshness; but when I made her acquaintance, she suggested involuntarily to the mind a good-sized piece of meat, freshly laid by the butcher on a clean marble table. Designedly I used the word ' clean '; not only our hostess herself seemed a model of cleanliness, but everything about her, everything in the house positively shone, and glittered; everything had been scoured, and polished, and washed: the samovar on the round table flashed like fire; the curtains before the windows, the table-napkins were crisp with starch, as were also the little frocks and shirts of Mr. Ratsch's four children sitting there, stout, chubby little creatures, exceedingly like their mother, with coarsely moulded, sturdy faces, curls on their foreheads, and red, shapeless fingers. All the four of them had rather flat noses, large, swollen-looking lips, and tiny, light-grey eyes.

'Here's my squadron! ' cried Mr. Ratsch, laying his heavy hand on the children's heads one after another. 'Kolia, Olga, Sashka and Mashka! This one's eight, this one's seven, that one's four, and this one's only two! Ha! ha! ha! As you can see, my wife and I haven't wasted our time! Eh, Eleonora Karpovna? '

'You always say things like that,' observed Eleonora Karpovna and she turned away.

'And she's bestowed such Russian names on her squallers! ' Mr. Ratsch pursued. 'The next thing, she'll have them all baptized into the Orthodox Church! Yes, by Jove! She's so Slavonic in her sympathies, 'pon my soul, she is, though she is of German blood! Eleonora Karpovna, are you Slavonic? '

Eleonora Karpovna lost her temper.

'I'm a petty councillor's wife, that's what I am! And so I'm a Russian lady and all you may say . . .'

'There, the way she loves Russia, it's simply awful! ' broke in Ivan Demianitch. 'A perfect volcano, ho, ho! '

'Well, and what of it? ' pursued Eleonora Karpovna. 'To be sure I love Russia, for where else could I obtain noble rank? And my children too are nobly born, you know. Kolia, sitze ruhig mit den Füssen! '

Ratsch waved his hand to her.

'There, there, princess, don't excite yourself! But where's the nobly born Viktor? To be sure, he's always gadding about! He'll come across the inspector one of these fine days! He'll give him a talking-to! Das ist ein Bummler, Fiktor! '

'Dem Fiktov kann ich nicht kommandieren, Ivan Demianitch. Sie wissen wohl! ' grumbled Eleonora Karpovna.

I looked at Fustov, as though wishing finally to arrive at what induced him to visit such people . . . but at that instant there came into the room a tall girl in a black dress, the elder daughter of Mr. Ratsch, to whom

Fustov had referred. . . . I perceived the explanation of my friend's frequent visits.

VII

THERE is somewhere, I remember, in Shakespeare, something about 'a white dove in a flock of black crows'; that was just the impression made on me by the girl, who entered the room. Between the world surrounding her and herself there seemed to be too little in common; she herself seemed secretly bewildered and wondering how she had come there. All the members of Mr. Ratsch's family looked self-satisfied, simple-hearted, healthy creatures; her beautiful, but already careworn, face bore the traces of depression, pride and morbidity. The others, unmistakable plebeians, were unconstrained in their manners, coarse perhaps, but simple; but a painful uneasiness was manifest in all her indubitably aristocratic nature. In her very exterior there was no trace of the type characteristic of the German race; she recalled rather the children of the south. The excessively thick, lustreless black hair, the hollow, black, lifeless but beautiful eyes, the low, prominent brow, the aquiline nose, the livid pallor of the smooth skin, a certain tragic line near the delicate lips, and in the slightly sunken cheeks, something abrupt, and at the same time helpless in the movements, elegance without gracefulness . . . in Italy all this would not have struck me as exceptional, but in Moscow, near the Pretchistensky boulevard, it simply astonished me! I got up from my seat on her entrance; she flung me a swift, uneasy glance, and dropping her black eyelashes, sat down near the window 'like Tatiana.' (Pushkin's *Oniegin* was then fresh in every one's mind.) I glanced at Fustov, but my friend was standing with his back to me, taking a cup of tea from the plump hands of Eleonora Karpovna. I noticed further that the girl as she came in seemed to bring with her a breath of slight physical chillness . . . 'What a statue!' was my thought.

VIII

'PIOTR GAVRILITCH,' thundered Mr. Ratsch, turning to me, 'let me introduce you to my . . . to my . . . my number one, ha, ha, ha! to Susanna Ivanovna!'

I bowed in silence, and thought at once: 'Why, the name too is not the same sort as the others,' while Susanna rose slightly, without smiling or loosening her tightly clasped hands.

'And how about the duet?' Ivan Demianitch pursued: 'Alexander Daviditch? eh? benefactor! Your zither was left with us, and I've got the bassoon out of its case already. Let us make sweet music for the honourable company!' (Mr. Ratsch liked to display his Russian; he was continually bursting out with expressions, such as those which are strewn broadcast about the ultra-national poems of Prince Viazemsky.) 'What do you say? Carried?'

cried Ivan Demianitch, seeing Fustov made no objection. 'Kolka, march
into the study, and look sharp with the music-stand! Olga, this way with the
zither! And oblige us with candles for the stands, better-half!' (Mr. Ratsch
turned round and round in the room like a top.) 'Piotr Gavrilitch, you like
music, hey? If you don't care for it, you must amuse yourself with conversation, only mind, not above a whisper! Ha, ha, ha! But what ever's become
of that silly chap, Viktor? He ought to be here to listen too! You spoil
him completely, Eleonora Karpovna.'

Eleonora Karpovna fired up angrily.

'Aber was kann ich denn, Ivan Demianitch . . .'

'All right, all right, don't squabble! Bleibe ruhig, hast verstanden? Alexander Daviditch! at your service, sir!'

The children had promptly done as their father had told them. The
music-stands were set up, the music began. I have already mentioned that
Fustov played the zither extremely well, but that instrument has always
produced the most distressing impression upon me. I have always fancied, and I fancy still, that there is imprisoned in the zither the soul
of a decrepit Jew money-lender, and that it emits nasal whines and complaints against the merciless musician who forces it to utter sounds.
Mr. Ratsch's performance, too, was not calculated to give me much
pleasure; moreover, his face became suddenly purple, and assumed a malignant expression, while his whitish eyes rolled viciously, as though he were
just about to murder some one with his bassoon, and were swearing and
threatening by way of preliminary, puffing out chokingly husky, coarse
notes one after another. I placed myself near Susanna, and waiting for a
momentary pause, I asked her if she were as fond of music as her papa.

She turned away, as though I had given her a shove, and pronounced
abruptly, 'Who?'

'Your father,' I repeated, 'Mr. Ratsch.'

'Mr. Ratsch is not my father.'

'Not your father! I beg your pardon . . . I must have misunderstood
. . . But I remember, Alexander Daviditch . . .'

Susanna looked at me intently and shyly.

'You misunderstood Mr. Fustov. Mr. Ratsch is my stepfather.'

I was silent for a while.

'And you don't care for music?' I began again.

Susanna glanced at me again. Undoubtedly there was something suggest-
ing a wild creature in her eyes. She obviously had not expected nor desired
the continuation of our conversation.

'I did not say that,' she brought out slowly.

'Troo-too-too-too-too-oo-oo . . .' the bassoon growled with startling
fury, executing the final flourishes. I turned round, caught sight of the
red neck of Mr. Ratsch, swollen like a boa-constrictor's, beneath his projecting ears, and very disgusting I thought him.

'But that . . . instrument you surely do not care for,' I said in an undertone.

'No . . . I don't care for it,' she responded, as though catching my secret hint.

'Oho!' thought I, and felt, as it were, delighted at something.

'Susanna Ivanovna,' Eleonora Karpovna announced suddenly in her German Russian, 'music greatly loves, and herself very beautifully plays the piano, only she likes not to play the piano when she is greatly pressed to play.'

Susanna made Eleonora Karpovna no reply—she did not even look at her —only there was a faint movement of her eyes, under their dropped lids, in her direction. From this movement alone—this movement of her pupils— I could perceive what was the nature of the feeling Susanna cherished for the second wife of her stepfather. . . . And again I was delighted at something.

Meanwhile the duet was over. Fustov got up and with hesitating footsteps approached the window, near which Susanna and I were sitting, and asked her if she had received from Lengold's the music that he had promised to order her from Petersburg.

'Selections from *Robert le Diable*,' he added, turning to me, 'from that new opera that every one's making such a fuss about.'

'No, I haven't got it yet,' answered Susanna, and turning round with her face to the window she whispered hurriedly, 'Please, Alexander Daviditch, I entreat you, don't make me play to-day. I don't feel in the mood a bit.'

'What's that? Robert le Diable of Meyerbeer?' bellowed Ivan Demianitch, coming up to us: 'I don't mind betting it's a first-class article! He's a Jew, and all Jews, like all Czechs, are born musicians. Especially Jews. That's right, isn't it, Susanna Ivanovna? Hey? Ha, ha, ha, ha!'

In Mr. Ratsch's last words, and this time even in his guffaw, there could be heard something more than his usual bantering tone—the desire to wound was evident. So, at least, I fancied, and so Susanna understood him. She started instinctively, flushed red, and bit her lower lip. A spot of light, like the gleam of a tear, flashed on her eyelash, and rising quickly, she went out of the room.

'Where are you off to, Susanna Ivanova?' Mr. Ratsch bawled after her.

'Let her be, Ivan Demianitch,' put in Eleonora Karpovna. 'Wenn sie einmal so etwas im Kopfe hat . . .'

'A nervous temperament,' Ratsch pronounced, rotating on his heels, and slapping himself on the haunch, 'suffers with the *plexus solaris*. Oh! you needn't look at me like that, Piotr Gavrilitch! I've had a go at anatomy too, ha, ha! I'm even a bit of a doctor! You ask Eleonora Karpovna . . . I cure all her little ailments! Oh, I'm a famous hand at that!'

'You must for ever be joking, Ivan Demianitch,' the latter responded with displeasure, while Fustov, laughing and gracefully swaying to and fro, looked at the husband and wife.

'And why not be joking, mein Mütterchen?' retorted Ivan Demianitch. 'Life's given us for use, and still more for beauty, as some celebrated poet has observed. Kolka, wipe your nose, little savage!'

IX

'I was put in a very awkward position this evening through your doing,' I said the same evening to Fustov, on the way home with him. 'You told me that that girl—what's her name?—Susanna, was the daughter of Mr. Ratsch, but she's his stepdaughter.'

'Really! Did I tell you she was his daughter? But . . . isn't it all the same?'

'That Ratsch,' I went on. . . . 'O Alexander, how I detest him! Did you notice the peculiar sneer with which he spoke of Jews before her? Is she . . . a Jewess?'

Fustov walked ahead, swinging his arms; it was cold, the snow was crisp, like salt, under our feet.

'Yes, I recollect, I did hear something of the sort,' he observed at last. . . . 'Her mother, I fancy, was of Jewish extraction.'

'Then Mr. Ratsch must have married a widow the first time?'

'Probably.'

'H'm! . . . And that Viktor, who didn't come in this evening, is his stepson too?'

'No . . . he's his real son. But, as you know, I don't enter into other people's affairs, and I don't like asking questions. I'm not inquisitive.'

I bit my tongue. Fustov still pushed on ahead. As we got near home, I overtook him and peeped into his face.

'Oh!' I queried, 'is Susanna really so musical?'

Fustov frowned.

'She plays the piano well,' he said between his teeth. 'Only she's very shy, I warn you!' he added with a slight grimace. He seemed to be regretting having made me acquainted with her.

I said nothing and we parted.

X

Next morning I set off again to Fustov's. To spend my mornings at his rooms had become a necessity for me. He received me cordially, as usual, but of our visit of the previous evening—not a word! As though he had taken water into his mouth, as they say. I began turning over the pages of the last number of the *Telescope*.

A person, unknown to me, came into the room. It turned out to be Mr. Ratsch's son, the Viktor whose absence had been censured by his father the evening before.

He was a young man, about eighteen, but already looked dissipated and unhealthy, with a mawkishly insolent grin on his unclean face, and an expression of fatigue in his swollen eyes. He was like his father, only his features were smaller and not without a certain prettiness. But in this very prettiness there was something offensive. He was dressed in a very slovenly way; there were buttons off his undergraduate's coat, one of his boots had a hole in it, and he fairly reeked of tobacco.

'How d'ye do,' he said in a sleepy voice, with those peculiar twitchings of the head and shoulders which I have always noticed in spoilt and conceited young men. 'I meant to go to the University, but here I am. Sort of oppression on my chest. Give us a cigar.' He walked right across the room, listlessly dragging his feet, and keeping his hands in his trouser-pockets, and sank heavily upon the sofa.

'Have you caught cold?' asked Fustov, and he introduced us to each other. We were both students, but were in different faculties.

'No! . . . Likely! Yesterday, I must own . . .' (here Ratsch junior smiled, again not without a certain prettiness, though he showed a set of bad teeth) 'I was drunk, awfully drunk. Yes'—he lighted a cigar and cleared his throat—'Obihodov's farewell supper.'

'Where's he going?'

'To the Caucasus, and taking his young lady with him. You know the black-eyed girl, with the freckles. Silly fool!'

'Your father was asking after you yesterday,' observed Fustov.

Viktor spat aside. 'Yes, I heard about it. You were at our den yesterday. Well, music, eh?'

'As usual.'

'And *she* . . . with a new visitor' (here he pointed with his head in my direction) 'she gave herself airs, I'll be bound. Wouldn't play, eh?'

'Of whom are you speaking?' Fustov asked.

'Why, of the most honoured Susanna Ivanovna, of course!'

Viktor lolled still more comfortably, put his arm up round his head, gazed at his own hand, and cleared his throat hoarsely.

I glanced at Fustov. He merely shrugged his shoulders, as though giving me to understand that it was no use talking to such a dolt.

XI

VIKTOR, staring at the ceiling, fell to talking, deliberately and through his nose, of the theatre, of two actors he knew, of a certain Serafrina Serafrinovna, who had 'made a fool' of him, of the new professor, R., whom he called a brute. 'Because, only fancy, what a monstrous notion! Every lecture he begins with calling over the students' names, and he's reckoned a liberal too! I'd have all your liberals locked up in custody!' and turning at last his full face and whole body towards Fustov, he brought out in a half-plaintive, half-ironical voice: 'I wanted to ask you something, Alexander Daviditch. . . . Couldn't you talk my governor round somehow? . . . You play duets with him, you know. . . . Here he gives me five miserable blue notes a month. . . . What's the use of that! Not enough for tobacco. And then he goes on about my not making debts! I should like to put him in my place, and then we should see! I don't come in for pensions, not like *some people*.' (Viktor pronounced these last words with peculiar emphasis.) 'But he's got a lot of tin, I know! It's no use his whining about hard times, there's no taking me in. No fear! He's made a snug little pile!'

Fustov looked dubiously at Viktor.

'If you like,' he began, 'I'll speak to your father. Or, if you like . . . meanwhile . . . a trifling sum. . . .'

'Oh, no! Better get round the governor . . . Though,' added Viktor, scratching his nose with all his fingers at once, 'you might hand over five-and-twenty roubles, if it's the same to you. . . . What's the blessed total I owe you?'

'You've borrowed eighty-five roubles of me.'

'Yes. . . . Well, that's all right, then . . . make it a hundred and ten. I'll pay it all in a lump.'

Fustov went into the next room, brought back a twenty-five-rouble note and handed it in silence to Viktor. The latter took it, yawned with his mouth wide open, grumbled thanks, and, shrugging and stretching, got up from the sofa.

'Foo! though . . . I'm bored,' he muttered, 'might as well turn in to the "Italie." '

He moved towards the door.

Fustov looked after him. He seemed to be struggling with himself.

'What pension were you alluding to just now, Viktor Ivanitch?' he asked at last.

Viktor stopped in the doorway and put on his cap.

'Oh, don't you know? Susanna Ivanovna's pension. . . . She gets one. An awfully curious story, I can tell you! I'll tell it you one of these days. Quite an affair, 'pon my soul, a queer affair. But, I say, the governor, you won't forget about the governor, please! His hide is thick, of course— German, and it's had a Russian tanning too, still you can get through it. Only, mind my step-mother Elenorka's nowhere about! Dad's afraid of her, and she wants to keep everything for her brats! But there, you know your way about! Good-bye!'

'Ugh, what a low beast that boy is!' cried Fustov, as soon as the door had slammed-to.

His face was burning, as though from the fire, and he turned away from me. I did not question him, and soon retired.

XII

ALL THAT DAY I spent in speculating about Fustov, about Susanna, and about her relations. I had a vague feeling of something like a family drama. As far as I could judge, my friend was not indifferent to Susanna. But she? Did she care for him? Why did she seem so unhappy? And altogether, what sort of creature was she? These questions were continually recurring to my mind. An obscure but strong conviction told me that it would be no use to apply to Fustov for the solution of them. It ended in my setting off the next day alone to Mr. Ratsch's house.

I felt all at once very uncomfortable and confused directly I found myself in the dark little passage. 'She won't appear even, very likely,' flashed into my mind. 'I shall have to stop with the repulsive veteran and his cook of a wife. . . . And indeed, even if she does show herself, what of it? She won't even take part in the conversation. . . . She was anything but warm in her manner to me the other day. Why ever did I come? ' While I was making these reflections, the little page ran to announce my presence, and in the adjoining room, after two or three wondering ' Who is it? Who, do you say? ' I heard the heavy shuffling of slippers, the folding-door was slightly opened, and in the crack between its two halves was thrust the face of Ivan Demianitch, an unkempt and grim-looking face. It stared at me and its expression did not immediately change. . . . Evidently, Mr. Ratsch did not at once recognise me; but suddenly his cheeks grew rounder, his eyes narrower, and from his opening mouth, there burst, together with a guffaw, the exclamation: ' Ah! my dear sir! Is it you? Pray walk in! '

I followed him all the more unwillingly, because it seemed to me that this affable, good-humoured Mr. Ratsch was inwardly wishing me at the devil. There was nothing to be done, however. He led me into the drawing-room, and in the drawing-room who should be sitting but Susanna, bending over an account-book? She glanced at me with her melancholy eyes, and very slightly bit the finger-nails of her left hand. . . . It was a habit of hers, I noticed, a habit peculiar to nervous people. There was no one else in the room.

' You see, sir,' began Mr. Ratsch, dealing himself a smack on the haunch, ' what you've found Susanna Ivanovna and me busy upon: we're at our accounts. My spouse has no great head for arithmetic, and I, I must own, try to spare my eyes. I can't read without spectacles, what am I to do? Let the young people exert themselves, ha-ha! That's the proper thing. But there's no need of haste. . . . More haste, worse speed in catching fleas, he-he! '

Susanna closed the book, and was about to leave the room.

' Wait a bit, wait a bit,' began Mr. Ratsch. ' It's no great matter if you're not in your best dress. . . .' (Susanna was wearing a very old, almost child-ish, frock with short sleeves.) ' Our dear guest is not a stickler for cere-mony, and I should like just to clear up last week. . . . You don't mind? '— he addressed me. ' We needn't stand on ceremony with you, eh? '

' Please don't put yourself out on my account! ' I cried.

' To be sure, my good friend. As you're aware, the late Tsar Alexey Nikolavitch Romanoff used to say, " Time is for business, but a minute for recreation! " We'll devote one minute only to that same business . . . ha-ha! What about that thirteen roubles and thirty kopecks? ' he added in a low voice, turning his back on me.

'Viktor took it from Eleonora Karpovna; he said that it was with your leave,' Susanna replied, also in a low voice.

'He said . . . he said . . . my leave . . .' growled Ivan Demianitch. 'I'm on the spot myself, I fancy. Might be asked. And who's had that seventeen roubles?'

'The upholsterer.'

'Oh . . . the upholsterer. What's that for?'

'His bill.'

'His bill. Show me!' He pulled the book away from Susanna, and planting a pair of round spectacles with silver rims on his nose, he began passing his finger along the lines. 'The upholsterer . . . the upholsterer . . . You'd chuck all the money out of doors! Nothing pleases you better! . . . Wie die Croaten! A bill indeed! But, after all,' he added aloud, and he turned round facing me again, and pulled the spectacles off his nose, 'why do this now? I can go into these wretched details later. Susanna Ivanovna, be so good as to put away that account-book, and come back to us and enchant our kind guest's ears with your musical accomplishments, to wit, playing on the pianoforte . . . Eh?'

Susanna turned away her head.

'I should be very happy,' I hastily observed; 'it would be a great pleasure for me to hear Susanna Ivanovna play. But I would not for anything in the world be a trouble . . .'

'Trouble, indeed, what nonsense! Now then, Susanna Ivanovna, eins, zwei, drei!'

Susanna made no response, and went out.

XIII

I HAD not expected her to come back; but she quickly reappeared. She had not even changed her dress, and sitting down in a corner, she looked twice intently at me. Whether it was that she was conscious in my manner to her of the involuntary respect, inexplicable to myself, which, more than curiosity, more even than sympathy, she aroused in me, or whether she was in a softened frame of mind that day, any way, she suddenly went to the piano, and laying her hand irresolutely on the keys, and turning her head a little over her shoulder towards me, she asked what I would like her to play. Before I had time to answer she had seated herself, taken up some music, hurriedly opened it, and begun to play. I loved music from childhood, but at that time I had but little comprehension of it, and very slight knowledge of the works of the great masters, and if Mr. Ratsch had not grumbled with some dissatisfaction, 'Aha! wieder dieser Beethoven!' I should not have guessed what Susanna had chosen. It was, as I found out afterwards, the celebrated sonata in F minor, opus 57. Susanna's playing impressed me more than I can say; I had not expected such force, such fire, such bold execution. At the very first bars of the intensely passionate allegro, the beginning of the sonata, I felt that numbness, that chill and sweet terror of ecstasy, which instantaneously enwrap the soul when beauty bursts with sudden flight upon it. I did not stir a limb till the very end. I kept wanting—and not daring—to sigh. I was sitting behind Susanna; I could not see her face; I saw only from time to time her long dark hair tossed up and down on her shoulders, her figure swaying impulsively, and her delicate arms and bare elbows swiftly, and rather angularly, moving. The last notes died away. I sighed at last. Susanna still sat before the piano.

' Ja, ja,' observed Mr. Ratsch, who had also, however, listened with attention; ' romantische Musik! That's all the fashion nowadays. Only, why not play correctly? Eh? Put your finger on two notes at once—what's that for? Eh? To be sure, all we care for is to go quickly, quickly! Turns it out hotter, eh? Hot pancakes! ' he bawled like a street seller.

Susanna turned slightly towards Mr. Ratsch. I caught sight of her face in profile. The delicate eyebrow rose high above the downcast eyelid, an unsteady flush overspread the cheek, the little ear was red under the lock pushed behind it.

' I have heard all the best performers with my own ears,' pursued Mr. Ratsch, suddenly frowning, ' and compared with the late Field they were all—tfoo! nil! zero!! Das war ein Kerl! Und ein so reines Spiel! And his own compositions the finest things! But all those now " tloo-too-too," and " tra-ta-ta," are written, I suppose, more for beginners. Da braucht man keine Delicatesse! Bang the keys anyhow . . . no matter! It'll turn out somehow! Janitscharen Musik! Pugh! ' (Ivan Demianitch wiped his forehead with his handkerchief.) ' But I don't say that for you, Susanna Ivanovna; you played well, and oughtn't to be hurt by my remarks.'

' Every one has his own taste,' Susanna said in a low voice, and her lips were trembling; ' but your remarks, Ivan Demianitch, you know, cannot hurt me.'

' Oh! of course not! Only don't you imagine '—Mr. Ratsch turned to me— ' don't you imagine, my young friend, that that comes from our excessive good-nature and meekness of spirit; it's simply that we fancy ourselves so highly exalted that—oo-oo!—we can't keep our cap on our head, as the Russian proverb says, and, of course, no criticism can touch us. The conceit, my dear sir, the conceit! '

I listened in surprise to Mr. Ratsch. Spite, the bitterest spite, seemed as it were boiling over in every word he uttered. . . . And long it must have been rankling! It choked him. He tried to conclude his tirade with his usual laugh, and fell into a husky, broken cough instead. Susanna did not let drop a syllable in reply to him, only she shook her head, raised her face, and clasping her elbows with her hands, stared straight at him. In the depths of her fixed, wide-open eyes the hatred of long years lay smouldering with dim, unquenchable fire. I felt ill at ease.

' You belong to two different musical generations,' I began, with an effort at lightness wishing by this lightness to suggest that I noticed nothing, ' and so it is not surprising that you do not agree in your opinions. . . . But,

Ivan Demianitch, you must allow me to take rather . . . the side of the younger generation. I'm an outsider, of course; but I must confess nothing in music has ever made such an impression on me as the . . . as what Susanna Ivanovna has just played us.'

Ratsch pounced at once upon me.

'And what makes you suppose,' he roared, still purple from the fit of coughing, 'that we want to enlist you on our side? We don't want that at all! Freedom for the free, salvation for the saved! But as to the two generations, that's right enough; we old folks find it hard to get on with you young people, very hard! Our ideas don't agree in anything: neither in art, nor in life, nor even in morals; do they, Susanna Ivanovna?'

Susanna smiled a contemptuous smile.

'Especially in regard to morals, as you say, our ideas do not agree, and cannot agree,' she responded, and something menacing seemed to flit over her brows, while her lips were faintly trembling as before.

'Of course! of course!' Ratsch broke in, 'I'm not a philosopher! I'm not capable of . . . rising so superior! I'm a plain man, swayed by prejudices— oh yes!'

Susanna smiled again.

'I think, Ivan Demianitch, you too have sometimes been able to place yourself above what are called prejudices.'

'Wie so? How so, I mean? I don't know what you mean.'

'You don't know what I mean? Your memory's so bad!'

Mr. Ratsch seemed utterly taken aback.

'I . . . I . . .' he repeated, 'I . . .'

'Yes, you, Mr. Ratsch.'

There followed a brief silence.

'Really, upon my word . . .' Mr. Ratsch was beginning; 'how dare you . . . such insolence . . .'

Susanna all at once drew herself up to her full height, and still holding her elbows, squeezing them tight, drumming on them with her fingers, she stood still facing Ratsch. She seemed to challenge him to conflict, to stand up to meet him. Her face was changed; it became suddenly, in one instant, extraordinarily beautiful, and terrible too; a sort of bright, cold brilliance— the brilliance of steel—gleamed in her lustreless eyes; the lips that had been quivering were compressed in one straight, mercilessly stern line. Susanna challenged Ratsch, but he gazed blankly, and suddenly subsiding into silence, all of a heap, so to say, drew his head in, even stepped back a pace. The veteran of the year twelve was afraid; there could be no mistake about that.

Susanna slowly turned her eyes from him to me, as though calling upon me to witness her victory, and the humiliation of her foe, and, smiling once more, she walked out of the room.

The veteran remained a little while motionless in his arm-chair; at last, as though recollecting a forgotten part, he roused himself, got up, and, slapping me on the shoulder, laughed his noisy guffaw.

'There, 'pon my soul! fancy now, it's over ten years I've been living with that young lady, and yet she never can see when I'm joking, and when I'm in earnest! And you too, my young friend, are a little puzzled, I do believe. . . . Ha-ha-ha! That's because you don't know old Ratsch!'

'No. . . . I do know you now,' I thought, not without a feeling of some alarm and disgust.

'You don't know the old fellow, you don't know him,' he repeated, stroking himself on the stomach, as he accompanied me into the passage. 'I may be a tiresome person, knocked about by life, ha-ha! But I'm a good-hearted fellow, 'pon my soul, I am!'

I rushed headlong from the stairs into the street. I longed with all speed to get away from that good-hearted fellow.

XIV

'THEY hate one another, that's clear,' I thought, as I returned homewards; 'there's no doubt either that he's a wretch of a man, and she's a good girl. But what has there been between them? What is the reason of this continual exasperation? What was the meaning of those hints? And how suddenly it broke out! On such a trivial pretext!'

Next day Fustov and I had arranged to go to the theatre, to see Shtchepkin in 'Woe from Wit.' Griboyedov's comedy had only just been licensed for performance after being first disfigured by the censors' mutilations. We warmly applauded Famusov and Skalozub. I don't remember what actor took the part of Tchatsky, but I well remember that he was indescribably bad. He made his first appearance in a Hungarian jacket, and boots with tassels, and came on later in a frockcoat of the colour 'flamme du punch,' then in fashion, and the frockcoat looked about as suitable as it would have done on our old butler. I recollect too that we were all in ecstasies over the ball in the third act. Though, probably, no one ever executed such steps in reality, it was accepted as correct and I believe it is acted in just the same way to-day. One of the guests hopped excessively high, while his wig flew from side to side, and the public roared with laughter. As we were coming out of the theatre, we jostled against Viktor in a corridor.

'You were in the theatre!' he cried, flinging his arms about. 'How was it I didn't see you? I'm awfully glad I met you. You must come and have supper with me. Come on; I'll stand the supper!'

Young Ratsch seemed in an excited, almost ecstatic, frame of mind. His little eyes darted to and fro; he was grinning, and there were spots of red on his face.

'Why this gleefulness?' asked Fustov.

'Why? Wouldn't you like to know, eh?'

Viktor drew us a little aside, and pulling out of his trouser-pocket a whole bundle of the red and blue notes then in use waved them in the air.

Fustov was surprised.

'Has your governor been so liberal?'

Viktor chuckled.

'He liberal! You just try it on! . . . This morning, relying on your inter-cession, I asked him for cash. What do you suppose the old skinflint an-swered? "I'll pay your debts," says he, "if you like. Up to twenty-five roubles inclusive!" Do you hear, inclusive! No, sir, this was a gift from God in my destitution. A lucky chance.'

'Been robbing some one?' Fustov hazarded carelessly.

Viktor frowned.

'Robbing, no indeed! I won it, won it from an officer, a guardsman. He only arrived from Petersburg yesterday. Such a chain of circumstances! It's worth telling . . . only this isn't the place. Come along to Yar's; not a couple of steps. I'll stand the show, as I said!'

We ought, perhaps, to have refused; but we followed without making any objection.

XV

AT YAR'S we were shown into a private room; supper was served, cham-pagne was brought. Viktor related to us, omitting no detail, how he had in a certain 'gay' house met this officer of the guards, a very nice chap and of good family, only without a hap'orth of brains; how they had made friends, how he, the officer that is, had suggested as a joke a game of 'fools' with Viktor with some old cards, for next to nothing, and with the con-dition that the officer's winnings should go to the benefit of Wilhelmina, but Viktor's to his own benefit; how afterwards they had got on to betting on the games.

'And I, and I,' cried Viktor, and he jumped up and clapped his hands, 'I hadn't more than six roubles in my pocket all the while. Fancy! And at first I was completely cleaned out. . . . A nice position! Only then —in answer to whose prayers I can't say—fortune smiled. The other fellow began to get hot and kept showing all his cards. . . . In no time he'd lost seven hundred and fifty roubles! He began begging me to go on playing, but I'm not quite a fool, I fancy! no, one mustn't abuse such luck; I popped on my hat and cut away. So now I've no need to eat humble pie with the governor, and can treat my friends. . . . Hi waiter! Another bottle! Gentlemen, let's clink glasses!'

We did clink glasses with Viktor, and continued drinking and laughing with him, though his story was by no means to our liking, nor was his society a source of any great satisfaction to us either. He began being very affable, playing the buffoon, unbending, in fact, and was more loathsome than ever. Viktor noticed at last the impression he was making on us, and began to get sulky; his remarks became more disconnected and his looks gloomier. He began yawning, announced that he was sleepy, and after swearing with his characteristic coarseness at the waiter for a badly cleaned pipe, he suddenly accosted Fustov, with a challenging expression on his distorted face.

'I say, Alexander Daviditch,' said he, 'you tell me, if you please, what do you look down on me for?'

'How so?' My friend was momentarily at a loss for a reply.

'I'll tell you how. . . . I'm very well aware that you look down on me, and that person does too' (he pointed at me with his finger), 'so there! As though you were yourself remarkable for such high and exalted principles, and weren't just as much a sinner as the rest of us. Worse even. Still waters . . . you know the proverb?'

Fustov turned rather red.

'What do you mean by that?' he asked.

'Why, I mean that I'm not blind yet, and I see very clearly everything that's going on under my nose. . . . And I have nothing against it: first it's not my principle to interfere, and secondly, my sister Susanna Ivanovna hasn't always been so exemplary herself. . . . Only, why look down on me?'

'You don't understand what you're babbling there yourself! You're drunk,' said Fustov, taking his overcoat from the wall. 'He's swindled some fool of his money, and now he's telling all sorts of lies!'

Viktor continued reclining on the sofa, and merely swung his legs, which were hanging over its arm.

'Swindled! Why did you drink the wine, then? It was paid for with the money I won, you know. As for lies, I've no need for lying. It's not my fault that in her past Susanna Ivanovna . . .'

'Hold your tongue!' Fustov shouted at him, 'hold your tongue . . . or . . .'

'Or what?'

'You'll find out what. Come along, Piotr.'

'Aha!' pursued Viktor; 'our noble-hearted knight takes refuge in flight. He doesn't care to hear the truth, that's evident! It stings—the truth does, it seems!'

'Come along, Piotr,' Fustov repeated, completely losing his habitual coolness and self-possession. 'Let's leave this wretch of a boy!'

'The boy's not afraid of you, do you hear,' Viktor shouted after us, 'he despises you, the boy does! Do you hear!'

Fustov walked so quickly along the street that I had difficulty in keeping up with him. All at once he stopped short and turned sharply back.

'Where are you going?' I asked.

'Oh, I must find out what the idiot. . . . He's drunk, no doubt, God knows what. . . . Only don't you follow me . . . we shall see each other to-morrow. Good-bye!'

And hurriedly pressing my hand, Fustov set off towards Yar's hotel.

Next day I missed seeing Fustov; and on the day after that, on going to his rooms, I learned that he had gone into the country to his uncle's, near Moscow. I inquired if he had left no note for me, but no note was forthcoming. Then I asked the servant whether he knew how long Alexander Daviditch would be away in the country. 'A fortnight, or a little more, probably,' replied the man. I took at any rate Fustov's exact address, and sauntered home, meditating deeply. This unexpected absence from Moscow, in the winter, completed my utter perplexity. My good aunt observed to me at dinner that I seemed continually expecting something, and gazed at the cabbage pie as though I were beholding it for the first time in my life. 'Pierre, vous n'êtes pas amoureux?' she cried at last, having previously got rid of her companions. But I reassured her: no, I was not in love.

XVI

THREE DAYS PASSED. I had a secret prompting to go to the Ratschs'. I fancied that in their house I should be sure to find a solution of all that absorbed my mind, that I could not make out. . . . But I should have had to meet the veteran. . . . That thought pulled me up. One tempestuous evening—the February wind was howling angrily outside, the frozen snow tapped at the window from time to time like coarse sand flung by a mighty hand—I was sitting in my room, trying to read. My servant came, and, with a mysterious air, announced that a lady wished to see me. I was surprised . . . ladies did not visit me, especially at such a late hour; however, I told him to show her in. The door opened and with swift step there walked in a woman, muffled up in a light summer cloak and a yellow shawl. Abruptly she cast off the cloak and the shawl, which were covered with snow, and I saw standing before me Susanna. I was so astonished that I did not utter a word, while she went up to the window, and leaning her shoulder against the wall, remained motionless; only her bosom heaved convulsively and her eyes moved restlessly, and the breath came with a faint moan from her white lips. I realised that it was no slight trouble that had brought her to me; I realised, for all my youth and shallowness, that at that instant before my eyes the fate of a whole life was being decided—a bitter and terrible fate.

'Susanna Ivanovna,' I began, 'how . . .'

She suddenly clutched my hand in her icy fingers, but her voice failed her. She gave a broken sigh and looked down. Her heavy coils of black hair fell about her face. . . . The snow had not melted from off it.

'Please, calm yourself, sit down,' I began again, 'see here, on the sofa. What has happened? Sit down, I entreat you.'

'No,' she articulated, scarcely audibly, and she sank on to the window-seat. 'I am all right here. . . . Let me be. . . . You could not expect . . . but if you knew . . . if I could . . . if . . .'

She tried to control herself, but the tears flowed from her eyes with a violence that shook her, and sobs, hurried, devouring sobs, filled the room. I felt a tightness at my heart. . . . I was utterly stupefied. I had seen Susanna only twice; I had conjectured that she had a hard life, but I had regarded her as a proud girl, of strong character, and all at once these violent, despairing tears. . . . Mercy! Why, one only weeps like that in the presence of death!

I stood like one condemned to death myself.

'Excuse me,' she said at last, several times, almost angrily, wiping first one eye, then the other. 'It'll soon be over. I've come to you. . . .' She was still sobbing, but without tears. 'I've come. . . . You know that Alexander Daviditch has gone away?'

In this single question Susanna revealed everything, and she glanced at me, as though she would say: 'You understand, of course, you will have pity, won't you?' Unhappy girl! There was no other course left to her then!

I did not know what answer to make. . . .

'He has gone away, he has gone away . . . he believed him!' Susanna was saying meanwhile. 'He did not care even to question me; he thought I should not tell him all the truth, he could think that of me! As though I had ever deceived him!'

She bit her lower lip, and bending a little, began to scratch with her nail the patterns of ice that covered the window-pane. I went hastily into the next room, and sending my servant away, came back at once and lighted another candle. I had no clear idea why I was doing all this. . . . I was greatly overcome.

Susanna was sitting as before on the window-seat, and it was at this moment that I noticed how lightly she was dressed: a grey gown with white buttons and a broad leather belt, that was all. I went up to her, but she did not take any notice of me.

'He believed it, . . . he believed it,' she whispered, swaying softly from side to side. 'He did not hesitate, he dealt me this last . . . last blow!' She turned suddenly to me. 'You know his address?'

'Yes, Susanna Ivanovna . . . I learnt it from his servants . . . at his house. He told me nothing of his intention; I had not seen him for two days—went to inquire and he had already left Moscow.'

'You know his address?' she repeated. 'Well, write to him then that he has killed me. You are a good man, I know. He did not talk to you of me, I dare say, but he talked to me about you. Write . . . ah, write to him to come back quickly, if he wants to find me alive! . . . No! He will not find me! . . .'

Susanna's voice grew quieter at each word, and she was quieter altogether. But this calm seemed to me more awful than the previous sobs.

'He believed him, . . .' she said again, and rested her chin on her clasped hands.

A sudden squall of wind beat upon the window with a sharp whistle and a thud of snow. A cold draught passed over the room. . . . The candles flickered. . . . Susanna shivered.

Again I begged her to sit on the sofa.

'No, no, let me be,' she answered, 'I am all right here. Please.' She huddled up to the frozen pane, as though she had found herself a refuge in the recesses of the window. 'Please.'

'But you're shivering, you're frozen,' I cried. 'Look, your shoes are soaked.'

'Let me be . . . please . . .' she whispered, and closed her eyes.

A panic seized me.

'Susanna Ivanovna!' I almost screamed: 'do rouse yourself, I entreat you! What is the matter with you? Why such despair? You will see, everything will be cleared up, some misunderstanding . . . some unlooked-for chance. . . . You will see, he will soon be back. I will let him know. . . . I will write to him to-day. . . . But I will not repeat your words. . . . Is it possible!'

'He will not find me,' Susanna murmured, still in the same subdued voice. 'Do you suppose I would have come here, to you, to a stranger, if I had not known I should not long be living? Ah, all my past has been swept away beyond return! You see, I could not bear to die so, in solitude, in silence, without saying to some one, "I've lost every thing . . . and I'm dying. . . . Look!"'

She drew back into her cold little corner. . . . Never shall I forget that head, those fixed eyes with their deep, burnt-out look, those dark, disordered tresses against the pale window-pane, even the grey, narrow gown, under every fold of which throbbed such young, passionate life!

Unconsciously I flung up my hands.

'You . . . you die, Susanna Ivanovna! You have only to live. . . . You must live!'

She looked at me. . . . My words seemed to surprise her.

'Ah, you don't know,' she began, and she softly dropped both her hands. 'I cannot live. Too much, too much I have had to suffer, too much! I lived through it. . . . I hoped . . . but now . . . when even this is shattered . . . when . . .'

She raised her eyes to the ceiling and seemed to sink into thought. The tragic line, which I had once noticed about her lips, came out now still more clearly; it seemed to spread across her whole face. It seemed as though some relentless hand had drawn it immutably, had set a mark for ever on this lost soul.

She was still silent.

'Susanna Ivanovna,' I said, to break that awful silence with anything; 'he will come back, I assure you!'

Susanna looked at me again.

'What do you say?' she enunciated with visible effort.

'He will come back, Susanna Ivanovna, Alexander will come back!'

'He will come back?' she repeated. 'But even if he did come back, I cannot forgive him this humiliation, this lack of faith. . . .'

She clutched at her head.

'My God! my God! what am I saying, and why am I here? What is it all? What . . . what did I come to ask . . . and whom? Ah, I am going mad! . . .'

Her eyes came to a rest.

'You wanted to ask me to write to Alexander,' I made haste to remind her.

She started.

'Yes, write, write to him . . . what you like. . . . And here . . .' She hurriedly fumbled in her pocket and brought out a little manuscript book. 'This I was writing for him . . . before he ran away. . . . But he believed . . . he believed him!'

I understood that her words referred to Viktor; Susanna would not mention him, would not utter his detested name.

'But, Susanna Ivanovna, excuse me,' I began, 'what makes you suppose that Alexander Daviditch had any conversation . . . with that person?'

'What? Why, he himself came to me and told me all about it, and bragged of it . . . and laughed just as his father laughs! Here, here, take it,' she went on, thrusting the manuscript into my hand, 'read it, send it to him, burn it, throw it away, do what you like, as you please. . . . But I can't die like this with no one knowing. . . . Now it is time. . . . I must go.'

She got up from the window-seat. . . . I stopped her.

'Where are you going, Susanna Ivanovna, mercy on us! Listen, what a storm is raging! You are so lightly dressed. . . . And your home is not near here. Let me at least go for a carriage, for a sledge. . . .'

'No, no, I want nothing,' she said resolutely, repelling me and taking up her cloak and shawl. 'Don't keep me, for God's sake! or . . . I can't answer for anything! I feel an abyss, a dark abyss under my feet. . . . Don't come near me, don't touch me!' With feverish haste she put on her cloak, arranged her shawl. . . . 'Good-bye . . . good-bye. . . . Oh, my unhappy people, for ever strangers, a curse lies upon us! No one has ever cared for me, was it likely he . . .' She suddenly ceased. 'No; one man loved me,' she began again, wringing her hands, 'but death is all about me, death and no escape! Now it is my turn. . . . Don't come after me,' she cried shrilly. 'Don't come! don't come!'

I was petrified, while she rushed out; and an instant later, I heard the slam downstairs of the heavy street door, and the window panes shook again under the violent onslaught of the blast.

I could not quickly recover myself. I was only beginning life in those days: I had had no experience of passion nor of suffering, and had rarely witnessed any manifestation of strong feeling in others. . . . But the sincerity of this suffering, of this passion, impressed me. If it had not been for the manuscript in my hands, I might have thought that I had dreamed it all—it was all so unlikely, and swooped by like a passing storm. I was till midnight reading the manuscript. It consisted of several sheets of letter-paper, closely covered with a large, irregular writing, almost without an erasure. Not a single line was quite straight, and one seemed in every one of them to feel the excited trembling of the hand that held the pen. Here follows what was in the manuscript. I have kept it to this day.

XVII

MY STORY

I AM this year twenty-eight years old. Here are my earliest recollections; I was living in the Tambov province, in the country house of a rich landowner, Ivan Matveitch Koltovsky, in a small room on the second storey. With me lived my mother, a Jewess, daughter of a dead painter, who had come from abroad, a woman always ailing, with an extraordinarily beautiful face, pale as wax, and such mournful eyes, that sometimes when she gazed long at me, even without looking at her, I was aware of her sorrowful, sorrowful eyes, and I would burst into tears and rush to embrace her. I had tutors come to me; I had music lessons, and was called ' miss.' I dined at the master's table together with my mother. Mr. Koltovsky was a tall, handsome old man with a stately manner; he always smelt of *ambre*. I stood in mortal terror of him, though he called me Suzon and gave me his dry, sinewy hand to kiss under its lace-ruffles. With my mother he was elaborately courteous, but he talked little even with her. He would say two or three affable words, to which she promptly made a hurried answer; and he would be silent and sit looking about him with dignity, and slowly picking up a pinch of Spanish snuff from his round, golden snuff-box with the arms of the Empress Catherine on it.

My ninth year has always remained vivid in my memory. . . . I learnt then, from the maids in the servants' room, that Ivan Matveitch Koltovsky was my father, and almost on the same day, my mother, by his command, was married to Mr. Ratsch, who was something like a steward to him. I was utterly unable to comprehend the possibility of such a thing, I was bewildered, I was almost ill, my brain suffered under the strain, my mind was overclouded. ' Is it true, is it true, mamma,' I asked her, ' that scented bogey ' (that was my name for Ivan Matveitch) ' is my father? ' My mother was terribly scared, she shut my mouth. . . . ' Never speak to any one of that, do you hear, Susanna, do you hear, not a word! ' . . . she repeated in a shaking voice, pressing my head to her bosom. . . . And I never did speak to any one of it. . . . That prohibition of my mother's I understood. . . . I understood that I must be silent, that my mother begged my forgiveness!

My unhappiness began from that day. Mr. Ratsch did not love my mother, and she did not love him. He married her for money, and she was obliged to submit. Mr. Koltovsky probably considered that in this way everything had been arranged for the best, *la position était régularisée*. I remember the day before the marriage my mother and I—both locked in each other's arms—wept almost the whole morning—bitterly, bitterly—and silently. It is not strange that she was silent. . . . What could she say to me? But that I did not question her shows that unhappy children learn wisdom sooner than happy ones . . . to their cost.

Mr. Koltovsky continued to interest himself in my education, and even by degrees put me on a more intimate footing. He did not talk to me . . . but morning and evening, after flicking the snuff from his jabot with two fingers, he would with the same two fingers—always icy cold—pat me on the cheek and give me some sort of dark-coloured sweetmeats, also smelling of *ambre*, which I never ate. At twelve years old I became his reader —*sa petite lectrice.* I read him French books of the last century, the memoirs of Saint Simon, of Mably, Renal, Helvetius, Voltaire's correspondence, the encyclopædists, of course without understanding a word, even when, with a smile and a grimace, he ordered me, ' relire ce dernier paragraphe, qui est bien remarquable! ' Ivan Matveitch was completely a Frenchman. He had lived in Paris till the Revolution, remembered Marie Antoinette, and had received an invitation to Trianon to see her. He had also seen Mirabeau, who, according to his account, wore very large buttons—*exagêré en tout,* and was altogether a man of *mauvais ton, en dépit de sa naissance!* Ivan Matveitch, however, rarely talked of that time; but two or three times a year, addressing himself to the crooked old emigrant whom he had taken into his house, and called for some unknown reason ' M. le Commandeur,' he recited in his deliberate, nasal voice, the impromptu he had once delivered at a soiree of the Duchesse de Polignac. I remember only the first two lines. . . . It had reference to a comparison between the Russians and the French:

> ' *L'aigle se plaît aux régions austères*
> *Où le ramier ne saurait habiter . . .* '

' Digne de M. de Saint Aulaire! ' M. le Commandeur would every time exclaim.

Ivan Matveitch looked youngish up to the time of his death: his cheeks were rosy, his teeth white, his eyebrows thick and immobile, his eyes agreeable and expressive, clear, black eyes, perfect agate. He was not at all unreasonable, and was very courteous with every one, even with the servants. . . . But, my God! how wretched I was with him, with what joy I always left him, what evil thoughts confounded me in his presence! Ah, I was not to blame for them! . . . I was not to blame for what they had made of me. . . .

Mr. Ratsch was, after his marriage, assigned a lodge not far from the big house. I lived there with my mother. It was a cheerless life I led there. She soon gave birth to a son, Viktor, this same Viktor whom I have every right to think and to call my enemy. From the time of his birth my mother never regained her health, which had always been weak. Mr. Ratsch did not think fit in those days to keep up such a show of good spirits as he maintains now: he always wore a morose air and tried to pass for a busy, hardworking person. To me he was cruel and rude. I felt relief when I retired from Ivan Matveitch's presence; but my own home too I was glad to leave. . . . Unhappy was my youth! For ever tossed from one shore to the other, with no desire to anchor at either! I would run across the courtyard in winter, through the deep snow, in a thin frock—run to the big house to read to Ivan Matveitch, and as it were be glad to go. . . . But when I was there, when I saw those great cheerless rooms, the bright-coloured, upholstered furniture, that courteous and heartless old man in the open silk wadded jacket, in the white jabot and white cravat, with lace ruffles falling over his fingers, with a *soupçon* of powder (so his valet expressed it) on his combed-back hair, I felt choked by the stifling scent of *ambre*, and my heart sank. Ivan Matveitch usually sat in a large low chair; on the wall behind his head hung a picture, representing a young woman, with a bright and bold expression of face, dressed in a sumptuous Hebrew costume, and simply covered with precious stones, with diamonds. . . . I often stole a glance at this picture, but only later on I learned that it was the portrait of my mother, painted by her father at Ivan Matveitch's request. She had changed indeed since those days! Well had he succeeded in subduing and crushing her! ' And she loved him! Loved that old man! ' was my thought. . . . ' How could it be! Love him! ' And yet, when I recalled some of my mother's glances, some half-uttered phrases and unconscious gestures. . . . ' Yes, yes, she did love him! ' I repeated with horror. Ah, God, spare others from knowing aught of such feelings!

Every day I read to Ivan Matveitch, sometimes for three or four hours together. . . . So much reading in such a loud voice was harmful to me. Our doctor was anxious about my lungs and even once communicated his fears to Ivan Matveitch. But the old man only smiled—no; he never smiled, but somehow sharpened and moved forward his lips—and told him: ' Vous ne savez pas ce qu'il y a de ressources dans cette jeunesse.' ' In former years, however, M. le Commandeur,' . . . the doctor ventured to observe. Ivan Matveitch smiled as before. ' Vous rêvez, mon cher,' he interposed: ' le commandeur n'a plus de dents, et il crache à chaque mot. J'aime les voix jeunes.'

And I still went on reading, though my cough was very troublesome in the mornings and at night. . . . Sometimes Ivan Matveitch made me play the piano. But music always had a soporific influence on his nerves. His eyes closed at once, his head nodded in time, and only rarely I heard, ' C'est du Steibelt, n'est-ce pas? Jouez-moi du Steibelt! ' Ivan Matveitch looked upon Steibelt as a great genius, who had succeeded in overcoming in himself ' la grossière lourdeur des Allemands,' and only found fault with him for one thing: ' trop de fougue! trop d'imagination! ' . . . When Ivan Matveitch noticed that I was tired from playing he would offer me ' du cachou de Bologne.' So day after day slipped by. . . .

And then one night—a night never to be forgotten!—a terrible calamity fell upon me. My mother died almost suddenly. I was only just fifteen. Oh, what a sorrow that was, with what cruel violence it swooped down upon me! How terrified I was at that first meeting with death! My poor mother! Strange were our relations; we passionately loved each other . . . passionately and hopelessly; we both as it were treasured up and hid from each other our common secret, kept obstinately silent about it, though we

knew all that was passing at the bottom of our hearts! Even of the past, of
her own early past, my mother never spoke to me, and she never complained in words, though her whole being was nothing but one dumb
complaint. We avoided all conversation of any seriousness. Alas! I kept
hoping that the hour would come, and she would open her heart at last,
and I too should speak out, and both of us would be more at ease. . . . But
the daily little cares, her irresolute, shrinking temper, illnesses, the presence
of Mr. Ratsch, and most of all the eternal question,—what is the use? and
the relentless, unbroken flowing away of time, of life. . . . All was ended
as though by a clap of thunder, and the words which would have loosed
us from the burden of our secret—even the last dying words of leave-
taking—I was not destined to hear from my mother! All that is left in my
memory is Mr. Ratsch's calling, 'Susanna Ivanovna, go, please, your mother
wishes to give you her blessing!' and then the pale hand stretched out
from the heavy counterpane, the agonised breathing, the dying eyes. . . .
Oh, enough! enough!

With what horror, with what indignation and piteous curiosity I looked
next day, and on the day of the funeral, into the face of my father . . .
yes, my father! In my dead mother's writing-case were found his letters.
I fancied he looked a little pale and drawn . . . but no! Nothing was stirring in that heart of stone. Exactly as before, he summoned me to his
room, a week later; exactly in the same voice he asked me to read:
'Si vous le voulez bien, les observations sur l'histoire de France de Mably,
à la page 74 . . . là où nous avons été interrompus.' And he had not even
had my mother's portrait moved! On dismissing me, he did indeed call me
to him, and giving me his hand to kiss a second time, he observed:
'Suzanne, la mort de votre mère vous a privée de votre appui naturel; mais
vous pourrez toujours compter sur ma protection,' but with the other hand
he gave me at once a slight push on the shoulder, and, with the sharpening of the corners of the mouth habitual with him, he added, 'Allez, mon
enfant.' I longed to shriek at him: 'Why, but you know you're my
father!' but I said nothing and left the room.

Next morning, early, I went to the graveyard. May had come in all its
glory of flowers and leaves, and a long while I sat on the new grave. I did
not weep, nor grieve; one thought was filling my brain: 'Do you hear,
mother? He means to extend his protection to me, too!' And it seemed
to me that my mother ought not to be wounded by the smile which it
instinctively called up on my lips.

At times I wonder what made me so persistently desire to wring—not
a confession . . . no, indeed! but, at least, one warm word of kinship from
Ivan Matveitch? Didn't I know what he was, and how little he was like
all that I pictured in my dreams as *a father?* . . . But I was so lonely, so
alone on earth! And then, that thought, ever recurring, gave me no rest:
'Did not she love him? She must have loved him for something?'.

Three years more slipped by. Nothing changed in the monotonous round
of life, marked out and arranged for us. Viktor was growing into a boy. I

was eight years older and would gladly have looked after him, but Mr. Ratsch opposed my doing so. He gave him a nurse, who had orders to keep strict watch that the child was not 'spoilt,' that is, not to allow me to go near him. And Viktor himself fought shy of me. One day Mr. Ratsch came into my room, perturbed, excited, and angry. On the previous evening unpleasant rumours had reached me about my stepfather; the servants were talking of his having been caught embezzling a considerable sum of money, and taking bribes from a merchant.

'You can assist me,' he began, tapping impatiently on the table with his fingers. 'Go and speak for me to Ivan Matveitch.'

'Speak for you? On what ground? What about?'

'Intercede for me. . . . I'm not like a stranger any way . . . I'm accused . . . well, the fact is, I may be left without bread to eat, and you, too.'

'But how can I go to him? How can I disturb him?'

'What next! You have *a right* to disturb him!'

'What right, Ivan Demianitch?'

'Come, no humbug. . . . He cannot refuse you, for many reasons. Do you mean to tell me you don't understand that?'

He looked insolently into my eyes, and I felt my cheeks simply burning. Hatred, contempt, rose up within me, surged in a rush upon me, drowning me.

'Yes, I understand you, Ivan Demianitch,' I answered at last—my own voice seemed strange to me—'and I am not going to Ivan Matveitch, and I will not ask him for anything. Bread, or no bread!'

Mr. Ratsch shivered, ground his teeth, and clenched his fists.

'All right, wait a bit, your highness!' he muttered huskily. 'I won't forget it!'

That same day, Ivan Matveitch sent for him, and, I was told, shook his cane at him, the very cane which he had once exchanged with the Duc de la Rochefoucauld, and cried, 'You be a scoundrel and extortioner! I put you outside!' Ivan Matveitch could hardly speak Russian at all, and despised our 'coarse jargon,' *ce jargon vulgaire et rude.* Some one once said before him, 'That same's self-understood.' Ivan Matveitch was quite indignant, and often afterwards quoted the phrase as an example of the senselessness and absurdity of the Russian tongue. 'What does it mean, that same's self-understood?' he would ask in Russian, with emphasis on each syllable. 'Why not simply that's understood, and why same and self?'

Ivan Matveitch did not, however, dismiss Mr. Ratsch, he did not even deprive him of his position. But my stepfather kept his word: he never forgot it.

I began to notice a change in Ivan Matveitch. He was low-spirited, depressed, his health broke down a little. His fresh, rosy face grew yellow and wrinkled; he lost a front tooth. He quite ceased going out, and gave up the reception-days he had established for the peasants, without the assistance of the priest, *sans le concours du clergé.* On such days Ivan

Matveitch had been in the habit of going in to the peasants in the hall or
on the balcony, with a rose in his buttonhole, and putting his lips to a silver
goblet of vodka, he would make them a speech something like this: ' You
are content with my actions, even as I am content with your zeal, whereat
I rejoice truly. We are all *brothers;* at our birth we are equal; I drink your
health! ' He bowed to them, and the peasants bowed to him, but only from
the waist, no prostrating themselves to the ground, that was strictly forbidden. The peasants were entertained with good cheer as before, but Ivan
Matveitch no longer showed himself to his subjects. Sometimes he interrupted my reading with exclamations: ' La machine se détraque! Cela
se gâte! ' Even his eyes—those bright, stony eyes—began to grow dim and,
as it were, smaller; he dozed oftener than ever and breathed hard in his
sleep. His manner with me was unchanged; only a shade of chivalrous
deference began to be perceptible in it. He never failed to get up—though
with difficulty—from his chair when I came in, conducted me to the door,
supporting me with his hand under my elbow, and instead of Suzon began
to call me sometimes, ' ma chère demoiselle,' sometimes, ' mon Antigone.'
M. le Commandeur died two years after my mother's death; his death
seemed to affect Ivan Matveitch far more deeply. A contemporary had
disappeared: that was what distressed him. And yet in later years M. le
Commandeur's sole service had consisted in crying, ' Bien joué, mal réussi! '
every time Ivan Matveitch missed a stroke, playing billiards with Mr.
Ratsch; though, indeed, too, when Ivan Matveitch addressed him at table
with some such question as : ' N'est-ce pas, M. le Commandeur, c'est Montesquieu qui a dit cela dans ses *Lettres Persanes?* ' he had still, sometimes
dropping a spoonful of soup on his ruffle, responded profoundly: ' Ah,
Monsieur de Montesquieu? Un grand écrivain, monsieur, un grand écrivain! '
Only once, when Ivan Matveitch told him that ' les théophilanthropes ont
eu pourtant du bon! ' the old man cried in an excited voice, ' Monsieur de
Kolontouskoi ' (he hadn't succeeded in the course of twenty years in
learning to pronounce his patron's name correctly), ' Monsieur de Kolontouskoi! Leur fondateur, l'instigateur de cette secte, ce La Reveillère
Lepeaux était un bonnet rouge! ' ' Non, non,' said Ivan Matveitch, smiling
and rolling together a pinch of snuff: ' des fleurs, des jeunes vierges, le
culte de la Nature . . . ils ont eu du bon, ils ont eu du bon! ' . . . I was
always surprised at the extent of Ivan Matveitch's knowledge, and at the
uselessness of his knowledge to himself.

Ivan Matveitch was perceptibly failing, but he still put a good face on it.
One day, three weeks before his death, he had a violent attack of giddiness
just after dinner. He sank into thought, said, ' C'est la fin,' and pulling himself together with a sigh, he wrote a letter to Petersburg to his sole heir,
a brother with whom he had had no intercourse for twenty years. Hearing
that Ivan Matveitch was unwell, a neighbour paid him a visit—a German,
a Catholic—once a distinguished physician, who was living in retirement
in his little place in the country. He was very rarely at Ivan Matveitch's,
but the latter always received him with special deference, and in fact had

a great respect for him. He was almost the only person in the world he did respect. The old man advised Ivan Matveitch to send for a priest, but Ivan Matveitch responded that 'ces messieurs et moi, nous n'avons rien à nous dire,' and begged him to change the subject. On the neighbour's departure, he gave his valet orders to admit no one in future.

Then he sent for me. I was frightened when I saw him; there were blue patches under his eyes, his face looked drawn and stiff, his jaw hung down. 'Vous voilà grande, Suzon,' he said, with difficulty articulating the consonants, but still trying to smile (I was then nineteen), 'vous allez peut-être bientôt rester seule. Soyez toujours sage et vertueuse. C'est la dernière récommandation d'un '—he coughed—'d'un vieillard qui vous veut du bien. Je vous ai recommandé à mon frère et je ne doute pas qu'il ne respecte mes volontés. . . .' He coughed again, and anxiously felt his chest. 'Du reste, j'espère encore pouvoir faire quelque chose pour vous . . . dans mon testament.' This last phrase cut me to the heart, like a knife. Ah, it was really too . . . too contemptuous and insulting! Ivan Matveitch probably ascribed to some other feeling—to a feeling of grief or gratitude—what was expressed in my face, and as though wishing to comfort me, he patted me on the shoulder, at the same time, as usual, gently repelling me, and observed: 'Voyons, mon enfant, du courage! Nous sommes tous mortels! Et puis il n'y a pas encore de danger. Ce n'est qu'une précaution que j'ai cru devoir prendre. . . . Allez!'

Again, just as when he had summoned me after my mother's death, I longed to shriek at him, 'But I'm your daughter! your daughter!' But I thought in those words, in that cry of the heart, he would doubtless hear nothing but a desire to assert my rights, my claims on his property, on his money. . . . Oh, no, for nothing in the world would I say a word to this man, who had not once mentioned my mother's name to me, in whose eyes I was of so little account that he did not even trouble himself to ascertain whether I was aware of my parentage! Or, perhaps, he suspected, even knew it, and did not wish 'to raise a dust' (a favourite saying of his, almost the only Russian expression he ever used), did not care to deprive himself of a good reader with a young voice! No! no! Let him go on wronging his daughter, as he had wronged her mother! Let him carry both sins to the grave! I swore it, I swore he should not hear from my lips the word which must have something of a sweet and holy sound in every ear! I would not say to him father! I would not forgive him for my mother and myself! He felt no need of that forgiveness, of that name. . . . It could not be, it could not be that he felt no need of it! But he should not have forgiveness, he should not, he should not!

God knows whether I should have kept my vow, and whether my heart would not have softened, whether I should not have overcome my shyness, my shame, and my pride . . . but it happened with Ivan Matveitch just as with my mother. Death carried him off suddenly, and also in the night. It was again Mr. Ratsch who waked me, and ran with me to the big house, to Ivan Matveitch's bedroom. . . . But I found not even the last dying gestures, which had left such a vivid impression on my memory at my mother's bedside. On the embroidered, lace-edged pillows lay a sort of withered, dark-coloured doll, with sharp nose and ruffled grey eyebrows. . . . I shrieked with horror, with loathing, rushed away, stumbled in doorways against bearded peasants in smocks with holiday red sashes, and found myself, I don't remember how, in the fresh air. . . .

I was told afterwards that when the valet ran into the bedroom, at a violent ring of the bell, he found Ivan Matveitch not in the bed, but a few feet from it. And that he was sitting huddled up on the floor, and that twice over he repeated, 'Well, granny, here's a pretty holiday for you!' And that these were his last words. But I cannot believe that. Was it likely he would speak Russian at such a moment, and such a homely old Russian saying too!

For a whole fortnight afterwards we were awaiting the arrival of the new master, Semyon Matveitch Koltovsky. He sent orders that nothing was to be touched, no one was to be discharged, till he had looked into everything in person. All the doors, all the furniture, drawers, tables—all were locked and sealed up. All the servants were downcast and apprehensive. I became suddenly one of the most important persons in the house, perhaps the most important. I had been spoken of as 'the young lady' before; but now this expression seemed to take a new significance, and was pronounced with a peculiar emphasis. It began to be whispered that 'the old master had died suddenly, and hadn't time to send for a priest, indeed and he hadn't been at confession for many a long day; but still, a will doesn't take long to make.'

Mr. Ratsch, too, thought well to change his mode of action. He did not affect good-nature and friendliness; he knew he would not impose upon me, but his face wore an expression of sulky resignation. 'You see, I give in,' he seemed to say. Every one showed me deference, and tried to please me . . . while I did not know what to do or how to behave, and could only marvel that people failed to perceive how they were hurting me. At last Semyon Matveitch arrived.

Semyon Matveitch was ten years younger than Ivan Matveitch, and his whole life had taken a completely different turn. He was a government official in Petersburg, filling an important position. . . . He had married and been left early a widower; he had one son. In face Semyon Matveitch was like his brother, only he was shorter and stouter, and had a round bald head, bright black eyes, like Ivan Matveitch's, only more prominent, and full red lips. Unlike his brother, whom he spoke of even after his death as a French philosopher, and sometimes bluntly as a queer fish, Semyon Matveitch almost invariably talked Russian, loudly and fluently, and he was constantly laughing, completely closing his eyes as he did so and shaking all over in an unpleasant way, as though he were shaking with rage. He looked after things very sharply, went into everything himself, exacted the strictest account from every one. The very first day of his arrival he ordered a service with holy water, and sprinkled everything with water, all the rooms in the house, even the lofts and the cellars, in order, as he put it, 'radically to expel the Voltairean and Jacobin spirit.' In the first week several of Ivan Matveitch's favourites were sent to the right-about, one was even banished to a settlement, corporal punishment was inflicted on others; the old valet—he was a Turk, knew French, and had been given to Ivan Matveitch by the late field-marshal Kamensky—received his freedom, indeed, but with it a command to be gone within twenty-four hours, 'as an example to others.' Semyon Matveitch turned out to be a harsh master; many probably regretted the late owner.

'With the old master, Ivan Matveitch,' a butler, decrepit with age, wailed in my presence, 'our only trouble was to see that the linen put out was clean, and that the rooms smelt sweet, and that the servants' voices weren't heard in the passages—God forbid! For the rest, you might do as you pleased. The old master never hurt a fly in his life! Ah, it's hard times now! It's time to die!'

Rapid, too, was the change in my position, that is to say in the position in which I had been placed for a few days against my own will. . . . No sort of will was found among Ivan Matveitch's papers, not a line written for my benefit. At once every one seemed in haste to avoid me. . . . I am not speaking of Mr. Ratsch . . . every one else, too, was angry with me, and tried to show their anger, as though I had deceived them.

One Sunday after matins, in which he invariably officiated at the altar, Semyon Matveitch sent for me. Till that day I had seen him by glimpses, and he seemed not to have noticed me. He received me in his study, standing at the window. He was wearing an official uniform with two stars. I stood still, near the door; my heart was beating violently from fear and from another feeling, vague as yet, but still oppressive. 'I wish to see you, young lady,' began Semyon Matveitch, glancing first at my feet, and then suddenly into my eyes. The look was like a slap in the face. 'I wished to see you to inform you of my decision, and to assure you of my unhesitating inclination to be of service to you.' He raised his voice. 'Claims, of course, you have none, but as . . . my brother's reader you may always reckon on my . . . my consideration. I am . . . of course convinced of your good sense and of your principles. Mr. Ratsch, your stepfather, has already received from me the necessary instructions. To which I must add that your attractive exterior seems to me a pledge of the excellence of your sentiments.' Semyon Matveitch went off into a thin chuckle, while I . . . I was not offended exactly . . . but I suddenly felt very sorry for myself . . . and at that moment I fully realised how utterly forsaken and alone I was. Semyon Matveitch went with short, firm steps to the table, took a roll of notes out of the drawer, and putting it in my hand, he added: 'Here is a small sum from me for pocket-money. I won't forget you in future, my pretty; but good-bye for the present, and be a good girl.' I took the roll mechanically: I should have taken anything he had offered me, and going back to my own room, a long while I wept, sitting on my bed. I did not notice that I had dropped the roll of notes on the floor. Mr. Ratsch found it and picked it up, and, asking me what I meant to do with it, kept it for himself.

An important change had taken place in his fortunes too in those days. After a few conversations with Semyon Matveitch, he became a great favourite, and soon after received the position of head steward. From that time dates his cheerfulness, that eternal laugh of his; at first it was an effort to adapt himself to his patron . . . in the end it became a habit. It was then, too, that he became a Russian patriot. Semyon Matveitch was an admirer of everything national, he called himself ' a true Russian bear,' and ridiculed the European dress, which he wore however. He sent away to a remote village a cook, on whose training Ivan Matveitch had spent vast sums: he sent him away because he had not known how to prepare pickled giblets.

Semyon Matveitch used to stand at the altar and join in the responses with the deacons, and when the serf-girls were brought together to dance and sing choruses, he would join in their songs too, and beat time with his feet, and pinch their cheeks. . . . But he soon went back to Petersburg, leaving my stepfather practically in complete control of the whole property.

Bitter days began for me. . . . My one consolation was music, and I gave myself up to it with my whole soul. Fortunately Mr. Ratsch was very fully occupied, but he took every opportunity to make me feel his hostility; as he had promised, he ' did not forget ' my refusal. He ill-treated me, made me copy his long and lying reports to Semyon Matveitch, and correct for him the mistakes in spelling. I was forced to obey him absolutely, and I did obey him. He announced that he meant to tame me, to make me as soft as silk. ' What do you mean by those mutinous eyes? ' he shouted sometimes at dinner, drinking his beer, and slapping the table with his hand. ' You think, maybe, you're as silent as a sheep, so you must be all right. . . . Oh, no! You'll please look at me like a sheep too! ' My position became a torture, insufferable, . . . my heart was growing bitter. Something dangerous began more and more frequently to stir within it. I passed nights without sleep and without a light, thinking, thinking incessantly; and in the darkness without and the gloom within, a fearful determination began to shape itself. The arrival of Semyon Matveitch gave another turn to my thoughts.

No one had expected him. It turned out that he was retiring in unpleasant circumstances; he had hoped to receive the Alexander ribbon, and they had presented him with a snuff-box. Discontented with the government, which had failed to appreciate his talents, and with Petersburg society, which had shown him little sympathy, and did not share his indignation, he determined to settle in the country, and devote himself to the management of his property. He arrived alone. His son, Mihail Semyonitch, arrived later, in the holidays for the New Year. My stepfather was scarcely ever out of Semyon Matveitch's room; he still stood high in his good graces. He left me in peace; he had no time for me then . . . Semyon Matveitch had taken it into his head to start a paper factory. Mr. Ratsch had no knowledge whatever of manufacturing work, and Semyon Matveitch was aware of the fact; but then my stepfather was an active man (the favourite expression just then), an 'Araktcheev!' That was just what Semyon Matveitch used to call him—'my Araktcheev!' 'That's all I want,' Semyon Matveitch maintained; 'if there is zeal, I myself will direct it.' In the midst of his numerous occupations—he had to superintend the factory, the estate, the foundation of a counting-house, the drawing up of counting-house regulations, the creation of new offices and duties—Semyon Matveitch still had time to attend to me.

I was summoned one evening to the drawing-room, and set to play the piano. Semyon Matveitch cared for music even less than his brother; he praised and thanked me, however, and next day I was invited to dine at the master's table. After dinner Semyon Matveitch had rather a long conversation with me, asked me questions, laughed at some of my replies, though there was, I remember, nothing amusing in them, and stared at me so strangely . . . I felt uncomfortable. I did not like his eyes, I did not like their open expression, their clear glance. . . . It always seemed to me that this very openness concealed something evil, that under that clear brilliance it was dark within in his soul. 'You shall not be my reader,' Semyon Matveitch announced to me at last, prinking and setting himself to rights in a repulsive way. 'I am, thank God, not blind yet, and can read myself; but coffee will taste better to me from your little hands, and I shall listen to your playing with pleasure.' From that day I always went over to the big house to dinner, and sometimes remained in the drawing-room till evening. I too, like my stepfather, was in favour: it was not a source of joy for me. Semyon Matveitch, I am bound to own, showed me a certain respect, but in the man there was, I felt it, something that repelled and alarmed me. And that 'something' showed itself not in words, but in his eyes, in those wicked eyes, and in his laugh. He never spoke to me of my father, of his brother, and it seemed to me that he avoided the subject, not because he did not want to excite ambitious ideas or pretensions in me, but from another cause, to which I could not give a definite shape, but which made me blush and feel bewildered. . . . Towards Christmas came his son, Mihail Semyonitch.

Ah, I feel I cannot go on as I have begun; these memories are too painful. Especially now I cannot tell my story calmly. . . . But what is the use of concealment? I loved Michel, and he loved me.

How it came to pass—I am not going to describe that either. From the very evening when he came into the drawing-room—I was at the piano, playing a sonata of Weber's when he came in—handsome and slender, in a velvet coat lined with sheepskin and high gaiters, just as he was, straight from the frost outside, and shaking his snow-sprinkled, sable cap, before he had greeted his father, glanced swiftly at me, and wondered—I knew that from that evening I could never forget him—I could never forget that good, young face. He began to speak . . . and his voice went straight to my heart. . . . A manly and soft voice, and in every sound such a true, honest nature!

Semyon Matveitch was delighted at his son's arrival, embraced him, but at once asked, 'For a fortnight, eh? On leave, eh?' and sent me away.

I sat a long while at my window, and gazed at the lights flitting to and fro in the rooms of the big house. I watched them, I listened to the new, unfamiliar voices; I was attracted by the cheerful commotion, and something new, unfamiliar, bright, flitted into my soul too. . . . The next day before dinner I had my first conversation with him. He had come across to see my stepfather with some message from Semyon Matveitch, and he found me in our little sitting-room. I was getting up to go; he detained me. He was very lively and unconstrained in all his movements and words, but of superciliousness or arrogance, of the tone of Petersburg superiority, there was not a trace in him, and nothing of the officer, of the guardsman. . . . On the contrary, in the very freedom of his manner there was something appealing, almost shamefaced, as though he were begging you to overlook something. Some people's eyes are never laughing, even at the moment of laughter; with *him* it was the lips that almost never changed their beautiful line, while his eyes were almost always smiling. So we chatted for about an hour . . . what about I don't remember; I remember only that I looked him straight in the face all the while, and oh, how delightfully at ease I felt with him!

In the evening I played on the piano. He was very fond of music, and he sat down in a low chair, and laying his curly head on his arm, he listened intently. He did not once praise me, but I felt that he liked my playing, and I played with ardour. Semyon Matveitch, who was sitting near his son, looking through some plans, suddenly frowned. 'Come, madam,' he said, smoothing himself down and buttoning himself up, as his manner was, 'that's enough; why are you trilling away like a canary? It's enough to make one's head ache. For us old folks you wouldn't exert yourself so, no fear . . .' he added in an undertone, and again he sent me away. Michel followed me to the door with his eyes, and got up from his seat. 'Where are you off to? Where are you off to?' cried Semyon Matveitch, and he suddenly laughed, and then said something more . . . I could not catch his words; but Mr. Ratsch, who was present, sitting in a corner of the drawing-room (he was always 'present,' and that time he had brought in the plans), laughed, and his laugh reached my ears. . . . The same thing, or almost the same thing, was repeated the following evening . . . Semyon Matveitch grew suddenly cooler to me.

Four days later I met Michel in the corridor that divided the big house in two. He took me by the hand, and led me to a room near the dining-room, which was called the portrait gallery. I followed him, not without emotion, but with perfect confidence. Even then, I believe, I would have followed him to the end of the world, though I had as yet no suspicion of all that he was to me. Alas, I loved him with all the passion, all the despair of a young creature who not only has no one to love, but feels herself an uninvited and unnecessary guest among strangers, among enemies! . . .

Michel said to me—and it was strange! I looked boldly, directly in his face, while he did not look at me, and flushed slightly—he said to me that he understood my position, and sympathised with me, and begged me to forgive his father. . . . 'As far as I'm concerned,' he added, 'I beseech you always to trust me, and believe me, to me you're a sister—yes, a sister.' Here he pressed my hand warmly. I was confused, it was my turn to look down; I had somehow expected something else, some other word. I began to thank him. 'No, please,'—he cut me short—'don't talk like that . . . But remember, it's a brother's duty to defend his sister, and if you ever need protection, against any one whatever, rely upon me. I have not been here long, but I have seen a good deal already . . . and among other things, I see through your stepfather.' He squeezed my hand again, and left me.

I found out later that Michel had felt an aversion for Mr. Ratsch from his very first meeting with him. Mr. Ratsch tried to ingratiate himself with him too, but becoming convinced of the uselessness of his efforts, promptly took up himself an attitude of hostility to him, and not only did not disguise it from Semyon Matveitch, but, on the contrary, lost no opportunity of showing it, expressing, at the same time, his regret that he had been so unlucky as to displease the young heir. Mr. Ratsch had carefully studied Semyon Matveitch's character; his calculations did not lead him astray. 'This man's devotion to me admits of no doubt, for the very reason that after I am gone he will be ruined; my heir cannot endure him.' . . . This idea grew and strengthened in the old man's head. They say all persons in power, as they grow old, are readily caught by that bait, the bait of exclusive personal devotion. . . .

Semyon Matveitch had good reason to call Mr. Ratsch his Araktcheev. . . . He might well have called him another name too. 'You're not one to make difficulties,' he used to say to him. He had begun in this condescendingly familiar tone with him from the very first, and my stepfather would gaze fondly at Semyon Matveitch, let his head droop deprecatingly on one side, and laugh with good-humoured simplicity, as though to say, 'Here I am, entirely in your hands.'

Ah, I feel my hands shaking, and my heart's thumping against the table on which I write at this moment. It's terrible for me to recall those days, and my blood boils. . . . But I will tell everything to the end . . . to the end!

A new element had come into Mr. Ratsch's treatment of me during my brief period of favour. He began to be deferential to me, to be respectfully familiar with me, as though I had grown sensible, and become more on a level with him. 'You've done with your airs and graces,' he said to me one day, as we were going back from the big house to the lodge. 'Quite right too! All those fine principles and delicate sentiments—moral precepts in fact —are not for us, young lady, they're not for poor folks.'

When I had fallen out of favour, and Michel did not think it necessary to disguise his contempt for Mr. Ratsch and his sympathy with me, the latter suddenly redoubled his severity with me; he was continually following me about, as though I were capable of any crime, and must be sharply looked after. 'You mind what I say,' he shouted, bursting without knocking into my room, in muddy boots and with his cap on his head; 'I won't put up with such goings on! I won't stand your stuck-up airs! You're not going to impose on me. I'll break your proud spirit.'

And accordingly, one morning he informed me that the decree had gone forth from Semyon Matveitch that I was not to appear at the dinner-table for the future without special invitation. . . . I don't know how all this would have ended if it had not been for an event which was the final turning-point of my destiny. . . .

Michel was passionately fond of horses. He took it into his head to break in a young horse, which went well for a while, then began kicking and flung him out of the sledge. . . . He was brought home unconscious, with a broken arm and bruises on his chest. His father was panic-stricken; he sent for the best doctors from the town. They did a great deal for Michel; but he had to lie down for a month. He did not play cards, the doctor forbade him to talk, and it was awkward for him to read, holding the book up in one hand all the while. It ended by Semyon Matveitch sending me in to his son, in my old capacity of reader.

Then followed hours I can never forget! I used to go in to Michel directly after dinner, and sit at a little round table in the half-darkened window. He used to be lying down in a little room out of the drawing-room, at the further end, on a broad leather sofa in the Empire style, with a gold bas-relief on its high, straight back. The bas-relief represented a marriage procession among the ancients. Michel's head, thrown a little back on the pillow, always moved at once, and his pale face turned towards me: he smiled, his whole face brightened, he flung back his soft, damp curls, and said to me softly, 'Good-morning, my kind sweet girl.' I took up the book —Walter Scott's novels were at the height of their fame in those days—the reading of *Ivanhoe* has left a particularly vivid recollection in my mind. . . . I could not help my voice thrilling and quivering as I gave utterance to Rebecca's speeches. I, too, had Jewish blood, and was not my lot like hers? Was I not, like Rebecca, waiting on a sick man, dear to me? Every time I removed my eyes from the page and lifted them to him, I met his eyes with the same soft, bright smile over all his face. We talked very little; the door into the drawing-room was invariably open and some one was always sitting there; but whenever it was quiet there, I used, I don't know why, to cease reading and look intently at Michel, and he looked at me, and we both felt happy then and, as it were, glad and shamefaced, and everything, everything we told each other then without a gesture or a word! Alas! our hearts came together, ran to meet each other, as underground streams flow together, unseen, unheard . . . and irresistibly.

'Can you play chess or draughts?' he asked me one day.

'I can play chess a little,' I answered.

'That's good. Tell them to bring a chessboard and push up the table.'

I sat down beside the sofa, my heart was throbbing, I did not dare glance at Michel. . . . Yet from the window, across the room, how freely I had gazed at him!

I began to set the chessmen . . . My fingers shook.

'I suggested it . . . not for the game,' . . . Michel said in an undertone, also setting the pieces, 'but to have you nearer me.'

I made no answer, but, without asking which should begin, moved a pawn . . . Michel did not move in reply . . . I looked at him. His head was stretched a little forward; pale all over, with imploring eyes he signed towards my hand . . .

Whether I understood him . . . I don't remember, but something instantaneously whirled into my head. . . . Hesitating, scarcely breathing, I took up the knight and moved it right across the board. Michel bent down swiftly, and catching my fingers with his lips, and pressing them against the board, he began noiselessly and passionately kissing them. . . . I had no power, I had no wish to draw them back; with my other hand I hid my face, and tears, as I remember now, cold but blissful . . . oh, what blissful tears! . . . dropped one by one on the table. Ah, I knew, with my whole heart I felt at that moment, all that he was who held my hand in his power! I knew that he was not a boy, carried away by a momentary impulse, not a Don Juan, not a military Lovelace, but one of the noblest, the best of men . . . and he loved me!

'Oh, my Susanna!' I heard Michel whisper, 'I will never make you shed other tears than these.'

He was wrong . . . he did.

But what use is there in dwelling on such memories . . . especially, especially now?

Michel and I swore to belong to each other. He knew that Semyon Matveitch would never let him marry me, and he did not conceal it from me. I had no doubt about it myself and I rejoiced, not that he did not deceive me—he *could not* deceive—but that he did not try to delude himself. For myself I asked for nothing, and would have followed where and how he chose. 'You shall be my wife,' he repeated to me. 'I am not Ivanhoe; I know that happiness is not with Lady Rowena.'

Michel soon regained his health. I could not continue going to see him, but everything was decided between us. I was already entirely absorbed in the future; I saw nothing of what was passing around me, as though I were floating on a glorious, calm, but rushing river, hidden in mist. But we were watched, we were being spied upon. Once or twice I noticed my stepfather's malignant eyes, and heard his loathsome laugh. . . . But that laugh, those eyes as it were emerged for an instant from the mist . . . I shuddered, but forgot it directly, and surrendered myself again to the glorious, swift river . . .

On the day before the departure of Michel—we had planned together that he was to turn back secretly on the way and fetch me—I received from him through his trusted valet a note, in which he asked me to meet him at half-past nine in the summer billiard-room, a large, low-pitched room, built on to the big house in the garden. He wrote to me that he absolutely must speak with me and arrange things. I had twice already met Michel in the billiard-room . . . I had the key of the outer door. As soon as it struck half-past nine I threw a warm wrap over my shoulders, stepped quietly out of the lodge, and made my way successfully over the crackling snow to the billiard-room. The moon, wrapped in vapour, stood a dim blur just over the ridge of the roof, and the wind whistled shrilly round the corner of the wall. A shiver passed over me, but I put the key into the lock, went into the room, closed the door behind me, turned round . . . A dark figure became visible against one of the walls, took a couple of steps forward, stopped . . .

'Michel,' I whispered.

'Michel is locked up by my orders, and this is I!' answered a voice, which seemed to rend my heart . . .

Before me stood Semyon Matveitch!

I was rushing to escape, but he clutched at my arm.

'Where are you off to, vile hussy?' he hissed. 'You're quite equal to stolen interviews with young fools, so you'll have to be equal to the consequences.'

I was numb with horror, but still struggled towards the door . . . In vain! Like iron hooks the fingers of Semyon Matveitch held me tight.

'Let me go, let me go,' I implored at last.

'I tell you you shan't stir!'

Semyon Matveitch forced me to sit down. In the half-darkness I could not distinguish his face. I had turned away from him too, but I heard him breathing hard and grinding his teeth. I felt neither fear nor despair, but a sort of senseless amazement . . . A captured bird, I suppose, is numb like that in the claws of the kite . . . and Semyon Matveitch's hand, which still held me as fast, crushed me like some wild, ferocious claw. . . .

'Aha!' he repeated; 'aha! So this is how it is . . . so it's come to this . . . Ah, wait a bit!'

I tried to get up, but he shook me with such violence that I almost shrieked with pain, and a stream of abuse, insult, and menace burst upon me . . .

'Michel, Michel, where are you? save me,' I moaned.

Semyon Matveitch shook me again . . . That time I could not control myself . . . I screamed.

That seemed to have some effect on him. He became a little quieter, let go my arm, but remained where he was, two steps from me, between me and the door.

A few minutes passed . . . I did not stir; he breathed heavily as before.

'Sit still,' he began at last, 'and answer me. Let me see that your morals are not yet utterly corrupt, and that you are still capable of listening to the voice of reason. Impulsive folly I can overlook, but stubborn obstinacy —never! My son . . .' there was a catch in his breath . . . 'Mihail Semyonitch has promised to marry you? Hasn't he? Answer me! Has he promised, eh? '

I answered, of course, nothing.

Semyon Matveitch was almost flying into fury again.

' I take your silence as a sign of assent,' he went on, after a brief pause. 'And so you were plotting to be my daughter-in-law? A pretty notion! But you're not a child of four years old, and you must be fully aware that young boobies are never sparing of the wildest promises, if only they can gain their ends . . . but to say nothing of that, could you suppose that I—a noble gentleman of ancient family, Semyon Matveitch Koltovsky— would ever give my consent to such a marriage? Or did you mean to dispense with the parental blessing? . . . Did you mean to run away, get married in secret, and then come back, go through a nice little farce, throw yourself at my feet, in the hope that the old man will be touched? . . . Answer me, damn you! '

I only bent my head. He could kill me, but to force me to speak— that was not in his power.

He walked up and down a little.

' Come, listen to me,' he began in a calmer voice. ' You mustn't think . . . don't imagine . . . I see one must talk to you in a different manner. Listen; I understand your position. You are frightened, upset. . . . Pull yourself together. At this moment I must seem to you a monster . . . a despot. But put yourself in my position too; how could I help being indignant, saying too much? And for all that I have shown you that I am not a monster, that I too have a heart. Remember how I treated you on my arrival here and afterwards till . . . till lately . . . till the illness of Mihail Semyonitch. I don't wish to boast of my beneficence, but I should have thought simple gratitude ought to have held you back from the slippery path on which you were determined to enter! '

Semyon Matveitch walked to and fro again, and standing still patted me lightly on the arm, on the very arm which still ached from his violence, and was for long after marked with blue bruises.

' To be sure,' he began again, ' we're headstrong . . . just a little head-strong! We don't care to take the trouble to think, we don't care to consider what our advantage consists in and where we ought to seek it. You ask me: where that advantage lies? You've no need to look far. . . . It's, maybe, close at hand. . . . Here am I now. As a father, as head of the family I am bound to be particular. . . . It's my duty. But I'm a man at the same time, and you know that very well. Undoubtedly I'm a practical person and of course cannot tolerate any sentimental nonsense; expectations that are quite inconsistent with everything, you must of course dismiss from your mind for really what sense is there in them?—not to speak of the immorality of such a proceeding. . . . You will assuredly realise all this yourself, when you have thought it over a little. And I say, simply and straightforwardly, I wouldn't confine myself to what I have done for you. I have always been prepared—and I am still prepared—to put your welfare on a sound footing, to guarantee you a secure position, because I know your value, I do justice to your talents, and your intelligence, and in fact . . . (here Semyon Matveitch stooped down to me a little) . . . you have such eyes that, I confess . . . though I am not a young man, yet to see them quite unmoved . . . I understand . . . is not an easy matter, not at all an easy matter.'

These words sent a chill through me. I could scarcely believe my ears. For the first minute I fancied Semyon Matveitch meant to bribe me to break with Michel, to pay me ' compensation.' . . . But what was he saying? My eyes had begun to get used to the darkness and I could make out Semyon Matveitch's face. It was smiling, that old face, and he was walking to and fro with little steps, fidgeting restlessly before me. . . .

' Well, what do you say,' he asked at last, ' does my offer please you? '

' Offer? ' . . . I repeated unconsciously, . . . I simply did not understand a word.

Semyon Matveitch laughed . . . actually laughed his revolting thin laugh.

' To be sure,' he cried, ' you're all alike you young women '—he corrected himself—' young ladies . . . young ladies . . . you all dream of nothing else . . . you must have young men! You can't live without love! Of course not. Well, well! Youth's all very well! But do you suppose that it's only young men that can love? . . . There are some older men, whose hearts are warmer . . . and when once an old man does take a fancy to any one, well—he's simply like a rock! It's for ever! Not like these beardless, feather-brained young fools! Yes, yes; you mustn't look down on old men! They can do so much! You've only to take them the right way! Yes . . . yes! And as for kissing, old men know all about that too, he-he-he . . .' Semyon Matveitch laughed again. ' Come, please . . . your little hand . . . just as a proof . . . that's all. . . .'

I jumped up from the chair, and with all my force I gave him a blow in the chest. He tottered, he uttered a sort of decrepit, scared sound, he almost fell down. There are no words in human language to express how loathsome and infinitely vile he seemed to me. Every vestige of fear had left me.

' Get away, despicable old man,' broke from my lips; ' get away, Mr. Koltovsky, you noble gentleman of ancient family! I, too, am of your blood, the blood of the Koltovskys, and I curse the day and the hour when I was born of that ancient family! '

' What! . . . What are you saying! . . . What! ' stammered Semyon Matveitch, gasping for breath. ' You dare . . . at the very minute when I've caught you . . . when you came to meet Misha . . . eh? eh? eh? '

But I could not stop myself. . . . Something relentless, desperate was roused up within me.

' And you, you, the brother . . . of your brother, you had the insolence, you dared . . . What did you take me for? Can you be so blind as not to have seen long ago the loathing you arouse in me? . . . You dare use the word offer! . . . Let me out at once, this instant! '

I moved towards the door.

'Oh, indeed! oh, oh! so this is what she says!' Semyon Matveitch piped shrilly, in a fit of violent fury, but obviously not able to make up his mind to come near me. . . . 'Wait a bit, Mr. Ratsch, Ivan Demianitch, come here!'

The door of the billiard-room opposite the one I was near flew wide open, and my stepfather appeared, with a lighted candelabrum in each hand. His round, red face, lighted up on both sides, was beaming with the triumph of satisfied revenge, and slavish delight at having rendered valuable service. . . . Oh, those loathsome white eyes! when shall I cease to behold them?

'Be so good as to take this girl at once,' cried Semyon Matveitch, turning to my stepfather and imperiously pointing to me with a shaking hand. 'Be so good as to take her home and put her under lock and key . . . so that she . . . can't stir a finger, so that not a fly can get in to her! Till further orders from me! Board up the windows if need be! You'll answer for her with your head!'

Mr. Ratsch set the candelabra on the billiard-table, made Semyon Matveitch a low bow, and with a slight swagger and a malignant smile, moved towards me. A cat, I imagine, approaches a mouse who has no chance of escape in that way. All my daring left me in an instant. I knew the man was capable of . . . beating me. I began to tremble; yes; oh, shame! oh ignominy! I shivered.

'Now, then, madam,' said Mr. Ratsch, 'kindly come along.'

He took me, without haste, by the arm above the elbow. . . . He saw that I should not resist. Of my own accord I pushed forward towards the door; at that instant I had but one thought in my mind, to escape as quickly as possible from the presence of Semyon Matveitch.

But the loathsome old man darted up to us from behind, and Ratsch stopped me and turned me round face to face with his patron.

'Ah!' the latter shouted, shaking his fist; 'ah! So I'm the brother . . . of my brother, am I? Ties of blood! eh? But a cousin, a first cousin you could marry? You could? eh? Take her, you!' he turned to my stepfather. 'And remember, keep a sharp look-out! The slightest communication with her— and no punishment will be too severe. . . . Take her!'

Mr. Ratsch conducted me to my room. Crossing the courtyard, he said nothing, but kept laughing noiselessly to himself. He closed the shutters and the doors, and then, as he was finally returning, he bowed low to me as he had to Semyon Matveitch, and went off into a ponderous, triumphant guffaw!

'Good-night to your highness,' he gasped out, choking: 'she didn't catch her fairy prince! What a pity! It wasn't a bad idea in its way! It's a lesson for the future: not to keep up correspondence! Ho-ho-ho! How capitally it has all turned out though!' He went out, and all of a sudden poked his head in at the door. 'Well? I didn't forget you, did I? Hey? I kept my promise, didn't I? Ho-ho!' The key creaked in the lock. I breathed freely. I had been afraid he would tie my hands . . . but they were my own, they were free! I instantly wrenched the silken cord off my dressing-gown, made a noose, and was putting it on my neck, but I flung the cord aside again at once. 'I won't please you!' I said aloud. 'What madness, really! Can I dispose of my life without Michel's leave, my life, which I have surrendered into his keeping? No, cruel wretches! No! You have not won your game yet! He will save me, he will tear me out of this hell, he . . . my Michel!'

But then I remembered that he was shut up just as I was, and I flung myself, face downwards, on my bed, and sobbed . . . and sobbed. . . . And only the thought that my tormentor was perhaps at the door, listening and triumphing, only that thought forced me to swallow my tears. . . .

I am worn out. I have been writing since morning, and now it is evening; if once I tear myself from this sheet of paper, I shall not be capable of taking up the pen again. . . . I must hasten, hasten to the finish! And besides, to dwell on the hideous things that followed that dreadful day is beyond my strength!

Twenty-four hours later I was taken in a closed cart to an isolated hut, surrounded by peasants, who were to watch me, and kept shut up for six whole weeks! I was not for one instant alone. . . . Later on I learnt that my stepfather had set spies to watch both Michel and me ever since his arrival, that he had bribed the servant, who had given me Michel's note. I ascertained too that an awful, heart-rending scene had taken place the next morning between the son and the father. . . . The father had cursed him. Michel for his part had sworn he would never set foot in his father's house again, and had set off to Petersburg. But the blow aimed at me by my stepfather rebounded upon himself. Semyon Matveitch announced that he could not have him remaining there, and managing the estate any longer. Awkward service, it seems, is an unpardonable offence, and some one must be fixed upon to bear the brunt of the *scandal*. Semyon Matveitch recompensed Mr. Ratsch liberally, however: he gave him the necessary means to move to Moscow and to establish himself there. Before the departure for Moscow, I was brought back to the lodge, but kept as before under the strictest guard. The loss of the 'snug little berth,' of which he was being deprived 'thanks to me,' increased my stepfather's vindictive rage against me more than ever.

'Why did you make such a fuss?' he would say, almost snorting with indignation; 'upon my word! The old chap, of course, got a little too hot, was a little too much in a hurry, and so he made a mess of it; now, of course, his vanity's hurt, there's no setting the mischief right again now! If you'd only waited a day or two, it'd all have been right as a trivet; you wouldn't have been kept on dry bread, and I should have stayed what I was! Ah, well, women's hair is long . . . but their wit is short! Never mind; I'll be even with you yet, and that pretty young gentleman shall smart for it too!'

I had, of course, to bear all these insults in silence. Semyon Matveitch I did not once see again. The separation from his son had been a shock to him too. Whether he felt remorse or—which is far more likely—wished to bind me for ever to my home, to my family—my family!—anyway, he assigned me a pension, which was to be paid into my stepfather's hands, and to be given to me till I married. . . . This humiliating alms, this pension I still receive . . . that is to say, Mr. Ratsch receives it for me. . . .

We settled in Moscow. I swear by the memory of my poor mother, I would not have remained two days, not two hours, with my stepfather, after once reaching the town . . . I would have gone away, not knowing where . . . to the police; I would have flung myself at the feet of the governor-general, of the senators; I don't know what I would have done, if it had not happened, at the very moment of our starting from the country, that the girl who had been our maid managed to give me a letter from Michel! Oh, that letter! How many times I read over each line, how many times I covered it with kisses! Michel besought me not to lose heart, to go on hoping, to believe in his unchanging love; he swore that he would never belong to any one but me; he called me his wife, he promised to overcome all hindrances, he drew a picture of our future, he asked of me only one thing, to be patient, to wait a little. . . .

And I resolved to wait and be patient. Alas! what would I not have agreed to, what would I not have borne, simply to do his will! That letter became my holy thing, my guiding star, my anchor. Sometimes when my stepfather would begin abusing and insulting me, I would softly lay my hand on my bosom (I wore Michel's letter sewed into an amulet) and only smile. And the more violent and abusive was Mr. Ratsch, the easier, lighter, and sweeter was the heart within me. . . . I used to see, at last, by his eyes, that he began to wonder whether I was going out of my mind. . . . Following on this first letter came a second, still more full of hope. . . . It spoke of our meeting soon.

Alas! instead of that meeting there came a morning . . . I can see Mr. Ratsch coming in—and triumph again, malignant triumph, in his face—and in his hands a page of the *Invalid*, and there the announcement of the death of the Captain of the Guards—Mihail Koltovsky.

What can I add? I remained alive, and went on living in Mr. Ratsch's house. He hated me as before—more than before—he had unmasked his black soul too much before me, he could not pardon me that. But that was of no consequence to me. I became, as it were, without feeling; my own fate no longer interested me. To think of him, to think of him! I had no interest, no joy, but that. My poor Michel died with my name on his lips. . . . I was told so by a servant, devoted to him, who had been with him when he came into the country. The same year my stepfather married Eleonora Karpovna. Semyon Matveitch died shortly after. In his will he secured to me and increased the pension he had allowed me. . . . In the event of my death, it was to pass to Mr. Ratsch. . . .

Two—three—years passed . . . six years, seven years. . . . Life has been passing, ebbing away . . . while I merely watched how it was ebbing. As in childhood, on some river's edge one makes a little pond and dams it up, and tries in all sorts of ways to keep the water from soaking through, from breaking in. But at last the water breaks in, and then you abandon all your vain efforts, and you are glad instead to watch all that you had guarded ebbing away to the last drop. . . .

So I lived, so I existed, till at last a new, unhoped-for ray of warmth and light . . .

The manuscript broke off at this word; the following leaves had been torn off, and several lines completing the sentence had been crossed through and blotted out.

XVIII

THE READING of this manuscript so upset me, the impression made by Susanna's visit was so great, that I could not sleep all night, and early in the morning I sent an express messenger to Fustov with a letter, in which I besought him to come to Moscow as soon as possible, as his absence might have the most terrible results. I mentioned also my interview with Susanna, and the manuscript she had left in my hands. After having sent off the letter, I did not go out of the house all day, and pondered all the time on what might be happening at the Ratsches'. I could not make up my mind to go there myself. I could not help noticing though that my aunt was in a continual fidget; she ordered pastilles to be burnt every minute, and dealt the game of patience, known as ' the traveller,' which is noted as a game in which one can never succeed. The visit of an unknown lady, and at such a late hour, had not been kept secret from her: her imagination at once pictured a yawning abyss on the edge of which I was standing, and she was continually sighing and moaning and murmuring French sentences, quoted from a little manuscript book entitled *Extraits de Lecture*. In the evening I found on the little table at my bedside the treatise of De Girando, laid open at the chapter: On the evil influence of the passions. This book had been put in my room, at my aunt's instigation of course, by the elder of her companions, who was called in the household Amishka, from her resemblance to a little poodle of that name, and was a very sentimental, not to say romantic, though elderly, maiden lady. All the following day was spent in anxious expectation of Fustov's coming, of a letter from him, of news from the Ratsches' house . . . though on what ground could they have sent to me? Susanna would be more likely to expect me to visit her. . . . But I positively could not pluck up courage to see her without first talking to Fustov. I recalled every expression in my letter to him. . . . I thought it was strong enough; at last, late in the evening, he appeared.

XIX

HE CAME into my room with his habitual, rapid, but deliberate step. His face struck me as pale, and though it showed traces of the fatigue of the

journey, there was an expression of astonishment, curiosity, and dissatisfaction—emotions of which he had little experience as a rule. I rushed up to
him, embraced him, warmly thanked him for obeying me, and after briefly
describing my conversation with Susanna, handed him the manuscript. He
went off to the window, to the very window in which Susanna had sat two
days before, and without a word to me, he fell to reading it. I at once
retired to the opposite corner of the room, and for appearance' sake took up
a book; but I must own I was stealthily looking over the edge of the cover
all the while at Fustov. At first he read rather calmly, and kept pulling with
his left hand at the down on his lip; then he let his hand drop, bent forward
and did not stir again. His eyes seemed to fly along the lines and his mouth
slightly opened. At last he finished the manuscript, turned it over, looked
round, thought a little, and began reading it all through a second time from
beginning to end. Then he got up, put the manuscript in his pocket and
moved towards the door; but he turned round and stopped in the middle of
the room.

'Well, what do you think?' I began, not waiting for him to speak.

'I have acted wrongly towards her,' Fustov declared thickly. 'I have
behaved . . . rashly, unpardonably, cruelly. I believed that . . . Viktor——'

'What!' I cried; 'that Viktor whom you despise so! But what could he
say to you?'

Fustov crossed his arms and stood obliquely to me. He was ashamed, I
saw that.

'Do you remember,' he said with some effort, 'that . . . Viktor alluded
to . . . a pension. That unfortunate word stuck in my head. It's the cause
of everything. I began questioning him. . . . Well, and he——'

'What did he say?'

'He told me that the old man . . . what's his name? . . . Koltovsky, had
allowed Susanna that pension because . . . on account of . . . well, in
fact, by way of damages.'

I flung up my hands.

'And you believed him?'

Fustov nodded.

'Yes! I believed him. . . . He said, too, that with the young one . . .
In fact, my behaviour is unjustifiable.'

'And you went away so as to break everything off?'

'Yes; that's the best way . . . in such cases. I acted savagely, savagely,'
he repeated.

We were both silent. Each of us felt that the other was ashamed; but
it was easier for me; I was not ashamed of myself.

XX

'I would break every bone in that Viktor's body now,' pursued Fustov,
clenching his teeth, 'if I didn't recognise that I'm in fault. I see now what

the whole trick was contrived for, with Susanna's marriage they would lose the pension. . . . Wretches! '

I took his hand.

' Alexander,' I asked him, ' have you been to her? '

' No; I came straight to you on arriving. I'll go to-morrow . . . early to-morrow. Things can't be left so. On no account! '

' But you . . . love her, Alexander? '

Fustov seemed offended.

' Of course I love her. I am very much attached to her.'

' She's a splendid, true-hearted girl! ' I cried.

Fustov stamped impatiently.

' Well, what notion have you got in your head? I was prepared to marry her—she's been baptized—I'm ready to marry her even now, I'd been thinking of it, though she's older than I am.'

At that instant I suddenly fancied that a pale woman's figure was seated in the window, leaning on her arms. The lights had burnt down; it was dark in the room. I shivered, looked more intently, and saw nothing, of course, in the window seat; but a strange feeling, a mixture of horror, anguish and pity, came over me.

' Alexander! ' I began with sudden intensity, ' I beg you, I implore you, go at once to the Ratsches', don't put it off till to-morrow! An inner voice tells me that you really ought to see Susanna to-day! '

Fustov shrugged his shoulders.

' What are you talking about, really! It's eleven o'clock now, most likely they're all in bed.'

' No matter. . . . Do go, for goodness' sake! I have a presentiment. . . . Please do as I say! Go at once, take a sledge. . . .'

' Come, what nonsense! ' Fustov responded coolly; ' how could I go now? To-morrow morning I will be there, and everything will be cleared up.'

' But, Alexander, remember, she said that she was dying, that you would not find her . . . And if you had seen her face! Only think, imagine, to make up her mind to come to me . . . what it must have cost her. . . .'

' She's a little high-flown,' observed Fustov, who had apparently regained his self-possession completely. ' All girls are like that . . . at first. I repeat, everything will be all right to-morrow. Meanwhile, good-bye. I'm tired, and you're sleepy too.'

He took his cap, and went out of the room.

' But you promise to come here at once, and tell me all about it? ' I called after him.

' I promise. . . . Good-bye! '

I went to bed, but in my heart I was uneasy, and I felt vexed with my friend. I fell asleep late and dreamed that I was wandering with Susanna along underground, damp passages of some sort, and crawling along narrow, steep staircases, and continually going deeper and deeper down, though we were trying to get higher up out into the air. Some one was all the while incessantly calling us in monotonous, plaintive tones.

XXI

SOME ONE'S HAND lay on my shoulder and pushed it several times. . . . I opened my eyes and in the faint light of the solitary candle, I saw Fustov standing before me. He frightened me. He was staggering; his face was yellow, almost the same colour as his hair; his lips seemed hanging down, his muddy eyes were staring senselessly away. What had become of his invariably amiable, sympathetic expression? I had a cousin who from epilepsy was sinking into idiocy. . . . Fustov looked like him at that moment.

I sat up hurriedly.

'What is it? What is the matter? Heavens!'

He made no answer.

'Why, what has happened? Fustov! Do speak! Susanna? . . .'

Fustov gave a slight start.

'She . . .' he began in a hoarse voice, and broke off.

'What of her? Have you seen her?'

He stared at me.

'She's no more.'

'No more?'

'No. She is dead.'

I jumped out of bed.

'Dead? Susanna? Dead?'

Fustov turned his eyes away again.

'Yes; she is dead; she died at midnight.'

'He's raving!' crossed my mind.

'At midnight! And what's the time now?'

'It's eight o'clock in the morning now. They sent to tell me. She is to be buried to-morrow.'

I seized him by the hand.

'Alexander, you're not delirious? Are you in your senses?'

'I am in my senses,' he answered. 'Directly I heard it, I came straight to you.'

My heart turned sick and numb, as always happens on realising an irrevocable misfortune.

'My God! my God! Dead! Dead!' I repeated. 'How is it possible? So suddenly! Or perhaps she took her own life?'

'I don't know,' said Fustov, 'I know nothing. They told me she died at midnight. And to-morrow she will be buried.'

'At midnight!' I thought. . . . 'Then she was still alive yesterday when I fancied I saw her in the window, when I entreated him to hasten to her. . . .'

'She was still alive yesterday, when you wanted to send me to Ivan Demianitch's,' said Fustov, as though guessing my thought.

'How little he knew her!' I thought again. 'How little we both knew her! " High-flown," said he, " all girls are like that." . . . And at that very minute, perhaps, she was putting to her lips . . . Can one love any one and be so grossly mistaken in them? '

Fustov stood stockstill before my bed, his hands hanging, like a guilty man.

XXII

I DRESSED HURRIEDLY.

' What do you mean to do now, Alexander? ' I asked.

He gazed at me in bewilderment, as though marvelling at the absurdity of my question. And indeed what was there to do?

' You simply must go to them, though,' I began. ' You're bound to ascertain how it happened; there is, possibly, a crime concealed. One may expect anything of those people. . . . It is all to be thoroughly investigated. Remember the statement in her manuscript, the pension was to cease on her marriage, but in event of her death it was to pass to Ratsch. In any case, one must render her the last duty, pay homage to her remains! '

I talked to Fustov like a preceptor, like an elder brother. In the midst of all that horror, grief, bewilderment, a sort of unconscious feeling of superiority over Fustov had suddenly come to the surface in me. . . . Whether from seeing him crushed by the consciousness of his fault, distracted, shattered, whether that a misfortune befalling a man almost always humiliates him, lowers him in the opinion of others, ' you can't be much,' is felt, ' if you hadn't the wit to come off better than that! ' God knows! Any way, Fustov seemed to me almost like a child, and I felt pity for him, and saw the necessity of severity. I held out a helping hand to him, stooping down to him from above. Only a woman's sympathy is free from condescension.

But Fustov continued to gaze with wild and stupid eyes at me—my authoritative tone obviously had no effect on him, and to my second question, ' You're going to them, I suppose? ' he replied—

' No, I'm not going.'

' What do you mean, really? Don't you want to ascertain for yourself, to investigate, how, and what? Perhaps, she has left a letter . . . a document of some sort. . . .'

Fustov shook his head.

' I can't go there,' he said. ' That's what I came to you for, to ask you to go . . . for me . . . I can't . . . I can't. . . .'

Fustov suddenly sat down to the table, hid his face in both hands, and sobbed bitterly.

' Alas, alas! ' he kept repeating through his tears; ' alas, poor girl . . . poor girl . . . I loved . . . I loved her . . . alas! '

I stood near him, and I am bound to confess, not the slightest sympathy was excited in me by those incontestably sincere sobs. I simply marvelled that Fustov could cry *like that,* and it seemed to me that *now* I knew what a small person he was, and that I should, in his place, have acted quite differently. What's one to make of it? If Fustov had remained quite unmoved, I should perhaps have hated him, have conceived an aversion for him, but he would not have sunk in my esteem. . . . He would have kept his prestige. Don Juan would have remained Don Juan! Very late in life, and only after many experiences, does a man learn, at the sight of a fellow-creature's real failing or weakness, to sympathise with him, and help him without a secret self-congratulation at his own virtue and strength, but on the contrary, with every humility and comprehension of the naturalness, almost the inevitableness, of sin.

XXIII

I was very bold and resolute in sending Fustov to the Ratsches'; but when I set out there myself at twelve o'clock (nothing would induce Fustov to go with me, he only begged me to give him an exact account of everything), when round the corner of the street their house glared at me in the distance with a yellowish blur from the coffin candles at one of the windows, an indescribable panic made me hold my breath, and I would gladly have turned back. . . . I mastered myself, however, and went into the passage. It smelt of incense and wax; the pink cover of the coffin, edged with silver lace, stood in a corner, leaning against the wall. In one of the adjoining rooms, the dining-room, the monotonous muttering of the deacon droned like the buzzing of a bee. From the drawing-room peeped out the sleepy face of a servant girl, who murmured in a subdued voice, ' Come to do homage to the dead? ' She indicated the door of the dining-room. I went in. The coffin stood with the head towards the door; the black hair of Susanna under the white wreath, above the raised lace of the pillow, first caught my eyes. I went up sidewards, crossed myself, bowed down to the ground, glanced . . . Merciful God! what a face of agony! Unhappy girl! even death had no pity on her, had denied her—beauty, that would be little—even that peace, that tender and impressive peace which is often seen on the faces of the newly dead. The little, dark, almost brown, face of Susanna recalled the visages on old, old holy pictures. And the expression on that face! It looked as though she were on the point of shrieking—a shriek of despair—and had died so, uttering no sound . . . even the line between the brows was not smoothed out, and the fingers on the hands were bent back and clenched. I turned away my eyes involuntarily; but, after a brief interval, I forced myself to look, to look long and attentively at her. Pity filled my soul, and not pity alone. ' That girl died by violence,' I decided inwardly; ' that's beyond doubt.' While I was standing looking at the dead girl, the deacon, who on my entrance had raised his voice and uttered a few disconnected sounds, relapsed into droning again, and yawned twice. I bowed to the ground a second time, and went out into the passage.

In the doorway of the drawing-room Mr. Ratsch was already on the look-out for me, dressed in a gay-coloured dressing-gown. Beckoning to me with his hand, he led me to his own room—I had almost said, to his lair. The room, dark and close, soaked through and through with the sour smell of stale tobacco, suggested a comparison with the lair of a wolf or a fox.

XXIV

'Rupture! rupture of the external . . . of the external covering. . . . You understand . . . the envelopes of the heart!' said Mr. Ratsch, directly the door closed. 'Such a misfortune! Only yesterday evening there was nothing to notice, and all of a sudden, all in a minute, all was over! It's a true saying, "heute roth, morgen todt!" It's true; it's what was to be expected. I always expected it. At Tambov the regimental doctor, Galimbovsky, Vikenty Kasimirovitch . . . you've probably heard of him . . . a first-rate medical man, a specialist——'

'It's the first time I've heard the name,' I observed.

'Well, no matter; any way he was always,' pursued Mr. Ratsch, at first in a low voice, and then louder and louder, and, to my surprise, with a perceptible German accent, 'he was always warning me: "Ay, Ivan Demianitch! ay! my dear boy, you must be careful! Your stepdaughter has an organic defect in the heart—hypertrophia cordialis! The least thing and there'll be trouble! She must avoid all exciting emotions above all. . . . You must appeal to her reason." . . . But, upon my word, with a young lady . . . can one appeal to reason? Ha . . . ha . . . ha . . .'

Mr. Ratsch was, through long habit, on the point of laughing, but he recollected himself in time, and changed the incipient guffaw into a cough.

And this was what Mr. Ratsch said! After all that I had found out about him! . . . I thought it my duty, however, to ask him whether a doctor was called in.

Mr. Ratsch positively bounced into the air.

'To be sure there was. . . . Two were summoned, but it was already over—abgemacht! And only fancy, both, as though they were agreeing' (Mr. Ratsch probably meant, as though they had agreed), 'rupture! rupture of the heart! That's what, with one voice, they cried out. They proposed a post-mortem; but I . . . you understand, did not consent to that.'

'And the funeral's to-morrow?' I queried.

'Yes, yes, to-morrow, to-morrow we bury our dear one! The procession will leave the house precisely at eleven o'clock in the morning. . . . From here to the church of St. Nicholas on Hen's Legs . . . what strange names your Russian churches do have, you know! Then to the last resting-place in mother earth. You will come! We have not been long acquainted, but I make bold to say, the amiability of your character and the elevation of your sentiments! . . .'

I made haste to nod my head.

'Yes, yes, yes,' sighed Mr. Ratsch. 'It . . . it really has been, as they say, a thunderbolt from a clear sky! Ein Blitz aus heiterem Himmel! '

'And Susanna Ivanovna said nothing before her death, left nothing? '

'Nothing, positively! Not a scrap of anything! Not a bit of paper! Only fancy, when they called me to her, when they waked me up—she was stiff already! Very distressing it was for me; she has grieved us all terribly! Alexander Daviditch will be sorry too, I dare say, when he knows. . . . They say he is not in Moscow.'

'He did leave town for a few days . . .' I began.

'Viktor Ivanovitch is complaining they're so long getting his sledge harnessed,' interrupted a servant girl coming in—the same girl I had seen in the passage. Her face, still looking half-awake, struck me this time by the expression of coarse insolence to be seen in servants when they know that their masters are in their power, and that they do not dare to find fault or be exacting with them.

'Directly, directly,' Ivan Demianitch responded nervously. 'Eleonora Karpovna! Leonora! Lenchen! come here! '

There was a sound of something ponderous moving the other side of the door, and at the same instant I heard Viktor's imperious call: 'Why on earth don't they put the horses in? You don't catch me trudging off to the police on foot! '

'Directly, directly,' Ivan Demianitch faltered again. 'Eleonora Karpovna, come here! '

'But, Ivan Demianitch,' I heard her voice, 'ich habe keine Toilette gemacht! '

'Macht nichts. Komm herein! '

Eleonora Karpovna came in, holding a kerchief over her neck with two fingers. She had on a morning wrapper, not buttoned up, and had not yet done her hair. Ivan Demianitch flew up to her.

'You hear, Viktor's calling for the horses,' he said, hurriedly pointing his finger first to the door, then to the window. 'Please, do see to it, as quick as possible! Der Kerl schreit so! '

'Der Viktor schreit immer, Ivan Demianitch, Sie wissen wohl,' responded Eleonora Karpovna, 'and I have spoken to the coachman myself, but he's taken it into his head to give the horses oats. Fancy, what a calamity to happen so suddenly,' she added, turning to me; 'who could have expected such a thing of Susanna Ivanovna? '

'I was always expecting it, always! ' cried Ratsch, and threw up his arms, his dressing-gown flying up in front as he did so, and displaying most repulsive unmentionables of chamois leather, with buckles on the belt. 'Rupture of the heart! rupture of the external membrane! Hypertrophy! '

'To be sure,' Eleonora Karpovna repeated after him, 'hyper . . . Well, so it is. Only it's a terrible, terrible grief to me, I say again . . .' And her coarse-featured face worked a little, her eyebrows rose into the shape of triangles, and a tiny tear rolled over her round cheek, that looked varnished like a doll's. . . . 'I'm very sorry that such a young person who ought to have lived and enjoyed everything . . . everything . . . And to fall into despair so suddenly! '

'Na! gut, gut . . . geh, alte! ' Mr. Ratsch cut her short.

'Geh' schon, geh' schon,' muttered Eleonora Karpovna, and she went away, still holding the kerchief with her fingers, and shedding tears.

And I followed her. In the passage stood Viktor in a student's coat with a beaver collar and a cap stuck jauntily on one side. He barely glanced at me over his shoulder, shook his collar up, and did not nod to me, for which I mentally thanked him.

I went back to Fustov.

XXV

I FOUND MY FRIEND sitting in a corner of his room with downcast head and arms folded across his breast. He had sunk into a state of numbness, and he gazed around him with the slow, bewildered look of a man who has slept very heavily and has only just been waked. I told him all about my visit to Ratsch's, repeated the veteran's remarks and those of his wife, described the impression they had made on me and informed him of my conviction that the unhappy girl had taken her own life. . . . Fustov listened to me with no change of expression, and looked about him with the same bewildered air.

'Did you see her? ' he asked me at last.

'Yes.'

'In the coffin? '

Fustov seemed to doubt whether Susanna were really dead.

'In the coffin.'

Fustov's face twitched and he dropped his eyes and softly rubbed his hands.

'Are you cold? ' I asked him.

'Yes, old man, I'm cold,' he answered hesitatingly, and he shook his head stupidly.

I began to explain my reasons for thinking that Susanna had poisoned herself or perhaps had been poisoned, and that the matter could not be left so. . . .

Fustov stared at me.

'Why, what is there to be done? ' he said, slowly opening his eyes wide and slowly closing them. 'Why, it'll be worse . . . if it's known about. They won't bury her. We must let things . . . alone.'

This idea, simple as it was, had never entered my head. My friend's practical sense had not deserted him.

'When is . . . her funeral? ' he went on.

'To-morrow.'

'Are you going? '

'Yes.'

'To the house or straight to the church?'

'To the house and to the church too; and from there to the cemetery.'

'But I shan't go . . . I can't, I can't!' whispered Fustov and began crying.
It was at these same words that he had broken into sobs in the morning. I
have noticed that it is often so with weeping; as though to certain words,
for the most of no great meaning,—but just to these words and to no others—
it is given to open the fount of tears in a man, to break him down, and to
excite in him the feeling of pity for others and himself . . . I remember
a peasant woman was once describing before me the sudden death of her
daughter, and she fairly dissolved and could not go on with her tale as soon
as she uttered the phrase, 'I said to her, Fekla. And she says, "Mother, where
have you put the salt . . . the salt . . . sa-alt?"' The word 'salt' over-
powered her.

But again, as in the morning, I was but little moved by Fustov's tears.
I could not conceive how it was he did not ask me if Susanna had not left
something for him. Altogether their love for one another was a riddle to
me; and a riddle it remained to me.

After weeping for ten minutes Fustov got up, lay down on the sofa, turned
his face to the wall, and remained motionless. I waited a little, but seeing that
he did not stir, and made no answer to my questions, I made up my mind
to leave him. I am perhaps doing him injustice, but I almost believe he was
asleep. Though indeed that would be no proof that he did not feel sorrow
. . . only his nature was so constituted as to be unable to support painful
emotions for long . . . His nature was too awfully well-balanced!

XXVI

THE NEXT DAY exactly at eleven o'clock I was at the place. Fine hail was
falling from the low-hanging sky, there was a slight frost, a thaw was close
at hand, but there were cutting, disagreeable gusts of wind flitting across
in the air. . . . It was the most thoroughly Lenten, cold-catching weather.
I found Mr. Ratsch on the steps of his house. In a black frock-coat adorned
with crape, with no hat on his head, he fussed about, waved his arms, smote
himself on the thighs, shouted up to the house, and then down into the street,
in the direction of the funeral car with a white catafalque, already standing
there with two hired carriages. Near it four garrison soldiers, with mourning capes over their old coats, and mourning hats pulled over their screwed-
up eyes, were pensively scratching in the crumbling snow with the long
stems of their unlighted torches. The grey shock of hair positively stood
up straight above the red face of Mr. Ratsch, and his voice, that brazen
voice, was cracking from the strain he was putting on it. 'Where are the
pine branches? pine branches! this way! the branches of pine!' he yelled.
'They'll be bearing out the coffin directly! The pine! Hand over those pine
branches! Look alive!' he cried once more, and dashed into the house. It
appeared that in spite of my punctuality, I was late: Mr. Ratsch had thought

fit to hurry things forward. The service in the house was already over; the priests—of whom one wore a calotte, and the other, rather younger, had most carefully combed and oiled his hair—appeared with all their retinue on the steps. The coffin too appeared soon after, carried by a coachman, two door-keepers, and a water-carrier. Mr. Ratsch walked behind, with the tips of his fingers on the coffin lid, continually repeating, 'Easy, easy!' Behind him waddled Eleonora Karpovna in a black dress, also adorned with crape, surrounded by her whole family; after all of them, Viktor stepped out in a new uniform with a sword with crape round the handle. The coffin-bearers, grumbling and altercating among themselves, laid the coffin on the hearse; the garrison soldiers lighted their torches, which at once began crackling and smoking; a stray old woman, who had joined herself on to the party, raised a wail; the deacons began to chant, the fine snow suddenly fell faster and whirled round like 'white flies.' Mr. Ratsch bawled, 'In God's name! start!' and the procession started. Besides Mr. Ratsch's family, there were in all five men accompanying the hearse: a retired and extremely shabby officer of roads and highways, with a faded Stanislas ribbon—not improbably hired—on his neck; the police superin- tendent's assistant, a diminutive man with a meek face and greedy eyes; a little old man in a fustian smock; an extremely fat fishmonger in a trades- man's blue jacket, smelling strongly of his calling, and I. The absence of the female sex (for one could hardly count as such two aunts of Eleonora Kar- povna, sisters of the sausage-maker, and a hunchback old maiden lady with blue spectacles on her blue nose), the absence of girl friends and acquaint- ances struck me at first; but on thinking it over I realised that Susanna, with her character, her education, her memories, could not have made friends in the circle in which she was living. In the church there were a good many people assembled, more outsiders than acquaintances, as one could see by the expression of their faces. The service did not last long. What surprised me was that Mr. Ratsch crossed himself with great fervour, quite as though he were of the orthodox faith, and even chimed in with the deacons in the responses, though only with the notes not with the words. When at last it came to taking leave of the dead, I bowed low, but did not give the last kiss. Mr. Ratsch, on the contrary, went through this terrible ordeal with the utmost composure, and with a deferential inclination of his person invited the officer of the Stanislas ribbon to the coffin, as though offering him entertainment, and picking his children up under the arms swung them up in turn and held them up to the body. Eleonora Karpovna, on taking fare- well of Susanna, suddenly broke into a roar that filled the church; but she was soon soothed and continually asked in an exasperated whisper, 'But where's my reticule?' Viktor held himself aloof, and seemed to be trying by his whole demeanour to convey that he was out of sympathy with all such customs and was only performing a social duty. The person who showed the most sympathy was the little old man in the smock, who had been, fifteen years before, a land surveyor in the Tambov province, and had not seen Ratsch since then. He did not know Susanna at all, but had drunk a couple of glasses of spirits at the sideboard before starting. My aunt had also come to the church. She had somehow or other found out that the deceased woman was the very lady who had paid me a visit, and had been thrown into a state of indescribable agitation! She could not bring herself to suspect me of any sort of misconduct, but neither could she explain such a strange chain of circumstances. . . . Not improbably she imagined that Susanna had been led by love for me to commit suicide, and attired in her darkest garments, with an aching heart and tears, she prayed on her knees for the peace of the soul of the departed, and put a rouble candle before the picture of the Consolation of Sorrow. . . . 'Amishka' had come with her too, and she too prayed, but was for the most part gazing at me, horror-stricken. . . . That elderly spinster, alas! did not regard me with indifference. On leaving the church, my aunt distributed all her money, more than ten roubles, among the poor.

At last the farewell was over. They began closing the coffin. During the whole service I had not courage to look straight at the poor girl's distorted face; but every time that my eyes passed by it—'he did not come, he did not come,' it seemed to me that it wanted to say. They were just going to lower the lid upon the coffin. I could not restrain myself: I turned a rapid glance on to the dead woman. 'Why did you do it?' I was unconsciously asking. . . . 'He did not come!' I fancied for the last time. . . . The hammer was knocking in the nails, and all was over.

XXVII

We followed the hearse towards the cemetery. We were forty in number, of all sorts and conditions, nothing else really than an idle crowd. The wearisome journey lasted more than an hour. The weather became worse and worse. Halfway there Viktor got into a carriage, but Mr. Ratsch stepped gallantly on through the sloppy snow; just so must he have stepped through the snow when, after the fateful interview with Semyon Matveitch, he led home with him in triumph the girl whose life he had ruined for ever. The 'veteran's' hair and eyebrows were edged with snow; he kept blowing and uttering exclamations, or manfully drawing deep breaths and puffing out his round, dark-red cheeks. . . . One really might have thought he was laughing. 'On my death the pension was to pass to Ivan Demianitch'; these words from Susanna's manuscript recurred again to my mind. We reached the cemetery at last; we moved up to a freshly dug grave. The last ceremony was quickly performed; all were chilled through, all were in haste. The coffin slid on cords into the yawning hole; they began to throw earth on it. Mr. Ratsch here too showed the energy of his spirit, so rapidly, with such force and vigour, did he fling clods of earth on to the coffin lid, throwing himself into an heroic pose, with one leg planted firmly before him . . . he could not have shown more energy if he had been stoning his bitterest foe. Viktor, as before, held himself aloof; he kept muffling himself up in his coat, and rubbing his chin in the fur of his collar. Mr. Ratsch's other children eagerly imitated their father. Flinging sand and earth was a source of great enjoyment to them, for which, of course, they were in no way to blame. A mound began to rise up where the hole had been; we were on the point of separating, when Mr. Ratsch, wheeling round to the left in soldierly fashion, and slapping himself on the thigh, announced to all of us 'gentlemen present,' that he invited us, and also the 'reverend clergy,' to a 'funeral banquet,' which had been arranged at no great distance from the cemetery, in the chief saloon of an extremely superior restaurant, 'thanks to the kind offices of our honoured friend Sigismund Sigismundo- vitch.' . . . At these words he indicated the assistant of the police super- intendent, and added that for all his grief and his Lutheran faith, he, Ivan Demianitch Ratsch, as a genuine Russian, put the old Russian usages before everything. 'My spouse,' he cried, 'with the ladies that have accompanied her, may go home, while we gentlemen commemorate in a modest repast the shade of Thy departed servant!' Mr. Ratsch's proposal was received with genuine sympathy; 'the reverend clergy' exchanged expressive glances with one another, while the officer of roads and highways slapped Ivan Demianitch on the shoulder, and called him a patriot and the soul of the company.

We set off all together to the restaurant. In the restaurant, in the middle of a long, wide, and quite empty room on the first storey, stood two tables laid for dinner, covered with bottles and eatables, and surrounded by chairs. The smell of whitewash, mingled with the odours of spirits and salad oil, was stifling and oppressive. The police superintendent's assistant, as the organiser of the banquet, placed the clergy in the seats of honour, near which the Lenten dishes were crowded together conspicuously; after the priests the other guests took their seats; the banquet began. I would not have used such a festive word as banquet by choice, but no other word would have corresponded with the real character of the thing. At first the proceedings were fairly quiet, even slightly mournful; jaws munched busily, and glasses were emptied, but sighs too were audible—possibly sighs of digestion, but possibly also of feeling. There were references to death, allusions to the brevity of human life, and the fleeting nature of earthly hopes. The officer of roads and highways related a military but still edifying anecdote. The priest in the calotte expressed his approval, and himself contributed an interesting fact from the life of the saint, Ivan the Warrior. The priest with the superbly arranged hair, though his attention was chiefly engrossed by the edibles, gave utterance to something improving on the sub- ject of chastity. But little by little all this changed. Faces grew redder, and voices grew louder, and laughter reasserted itself; one began to hear discon- nected exclamations, caressing appellations, after the manner of 'dear old boy,' 'dear heart alive,' 'old cock,' and even 'a pig like that'—everything, in fact, of which the Russian nature is so lavish, when, as they say, 'it comes unbuttoned.' By the time that the corks of home-made champagne were popping, the party had become noisy; some one even crowed like a cock, while another guest was offering to bite up and swallow the glass out of which he had just been drinking. Mr. Ratsch, no longer red but purple, suddenly rose from his seat; he had been guffawing and making a great noise before, but now he asked leave to make a speech. 'Speak! Out with it!' every one roared; the old man in the smock even bawled 'bravo!' and clapped his hands . . . but he was already sitting on the floor. Mr. Ratsch lifted his glass high above his head, and announced that he proposed in brief but 'impressionable' phrases to refer to the qualities of the noble soul which, 'leaving here, so to say, its earthly husk (die irdische Hülle) has soared to heaven, and plunged . . .' Mr. Ratsch corrected himself: 'and plashed. . . .' He again corrected himself: 'and plunged . . .'

'Father deacon! Reverend sir! My good soul!' we heard a subdued but insistent whisper, 'they say you've a devilish good voice; honour us with a song, strike up: "We live among the fields!"'

'Sh! sh! . . . Shut up there!' passed over the lips of the guests.

. . . 'Plunged all her devoted family,' pursued Mr. Ratsch, turning a severe glance in the direction of the lover of music, 'plunged all her family into the most irreplaceable grief! Yes!' cried Ivan Demianitch, 'well may the Russian proverb say, "Fate spares not the rod." . . .'

'Stop! Gentlemen!' shouted a hoarse voice at the end of the table, 'my purse has just been stolen! . . .'

'Ah, the swindler!' piped another voice, and slap! went a box on the ear.

Heavens! What followed then! It was as though the wild beast, till then only growling and faintly stirring within us, had suddenly broken from its chains and reared up, ruffled and fierce in all its hideousness. It seemed as though every one had been secretly expecting 'a scandal,' as the natural outcome and sequel of a banquet, and all, as it were, rushed to welcome it, to support it. . . . Plates, glasses clattered and rolled about, chairs were upset, a deafening din arose, hands were waving in the air, coat-tails were flying, and a fight began in earnest.

'Give it him! give it him!' roared like mad my neighbour, the fishmonger, who had till that instant seemed to be the most peaceable person in the world; it is true he had been silently drinking some dozen glasses of spirits. 'Thrash him! . . .'

Who was to be thrashed, and what he was to be thrashed for, he had no idea, but he bellowed furiously.

The police superintendent's assistant, the officer of roads and highways, and Mr. Ratsch, who had probably not expected such a speedy termination to his eloquence, tried to restore order . . . but their efforts were unavailing. My neighbour, the fishmonger, even fell foul of Mr. Ratsch himself.

'He's murdered the young woman, the blasted German,' he yelled at him, shaking his fists; 'he's bought over the police, and here he's crowing over it!!'

At this point the waiters ran in. . . . What happened further I don't know; I snatched up my cap in all haste, and made off as fast as my legs would carry me! All I remember is a fearful crash; I recall, too, the remains of a herring in the hair of the old man in the smock, a priest's hat flying right across the room, the pale face of Viktor huddled up in a corner, and a red beard in the grasp of a muscular hand. . . . Such were the last impressions I carried away of the 'memorial banquet,' arranged by the excellent Sigismund Sigismundovitch in honour of poor Susanna.

After resting a little, I set off to see Fustov, and told him all of which I had been a witness during that day. He listened to me, sitting still, and not raising his head, and putting both hands under his legs, he murmured again, 'Ah! my poor girl, my poor girl!' and again lay down on the sofa and turned his back on me.

A week later he seemed to have quite got over it, and took up his life as before. I asked him for Susanna's manuscript as a keepsake: he gave it me without raising any objection.

XXVIII

SEVERAL YEARS PASSED BY. My aunt was dead; I had left Moscow and settled in Petersburg. Fustov too had moved to Petersburg. He had entered the department of the Ministry of Finance, but we rarely met and I saw nothing much in him then. An official like every one else, and nothing more! If he is still living and not married, he is, most likely, unchanged to this day; he carves and carpenters and uses dumb-bells, and is as much a lady-killer as ever, and sketches Napoleon in a blue uniform in the albums of his lady friends. It happened that I had to go to Moscow on business. In Moscow I learned, with considerable surprise, that the fortunes of my former acquaintance, Mr. Ratsch, had taken an adverse turn. His wife had, indeed, presented him with twins, two boys, whom as a true Russian he had christened Briacheslav and Viacheslav, but his house had been burnt down, he had been forced to retire from his position, and worst of all, his eldest son, Viktor, had become practically a permanent inmate of the debtors' prison. During my stay in Moscow, among a company at a friendly gathering, I chanced to hear an allusion made to Susanna, and a most slighting, most insulting allusion! I did all I could to defend the memory of the unhappy girl, to whom fate had denied even the charity of oblivion, but my arguments did not make much impression on my audience. One of them, a young student poet, was, however, a little moved by my words. He sent me next day a poem, which I have forgotten, but which ended in the following four lines:

> 'Her tomb lies cold, forlorn, but even death
> Her gentle spirit's memory cannot save
> From the sly voice of slander whispering on,
> Withering the flowers on her forsaken tomb. . . .'

I read these lines and unconsciously sank into musing. Susanna's image rose before me; once more I seemed to see the frozen window in my room; I recalled that evening and the blustering snowstorm, and those words, those sobs. . . . I began to ponder how it was possible to explain Susanna's love for Fustov, and why she had so quickly, so impulsively given way to despair, as soon as she saw herself forsaken. How was it she had had no desire to wait a little, to hear the bitter truth from the lips of the man she loved, to write to him, even? How could she fling herself at once headlong into the abyss? Because she was passionately in love with Fustov, I shall be told; because she could not bear the slightest doubt of his devotion, of his respect for her. Perhaps; or perhaps because she was not at all so passionately in love with Fustov; that she did not deceive herself about him, but simply rested her last hopes on him, and could not get over the thought that even this man had at once, at the first breath of slander, turned away from her with contempt! Who can say what killed her; wounded pride, or the wretchedness of her helpless position, or the very memory of that first, noble, true-hearted nature to whom she had so joyfully pledged herself in the morning of her early days, who had so deeply trusted her, and so honoured her? Who knows; perhaps at the very instant when I fancied that her dead lips were murmuring, ' he did not come! ' her soul was rejoicing that she had gone herself to him, to her Michel? The secrets of human life are great, and love itself, the most impenetrable of those secrets. . . . Anyway, to this day, whenever the image of Susanna rises before me, I cannot overcome a feeling of pity for her, and of angry reproach against fate, and my lips whisper instinctively, ' Unhappy girl! unhappy girl! '

1868.

THREE PORTRAITS

'NEIGHBOURS' CONSTITUTE one of the most serious drawbacks of life in the country. I knew a country gentleman of the Vologodsky district, who used on every suitable occasion to repeat the following words, 'Thank God, I have no neighbours,' and I confess I could not help envying that happy mortal. My own little place is situated in one of the most thickly peopled provinces of Russia. I am surrounded by a vast number of dear neighbours, from highly respectable and highly respected country gentlemen, attired in ample frockcoats and still more ample waistcoats, down to regular loafers, wearing jackets with long sleeves and a so-called shooting-bag on their back. In this crowd of gentlefolks I chanced, however, to discover one very pleasant fellow. He had served in the army, had retired and settled for good and all in the country. According to his story, he had served for two years in the B— regiment. But I am totally unable to comprehend how that man could have performed any sort of duty, not merely for two years, but even for two days. He was born 'for a life of peace and country calm,' that is to say, for lazy, careless vegetation, which, I note parenthetically, is not without great and inexhaustible charms. He possessed a very fair property, and without giving too much thought to its management, spent about ten thousand roubles a year, had obtained an excellent cook—my friend was fond of good fare—and ordered too from Moscow all the newest French books and magazines. In Russian he read nothing but the reports of his bailiff, and that with great difficulty. He used, when he did not go out shooting, to wear a dressing-gown from morning till dinner-time and at dinner. He would look through plans of some sort, or go round to the stables or to the threshing barn, and joke with the peasant women, who, to be sure, in his presence wielded their flails in leisurely fashion. After dinner my friend would dress very carefully before the looking-glass, and drive off to see some neighbour possessed of two or three pretty daughters. He would flirt serenely and unconcernedly with one of them, play blind-man's-buff with them, return home rather late and promptly fall into a heroic sleep. He could never be bored, for he never gave himself up to complete inactivity; and in the choice of occupations he was not difficult to please, and was amused like a child with the smallest trifle. On the other hand, he cherished no particular attachment to life, and at times, when he chanced to get a glimpse of the track of a wolf or a fox, he would let his horse go at full gallop over such ravines that to this day I cannot understand how it was he did not break his neck a hundred times over. He belonged to that class of persons who inspire in one the idea that they do not know their own value, that under their appearance of indifference strong and violent passions lie concealed. But he would have laughed in one's face if he could have guessed that one cherished such an opinion of him. And indeed I must own I believe myself that even supposing my friend had had in youth some strong impulse, however vague, towards what is so sweetly called 'higher things,' that impulse had long, long ago died out. He was rather stout and enjoyed superb health. In our day one cannot help liking people who think little about themselves, because they are exceedingly rare . . . and my friend had almost forgotten his own personality. I fancy, though, that I have said too much about him already, and my prolixity is the more uncalled for as he is not the hero of my story. His name was Piotr Fedorovitch Lutchinov.

One autumn day there were five of us, ardent sportsmen, gathered together at Piotr Fedorovitch's. We had spent the whole morning out, had run down a couple of foxes and a number of hares, and had returned home in that supremely agreeable frame of mind which comes over every well-regulated person after a successful day's shooting. It grew dusk. The wind was frolicking over the dark fields and noisily swinging the bare tops of the birches and lime-trees round Lutchinov's house. We reached the house, got off our horses. . . . On the steps I stood still and looked round: long storm-clouds were creeping heavily over the grey sky; a dark-brown bush was writhing in the wind, and murmuring plaintively; the yellow grass helplessly and forlornly bowed down to the earth; flocks of thrushes were fluttering in the mountain-ashes among the bright, flame-coloured clusters of berries. Among the light brittle twigs of the birch-trees blue-tits hopped whistling. In the village there was the hoarse barking of dogs. I felt melancholy . . . but it was with a genuine sense of comfort that I walked into the dining-room. The shutters were closed; on a round table, covered with a tablecloth of dazzling whiteness, amid cut-glass decanters of red wine, there were eight lighted candles in silver candlesticks; a fire glowed cheerfully on the hearth, and an old and very stately-looking butler, with a huge bald head, wearing an English dress, stood before another table on which was pleasingly conspicuous a large soup-tureen, encircled by light savoury-smelling steam. In the hall we passed by another venerable man, engaged in icing champagne—'according to the strictest rules of the art.' The dinner was, as is usual in such cases, exceedingly pleasant. We laughed and talked of the incidents of the day's shooting, and recalled with enthusiasm two glorious 'runs.' After dining pretty heartily, we settled comfortably into ample arm-chairs round the fire; a huge silver bowl made its appearance on the table, and in a few minutes the white flame of the burning rum announced our host's agreeable intention 'to concoct a punch.' Piotr Fedoritch was a man of some taste; he was aware, for instance, that nothing has so fatal an influence on the fancy as the cold, steady, pedantic light of a lamp, and so he gave orders that only two candles should be left in the room. Strange half-shadows quivered on the walls, thrown by the fanciful play of the fire in the hearth and the flame of the punch . . . a soft, exceedingly agreeable sense of soothing comfort replaced in our hearts the somewhat boisterous gaiety that had reigned at dinner.

Conversations have their destinies, like books, as the Latin proverb says, like everything in the world. Our conversation that evening was particularly many-sided and lively. From details it passed to rather serious general

questions, and lightly and casually came back to the daily incidents of life.
. . . After chatting a good deal, we suddenly all sank into silence. At such
times they say an angel of peace is flying over.

I cannot say why my companions were silent, but I held my tongue
because my eyes had suddenly come to rest on three dusty portraits in
black wooden frames. The colours were rubbed and cracked in places,
but one could still make out the faces. The portrait in the centre was that
of a young woman in a white gown with lace ruffles, her hair done up high,
in the style of the eighties of last century. On her right, upon a perfectly
black background, there stood out the full, round face of a good-natured
country gentleman of five-and-twenty, with a broad, low brow, a thick
nose, and a good-humoured smile. The French powdered coiffure was
utterly out of keeping with the expression of his Slavonic face. The artist
had portrayed him wearing a long loose coat of crimson colour with large
paste buttons; in his hand he was holding some unlikely-looking flower.
The third portrait, which was the work of some other more skilful hand,
represented a man of thirty, in the green uniform, with red facings, of the
time of Catherine, in a white shirt, with a fine cambric cravat. One hand
leaned on a gold-headed cane, the other lay on his shirt front. His dark,
thinnish face was full of insolent haughtiness. The fine long eyebrows
almost grew together over the pitch-black eyes, about the thin, scarcely
discernible lips played an evil smile.

'Why do you keep staring at those faces?' Piotr Fedoritch asked me.

'Oh, I don't know!' I answered, looking at him.

'Would you care to hear a whole story about those three persons?'

'Oh, please tell it,' we all responded with one voice.

Piotr Fedoritch got up, took a candle, carried it to the portraits, and
in the tone of a showman at a wild beast show, 'Gentlemen!' he boomed,
'this lady was the adopted child of my great-grandfather, Olga Ivanovna N.N., called Lutchinov, who died forty years ago unmarried. This
gentleman,' he pointed to the portrait of a man in uniform, 'served as a
lieutenant in the Guards, Vassily Ivanovitch Lutchinov, expired by the will
of God in the year seventeen hundred and ninety. And this gentleman, to
whom I have not the honour of being related, is a certain Pavel Afanasiitch
Rogatchov, serving nowhere, as far as I'm aware. . . . Kindly take note of
the hole in his breast, just on the spot where the heart should be. That hole,
you see, a regular three-sided hole, would be hardly likely to have come
there by chance. . . . Now,' he went on in his usual voice, 'kindly seat
yourselves, arm yourselves with patience, and listen.'

Gentlemen! (he began) I come of a rather old family. I am not proud of
my descent, seeing that my ancestors were all fearful prodigals. Though
that reproach cannot indeed be made against my great-grandfather, Ivan
Andreevitch Lutchinov; on the contrary, he had the character of being excessively careful, even miserly—at any rate, in the latter years of his life. He
spent his youth in Petersburg, and lived through the reign of Elizabeth. In

Petersburg he married, and had by his wife, my great-grandmother, four children, three sons, Vassily, Ivan, and Pavel, my grandfather, and one daughter, Natalia. In addition, Ivan Andreevitch took into his family the daughter of a distant relation, a nameless and destitute orphan—Olga Ivanovna, of whom I spoke just now. My great-grandfather's serfs were probably aware of his existence, for they used (when nothing particularly unlucky occurred) to send him a trifling rent, but they had never seen his face. The village of Lutchinovka, deprived of the bodily presence of its lord, was flourishing exceedingly, when all of a sudden one fine morning a cumbrous old family coach drove into the village and stopped before the elder's hut. The peasants, alarmed at such an unheard-of occurrence, ran up and saw their master and mistress and all their young ones, except the eldest, Vassily, who was left behind in Petersburg. From that memorable day down to the very day of his death, Ivan Andreevitch never left Lutchinovka. He built himself a house, the very house in which I have the pleasure of conversing with you at this moment. He built a church too, and began living the life of a country gentleman. Ivan Andreevitch was a man of immense height, thin, silent, and very deliberate in all his movements. He never wore a dressing-gown, and no one but his valet had ever seen him without powder. Ivan Andreevitch usually walked with his hands clasped behind his back, turning his head at each step. Every day he used to walk in a long avenue of lime-trees, which he had planted with his own hand; and before his death he had the pleasure of enjoying the shade of those trees. Ivan Andreevitch was exceedingly sparing of his words; a proof of his taciturnity is to be found in the remarkable fact that in the course of twenty years he had not said a single word to his wife, Anna Pavlovna. His relations with Anna Pavlovna altogether were of a very curious sort. She directed the whole management of the household; at dinner she always sat beside her husband—he would mercilessly have chastised any one who had dared to say a disrespectful word to her—and yet he never spoke to her, never touched her hand. Anna Pavlovna was a pale, broken-spirited woman, completely crushed. She prayed every day on her knees in church, and she never smiled. There was a rumour that they had formerly, that is, before they came into the country, lived on very cordial terms with one another. They did say too that Anna Pavlovna had been untrue to her matrimonial vows; that her conduct had come to her husband's knowledge. . . . Be that as it may, any way Ivan Andreevitch, even when dying, was not reconciled to her. During his last illness, she never left him; but he seemed not to notice her. One night, Anna Pavlovna was sitting in Ivan Andreevitch's bedroom—he suffered from sleeplessness— a lamp was burning before the holy picture. My grandfather's servant, Yuditch, of whom I shall have to say a few words later, went out of the room. Anna Pavlovna got up, crossed the room, and sobbing flung herself on her knees at her husband's bedside, tried to say something—stretched out her hands . . . Ivan Andreevitch looked at her, and in a faint voice, but resolutely, called, 'Boy!' The servant went in; Anna Pavlovna hurriedly rose, and went back, tottering, to her place.

Ivan Andreevitch's children were exceedingly afraid of him. They grew up in the country, and were witnesses of Ivan Andreevitch's strange treatment of his wife. They all loved Anna Pavlovna passionately, but did not dare to show their love. She seemed of herself to hold aloof from them. . . . You remember my grandfather, gentlemen; to the day of his death he always walked on tiptoe, and spoke in a whisper . . . such is the force of habit! My grandfather and his brother, Ivan Ivanovitch, were simple, good-hearted people, quiet and depressed. My grand'tante Natalia married, as you are aware, a coarse, dull-witted man, and all her life she cherished an unutterable, slavish, sheep-like passion for him. But their brother Vassily was not of that sort. I believe I said that Ivan Andreevitch had left him in Petersburg. He was then twelve. His father confided him to the care of a distant kinsman, a man no longer young, a bachelor, and a terrible Voltairean.

Vassily grew up and went into the army. He was not tall, but was well-built and exceedingly elegant; he spoke French excellently, and was renowned for his skilful swordsmanship. He was considered one of the most brilliant young men of the beginning of the reign of Catherine. My father used often to tell me that he had known more than one old lady who could not refer to Vassily Ivanovitch Lutchinov without heartfelt emotion. Picture to yourselves a man endowed with exceptional strength of will, passionate and calculating, persevering and daring, reserved in the extreme, and—according to the testimony of all his contemporaries—fascinatingly, captivatingly attractive. He had no conscience, no heart, no principle, though no one could have called him positively a bad-hearted man. He was vain, but knew how to disguise his vanity, and passionately cherished his independence. When Vassily Ivanovitch would half close his black eyes, smiling affectionately when he wanted to fascinate any one, they say it was impossible to resist him; and even people, thoroughly convinced of the coldness and hardness of his heart, were more than once vanquished by the bewitching power of his personal influence. He served his own interests devotedly, and made other people, too, work for his advantage; and he was always successful in everything, because he never lost his head, never disdained using flattery as a means, and well understood how to use it.

Ten years after Ivan Andreevitch had settled in the country, he came for a four months' visit to Lutchinovka, a brilliant officer of the Guards, and in that time succeeded positively in turning the head of the grim old man, his father. Strange to say, Ivan Andreevitch listened with enjoyment to his son's stories of some of his *conquests*. His brothers were speechless in his presence, and admired him as a being of a higher order. And Anna Pavlovna herself became almost fonder of him than any of her other children who were so sincerely devoted to her.

Vassily Ivanovitch had come down into the country primarily to visit his people, but also with the second object of getting as much money as possible from his father. He lived sumptuously in the glare of publicity in Petersburg, and had made a mass of debts. He had no easy task to get round his father's miserliness, and though Ivan Andreevitch gave him on this one visit probably far more money than he gave all his other children together during twenty years spent under his roof, Vassily followed the well-known Russian rule, ' Get what you can! '

Ivan Andreevitch had a servant called Yuditch, just such another tall, thin, taciturn person as his master. They say that this man Yuditch was partly responsible for Ivan Andreevitch's strange behaviour with Anna Pavlovna; they say he discovered my great-grandmother's guilty intrigue with one of my great-grandfather's dearest friends. Most likely Yuditch deeply regretted his ill-timed jealousy, for it would be difficult to conceive a more kind-hearted man. His memory is held in veneration by all my house-serfs to this day. My great-grandfather put unbounded confidence in Yuditch. In those days landowners used to have money, but did not put it into the keeping of banks, they kept it themselves in chests, under their floors, and so on. Ivan Andreevitch kept all his money in a great wrought-iron coffer, which stood under the head of his bed. The key of this coffer was intrusted to Yuditch. Every evening as he went to bed Ivan Andreevitch used to bid him open the coffer in his presence, used to tap in turn each of the tightly filled bags with a stick, and every Saturday he would untie the bags with Yuditch, and carefully count over the money. Vassily heard of all these doings, and burned with eagerness to overhaul the sacred coffer. In the course of five or six days he had *softened* Yuditch, that is, he had worked on the old man till, as they say, he worshipped the ground his young master trod on. Having thus duly prepared him, Vassily put on a careworn and gloomy air, for a long while refused to answer Yuditch's questions, and at last told him that he had lost at play, and should make an end of himself if he could not get money somehow. Yuditch broke into sobs, flung himself on his knees before him, begged him to think of God, not to be his own ruin. Vassily locked himself in his room without uttering a word. A little while after he heard some one cautiously knocking at his door; he opened it, and saw in the doorway Yuditch pale and trembling, with the key in his hand. Vassily took in the whole position at a glance. At first, for a long while, he refused to take it. With tears Yuditch repeated, ' Take it, your honour, graciously take it! ' . . . Vassily at last agreed. This took place on Monday. The idea occurred to Vassily to replace the money taken out with broken bits of crockery. He reckoned on Ivan Andreevitch's tapping the bags with his stick, and not noticing the hardly perceptible difference in the sound, and by Saturday he hoped to obtain and to replace the sum in the coffer. As he planned, so he did. His father did not, in fact, notice anything. But by Saturday Vassily had not procured the money; he had hoped to win the sum from a rich neighbour at cards, and instead of that, he lost it all. Meantime, Saturday had come; it came at last to the turn of the bags filled with broken crocks. Picture, gentlemen, the amazement of Ivan Andreevitch!

' What does this mean? ' he thundered.

Yuditch was silent.

' You stole the money? '

'No, sir.'

'Then some one took the key from you?'

'I didn't give the key to any one.'

'Not to any one? Well then, you are the thief. Confess!'

'I am not a thief, Ivan Andreevitch.'

'Where the devil did these potsherds come from then? So you're deceiving me! For the last time I tell you—confess!'

Yuditch bowed his head and folded his hands behind his back.

'Hi, lads!' shrieked Ivan Andreevitch in a voice of frenzy. 'A stick!'

'What, beat . . . me?' murmured Yuditch.

'Yes, indeed! Are you any better than the rest? You are a thief! O Yuditch! I never expected such dishonesty of you!'

'I have grown grey in your service, Ivan Andreevitch,' Yuditch articulated with effort.

'What have I to do with your grey hairs? Damn you and your service!'

The servants came in.

'Take him, do, and give it him thoroughly.' Ivan Andreevitch's lips were white and twitching. He walked up and down the room like a wild beast in a small cage.

The servants did not dare to carry out his orders.

'Why are you standing still, children of Ham? Am I to undertake him myself, eh?'

Yuditch was moving towards the door . . .

'Stay!' screamed Ivan Andreevitch. 'Yuditch, for the last time I tell you, I beg you, Yuditch, confess!'

'I can't!' moaned Yuditch.

'Then take him, the sly old fox! Flog him to death! His blood be on my head!' thundered the infuriated old man. The flogging began. . . . The door suddenly opened, and Vassily came in. He was almost paler than his father, his hands were shaking, his upper lip was lifted, and laid bare a row of even, white teeth.

'I am to blame,' he said in a thick but resolute voice. 'I took the money.'

The servants stopped.

'You! what? you, Vaska! without Yuditch's consent?'

'No!' said Yuditch, 'with my consent. I gave Vassily Ivanovitch the key of my own accord. Your honour, Vassily Ivanovitch! why does your honour trouble?'

'So this is the thief!' shrieked Ivan Andreevitch. 'Thanks, Vassily, thanks! But, Yuditch, I'm not going to forgive you anyway. Why didn't you tell me all about it directly? Hey, you there! why are you standing still? do you too resist my authority? Ah, I'll settle things with you, my pretty gentleman!' he added, turning to Vassily.

The servants were again laying hands on Yuditch. . . .

'Don't touch him!' murmured Vassily through his teeth. The men did not heed him. 'Back!' he shrieked and rushed upon them. . . . They stepped back.

'Ah! mutiny!' moaned Ivan Andreevitch, and, raising his stick, he approached his son.

Vassily leaped back, snatched at the handle of his sword, and bared it to half its length. Every one was trembling. Anna Pavlovna, attracted by the noise, showed herself at the door, pale and scared.

A terrible change passed over the face of Ivan Andreevitch. He tottered, dropped the stick, and sank heavily into an arm-chair, hiding his face in both hands. No one stirred, all stood rooted to the spot, Vassily like the rest. He clutched the steel sword-handle convulsively, and his eyes glittered with a weary, evil light. . . .

'Go, all of you . . . all, out,' Ivan Andreevitch brought out in a low voice, not taking his hands from his face.

The whole crowd went out. Vassily stood still in the doorway, then suddenly tossed his head, embraced Yuditch, kissed his mother's hand . . . and two hours later he had left the place. He went back to Petersburg.

In the evening of the same day Yuditch was sitting on the steps of the house serfs' huts. The servants were all round him, sympathising with him and bitterly reproaching their young master.

'That's enough, lads,' he said to them at last, 'give over . . . why do you abuse him? He himself, the young master, I dare say is not very happy at his audacity. . . .'

In consequence of this incident, Vassily never saw his father again. Ivan Andreevitch died without him, and died probably with such a load of sorrow on his heart as God grant none of us may ever know. Vassily Ivanovitch, meanwhile, went into the world, enjoyed himself in his own way, and squandered money recklessly. How he got hold of the money, I cannot tell for certain. He had obtained a French servant, a very smart and intelligent fellow, Bourcier, by name. This man was passionately attached to him and aided him in all his numerous manœuvres. I do not intend to relate in detail all the exploits of my grand-uncle; he was possessed of such unbounded daring, such serpent-like resource, such inconceivable wiliness, such a fine and ready wit, that I must own I can understand the complete sway that unprincipled person exercised even over the noblest natures.

Soon after his father's death, in spite of his wiliness, Vassily Ivanovitch was challenged by an injured husband. He fought a duel, seriously wounded his opponent, and was forced to leave the capital; he was banished to his estate, and forbidden to leave it. Vassily Ivanovitch was thirty years old. You may easily imagine, gentlemen, with what feelings he left the brilliant life in the capital that he was used to, and came into the country. They say that he got out of the hooded cart several times on the road, flung himself face downwards in the snow and cried. No one in Lutchinovka would have known him as the gay and charming Vassily Ivanovitch they had seen before. He did not talk to any one; went out shooting from morning to night; endured his mother's timid caresses with undisguised impatience, and was merciless in his ridicule of his brothers, and of their wives (they were both married by that time). . . .

I have not so far, I think, told you anything about Olga Ivanovna. She had been brought as a tiny baby to Lutchinovka; she all but died on the road. Olga Ivanovna was brought up, as they say, in the fear of God and her betters. It must be admitted that Ivan Andreevitch and Anna Pavlovna both treated her as a daughter. But there lay hid in her soul a faint spark of that fire which burned so fiercely in Vassily Ivanovitch. While Ivan Andreevitch's own children did not dare even to wonder about the cause of the strange, dumb feud between their parents, Olga was from her earliest years disturbed and tormented by Anna Pavlovna's position. Like Vassily, she loved independence; any restriction fretted her. She was devoted with her whole soul to her benefactress; old Lutchinov she detested, and more than once, sitting at table, she shot such black looks at him, that even the servant handing the dishes felt uncomfortable. Ivan Andreevitch never noticed these glances, for he never took the slightest notice of his family.

At first Anna Pavlovna had tried to eradicate this hatred, but some bold questions of Olga's forced her to complete silence. The children of Ivan Andreevitch adored Olga, and the old lady too was fond of her, but not with a very ardent affection.

Long continued grieving had crushed all cheerfulness and every strong feeling in that poor woman; nothing is so clear a proof of Vassily's captivating charm as that he had made even his mother love him passionately. Demonstrations of tenderness on the part of children were not in the spirit of the age, and so it is not to be wondered at that Olga did not dare to express her devotion, though she always kissed Anna Pavlovna's hand with special reverence, when she said good-night to her. Twenty years later, Russian girls began to read romances of the class of *The Adventures of Marquis Glagol, Fanfan and Lolotta, Alexey or the Cottage in the Forest;* they began to play the clavichord and to sing songs in the style of the once very well-known:

> ' *Men like butterflies in sunshine*
> *Flutter round us opening blossoms,*' etc.

But in the seventies of last century (Olga Ivanovna was born in 1757) our country beauties had no notion of such accomplishments. It is difficult for us now to form a clear conception of the Russian miss of those days. We can indeed judge from our grandmothers of the degree of culture of girls of noble family in the time of Catherine; but how is one to distinguish what they had gradually gained in the course of their long lives from what they were in the days of their youth?

Olga Ivanovna spoke French a little, but with a strong Russian accent: in her day there was as yet no talk of French emigrants. In fact, with all her fine qualities, she was still pretty much of a savage, and I dare say in the simplicity of her heart, she had more than once chastised some luckless servant girl with her own hands. . . .

Some time before Vassily Ivanovitch's arrival, Olga Ivanovna had been betrothed to a neighbour, Pavel Afanasievitch Rogatchov, a very good-natured and straightforward fellow. Nature had forgotten to put any spice of ill-temper into his composition. His own serfs did not obey him, and would sometimes all go off, down to the least of them, and leave poor Rogatchov without any dinner ... but nothing could trouble the peace of his soul. From his childhood he had been stout and indolent, had never been in the government service, and was fond of going to church and singing in the choir. Look, gentlemen, at this round, good-natured face; glance at this mild, beaming smile ... don't you really feel it reassuring, yourselves? His father used at long intervals to drive over to Lutchinovka, and on holidays used to bring with him his Pavlusha, whom the little Lutchinovs teased in every possible way. Pavlusha grew up, began driving over to call on Ivan Andreevitch on his own account, fell in love with Olga Ivanovna, and offered her his hand and heart—not to her personally, but to her benefactors. Her benefactors gave their consent. They never even thought of asking Olga Ivanovna whether she liked Rogatchov. In those days, in the words of my grandmother, ' such refinements were not the thing.' Olga soon got used to her betrothed, however; it was impossible not to feel fond of such a gentle and amiable creature. Rogatchov had received no education whatever; his French consisted of the one word *bonjour*, and he secretly considered even that word improper. But some jocose person had taught him the following lines, as a French song: ' Sonitchka, Sonitchka! Ke-voole-voo-de-mwa—I adore you—me-je-ne-pyoo-pa. . . . ' This supposed song he always used to hum to himself when he felt in good spirits. His father was also a man of incredible good-nature, always wore a long nankin coat, and whatever was said to him he responded with a smile. From the time of Pavel Afanasievitch's betrothal, both the Rogatchovs, father and son, had been tremendously busy. They had been having their house entirely transformed adding various ' galleries,' talking in a friendly way with the workmen, encouraging them with drinks. They had not yet completed all these additions by the winter; they put off the wedding till the summer. In the summer Ivan Andreevitch died; the wedding was deferred till the following spring. In the winter Vassily Ivanovitch arrived. Rogatchov was presented to him; he received him coldly and contemptuously, and as time went on, he so alarmed him by his haughty behaviour that poor Rogatchov trembled like a leaf at the very sight of him, was tongue-tied and smiled nervously. Vassily once almost annihilated him altogether—by making him a bet, that he, Rogatchov, was not able to stop smiling. Poor Pavel Afanasievitch almost cried with embarrassment, but—actually!—a smile, a stupid, nervous smile refused to leave his perspiring face! Vassily toyed deliberately with the ends of his neckerchief, and looked at him with supreme contempt. Pavel Afanasievitch's father heard too of Vassily's presence, and after an interval of a few days—' for the sake of greater formality '—he sallied off to Lutchinovka with the object of ' felicitating our honoured guest on his advent to the halls of his ancestors.' Afanasey Lukitch was famed all over the countryside for his eloquence—that is to say, for his capacity for enunciating without faltering a rather long and complicated speech, with a sprinkling of bookish phrases in it. Alas! on this occasion he did not sustain his reputation; he was even more disconcerted than his son, Pavel Afanasievitch; he mumbled something quite inarticulate, and though he had never been used to taking vodka, he at once drained a glass 'to carry things off'—he found Vassily at lunch,—tried at least to clear his throat with some dignity, and did not succeed in making the slightest sound. On their way home, Pavel Afanasievitch whispered to his parent, 'Well, father?' Afanasey Lukitch responded angrily also in a whisper, 'Don't speak of it!'

The Rogatchovs began to be less frequent visitors at Lutchinovka. Though indeed they were not the only people intimidated by Vassily; he awakened in his own brothers, in their wives, in Anna Pavlovna herself, an instinctive feeling of uneasiness and discomfort . . . they tried to avoid him in every way they could. Vassily must have noticed this, but apparently had no intention of altering his behaviour to them. Suddenly, at the beginning of the spring, he became once more the charming, attractive person they had known of old . . .

The first symptom of this sudden transformation was Vassily's unexpected visit to the Rogatchovs. Afanasey Lukitch, in particular, was fairly disconcerted at the sight of Lutchinov's carriage, but his dismay very quickly vanished. Never had Vassily been more courteous and delightful. He took young Rogatchov by the arm, went with him to look at the new buildings, talked to the carpenters, made some suggestions, with his own hands chopped a few chips off with the axe, asked to be shown Afanasey Lukitch's stud horses, himself trotted them out on a halter, and altogether so affected the good-hearted children of the steppes by his gracious affability that they both embraced him more than once. At home, too, Vassily managed, in the course of a few days, to turn every one's head just as before. He contrived all sorts of laughable games, got hold of musicians, invited the ladies and gentlemen of the neighbourhood, told the old ladies the scandals of the town in the most amusing way, flirted a little with the young ones, invented unheard-of diversions, fireworks and such things, in short, he put life into every thing and every one. The melancholy, gloomy house of the Lutchinovs was suddenly converted into a noisy, brilliant, enchanted palace of which the whole countryside was talking. This sudden transformation surprised many and delighted all. All sorts of rumours began to be whispered about. Sagacious persons opined that Vassily Ivanovitch had till then been crushed under the weight of some secret trouble, that he saw chances of returning to the capital . . . but the true cause of Vassily Ivanovitch's metamorphosis was guessed by no one.

Olga Ivanovna, gentlemen, was rather pretty; though her beauty consisted rather in the extraordinary softness and freshness of her shape, in the quiet grace of her movements than in the strict regularity of her features. Nature had bestowed on her a certain independence; her bringing up—she had grown up without father or mother—had developed in her reserve and determination. Olga did not belong to the class of quiet and tame-spirited young ladies; but only one feeling had reached its full possibilities in her as yet—hatred for her benefactor. Other more feminine passions might indeed flare up in Olga Ivanovna's heart with abnormal and painful violence . . . but she had not the cold pride, nor the intense strength of will, nor the self-centred egoism, without which any passion passes quickly away.

The first rush of feeling in such half-active, half-passive natures is sometimes extremely violent; but they give way very quickly, especially when it is a question of relentless conformity with accepted principles; they are afraid of consequences. . . . And yet, gentlemen, I will frankly confess, women of that sort always make the strongest impression on me. . . . (At these words the speaker drank a glass of water. Rubbish! rubbish! thought I, looking at his round chin; nothing in the world makes a strong impression on you, my dear fellow!)

Piotr Fedoritch resumed: Gentlemen, I believe in blood, in race. Olga Ivanovna had more blood than, for instance, her foster sister, Natalia. How did this blood show itself, do you ask? Why, in everything; in the lines of her hands, in her lips, in the sound of her voice, in her glance, in her carriage, in her hair, in the very folds of her gown. In all these trifles there lay hid something special, though I am bound to admit that the—how can one express it?—*la distinction*, which had fallen to Olga Pavlovna's share would not have attracted Vassily's notice had he met her in Petersburg. But in the country, in the wilds, she not only caught his attention, she was positively the sole cause of the transformation of which I have just been speaking.

Consider the position. Vassily Ivanovitch liked to enjoy life; he could not but be bored in the country; his brothers were good-natured fellows, but extremely limited people: he had nothing in common with them. His sister, Natalia, with the assistance of her husband, had brought into the world in the course of three years no less than four babies; between her and Vassily was a perfect gulf. . . . Anna Pavlovna went to church, prayed, fasted, and was preparing herself for death. There remained only Olga—a fresh, shy, pretty girl. . . . Vassily did not notice her at first . . . indeed, who does notice a dependent, an orphan girl kept from charity in the house? . . . One day, at the very beginning of spring, Vassily was walking about the garden, and with his cane slashing off the heads of the dandelions, those stupid yellow flowers, which come out first in such numbers in the meadows, as soon as they begin to grow green. He was walking in the garden in front of the house; he lifted his head, and caught sight of Olga Ivanovna.

She was sitting sideways at the window, dreamily stroking a tabby kitten, who, purring and blinking, nestled on her lap, and with great satisfaction held up her little nose into the rather hot spring sunshine. Olga Ivanovna was wearing a white morning gown, with short sleeves; her bare, pale-pink, girlish shoulders and arms were a picture of freshness and health. A little red cap discreetly restrained her thick, soft, silky curls. Her face was a little flushed; she was only just awake. Her slender, flexible neck bent forward so charmingly; there was such seductive negligence, such modesty in the restful pose of her figure, free from corsets, that Vassily Ivanovitch (a great connoisseur!) halted involuntarily and peeped in. It suddenly occurred to him that Olga Ivanovna ought not to be left in her primitive ignorance; that she might with time be turned into a very sweet and charming woman. He stole up to the window, stretched up on tiptoe, and imprinted a silent kiss on Olga Ivanovna's smooth, white arm, a little below the elbow.

Olga shrieked and jumped up, the kitten put its tail in the air and leaped into the garden. Vassily Ivanovitch with a smile kept her by the arm. . . . Olga flushed all over, to her ears; he began to rally her on her alarm . . . invited her to come a walk with him. But Olga Ivanovna became suddenly conscious of the negligence of her attire, and 'swifter than the swift red deer' she slipped away into the next room.

The very same day Vassily set off to the Rogatchovs. He was suddenly happy and light-hearted. Vassily was not in love with Olga, no! the word 'love' is not to be used lightly. . . . He had found an occupation, had set himself a task, and rejoiced with the delight of a man of action. He did not even remember that she was his mother's ward, and another man's betrothed. He never for one instant deceived himself; he was fully aware that it was not for her to be his wife. . . . Possibly there was passion to excuse him— not a very elevated nor noble passion, truly, but still a fairly strong and tormenting passion. Of course he was not in love like a boy; he did not give way to vague ecstasies; he knew very well what he wanted and what he was striving for.

Vassily was a perfect master of the art of winning over, in the shortest time, any one however shy or prejudiced against him. Olga soon ceased to be shy with him. Vassily Ivanovitch led her into a new world. He ordered a clavichord for her, gave her music lessons (he himself played fairly well on the flute), read books aloud to her, had long conversations with her. . . . The poor child of the steppes soon had her head turned completely. Vassily dominated her entirely. He knew how to tell her of what had been till then unknown to her, and to tell her in a language she could understand. Olga little by little gained courage to express all her feelings to him: he came to her aid, helped her out with the words she could not find, did not alarm her, at one moment kept her back, at another encouraged her confidences. . . . Vassily busied himself with her education from no disinterested desire to awaken and develop her talents. He simply wanted to draw her a little closer to himself; and he knew too that an innocent, shy, but vain young girl is more easily seduced through the mind than the heart. Even if Olga had been an exceptional being, Vassily would never have perceived it, for he treated her like a child. But as you are aware, gentlemen, there was nothing specially remarkable in Olga. Vassily tried all he could to work on her imagination, and often in the evening she left his side with such a whirl of new images, phrases and ideas in her head that she could not sleep all night, but lay breathing uneasily and turning her burning cheeks from side to side on the cool pillows, or got up, went to the window and gazed fearfully and eagerly into the dark distance. Vassily filled every moment of her life; she could not think of any one else. As for Rogatchov, she soon positively ceased to notice his existence. Vassily had the tact and shrewdness not to talk to Olga in his presence; but he either made him laugh till he was ready to cry, or arranged some noisy entertainment, a riding expedition, a boating party by night with torches and music—he did not in fact let Pavel Afanasievitch have a chance to think clearly.

But in spite of all Vassily Ivanovitch's tact, Rogatchov dimly felt that he, Olga's betrothed and future husband, had somehow become as it were an outsider to her . . . but in the boundless goodness of his heart, he was afraid of wounding her by reproaches, though he sincerely loved her and prized her affection. When left alone with her, he did not know what to say, and only tried all he could to follow her wishes. Two months passed by. Every trace of self-reliance, of will, disappeared at last in Olga. Rogatchov, feeble and tongue-tied, could be no support to her. She had no wish even to resist the enchantment, and with a sinking heart she surrendered unconditionally to Vassily. . . .

Olga Ivanovna may very likely then have known something of the bliss of love; but it was not for long. Though Vassily—for lack of other occupation—did not drop her, and even attached himself to her and looked after her fondly, Olga herself was so utterly distraught that she found no happiness even in love and yet could not tear herself away from Vassily. She began to be frightened at everything, did not dare to think, could talk of nothing, gave up reading, and was devoured by misery. Sometimes Vassily succeeded in carrying her along with him and making her forget everything and every one. But the very next day he would find her pale, speechless, with icy hands, and a fixed smile on her lips. . . . There followed a time of some difficulty for Vassily; but no difficulties could dismay him. He concentrated himself like a skilled gambler. He could not in the least rely upon Olga Ivanovna; she was continually betraying herself, turning pale, blushing, weeping . . . her new part was utterly beyond her powers. Vassily toiled for two: in his restless and boisterous gaiety, only an experienced observer could have detected something strained and feverish. He played his brothers, sisters, the Rogatchovs, the neighbours, like pawns at chess. He was everlastingly on the alert. Not a single glance, a single movement, was lost on him, yet he appeared the most heedless of men. Every morning he faced the fray, and every evening he scored a victory. He was not the least oppressed by such a fearful strain of activity. He slept four hours out of the twenty-four, ate very little, and was healthy, fresh, and good-humoured.

Meantime the wedding-day was approaching. Vassily succeeded in persuading Pavel Afanasievitch himself of the necessity of delay. Then he despatched him to Moscow to make various purchases, while he was himself in correspondence with friends in Petersburg. He took all this trouble, not so much from sympathy for Olga Ivanovna, as from a natural bent and liking for bustle and agitation. . . . Besides, he was beginning to be sick of Olga

Ivanovna, and more than once after a violent outbreak of passion for her, he would look at her, as he sometimes did at Rogatchov. Lutchinov always remained a riddle to every one. In the coldness of his relentless soul you felt the presence of a strange almost southern fire, and even in the wildest glow of passion a breath of icy chill seemed to come from the man.

Before other people he supported Olga Ivanovna as before. But when they were alone, he played with her like a cat with a mouse, or frightened her with sophistries, or was wearily, malignantly bored, or again flung himself at her feet, swept her away, like a straw in a hurricane . . . and there was no feigning at such moments in his passion . . . he really was moved himself.

One day, rather late in the evening, Vassily was sitting alone in his room, attentively reading over the last letters he had received from Petersburg, when suddenly he heard a faint creak at the door, and Olga Ivanovna's maid, Palashka, came in.

'What do you want?' Vassily asked her rather crossly.

'My mistress begs you to come to her.'

'I can't just now. Go along. . . . Well, what are you standing there for?' he went on, seeing that Palashka did not go away.

'My mistress told me to say that she very particularly wants to see you,' she said.

'Why, what's the matter?'

'Would your honour please to see for yourself. . . .'

Vassily got up, angrily flung the letters into a drawer, and went in to Olga Ivanovna. She was sitting alone in a corner, pale and passive.

'What do you want?' he asked her, not quite politely.

Olga looked at him and closed her eyes.

'What's the matter? what is it, Olga?'

He took her hand. . . . Olga Ivanovna's hand was cold as ice . . . She tried to speak . . . and her voice died away. The poor woman had no possible doubt of her condition left her.

Vassily was a little disconcerted. Olga Ivanovna's room was a couple of steps from Anna Pavlovna's bedroom. Vassily cautiously sat down by Olga, kissed and chafed her hands, comforted her in whispers. She listened to him, and silently, faintly, shuddered. In the doorway stood Palashka, stealthily wiping her eyes. In the next room they heard the heavy, even ticking of the clock, and the breathing of some one asleep. Olga Ivanovna's numbness dissolved at last into tears and stifled sobs. Tears are like a storm; after them one is always calmer. When Olga Ivanovna had quieted down a little, and only sobbed convulsively at intervals, like a child, Vassily knelt before her with caresses and tender promises, soothed her completely, gave her something to drink, put her to bed, and went away. He did not undress all night; wrote two or three letters, burnt two or three papers, took out a gold locket containing the portrait of a black-browed, black-eyed woman with a bold, voluptuous face, scrutinised her features slowly, and walked up and down the room pondering.

Next day, at breakfast, he saw with extreme displeasure poor Olga's red and swollen eyes and pale, agitated face. After breakfast he proposed a stroll in the garden to her. Olga followed Vassily, like a submissive sheep. When two hours afterwards she came in from the garden she quite broke down; she told Anna Pavlovna she was unwell, and went to lie down on her bed. During their walk Vassily had, with a suitable show of remorse, informed her that he was secretly married—he was really as much a bachelor as I am. Olga Ivanovna did not fall into a swoon—people don't fall into swoons except on the stage—but she turned all at once stony, though she herself was so far from hoping to marry Vassily Ivanovitch that she was even afraid to think about it. Vassily had begun to explain to her the inevitableness of her parting from him and marrying Rogatchov. Olga Ivanovna looked at him in dumb horror. Vassily talked in a cool, business-like, practical way, blamed himself, expressed his regret, but concluded all his remarks with the following words: 'There's no going back on the past; we've got to act.'

Olga was utterly overwhelmed; she was filled with terror and shame; a dull, heavy despair came upon her; she longed for death, and waited in agony for Vassily's decision.

'We must confess everything to my mother,' he said to her at last.

Olga turned deadly pale; her knees shook under her.

'Don't be afraid, don't be afraid,' repeated Vassily, 'trust to me, I won't desert you . . . I will make everything right . . . rely upon me.'

The poor woman looked at him with love . . . yes, with love, and deep, but hopeless devotion.

'I will arrange everything, everything,' Vassily said to her at parting . . . and for the last time he kissed her chilly hands. . . .

Next morning—Olga Ivanovna had only just risen from her bed—her door opened . . . and Anna Pavlovna appeared in the doorway. She was supported by Vassily. In silence she got as far as an arm-chair, and in silence she sat down. Vassily stood at her side. He looked composed; his brows were knitted and his lips slightly parted. Anna Pavlovna, pale, indignant, angry, tried to speak, but her voice failed her. Olga Ivanovna glanced in horror from her benefactress to her lover, with a terrible sinking at her heart . . . she fell on her knees with a shriek in the middle of the room, and hid her face in her hands.

'Then it's true . . . is it true?' murmured Anna Pavlovna, and bent down to her. . . . 'Answer!' she went on harshly, clutching Olga by the arm.

'Mother!' rang out Vassily's brazen voice, 'you promised me not to be hard on her.'

'I want . . . confess . . . confess . . . is it true? is it true?'

'Mother . . . remember . . .' Vassily began deliberately.

This one word moved Anna Pavlovna greatly. She leaned back in her chair, and burst into sobs.

Olga Ivanovna softly raised her head, and would have flung herself at the old lady's feet, but Vassily kept her back, raised her from the ground, and led her to another arm-chair. Anna Pavlovna went on weeping and muttering disconnected words. . . .

'Come, mother,' began Vassily, 'don't torment yourself, the trouble may yet be set right. . . . If Rogatchov . . .'

Olga Ivanovna shuddered, and drew herself up.

'If Rogatchov,' pursued Vassily, with a meaning glance at Olga Ivanovna, 'imagines that he can disgrace an honourable family with impunity . . .'

Olga Ivanovna was overcome with horror.

'In my house,' moaned Anna Pavlovna.

'Calm yourself, mother. He took advantage of her innocence, her youth, he—you wish to say something'—he broke off, seeing that Olga made a movement towards him. . . .

Olga Ivanovna sank back in her chair.

'I will go at once to Rogatchov. I will make him marry her this very day. You may be sure I will not let him make a laughingstock of us. . . .'

'But . . . Vassily Ivanovitch . . . you . . .' whispered Olga.

He gave her a prolonged, cold stare. She sank into silence again.

'Mother, give me your word not to worry her before I return. Look, she is half dead. And you, too, must rest. Rely upon me; I answer for everything; in any case, wait till I return. I tell you again, don't torture her, or yourself, and trust to me.'

He went to the door and stopped. 'Mother,' said he, 'come with me, leave her alone, I beg of you.'

Anna Pavlovna got up, went up to the holy picture, bowed down to the ground, and slowly followed her son. Olga Ivanovna, without a word or a movement, looked after them. Vassily turned back quickly, snatched her hand, whispered in her ear, 'Rely on me, and don't betray us,' and at once withdrew. . . . 'Bourcier!' he called, running swiftly down the stairs, 'Bourcier!'

A quarter of an hour later he was sitting in his carriage with his valet.

That day the elder Rogatchov was not at home. He had gone to the district town to buy cloth for the liveries of his servants. Pavel Afanasievitch was sitting in his own room, looking through a collection of faded butterflies. With lifted eyebrows and protruding lips, he was carefully, with a pin, turning over the fragile wings of a 'night sphinx' moth, when he was suddenly aware of a small but heavy hand on his shoulder. He looked round. Vassily stood before him.

'Good-morning, Vassily Ivanovitch,' he said in some amazement.

Vassily looked at him, and sat down on a chair facing him.

Pavel Afanasievitch was about to smile . . . but he glanced at Vassily, and subsided with his mouth open and his hands clasped.

'Tell me, Pavel Afanasievitch,' said Vassily suddenly, 'are you meaning to dance at your wedding soon?'

'I? . . . soon . . . of course . . . for my part . . . though as you and your sister . . . I, for my part, am ready to-morrow even.'

'Very good, very good. You're a very impatient person, Pavel Afanasie-vitch.'

'How so?'

'Let me tell you,' pursued Vassily Ivanovitch, getting up, 'I know all; you understand me, and I order you without delay to-morrow to marry Olga.'

'Excuse me, excuse me,' objected Rogatchov, not rising from his seat; 'you order me. I sought Olga Ivanovna's hand of myself and there's no need to give me orders. . . . I confess, Vassily Ivanovitch, I don't quite understand you.'

'You don't understand me?'

'No, really, I don't understand you.'

'Do you give me your word to marry her to-morrow?'

'Why, mercy on us, Vassily Ivanovitch . . . haven't you yourself put off our wedding more than once? Except for you it would have taken place long ago. And now I have no idea of breaking it off. What is the meaning of your threats, your insistence?'

Pavel Afanasievitch wiped the sweat off his face.

'Do you give me your word? Say yes or no!' Vassily repeated emphatically.

'Excuse me . . . I will . . . but . . .'

'Very good. Remember then . . . She has confessed everything.'

'Who has confessed?'

'Olga Ivanovna.'

'Why, what has she confessed?'

'Why, what are you pretending to me for, Pavel Afanasievitch? I'm not a stranger to you.'

'What am I pretending? I don't understand you, I don't, I positively don't understand a word. What could Olga Ivanovna confess?'

'What? You are really too much! You know what.'

'May God slay me . . .'

'No, I'll slay you, if you don't marry her . . . do you understand?'

'What! . . .' Pavel Afanasievitch jumped up and stood facing Vassily. 'Olga Ivanovna . . . you tell me . . .'

'You're a clever fellow, you are, I must own'—Vassily with a smile patted him on the shoulder—'though you do look so innocent.'

'Good God! . . . You'll send me out of my mind. . . . What do you mean, explain, for God's sake!'

Vassily bent down and whispered something in his ear.

Rogatchov cried out, 'What! . . . I?'

Vassily stamped.

'Olga Ivanovna? Olga? . . .'

'Yes . . . your betrothed . . .'

'My betrothed . . . Vassily Ivanovitch . . . she . . . she . . . Why, I never wish to see her again,' cried Pavel Afanasievitch. 'Good-bye to her for ever! What do you take me for? I'm being duped . . . I'm being duped . . . Olga Ivanovna, how wrong of you, have you no shame? . . .'

(Tears gushed from his eyes.) 'Thanks, Vassily Ivanovitch, thanks very much . . . I never wish to see her again now! no! no! don't speak of her. . . . Ah, merciful Heavens! to think I have lived to see this! Oh, very well, very well! '

' That's enough nonsense,' Vassily Ivanovitch observed coldly. 'Remember, you've given me your word: the wedding's to-morrow.'

' No, that it won't be! Enough of that, Vassily Ivanovitch. I say again, what do you take me for? You do me too much honour. I'm humbly obliged. Excuse me.'

' As you please! ' retorted Vassily. ' Get your sword.'

' Sword . . . what for? '

' What for? . . . I'll show you what for.'

Vassily drew out his fine, flexible French sword and bent it a little against the floor.

' You want . . . to fight . . . me? '

' Precisely so.'

' But, Vassily Ivanovitch, put yourself in my place! How can I, only think, after what you have just told me. . . . I'm a man of honour, Vassily Ivanovitch, a nobleman.'

' You're a nobleman, you're a man of honour, so you'll be so good as to fight with me.'

' Vassily Ivanovitch! '

' You are frightened, I think, Mr. Rogatchov.'

' I'm not in the least frightened, Vassily Ivanovitch. You thought you would frighten me, Vassily Ivanovitch. I'll scare him, you thought, he's a coward, and he'll agree to anything directly. . . No, Vassily Ivanovitch, I am a nobleman as much as you are, though I've not had city breeding, and you won't succeed in frightening me into anything, excuse me.'

' Very good,' retorted Vassily; ' where is your sword then? '

' Eroshka! ' shouted Pavel Afanasievitch. A servant came in.

' Get me the sword—there—you know, in the loft . . . make haste. . . .'

Eroshka went out. Pavel Afanasievitch suddenly became exceedingly pale, hurriedly took off his dressing-gown, put on a reddish coat with big paste buttons . . . twisted a cravat round his neck . . . Vassily looked at him, and twiddled the fingers of his right hand.

' Well, are we to fight then, Pavel Afanasievitch? '

' Let's fight, if we must fight,' replied Rogatchov, and hurriedly buttoned up his shirt.

' Ay, Pavel Afanasievitch, you take my advice, marry her . . . what is it to you . . . And believe me, I'll . . .'

' No, Vassily Ivanovitch,' Rogatchov interrupted him. ' You'll kill me or maim me, I know, but I'm not going to lose my honour; if I'm to die then I must die.'

Eroshka came in, and trembling, gave Rogatchov a wretched old sword in a torn leather scabbard. In those days all noblemen wore swords with powder, but in the steppes they only put on powder twice a year. Eroshka moved away to the door and burst out crying. Pavel Afanasievitch pushed him out of the room.

'But, Vassily Ivanovitch,' he observed with some embarrassment, 'I can't fight with you on the spot: allow me to put off our duel till to-morrow. My father is not at home, and it would be as well for me to put my affairs in order to—to be ready for anything.'

'I see you're beginning to feel frightened again, sir.'

'No, no, Vassily Ivanovitch; but consider yourself . . .'

'Listen!' shouted Lutchinov, 'you drive me out of patience. . . . Either give me your word to marry her at once, or fight . . . or I'll thrash you with my cane like a coward,—do you understand?'

'Come into the garden,' Rogatchov answered through his teeth.

But all at once the door opened, and the old nurse, Efimovna, utterly distracted, broke into the room, fell on her knees before Rogatchov, and clasped his legs. . . .

'My little master!' she wailed, 'my nursling . . . what is it you are about? Will you be the death of us poor wretches, your honour? Sure, he'll kill you, darling! Only you say the word, you say the word, and we'll make an end of him, the insolent fellow. . . . Pavel Afanasievitch, my baby-boy, for the love of God!'

A number of pale, excited faces showed in the door . . . there was even the red beard of the village elder . . .

'Let me go, Efimovna, let me go!' muttered Rogatchov.

'I won't, my own, I won't. What are you about, sir, what are you about? What'll Afanasey Lukitch say? Why, he'll drive us all out of the light of day. . . . Why are you fellows standing still? Take the uninvited guest in hand and show him out of the house, so that not a trace be left of him.'

'Rogatchov!' Vassily Ivanovitch shouted menacingly.

'You are crazy, Efimovna, you are shaming me, come, come . . .' said Pavel Afanasievitch. 'Go away, go away, in God's name, and you others, off with you, do you hear? . . .'

Vassily Ivanovitch moved swiftly to the open window, took out a small silver whistle, blew lightly . . . Bourcier answered from close by. Lutchinov turned at once to Pavel Afanasievitch.

'What's to be the end of this farce?'

'Vassily Ivanovitch, I will come to you to-morrow. What can I do with this crazy old woman? . . .'

'Oh, I see it's no good wasting words on you,' said Vassily, and he swiftly raised his cane . . .

Pavel Afanasievitch broke loose, pushed Efimovna away, snatched up the sword, and rushed through another door into the garden.

Vassily dashed after him. They ran into a wooden summerhouse, painted cunningly after the Chinese fashion, shut themselves in, and drew their swords. Rogatchov had once taken lessons in fencing, but now he was scarcely capable of drawing a sword properly. The blades crossed. Vassily was obviously playing with Rogatchov's sword. Pavel Afanasievitch was breathless and pale, and gazed in consternation into Lutchinov's face.

Meanwhile, screams were heard in the garden; a crowd of people were running to the summerhouse. Suddenly Rogatchov heard the heart-rending wail of old age . . . he recognised the voice of his father. Afanasey Lukitch, bare-headed, with dishevelled hair, was running in front of them all, frantically waving his hands. . . .

With a violent and unexpected turn of the blade Vassily sent the sword flying out of Pavel Afanasievitch's hand.

'Marry her, my boy,' he said to him: 'give over this foolery!'

'I won't marry her,' whispered Rogatchov, and he shut his eyes, and shook all over.

Afanasey Lukitch began banging at the door of the summerhouse.

'You won't?' shouted Vassily.

Rogatchov shook his head.

'Well, damn you, then!'

Poor Pavel Afanasievitch fell dead: Lutchinov's sword stabbed him to the heart . . . The door gave way; old Rogatchov burst into the summerhouse, but Vassily had already jumped out of window . . .

Two hours later he went into Olga Ivanovna's room . . . She rushed in terror to meet him. . . . He bowed to her in silence; took out his sword and pierced Pavel Afanasievitch's portrait in the place of the heart. Olga shrieked and fell unconscious on the floor . . . Vassily went in to Anna Pavlovna. He found her in the oratory. 'Mother,' said he, 'we are avenged.' The poor old woman shuddered and went on praying.

Within a week Vassily had returned to Petersburg, and two years later he came back stricken with paralysis—tongue-tied. He found neither Anna Pavlovna nor Olga living, and soon after died himself in the arms of Yuditch, who fed him like a child, and was the only one who could understand his incoherent stuttering.

1846.